THE REVENGE OF THE
DWARVES

MARKUS HEITZ

Translated by Sheelagh Alabaster

orbit

www.orbitbooks.net

ORBIT

First English-language edition 2011
Originally published in Germany as *Die Rache der Zwerge*
by Heyne Verlag in 2005
First published in Great Britain in 2011 by Orbit

9 11 12 10

A CIP catalogue record for this book
is available from the British Library.

ISBN 978-1-84149-935-2

Typeset in Sabon by Palimpsest Book Production Limited,
Falkirk, Stirlingshire
Printed and bound by CPI Group (UK) Ltd, Croydon, CR0 4YY

Papers used by Orbit are from well-managed forests
and other responsible sources.

MIX
Paper from
responsible sources
FSC® C104740

Orbit
An imprint of
Little, Brown Book Group
Carmelite House
50 Victoria Embankment
London EC4Y 0DZ

An Hachette UK Company
www.hachette.co.uk

www.orbitbooks.net

The Third *I dedicate*
to those who read my dedication;
without the dedication you have shown,
its sister volumes would have stood alone.

"Impressive height or exceptional length of a limb is not the be all and end all of a creature. What I say is: the taller you are, the more likely you are to get hit!"
—Boïndil "Ireheart", Doubleblade of the Secondling Clan of the Swinging Axes.

"Now and then you hear malicious remarks about dwarves. They are said to be of inferior build, to be cranky, to have a weird sense of humor; it is told that they only drink beer that is as black as night and are not able to appreciate music unless a hundred voices are bellowing in unison. But I say: only when you have been a guest in their majestic halls, as once I was, should you have the right to pronounce on these rumors and confirm them all to be true. Let us not laugh at them as if they were lovable children with long beards, but, on the contrary, let us praise the magnificent way they have preserved all of us from total destruction. More than once."
—Excerpts from the ten-volume work *My Life and Uniquely Heroic Exploits*—the memoirs of the Incredible Rodario.

"Ih did aforetimes ask a dwerff as what, other than such dwerff, he fain had byn born. Ih offert the chois of myghtie draggon, all seeing magus or his own god vraccas. He did look at me in wonder and did shayk his hed, saying: ye myghtie draggons were perforce slain by a dwerff, syns draggons are no more; ye all

seeing magus lykewyse was vanquysht by a dwerff, syns he is no more. And vraccas neyther schal ih be, for ther be no thing left to mak, better than his dwerffis"

—Taken from "Descryptions of ye Ffolk of Girdlegyrd: Manneris and Karacterystycks" in the Great Archive of Viransiénsis, drawn up by Tanduweyt, collected by M.A. Het, Magister Folkloricum, in the the 4299th solar cycle.

Girdlegard

200 Miles

N

FOURTHLING KINGDOM (GOÏMDIL'S FOLK)

THIRDLING KINGDOM (LORIMBUR'S FOLK)

Silverfast

Borwôl

Urgon

Pendleburg

Idoslane

Lot-Ionan's Vaults

Calmstead

TOBORIBOR

Deichsel-dorf

SECONDLING KINGDOM (BEROÏN'S FOLK)

FIFTHLING KINGDOM (GISELBERT'S FOLK)

Stone Gateway

Elven Kingdom of Âlandur

Gauragar

Porista

Paland

Blacksaddle

Sangpûr

Tabâin

Goldensheaf

Storm Valley

Weyurn

Lake

Windsport

Mifurdania

Lake

Lake

Rân Ribastur

FIRSTLING KINGDOM (BORENGAR'S FOLK)

Prologue

Girdlegard,
Gray Range on the border of the Fifthling Kingdom,
Spring, 6234th Solar Cycle

Gronsha stood still, listening intently in the swirling fog that his yellow eyes were quite unable to penetrate, though he was one of the finest scouts in Prince Ushnart's army. To tell the truth, he was one of only three scouts still left to Prince Ushnart. The others who had set off to reconnoiter for the Prince now lay at the Stone Gate, their heads struck clean from their shoulders.

He could hear footsteps. Many footsteps.

Swiftly he grabbed hold of his jagged two-handed sword, ready to wield it. He and his troop had made the fatal error of being over-confident when they had left the Subterranean Kingdom by way of the Stone Gate and seen the enemy recoiling before their superior numbers. And now the Bearded Ones were clinging to their heels as tenaciously as gnome excrement sticks to your boots.

Not that he was frightened of the Groundlings. Black Water, blood of the Perished Lands, flowed now in his veins and rendered him immortal. Unless, of course, someone were to strike his head clean off his shoulders.

But the enemy, unfortunately, were very good at that: even their stunted physique was no handicap there.

If they couldn't reach the neck with their axes, they

would slice at the legs. An opponent sunk to his knees was easy to decapitate.

In the Groundlings' northern kingdom, a place thought more or less deserted, they had come upon an unexpectedly large enemy band. He and his two fellow scouts, facing defeat, had chosen to turn tail, heading back to the Outer Lands. Maybe they could locate another escape route back to Prince Ushnart's camp to warn him about the Groundlings; could they manage to find an exit that did not involve a battle with a horde of ax-wielding warriors?

In the Outer Lands, it was said, it was his own tribe that reigned—the orcs. So far he had not come across any, but he wouldn't object to a little support.

"It's steamy as wash-day. You can't see a thing in this fog," he overheard one of the Groundlings complain. It was essential for any self-respecting scout that he be able to understand the language spoken by the enemy.

"You'd think the wretched fog itself was wanting to help the swine."

Gronsha objected to the term swine—it was an insult indeed to be called a pig by that barrel-sized runt of a creature. Pigs were all right to eat, but they were nothing much to look at. And he, after all, was well built, twice the size of one of those Beard-Faces. Instinctively he tensed his muscles in anger. This made his armor grate against the rock behind, signaling his whereabouts to the dwarves.

They'd heard it.

"Ah, we've got him."

Oh no, you haven't, Beard-Face. Gronsha sprinted away to shake off his pursuers, but again the dull metallic clank betrayed him.

He'd no idea how far he'd gone or in which direction he'd been running. And where on earth were his companions?

He only knew that it was dark all around him. Was he in a cave? He pressed up against the nearest wall, holding his breath to listen out for the enemy.

"Halt!" one of them ordered, quite close. He could hear the creak of boots as his pursuer stood still. "Can you hear him?"

No answer.

Gronsha gave an evil grin. So the Groundlings were as helpless in this fog as he was himself.

Carefully he sniffed the air, noting his opponent's position by the unmistakable smell. He moved off, sword raised in his two hands above his head, ready to strike: he could split the creature in two with a single blow.

"Boïndil?"—he heard the voice of the Groundling querying his approach. A stocky shadowy figure emerged from the fog, and Gronsha launched his attack, sure of his target.

"Aha, so somebody's listening to me, at least," said the dwarf, stepping neatly to one side and wielding his own weapon in his turn. The ax-blade slashed into Gronsha's right buttock. He let out a yell and disappeared into the wall of fog.

This was no way to fight. This was not the type of encounter he enjoyed.

This accursed fog.

He decided to retreat rather than stumble around hoping for a chance hit before one of them managed to strike him again.

The wound on his backside was quickly closing up. The Black Immortality draught that he had been taken would heal him instantaneously, though the cut had been in a sensitive and undignified area. Typical of those devious Groundlings. They would always avoid honorable combat and sneak off and hide in their strongholds and caves.

Gronsha turned and headed back through the thick mist. Behind him he heard the screams of a dying orc, felled by a Groundling. The ghastly sound curdled his blood.

He caught sight of a small figure backing into view through the mist. Without pause for thought he raised his weapon and smashed the blade right down on the enemy's helmet. Death struck so fast that not a single cry was uttered. Blood sprayed out on all sides.

Gronsha was not yet satisfied. "You scummy rockslime worm. I'll cut you to ribbons!" He hacked away at the corpse in a blind rage, oblivious to the din. Laughing, he severed the bearded head and booted it off into the fog: this was his way to take revenge. His victim's helmet and shield he took with him. They would serve him well.

As he lifted the shield the next dwarf rushed up ready to kill. "Here!" the dwarf shouted, ax upraised. "Here he is. This way!"

"Damnable maggot," croaked Gronsha, taking the blow on his shield. The blade skidded over the edge of the metal, hitting him on the shoulder. The thick layer of lard on his body armor, designed to foil enemy weapons, had failed him this time.

Gronsha sprang back, but his adversaries were attacking from all sides. Running straight ahead he crashed against a rough granite wall that tore at his skin as he slid along it.

His discovery of the wall was no real help. He felt he was going round in circles. The enveloping mist allowed no escape and seemed to be mocking him as it imprisoned him in the swirling darkness. The combat zone for him and the Groundlings must be a cave with many interconnecting tunnels.

His shoulders throbbed and burned. The Black Immortality healed him fast but even so the pain was intense. He attempted a cautious movement of his arm, which obeyed him dutifully. Gronsha would have to rely on that arm because his enemies were still at large.

He could smell their presence despite the hateful damp cold gray vapor that was like a blindfold on his eyes. The further in you ventured, the less you could hear in this fog. Even his own armor had ceased to give off any sound. He was swathed in a cold damp blanket of the stuff.

Those other caves, the ones in the land of Toboribor, Realm of the Orcs to the southwest of Girdlegard, were always warm and dry: you could move about unhampered. This cavern was the exact opposite: cold, eerie and forbidding.

The gray veils swirled about wildly, making him think there were Groundlings on all sides about to attack as he felt his way along the wall searching for an exit. Three times he was fooled by his imagination and stabbed furiously at empty air.

At last Tion and Samusin, the gods of his people, took pity on him and showed him a way out—a black opening in the rock wall.

All at once a Groundling was in his path, jumping out at him from the fog and wielding a deadly ax. "Perish, fiend!"

This time Gronsha was ready for him, parrying the blow and kicking his attacker in the face so that the dwarf lurched back into the wall of mist, spitting blood and teeth. "You shall die first, rock-louse!"

Time to apply some trickery. Gronsha squatted down low, put the battered dwarf helmet on his head, took up the captured shield and altered his voice as he lurched from side to side, gurgling in desperation. "Help! He's done for me." He groaned and whimpered. "For the sake of Vraccas, friends, come to my aid!"

"Bendagar? Are you injured?"

"My leg," moaned Gronsha, battling with the urge to laugh. This was no time for laughter—not yet.

"Hold on, we're coming," he heard the Groundling's comrade call. The dwarf's outline appeared in the fog. "Mind you keep quiet. There's another of those snout-faces round here somewhere. He—"

Gronsha did not wait. He thrust the sword tip violently through the chain mail and into the belly of his enemy. "Well, well, Beard-Face, you don't say?" His laugh was full of malice as he twisted the blade. The dwarf groaned and tried to strike at him but Gronsha fended off the blow, grabbing the ax handle and forcing it out of the weakening grasp of the other. "Bite on your own blade," he growled, slicing into the bearded face.

The Groundling sank back into the wall of fog. This time forever.

Gronsha leaped over the body and raced into the

swirling mist of the tunnels through which he hoped to make his escape.

It was a leap into the unknown and nothing like the sort of exploring he was used to.

He was aware of a feeling of great unease. *I am in the Outer Lands*, he thought, quaking with fear but unable to name the source of his terror.

In Toboribor there were legends about the mighty territories of the orcs. One place alone was as big as the whole of Girdlegard and could sustain a vast population of orcs—more orcs than there were stars in the heavens.

He thought the myths were exaggerated. But still, there *must* be orcs in the Outer Lands. Many thousands of solar cycles ago the first and only ever successful raid had started from the north.

Of course it was thanks to his people that the Northern Gateway had been breached. Every orc descendant knew the legend of the glorious orbit that celebrated the victory over the Groundlings. Only orcs had the necessary stamina, strength and courage. Cycle after cycle, the memorable event was honored in Toboribor.

How wonderful, thought Gronsha, to have celebrated the next festival in a conquered dwarf kingdom. And with the severed head of a Groundling to serve as a missile for the shot-put event, the way they used to at the festival commemorating the fall of Girdlegard. The feasts they provided had been enormous; this time he'd certainly have carried off the prize for competitive belching. Instead of enjoying the games, though, there he was, on his own, stuck in the Outer Lands. He had been born in the caves of Toboribor and knew nothing of the land of his fore-bears. The same as all the orcs in Toboribor.

But it wasn't just orcs he was hoping to come across; there would be ogres, trolls, älfar and all the other crea-tures that worshipped the gods Samusin and Tion.

"Those were the days," he grumbled. Since the defeat of their ally Magus Nôd'onn there was no chance of any more good times for him and Prince Ushnotz, who was wanting to establish a new empire; they were constantly running away from the Red-Bloods, they had no home anymore and the prince was weak and treated them unfairly.

He still didn't dare to stand up to Ushnotz, to kill him and take over. Others, those with more experience, he was sure, would be getting there first with their plans for a coup. Whoever managed to vanquish the prince would replace him—that was always the way with his people. The best man would take power. So Groshna went on waiting. He was waiting for his chance.

The only good thing about his position was his immor-tality, granted him by the Black Water. But immortality without power was like a bone with no meat.

Gronsha's plan was changing, the further he advanced and the more the mist lifted. "Why should I go back and serve Ushnotz at all?" he asked into the empty air, and his words echoed back from the cavern walls. Reflections from the glistening moss gave enough light for his sensi-tive vision. He could see nearly as well as in bright daylight. His confidence grew. "I'm as good a prince as any."

Perhaps he would be able to drum up a small band of mercenaries in the Outer Lands and get them to attack the Stone Gate. He and his troopers had managed to inflict substantial damage on the gates before having to retreat; the Groundlings would not be able to secure the gates easily. A few hundred orcs and they'd soon dispense with that puny handful of defenders. He'd have to act quickly and find allies enough to launch an attack before the Groundlings got their repairs underway.

Gronscha grinned. He, the immortal orc, would be the one to take the Groundlings' stronghold. All he needed were comrades in arms. No point in being choosy. Anything that could hold a weapon would be fine with him. Now he was convinced: it had been *Tion's will* that he should go into the Outer Lands.

His eyes picked out a sign on the cave wall. It was a rune, elaborate and strange and revoltingly dwarfish. The shape couldn't be from the Sharp-Ears.

"Are those confounded bearded boils on this side, too?" cursed Gronsha. He couldn't work out whether the marks on the stone were recent or had been etched a thousand cycles previously. He would have to be careful.

He carried on, following the tunnel that soon branched into two, and strode along after a moment's hesitation, taking the passageway that had the slightly warmer air.

Soon the passage fanned out into a dozen corridors. Gronsha was entering a maze.

He marked his chosen path, scratching a large orc rune: two vertical lines with two dots between them. He might need to find his way back. Before long he was faced with the same decision about which direction to take. This happened eight times.

It was deathly quiet.

His footsteps made no sound now; the layer of grease

on his armor had melted into the gaps and was lubricating the metal so there was no noise from the plates grating together. You couldn't even hear a pebble dislodging from the roof, or a drop of water splashing down. In the Outer Lands there was neither sound nor life. Nothing but him and the passageways, sometimes high and wide as barn doors, sometimes as small as a human female.

Fear started to take hold of him.

He began to sweat. He was seeing hundreds of shadows surrounding him, then he thought his own shadow was moving when he was standing still. In no time he was so far gone he'd have welcomed even the sound of an orc's death scream. At least he'd have been able to hear *something*.

Finally he broke into a run, not knowing what he was running from or running towards. He was so desperate to get away from the silence, he forgot to mark his way. No matter how tired he was, no matter how much time had passed: nothing else was important.

Then the passage opened up into a cavern.

Gronsha stopped on the threshold, gasping, in his left side a piercing pain each time he drew breath. He reckoned the cave was about forty paces long and over a hundred in height. Great shafts of sunlight, wide as tree trunks, fell through. It looked as if they were columns supporting the roof. The bright light cut through the gloom, tearing pale holes in the darkness of the floor.

He stopped short. Bones . . . heaps of bones. Orc bones!

Either he had found a burial chamber where cowards' remains were unceremoniously thrown to rot away, or else these caves were home to some creature that was preying on his people for food.

Gronsha took a few careful steps into the cave, went down on one knee and poked around with the tip of his sword in a pile of bones the light had caught.

The bones did indeed show knife marks. Someone had painstakingly scraped off the flesh. They had broken open the larger bones to get at the marrow. Nobody had touched the skulls. He had the distinct impression that these remains were quite fresh.

He breathed out, stood up and tested the air. Perhaps the Groundlings had been, in all senses of the words, the smaller evil.

He strode on across the cavern, instinctively avoiding the patches of light. On the other side he took the next passageway and followed it, his stomach rumbling. All this running around had made him really hungry.

Gronsha's trusty nose warned him.

A familiar smell told him that some of his own people were hereabouts, even though he could neither see nor hear them. It was strange that here the whiff of rancid fat from the armor was missing.

Then he saw the firelight at the end of the passage.

Not wanting to get himself shot full of arrows by some over-eager guard, Gronsha did not try to muffle the sound of his approach. "Ho," he called out, the cave walls echoing and funneling his strong dark voice. "I am an orc. From Toboribor! I need your help, Brothers, against the Groundlings!"

Two large solidly built forms became visible at the end of the passage, blocking out the fire's light. The vague smell he knew so well was getting stronger, and shadows flew along the cave wall toward him. He could not yet see any details, but it seemed that the orcs from the Outer Lands were no less tall than those from southern Girdlegard.

They approached him, their deadly barbed spear points facing the ground. Gronsha assumed the vicious metal hooks would simply rip off under pressure and stick in the victim's flesh. He regarded the weapon with respect.

A third shape joined them, hurrying up with a lantern to shine on him.

Soon they were in front of him—he saw to his surprise one of them was a female. Not only did the sight of her, with all those rings in her ears and the unusually delicate nose, excite him, but he wondered what she was doing casting her lot in with these warriors. It wouldn't happen back in Toboribor. Women should be seeing to the food and the kids. And to the needs of the fighting men, to his own needs, at once, right here.

"Don't move your hands," she ordered in her husky voice. The lance point was placed at his throat and forced him over toward the wall. "Stay there. *Brother*." The other orcs laughed.

Gronsha studied their armor and the helmets. They really weren't using the life-saving coating of fat on the metal plates. They'd stand no chance like that in a proper fight. He couldn't see the point of making your enemy's job easier. All in all they looked fairly clean. At any rate they were much cleaner than him. Unhealthily clean.

He started to feel envious. That armor indisputably came from an orc forge. But the quality of the metal and handiwork was way above anything that he had ever seen made by Prince Ushnotz's smiths. Could that be why they were able to dispense with the coating of fat?

"I am Gronsha. Take me to your leader," he commanded, stretching to his full height. "It is possible that I am being followed. It would be as well for you to watch out."

The woman looked along the passageway he had come down and then sent the two warriors out to check. "You're from . . . where?"

"Toboribor."

"Toboribor?" She did not even look at him; she was watching what was going on down the passage. "What kind of a name is that?"

"*What kind of a name is that?*" he grunted indignantly. He was surprised. "It is a mighty orc kingdom, far to the south of Girdlegard."

Now she did grace him with a glance. The expression in her pink eyes hovered between indifference and disdain. "An orc kingdom? That is good news for once. If it's in the south, what are you doing in the north?" Her accent was painful for him: too clear and sharp. Arrogant, more like. "So you're lost?"

"I command the troops of Prince Ushnotz, who rules Toboribor. I am here to look for allies to help us fight the Groundlings . . ." He bent the truth a little and noted from her face that she did not get his meaning. "You don't know who the *Groundlings* are?" It was getting more and more difficult. "Then you are indeed blessed by Tion and Samusin, if you haven't met this plague of ax monsters," he snorted. He held his hands at hip level to show their height. "This size without their helmets. We call them Beard-Faces and Rock-Lice and usually—"

"Oh, of course. I know them," she interrupted. The two orcs she'd sent out to reconnoiter were back and gave the all-clear. Nobody had followed him. "Our names for them are different. It's not often that one of our *Brothers*"—she emphasized the word and smiled— "takes the path and comes to Fon Gala."

"To where?" Gronsha asked.

"Here."

"Oh, the Outer Lands. That's what we call it."

"Welcome." She widened her smile, baring her teeth and showing her fangs.

Gronsha liked her. He wanted her. When he had captured the stronghold he would take her for his wife and breed many children on her. He bet she'd never had an orc like him. He would break her in and teach her how a woman should behave.

"You may come with me, Gronsha. I'll take you to our prince. He will be pleased to hear news of Toboribor." At long last she removed the spear point from his throat and gestured toward the end of the tunnel where the light was coming from. "After you. *Brother*." That set the orcs off laughing again.

They reached a large cavern that was part natural, part artificial. A hundred paces wide and two hundred in length, as high as the tallest tower on the Stone Gateway. In the middle a small stream flowed and along its banks black, five-cornered tents had been erected. There were several kinds of smell he noted in the air: food was cooking, and there was beer brewing somewhere. There were coal fires burning in glowing iron braziers.

Gronsha wondered why the normal unmistakable smell

of his own people was absent—that heady mix of strength and presence and superiority, that the Red-Bloods said "stank." The brother and sister orcs from the Outer Lands couldn't have been here long.

He could not suppress a grin. Guessing at their number, he arrived at a couple of thousand. At least. With a force of that size it would be easy to wipe out the Groundlings.

His companion pointed to the largest black tent. "In there."

Together they crossed the campsite, followed by the curious gaze of the many orcs gathered there. Gronsha tried to make himself look impressive. He spread his arms a little and made his gait powerful. He bared his teeth and rolled his eyes.

"I'm bringing the prince a phottòr," the orc woman called out merrily. "He's from an orc kingdom far away." The others standing around put their heads together and were talking amongst themselves, glancing now and then at the newcomer in admiration. At least, that is how he interpreted their behavior.

"What is a phottòr?" he wanted to know, without changing his demeanor. Two of the females were making eyes at him and he puffed himself up even more to impress them.

"That's what we call you people. In our language it's a term of honor."

Gronsha raised his broad chin. He liked honors; they suited him.

As they stopped at the entrance, the orc woman held fast to his arm, warning him, "You must be courteous,

Gronsha. Maybe our ways will be different from your own." Then she pushed him into the tent ahead of herself.

The interior was illuminated by hundreds of lamps. Gronsha saw an orc of mighty physique four paces away, reclining on luxurious bright-coloured rugs as he dined. A mantle of black silk was draped around his shoulders; it was the kind of thing an effete Red-Blood would wear. The weapons arrayed behind him on a wooden stand could have equipped a small army. On three of his fingers gold rings reflected the light.

This prince was certainly the biggest orc Gronsha had ever seen. He felt the size of an adolescent in comparison to this giant. His face was broad, with a narrow moustache, and he had a high slanting forehead. The black hair was braided. The prince stopped eating, his curiosity roused. "Kamdra, my dear. What have you got there?"

"Noble Lord Flagur," she said, bowing to the prince. Gronsha followed suit. "I bring you a gift, Illustrious One. He was found in one of the passageways we thought was defunct." She pushed Gronsha forward. "He is called Gronsha. His speech is difficult to understand. A degenerate, my lord. But he speaks of an orc kingdom."

Flagur sat up and placed one hand on his knee, gesturing with the other for Gronsha to approach. "Fine. Gronsha," he repeated slowly, trying out the sound. "It suits him." The look in his pink eyes was considerably sharper and more severe than that in the woman's.

By now Gronsha had got over his surprise, though he was still having to contend with the revoltingly sweet perfumes wafting around inside the tent. Scents, cleanliness and an unfamiliar way of speech. These orcs were not behaving normally at all; certainly not in their treatment of him. It pricked at his pride and he drew himself up. "I am not a thing. And definitely not deg . . . delg . . ."

"Degenerate?" suggested Flagur.

Gronsha made to take a step forward, his pride stung to boiling anger. "Prince Flagur. You must give me your . . ." A burning pain bit at the back of his neck. He whirled around, spitting, and saw Kamdra. There was blood on the point of her spear—his blood. "You—"

"No. *You* will address the prince as *Your Lordship* and *Noble Lord*, as you ought." She held her weapon ready. "I will teach you our ways, phottòr."

He growled at her but made as if to obey. Now he was resolute: he would take this woman, would break her will and make her his slave. He turned back to Flagur. "Give me your support, My Lord," he repeated. " We must attack the stronghold of the Groundlings—"

"He means the ubariu, Illustrious One," Kamdra interpreted.

"Ours?"

"No, *their* ubariu, Noble Lord." The orc woman sounded highly amused. "It seems they have them over there on the other side of the mountains as well. But they have nothing to do with the phottòr, I'm sure."

Flagur nodded and seemed good-humored now. "We'll find out about that soon." He nodded to Gronsha. "And you. Tell me about this orc kingdom of yours."

Gronsha spoke of Toboribor, about the caves, about his master Ushnotz's army, about the ineffective bastion clumsily erected by the Groundlings at the Stone Gate, and he told Flagur of the desperate state of the army of men and of elves.

He asked for charcoal and paper to draw a rough map. Pen and ink he left untouched. Unschooled in their use, he would only end up breaking the nib and leaving blotches everywhere. "Girdlegard is easily conquered, Prince Flagur," he enticed. "I know the territory inside out. Give me your best warriors and I will take the Groundlings' stronghold." Another sharp jab in the neck, and Gronsha quickly added a yelled "Your Lordship." Oh, he had plans for breaking Kamdra's resistance.

"So that you can hand the stronghold to your own prince?" Flagur laughed outright. "Never."

Gronsha bowed his head. Blood was trickling down his back inside his armor. "No. I thought that Your Lordship could become the new leader of all the Orcs. Think of it: at least five thousand more fighting men at your disposal. Your Lordship."

The orc prince's eyes narrowed. "Why would they follow *me*?"

"Because I would support you."

Flagur exploded into hysterical laughter, and then Kamdra joined in, forgetting this time to punish Gronsha for the missing *Your Lordship*. "Exquisite," he roared. "Tell me, how are you going to get them to follow a stranger's command? Would you take over their minds? Even my best rune master would not be able to do that. Not with five thousand."

Gronsha did not answer, caught unawares. "Rune master?" He blinked.

Kamdra helped him with the word: "A rune master uses invisible powers. You wouldn't understand, phottòr."

Gronsha understood only too well. He was dealing here with orcs that had their own magus. A *magus*.

Now it was clear that with their help he would be able to crown himself ruler of all Girdlegard. But for that he needed power over the tribe.

His plan was simple and effective: he would kill Flagur when he got the chance and then he would proclaim himself ruler, according to the custom of the orcs. No one would doubt his superiority ever again, if he were able to kill this giant of an orc. "Illustrious One, do I get your warriors or not?" he asked, adding emphasis to his words.

Flagur, who had by now managed to stop laughing, fell into hysterics again and collapsed onto the rugs and cushions.

That was what Gronsha was waiting for. He hurled himself forward, reaching for his dagger, aiming the blade directly at the prince's heart.

Still laughing, Flagur grabbed his sword from behind and slashed at the attacker.

It was a brutal blow. Not only was Gronsha thrown off his stroke, but the short sword sliced through his armor and the flesh beneath; streams of his dark green blood were spilling fast and he tipped forward onto the couch where Flagur lay.

"I knew he would try that," grinned the prince, wiping his blade on the dead orc's clothing. "It's a classic move for them. Violence. That's all they know how to do."

To make sure, Kamdra stabbed Gronsha in the back with her lance, inserting the barbed tip and using it to haul the corpse off to the door. "Your Noble Lordship was brilliant, as ever," she said, bowing to him.

But Gronsha was not dead in the least. He used his dagger to slash away behind him, severing the shaft of the lance; he jumped up. The gaping wound in his chest had closed up, with the Blood of the Perished Lands effective as always.

He hurled the dagger at Kamdra and hit her in the left shoulder. Three swift paces brought him face to face with Flagur. He pulled one of the swords out of the weapons stand and brandished it. The prince used his short sword to hit at him and Gronsha stood firm to demonstrate his limitless superiority, taking the blow on his left forearm.

The wound was deep and painful, but it healed over in front of Flagur's very eyes.

"Look what I can do!" Grunting he turned to Kamdra. "Pull my dagger out of your shoulder and see if you can do the same thing."

But Flagur, rolling back over his shoulder away from the carpets, selected a spiked mace from the stand, wielding this in one hand and the short sword in the other. "It has a little secret," he grunted with delight, his pink eyes shining. "You're not immortal, are you?"

"Yes," squeaked Gronsha in his excitement, his voice too high and too loud. One stroke, another, and he would be leader of all the orcs. "Unlike you!"

His opponent grinned like a wild animal. "Let us find out."

He attacked Flagur, who swerved out of the way and had the mace raised in his hand to strike at Gronsha's back.

Expecting the move, Gronsha dived underneath the whirling flail and rammed his sword up to the hilt deep into his enemy's belly. "Die!" he rejoiced. "I am the new ruler."

His joy died abruptly as Flagur dropped the sword and grasped Gronsha's throat in both hands, lifting him bodily into the air, right up to the roof of the tent, at full stretch. The sword in his belly didn't worry him at all.

Gronsha kicked the hilt of the sword. His foe should have been screaming with pain, but he gave not a murmur.

"Let us talk, Noble One," Gronsha gasped, terrified for his life. He didn't attempt to struggle his way out of the vice-like grip. He groped for the leather flask he carried at his belt. "There, in there. That's my secret. The Black Immortality."

The fingers pressed harder still and he could feel the vertebrae grating in protest.

Gronsha threw the flask onto the floor. "Take it, by the dark forces of Tion, take it! Take it but let me live," he whispered. "I want . . ." His voice failed him; he could get no breath.

Suddenly his neck broke under the enormous pressure. The undead life of Gronsha, the last of the scouting force sent out by Ushnotz, seeped away in the powerful hands of Flagur. The prince threw the cadaver to one side. "Kamdra, get the healer and the rune master," he said, his voice strong, and he sat himself back onto the cushions, careful to ensure the sword did not snag in the fabric. Only now did he permit himself to show any sign of weakness: he grimaced. The excitement of combat and killing faded away.

"What happens to him?" asked Kamdra, indicating the corpse.

Flagur took up his short sword gingerly, sliced off a strip of calf-flesh from the dead Gronsha, and swirled it around in a bowl of water to get the dirt off. Then he put it in his mouth and chewed. The flavor was a strange one. "Delicious," he said, and invited her to try the meat.

Kamdra took a taste and her eyes widened. "I'd never have expected that. He stank so strongly I thought we'd have to leave the meat to soak for seven moons." She bowed and hurried out to fetch the rune master and the healer for her lord.

"Wait," he called her back. "Send to the ubariu to say we have news for them. They will be very keen to learn what is happening in Girdlegard." She nodded and left.

Flagur couldn't control his appetite and he ate several more strips of flesh from the delicacy he himself had selected and slaughtered. With prizes like that, Girdlegard held a definite attraction for himself and his followers.

He stretched out his hand for the leather flask, opened it and sniffed the contents. The smell was appalling, and the fumes made his eyes water. Revolted, he tipped the liquid into the rubbish, throwing the empty flask along with it.

The weapon piercing his body was torturing him, but he would survive. He put his faith in the help of Ubar, his god, and creator of his people.

Around him everything started to swim. His pink eyes slid over toward the tent door, whence several vague shapes were drawing near. A voice close to his ear said, "Noble Lord, we are about to start. Be strong and may Ubar be with you."

"He will be," muttered Flagur, tensing his muscles. "Get on with it."

I

Girdlegard,
The Gray Range on the Southern Boundary of the
Fifthling Kingdom,
Spring, 6241st Solar Cycle

"The last time I was here everything lay in ruins, Keen-Ears. But this ... I'd never have expected *this*." Tungdil Goldhand ruffled his gray pony's mane. Amazed, he took the last bend in the mountain track, stopped and looked up to the top of the five-cornered tower that reached, imposing and impregnable, into the sky. "Not after just five sun cycles." He used the impromptu halt to put his drinking flask, now nearly empty, to his parched mouth, letting the last few drops of brandy trickle down his throat. The alcohol stung his cracked lips.

Passing the immense building that would have made even an ogre look small, he reached the plain in front of the entrance to the fifthling kingdom, ruled by the descendants of Giselbart Ironeye.

It seemed only yesterday that he had led the twenty-strong reconnaissance troop here with his friend Boïndil and his current life-partner, Balyndis.

On that journey they had made their way through a devastated landscape of ruins and moss-covered stones. Most of the fifthlings' fortifications had been turned to rubble.

Today a completely different scene met his eyes, a scene to gladden the proud heart of any child of the Smith.

He was riding now past where they had drowned some of Ushnotz's orc army. He saw that the pit had been filled in and covered over with black marble slabs bearing inscriptions in gold and in vraccasium to commemorate the glorious battle and honor the fallen dwarves. Each one of them a hero, they lived on in songs about the war.

Nowhere was there the slightest trace of the weathered ruins Tungdil had once struggled through. All the old stones had been moved elsewhere. Blocks of light-coloured granite and dark basalt rock formed a continuous encircling wall the height of twenty paces: a protective arm surrounding the entrance itself.

Three towers of black basalt rose above the main structure; from the platforms the dwarves could overlook the length of the steep winding path and could see probably a hundred miles in the other direction into the kingdom of Gauragar. The banner of the fifthlings—a circle of vraccasium chain-links to represent the work of the goldsmiths and the unity of the people—was flying from the flagpole to show who was on guard.

Tungdil felt moisture on his face. Turning his head he looked over at the nearby waterfall, still crashing and thundering as it had five cycles ago. The white cascade with its clouds of vapour sparkled and shimmered like crystal in the spring sunshine. All in all, the view was spectacular.

The pony Keen-Ears snorted, looking for grazing at the foot of the forbidding fortress, but found nothing to his liking on the bare rock. He pawed the ground impatiently.

"I know. You're hungry. They'll let us in soon." Tungdil did not get a chance to stand around admiring the skill of the secondling stone masons in the construction of this impressive building.

Tall as a house, the two doors of the great portal opened slowly. Iron plating had been fixed to the outside of the gate to withstand attacks with battering rams and other siege engines.

A dwarf came out, his helmet sparkling like diamonds. Tungdil knew who wore elaborate headgear like that. The high king, Gandogar Silverbeard of the Clan of the Silver Beards of the fourthling folk, had come out in person and was hastening forward to welcome him.

"King Gandogar." Tungdil fell on one knee and reached for the ax called Keenfire to proffer to the king in the time-honored dwarven greeting. This was the silent renewal of the vow, pledging one's life for the sake of all dwarves and for Girdlegard.

Gandogar stopped him with a gesture. "No, Tungdil Goldhand. Do not kneel to me. Let me shake your hand. You are our greatest hero. Your deeds are beyond measure. It should be I who—"

Tungdil rose to his feet, grasping the king's hand and interrupting the flow of praise. As he and the high king shook hands, Tungdil's rusty chain mail grated.

Gandogar concealed his sense of shock as best he could. Tungdil was looking old, older than he really was. The brown eyes were dull, as if all simple joy of life were lost. His face was swollen, beard and hair matted and unkempt. The change in him could not all be from the long journey. "It should be I who kneel before you," he finished.

"Don't praise me so much," smiled Tungdil. "You are embarrassing me." The one-time rivals had become friends.

"Let us go in so you can see with your own eyes what the best of the firstlings, secondlings and fourthlings have achieved." Gandogar hoped that his surprise at Tungdil's state had not been too obvious, as he gestured toward the entrance. "After you, Tungdil."

"And the thirdlings, king? What have they contributed?" asked Tungdil as he untied his pony to lead behind him.

"Apart from your own contribution, you who made everything possible?" returned Gandogar. It was not easy for him to see in Tungdil the dwarf of five sun cycles ago. If a child of the Smith ever let his chain mail rust it was a bad sign. There would be a chance later on to speak of that. Not now. He took off his helmet, revealing his long dark brown hair. "The thirdlings do what they do best: training us in warfare. And they are unbelievable at it." He smiled. "Come. We have a surprise for you."

They strode through the gate.

On the other side a rousing reception awaited him, with dwarves of all ages lining the way into the mountain, their laughing faces aglow. They were celebrating his visit, honoring him, applauding. There were musicians in the crowd and up on the towers and the walls. Flutes and crumhorns sounded out and the rhythm was given by the dwarves beating on their shields. The enthusiasm was palpable; it was all in his honor, and the crowd's welcome flowed round him like liquid gold.

"Word got round quickly that you were on your way," grinned Gandogar. He was pleased at the success of the surprise welcome. "They've been longing to see their great hero."

"By Vraccas!" Tungdil was so moved by the reception

that his throat went dry. "Anyone would think I was returning in victory from a great battle." His gaze swept over the crowd, noting the laughing faces of men, women and children who had turned out eagerly to meet him. And they had come despite his five-cycle absence away in the vaults of his foster-father. On the other hand, for a dwarf five solar cycles were not long.

He waved at them all, responding to their hearty welcome as he strode at the high king's side through their ranks. "My thanks," he called joyfully. "Thanks to you all."

The applause swelled and he heard his name shouted.

He could easily have been running the gauntlet of their disapproval, it struck him. For his wife Balyndis was once married to Glaïmbar Sharpax from the Iron Beater clan of Borengar's people: the same man who now held no less a title than ruler of all the fifthlings.

Meeting Glaïmbar would be the biggest challenge. The people of the Gray Range had seemingly forgiven him for being with Balyndis now, but did there have to be so many of them? He smiled at them bravely and breathed a sigh of relief when safely within the enormous corridor that led inside the mountain.

Gandogar stopped at the entrance; he noticed that Tungdil's joy was not unmixed. "Are you all right?"

The dwarf did not answer at first. "It's strange. On the one hand my heart sings like sounding iron smitten on the smith's anvil. But on the other . . ." He broke off, fell silent, then cleared his throat. "I think it's just that I am not used to having so many dwarves around me all at once, Gandogar." He smiled, lifting his hand in excuse. "Normally it's just the one dwarf, my wife."

"I understand. In part," responded Gandogar. "How you can live so isolated, far from any company—that's a mystery to me. All those strangers around one can be frightening." He winked. "I know what it is like. My wife's clan is enormous. I'm always terrified of their family visits."

Tungdil laughed. Meanwhile one of the dwarves had taken the reins of his loyal pony, promising the best of grooming and care. Tungdil and the high king progressed through the corridors, passages and rooms; the music and the sounds of rejoicing from the crowds grew quieter now.

Tungdil recalled . . . Here he and his comrades had encountered nothing but dust and rubbish. After the defeat of the fifthlings, Tion's monsters had ruled in these mountains for hundreds of cycles.

But now it was over. Delegations of all the dwarf folk had come and brought new life after the victory. The Gray Range pulsated; Tungdil could hear children's laughter. What pain he felt at that sound.

"We haven't been content merely to make good the damage to the stonework on the walls and in the rooms," he heard a man's voice in the adjacent passageway. A dwarf came out with his retinue. "We have created new halls. New halls for the children growing up in the light of the sun that rises up over the Dragon's Tongue, the Great Blade and the other mountain peaks."

Tungdil recognized the impressive figure and the characteristic voice at once; he would have preferred not to meet this dwarf until later on. "Greetings, King Glaïmbar Sharpax," he said, bowing. He was surprised to see a female dwarf in an embroidered brown robe standing behind the ruler, a newborn baby on her arm. "May I congratulate you on the birth of your child?"

Glaïmbar, taller and more solid in stature than Gandogar, ran a hand over his luxuriant black beard. "My thanks, Tungdil Goldhand, and welcome to my kingdom." He pointed to the baby. "These are the true fifthlings. The rest of us will keep their kingdom safe until they are old enough to defend it for themselves." He held out his hand; the metal plates on his elaborate armor clinked as he moved. "I can see the concern in your eyes, Tungdil. We shall let bygones be bygones. My heart has found another and I harbor no grudge, neither against you nor against Balyndis. Tell her so when you return."

In spite of the many adventures he had experienced in his short life, and the many lucky escapes from perilous situations, Tungdil had seldom felt so strong a sense of relief as now. He grasped the king's hand in both his own, shaking it so vigorously that Gandogar restrained him. "Stop, my friend. Glaïmbar will need that arm again," he laughed indulgently; he knew the history these two shared.

A swift glance at Glaïmbar's face showed Gandogar that the king of the fifthlings was also taken aback by the lack of care in Tungdil's appearance. This was not how a hero should look, even if he had withdrawn from society and lived away from them all for such a long time.

"Sadly, I don't need my arms for fighting anymore," added Glaïmbar after a pause. "It has grown quiet on the Northern Pass."

"Be content, King Glaïmbar," said Tungdil. He felt as if a leaden weight had been lifted from his shoulders. Following on from the rapturous welcome he'd been met with, here were words of forgiveness from a former rival; two of his greatest fears were resolved. But still he warned himself not to be too trusting. Until he saw deeds to back up the words of reconciliation, he must remain on his guard. "Your arms will soon be tired from rocking the child."

"Come. I will show you the new treasures of our flourishing dwarf kingdom." Gandogar, Glaïmbar and Tungdil walked away together to explore the fortress.

Each dwarven folk had contributed the finest of its handiwork and skills. The secondling stonemasons had executed immaculate repairs and excavated new accommodation quarters and halls, forming pillars and bridges of stone with an accuracy that beggared belief.

The smithies of the firstlings had supplied decorative strengthening girders, fretted screens, metal furniture and fencing, lamps and other articles.

The fourthlings brought the arts of their colleagues to perfection by studding them with precious stones, polished for sparkle.

Together with artistic murals in gold and vraccasium and other precious metals from the devastated remains of the vanquished fifthling realm, the new occupants had created the finest of dwarf kingdoms. Here, all the best had been brought together.

Glaïmbar enjoyed the admiration he saw in the eyes of his high-ranking guests. "You see how the whole of the Gray Range territories have become a center of excellence. And the cream of the thirdling warriors are training us in new methods of combat, so we may better protect our wealth and the land of Girdlegard," he concluded as they completed their tour and made for the assembly hall.

Tungdil remembered this unusual room clearly; it was constructed like a theatre with a circular floor area, twenty paces across. The walls had a broad ledge at waist height—about four paces wide—then continued in the vertical plane.

Here was the place he had made the proposal that Glaïmbar should be crowned king. Here it was he had renounced his own claim. *What would have happened if I had been king of the fifthlings?* he wondered, gazing at the empty rows. *Would things have turned out better, or worse?*

There was to be no voting in the chamber today. Instead, the clan leaders were waiting to feast with them. They were all sitting in the center of the first level at a long table that seemed to bear every dish the dwarven cuisines could offer.

When the three stepped into the room, conversations ebbed away and all those present got to their feet. Knees were bent in homage, swords held aloft, heads bowed. It was the silent pledge, a promise to give life and limb for the high king. "Rise and eat," spoke Gandogar, taking his place at the end of the table. "Let us enjoy our meal. I am hungry from our walk. Thirsty, too. Let us talk later." Tungdil sat at his left side, Glaïmbar at his right. The meal began and the musicians struck up.

Tungdil partook of the feast with delight, his palate enchanted by the variety of tastes: spiced root jelly, roast goat meat, kimpa mushrooms, sour cheese with herbs, and steaming hot dumplings made of root flour. The feast was such a contrast to the simple fare of his life in the mines—neither he nor Balyndis were accomplished cooks—the other thing was that he liked the food of humans, but she preferred a more traditional diet. The compromises usually tasted rather disappointing.

He wiped his fingers on his dirty beard. So enthusiastically was he attacking his food that he missed the horrified glances of the clan leaders. They were disturbed at his lack of grooming.

Gandogar passed him a tankard of beer. "Here, taste this. You don't have stuff like that back home, do you?"

It won't have been meant unkindly, but it made its mark through the wafer-thin mental armor. His expression clouded over. "I am content with what I have." He took a helping of the roast, sinking his teeth into the goat flesh; brownish-red gravy dripped through his matted beard as if it were blood trickling down. His abrupt movements were at odds with his words.

"Do you have any children yet?" asked Glaïmbar, not knowing that this was another sensitive area. "Who knows when we will need the next heroes, and if your children—"

Tungdil threw down the piece of meat, wiped his mouth on the sleeve of his mail shirt and gulped down his beer. Then he motioned to a dwarf standing by to bring him more. "Please, tell me why you have summoned me, King Gandogar," he said, changing the subject so emphatically that even the simplest of minds got the point.

Glaïmbar and the high king exchanged looks. "As I said before, it is all very quiet now, Tungdil," said the king, continuing to eat. "This makes me uneasy."

"Rightly so," agreed the other. "For a whole cycle now we've been seeing a lot of orc activity in the Brown Ranges;

they're all surging over the pass as if the forces of goodness were pursuing them." He was served dessert. "But at the Stone Gate it's as quiet as the grave."

"These last four cycles we could have safely left the gates open and nothing would have happened," added Glaïmbar.

Tungdil recognized the pudding at once and took some. It was a light sweet cream that he'd had before, back with the freelings of Trovegold—in the house of the dwarf Myr, who had betrayed him and paid for it with her life. The woman he had loved.

The choice of dessert was a mistake. The first spoonful brought back the bitter-tasting memories that wrecked his appetite. He reached for the beer again.

"That is strange indeed," he grunted rather than said. He cleared his throat and swallowed down the images of the past. A lot of beer would be needed to keep those pictures in their place. "Have you sent out scouts?"

"No," answered Glaïmbar. "We didn't want to waken any sleeping ogres until we had completed and extended our defenses."

"That's why you are here. We thought of sending out a small party and we thought of you, Tungdil Goldhand, to lead it." Gandogar took over. "You've been to the Outer Lands, I hear." He pointed to the hero's ax, resting next to his chair. "You have the ax Keenfire to overcome all adversaries. You are the best choice for such an undertaking."

Tungdil pushed his full plate away and asked for a third tankard of beer. He was stilling his hunger with the barley now. As so often in the recent past. "Yes, Your Majesty.

I have been to the Outer Lands. I stayed about the length of an orbit. It was foggy; I lost three men to the orcs and in one of the caves I discovered a rune that I couldn't decipher. It wasn't worth going." He poured the beer down his throat, clanged the tankard down and suppressed a belch. "You must admit, it's not a lot of experience."

"Nevertheless, we need to find out what's happening there." The high king did not sound as if he would accept a refusal on Tungdil's part, not even an implied one. "I want you to set off tomorrow for the Stone Gate. You'll take a group of our best warriors with you to the Outer Lands, and you'll see what's what."

Tungdil had started on the fourth tankard, but put it back down on the table. "It'll be foggy, king, that's what. You know what fog is like. How many shades of gray do you want me to describe when I get back?"

"Hang on, Goldhand," warned Glaïmbar, delicately eating his dessert. "You may have to offer the high king an apology if you see hordes of monsters assembling there to attack us."

Tungdil turned back to his beer and then looked at Glaïmbar. So he was keen to send him to the Outer Lands, was he? Perhaps the mooted reconciliation hadn't been so genuine, after all? He was ashamed of harboring this uncharitable thought. He was as suspicious as a gnome.

Cursing, he put down his beer. "Excuse my surly tone, King Gandogar," he said quietly. "Of course I will go to the Northern Pass." Turning to Glaïmbar, "I'll be happy to encounter Tion's creatures. And if I die in battle, I don't care! Because . . ." He pressed his lips together. "Forgive me. I am too tired to be good company." He got up, bowed to the two rulers, grabbed the tankard and left the dining hall.

The dwarves all followed him with their eyes, chewing their food in silence. No one spoke. No one wanted to voice the growing doubts about their hero.

Gandogar regarded Tungdil's uneaten food with concern. "Something has changed him."

"Changed him?" echoed Glaïmbar. "I'm sure it's to do with Balyndis."

"He will find someone at the Stone Gate he can talk to about it. Someone that's closer to him than we are." Gandogar took a mouthful of beer, while Glaïmbar stared at him.

"*He* is coming?"

"No," the king's answer rang hollow in the tankard. Gandogar blinked over the rim, set the tankard down, swirled the remaining liquid round the sides to clear the froth and downed the rest of the beer in one. "He is already here, my good Glaïmbar."

Girdlegard,
In the Red Mountains on the Eastern Border of the
Firstling Kingdom
Spring, 6241st Solar Cycle

Fidelgar Strikefast, a well-built dwarf with a bright yellow beard, sat down, took the small metal box out of his ruck-sack and placed it in front of him on the stone table. He had completed his first round and was granting himself a rest in the extensive cavern whose high roof rested on

stone pillars. In the old days there had been wagons
running here on the rails, but in recent cycles there had
been little call for them. His task was to check out the
passages, and they were all long.

Baigar Fourhand, working away with a hammer and a
hook at an upturned wagon, turned to look at him. He
had draped the braids of his brown beard over his shoulder
to keep them out of the way of the red-hot forge. Next
to him there was a portable smithy as used by traveling
craftsmen. It was large enough to let him carry out minor
repairs. "Everything nice and quiet?" he asked and looked
at the box with curiosity.

"Now that I've killed four orcs and wiped out a troll,
yes," he joked, taking out two beakers and a flask engraved
with the sign for gold. "No, it's all quiet."

Now Baigar put his tools on one side and nosed his
way forward. "What have you got there?"

"A Trovegold novelty." Fidelgar stroked the edges of
the little box, opened the clasps and lifted the lid with
care. The smell of spices and brandy wafted out. Baigar
saw some brown objects inside that were about the size
and shape of a finger. "Smoke rolls."

"From Trovegold? The city where the freelings live?"

"Exactly. One of their traders passed through. I just
had to buy some." He took a smoke roll out and held it
out to Baigar. "Rolled tobacco leaves stored in spices. Or
maybe they put the spices in."

As Baigar sniffed at the smoke roll his beard braids slid
back down over his chest. "So you cut a bit off and stick
it in your pipe?"

"No. You don't need a pipe. The freelings have thought

up something to save time." Fidelgar stood up, went over to the forge and used the tongs to extract a red-hot coal. He put one end of the smoke roll in his mouth and held the other end to the glowing coal. There was a hissing sound as the tobacco caught. "Then you drag on it like with a pipe," he explained indistinctly. Several quick puffs and he was closing his eyes in pleasure. It smelled good, like vanilla and honey and some other aromas he could not name.

"That looks like a great idea." Baigar took a roll out and copied what the other dwarf had done. The smoke was stronger-tasting, and hotter, than what he was used to from his pipe. And the effect was more powerful. His head was spinning. "I would never have thought that trading with the freelings would bring us so many advantages." He waved the glowing smoke roll in the air. "And I don't just mean this thing here. What about gugul meat? And then their herbs are really useful, I'm told."

Fidelgar moved his smoke roll to the side of his mouth and opened the flask, pouring a clear liquid into the two beakers. "And they have this Trovegold goldwater. It's a liquor with flakes of gold in it." He nodded encouragingly. "Tastes great."

"Flakes of gold? In liquor?" Baigar sipped at it, trying out the thin flakes on his tongue. "Tastes like . . ." He smacked his lips as he searched for the right word. "Gold . . . Nothing else can describe that exquisite taste." He gave a contented sigh. "Incredible. I can feel it coursing through me; the tiredness is disappearing and my mood is lifting. Seems like a miracle cure."

"The gold or the alcohol?" Fidelgar grinned. "They can adapt the taste according to which spirits you have and what type of gold you use. You can't get nearer to gold than that, now can you?" He took another mouthful of it and pulled on the smoke roll again. He took a look around. "Incredible how peaceful everything is."

Baigar puffed away and tried making smoke rings. "Sure about that? No rock gnomes?"

"Would I be sitting here smoking?" Fidelgar glanced at the broken wagon Baigar had been working at. "Why bother mending the cars if we don't use the tunnels anymore?"

"You never know," replied Baigar. "And anyway, we do use them. We send out the building squads in them to do repairs. And why do you do your guard rounds if there are no monsters left in Girdlegard?"

"Because you never know," laughed Fidelgar. He pointed to the four tunnels the rails ran into. "It's a shame. Just when our dwarf folks are united, these underground networks are still lying useless. Curse that earthquake the Judgment Star caused."

"Never fear. Vraccas is on our side." Baigar shook his head. "We're getting round to mending the main tracks. Just yesterday one of the gangs managed to clear a good half-mile of tunnel." He sighed. "The rubble is just the half of it. It's an enormous job renewing the rails that were damaged in the rockfalls. Some of the rails have to be forged new on site." He pointed over to the wagon. "If you have rails that are bent like that then the axles get out of shape. That's happening all the time when the work squads use them. All means more work for me."

"Those were the days when you could travel from one dwarf kingdom to another in the blink of an eye," enthused

Fidelgar, sending up a perfect smoke ring. He apparently had had a lot more practice at this than Baigar. "The cars would fly along the rails and the wind would whistle in your hair and beard and tickle your stomach."

"So you travelled that way?" asked the astonished Baigar.

"Yes, I was there when Queen Xamtys II left for the secondling kingdom and we fought Nôd'onn's hordes. That was a battle!" He blew at the glowing tip of the smoke roll so that the tobacco would not go out. "I can see it as if it were yesterday, how we—"

Baigar raised his hand abruptly. "Hush!" He listened at the black tunnel entrances. "Thought I heard something." He removed his smoke roll and put it on the stone table.

"Could be. The work gang must still be out and—"

They heard a terrible scream coming from the furthest left of the four tunnels.

Fidelgar recognized the sound of death. A dwarf had that moment died. Then came the second scream, followed by cries of panic. "Come with me!" He jammed the smoke roll in the side of his mouth. It had been expensive and he did not want to let it go to waste. Hastily he grabbed his shield and ax and strode over to the tunnels.

Baigar took up his bag of tools and two flaming torches and ran after Fidelgar. In the old days he would have immediately thought of an orc attack, but now he assumed there must have been an accident.

They both ran into the straight passageway meant to let the wagons brake safely before reaching the halls at the end of their journey.

The shouts were getting nearer, and the rattlings and clankings of machinery could be heard. It sounded to Baigar like winding gear running, cogwheels spinning and then the dwarves' stone-mill grinding. But he had never heard all those sounds at the same time before now.

Ahead they discerned a glow of light, in the middle of which a monstrous creature was rearing up, completely blocking the tunnel. It was whirling its many shining claws and bronze-coloured arms, while the dwarves of the work gang were desperately attempting to hold it back. But their picks had not the slightest effect on the skin of this monster, and the handles broke like matchwood.

Every time a claw hit home there was a bloodcurdling scream from the victim. Dwarves flew through the air to lie motionless on the passage floor.

"Vraccas, help us! What on earth is this?" Horrified, Fidelgar had to watch as a hideous claw penetrated one dwarf, exiting on the other side of his body; then the arm was withdrawn, pulling the quivering prey close enough to reach with another set of claws. The living dwarf was quartered as he lay and torn to shreds.

Only one of the work squad was still alive, and badly injured, lying groaning on the ground, trying to crawl to safety. Meanwhile the monster made its way forward.

"We must help him," said Baigar, running to the injured dwarf. Fidelgar had no hesitation in following.

As the pair approached the monster they realized their error. This was not some creature of flesh and blood but a diamond-shaped thing advancing, point foremost.

Its skin was a covering of riveted armour plating. The

arms, a good two paces in length, were made of metal, too, ending in blades and toothed claws, which were grabbing and snapping shut randomly. They could not see the monster's means of locomotion. Below, there was a metal skirt protecting the mechanism from attack.

"This is not a living beast," cried Baigar in horror, staring at the victims' blood that dripped from the claws and coated the metal surfaces. He could make out runes on the plating, and their meaning sent shudders through him. He needed to get out alive to report to his queen.

"Mind out!" Fidelgar pulled him back by the sleeve, so that a grabbing claw missed him by a beard-hair's breadth. He stumbled backwards. "We need to get out. Here, take hold." The two dwarves lifted the injured man up and helped him along.

The thing hissed and covered them with a cloud of steam that stank of oil, making breathing impossible. Coughing and spluttering, they dragged their comrade back with them away from the machine come alive that was following them.

The beast had no intention of giving up, but thrust its bloody claws into the heavy repair vehicle that carried the tools and the portable forge, simply pushing it backwards along the rails.

"Stop it!" called Fidelgar, jumping into the wagon and pulling hard on the brake. At once the advance of their unearthly opponent was slowed but the wagon was still moving relentlessly on. The strength of the thing was enormous.

"That should give us enough of a start," said Fidelgar and he hopped out of the wagon on his way back to

Baigar and the injured dwarf. They hurried along the tunnel as fast as they could with their burden.

When they had reached the open hall, Baigar prepared to leave them. Fidelgar handed him his smoke roll. "I'll maneuver another wagon into the tunnel," he explained breathlessly. "Get him to a healer as quickly as you can and alert more of the guards." He made one of the wagons fast with an iron hook attached to a chain that they used for the giant pulley. Because it would take too long to start the steam engine that normally dealt with the heavy lifting, he had to rely on the strength of his own muscles. He used the emergency winding gear; the chain clanked slowly into place and took up the slack.

"Tell them to bring long iron rods," he called after Fidelgar.

The guard dragged the wounded dwarf out. "What shall I say when they ask what sort of monster it is?"

"Tell them it is a new fiendish device of the thirdlings' design," answered Baigar.

Fidelgar could not believe it. "How can that—"

"I saw dwarf runes on the armour plating." Baigar was sweating heavily from the exertion and just managed to lift the wagon with the help of a pulley. "*Beaten but not destroyed, we bring destruction,*" he quoted through gritted teeth. "It can only be the thirdlings. Tell the queen this for me if I should die." The muscles of his arms and upper body swelled and flexed as he pushed the heavy wagon over to the rails.

In the nick of time. Hissing sounded out of the passage and a white cloud flew out through the mouth of the tunnel, signaling the murderous monster's approach.

"Off you go!" yelled Baigar. "I don't know how long it can be held back!" He made ready to let the wagon down.

"Vraccas protect you!" Fidelgar nodded, took the wounded dwarf over his shoulder and ran off.

He had never moved faster in his life and for the first time it struck him that the vast extent of the dwarf kingdoms was not an advantage. He shouted out to attract attention. The other dwarves left their work and rushed to arm themselves, so that he had soon collected fifty warriors about him. He left the wounded dwarf in someone's care and then hastened back to the hall with his companions.

Yet they arrived too late.

The wagons lay overturned on the rails blocking the tunnel mouth diagonally like a barricade. They had prevented the monster from passing into the hall and thus into the firstling kingdom.

But they could not find the courageous Baigar—only part of his leg, a scrap of his jerkin and the blood-soaked smoke roll. It was impossible to make out where the rest of him was amongst the remains of the other dwarf corpses, in scattered heaps against the walls and piled up to the roof.

Fidelgar looked back along the tunnel but could see no sign of the monster.

Their new enemy had retreated and must be waiting in one of the passages, ready to attack. The thirdlings had declared war on their brothers and sisters again after an armistice that had lasted five cycles. He would inform the queen of this himself, as Baigar had asked.

Girdlegard,
The Gray Range on the Northern Border of the
Fifthling Kingdom,
Spring, 6241st Solar Cycle

Tungdil set out on his way through Glaïmbar's kingdom toward the Stone Gateway, on the same road as before, when he had travelled with Balyndis and Boïndil.

The beauty of the landscape distracted him from his usual worries, and from the discontent that had insinuated itself into his mind. But not from the pain which waited in some corner of his brain ready to pounce like a vicious animal; all too often it emerged, fixing its cruel claws into the most vulnerable part of his being, into his very soul. Ever since that fateful day the two had been his constant companions: discontent and pain.

The slight distraction that let him forget momentarily was shattered when his ear caught the sound of a child's carefree laughter. It cut through his heart and tore at his soul so that it bled afresh until Tungdil stilled the bleeding with alcohol. But beer was too fluid a bung to stop the loss and it had to be constantly topped up. That was how habits started.

Swaying slightly, Tungdil reached the great gate with its two huge doors that only once had been breached by treachery. Apart from that one time the doors had withstood all monster attacks for thousands of cycles.

And that was how it would be again. The damage had been repaired by the stonemasons; the five bolts were in place, only to be moved when the secret password was spoken.

"If you had only one eye and were singing I'd take you for Bavragor Hammerfist," bawled a voice behind him, jolting him out of his reverie.

"One dead man speaks about another?" he replied, whirling round too quickly for his own feet. Two strong arms held him fast to save him from falling.

"Well, Scholar, does a dead man look like this?"

Tungdil took in every detail of the muscular, stocky build. The dwarf's long black hair had been shaved away at the sides of his head and a plait hung down his back; the beard of the same colour reached to the buckle of his belt. Chain mail shirt, jerkin, boots and helmet completed the warrior look. A hooked crow's beak war hammer with a spur as long as a forearm was propped next to him on the rock, handle against his hip.

"Boïndil?" he whispered incredulously. "Boïndil Doubleblade!" he called out in delight, pulling his friend toward him. They had not seen each other for five long cycles. He was not ashamed of his tears, and the loud snuffles by his ear told him that even the other veteran fighter was not holding back his feelings.

"At the grave of my brother Boëndal at the High Gate— that was the last time we met." Boïndil was crying with joy.

"Then too we wept in each other's arms," said Tungdil, clapping him on the back. "Boïndil! How I've missed you!" He released the friend with whom he had shared bold adventures; they had gone through so much together—good things and bad, sadness and wonder.

The warrior twin wiped away the tears that were coursing down his beard like drops running off a bird's plumage. "I keep oiling the beard, you know," he said, grinning. "Scholar, I have missed you." Tungdil looked for signs of the furious madness that slept within the dwarf and sometimes escaped to the surface. But the brown gaze was friendly and warm with no trace of wildness. "Death changes the living, too, you told me once." He patted Tungdil's chain shirt. "But if you go on like this when you're alive, the change will be your death," he teased. "Does Balyndis brew you such good beer?"

"Our beer is bought from traders, and it's nowhere near as good as the dwarf beer. Same effect, though, and a worse hangover the next day." Tungdil did not take offence at the remarks about the size of his belly.

But his friend's thick eyebrows were raised in remonstration. "In other words, you've turned into a drinker, like Bavragor," he summed up. He noted the strong smell of sweat, the matted hair and the face, old before its time. "You have let yourself go, my fat hero. What has happened?"

"We haven't seen each other for over five cycles and you're preaching a sermon," complained Tungdil. "Why don't you tell me what's brought you here to the High Gate?" He looked around and saw all the fighting men, arrayed in ranks behind them, ready to practice their combat techniques.

"Nothing has driven me here. I no longer lust after battle and the fire in my blood has lessened. It was the Great King himself who asked me to go with you. Somebody's got to look after you, after all." He touched the handle of his crow's beak. "And somebody must see that my brother's memory is honored. The hammer spur wants to fight, even if I don't. It is burning to sink itself into a snout-face's belly."

A thirdling was running up and down in front of the ranks of warriors; the black tattoos on his face told of his origins and of the skilled profession he followed. A few cycles earlier this thirdling and these very dwarves he now commanded had faced each other as opponents on the field of battle. That boundless hatred was no longer around. Not everywhere.

Boïndil followed his gaze. "I'm still amazed," he admitted. "Apart from a few exceptions," he laid his hand on his friend's shoulder, "I really can't stand thirdlings. I can't forget that some of them vowed to destroy us, to annihilate us. I am afraid of their deviousness."

"Yes. But there's only a handful of them now, not a whole tribe any more like in Lorimbas's day. The misguided ones will die out," pronounced Tungdil confidently. "Are these my men?" He walked over to the group, his friend following him.

The thirdling noticed them approaching. "Greetings, Tungdil Goldhand and Boïndil Doubleblade," he said, bowing. "I am Manon Hardfoot of the Death Ax clan. Here are the two dozen warriors I have trained for the excursion into the Outer Lands." His brown eyes displayed conviction. "They are afraid of nothing."

Boïndil gave a friendly laugh, "Believe me, Manon, there is always something that can make a warrior afraid. Which is not saying that it cannot be overcome."

Manon grinned in challenge. "Then my troops will show you that there are dwarves without fear."

"We won't find anything except rubble and stones," replied Tungdil calmly. "When can we set off?"

"As soon as you want," Manon responded.

"Tomorrow, then, at daybreak," Tungdil decided, walking over to the tower. He climbed up to the top and went out onto the ramparts above the gate. Boïndil remained at his side.

Together they contemplated the Outer Lands bathed in the clear light of late afternoon. In front of the gate was the abandoned plain from whence in past times monsters and other fiendish creatures had regularly launched their onslaughts on these walls.

"It's hard to believe they've given up their attacks," said Tungdil quietly. He relished the feel of the cold wind clearing his head from the last effects of the beer. The air was icy sharp and pure: no trace of monsters here. "Only these ancient mountains can still remember how the armies of Tion's accursed followers advanced on us in relentless assaults."

"It will have been the Star of Judgment," supposed his friend. "It didn't merely eradicate evil in Girdlegard, but beyond the mountain boundaries as well." He gave a sigh. "Imagine it, Scholar. Peace." The tone of his voice revealed that he did not dare to believe it wholeheartedly.

"I remember that day." The magic wave of light that had rolled over Girdlegard, summoned by the eoîl, had burned all the evil to ashes and captured its energy in the form of a diamond. Anyone possessing this artifact and able to use its magic powers would be the most powerful being ever in existence. For safety's sake the dwarves had made meticulously crafted copies and sent them out to the various dwarf kingdoms; Tungdil held such a stone himself, not knowing if it were real or false. One of the stones had got lost. He asked Boïndil about it.

"It remains a mystery. The stone destined for Queen Isika of Rân Ribastur disappeared completely. To this very day no one has found the messenger or the escort sent to protect the diamond. The stone itself never turned up." He looked up at the cloud-hung summit of the Dragon's Tongue; no artist could have rendered the beauty of the mountain slopes as they reflected the setting sun. Shadows were lengthening and the breeze grew icier with each breath. "All investigations were fruitless."

"That was five whole cycles ago," reflected Tungdil, shivering. "Have attempts been made on any of the other stones?"

"Not as far as I know," said Boïndil. He shook his head. The long plait of black hair swayed like a rope down his back. "Girdlegard has neither magus nor maga now, so there is none that could ever use the power."

"Except for the handful of initiates serving the traitor Nôd'onn," Tungdil corrected him.

"They have no powers. The eoîl dried up the magic source, they say. Where would the famuli draw their strength? And they did not even complete their training. What can they achieve, Scholar?"

Tungdil did not trouble to reply. When growing up, he had been through the school of the magus Lot-Ionan; he was familiar with the power of magic. But since nothing untoward had occurred for such a long time, he was prepared to share his friend's optimism. There could be too much dwelling on dark thoughts. It wasn't good for you. "Let's go down. Spring is a long time coming here at the Northern Pass." He took a last look at the majestic ridges where the wind was blowing the snow from the rocks in long white banners. "I could do with a warm beer with mead." They went down the steps.

"How is Balyndis?" enquired Boïndil as they left the tower to go to the tunnels. "Girdlegard's best smith?"

"She's in mourning," said Tungdil bitterly. And his response was so adamant that the warrior did not dare to repeat his question. Not yet. In silence they walked over side by side to find their quarters for the night.

"Psst! Tungdil Goldhand!" came a whisper through the crack of an open door. "Have you got a minute?"

Boïndil wrinkled his brow. "What's all the secrecy for?" He pushed open the door, one hand on the crow's beak hammer he carried. "Show yourself, if your intentions are honest!" A woman yelped in fright; she had not seen the dwarf-twin approach. "You can come in, Scholar. She is harmless," he said over his shoulder.

Tungdil stepped past him and entered the room where a female dwarf was standing. She was wearing simple clothing and must have seen all of three hundred cycles in her time. "What do you want?"

She bent her gray head in greeting. "Forgive me for addressing you, but . . . Is it true what I've heard? That you are going to the Outer Lands?"

"It is no secret."

"I am Saphira Ironbite." She hesitated and cast her eyes down. "May I request a favor?"

"You want him to bring you a souvenir?" mocked the dwarf-twin.

"Bring me my son, if you find him," she blurted out, grasping Tungdil's hand in desperation. "I beg you, look out for him! His name is Gremdulin Ironbite of the Iron Biters clan. He is of your height and wears a helmet with a golden moon on the front . . ."

"I thought no scouts had gone out?" Tungdil's curiosity was roused. He was skeptical now. He would not have been surprised if Glaïmbar were sending him into a trap, perhaps from delayed revenge for his having carried Balyndis off so far away from all the dwarven customs.

"He was not a scout, he was a guard at the gate," she responded quietly, fighting with her emotions. "His friends told me he heard a suspicious noise and went off to investigate."

"At the gate itself?" Boïndil broke in.

"No, the noise had come from above. A loose stone rolling or something." There were tears in her eyes. "That's the last they saw of him."

Tungdil was touched, but not unduly affected. He did not even know the dwarf they were talking of. "When was this?"

"Half a sun cycle ago," she sobbed. "Tion's monsters have him, I am sure. Tungdil Goldhand, if any dwarf can free him, it is you." She kissed his hand. "I beg you, for the sake of Vraccas. Save him if you can." She wept, sinking down on her knees at his feet.

Boïndil regretted his harsh words, so swiftly spoken. He had wrongly assumed she was approaching his friend with some trivial request. "We shall keep our eyes peeled, good Saphira. Forgive me."

Tungdil helped her up. "Don't kneel to me. There is no

need to beg for help. I will do what any dwarf would do."

She smiled at him and wiped the tears from her wrinkled cheeks. "May Vraccas bless you, Tungdil Goldhand." She drew a golden amulet from her pocket and hung it round his neck. "This belongs to my son. He will know that I have sent you. And if you cannot find him, keep it still, for having tried. He would be proud to know a hero was wearing it."

The pendant showed a silver moon in front of golden mountains. "I thank you. How is it that the king did not send to search for your son?"

Fire sparked in her eyes. "He had them searching half a cycle long. They found his shield up by a deep ravine and they presumed that he had fallen there."

"What makes you so sure that this is not the case?" Boïndil stared at her. "Not, of course, that I wish him dead."

"A mother feels it when her own child dies." She gave a faint smile. "He is not dead. I know he lives and is in need of help."

Tungdil gave a start when he heard her words, as if pierced by an älfar arrow. He turned away. "Trust her feeling," was all he said to Boïndil. Then he left the chamber, turning once more at the doorway. "We shall bring you back your son. Dead or alive."

Next morning the small band left the safety of the dwarf lands and marched to the Northern Pass, where biting winds awaited. The icy gusts sang many-voiced along the edges of the cliffs. Tungdil wondered if the wind was mocking them or issuing a warning.

"The wind is good. It will blow away the mist," said Boïndil, muttering into the scarf he had wrapped around his face. He peered out, even if it felt as if his eyes might turn to balls of ice in the cold.

"Out here it will," corrected Tungdil. "As soon as we reach the tunnels we'll meet the wretched fog. I'm sure of it." He fell silent for a while and looked up at the walls. "I wonder what the monsters want with Gremdulin."

"They'll want the password from him," Boïndil guessed. "The snout-faces are getting cleverer. But it won't help them. Only the king and two of his closest men know the words that will unlock the bolts."

"They are welcome to that." Tungdil pointed to the cliffs. "Can you think of a creature that doesn't fly and still can survive on rocks like that? And if it's orcs, why didn't more of them climb up along there, take over the ramparts and let down ropes for the others?" His brown gaze swept searching over the grass that bore patches of snow in places. "Boïndil, something's not right here."

"A new adventure, Scholar," grinned Boïndil. "Like the old days."

"No," replied Tungdil, shaking his head. Then he took a mouthful of brandy from his leather flask. "Not like the old days. It will never be like the old days. Too many of our comrades have died." Hastening his pace, he took over the head of the contingent.

"Was Tungdil Goldhand always . . . like that?" asked Manon cautiously. He had moved up to march at Boïndil's side.

"What do you mean?" thundered the dwarf-twin.

"Don't get me wrong. He will be a good leader for us,

but . . . the men are surprised at him. We have heard tales of his deeds. We had heard of his appearance." He looked over at Tungdil carefully. It was hard for him to voice the concerns his troops had spoken of. "The way he looks—it's not like the hero they imagined. And there are rumors going round about the way he behaved at the high king's feast. They say he is drunk all the time." Manon let his gaze fall. "My men think these rumors are not unfounded."

They are not alone in that, thought Boïndil to himself. "Call them to order," he growled. "They shouldn't be spreading gossip like washerwomen. You will soon see that Tungdil is a hero still." He could only hope his words were true. Silently he wished for strength for his friend, so that he could again be the dwarf he once had been. A dwarf like Vraccas had intended.

Manon nodded and returned to his place in the troop.

After more than half an orbit they entered a passage, which filled up with fog when they had hardly gone a hundred paces.

Boïndil nodded. "This is the right place. I remember it exactly." He sniffed at the murky air. "That's the one: damp, cold, revolting."

"Only the orcs missing," said Tungdil quietly and he motioned to his companions to draw their weapons. "Take care. In this pea-souper you won't see the enemy until he's right in front of you. And be quiet. The more noise we make, the more you're telling them about your where-abouts."

They crept along in the fog. It brought back memories for Tungdil and Boïndil. "There were three of the snout-faces," whispered Ireheart. "Two we finished off, but one escaped, remember?"

Indeed, how could he have forgotten that sight of mutilated dwarf corpses? The orc that got away had laid about himself horrifically, mowing down their comrades. "Be quiet!"

"Perhaps that orc is still around?" murmured Boïndil, and drew back: his companion's breath was heavy and sour with alcohol. "Oh, you know what? Maybe I do feel like a fight, after all."

"Boïndil! Just keep quiet, for once!"

"All right. I won't say another word. Until we find the orc, that is." He wielded his war hammer in a trial move. He had missed this sense of excitement.

They made their tortuous way through the mist that was dampening their beards and hair; drops of moisture had collected on their armor. The dwarves pricked up their ears to listen for sounds in the gray murk; you could detect nothing but the steps of the dwarf directly ahead, or the one behind you. The monsters were not showing themselves, which was not making progress any easier.

"When's this fog going to stop? I'd rather face an attack and use my crow's beak to slash through. I can't stand this creeping around," Boïndil complained.

"Have you seen an orc?" asked the wraithlike figure of Tungdil bad-temperedly.

"No, why?"

"Then why are you talking about it?"

Ireheart fell silent again and he heard Tungdil take another draft from his flask; there was a smell of brandy.

After endless walking they discovered they had reached

a cave. They felt their away round the walls. Tungdil located the rune and then they found a tunnel leading deeper into the Outer Lands. Nobody dared raise his voice. Now they were really in a place no dwarf had been before.

Suddenly, round a turning, the fog thinned as if a wet gray curtain had been torn away and discarded.

The quiet made them nervous. The dwarves would have been keen to hear the slightest sound, any sound to indicate life here in the tunnels—it didn't matter if it came from friend or foe.

"This is a ruddy labyrinth." Manon spoke. "There are more and more forks to the path."

"I know," replied Tungdil. "And someone has been here before us." He pointed to scratches on the rock wall that no one else had noticed. "It's an orc rune from Girdlegard. It stands for *gr*. We've been following the marks for some time."

"We're on the tracks of the pig-face that escaped us that time!" Boïndil nodded to Manon as if to say, *You see? This is a fine leader we have.* "Wonder where it's taking us?"

Tungdil shrugged his shoulders and moved on. The runes he found now were less carefully scratched, and soon they petered out altogether. Tungdil led the troop along the passage, leaving his own marks on the wall as he went.

A cave," he said after the last turning. He pointed. In front of them slanting light filtered through, shining on the bones that covered the floor. They entered the chamber cautiously.

"Ho, so somebody doesn't like orcs," said Ireheart, looking at the remains scattered around. He crouched down to examine his finds. "They've been dissected. The kind of monster that pulls an orc apart is my kind of monster," he joked. He spat on the bones. "They've been here for some time, it looks like."

"This may be why there've been no more attacks on the gate," chipped in Manon, picking up a thigh bone and checking out the knife marks on it.

"There are too many orcs. Nothing could eat all of them," said Boïndil doubtfully.

Manon looked at the huge cavern and held his hand out in a beam of light. "What if it's a really big monster? A dragon?"

"I don't think so," contradicted Tungdil. "We would have seen tracks: marks on the rock, discarded scales, broken teeth." He had located the way out.

"And a dragon could never have got through the narrow passageways."

"There used to be smaller dragons in the old days," objected Manon.

"I know. I've seen the books and the drawings. I've studied them all." Tungdil wanted to show the thirdling that he was indeed the educated dwarf here. "That is why I am dismissing the possibility of a dragon." He turned and walked on.

The others followed him to the next tunnel and then they got to a further cave that had a stream running through it. The dwarves spread out. It was clear from the tracks on the ground that there had been an encampment here. And a very big one, at that.

The number of fires that had been lit here in the past indicated to Boïndil that perhaps two thousand people had made camp here. "They were here for quite some time," he said, looking at the marks. "And they haven't been gone long." He ran his gloved hands through the ash. "Cold, but fairly fresh."

"The question is, were they orcs or something else entirely for whom our deadly enemies are food?" Tungdil pointed over to the opening of a wide naturally formed tunnel. "That way. Let's see if we can find more clues as to where they've gone."

They moved on, weapons at the ready, and muscles tensed. Just because a creature had developed a taste for orc flesh did not mean that a dwarf would be considered a friend.

The tunnel ended at a heap of stones blocking their path.

Tungdil looked up, then at the stones in front of him. "These boulders haven't fallen from the roof. They've been piled here on purpose to close off the tunnel." He looked at Boïndil. "Maybe the army camping here did this to cover its retreat."

"Or perhaps they were trying to stop more monsters coming through," suggested Manon.

"It's all very peculiar," was Ireheart's view. "Easier in the old days, wasn't it, Scholar? The pig-faces came, we wiped them out, all done, finished." He sat down on a rock ledge, and slipped off his helmet, scratching his head; it was one of the few days he wore his hair unbraided, and it looked strange on him. "Now we're right back at square one."

"Except we know now that someone has a fancy for orc flesh," Manon chipped in. "I'm sticking to my dragon theory. We're in the Outer Lands here . . ."

"No. There are no more dragons. Or they're never seen nowadays." Tungdil sat down, too, and ordered the troops to take a rest; they all relaxed and had something to eat. "No dragon would take the trouble to collect its prey together in this way." His clothing stuck to him; he was dripping with sweat. He was not used to the exertion of a long march any more.

"Those beasts are clever. They would never put orc-snout flesh in their mouths," laughed Boïndil, as he bit into his bread and stinking cheese. All of a sudden his gaze fastened on the heap of stones behind Tungdil. "What's that? Isn't there something catching the light?" Boïndil jumped to his feet and began to pull away the rubble. He called five of the warriors over and got them to dig. He was too tired.

It took quite some time before the hidden object was revealed. Rubble kept slipping back down over where they were working whenever they removed a sizeable boulder, and there was dust everywhere by now. Finally Tungdil was handed a flattened helmet. A helmet with a golden moon on the front; black bloodied hairs stuck still to the rim.

"So that will be her son we have found," said Ireheart under his breath.

Tungdil put the helmet in his pack. "It's his helmet we've found. Not him. Don't make the same mistake as the search party the king sent out. They might have placed the helmet there on purpose, so it gets found and it's assumed that he's dead."

"Why on earth would anyone do that?"

"Exactly. Why? Orcs would never have taken the

trouble. It must have been something with a brain," insisted Tungdil.

Ireheart leaned back and looked at the stone barricade. "Are you thinking of dismantling it to find out?"

Tungdil shook his head. "No. I'm sure that would be a waste of effort. We—"

They all heard the clinking noise that travelled out along the tunnel toward them from the cave; metal had come into contact with stone.

"So we are not alone," whispered Boïndil, stuffing his food back into his knapsack.

"Let's go and see," agreed Tungdil, getting the troop to assemble.

While they crept silently back through the tunnel to the cave they picked up that same sound again. It was nearer now.

Tungdil, Boïndil and Manon took a cautious look out of the tunnel mouth. At first glance there was little to see. The cave was empty and abandoned. Dust circulated in the air, and there in the center of the cave was a pile of rubble that had not been there before.

"A ghost?" Ireheart mouthed to Tungdil.

"Well, we are in the Outer Lands, but I wouldn't jump to conclusions like that," he said thoughtfully. "Whatever it is, it's—"

"Up there!" called Manon, pointing out a dwarf-sized form up by the roof.

"Who can that be?" Tungdil asked him.

Ireheart looked up. "What, by all the gods, is he doing up there?"

To all intents and purposes the dwarf seemed to have

hauled himself up on a pulley hoist attached by chain to the top of the rocks. Now he was settled in a leather bucket-seat arrangement, working away with a long iron chisel.

Manon shook his head. "He's not one of ours. I've heard nothing about any other missions, and I haven't got the faintest idea what he's up to up there. Or how on earth he got there."

The stranger positioned the iron bar, pulled a hammer out of his belt and whacked it on the end, pushing the tip of the chisel into the rock. Large chunks of rock splintered off, falling noisily to the ground, with granite dust clouding after. Now they knew what had caused the new pile of rubble they had seen.

Boïndil cursed. "Look at the roof," he called out in alarm. "There are cracks everywhere."

"Can you do all that with an iron bar?" laughed Manon in disbelief.

"False granite," explained Ireheart. "I'm a secondling, and even if I was never much good at handling stone, I know my minerals better than a thirdling." He indicated the place where the clumps of stone had collected. "See how the chunks break open when they fall? Looks like granite, but it's nowhere near as hard. The older the stone the more porous it gets."

"That fellow is trying to bring down the whole cave!" Tungdil turned. "Let's get out of here, or we'll have no way back!" The others followed him at speed.

The dwarf working overhead had noticed the approach of the uninvited newcomers and was redoubling his efforts. One last mighty blow with the hammer and a boulder the size of a house broke free. It crashed to the floor and sent a great cloud of dust right up to the roof of the cave.

Immediately, the unknown dwarf shimmied down the chain and disappeared in the dry cloud of powdered stone. Only visible as a vague shape, he ran off in front of Tungdil and his troop as they coughed their way through the dust cloud to reach the safety of the side tunnel.

Above them the work of destruction continued. Perhaps the best comparison is with a vaulted roof whose keystone has been kicked out by the actions of a madman. There was no support left in place to take the immense weight of the massive ceiling and to transfer the pressure to the side walls.

More huge stones fell; two of the warriors were buried, crushed under the stone slabs as if they had been soft kashti mushrooms. Their helmets rolled between the legs of the remaining soldiers, tripping one of them up. His comrade was just in time to pull him back onto his feet. Not even the largest monster could have withstood this rockfall; perhaps even a full-grown dragon would have been brought to its knees.

The fine granite dust got into the dwarves' airways and lungs and made it impossible for them to breathe properly. The cliff shook under them, cracking and roaring. The mountain screamed its distress out loud, outraged at the destruction.

"The bastard," spluttered Manon as he rushed past Tungdil and Boïndil to try to catch the dwarf who had brought the roof of the cave thundering down. "I'll kill the bastard!"

Tungdil did not doubt the earnestness of Manon's words. The thirdling had lost two of his men for no good reason.

"No, Manon!" he wanted to call out, but from his dust-stopped throat he could only produce a croak in protest. The only way to stop a murder now was to run after the two of them himself.

In the tunnel they ran into the air was clear; no clouds of dirt obscured their view. They hastened after one another as if they were threaded like pearls on a string: the dwarf first, then Manon and last of all, Tungdil, losing ground all the time. He was out of condition and had no energy left.

"Stop," he groaned, spitting out saliva that could well have served as mortar. "Manon, wait for me! He could be leading you into a trap." He set off again in pursuit, with the rest of the troop and Boïndil following behind. "What a hothead!"

As they reached the cave where they had first seen the orc bones they caught sight of Manon disappearing down another tunnel they had not noticed before.

The chase continued.

Tungdil had a terrible stitch in his side. He gasped and his breath whistled like an old kettle; even the older Ireheart, who had bidden farewell to battles and other exertions now at his advanced age, had more stamina than he did. "Run on ahead," he panted, falling back to a walking pace. "I'll be along shortly. I don't want to hold you up."

"No need, Scholar," said Boïndil, pointing to a fork in the tunnel.

There Manon lay, his drawn sword in his left hand. He

sported a bad cut just below the eye. Ireheart and Tungdil bent down to help him while the warriors provided cover. Of the dwarf they had been chasing there was no trace.

Tungdil checked the jugular vein. "He's not dead," he reported with a huge sigh of relief.

Boïndil was holding up a stone the size of a small egg that had the thirdling's blood dripping from it. "They got him with a slingshot!"

"Begone!" A voice echoed round the tunnel. "There is nothing here for you to find." They could make out something the size of a dwarf, wearing nothing but a loincloth and a chain mail shirt. In its right hand the figure held a large hammer aloft. The smoke from its torch made it hard to distinguish facial features.

Tungdil stood up and made his way to the front of the band, while two of the warriors saw to Manon. "Who are you? And why did you bring down the cave—?"

Behind the figure a huge shadow filled the entire cave. Cogwheels grated and whirred loudly, mechanical parts screeched. The thing was getting closer.

"Get away from here!" the figure called to them, dropping the torch and hurling the hammer at them.

One of the warriors fielded the missile, catching it on his shield, which deflected it to crash against the low stone roof.

The events of the cave were repeated: great fragments of false granite fell onto the rock floor, and the passageway split open with a gaping hole several paces wide.

"Back! It's too dangerous to try anything here." In frustration, Tungdil clenched his fists. This time he stood no chance of discovering the secret of the Outer Lands.

Boïndil and three warriors grabbed the unconscious Manon and ran for their lives. Not all of them escaped the fatal rain of stones. Two more were buried under the false granite and the rest managed by the skin of their teeth, coughing and gasping, to reach the cave of bones. Behind them the tunnel collapsed and belched out a fountain of deadly dust that covered the dwarves.

And that was not all.

The mountain shook in rage as if angry at what was happening within; it seemed to want to punish those who were inside it. Above their heads they could hear cracking and twisting noises, as splinters of rock started to fall.

"What have we done to make Vraccas so angry? This chamber won't hold much longer," guessed Ireheart, worried about his friend. "Can you go on?" he asked the gasping Tungdil.

"I'll have to," he groaned, fighting for breath as he struggled to his feet. "I never wanted to die like this." He thought about the strange shape he had seen behind the figure of the dwarf. "What was that thing he had with him?"

"I don't know. Whatever it was, he would have set it on us if the tunnel hadn't collapsed." Boïndil shook the dust out of his beard, which had turned gray. "You're the scholar, Tungdil. Have you ever seen anything like that before?"

On the opposite side of the cave, parts of the walls were starting to burst, with stone shrapnel flying hundreds of feet through the air. One of the warriors was hit in the face. Blood shot out of the wound on his cheek.

Tungdil did not answer, but gave the signal for them to set off. Things were no longer clear at all.

They hurried back through the fog-filled tunnel, while the stone under their feet shook and would not come to rest. Tungdil was convinced that the rock was furious at the intrusion: the insides of the mountain had been vandalized, and its caves destroyed.

But they escaped the anger of the mountain, finally reached the Northern Pass and made their way home through the frost and fog. Hoar frost formed on their helmets, their chain mail, their shields, and their beards, turning the dwarfs completely white.

When they arrived back at the gate, they were expected.

II

Girdlegard,
Kingdom of Gauragar,
Spring, 6241st Solar Cycle

"Make way! Make way for the King of the Players!" shouted the herald in his multi-colored garb, one hand beating the drum he carried on a strap round his neck. Then he raised the trumpet to blow the fanfare, a tune vaguely reminiscent of Gauragar's royal anthem. He strode noisily through the crowd; eager to see what the approaching high-born personage might look like, people fell back to let the herald pass.

Following the herald came an arrogant figure wearing what were surely priceless robes; he wore a conspicuous blue hat sporting three feathers and held a silver-headed cane in his hand. A goatee beard suited his aristocratic visage well and the long dark brown hair rested on the collar of his mantle. He waved to all sides majestically; to emphasize the royal gesture he had fastened a white silk cloth to the ring on his middle finger and it fluttered like a miniature standard.

"May the gods love you and protect you, people of Storm Valley!" He walked to this side and that, and even risked a smile to a young woman. "Especially you, my lovely child. If the gods do not comply, call for me and I will gladly take on the duty myself." The girl blushed and some in the crowd around her laughed out loud.

Arriving at the center of the marketplace, he jumped up onto the rim of the fountain.

"Now, come, honored spectators! Come and see for yourselves in my traveling collection of curiosities the most wonderful adventures ever witnessed in Girdlegard. It will be as if you had been there in person," he enticed them. He ran round the low circular wall of the fountain, the buckles on his shoes clinking as he did so. "The battle with the orcs, the fight against the eoîl and the avatars, the cruelty of the unslayable siblings that governed Dsôn Balsur—you will see it all with your very own eyes. Heroes, villains, Death and Love. I, the renowned Rodario, whom once they called Rodario the Incredible and Lover of the Maga Andôkai, shall tell you of grand deeds. I have tales to tell of why Andôkai was also known as the Tempestuous One." A few laughed at this innuendo. "And I fought side by side with Tungdil Goldhand in combat with the eoîl," and here he swished his cane through the air in imitation, "until the mist-shape lay dead at our feet!" He stood up at his full height and stretched out his arms. "For I, myself, cherished spectators, have lived through these very events. Can there be another such who could recount in more detail, with more verisimilitude? Who could report to you with greater honesty than I?" Blue and gray flames shot from his fingertips, to the shock and surprise of the bystanders. "This was merely a foretaste," he promised, looking at a young boy. "You will have to cover your eyes during the show, little man, to stop them jumping out of your skull," he said in a conspiratorial undertone.

The boy went pale and crept closer to his mother, who laughed and ran her fingers through his hair. Rodario fired off another batch of flames against a darkening sky which was indicating the approach of a spring storm. A few thunderclaps and some lightning would not harm the atmosphere in the great marquee one little bit. "Listen! The first twenty spectators to arrive will receive a free cup of wine, and also a glass jar with a breath of eoîl fog. Watch it and wonder! But never dare to remove the cork, else otherwise . . ." He left the threat hanging unspoken in the air, and restricted himself to displaying a mysterious warning expression.

His brown-eyed gaze swept over the throng, who were hanging on his every word. As always, he had been able to win over the crowd by a mixture of personal charm and free offers. In every place he visited he would look around for a familiar face; but as always in these last five cycles that face was still missing.

Finally he noticed a beautiful woman in the second row watching him. This cheered his mood considerably and combatted his disappointment.

She looked to be about twenty, tall and attractive. Everything was in the right place for a woman, though a little more substance in the décolleté would not have come amiss. She wore her long blond hair down; her face was narrow and full of expression; her green eyes were following him intently. He would have judged her to be of noble birth, had she not been so simply attired and had it not been for the laundry bundle in her arms.

Her visage showed a strange longing; it was less a matter of desire for himself as a man, more a question of sharp interest in what he was doing. Rodario was well acquainted with this effect. He had stood at the doors of a theater

70 *Markus Heitz*

four cycles earlier with the same expression on his face, with no other thought in his mind than the need to appear on stage. And he had achieved his dream.

He took it as a sign from the gods. Following his instincts, he jumped down from the fountain edge and landed directly in front of her. Then he made her a deep bow and, thanks to amazing dexterity and meticulous preparation, conjured up a black paper flower as if from nowhere.

"Bring this flower this evening and you shall see the show for free," he told her with a smile, raising one eyebrow and treating her to his famous stare no female yet had been able to withstand. "Tell me your name, my Storm Valley beauty."

After a moment's hesitation she accepted the paper flower. Then a young man pushed his way through in front of her, tore the gift from her hand and trampled it underfoot. "Keep your flattery to yourself," he threatened.

"Sir, it is not courteous to interrupt the entertainment in this way," Rodario responded smoothly.

"It's not entertainment, you clown! You were flirting with my wife," the man retorted angrily, shoving his balled fist into Rodario's face. "Try that again and it'll be a black eye you get, and not a black paper flower."

"No?" Rodario bent forward swiftly, pretending to pull something out of the young man's ear. To the delight of the watching crowd he extracted a second paper flower. "You see? You already had one." He handed the flower to the young woman. "Here, madam, with your husband's compliments. He is a lucky man to have such flowers growing in his head. It must be the futility, I mean the *fertility*, of his earwax that does it, methinks."

Furiously the man snatched at the flower before his wife could grasp the stem. He hurled it into the dirt. "Enough!" he shouted. "You will pay for this!"

Rodario even pretended to extract something out of the man's open mouth. He waved a coin in the air. "But why? You are so rich already. There is gold in your gullet."

Now the crowd was laughing heartily at the performance: they shouted and whistled. The young man was the focus of their ridicule. For his honor's sake he had to put a stop to this mockery.

"I'll stick the money in your powdered arse," he yelled, attacking.

Rodario avoided the wild blow and poked his walking cane neatly between the young man's legs, bringing him down against the wall of the fountain. His own momentum swept the man into the water. Children roared with laughter and applauded, and all the grown-ups were joining in the fun by now.

Spluttering, the victim stood up and shook himself. Rodario helpfully held out his cane.

"Out you come now and let us forget our little quarrel," he offered. "I'll stand you a drink; what do you say?"

The humiliated husband wiped the water out of his eyes. He did not look any happier. Uttering a loud cry he launched himself at the showman, who again proved the niftier on his feet.

The man landed in the dust, which immediately caked his wet clothing. He clenched his fists, his fingers scrabbling in the dirt. "Wait, I'll kill you, you jumped-up . . ."

Rodario bent down and fiddled behind the man's ear, producing another flower. "See, the water has made the seeds sprout." The crowd rocked with laughter and Rodario tossed the third flower to the pretty young wife. "Now that's enough, my good man." He stood up straight. "I don't want you getting hurt just because you lost your temper."

Enraged, the man got to his feet, wiped his filthy face and stomped off; his wet shoes squelched and leaked as he walked away. As he went past he grabbed his wife by the wrist and pulled her away.

The unhappy glance she gave Rodario was the loudest silent cry for help he had ever witnessed. The gap in the crowd closed up again after them, and the showman lost sight of the couple.

"There, you see what happens if you cross a hero," he triumphed, grinning. He bowed. "Come to the show this evening and let me enchant you all. Until then, fare you well." Like the noblest of courtiers, he whirled his hat around and indicated with a motion of the shoulder that the performance, for now, was over.

The audience applauded again and returned to their market-day tasks.

Rodario grinned at his herald. "Well cried, cryer. Do a couple more rounds through the back streets and make lots of noise. Let's make sure the whole world knows who's in Storm Valley tonight."

His man returned the grin: "After a session like that word will get around faster than a fart in the wind."

"Not a happy choice of simile, but accurate enough in the circumstances," said Rodario as he went over to a market stall selling wine. He got himself a beaker, tasted it and nodded. "Exquisite little drop. Worthy of an emperor. Send me a barrel of this to the road that leads

south out of here. That's where we've put up our tents,"
he told the wine merchant, handing him a heap of Bruron's
coins. "Will that cover it?"

"Of course, sir," The man bent over the money to count
it. With these show folk you could never quite be sure.
He even took the trouble to scratch at the surface of one
of the coins with a knife to check whether perhaps it was
merely lead coated with silver. Satisfied, he shoveled the
money into his pocket.

Rodario grinned, leaning back against the makeshift
bar—a plank balanced on two wine barrels. "Don't you
trust me?"

"No," replied the vintner in a friendly enough manner.
"You wanted to try the wine before you ordered the barrel,
didn't you?" He filled Rodario's beaker again. "There,
that cup and the next for free as a bonus."

"Too kind, my good man," laughed the showman and
he looked around, secretly hoping he might catch sight of
the pretty girl again. "If you saw my little contretemps
just now, have you any idea who my opponent might be?"
he enquired, and called a lad over who was peddling deli-
cacies from a tray; he was offering freshly baked black
bread with cream, ham and a layer of melted cheese.
Rodario knew he must eat something or the wine would
have a devastating effect. He didn't want to turn up that
evening the worse for wear, let alone to fall off the stage
drunk and incapable when he faced his audience. He'd
seen that happen to others. He bought himself one of the
savory snacks in exchange for a quarter. He contemplated
his purchase and thought of his good friend who had so
loved these flatbreads.

"Sure I know who it is." The vintner topped up the jug from the barrel and thus prevented Rodario's thoughts becoming too melancholy. "Nolik, son of Leslang, the richest man in Storm Valley. The two of them own a quarry that supplies the finest marble in Gauragar. King Bruron is a personal friend of theirs."

"And yet the man has no breeding." Rodario took a bite. "He gets his wife to work as a washerwoman?"

The wine seller took a quick look around before answering. "Nolik is a bad man. No idea how he won Tassia's heart. Can't have been honestly."

"Who will ever understand women? Perhaps his inner virtues are as gold compared to his behavior?" Rodario rolled his eyes. "This savory flatbread is de-li-cious," he praised, his mouth full, as he juggled the snack from one hand to the other, "but it's still too hot!" He gulped some wine to quench the burning and sighed happily.

The other man laughed so loud that the folk around them turned their heads. "Nolik and inner values? No, definitely not." Quietly he added, "Tassia's family owed his father money. Need I say more?"

"No." Rodario chewed his last morsel, picked up the jug and the beaker and moved on. "Don't forget my wine!" He raised his two prizes in the air. "You'll have these back this evening if the barrel gets delivered," he placated the man.

Rodario loved to wander through a busy throng of people; this was life. He had had enough of death, heroic deeds or not. He was a showman: a skilled mimic and an excellent lover—better than any other in Girdlegard. And for both areas of expertise he needed real people around him to appreciate his god-given gifts.

There was another reason he had been obliged to give up his theatre in Porista: the face he had been seeking in the crowd. The face of Furgas.

The friend who had been his companion on those long theater tours was in despair over the death of his beloved Narmora and had completely disappeared since the victory over the eoîl and the conversation they had subsequently had with Tungdil.

That was five cycles ago now.

Since that time Rodario had been traveling through the Girdlegard kingdoms, doing the same thing in each town, village or hamlet he passed through: He asked about Furgas and showed people the likeness he had had made. Without success.

But he was not giving up. Not in Storm Valley, where his enquiries had been met with shaking heads when he showed the miniature portrait of his friend in the inns and in the marketplace and at the town gates.

Rodario was very worried about his lost companion. Then there was the problem of the various pieces of complicated apparatus Furgas had invented and which Rodario used in all his performances, strapped to his body: burlap seed slings to shoot balls of fire, little leather bags where the black paper flowers waited, and all sorts of other containers for powders. These were such ingenious contraptions that they let him appear in the eyes of his audience like a magus—they formed the core of his whole act. He was afraid of the day that must come when one of these trusty utensils might give up and need repair. He had always managed to cope with small defects in his props, but patching up was not always going to work.

So Rodario returned to where his troupe had set up camp, that familiar feeling of disappointment with him again. He would get over it. Back on stage he could act away his worries and forget them. The crowd loved him and thought of him as the merry showman, always bright and ready with a quip, because they had no way of seeing behind the mask.

The performance ended in triumph and in one of the colossal thunderstorms that gave Storm Valley its name and which tested the strength of the marquee's guy-ropes to the utmost. The fabric billowed in and out, giving the audience the impression they were sitting inside some extremely unsettled intestines. Hardly had the applause died away than the audience rushed back to town for home and shelter. The sales of eoîl-breath in the little flacons could have gone better.

Rodario retired to his personal caravan with its mystical designs painted on the walls. This was where he prepared for his act before each performance and where he counted the takings after it. The coins were stacked on the traveling actor's make-up table. Little by little, we're getting there, he thought. It's a living.

He was still wearing the robe he always used; it had been his in Porista when, as a "Magus", he had used the name Rodario the Incredible. The tricks intended to confuse his enemies had now been downgraded to stage props. He took his make-up off and unstrapped the various trick devices from his body.

He poured himself some wine, drank it and took a look in the mirror; in the lamplight his face was much older now. "Every wrinkle is a cycle of worry." He toasted

Furgas's picture. "May you be safe and well, old friend, until I can find you. Who could compete with your masterful ingenuity?" He gulped down the wine, not hearing the knock at the door at first.

"I'm asleep," he called out crossly when the knocking did not stop.

"That's good. Let me bring you a nightmare, flatterer." A man's voice. The door burst open, sending up clouds of dust. On the threshold was Nolik with two men behind him. They all bore cudgels.

"Awake already, my strong friend. What is the hurry? I would have opened the door for you." Rodario jumped up, grabbing his sword. "This is a real weapon, Nolik," he warned, tossing the hair back out of his eyes. "Don't force me to give it your blood to taste."

"Hark at that fancy talk even now the curtain's down." Nolik laughed and stepped into the caravan, his companions at his heels. He pulled open the first cupboard he came to, wrenching clothes out and hurling them onto the ground. "Where the hell . . . ?"

"Looking for tonight's takings?" Rodario raised his sword. "I thought you were so very rich? Is the marble not selling?"

A second cupboard was pulled open and pots, bottles and bags were thrown around. They shattered or burst open and the contents ran into each other. "You know who I mean," yelled Nolik, taking a stride forward and crushing the valuable eoîl-breath ingredients underfoot.

Rodario set the point of his sword at Nolik's breast. "You, my good man, shall pay me for the wanton damage you have caused here. And by all the monsters of Tion, tell me what the blazes you and these highly intellectually underprivileged mates of yours are looking for."

"Tassia."

"Your wife?" he laughed. "Oh, now I understand. She's run away and you think I'm hiding her."

"Of course. She's always had these mad ideas, and you and your flattery have set her off again. The bed was empty yet again."

Rodario grinned and looked past the man to his two companions. "Then take yourself back there and cuddle up to these two delights. If I were your wife I'd have done a bunk ages ago. Now get off out of here!"

No one did as he suggested. Nolik was about to open one of the chests when the showman slammed the flat of his sword down on his fingers, making him jump back.

"Touch one more thing in my wagon and you'll be using the other hand forever and a day when you wipe your backside," hissed Rodario, trying hard to look very, very dangerous.

"Beat him to a pulp," Nolik ordered with a curse, holding up his bruised hand. "We'll take the caravan apart afterwards."

Hesitating somewhat, the henchmen pushed past their leader. They were strongly built, probably quarry workers, used to lifting great boulders as heavy as a cart. If one of them hit him with a cudgel, he would be a goner.

Then the first attack came.

Rodario deflected the club, which crashed into the side of the bed, shattering it. Underneath, Rodario caught sight of a woman's dress—and inside the dress—who but Tassia?

She slipped against the back wall and hid her head in her hands. The brief glimpse he gained of her face showed him the black eye she sported.

"So Nolik is not only stupid, he is a cowardly swine as well," he remarked scornfully. "If you were a pile of excrement you would stink so bad that people's noses would drop off." He thrust home suddenly with his sword, wounding the first of the heavies on his thigh. "But you, Nolik, are worse than excrement." Rodario continued the flow of words, pushing his visitors back as he talked; this time he caught the second man's arm with his blade. The two men took to their heels and made off into the storm.

Nolik glanced over his shoulder to see where they had got to, then threw his club away. "That's enough," he said, his voice normal now, the fury dissipated. "Tassia, get up. We owe the man an explanation."

The girl got to her feet, picked up the linen bundle she had hastily packed on leaving, and went over to stand by her husband. "Forgive the play-acting, Rodario," she said calmly. "I'm relieved you are not hurt, but we needed those two as independent witnesses."

Rodario did not know what to think, but willingly lowered his sword. "So you were putting on a bit of acting for me?" he asked cautiously. "And the name of the play in question?"

"*Lose the Girl and Keep your Reputation*," Nolik replied, pointing to Tassia. "It was her idea."

Tassia stepped forward, her blond head held low. "Forgive us," she entreated again. "Nolik and I do not care for each other and never have. His father insisted I marry him by way of repaying my family's debts."

"I don't find her attractive. Don't find any women attractive," Nolik explained. "We're both unhappy and have had to act out a pretense in the eyes of my father and of the whole town, until we saw a way to get out of this predicament." He nodded to the showman. "You and your traveling *Curiosum* exhibition will save us, if you can help, Rodario."

"A nice little plan," said Rodario, gesturing to them to sit down, while he locked the door and then sank down onto the wrecked bed. He was not sure yet whether he could trust this couple. The story was a bold one, a bit like a play itself. "So what happens next?"

Tassia drew breath. "You'll help us?"

Rodario took his time replying. Suspicion, desire and his own love of adventure were struggling inside him. If Tassia had been as ugly as a toad from a Weyurn pond he would probably have said no. As it was, desire was winning out. "How could I let such a talented actress go or, indeed, how could I leave her in distress, my esteemed Tassia?" He smiled. "You have the makings of a stage star." He held out his hand to her. "Agreed?"

"With all my heart," she said with joy, shaking his hand.

Nolik followed their example. "Here's how it goes: I'll tell my father you've beaten me and forced me to sell you Tassia," he suggested. "I've got the money so it won't cost you a penny. I'm free again and can get the marriage annulled, and she may go her own way. My father will have a fit, but he'll calm down eventually." He lifted the bag of coins. "The sight of this will cheer him. Even if it's his own gold."

Rodario slapped his thigh with delight; this was a fine

joke. "I'll have to write a play about this." He turned to Nolik. "I'm surprised at you. You know the townsfolk give you a bad reputation? Yet your deeds speak for you."

The young man grimaced. "No, it's true: I am a bad person, Rodario. The black eye I gave Tassia is genuine— I have a very quick temper. It's better if Tassia goes than if she were to stay." He strode out into the rain without looking round again.

She called out after him, "Good luck." Nolik lifted his hand in acknowledgment as he made his way back to Storm Valley.

"So, Tassia," said Rodario. He looked at her. "Welcome to the *Curiosum* company. You always wanted to be an actress. How did that come about?" He patted the bed and she sat down next to him.

"I don't really know. It's just an urge I have." She looked him straight in the eyes, raised her right hand and stroked his cheek. As she made the movement her shawl slipped from her shoulders, revealing bare skin. "Like the urge I have for you," she whispered. "I saw you at the fountain, with all that spurting water and the big black cloud behind you, and I was lost. You looked like a god in those robes and your jokes were like holy words." Her pretty face drew closer. "You are the wittiest, best-looking and most desirable man I have ever met, Rodario." She bent her head forward and parted her lips.

Rodario swallowed hard, regarded her immaculate tanned skin and wanted to kiss her. And wanted to do other things with her as well—things he excelled at. His desires were to be satisfied this very night. How most agreeable.

Then she pulled back her head and asked, "How was I?"

"What do you mean? We haven't done anything yet," he said in surprise, slipping nearer to her once more.

"I mean my improvised seduction scene, Master Rodario." She edged away, laughing as innocently as a child that has stuffed its pockets with stolen sweets and is blaming another for the theft. "You were certainly taken in, I know. It was fairly obvious."

Rodario felt Tassia had made a fool of him and it was a blow to his pride. He covered up his disappointment and transformed his surprise to laughter. "My compliments, dear Tassia!" He made her a bow and planted a soft kiss on the back of her hand. "You have mastered all the arts of declamation. It seems I should take lessons from you myself. It was magnificent how you pretended to bestow your favor on me." He stood up and took her hand. "Come, let me show you where you can sleep tonight. There's a bed free in Gesa's wagon. She is an enchanting matron who looks after our horses. We'll settle things about your wages and so on in the morning."

"Thank you." As she passed she caught sight of the picture of Furgas. "Who is that?" she wanted to know.

"He's a good friend. I miss him. He used to belong to my troupe and he is an expert in his field," said Rodario, standing as close to her as he could. She had certainly achieved one thing with her performance that evening. He had lost his heart a little bit more. "Have you ever seen him?"

"Maybe. I'm not sure," she said, shaking her head. Her answer took him by surprise.

Rodario took the picture and handed it to her. "Have a good look." He felt excitement and the first stirrings of joy.

Tassia took up a quill, opened the inkpot and altered the likeness slightly, giving the face longer hair and a short beard to go with the moustache. "He was thinner than on this picture," she said. "That's him all right. He was up by the quarry at the river where I do the washing. He wanted to know exactly where he was. So I told him."

Rodario grabbed her by the shoulders. "When was that? What else did he say?" He gave silent thanks to Palandiell for the inspired coincidence that had brought Tassia's path to cross his own. "It is really important. Where was he trying to get to?"

"He didn't say much. But I could see from his eyes that he was very sad." She tried to conjure up again the details of their meeting. "It must have been four cycles ago. I felt sorry for him. I'd never seen so much distress in a man. Sorrow had made deep lines on his face. That's why I remember him." She looked at Rodario. "He was driving a big cart with a tarpaulin over it. There was a lot of rattling coming from underneath the cover. I took him for a tinker." Tassia gave a start when a bolt of lightning struck the ground close to where they were standing. There was a terrifying crash and she clung to Rodario in fear. He put his arms round her. Unfortunately she did not remain like that for long and quickly moved away. "Forgive me. The thunderstorm . . ." she said quietly.

"Of course," he said, regretting that he could not hold her longer. "You were saying . . . ?"

"Your friend was watering his horses. I told him where

he was and he looked a bit happier then. I asked him if he had pans for sale, but he laughed and said he couldn't help me. He needed his things in Weyurn, in . . ." She thought hard. "I think he called it . . . Mafidina?"

"Mifurdania," Rodario corrected her. "We used to have a theatre there." At last he had got a hint, a clue, as to the whereabouts of his missing friend; the next stage of the *Curiosum* tour was now determined. He had a further question: "Did he say at all what he was going to be doing?"

"Trading," she answered. "Then to travel on." She suppressed a yawn but Rodario noticed. "Why did you split up if you were such friends?"

"Oh, sleep has you in its arms now, Tassia. I'll explain it all to you soon enough." He took her bag. "Here, I'll carry that."

A sudden gust of wind made the caravan shake. Rain rattled down. They would both of them be soaked through as soon as they put a foot outside.

Rodario looked at Tassia. "Right, you can sleep here. Let us share a broken bed," he offered and she smiled in acceptance. They both slipped under the sheets and listened in the dark to the sounds of nature. After a while Rodario felt a hand on his chest.

"When I called you witty, good-looking and desirable before, only one of those was a lie," she whispered and he heard her take off her dress.

"Be careful what you say next." He gave a quiet laugh. So his charm still worked. Even in the dark and without the use of words. She kissed his cheek. He got the feeling that Tassia was not entirely inexperienced.

"You are not the best-looking man I've ever seen," she said, snuggling close; he felt her warm skin and smelled the fragrance of her hair. "But the other two things are true."

"Then you could add the *one with the greatest stamina*," he laughed, kissing her on the mouth. Yet again a woman had chosen him to provide happiness. He was glad to be of service.

Girdlegard,
Kingdom of Tabaîn,
Two Miles South of the Capital Goldensheaf,
Spring, 6241st Solar Cycle

If the kingdom of Tabaîn had two defining features they were the almost infinite stretch of its sunshine-yellow rolling cornfields, and its squat low-lying houses built of blocks of stone as long as a man is tall, as high as a child may grow, as wide as an arm is long.

"It's like a sheet of gold-leaf a clumsy worker has torn holes in," was Prince Mallen of Idoslane's judgment as he surveyed the golden landscape. It lay as flat as a board at his horse's feet. There were a few hillocks, perhaps ten or twenty paces high, which, from wishful thinking and ignorance, the Tabaîner populace of the center and the south had designated mountains. None of them had ever seen the ranges proper, let alone another kingdom.

"It's perfect territory for our heavy cavalry to storm. We'd thunder through and conquer it all in a whirlwind attack," enthused Alvaro, companion to Mallen and commander of his bodyguard. He caught the disapproving look. "Of course, I don't mean that seriously, my prince," he added quickly, clearing his throat in embarrassment.

"Do you not see how they build their houses and their keeps, Alvaro?" Prince Mallen pointed to their destination, the city of Goldensheaf with its royal fortress, over to their left. The segments of his costly armor clanked as he moved. "How would we take that? There's not a single tree in sight to make a siege ladder, no rocks for our catapults. And, of course, no wood to make the catapults from in the first place." He patted the neck of his stallion reassuringly. "And I don't mean that seriously, either, of course." He grinned and clapped Alvaro on the shoulder. "King Nate is welcome to his smooth little country." He set his horse in motion again and the troop moved off. They would soon be in Goldensheaf itself, visiting in response to an invitation from the sovereign.

Alvaro still felt uneasy about what he had said. "Your Highness, forgive me my words, if you will." He rode at Mallen's side and searched for the right thing to say. "I was brought up to measure myself against orcs and other beasts and always to defend my beloved Idoslane against invading hordes, but now . . ." As he shrugged his shoulders in excuse, his harness clinked. ". . . now men like me have nothing to do. Idleness puts warlike schemes into our heads, my prince."

Mallen unfastened the old-fashioned helmet from his belt and set it on his blond head, securing it with the leather chin strap. "I know. There are many warriors who are kicking their heels."

"Palandiell knows the truth of that!" snorted Alvaro,

relieved to hear he was understood. "The odd robber and band of highwaymen really don't present the same challenge. I have fought against Nôd'onn, against the avatars, against marauding orcs." He hit himself on his armored breastplate. "My sword is rusting in its sheath; I put on my leather doublet and my arms hardly know what movements to make." He sighed. "It is good that Girdlegard and in particular that Idoslane no longer need fighting men. But it is hard for the likes of us."

"But instead of fighting battles you can travel with me and see new things," smiled Mallen. He was enjoying the sunshine and soaking up the fragrance of the ripening sun-drenched ears of corn. He looked up at the sky and saw two raptors were circling above the crops, searching the ground for prey. "You would never have been able to do that before. All thanks to those orcs you seem to be missing now."

"You are right, Your Highness. I am being selfish and unjust."

The route taken by the troop of forty horsemen and four wagons led to a generously broad road through the fields directly to the heart of Goldensheaf. The town was tucked down into the earth and even the fortifications looked as if they had purposely been made less high than one might expect.

The men admired the fields, heavy with ripening crops. This was the first winter barley, promising a rich harvest. Then the summer crop would be sown; it would fill Tabaîn's barns and storehouses up to the rafters and help to feed the neighboring kingdoms as well. That is, if they were spared the destructive storms notorious in these flat plains.

"It must be the way of the landscape itself that tremendous storms are such a feature. Not even in the mountains of the dwarves or in the kingdom of Urgon do they suffer the whirlwinds they get here, when everything is dragged up from the ground," mused Alvaro, watching the crops wave in the strong breeze.

"That's why their houses are made solid as fortresses," said Mallen. "Any normal house would get blown away at once. And the corpse of any man caught in a tornado like that might never be found."

Alvaro looked up at the clear blue sky. "Let's hope we're spared that spectacle."

They rode on, entering the city. Goldensheaf opened its gates in welcome. Hundreds of citizens lined the streets of the capital and waved flags and scarves; others strewed flower petals from windows and rooftops in honor of the guests. Strains of joyful, if unfamiliar, music interwove with the shouts and cheers of the townspeople.

Mallen noticed that none of the houses was taller than the occasional two-storey building. To lighten the overall impression of grayness, some of the stone blocks had been painted. Other people had taken the easier path and decorated their houses with colorful banners in various widths.

"It's good to feel so welcome," remarked Alvaro, thoroughly enjoying being the center of attention.

A delegation of youths and maidens in dazzling white robes and carrying sheaves and garlands drew near to serve the officers with refreshments: wine and slices of different types of fruit.

"This is what I call a reception," grinned Alvaro. "Don't worry about anything else, I'm happy just to travel through Girdlegard with you for the rest of my days, my prince."

Mallen tried the wine, surprised at how light it tasted. Idoslane's own wines were famous for their fullness, rich ruby-red color and a slight woody by-taste. Tabaîn, on the other hand, had learnt the skill of producing a wine so light you could drink it as easily as water. So deceptively light.

The delegation drew back when a mounted escort arrived to accompany them to the fortress. The next surprise awaited.

"They really have built right down below ground level. One easy jump and we'd be over the walls," Alvaro whispered to his prince when they had seen more of the construction. The walls were not more than five paces high, while the yard into which they were riding down the ramp lay a good ten paces down.

"We'd have quite a fall after your one easy jump," Prince Mallen laughed. Some of the walls had stone projections too symmetrical to be considered mistakes. He must ask King Nate about them later.

Once in the courtyard they dismounted and followed one of the royal courtiers into the palace, the exterior of which was an unprepossessing and unadorned box shape.

But this impression was more than compensated for as soon as they took their first glance inside. Splendidly decorated walls, ceilings and floors graced the building. Carpets deadened their footsteps and made walking a pleasure; wonderful mural depictions of landscapes gave the feeling not of a gray-walled castle but of rolling fields of corn.

There were no sharp corners here or mean passageways,

but generous corridors with curved lines and elegant dimensions. Likewise, none of the rooms they marched through was starkly geometrical. The whole building was a glorious feast of architecture, pleasing to the eye and to the soul.

King Nate, with his sparse wheaten-blond hair and eyes as green as fresh grass, received them in the throne room with open arms of welcome. The two rulers embraced. "So you have finally managed, after all these cycles, to come and visit us here in Goldensheaf," King Nate said, his voice joyful. "And what do you think of the corn-basket of the whole of Girdlegard, Prince Mallen?"

"The land is as even and smooth as the face of a beautiful woman," Mallen answered diplomatically, falling into step next to Nate, who walked him to a feast table loaded with a magnificent variety of fruit, vegetables and meat dishes, and many types of bread offered as an accompaniment.

"Don't tell me you think it is too flat?" laughed his host, inviting Mallen to sit at his right. The seat on his left remained empty. "Surely the flatness has the great advantage of not overtiring the horses, doesn't it?"

Mallen and Alvaro laughed. "Perhaps you would grant us a few moments to shake off the dust of the journey . . . ?" asked the prince, but Nate dismissed the request.

"No, leave the dust on your armor. You carry part of the riches of my kingdom into the palace for me. What possible objection could I have . . . ?" he smiled. "Take refreshment with me now, then you shall find a hot bath and a bed waiting."

"If you insist, Your Majesty," Mallen nodded, his

stomach rumbling. He was happy to comply. Plates were being heaped with food and wine served, together with the finest water from Tabaîn's deep wells.

"I have planned an interesting nine orbits' entertainment for you," announced Nate, eating surprisingly heartily for a man of his advanced years. "You shall come with me to the various farms where I can have you shown all our different agricultural skills; you shall see orchards that you will hardly believe."

Alvaro grinned at Mallen as he chewed at his food and the prince understood his smile. What was meant was: "Ah, so they do have trees enough to make wooden siege ladders and catapults, after all."

"And then this evening we shall have a masked ball here, to which all the nobles of the land have been invited. They are all eager to see the hero who has kept our realm safe from the evil powers on more than one occasion, prince."

Mallen lifted his hand. "Not so, King Nate. Modesty is called for. My soldiers and myself have, it is true, made a contribution. But it is the dwarf folk who deserve your praise. Without their stamina and stubborn determination, their strong arms and their belief in goodness, we should not both be sitting at a feast together as we are doing now. The dwarves have made many sacrifices in the past."

"True words indeed, Prince Mallen," said a soft voice from the doorway.

An elf in flowing light green and yellow robes stood there waiting for a sign to show she was allowed to join them.

The prince and Alvaro looked at each other in surprise. It was not often you got to see an elf face to face outside the realm of Âlandur: up to now it had only been in times of war.

"Come and join us, Rejalin," called the king and a servant pulled out the chair at Nate's left. Now it was obvious for whom the place had been reserved. "Keep us company."

"Gladly, Your Majesty." She approached, her every movement the essence of a grace that no other residents of Girdlegard could hope to attain. Rejalin wore her long, light hair woven into a plait around her head; delicate filigree jewelry sparkled from it. Mallen was admiring her already; when she bowed her head slightly and addressed him— "Greetings, Prince Mallen"—he was on the point of falling under her spell. No woman he knew had eyes of such a blue-green color.

"Rejalin is with a delegation from Âlandur, sent to me by Prince Liútasil," explained the king, as the elf maiden tasted the fruit in front of her. She elevated the normally banal act of eating to a simple but enchanting performance.

She lifted her head and smiled at Alvaro and Mallen. "It is time that my people start to share their great knowledge with others. Prince Liútasil has decided to impart what we have learned to all the rulers. Those that show themselves worthy."

Alvaro lowered the fork that was on its way to his mouth and challenged Rejalin with a look. "So one has to prove oneself worthy in order to receive favor from the elves?" He placed his hands together and watched her face. "What would one have to do in order to be able to belong to the select circle?"

Rejalin delicately plucked an early berry fruit from its stem. "I am not at liberty to tell you," she replied, her tone even and friendly and her voice melodious enough to subdue the most aggressive of orcs. "We see and we judge without words and then we report to our prince."

"Then tell me, Rejalin," he said, pointing at his own master, "how it may be that one of the greatest heroes of Girdlegard has not yet had the honor of an elven deputation?" He was listening for the smallest trace of insult or slight in her words.

She did not step onto this thin ice but instead sent a lingering glance to Mallen that had in it shades of the expression a woman might reserve for her lover. "They have certainly come to you, Prince Mallen, while you have been traveling here to Tabaîn," she said, addressing the ruler directly and ignoring the warrior. "You are awaited by a delegation of my brothers and sisters. The journey from Âlandur to Idoslane is of a considerable length." She smiled and he instinctively responded to her friendliness.

Alvaro had not given up by a long way. "This knowledge your people has," he went on, "what kind is it? How to make more beautiful music?"

"Progress," she said without turning to answer him— her gaze was fixed on Mallen. "It touches all areas of daily life. Including art." She lowered her eyes, paused, then regarded Alvaro. "Your manner is not very friendly, sir."

The warrior leaned back in his chair. "I should have been glad to see your pretty face when the battle of Porista was being fought. But the elves preferred to remain in the woods."

"We fought against the älfar, Alvaro," she corrected, speaking more sharply than before, which made him grin. She finally lost her patience.

"Of course you fought the älfar. We *all* fought the älfar at Dsôn Balsur and *nearly all* of us fought the avatars," he followed through. "We played a part in protecting Âlandur from your malicious relations, but how do you thank Girdlegard? This is a mystery I can't fathom out." He reached for his beaker and raised it to her. "May you be the first one to explain it to me, Rejalin."

Mallen looked at him angrily. "Stop this, Alvaro. It is obvious. The elves would have had to fight on the same side as the älfar. It would never have worked. Fire and water would be a better mix than that. They would have attacked each other and the avatars would have stormed off with the victory."

Rejalin inclined her head. "I see you have greater insight than your friend, Prince Mallen of Idoslane. It would have been like asking you to fight alongside the same orcs who had devastated your city and slaughtered its inhabitants the previous orbit. After they had raped your women and children and consumed their bodies before your very eyes."

"You may not believe me, but if it meant that as allies we were able to withstand a stronger enemy still, I would do it. There would be opportunities enough later on to destroy the orcs," Alvaro went on relentlessly. "Rejalin, you elves don't have any sense of what might be the appropriate time for action. Your turning up here is the best example: only after a full five cycles have passed does it occur to your ruler to want to share his knowledge. *Five cycles!*"

"Enough, now," said Mallen harshly. "I offer my apologies for my companion, Your Majesty," he continued, addressing King Nate in measured tones. "He is a warrior, longing to return to battle; when there is peace he does not know what to do with his sword." He stood up. "We will withdraw and refresh ourselves with a bath and then return rested to your presence."

"It is forgiven," said Nate; Rejalin nodded and met Mallen's eyes again with her gaze. "I shall have a selection of costumes brought to your chambers."

Mallen inclined his head and left the hall with his officer. They walked in silence, not even speaking when they reached their respective rooms. The dispute between Rejalin and Alvaro had spread to the two men.

By evening it was to be settled.

Not only was the masked ball about to begin, but the sky had suddenly changed, so when Prince Mallen awoke he found only lowering darkness as far as the eye could see.

From the window of his chamber just above the crenellated battlements he could discern the various shades of gray in the clouds, interspersed with strips of ragged black, racing across with the wind, and curtains of rain falling to the ground to soak the fields of Goldensheaf.

The wind had picked up noticeably, with the fresh breeze now a gale, undecided about whether it should get stronger still or start to die away. On the horizon lightning flashed, and Mallen heard a rumble of distant thunder.

There was a knock. "Excuse me, my prince. We are

awaited," called Alvaro from outside the door. "Put on your costume and let us go down."

"I'll be ready soon," Mallen replied, looking through the selection of masks King Nate had supplied. At first he could not find anything to suit his mood. He wanted neither to be an airy fantastical form in blue floating cloth and wire contraptions, nor to represent an oversized ear of barley; nor to wear a robe of gold pieces that would be heavier than his armor.

He decided on wearing his own armor instead and with it a black and white feathered mask studded with rubies. Then he went to open the door, to be met with a surprising vision of Alvaro. He laughed out loud.

The officer had forced himself into a gnome costume. The false nose of papier-mâché and a foolish cap with bells on showed how he was having to present himself at the ball. "There was no choice," he growled. "I'll wager this is King Nate's idea of revenge for the quarrel at table." He looked at his master enviously. "So what are you supposed to be?"

"I am going as my father. He wore this armor, and I'm about the size he was in the pictures," replied Mallen, not able to suppress his grin. "If there's a prize this evening you can be sure of my vote."

"Too kind, my prince." Alvaro waited until Mallen had started down the corridor, then followed him, a little to one side. "I wanted to ask you to forgive me," he said at last. "But I couldn't help saying what I did. You know I've got nothing against the elves. But as long as they can't provide any explanation apart from the one *you* gave to Rejalin, I'm staying on my guard."

"Let it go," said Mallen, clapping him on the shoulder. "You are forgiven. Just make sure you don't go on like that again when I'm around. Otherwise you're free to say what you like." He knew that many of the army veterans shared his officer's views. Forbidding them to voice their opinions would only encourage their prejudice against the elves.

"Thank you, my prince." Alvaro bowed. They reached the stairs down to the ballroom where the guests were assembling. The costumes were brightly colored, some eccentric, many daring in the extreme. There were animals in the throng as well as imaginary beings; even an orc or two and an älf were spotted by the visitors from Idoslane.

"Rejalin won't like that," grinned Alvaro, pointing to the älf.

"Now you're a gnome, the spitefulness suits you. Mind you don't stick like that."

They went down the steps and their arrival was announced. They were met with applause—it was a double honor to be bowing to a hero and to a prince.

Mallen found himself looking out for Rejalin. He caught sight of her near the door, wearing a dress that could only have been woven by elves: it seemed to consist of silver threads and stars. Together with the jewel-studded coronet of plaited hair her appearance was that of an elf goddess, a constellation of the night sky come to life and wandering now among mortals.

Rejalin smiled over at him and bowed.

For the prince the world stopped turning; he only had eyes for her. Even when King Nate in the costume of a magus arrived to bid him welcome and stood directly in front of him, Mallen's gaze slid round to where the elf maiden was. Nothing could match her immaculate beauty, not the flawless crystal on the tables, the shining gold on the walls or the wonderful paintings on the ceiling . . . Apart from her everything paled into ugly insignificance.

"Prince Mallen—can you hear me?" King Nate tried to get his attention. "I was telling you that you will be given an opportunity to admire the diamond."

Now he had to tear his eyes away. "What diamond?" he asked, distractedly. Then he remembered. "Oh, you mean *that* diamond?"

Nate's eyes smiled knowingly. "It is the only thing that could compete with Rejalin's own faultless beauty."

Mallen looked over to her again, but she had slipped from sight among the throng of guests. Disappointment filled him and he turned to Nate. "You would show me the stone? Why?"

"Do you fear a danger, Prince Mallen?" the king asked. "In this hall there are only people that I trust. None here would dare to lay a hand on my possessions." He raised his right hand, a movement noted on the dais nearby. The soft music died away, to be replaced by fanfares, calling the attention of all the guests to their royal host. Tabaîn's ruler mounted the steps to his throne. "Trusted friends! The winds may rage outside, but we shall not let them affect our welcome for our honored guest, Prince Mallen, ruler of Idoslane and hero of many battles fought to protect our land, and for whom this celebration ball is held." The crowd clapped enthusiastically. Nate gestured toward Rejalin, who had come to where Mallen was standing. "The people of Âlandur likewise have honored us by sending a wise and dazzling beauty. Rejalin is my guest and is having discussions with me about how our two realms can help each other with the knowledge we have each amassed." The crowd applauded once more.

"Dazzling beauty is usually to distract from some hidden flaw," muttered Alvaro. One of the guests in orc costume turned his head.

King Nate signed to the guards to open the door. As Tabaîn's anthem sounded, a servant brought out a velvet cushion bearing a diamond. The people held their breath. The stone caught the light from the chandeliers and glowed with cold fire.

"Humans and elves are here assembled. And so I want to complete the circle of peoples by repeating the words of Gandogar Silverbeard, the high king of the dwarves, when he handed this gift to me." Nate cleared his throat. "Just as this and thirteen further stones all resemble each other, may our thoughts henceforth be in harmony and our hearts beat for the benefit of all our lands. If doubts arise within the community of our peoples, let us look at the stone and remember." He lifted the diamond in both hands and held it above his head. "Let us remember these words! For Tabaîn! For Girdlegard!"

Cheers resounded as the assembled guests were swept on a wave of enthusiasm. But Alvaro grimaced. He thought the king's words were aimed at him.

"Though it shine never so brightly," said Mallen to Rejalin "it is a lifeless thing and cannot match your living beauty." He held out his hand. "Will you do me the honor of taking the floor with me?"

The elf nodded and laid her left hand on his outstretched

palm. "You will have to show me how. I am not familiar with the dance steps humans use."

The prince led her to the middle of the ballroom, oblivious to all else. "Simply follow my lead, Rejalin."

Nate came over to Alvaro, who was furiously watching the spellbound prince. "You will have taken note of my words, Alvaro?" enquired the king, holding out the stone. "Harmony is the order of the day."

The officer bowed. "Certainly, Your Majesty." He looked at the diamond. "But you are aware that only one of the fourteen gems is the real diamond," he said, so quietly that none of the others could hear. "That is the way with false beauty. Many allow themselves to be dazzled by it," he added regretfully, his eyes on the dance floor, "while others recognize it for what it is."

King Nate closed his fingers over the diamond, his voice angry now. "Alvaro, you are an incorrigible warrior, blinkered and unwilling to recognize goodness even when it is dancing in front of your nose. The costume of a gnome is indeed well suited to you tonight."

"Whereas the garb of a magus that you wear is pretentious on your shoulders," retorted Alvaro with anger. "I say what I mean, even to the most powerful in the land." He tapped himself on the chest. "For I have fought for this land. In the front line, man to man. It is to a blinkered, incorrigible warrior such as myself that you owe your title." He glanced over at the guest in the älfar costume. "Excuse me, I will join the other monsters. I have wise phrases, too: it was always mistrust that averted disaster, never trust." His heart beating fast, Alvaro made his bow, only too well aware of the enormity of the words he had spoken to the ruler.

At that moment the door of the ballroom balcony flew open as a mighty gust of wind blew out most of the candles; only those in glass lanterns resisted staunchly.

A fizzing, crackling object swept through, throwing off sparks, and clanking and clattering as it bounced down from step to step. It looked like two hemispherical iron braziers fused together, but in its center there was not burning charcoal but a strange figure. Stone flags cracked under the weight of the contraption.

The dancers pushed each other out of the way in horror and the guards rushed up with their halberds at the ready to protect the king.

The huge metal globe, a cage of strong iron bands each the width of two fingers, crashed through the crowd, mowing down two of the men; there was the sound of breaking bones. The guards were left screaming in agony.

In full view of the terrified spectators the grim object came to a halt. Locks clanked open and the metal bands folded away, disappearing into a kind of iron sack on the creature's back.

What the frightened guests had only vaguely been able to see up to now emerged grinning and baring its teeth. It was as tall and broad as an orc, with shimmering gray skin streaked with black and dark green. The creature's face had a terrifying grace and symmetry that the humans here had heard of in tales of quite another people: the älfar. Sharp ears protruded through the long black hair, and as it drew its mighty sword, it opened its mouth in a roar, revealing a powerful set of pointed teeth.

"Stay back!!" Mallen pushed Rejalin aside and ran over

to the king. There was no doubt in his mind that the creature wanted the diamond. *The* diamond.

He raced to the head of the line of guards who stood in front of their ruler with lowered spearpoints at the ready. Someone quickly handed him a shield.

The prince took a closer look at the strange monster. On its legs it wore a flexible armor covering so that its lower body looked to be made of iron. Chest, upper arms and throat were protected by metal plates with runic decorations: these plates, Mallen was shocked to notice, were fastened directly into the creature's skin by means of thick metal wire.

"Stone!" it commanded in a voice as clear as glass, thrusting its hand out toward King Nate. The fingers clicked open and reflected the lamplight; like the rest of the creature's forearm they were covered in metal. Mallen saw the countless bolts and thin rivets holding body and armor welded together.

"By Palandiell! Is the evil one reincarnated?" asked Alvaro, appearing at the prince's side and holding a sword he had grabbed from one of the injured guards. "Whatever it is, it should by rights be dead. Do you see what it has on its back?"

Mallen took a closer look. It was not a rucksack but a kind of metal box held in place by six long rods piercing the body. The ends protruded from the creature's chest and were reinforced with crossbeams so that they were not torn out of the flesh by the sheer weight of the metal. No living being could withstand such torture.

"Stone!" it repeated forcefully, stepping forward; an iron shoe landed with a crash on the flagstone, cracking it in half. The runes glowed an intimidating green—all except one. Mallen would not otherwise have noticed it, but it was very different in appearance from the others—namely, elvish!

"What are you?" asked King Nate, who continued steadfastly to hold the gemstone concealed in his hand. "What do you want with the stone?"

Mallen turned round to Rejalin, who had remained out on the dance floor, white-faced as a corpse, staring at the monster. He could read recognition in her eyes. *What can this mean?* he thought.

Then the monstrosity sprang. Without noticeable effort it jumped over the row of soldiers and landed next to the king; the marble cracked noisily where it came down. Before anyone could act, it had grabbed hold of the monarch, tearing the diamond out of his hands and taking three of Nate's fingers with it. He screamed and sank to his knees, blood gushing over his hand and staining the costly garments he wore.

Alvaro and Mallen both attacked at once: one from the right, one from the left.

The monster roared and parried Alvaro's blow with its bare hand. The runes on the armor glowed green, and the creature shattered the descending blade as easily as if it had been made of balsa wood. Then it kicked the officer in the chest so hard that he shot against the guards as if from a catapult, knocking three of them flying.

Mallen was sure at least his own attack would be successful, but his opponent turned with unbelievable speed, so that Mallen's blade landed on the armored breastplate. The sword thrust was deflected harmlessly.

The response was a flying iron fist.

Mallen ducked and the blow shattered his shield rather than his face. He had an idea how a wall might react to the blows of a battering ram. In spite of the weight of his armor it knocked him over so that he lost his footing and sailed two paces back through the air. He fell heavily against the wall and saw stars dancing before his eyes. "What are you waiting for?" he yelled. "It's taken the stone! Don't let it get away." He threw down the useless shield and launched another onslaught.

By this time the soldiers had been shaken out of their trance and were pinning their hopes on the superiority of their numbers.

The monstrous being thrashed around itself with a captured sword, bringing down one of the men. The rune-glow grew stronger, seeming to give the creature immense power. Picking up its victim by one leg, it screamed and hurled him against the attacking guards, who reeled back in horror to avoid the human cudgel. This provided the monster with the gap it needed to dash through and escape. It had what it had come for. The bloody cadaver of the unfortunate guard was dropped, horribly twisted and battered.

At the stairway Alvaro confronted the fleeing creature; crouched forward in readiness, he brandished his outstretched sword in the direction of the beast. "The face of an elf, the body of an orc and the magic runes of Dsôn Balsur on your armor; *what* are you?" he demanded to know.

Mallen raced after the monster, five guards in his wake. He was desperate to retrieve the stone. Alvaro knew he had no chance of vanquishing the beast on his own. He wanted to give his prince time to attack from behind.

But the monster had seen through the plan. It glanced back over its shoulder at its pursuers, bared its teeth, threw down its sword and dashed past Alvaro.

"Halt!" The officer raised his weapon to strike.

The ghastly thing touched him on the head with its left hand; runes flashed and a lightning bolt was released, incapacitating everyone in the room with the dazzling light.

When Mallen could see again it was clear that the intruder had disappeared. Rejalin was kneeling next to Alvaro cradling his head; blood gushed from his throat in a stream impossible to staunch.

The guards bolted up the steps to look outside for the escaped monster, while Mallen dropped on his haunches by the side of his mortally wounded comrade. "No, my friend. Do not let your soul depart." He pulled off the false gnome mask, took the man's hand in his own and pressed it hard. He tried to hide the depth of his concern at his friend's condition so that Alvaro would not realize how close he was to death. Hope was essential. "I beseech you."

Alvaro attempted to speak, his gaze sliding over to the elf maiden. But he was coughing blood and his croaking voice could not be understood; finally his body fell back and his eyes relinquished all signs of life.

Tears flowed down Mallen's cheeks. He was not ashamed to weep. He had lost a man at whose side he had ridden and fought through countless battles, against enormous odds—and yet they had always survived. What no orc sword had ever achieved this monster had brought about with a single touch of the hand. "There, you see what has come of your longing for combat," he murmured as he gently closed the dead man's eyelids. "You shall not be forgotten. Your death shall not stay unavenged." He nodded over to Rejalin, who was watching him, compassion in her gaze. "Is it true what he said?"

"What do you mean, Prince Mallen?" She carefully laid the officer's head back on the ground, dismayed at the sight of the blood sticking to her fingers. Mallen thought this must be the first time in her sheltered existence that she had been confronted with violent and brutal death in such a way. She had lived among art and poetry, not warfare.

"Alvaro recognized the runes on the armor as being of älfar origin. I, too, found them familiar in some way. They were similar to those I saw on enemy armor at Porista. What can you tell me?"

The elf maiden avoided his eyes.

Mallen let go of the dead man's hand. "Did I see elf runes on the armor?"

"You are mistaken."

Contrary to all rules of respect and courtly conduct he took fast hold of her arm and gently forced her to look him in the eyes. "Rejalin! What do you know?"

"Nothing," she said harshly, pulling free. "I was too far away to be able to recognize anything about the creature."

"You are lying. Your eyes—"

"You dare to accuse me, Rejalin of Âlandur, of speaking an untruth?" She sprang to her feet. "I should have known better. You are an uncultured yokel, no better than any other human I have ever met," she said with disdain. "I fear your realm must undergo intense scrutiny before it can be judged worthy to receive the gifts of our knowledge."

It seemed to Mallen that a mask concealing the elf's real nature had fallen from her countenance; her anger revealed her true attitude toward himself and his kind. The admiration he had been feeling for her started to ebb away. "One of the diamonds has been stolen, but this is all you can think of now?"

"It is one of fourteen."

"It is the *second* of fourteen," Mallen corrected, standing up. "Rejalin, you will tell me what you . . ."

Rejalin turned on her heel and went over to King Nate.

The prince started to follow her but was prevented by the two guests dressed as orcs. "Rejalin has no wish to continue speaking to you, Prince Mallen of Idoslane," came the voice from behind the papier-mâché. The man lifted his hand to remove the mask; the face underneath was that of an elf. It bore a smile, but a cool one. "She prefers to attend to the care of her host and to see what the elves' knowledge of healing can do to aid him."

"This is knowledge which you have yet to earn. Go and seek the diamond," said the other elf, slipping in his turn out of his disguise. "We shall inform you when Rejalin wishes to speak to you about what has occurred."

Mallen pushed them to one side, but they overtook him and barred his way. He stopped short and was about to raise his sword arm in earnest when he recalled the words spoken so recently by the king. Harmony; the peoples united. "Tell Rejalin that I expect an explanation and that

I shall inform all the other royal houses of Girdlegard about this event and the strange attitude an elf woman displayed. If she won't speak to me she will have to account for herself when her own ruler, Prince Liútasil of Âlandur, commands it."

"Certainly, Prince Mallen," the elf on the right nodded superciliously. "We shall pass on your words."

Mallen sheathed his sword, called some of his soldiers and gave the order for them to carry the body of his friend out of the ballroom.

As they laid him on a stretcher and bore him away up the steps, a thought occurred: Alvaro had been touched on the head by the monster's hand—not on the neck where the deadly wound had been. While all were blinded by the flash no one had been near him. No one save the elf woman.

An incredible idea came to him. Mallen stopped on the dais and turned to Rejalin, who was attending to the king. *Was she exacting revenge for his insults, he wondered, or was Alavaro too close to the truth in what he said today at the feast?*

The unique beauty of the elf woman had disappeared completely. From now on Mallen resolved to treat her with the strongest suspicion.

Her and all other elves.

III

Girdlegard,
The Mountains of the Gray Range on the Northern
Border of the Fifthling Kingdom
Spring, 6241st Solar cycle

Tungdil and Boïndil were in one of Gandogar's own chambers waiting impatiently for the high king to arrive. The dust of the Outer Lands was still chafing their skin and clinging to their beards, but nothing, not even the glimpse of a water trough, had kept them from the opportunity of an immediate meeting. There was simply too much to discuss.

"Did you see how she wept when we handed over her son's helmet?" asked Boïndil, filling a jug with water. For once he felt like quenching his thirst with water rather than beer—unlike Tungdil, who had already downed a tankard of the black stuff.

"It was better to let her assume that her son is dead," insisted Tungdil.

"But you said yourself that he might well be alive, and that you didn't trust those obvious signs."

"Better to find her son within the cycle and bring him back to her, than to leave her in this uncertainty."

Ireheart was silent. "And what do you think that figure was? And the strange thing behind it?"

"Maybe a gnome in disguise," said Tungdil, gulping down a draught. "Or a dwarf?"

"Or an Undergroundling?"

Tungdil had asked himself this question countless times on the way back from the Stone Gateway.

The fact was that they had found indecipherable runes on the tunnel walls. He and Boïndil had assumed they were of dwarf origin because of the perfection of the craft used in their execution.

It was also a known fact that old records and drawings described a race related to their own on the other side of the mountain chain encircling Girdlegard. It was they who had forged a first Keenfire so they must have loved working with red-hot metal and have been experts in the smithy. But regrettably it seemed that not a soul had ever seen one of them face to face. "I just don't know," admitted Tungdil honestly. "But if it was one of those dwarves, then we know now they don't like us."

The warrior's brow furrowed, his expression thunderous. "You think they're after our treasure?" He put the beaker down and ran his finger along the edge of his spurred ax. "Just let them try it," he growled aggressively.

"Let us see why Gandogar wanted us back here so swiftly," Tungdil said to calm him. "The messenger we found at the gate—he must have been sent out after us just after we left."

"It can't be anything terrible," said the warrior twin, "or the guards at the gates would have been on high alert."

The door opened to admit Gandogar. Three elves followed him, completely out of place here in their fine raiment, garments of delicate fabrics in the lightest of colors. In Tungdil's view their robes alone were disturbing enough, contrasting with the muted browns and subdued tones that the children of the Smith preferred to wear.

But really, he thought, it wasn't their apparel. It was the elves themselves he didn't like. Not elves in general: he had nothing against them in principle. Their way of life, from their buildings to their clothing and their language: it all formed an organic whole in Âlandur. But here their very presence struck a discordant note, like a shrill soprano singing out high above the mellow harmonies of a dwarf-voice choir.

Judging from the expression on Boïndil's face, he was of like mind. "It *is* something terrible," he murmured, half in earnest, half in jest. "It's delicate little elves."

"So the heroes have returned!" Gandogar greeted them warmly, shaking hands. "Were you pleased to find your old friend, Tungdil?"

"Your little surprise worked well, Your Majesty," Tungdil smiled.

Gandogar took a step to one side. "These are Eldrur, Irdosíl and Antamar. A delegation from the elf ruler, Prince Liútasil—not messengers but ambassadors to initiate co-operation between our hitherto hostile peoples." He presented the two dwarves.

The elves bowed to Tungdil and Ireheart. This gesture of respect would not have been so sincere ten cycles before—if indeed it would have been made at all. They had been warned about the likely state of Tungdil, other-wise the elf faces might have betrayed natural feelings of disgust.

Boïndil could not help himself. "Well, knock me down with a shovelful of coals!" he laughed out loud. "The . . ."

and he nearly said "pointy-ears", ". . . elves and dwarves living under one roof?" He dug Tungdil in the ribs. "What do you say to that, eh, Scholar?"

Eldrur joined in with the laughter. "It may seem strange to you, Boïndil Doubleblade, but our ruler considers it was high time this came about. He needed to wait until he had persuaded the last of the doubters in our ranks of the great benefits of close cooperation." He looked around. "I wouldn't go so far as to say we were moving in permanently. We shall be staying here for the next hundred orbits, as we shall do in all the dwarven kingdoms, to learn more about their land and culture."

"Sounds like spying to me," said Ireheart. "You want our formulae for iron and steel smelting, don't you?" He winked at Tungdil.

"No, on the contrary. We want to share our knowledge with you. We are not looking for recompense, but I am sure that your people," here Eldrur turned to Gandogar, "will reward us for our generosity. By this I do not mean with gifts of monetary value, but with the knowledge and rich experience of your forefathers."

"So, not spies but blackmailers," mouthed Boïndil. He was enjoying himself. "Even if their speech is flowery."

Tungdil answered, "At long last Girdlegard is uniting." He licked his dry lips, wanting his next beer. "It seems exactly the right time, because we have something to report from our excursion into the Outer Lands."

The elves exchanged glances. "The high king has already intimated something. You have shown courage again, Tungdil Goldhand," Eldrur said, according him respect.

"I asked him to," said Gandogar, inviting them over to

partake of the modest refreshments on the table in the middle of the room. The word "modest" in connection with dwarven cuisine is always to be interpreted generously, as is familiar from their classic dishes. The elves appreciated the simmered mushrooms but their palates were offended when it came to the strongly spiced cheese or the dessert prepared from the intestines of gugul larvae. Tungdil was particularly cheered by the sight of a small barrel of black beer.

"We acquire the beetles from the freeling markets in the south, and we process them here ourselves," explained the high king proudly. He had not noticed the faces of his elven guests, who were trying their best to appear hungry. Gandogar helped himself to the white cream. "If for nothing else, you have proved invaluable in opening up trade for us in this way," he said to Tungdil, who was also tucking in, careful, however, to avoid those dishes that reminded him too acutely of time spent in the city of the freelings and with Myr.

"A dwarf-woman had asked us to look out for her son, Gremdulin," said Tungdil, downing the next two tankards as he launched into his report on their trip to the Outer Lands. Ireheart had to signal to him that his speech was getting slurred. "We found piles of orc bones in a cave— the monsters had been slaughtered by the hundred, it seems. We were just about to investigate further when a dwarf we didn't know turned up and somehow brought the whole cave crashing down around us. He was working with the weirdest machine. Never seen the like . . ." He gestured with his arms to indicate the dimensions. "When we'd escaped the rockfall we headed straight back out to the gate," he said, hurriedly ending his report. He just managed to suppress a huge belch, disguising it as a long exhalation, but it was enough to shatter the equilibrium of the elves.

"I'll wager they regret they ever came," whispered Boïndil merrily. "Look, their pointy ears are drooping. Maybe I can cheer them up with the one about the dwarf and the orc."

Gandogar ignored the crude behavior of his heroes. "It sounds as if we have a completely new danger to contend with," he said, concerned, addressing them all. "Do your people know about these machines Tungdil is describing?"

Eldrur hesitated, his brown gaze fixed on Tungdil's empty tankard. "Forgive me if I speak bluntly, but can we really believe him? Is there not a possibility he may be exaggerating?" He glanced at Ireheart. "Is that exactly how it was, Boïndil Doublebade, or did you both perhaps succumb to your thirst on the way?"

Had it been spoken before the death of his brother, the politely voiced insult would have brought Boïndil vaulting over the table to grab the elf by the ears, using one hand to dunk the scoundrel's face in the soup while he wielded his ax in the other to cut him into tiny slices.

But nowadays his combat-fury was stilled, and the curse was broken that made his blood boil. "I would say only this, *Friend* Elf: even if a dwarf is too drunk to tie his shoelaces, he will never, ever tell a lie." And his laughter was as sharp-edged as the blade of an ax.

Eldrur realized his mistake and bowed in apology. "Forgive me, Tungdil Goldhand."

Tungdil waved his hand dismissively. Even if he remained calm on the surface, the words of the elf were eating into him. He had reached the point where his reports were not being believed! He looked down at himself, noting the belly, the bits of food he had dropped and the dirt on the chain mail shirt that now fitted him as tightly as a sausage skin. His eye fell on the empty tankards. *What has become of me?* he asked himself in desperation and disgust—and then reached out for the next beer.

"No, I have never heard of any machinery like that, High King Gandogar," said Eldrur. "Were there not some rumors once of a dwarf people known as the Undergroundlings? Perhaps—?"

The door opened and a messenger hurried in, drenched in sweat. "Excuse my bursting in, sire. My name is Beldobin Anvilstand from the Clan of the Steely Nails." He made a bow to the high king. "I am sent by my Queen, Xamtys the Second, with this message for you, King Gandogar," he said, out of breath. "You must read it at once! There are terrible things happening in the Red Mountain Range."

The leather wallet changed hands and Gandogar broke the seal; he quickly read the lines and raised his eyes from the paper. "My friends, here we have the answer to our riddle." He read the letter out:

Honored Majesty, High King Gandogar,

I fear we have underestimated the tenacity of our enemies.

  After more than five cycles of quiet they have again

set out to bring death and renewed destruction to our peoples with methods previously unknown.

I have already lost fifty-four good workers and ten of my warriors to an uncanny machine that travels through our tunnels attacking anything in its path. It has teeth, tongs, blades and other deadly weaponry with which it hacks and stabs. I have enclosed a drawing, in case your people or perhaps the fifthlings with whom you are staying currently, were to come across such a machine.

It is subverting any attempt on our part to repair the tunnel network, because no one dares enter the galleries. I understand the fear only too well. So far we have found nothing with which to combat this malign contraption, as it gives no warning when or where it may strike. We are not able to defend ourselves or prepare for its attacks. Traps we have tried have proved ineffective.

We know nothing about it. Only that it is immensely strong and heavy. It is partly steampowered. I assume it is of a similar construction to the hoists we use to lift the wagons onto the rails, but it is smaller and it is mobile.

The runes on the armor plating make it clear that a thirdling force is behind it: "Beaten yet not destroyed, we bring destruction."

I do not want the entire thirdling community blamed for the actions of an individual or of an ignorant and malicious minority. But they must all be interrogated to find out who is capable of constructing something like this.

I have sent warnings to all the other dwarf realms, because I do not know if the danger is targeted solely on us or whether—Vraccas help us—there are similar machines elsewhere.

The dwarf assembly must be called, so that we can decide on action.

May Vraccas bless you and keep you, High King Gandogar.

Queen Xamtys Stubbornstreak
of the Clan of the Stubbornstreaks,
in the Firstling Kingdom of Borengar's Folk

"There we are! That's the explanation. That figure in the tunnel was a thirdling," Ireheart exclaimed, slamming his hand down so hard that the spoons rattled. "We must have discovered their base in the Outer Lands."

Tungdil took a deep breath. He was not feeling well. He had swigged that beer far too quickly. "Why would they bother to dig to the outside and send their machines from the Outer Lands into our tunnels?" he objected, mumbling and burping.

"To advance unhindered—much less likely to be disturbed than coming overland from somewhere in the Outer Lands," said Gandogar, agreeing with the dwarf-twin.

"It would explain why they were making the tunnels collapse behind them, like you said," Eldrur chipped in. "They want to be sure they're not found." He continued the line of thought pursued by the previous speakers. "I think they must be based in the Outer Lands just on the other side of the border. They're sending the machines in from there."

Gandogar put the letter down on the table. "Xamtys is right. I'll call an assembly. All the dwarf folks and the freelings, too, must decide on what to do. We'll have to send a force out through the Northern Pass to find this fiendish workshop."

"We've seen *one* at least of these evil bastards," said Boïndil, clenching his fists in anger. "If only we had been quicker . . . Who knows? Perhaps we could have put a swift end to all this horror."

Tungdil was no longer in any condition to follow what was being said; the room was going round and his stomach was rebelling. "I must go," he mumbled, getting up and swaying off toward the door. Boïndil sprang to his aid in case he fell. "Leave me alone." Tungdil pushed his friend away, "I can manage." He stumbled off through the door and disappeared.

Ireheart watched in distress. He hardly recognized the good friend Tungdil once had been. Sighing deeply he returned to the table to face the disapproving elves and Gandogar's anger. "It's a fever he picked up on the journey," he said in excuse. "It's affecting his mind."

Irdosíl smiled; his light gray eyes said he believed not a single word yet he did not confront the lie, wanting to spare Boïndil's feelings. A dwarf did not tell lies.

"This is how we shall proceed," said the high king. "A summons will go out this very day to all the dwarves." He turned to the elves. "You are also welcome to attend our assembly."

Boïndil was about to object. He thought better of it

and put some food in his mouth instead. He did not like the open manner Gandogar used with the elves. Letting the pointy-ears see their customs and way of life was one thing, but to admit them to their innermost decision-making circle was a step too far, he thought. Then it occurred to him that the arrangement went both ways. "So, who will be going to Âlandur, Your Majesty?" he asked innocently, looking at Eldrur.

"I don't understand." Gandogar was irritated. "What do you mean?"

"Our return visit. Our elf friends are all out visiting at the moment, if I've got it right?" he expanded. "They are bound to expect the children of the Smith to send a delegation to Âlandur to pay our respects in turn."

Eldrur's smile came out crooked. "Prince Liútasil will not be insisting the visit be reciprocated, Boïndil Doubleblade. He is aware of the discomfort you face if you have to spend time under the open sky or in forests."

Ireheart folded his arms over his long black beard. "Not so fast, Friend Elf. If you can cope with spending time underground we can certainly manage to do the reverse. I'm not afraid of any tree."

Gandogar grinned. "A good idea, Boïndil. Why don't you take on that responsibility?"

"*Me?*" That was hardly the outcome the dwarf-twin had been expecting. "I think it's better if I stay here, High King Gandogar. If we're off to the Outer Lands you will have need of me."

"Of course, there was never any doubt about that. But it will be some time before all the dwarf clan delegates arrive," said Gandogar unwaveringly. "Âlandur is not far away, so I suggest you pay a courtesy visit to the realm of the elves. What more suitable ambassador than one of our greatest heroes?"

"Your Majesty, I . . ." Boïndil attempted to change his sovereign's mind. He and Eldrur were looking equally unhappy about this.

"No more objections, Boïndil," Gandogar said amicably. "It's settled. You shall leave at daybreak with gifts for Lord Liútasil to thank him for his efforts to further understanding between our peoples. I shall send for you when our assembly reaches consensus and we are ready to set off for the Outer Lands."

He stood up and nodded to the elves. "Eldrur, if you would be good enough to compose a document in your own language, explaining my ambassador's mission and stating that he bears with him the most cordial greetings of the high king of the dwarves."

"Certainly, Most High Majesty." The elf bowed as Gandogar withdrew, leaving Boïndil and the other guests to their meal.

Eldrur considered the warrior's bearded face. Ireheart was picking reluctantly at his food. "You are cursing yourself, aren't you?" he remarked, hitting the nail on the head.

"No," retorted Ireheart, chewing on a piece of mushroom. "I could hit myself in the face, though. With this weapon," he said, pointing at the crow's beak at his side.

The elves laughed. It was a soft melodious sound: more a refined, tinkling chorus than merry heartfelt laughter. False as gnome-gold. "You will certainly be something of a novelty for Âlandur," predicted Eldrur, sounding anything but pleased.

"That letter you're writing for me to take—why don't you tell your prince to send me straight home again?" Ireheart requested grimly.

"Are you maybe not as tough as you were telling us?" joked Irdasíl. "What wouldn't I give to be going in your place?"

"No chance." Ireheart gave him a disdainful glance, then looked back down at his plate. "You're far too tall for a dwarf," he muttered, shoving the plate away and getting up.

"I didn't mean I wished to go as a dwarf, I meant . . ."

"So you don't fancy being a dwarf, eh?" He looked out from under beetling black brows, laying hold of the handle of his weapon. "You got something against my race? Come right out and say it, *my friend*."

"No, no, not at all," protested Irdosíl. "What I was trying to say . . ."

Eldrur laughed. "He's taking a rise out of you, Irdosíl— he's joking, can't you see?"

Boïndil was grinning. "Took his time, didn't he?" He sauntered off toward the door, crow's beak hammer harmlessly shouldered. "Have you heard the one about the orc who stops to ask a dwarf the way?" The three elves shook their heads. "Then it's high time the forests were told some proper jokes." He winked and left them.

Antamar, who so far had said nothing, looked at Eldrur. "Stupid mess."

"I know." Eldrur was annoyed. "But what should we have done?"

"Just now? Nothing." Antamar regarded the others in turn. "But now you can compose a suitable letter for him to take with him."

Eldrur had noted the particular stress on the word "suitable". That was enough.

On the way to his room Tungdil had got lost a few times. Eventually someone showed him to a bed.

He had not the slightest idea where he was, but his drinking instinct immediately found the bottle of brandy on the shelf.

However much his stomach was protesting, he stood up and groped for the bottle, greedily pulling out the cork and taking a long swig.

The sharp liquor was hardly down his throat before he was sick. The food he had eaten came up again and again, and the pot he had grabbed in his haste could not hold it all.

He spluttered, gasping for air. Then he caught sight of his image in the large silver mirror. He saw himself in his full piteous glory: a bottle in one hand, a chamber pot in the other, beard and chain mail dripping with vomit, his body gross and his whole appearance utterly neglected. A fine figure of a hero now, indeed.

Tungdil sank down on his knees; he could not take his eyes off the mirror, which showed him his own reflection in such merciless clarity.

"No," he whispered, hurling the brandy at the polished silver; the glass bottle shattered, sending a film of alcohol all over his own image. That ugly Tungdil was still staring at him with red eyes. "No," he yelled, throwing the pot, but missing the mirror. He held his hands over his eyes. "Go away," he roared and started to weep. "Go away, murderer! You killed him . . ." He sank down onto the flagstones and gave in to grief, sobbing and moaning until sleep took over.

He never felt the strong arms lift him and carry him away.

Girdlegard,
Queendom of Weyurn, Mifurdania,
Late Spring, 6241st Solar Cycle

Dressed simply and comfortably, Rodario was sitting on the steps of the caravan musing over a new play he might put on.

He and his troupe were on a small island, camped just outside the town proper, which, ever since the earthquake, had been surrounded by Weyurn's extensive stretches of water. The small lakes had multiplied and many citizens had lost all their possessions. Rodario's company had done more of the journey by water or over islands than on terra firma, because relatively little of the queens' realm of Weyurn had escaped the floodwaters. It was a strange sight.

It was definitely time for a new heroic saga, now the old one about the victory over the eoîl and the avatars had lost its thrill for him. And the spectators were starting to feel the same way.

Or maybe a comedy this time? he wondered. The audiences were demanding more entertainment, more wit and less pathos and slaughter nowadays. Times were good; the people of Girdlegard were free of cares and they wanted to laugh at on-stage innuendo.

In thoughtful mood he watched Tassia hang out her washing between two of the caravans. The bright sun on her thin linen dress made it almost transparent in places. When she felt his eyes on her, desiring her, she stopped what she was doing, turned and gave him a wave.

He lifted the hand with the quill in greeting. There was no question about it: she would play the main role in his new play and men would come in droves to the theater marquee to see her.

"Yes, well, the men," he murmured. He was jealously noting how Reimar, one of the workers who helped put up the tents, was handing her a flower. Tassia laughed happily and gave Reimar a kiss. On the mouth. And she was letting him put his arm round her waist.

"Tassia, would you come over here, please?" he called, slightly louder than intended. "And you, Reimar—get off back to your work, now!"

"At once, Master of the Word." She pegged up a cotton bodice to dry, put her hand to Reimar's cheek and sauntered over, carrying her empty washing basket. "What can I do for you?"

"I need your advice." He invented something on the spot; in reality he wanted her away from Reimar's attentions. He held out his notes. "What do you think?"

She took the sheets of paper and skimmed what he had written. "Impossible."

"Impossible?" he repeated, horrified, grabbing back the pages. "But it's . . ."

"Impossible to read," she laughed, sitting herself on his lap. "Your handwriting is appalling. You'll have to tell me what it's all about." She curled a lock of his long dark brown hair playfully round her finger. Then she grinned. "It was only an excuse, wasn't it?"

"Just to get you in my arms, O thou most enchanting of Girdlegard's girls," he said with a false smile indistinguishable from the genuine article unless you had known the man for over ten cycles.

"Not just to drive poor Reimar away?" she needled. "He's such a sweetie. And so strong. Those muscles . . ."

"But no brains at all. And the manners of a pig." Rodario stroked his beard. "And I'm far better-looking. So you see, he can't compete at all."

Tassio kissed him on the forehead. "Sometimes, my dear stage-genius, a woman does not need a man with brains and fine manners," she replied, opening her eyes wide and pretending to look innocent. It told him everything.

He stood up abruptly, so she tumbled to the ground. "So you're taking your pleasures behind my back?"

"Do as you would be done by, my dear. Same standards for all," she laughed, lying back in the grass with her hands clasped behind her blond head. "I've heard tales about you that would shame a randy rabbit. And I've seen those besotted females lining the streets of Mifurdania to flutter their lashes at you." Tassia closed her eyes and turned her beautiful face toward the sun. "They may be a bit long in the tooth, but they seemed to have no objection to a dalliance with the Fabulous Rodario."

"Yes, you are right . . . women find me desirable." The

actor cleared his throat. "But since I've met you, Tassia, things have been different."

"Now, now," she warned, waving a forefinger in warning. "If I were you I wouldn't take an oath on that. I'm not blind, deaf or stupid, and I am definitely capable of identifying the sound of certain nocturnal activities."

Rodario was starting to perspire, and the spring sunshine was not the cause. His plan of attack was failing miserably. He was heading for a humiliating defeat. "I . . . I was practicing my swordplay."

"Is that why the caravan was rocking?"

"There were quite a few leaps and lunges to practice."

"And what sword were you using, my darling?" asked Tassia, as sweet as candy. "Or perhaps it was a dagger. Or only a little pocket knife, the same as all the men?" She opened her eyes wide and flashed him a smile. "Fencing must be so hard, when you're practicing lines for a woman's part at the same time—groaning and the occasional husky "Oh, *unbelievable*!"

Rodario stared at her; he opened his mouth but at first could only stammer and splutter before he was eventually overcome with laughter. Tassia joined in. "I think I'll have to give up my title to you," he said admiringly and sat down beside her on the fresh green grass.

"Which one? *Heart-breaker* or *Unbelievable*?"

"I must stop worrying about things I've always done," he said, more to himself than to her. He lay back, head on his arm, looking at her. "You, my poor dear, have a lot of catching up to do, what with your husband being so much more interested in men than women."

Her cheeriness faded away. "Yes," she said, close to

tears, her chin starting to wobble. "Oh, it's awful, isn't it? Oh, the shame." She hid her face in her hands. "Shame on me. The gods—"

"Stop! Stop!" he interrupted her. "You were far too quick with the tears."

She stopped sniffing immediately and looked up at him through her fingers. "Too quick?"

"More of a transition needed there, or no one will be convinced." He pulled her hands away from her face and kissed her on the forehead. "Apart from that, my dear Tassia, you with your body and face of a temptress elf, I was quite impressed by your performance. You just need a little more practice." She laughed and rolled over on top of him, giving him a good view down her front. He liked what he saw. "One day the *Curiosum* will belong to me and you'll be dancing to my tune," she threatened him jokingly.

"No doubt about that. You've won Reimar over already and you'll soon have all the others eating out of your hand. Even old Gesa." He nodded and pushed her off. She yelped, landing on her backside in one of the few puddles in the field. Rodario stood up. "Oh, I'm so sorry!"

"Come and get me out!" she demanded.

But that was when the idea for a storyline came to him. "Get yourself out, Tassia—I've got to go and write this down." He hurried over to the steps where he had paper, quill and ink. "Inspiration doesn't stick around—you have to get things written down when the ideas come."

The girl, swearing, clambered up and then came and stood by him, wringing the water out of her wet skirt over his head. "You should have some of this, too."

"Not now, Tassia." He really was working. "I've had an idea for a comedy."

"Oh?" She sat down next to him. "What's it about?" She wiped the drops off his face.

"About a man and woman."

"How original."

He stopped writing to look at her. "Or rather, it's about you and me."

Tassia looked interested. "Sounds like a love story."

"Exactly, my blond beauty. Our story will be the plot: a man, a girl married to a husband who prefers other men, an evil father, a swordfight, a relationship full of fire and passion, with wit and—"

". . . and some treasure," Tassia interrupted.

Rodario's quill hurried over the paper. "Good thinking, good thinking," he praised her. "But where do we get the treasure from?"

She smiled brightly. "I could have stolen a fortune from the evil father of my man-loving onetime spouse," she contributed.

It sank in. "Oh, Tassia, no."

"Why not?" she said with a bold smile.

"Tell me *that* bit isn't true!"

"But it is." She took him by the hand, pulled him into his caravan and lifted one of the floorboards. She took out a bundle and opened it up. Rodario knew perfectly well this was not a hiding place he had selected. "Close the door," she said. It was a necklace made of gold and in the middle there was a splendid gemstone that glittered and sparkled in the light from the window. Tassia held it out. "What do you say? Is that a treasure?"

"In the name of goodness," he breathed. "Is that . . . a diamond?" He took the jewel carefully and looked at it from all angles.

"No. Nolik's father is too much of a miser for that, even though he is drowning in gold. It's an imitation cut from the finest rock crystal, Nolik said."

"Did he give you the necklace?"

"Yes." Tassia grinned. "But first he stole it from his father. He gave it to me to make up for how I was being treated. He won't even know it's missing."

Rodario disagreed. He thought the gold was very fine, and he knew that a crystal like that was of considerable value. "We ought to send it back," he said.

She took the jewel back. "Never." She was adamant. "Anyway, we'll need it for the play. Why don't you write up the argument we've just had?" She ran her finger across his cheek. "Dearest, if Nolik's father hasn't sent his bullies after us by now, he's probably not going to. We're three hundred miles away now and nobody's tried to stop us. We've nothing to be afraid of."

He let himself be persuaded. Besides, he liked the idea of putting the necklace in his new drama. "In my play we shall be visited by evil villains who try and steal the necklace." He grinned at her and planted a wild kiss on her mouth. "Oh, I can see it all." He lifted his hand, painting in the air with dramatic gestures. "We are surrounded by villains but we fight our way free. Because the necklace, in reality, is far more than just a jewel." He was getting carried away, his thoughts glowing and throwing off sparks. "Of course. The necklace is a key! The crystal opens . . . a secret grotto, and inside, there's a chamber full of gold and diamonds." A dreamy look came into his eyes and he struck a heroic pose familiar from his stage appearances. "Tassia, I am a genius! Nobody can doubt it, not even the gods. And there will be a fantastic sword-fight in the final scene. Me against three, no, against seven men!"

"But I'll be in that fight, too," she said. "You'll have to give me fencing lessons."

Rodario gave a dirty laugh. "Which kind of sword-fighting were you thinking of?" He bent over and stroked her hair. "This is going to be a huge success—it'll soar like a comet." His exuberance faded suddenly as he remembered: "But we need Furgas. He's the only one who knows how to make all my ideas work."

Tassia wrapped the necklace back up and replaced it in the hiding place. "You're really worried, aren't you?" she said, surprised to note the seriousness so often lacking in the showman Rodario.

He nodded. "I've been searching for five cycles and I've never given up because I'm convinced my friend is still alive and in trouble," he explained, pulling her down to sit beside him on the bed. "Not physical danger, but I fear for his mind. He lost his partner and his two children in the battle at Porista. He was so bitter that in his fury against every living thing he just walked out. Never said goodbye or gave any idea where he was going."

She took his hand and pressed it in sympathy.

Rodario gave an anguished smile. "I've been searching for him all this time. And when you told me you had seen him, I felt hope blossom all of a sudden, you know, like poppies blooming in a cornfield. I'm going to turn

Mifurdania upside-down till someone tells me where he is."

"You will find him," she said, stroking his hand affectionately.

Rodario kissed her bare shoulder. He did not admit to her that he was also a little afraid of encountering his hitherto best friend. There was no way of knowing how Furgas would react. Tungdil had recounted a conversation and the Furgas he had described was not the one Rodario recognized. Someone had once said that death changes the living, too. Perhaps Furgas wouldn't want any more to do with him.

"I'll find him," he echoed Tassia's thought. "The gods know what else will happen."

A little while later, Rodario, dressed as befitted a self-proclaimed emperor of the acting profession, paraded through the streets of Mifurdania with Tassia at his side. Or rather, they walked unsteadily along the narrow wooden causeways and bridges between the houses, because the lakes of Weyurn had spread all this way now.

"They've turned the disaster to their advantage," Rodario said admiringly as they travelled through his old territory, which had been razed to the ground by the orc hordes of the traitor Nôd'onn. "A city on stilts." He pointed over to where a remnant of the wall could be seen above the water line. "That's where Furgas and I and Tungdil and the other dwarves escaped through the gate when the city was attacked." He was beginning to remember more and more about those events. "Come on, I'll show you where the old *Curiosum* used to be."

They made their way through a labyrinth of alleyways that Rodario did not know at all. The town had little in common with the old Mifurdania, because it was smaller and more maze-like now. More than once they ended up back where they had started, but eventually he thought he had found the place.

Disappointment hit him. There was nothing left of the once-imposing building—only a narrow house against whose walls the water was lapping gently.

"There's nothing left," he said. "I'm sorry, Tassia."

"Master Rodario?" called a voice behind him, and someone clapped him on the shoulder, nearly flooring him. Two strong arms swiveled him around. "It is! It's him! Ye gods help poor Mifurdania, the man's come back!"

The actor looked into the broad visage of a strongly built man of roughly fifty cycles. He looked vaguely familiar: thin shirt, dirty leather apron, forearms as thick as ax handles, short blond ash-covered hair—then he remembered. "Lambus!" he laughed. "My friend the smith!—still alive?"

"The orcs didn't finish me off, the waters didn't get me, so I'm still here," the man said merrily and glanced at Tassia. "When will we ever see you without a pretty girl at your side?" he joked.

"When he's dead," Tassia grinned, holding out her hand. "I'm Tassia, his wife. I'm an actress." Rodario looked extremely surprised and rolled his eyes, while she laughed, "We run the company together, the *Curiosum*."

"That's not strictly . . ." he objected, not taking to the role he had been allocated, but he felt a sharp kick to his foot and fell silent.

"It's great to hear our famous Incredible Rodario has come back. Laughter is good for us! I'm sure we've all forgiven you the previous escapades. The cuckolds of Mifurdania will have long forgotten the bedroom farces you played out at their expense." He grinned widely. "What a surprise to see you've settled down. But with a woman like her anyone would settle." He pointed to a wine-shop. "Come on, both of you, I'll buy you a drink."

"I can hardly believe it, either. I must have been drunk when I said yes," Rodario answered, digging Tassia in the ribs and making her gasp. She got her own back by kicking him on the shin.

Lambus noticed nothing. He led them into the inn, sat down at the first table he came to and ordered a jug of wine and some water.

"My broad-chested friend here," Rodario said as he introduced the smith, "used to make all the things we needed for the *Curiosum*: swords, iron bars, metalwork—for all the contraptions and illusions that our props man thought up."

Lambus nodded. "Those were the days! That Furgas was a master! He'd come up with the most amazing effects. Where did he get those spectacular ideas? The gods know how many hours I spent at the forge cursing when things didn't work right first time . . ." They raised their glasses. "Here's to the old days!"

"The old days!" Rodario chimed in. Tassia smiled.

The smith downed his wine and looked up at his actor-friend expectantly. "So what have you got for me this time? Has your magic props man had some new ideas? It's ages since I last saw him!"

Rodario shook his head. "He's not with the troupe now. That's why I'm looking for him."

Lambus furrowed his brow. "You don't say? So he's touring with a company of his own?"

"Why do you say that?"

"He was here. He had a child with him."

Rodario nearly jumped over the table in excitement. "When? When? Lambus, tell me!"

"Half a cycle ago—beginning of autumn."

"Go on!" encouraged Rodario, pouring the smith more wine. "Tell me everything! Where his house is, what he's doing . . ."

"He doesn't have a house. Well, not in Mifurdania. He came by boat, a kind of barge affair." Lambus thought hard. "He was buying stores for the winter, butter and lard, and then sacks of corn. He asked me for the old metal moulds we'd used for the cog-wheels for the shows." His face grew more thoughtful still. "Because of all the food I assumed it was for your troupe going into winter quarters on one of the islands, to rehearse a new play."

"I don't get it," said Rodario. "Has he really taken on new actors?"

"Perhaps he'd had enough of you?" said Lambus. "Did you have a fight? But I can't imagine you two falling out."

Rodario did not feel like telling the whole story. "Do you know which island it was?"

Lambus shrugged his shoulders. "I'm sorry. If you want to find him, it'll be a long search. Since the big flood, islands come and go. Every day there's something new on the waters."

Rodario sighed. At least he knew now that his friend

was alive. But no more than that. "Did he tell you anything?"

"No, not really." The smith was a little awkward. "That is, he wanted me to go with him for four dozen orbits," he admitted at last. "He offered me one hundred Weyurn crowns if I kept quiet about my work. I had to turn him down. I've got too many customers in the town I can't afford to lose." Lambus looked past Rodario and Tassia. "Is someone looking for you, do you think?"

The couple froze, the same thought in their minds. "How many? What do they look like?" asked Rodario without turning round. All he had on him was one pitiful dagger.

Lambus moved his head a little. "Eight. Tall. Big guys. I'd say they can carry heavy loads when they have to. Ordinary kind of clothes, but not from Weyurn."

"So much for that treasure no one was going to miss," Rodario hissed to Tassia. "*He won't even notice the necklace is missing*," he mocked in falsetto.

"Who says it's got to be *my* fault? Perhaps it's just some local fellows whose wives you seduced and they're after your pocket knife," she retorted sharply, exaggerating a deep, boasting voice: "*Roll up, ladies. I have the stamina, I am Unbelievable!*"

"No, my dear. These bruisers are from Nolik's father."

"Is this some new play you're rehearsing?" asked Lambus enthusiastically. "It sounds great!"

Rodario turned to the smith. "Lambus, my good man. The men behind us are not kindly disposed. Would you be good enough . . . ?" He passed him a coin.

The smith nodded. "Go out through the kitchen. I'll try to keep them occupied if they see you, Master Rodario."

The pair stood up slowly and went over to the land-lord, who let them out through the back. But two more of the heavies were standing out there with cudgels in their hands.

"There she is!" called one of them. He jumped at Tassia.

"See—they *are* here because of you!" Rodario couldn't resist the snide remark. He kicked the man in the groin, so that he collapsed in a moaning heap.

Tassia skirted round him as he fell, and grabbed his cudgel. Resolutely she landed a great thud with it on the chin of the second bully, stunning him. He tottered back-wards and before he could get his balance, Rodario hit him over the head with a crate of rotten fruit. He sank down motionless.

"We make a damn good team," he crowed. He was about to kiss Tassia when the back door flew open and four new opponents tumbled through.

The girl raised her club: "Be off with you! That neck-lace belongs to me!"

"Let's get out of here!" Rodario took her by the hand and pulled her after him. Together they raced around the corner, not stopping until they came to a landing stage. The path ended too abruptly for his liking.

However, the boats that had been tied up together formed a rudimentary if unstable bridge to the other side.

"Follow me!" Rodario jumped and, in danger of being thrown off, balanced on the boats that were bobbing on the water like a handful of walnut shells. He managed to reach the narrow footpath on the other side. "What are you waiting for?"

"Quiet, you!" Tassia made her way across after him.

It was harder for her because he had already set the boats rocking. She ripped her skirt to give herself more freedom of movement.

In the meantime Rodario had taken hold of the rope from the last of the barges and pulled it taut till she was by his side. Then he gave the boat a shove out onto the water. The bullies in hot pursuit were faced with a gap to jump.

Two of them fell off into the ice-cold water. The third was about to attempt a leap across. Then Tassia saw a shadow fall over her from behind. An older man in local Mifurdanian attire stood in the doorway, about to empty some slops into the canal. He saw Rodario on the deck. "You?" He lifted his bucket to strike. "This is the moment I've been waiting for, you damnable seducer I'll feed your manhood to the fishes!"

Girdlegard
Kingdom of Gauragar
Late Spring, 6241st Solar Cycle

Tungdil was rocking back and forth, his head fit to burst. His brain throbbed and thumped and seemed keen to escape by way of his ears, but his throat was as dry and dusty as if he had been eating sand for three long solar cycles.

He groaned, opening heavy lids, and blinked in the bright light, catching sight of his fingertips hanging an arm's length away and gravel and scree passing by just underneath them. There was a strong smell of pony and he could hear the sounds of at least one other horse.

If he put two and two together, he thought, he must be on a journey. Against his will.

"Where . . . ?" he croaked as he tried to sit up. This made him fall head first into the dust. His startled pony gave a leap to one side and the pack mule that was following bellowed in panic.

"Calm down," Boïndil soothed. "He won't hurt you—he's just fallen out of the saddle." A concerned face showed itself over his own, a black beard tickling Tungdil's nose. "Are you awake, Scholar?"

Tungdil sat up and brushed the dirt from his breeches; he took a look around and saw trees, bushes and grass. It was not like this in the middle of the mountain. "Where am I?" He pulled himself up on the saddle and felt his head was ready to explode.

"You're with me," was the dwarf-twin's roundabout answer.

"I can see that." He turned round and recognized the outline of the Gray Range in the distance. You could still see the stronghold, if you knew it was there. The tower reached up to the sky like a torch made of stone. "What are we doing here?"

"They've sent us on a mission. We're the high king's envoys to Âlandur," Ireheart finally admitted.

"Why? Is this punishment for my behavior?"

"Actually . . . it was only me he sent," Boïndil said awkwardly. "But I thought a scholar might come in useful with the Sharp . . . with the Elves." He swung himself up into the saddle. "So I brought you along."

"Gandogar doesn't know I'm here?"

"I left message for him."

"Have you *kidnapped* me?"

"No, by Vraccas, I certainly haven't." Ireheart was indignant. "I found you in your room and when I asked you if you would like to keep me company, you said yes."

"Loud and clear?"

Boïndil laughed. "Seemed like a yes to me!" He indicated Tungdil should get back up. "To be honest, I thought it would do you good to have a change—see something new. Going to pay our respects to the Lord of the Elves is not that bad a job. And anyway, you two know each other already. It's probably a good thing if their prince sees a dwarf face that's familiar." He quickly explained why they were heading for Âlandur. "As soon as all the dwarf delegates are assembled, Gandogar will send for us. We shan't be missing anything. They need heroes like us."

Tungdil looked in silence at the far Gray Mountains, then at the road ahead. "Right," he said and got clumsily back into the saddle.

The ponies trotted along next to each other and Tungdil drank some water out of the leather bottle at his side and kept quiet; his head hurt too much for him to want conversation.

Not till late afternoon did he come to life and start to think of what had been said back at the high king's court, and of what they had seen in the Outer Lands. He could not remember what Gandogar and the elves had said about the piles of orc bones, so he asked Ireheart, who looked at him in surprise. "Nothing at all. Eldrur stopped me and wanted to know how many snout-faced orcs had fallen foul of the unknown beasts." He made a face and tossed his black plait back over his shoulder. "Do you think the thirdlings just ate them?"

Tungdil saw an inn at the crossroads they were nearing: This had to mean a bed and a beer. At least one beer.. "We'll stop here," he decided. "Thirdlings wouldn't eat orc flesh any more than we would. Not even if they were starving."

"And . . . what about . . . the Undergroundlings?"

"Boïndil, what rubbish!" said Tungdil in surprise. "No dwarf would ever do such a thing." He thought of Djerûn, the bodyguard of Maga Andôkai. Himself sprung from the evil one, he had nevertheless devoured the creatures of Samusin and Tion. Tungdil gave voice to his thoughts: "We know there are more of them than merely Djerûn. Think of the one the avatars sent to kill Andôkai."

"That would explain why the other monsters haven't attempted the North Pass," grinned Ireheart. "If a whole family of Djerûns has set up home in the Outer Lands by the Stone Gateway then we've got nothing to worry about."

Tungdil nodded. "Perfect for the thirdlings, if it's them behind all this. They block the tunnels and dig passageways in secret right into our territory to send their machines through, while the likes of Djerûn fend off the orcs and other monsters."

His friend stayed silent for quite a while. "What do you think? Will the high king be sending an army to the Outer Lands to sniff out the thirdlings?"

"In my view Gandogar has no other choice," said Tungdil, reining his pony to a standstill outside the inn, which seemed to have extensive stabling. Obviously the crossroads was a popular place for travelers and merchants to get fresh horses.

A boy came running up to lead away their animals. "Good evening, Master Dwarves. May Vraccas be with you," he greeted them politely. "Fresh grass and oats for the ponies and a good room for the night for yourselves?"

Boïndil threw the boy a silver coin. "Will that get you to see to the animals and give them the best of care?"

"Of course, Master Dwarf," the boy said happily. "I'll soon have their coats shining!" He led them off to stand under the shelter and got to work grooming.

Tungdil and Boïndil stepped into the inn, amazed at the souvenirs and trophies displayed on the walls. The landlord had hung up old orc and älfar weapons and a collection of animal teeth. Long nails through the eye sockets fastened the skulls of monsters to the wooden beams.

"Take a look at that," murmured Boïndil, nodding toward the corner by the taproom bar. A life-sized stuffed orc was mounted on a stand, right arm lifted as if to strike; in its left hand was a shield that bore the words: GILSPAN KILLED ME. In large letters on the armor stood the prices for the drinks on offer.

"Not always easy to understand, these humans and their sense of humor," remarked Tungdil as he crossed the crowded taproom to sit at a table by the window where the setting sun shone through.

A wiry young man approached, wearing an apron and a smile that would have done the Incredible Rodario proud. "Welcome, Master Dwarves, welcome to Gilspan's Hunting Lodge."

Ireheart chuckled into his beard. "So, you, my fine linnet, are Gilspan."

"I most certainly am, Master Dwarf," the young man retorted indignantly.

"How old were you when you say you killed that snout-face? Four or five cycles?" He gave a friendly laugh and pinched Gilspan's arm. "Ha, your muscles are good enough for tray-carrying, but not for winning a fight, I'd wager. Did you find your orc lying dead on the battlefield?"

The first guests were turning round to see who it was, spoiling for a brawl by slighting mine host's valor.

"I stabbed him in the heart, Master Dwarf!"

"In the heart, eh?" Ireheart turned to look at the stuffed orc. "And where does a greenskin keep its heart, then?"

Gilspan went red.

"Give it a rest, Boïndil," interrupted Tungdil. "Bring us two strong beers, landlord, some hearty stew, and half a loaf to go with it." He slid the coins over the counter. Still smarting from the insult, Gilspan took the money and went off.

"If he were half the man he thinks he is, he'd have challenged me to a fight on the spot," muttered Ireheart. He searched for his pipe, filled it and lit it from a candle; molten wax formed a small puddle on the table as he did so. "He never killed that pig-face—I'd stake my beard on it!"

They were brought their drinks with bad grace. It might have been pure chance, but when Boïndil's tankard was set down, beer slopped over and spilled into his lap. Gilspan gave a false smile and an apology and hurried off.

"Bring me a jug of brandy," Tungdil called out after him, lifting his tankard to his lips and emptying it in a single draught. He started on its successor greedily; the beer ran dark down his beard, staining it.

"How did it happen, Scholar?"

Tungdil wiped his mouth and his beard. "I was drinking too fast."

"I meant, that you're tipping it down you as if that old drunkard Bavragor were your baby brother," Boïndil insisted sharply. "Tell me why you're like this now. And why Balyndis mourns."

Tungdil was angry with himself for having let that slip out. "Because of Balodil."

"Balodil." The dwarf-twin leaned forward so low toward his friend that his black beard was nearly in his tankard. "And who is Balodil?"

"He's our son." Tungdil took a mouthful of brandy. "Was our son."

Boïndil was careful not to say anything. Gradually Tungdil's words and his recent behavior merged to form distressing picture.

Gilspan brought their food. Neither of them touched it despite the delicious smell and despite their hunger after the long journey. The past must first be dealt with.

"He was born four cycles ago and was the crowning of our love: the apple of our eye," whispered Tungdil from a place far away, as he sat staring at the flicker of the candle flame. "I took him with me on an errand and I'd promised Balyndis I would look after him. But the wooden bridge I always used had been damaged in the flood." He gulped down the brandy. His face was a single grimace of disgust. "I am Tungdil Goldhand, victor over Nôd'onn and avatars, slaughterer of hundreds of orcs, and a scholar to boot. You'd think I could manage to cross a rickety bridge," he said caustically, looking his friend in the face. "That old bridge, Boïndil, showed me who was stronger. It collapsed under the cart and we were tipped into the river. My mail shirt pulled me down. I'd have drowned but for an empty barrel bobbing up under me." The laughter and loud voices in the taproom behind them swallowed his words. "So now here I am, telling you about Balodil. How do you think the story goes for him?" This time he did not even trouble to pour the brandy into his cup, but drank straight from the jug. He set it down, gasped for air and belched. "I never found his body, however long I searched. Since that day I've hated myself. Balyndis can never forgive me and I . . . and I've taken to drink. I'm going to drink till it kills me." He paused. "No, I'm going to drink so it kills me. Should have drowned with my son instead of living on like this. So I'm drowning my sorrows and myself in drink." Disgusted, he pushed away the plate of stew.

"Scholar, it was an accident. Rotten timber," objected Boïndil, wanting to wrest away his guilt. "Rotten wood and the curse of the goddess Elria. It was the curse that struck you, dragging you, your son and the cart to the bottom. It was not your fault."

"That's what Balyndis says, too." He lowered his head. "But I see that silent accusation in her eyes all the time. I fear our love went cold that very day. She thinks I don't notice her feelings—she tries to hide the hatred and disgust. It is so cold now back in our vaults, colder than ever before.

The grief in my heart has robbed me of any desire to live."
He rubbed his face with both hands. "So now you know
why I've changed. I'm off to bed, Boïndil." He got up,
swaying, stumbled off to the stairs and disappeared.

Ireheart wiped the tears away. He must help his friend
and restore his love of life. There was only one way to
do that.

"Vraccas, have mercy. And send your blessing to
Tungdil." He glanced at Gilspan, expansively welcoming
new arrivals and showing off the orc he had dispatched;
mine host was clapped heartily on the shoulder for his
deeds of daring.

Boïndil got up and plodded up the stairs. He had to
speak to Balyndis: he simply could not believe she was
harboring the feelings that Tungdil had described.

The night was already far advanced.

Gilspan was at the table entertaining the other guests
with yet another story about how he had killed his orc.
"And when the Toboribor hordes came through close to
our farm, I took up my weapon to defend my house. My
father was far away from home, but he'd left me his dagger.
I'd sworn on it that I'd protect my mother and all the
people on our land." He laid the dagger on the table as
evidence.

"That was all you had?" breathed a girl of sixteen
summers, traveling in the company of her parents and of
her betrothed.

"Yes. And the orcs were not stopping! They arrived in
the evening, a whole troop of them on the scavenge for
provisions." Gilspan sprang up. "I went up to their leader

and challenged him to a duel. He had his sword and I attacked him with my dagger . . ."

"Oh, you're so brave!" The girl clapped her hands and was lost in admiration.

"I thought the Blood of Girdlegard was supposed to render them immortal," objected her fiancé.

"It didn't help him," said Gilspan, waving his dagger in the air. "I got everywhere, stabbing away and slitting at him till I'd plunged the blade right into his heart and he fell dead at my feet." He posed with one foot on a chair. "The others fled and the farm was saved. Because he died before the time of the Judgment Star the cadaver has survived all this time."

The men gave him a round of applause, the women gave him some coins and the girl gave him a small silken square embroidered with her monogram.

"But how were you able to cut off its head with a dagger?" The jealous fiancé was not giving up.

"A knife-thrust to the heart was enough, sir."

The girl's betrothed looked over at the orc. "Excuse me, Gilspan, but the soldiers I've talked to always say you've got to cut the creatures' heads off to properly do away with them."

It went very quiet. Everyone was staring at the stuffed creature posed in the corner with its bared fangs, a remarkably lifelike figure in the dim light.

"Wasn't it standing a bit differently when we came in?" whispered the damsel fearfully, sliding nearer to Gilspan. Her betrothed took her arm and pulled her back to his side.

"Yes, you're right." Her father went pale. "I swear by

Palandiell he had his sword held upright before, not down in front of him."

"What's this? A horror story to frighten little children? I pulled his innards out through his doublet myself," said the landlord. He went up to the creature.

There was a loud creaking noise and the upper torso of the orc turned in Gilspan's direction.

The women screamed. The men drew their swords. "You idiot of a man! You've brought the evil one right into your own house!"

Gilspan was completely bewildered. He wanted to reply but the orc started making its way over, raising its sword arm and lunging at him.

The man disappeared screaming under the monster. He dropped his dagger, crawled out from beneath his attacker, slid under the nearest table and cried for help like an old spinster.

Upstairs, doors were opening, boots came clattering down the stairs and lanterns were brought to give a better light.

The orc lay motionless on the floor and laughed. And laughed and laughed . . . As more and more lamps came on the scene they saw it was not the monster, but a dwarf lying there, helpless with laughter. He got up and stood by the bar counter, slapping himself on the thigh.

His laughter infected the room, not least because of the relief everyone felt, and then because of Gilspan the hero quivering underneath the table.

Boïndil had played a joke on them all and had made the monster come to life by groaning a bit, pushing it and rocking it where it stood. "Now, my little linnet," he said, bending down to look under the table. "Where is your bold courage now? Where did you get the orc?"

"I . . ." Gilspan was obviously thinking up a new lie.

"Think hard who you're trying to trick here," warned Ireheart, shaking a fist in his face.

"Bought it. I bought it, four cycles ago," he admitted ruefully. "Like all the other stuff on the walls." The guests laughed at him as he crawled out from his hiding place.

"Rotten stinking dwarf! You've ruined everything!"

"Me? It's you who've ruined everything by your cowardice. If you'd been the man you pretend to be and had launched yourself at your attacker, everyone would be admiring you." Boïndil nodded to the girl's fiancé. "Well spotted. You do have to cut off their heads so that evil doesn't restore their powers." He raised his crow's beak hammer and slung it through the creature's head, severing the dried vertebrae so that the skull was caught on the weapon's long spike. "It'd be really dead now." He smashed the bone on the counter and fragments scattered far and wide. "Best to be on the safe side," he grinned, shouldering his hammer.

The next day they continued their journey to Âlandur.

Tungdil had slept through the tumultuous doings of the night. He got up in the morning, woken by Boïndil, and got ready for the journey in silence. Without stopping for breakfast they set off in a southwesterly direction.

The ponies trotted tirelessly on, following the road. They were surrounded by a richly varied landscape: it was still mountainous here, although a dwarf would call it hilly; sometimes they rode along the side of a ravine, sometimes through wide valleys, and then again across uplands from where they had a view over the wilder North Gauragar. They saw no thick forests: for that the soil was too poor.

Ireheart at the head of the column had some food on the way; Tungdil had bought a bottle of brandy from the innkeeper. He continued where he had left off the previous evening.

His friend looked back at him, shaking his head. "Do you really think drinking makes it better? You could have learned a lesson from Bavragor."

Tungdil paid no attention and lifted the bottle once more to his cracked lips.

"That's enough! It's not going to bring Balodil back, Scholar!" Boïndil turned his pony round and rode back. "Make use of your life and respect his memory instead of wallowing in self-pity and making a fool of yourself."

"No, it won't bring Balodil back," murmured Tungdil. "I told you, I'm drinking myself to death." He belched, spat, and drank again.

"You want to die?" Ireheart jumped down out of the saddle, grabbed the startled dwarf by the collar of his leather doublet under the mail shirt and pulled him to the ground. He dragged him over to the edge of the precipice they were on. "You really want to die?" In a fury he wrested the brandy bottle out of his grasp and hurled it down the cliff. After a long fall it shattered, leaving a dark stain on the rock. "Then go after it!" he thundered. "Put an end to your miserable existence. Do it right now. But stop the self-pity. The lowliest of creatures has more dignity than you."

Tungdil could not escape from Boïndil's steel-hard grip. Without mercy the dwarf-twin pressed his face down over the drop.

A warm breath of wind came up from below, playing gently around his face as if inviting him to jump.

"Well, Scholar?" fumed Ireheart. "You say you want to die. Get on with it!" He grabbed the mail shirt and pulled with all his amazing strength. From somewhere deep inside, Tungdil's instinct to resist awoke. It was a boundless urge, knowing neither rhyme nor reason. There was nothing to live for and yet still he held back and refused to take his place in the Eternal Smithy—if indeed there was a place for him there. He grasped the stunted grass, scraping his fingertips open on the stone. The pain cleared his alcohol-befuddled head.

"LET GO!" yelled Boïndil in his ear. "I'm making it easy for you and stopping you from wasting yet more money on brandy and beer." He gave Tungdil a mighty kick in the side.

Tungdil cowered in pain, losing his grip. The top half of his body now lay over the cliff edge. "No, no!" he called out in desperation. "You . . ."

"I'll tell them you were protecting me from bandits," Ireheart continued relentlessly. "People will think of you as a hero who died in time to salvage the meager remains of his reputation."

Another kick met Tungdil's ribs. Yelling, he slid forward. Stones broke away and rolled down the steep slope, raising small clouds of dust on the way.

"NO!" Gathering the last of his strength, Tungdil pushed himself up off the ground, throwing his weight backwards.

He hurled himself back, dragging Boïndil with him, and together they fell onto safer ground. "I've . . . changed . . . my mind," he panted.

"Oh, and where does this sudden change of heart come from?"

Tungdil took a deep breath. "I can't say. There's a voice inside that won't let me."

"A voice called fear?"

Tungdil shrugged his shoulders. "No. No, it was something else. Life itself, I expect."

"The voice of Vraccas," replied Boïndil, getting up and proffering his hand. "He will need you and your Keenfire blade soon enough. New enemies are threatening your race. Perhaps it is your destiny to defeat them."

Tungdil let himself be helped up, then he went over to the cliff edge and looked over. Only one small step and his troubles would be gone. He raised his foot . . . and again he felt the inner barrier.

"Still got a death wish?" growled his friend.

"No," answered Tungdil slowly. "I wanted to be sure that I really want to live." He turned away from the edge.

Ireheart held out the reins of his pony to him and Tungdil took them. "That is what you want. I would have pushed you over if you hadn't fought against me with all your strength." His voice was earnest. "It's the only way to find out if someone really wants to die." A crooked smile crossed his face. "Believe me—I've been through the same treatment as you."

"You were in despair at the death of your brother." Tungdil understood now and watched the warrior climb back into the saddle.

"Half of me died when he did. Perhaps it was the better half. The other half dissolved into pitiless grief until I was convinced I wanted to die. Someone did to me what I just did to you and that made me see I preferred to be amongst the living rather than the dead. Vraccas knows why." Grinning, he pointed to the road ahead. "But sending us to the elves is taking it a bit far." He spurred his pony onwards.

Tungdil laughed quietly. "You're right. Vraccas knows why."

The shock of his salvation gave Tungdil now an extreme clarity of thought he had not known since before the death of his son. He had done everything wrong. For the past four cycles he had done everything wrong.

There was only one way out. He vowed to himself that he would return to Balyndis as soon as he could and beg her forgiveness for everything. The bitter words, the constant drinking, the rejection whenever she had tried to touch him. He could not forgive himself. Deep in thought, he stroked his pony's soft muzzle.

Ireheart was a few paces ahead. "Coming, Scholar?" he called. "Or is the pony giving you some advice?"

"No," Tungdil called back. "It's telling me I'm too fat."

"You should have asked me. I could have told you that."

Tungdil took the pony by the reins and started to run. "You are a good friend," he said and it was not clear which of the two he meant. The exercise would not hurt him, and it was a good few miles still to Âlandur. Time to lose a few pounds.

IV

Girdlegard,
Queendom of Weyurn, Mifurdania,
Late Spring, 6241st Solar Cycle

"Mind out, Rodario!" He heard Tassia's warning just in time. He ducked, the slops aimed at his back missing him by inches and hitting the girl instead. She cried out and stumbled backwards into Mifurdania's floodwaters, which washed the pail's stinking contents from her dress.

"That's good luck," grinned Rodario, punching an injured pursuer full in the face as he was trying to jump onto the walkway from one of the boats. The thug landed in the water. Then the actor spun around, beaming. "Master Umtaschen? You haven't forgotten me? Delighted to find you still so lively."

"You foul seducer!" shouted the older man, who had attacked so suddenly with the bucket. "She was promised to the judge's son. He would have none of her with your bastard in her belly!" He swung the bucket again. "I'll have your balls off for that!"

"Master Umtaschen, it was your daughter who seduced me," retorted Rodario, fending off the pail. "And I wasn't the first. Believe me, I'd have noticed." He grabbed the bucket and hurled it at the last of the band of pursuers Nolik's father had sent after them.

The man, who had been balancing precariously debating

his next move, was sent flying into the water to join Tassia and his comrade in thuggery.

"At least the others didn't make her pregnant!" Umtaschen roared, swinging both fists.

"If that is the case, Master Umtaschen, I'll be happy to meet with her again and show her a good time. It seems I have your blessing as long as I'm careful where I aim this time," laughed Rodario as he took a sudden step forward.

Umtaschen sprang back out of range inside his house. "We're not done yet!" he threatened and disappeared as fast as he could when Rodario gave a warning stamp with his foot.

Someone splashed him. He turned round.

A girl's hand waved from below the edge of the landing stage. "Help me up before the other two get me," Tassia called and he hurried over to haul her out. As she stood in front of him soaked to the skin, he could see how the water had made her dress transparent.

The two who had been following them had given up and were swimming back to their three colleagues on the other side of the canal.

"What do we do now?" asked Tassia, smoothing back her wet fair hair. In Rodario's eyes she was temptation itself. "They're bound to have gone to the *Curiosum*."

"They didn't find the necklace there so they think one of us has it," Rodario said and nodded. "Hey, you block-heads!" he called out to the men, pretending to be holding something. "You want the necklace? Think again! Tell Nolik's father we're going to sell it. He can come to Mifurdania and buy it back." One of the heavies was about to clamber onto the string of tethered boats, but Rodario moved up to the end of the landing stage. "Stop right there! If anyone follows us we'll chuck the necklace into one of the canals and you can go diving for it." A gesture from his leader stopped the man in his tracks. "Well done," the actor praised him, taking Tassia's hand and running off. "Stay where you are!" he warned and ran off round the corner with a laugh.

When they were passing under an awning formed by garments drying on a washing line, Tassia stopped. "Wait! Give me a leg up!"

Rodario did as she asked, and she placed one foot on his locked hands and wedged her other foot against the wall; sprightly, as if on solid ground, she filched a dark yellow dress from the line and jumped down again. Without taking any note of her surroundings she stripped off her wet clothing and slipped into the stolen garment; then she gave Rodario a passionate kiss, laughed and ran off.

"This wild creature will be the end of me or the making of me," he grinned, hurrying after her.

Late in the afternoon they finally arrived at the forge where Lambus worked. Rodario wanted to thank him and to get a few more details about where Furgas might be.

The inner gate to the forge stood open. A fire burned in the furnace and two pieces of metal lay red-hot in the flames waiting to be worked on. They couldn't see the blacksmith.

"Lambus, you old iron-basher," called Rodario. "Are you here?" He stepped into the half light but before his eyes could adapt to the dark he tripped over something on the ground. "What the . . . ?" He bent down and saw what had nearly made him fall: a young man's outstretched legs. In the man's side there was a gaping hole. Blood had spread over the floor. "Mind out, Tassia," he warned the girl, who was hot on his heels. "There's been a murder."

"Perhaps one of the heavies sent by Nolik's father?" She peered over his shoulder and went pale. She stepped back, retching, then turned and fled for the door to get fresh air.

Rodario studied the brutal wounds: the work of a very sharp ax. "I don't think so. Those men didn't have weapons that could make injuries like these." Rodario got up and went over to look at the iron objects in the furnace. One of them could indeed have been an ax head. "Lambus?" he called out, taking a poker and moving slowly into the dark recesses at the back of the forge.

At that point a figure jumped out of the shadows at him.

With great presence of mind Rodario stepped to one side and a dagger just missed his throat. "Assassin!" he shouted and took a wild swing with the poker, hitting the dark-clad attacker full in the face so he collapsed in a groaning heap. The knife clattered to the floor. To be on the safe side he gave the man another blow with the poker, then grabbed him and dragged him over to the part of the outbuilding where there was better light. "Let's see what we've got here."

He saw a dirty face marked with burns. The man was a good fifty cycles old and looked more like a simple workman than a professional killer. The poker blow had broken his nose and knocked out two of his teeth. There was blood coming out of his nostrils and his mouth. In a daze, he was trying to break away, but couldn't.

"Tassia, bring me a red-hot iron!" Rodario requested. "We can pierce his tongue with it."

"No, let me go," he mumbled, terrified. "He'll kill them if I'm not back on time."

"Did you kill this man?" Rodario picked up the glowing metal and held it in the man's face. His eyes widened in fear. "Who sent you and where is Lambus?"

The man was trembling like a fish on a hook. "I don't know. Ilgar did it because the boy refused to come along and he threatened to betray us."

Each answer brought more questions in its wake. "Get the story out, old man, or I swear—by Samusin—I'll put out your eyes with this iron." Rodario threatened the man again, putting on his most villainous expression, a face that went down well on stage. Not for a moment did he really intend to harm the old man any further.

"Are you a friend of the blacksmith?" the man asked, coming to his senses. "If so, by the grace of Palandiell, don't tell anyone what you've seen. Tell them Lambus is off on his travels. Get rid of the boy's body. That's the only way your friend will ever be able to come back."

"Is Furgas in the power of whoever's got Lambus?" asked Rodario, guessing wildly. "He's about my size, black hair and . . ."

The man's face changed suddenly. He looked surprised. "You know the magister?"

"He's my best friend."

The man spat in his face. "May all the demons . . ."

Rodario heard a faint swishing noise, one he knew well

from his adventures outside the world of theater. A jolt—
and the man fell slack in his grip. An arrow shaft stuck
out from the man's back. Death had been instantaneous.

"Get down, Tassia. Get under cover," called Rodario,
going to one side to crouch down behind a heap of coal,
and wiping the bloody spittle out of his face. There had
been many times in his life when things had happened
beyond his understanding, but so far, this was the height
of not-understanding.

Quiet steps could be heard approaching; Rodario could
hear the creak of leather armor straps, and iron rings
clanked. There was the sound of a sword being drawn.
When he saw a boot next to him he took hold of the
tongs and dropped the red-hot metal down inside.

There was a hissing. The man yelled fit to bust and ran
out of the shed, smoke streaming after him. Immediately
after that they heard a splash. The man had jumped into
the water to cool the burned leg.

"Ha!" Grabbing a smaller hammer from the forge,
Rodario ran out in pursuit. But the man had disappeared.
Rings on the surface of the water showed where someone
had dived in.

Tassia came over to his side. "Drowned?" she asked in
surprise. "Must have hurt so bad he forgot he can't swim."
Out of the corner of his eye Rodario caught sight of a
boat that was pulling away from Mifurdania. It was a
squat little barge, heavily laden and so low in the water
that any small wave would have swamped it. The broad
sail was letting it pick up speed as it headed north.

At the stern of the barge stood a brunette in a simple
brown dress. She was looking over toward them through

a long tube, the sunlight glinting off glass. Then she put it down behind her.

"Tassia. We're off." Rodario kept his eye on the brown-haired woman. She reminded him of someone, but it couldn't be . . .

Tassia was staring at the circles on the water. "Perhaps he'll come up again for air?"

The other woman took out an arrow and fitted it to a bow.

"Tassia. Come with me."

The bowstring was drawn back, the arrow pointing straight at him and at his self-appointed "wife".

"What is it, O Fabulous One? Look over there on the left. That could be him. I can see something dark. Perhaps . . . ?"

Rodario had just enough time to throw himself at Tassia and tumble them both into the water to avoid the arrow. The waters surrounded him in a cold embrace. Spluttering, he came up to the surface again under the shelter of one of the walkways. Tassia came up cursing loudly and tried to hit him. "What on earth are you doing? To get me soaked twice in one day, Rodario; it's the limit!"

"Slow down, mermaid." He pointed over to the barge.

The woman was still at her post and fitting another arrow to her bow, waiting for a target.

When someone's head popped suddenly out of the water like a cork, she did not hesitate—the movement was fluid, steady and sure. The arrow flew and entered the side of the skull over the right temple. The scream turned to bubbling sound as water gushed into the mouth. Without realizing it she had killed one of her own henchman.

"Thanks be to Palandiell!" mouthed Tassia, not taking her eyes from the dead body that drifted past them, face down. An arrow stuck out like a dead branch. "And thanks be to you, too, Rodario. You've saved my life," she said in a serious voice and kissed him long and hard on the lips. In spite of the cold this was starting to give him a warm feeling.

When they looked for the barge again it had disappeared behind a row of houses. They clambered out onto dry land and made their way, soaked through as they were, to the *Curiosum*'s site.

What they left behind were three dead bodies and a whole lot of things that didn't make any sense. Most of the uncanny things that had happened that day seemed to be connected to his friend Furgas, and he was utterly determined to work out what was going on. He was going to write a play about it.

Girdlegard
Kingdom of Gauragar,
Porista,
Late Spring, 6241st Solar Cycle

Young Lia was sitting, a boyish figure, with the other workers. She gazed out over the pancake-flat plain in the middle of Porista, drank her cold tea and took an occasional mouthful of the stew they gave her. Her task was dangerous, but it was well paid: she was to gather information, scouting in a particular area.

In recent cycles Porista had undergone difficult changes.

Once it had been the center of Nudin's realm—Nudin the Knowledge-Lusty, one of Girdlegard's magi. But when he had turned into Nôd'onn the Treacherous it had become the field of a terrible battle, and had to a great extent been destroyed by a conflagration. People had only gradually been returning, salvaging what they could from the smoking ruins to build anew, when an army of avatars swept through the land, determined to secure for themselves the magic wellspring that lay underneath the palace of the magus. The rest of Girdlegard could not sit back and let that happen and so had hastened to its defense; the resulting fighting had left fresh scars on the new Porista. Even the grounds of the palace had become just an ugly heap of stones.

Then peace had arrived.

About five cycles earlier, after the defeat of all the great magae and magi, and after the resultant collapse of the magic fields, King Bruron had laid claim to the land and annexed the territory.

Since then the city had been growing steadily.

A friendly army of casual laborers had been sent out by the monarch to remove, stone by stone, the debris of the flattened palace to make way for his own new residence. They had just completed the work. Now all that remained were the foundations and the rubble-filled cellar entrances. This was all that told of the extent of the gigantic building that had previously stood on the site.

Lia's slim build had an advantage: it allowed her to slip down past the fallen stones into the interior of the cellars to reconnoiter. Once back in the daylight she would report to the king's construction masters so they could decide how work on the chambers should progress: fill them in with shale or excavate carefully by hand.

None of the overseers on the site had any idea that Lia was conducting her own research at the same time.

Franek, one of her friends, came over and offered her some flatbread. Like her he wore simple clothing, the material looking the worse for wear in places. His mop of dark blond hair was covered with a leather cap. "Have you found anything?" he whispered. He was one of the scouts, too, and was working in another part of the site. He also was on a higher mission.

The girl took the bread, placing it on the bowl of stew, and then rearranged the headscarf that protected her brown hair from the dust below ground. "No," she answered quietly, making gestures with her hands to imply that she was complaining about the quality of the baking.

Franek sighed. "Then I don't know how long we should carry on looking. There aren't many cellars still to search."

"I said straightaway that it must be broken. Have you seen how even the largest blocks of stone are split right through? That's how great the pressure was." Lia always looked on the black side. "There's nothing left of some walls but brick dust." She held the bread out to him again and he stuck it under his jacket.

"Samusin won't desert us," Franek said as he went off back to his work.

Lia finished her meal, wiped her hands on her breeches and went back to the opening, which was sheltered by a canvas awning to protect the workers from the sun. Tamàs and Ove, two of the building masters, were studying their plans. She greeted them as she passed.

Tamàs, the younger one, greeted her in return and looked at her. He liked what he saw and his inquiring gaze was no longer totally academic. "You're late. Two others have gone down already," he said, smiling. "I hope there's room for you all. If not, come back up here and keep us company drawing up the charts."

Lia stopped in her tracks. "Excuse me, sir. Who has gone down?"

"Two boys I just sent down," murmured Ove without lifting his eyes from the plans. "We haven't got much time. King Bruron wants to get started with the building. We need the last secrets of the vaults found quickly. And since you were on a break I sent down two young lads who were free." He turned a page and made a mark on the site plan.

"It's dangerous down there. I'll go and find them." She forced herself to smile and hurried down the cellar steps.

That was all she needed: children at work. She wasn't worried about any of the other people she worked with because they could not move in the cramped conditions underground. Young lithe bodies, on the other hand, were competition.

Lia could been the boys working their way forward outside where the domed roof had once been. They were chattering, talking about their wages and about how they hoped to find treasure buried by past occupants of the palace.

"Hey, you boys," she called, slithering through the narrowest of spaces like an eel. "Off with you! This is my cellar!"

"You wish!" laughed one of them.

"Master Ove sent us down here," called the other one. "Go and complain to him if you don't like the idea of us finding the treasure before you do."

Lia forced her way through under one of the fallen blocks of stone. It rocked worryingly while she was still underneath it. "There is no treasure to find," she said. "It's not safe here for you. The chamber hasn't settled."

"We've done this a lot," come the high-spirited response. "And anyway . . ."

Some of the rubble collapsed and clouds of dust rose up so she could not see. She coughed and cursed at the same time. "Are you all right?" she called, rubbing her eyes.

"Well I never! There's someone down here! An old man with a long beard!"

Lia tried to move more quickly. It had happened. Now there were things she must prevent. "Where are you?"

"Idiot!" snarled the other boy at his friend. "You pushed against that pillar and you nearly had me buried in dirt. And *that thing* is not a man," there was the sound of wooden boards clattering "—it's a *statue*."

"That wasn't me. It fell in on its own," came the defense. Now Lia could see both of the squabbling boys.

They were standing in a small cave-like space, no bigger than a store cupboard. It had somehow been formed when beams and pillars had twisted and collapsed. Between all the rubble lay a statue with its face uppermost. It was so true to life that Lia was not surprised the boy had thought it was real.

"So *that's* where you are!" She slipped under one of the supports without touching it, then stood up. Slowly she approached the two treasure-seekers, her eyes sliding over the statue's form. Everything was in place. Every fine detail of the clothing, each single beard hair, every fold and wrinkle in the old face could be recognized.

"It's as if they'd turned someone into stone," whispered the taller of the boys with respect. "It's amazing."

"It'll bring us a good bit of extra money. One of those rich guys will want it for his garden or in his study, I bet. A good day's work!" nodded his friend, giving a skeptical glance at the distance the statue would have to be heaved up. "We'll have to dig a way to the top and get a hoist set up. We won't be able to pull it through the rubble." He threw Lia a warning look. "The statue is ours. Got that?"

She was furious that she'd taken that lunch break. If only she'd got back to work a little bit sooner she wouldn't have run into trouble with these two kids at all. "Of course you found it. But it won't get you any money. It's already the property of Tomba Drinkfass," she said, inventing a name. "He gave the statue to Nudin originally."

"Even better," said the taller of the two. "We'll get a reward for finding it."

"Yes, *we* will," the other one stressed, pointing to his friend and himself. "You won't."

Lia had a quick think about how to make the best of the situation. She could go along with this and wait for her chance, follow the statue to its new owner and take it then. That would demand time and effort. And there'd be quite a to-do once any of Porista's older citizens got wind of what had been found. Or she could . . .

"Samusin is my witness I won't say a word about the

statue. Or about you." She spoke slowly before swiftly plunging her dagger into the throat of the boy at her left.

She cut his throat and then thrust her weapon into the other boy's chest. Eyes wide open in surprise, he sank onto the statue's base, blood gurgling. He stared at his murderess in complete astonishment at what she had done.

His friend grew weaker by the second and crumpled onto the floor, expiring soon afterwards. The blood from his slit throat no longer spurted out of the open gash, but overflowed much as a stew might boil over in an unwatched pot.

Lia watched them both die. The sacrifice was essential. For the greater good, more important than two young lives. Perhaps thousands would be saved. She dragged the two bodies, still warm and convulsing, into a small hollow under some debris and pushed away the supporting beams over where they lay.

Then she started on her way back, counting her steps so that she would be able to locate the statue again. Still gasping for air and sobbing she returned to the building supervisors and told them a terrible accident had happened.

"The cellar walls are soft as wax," she reported, bursting into tears again. "It would be madness to go back in there."

Ove and Tamàs conferred briefly, then stopped the works for the day out of respect for the two children who had died. On the next day, they decided, the bodies should be fetched up and then the cellar area filled in.

Lia returned to the building site that night with Franek and ten helpers.

They carried poles, pickaxes, pulleys, rope and cable winches with them. A cart with two horses waited in a side road to transport their prize away. They had placed watchers in strategic places to warn them if anyone should approach. They had to work quickly. And they had to succeed, whatever the cost, whatever lives might be lost.

On the surface Lia paced out the distance she had calculated. Then she placed a marker on the flagstone. "It must be right under here," she said to her companions. The men set to work.

Franek and Lia helped to shovel the debris to one side while the hole the men were digging grew steadily bigger. They had to take great care that none of the surface material broke off and fell back in.

"And to think I was ready to give up," said Lia, thrilled that the treasure would soon be salvaged.

Her joy triumphed over her guilty conscience about the murder of the two young boys. She had told Franek what she had done, hoping the confession would make her feel better, but it had not worked. At least he had agreed that she had done the right thing. She would have to leave Porista once and for all. If the bodies were found she would be accused of the murders.

"Samusin is on our side again," he nodded, watching the men shifting away the loose earth and hacking through the vaulted cellar roof.

"Don't speak too soon," said Lia. "Let's not thank the god of retribution until we've got the statue safely out of Porista."

With a crack, a section of the tunnel roof gave way;

two of the men fell though to the cellars, yelling out as they dropped down.

Franek looked round in alarm, checking with their watchers. Nobody seemed to have heard the noise. "Quick! Get them out of there!" Five others jumped down with lanterns in their hands.

"Get the statue first," called Lia after them anxiously, stepping a couple of paces back from the hole in case another section should cave in. "Then get the injured out."

The others worked at the entrance to make the opening wider while another group put the pulleys and the hoist together. They tossed ropes down to fasten round the stone figure.

Soon the statue was winched up, rising in the dark to the surface. It was covered in a fine coating of dust and there was a huge red stain—the blood of the young boys who had paid for their find with their lives. It looked as if it were the statue that was bleeding.

"Bring the cart over here," ordered Franek, lifting a lamp and giving the prearranged signal. Soon the wheels were turning, muffled with cloths to avoid making any sound; the horses' hooves had been wrapped in hessian as well.

Lia was getting more and more uneasy. "Come on up; hurry!" she called down into the vaults. "Let's get out of here."

The rope snagged, the pole bent under the weight, but did not break. The men climbed out of the hole and heaved the heavy statue onto the sacking that had been put on the wagon in readiness.

"The guards!" came a shout from across the site, echoing back to Franek and Lia.

"Stupid idiot!" Franek cursed their watchman, who had meant well with his warning, but had certainly risked alerting Bruron's soldiers. They saw pinpricks of light—torches coming nearer. "Take the rags off," he told the others and leaped up onto the wagon. "They've seen us now—the noise won't make it any worse."

Lia followed him and jumped up to crouch beside the statue. The whip cracked and the wheels rattled along.

"Halt!" They heard the challenge from the guards. "Stop in the name of King Bruron!" There were no more niceties—arrows were already flying in their direction, most of them falling short, but two buried themselves in the wood of the wagon, one hit the statue and broke, and one caught Lia in the leg. She cried out.

By the light of the torches they could see the guards falling on the men who had helped them with the statue. Anyone who put up a defense was killed outright—the rest were taken prisoner. Bruron had issued a strict new law five cycles ago, protecting people's property and condemning to death anyone suspected of pilfering. The fact that they had emptied the vaults belonging to a man who was dead made no difference.

Out of the darkness of the side streets four mounted guards came galloping up; they had heard the noise and it was simple for them to overtake the wagon.

"Stop!" the first rider shouted to Franek. "I can . . ."

Her friend turned, whip in hand, and caught the soldier full in the face. His eyeball burst under the force of the slashing leather and he fell from the saddle. The next rider had to swerve to avoid him, and lost ground.

One of the guards made a bold leap straight onto the

cart and hit Lia in the face with his balled fist to silence her, then climbed over the statue to get at Franek.

"Look out!" she croaked in warning, swallowing her own blood. Groaning, she drew her dagger and crawled across the swaying cart to reach the guard.

Another rode past them, heading for the gate to get the sentries to stop the unscrupulous thieves escaping with their plunder.

Franek had seen him. He hurled his sword at the man when he was three arms' lengths away from him, catching him in the side. At full gallop he fell to the ground, rolled over and over, and was crushed under the back wheel of the wagon.

Just as the last of them was attacking Franek from behind, Lia thrust her dagger into his upper arm.

She had been aiming for his neck, but the wagon was rocking so violently it was impossible for her, especially with the injury to her leg, to be more accurate. She swayed, falling on her opponent and dragging him down with her. Together they fell over the statue and tumbled off the speeding wagon.

This time Lia was out of luck.

She landed under the heavily armored man and broke his fall with her own body. As her head crashed against the cobblestones of Porista's streets, she felt her skull crack and a sharp pain in her breast. Warmth surrounded her head; then she was weightless, outside her body.

"Lia!" she heard her friend calling—she could just hear his voice above the noise of the hooves and the wheels.

"Keep going," she said, speaking with difficulty, and

knowing that he would be unable to hear her. "We have taken the first step, Samusin," she whispered up to the stars. "For that I gladly surrender my life, O god of retribution." Lia tried to smile before death turned her face to stone. She could not.

The guard who was lying half conscious a few steps away sat up slowly and reached for his bugle to warn the sentries at the gate. But the bugle was not hanging at his belt. He found it buried in the girl's breast. As they had fallen from the wagon it had pierced her flesh and bone and shattered. Blood was pouring out of it as if it were an upturned funnel. He would not be placing it to his lips again.

"Curses," he muttered angrily as he staggered to his feet. The thief had got away with his booty. And if he had seen aright back there on the wagon, the prize that had been stolen was something very special: it was the magus Lot-Ionan, turned to stone.

Girdlegard,
Black Mountain Range,
Realm of the Thirdlings,
Late Spring, 6241st Solar Cycle

King Malbalor White-Eye from the clan of the Bone Breakers in the thirdling folk of Lorimbur read through the message brought him by the envoy of Queen Xamtys. It spoke of a machine and of dwarf runes promising death. There was to be an assembly, and the rulers and freeling city kings were to travel to the Gray Range.

"This will open the old rifts," he said to the representatives of the clans of the four other dwarf tribes sitting round the table with him in the hall.

The realm of the thirdlings had survived in name only. At the demise of Lorimbas Steelheart and the almost complete annihilation of the thirdlings by the army of the now-deposed mad king Belletain, the other dwarves had sent warriors to the east to protect the passage into Girdlegard. There were only a few thirdlings remaining in the Black Range and they were in the minority. People said it was a minority that was tolerated.

"You know that most of the survivors of my race have made peace and now live side by side with you." Malbalor held the paper aloft. "These lines threaten our new community."

"If it ever was a new community," muttered somebody.

The king could not work out who had expressed those words. He rose up in anger, showing his impressive stature. He was a classic thirdling: tall, sturdily built and battle-hardened. Over his mail shirt he was dressed in armor formed of thin metal plates; his legs were protected by chain mail. His brown eyes sent out sparks of fire.

"It is remarks like that which open up the old rifts," he called out, pounding the table with his fist; his long blue-dyed beard quivered. "Don't you see it is a contrivance? The runes are intended to incite hatred and sow distrust of the thirdlings who live amongst you in peace. Have we not shown, we the descendants of the dwarf-killer Lorimbur, that we do not desire the death of the other dwarves?"

"What are five cycles?" came another objection.

This time the heckler was betrayed by his neighbor turning to him and asking, "Why don't you stand up and speak out, instead of hiding away like a coward, Ginsgar Unforce of the clan of the Nail Smiths of the firstling folk of Borengar?"

Thus exposed, the dwarf rose to his feet; he was broad in the chest and wore a fire-red beard and long locks of hair. In his left hand he held raised his war hammer, as befitted a dwarf from the clan of the best smiths. "I have never liked the thirdlings. I despise them for their base-ness, their trickery and their lack of honor," he spoke out fearlessly, looking the king in the face. "That it's one of your kind, Malbalor, that has invented this devilry of a machine, comes as no surprise to me. I see that thirdlings are at their killing again, and that is even less of a surprise." He turned to face all those present. "Let us send out an army to destroy the camp in the Outer Lands. Then let's drive all the thirdlings together and take them captive. Then we will have peace and quiet for once."

The neighbor who had placed him in the spotlight raised his eyebrows. "There are thirdlings who pretend to belong to another dwarf folk in order to stir up trouble. To hear you talking like that, and to see your physical appearance, one might reach strange conclusions."

Ginsgar whirled round and brandished his hammer. "You dare to call me a thirdling?" he yelled furiously. "My clan has been living in the Red Range for countless cycles and—"

"Enough!" ordered Malbalor. "Sit down again, Ginsgar. I couldn't care less who you belong to. I will not tolerate any such inflammatory talk. Not here in this hall and not here in this kingdom. We will all keep cool heads." He took a deep breath. "I have asked you all here for you to warn your people to keep their eyes open for danger, but to steer clear of making unfounded accusations. From today the mines and tunnels will only be entered by gangs of forty dwarves at a time to continue the repair work. They must take long iron poles, hooks and chains. So equipped I would hope that you will be able to bring down these machines." He looked at the assembled dwarves intently. "They are *machines*! If dwarf hand has made them then a dwarf hand can destroy them. May Vraccas help us to withstand this test. In two orbits' time I shall be setting off for the northwest, to take counsel with Gandogar and the others." He nodded to them all and dismissed them.

Malbalor waited until he was alone in the hall, then sank back like lead onto his seat. When Gandogar had asked him to become king and he was elected to the role, he had never for a moment thought the task would be so onerous.

Five dwarf folks had united to form an army—Glaïmbar Sharpax had managed it with no trouble at all in the Gray Range. It was a melting pot there, giving rise to a new form of dwarf. But in the Black Range it was not working. Nothing was melting in this pot, nothing integrating. On the contrary, the individual elements were getting harder and more determined than ever not to form new compounds and combinations.

The superstitious amongst their people said it was the curse of Lorimbur, the founding father of the thirdling race, that was invested deep in the stones of mountains here and preventing any chance of peaceful coexistence. Malbalor was starting to believe it.

He took some of the water in the carafe in front of him, and regarded the reflection of his tired countenance. Worry had driven deep furrows in his face, and chiseled out lines around his eyes and on his brow. The rest lay hidden behind his beard; that was best so. He had no wish to appear any older than he already felt.

The cool water ran down his throat; refreshed, he got up and left the hall in order to make preparations for his coming absence. As he strode through the high galleries he made the decision to appoint Ginsgar as his deputy, so the trouble-maker could experience first-hand what responsibility the role of king involved. He thought this would be suitable revenge.

When he turned the corner, a company of dwarves approached: having been hard at work, they looked and smelled as if they had just come out of a quarry after an orbit's solid laboring. They only wore short breeches and heavy knee-high boots; thighs and upper torsos were naked. To protect their heads from falling stones they also wore helmets, and they carried pickaxes and shovels. Over their mouths and noses they had bound cloths to keep the fine dust out; the ends of their beards peeked out below.

On the face of it the appearance of such a group had nothing strange about it. In any other part of the Black Range Malbalor would quickly have dismissed the memory of meeting a group of twenty dwarves.

But two things seemed wrong. For a start there was

no reason for them to be there; there was no dwarf accommodation near and no collapsed tunnels needing repair; and then not a single one of them greeted him as they passed, although he had nodded to them in acknowledgment.

Malbalor was not one of those rulers who absolutely had to see every head bowing in deference but a certain amount of respect he did demand. He stopped and turned. "Hey, you! Wait a moment!"

They went on walking.

Now his suspicions were aroused.

He caught up with the last of the group, grabbed him by the shoulder and spun him around. Seen from close up the helmets appeared unusual; their shape was different from any he knew. The nose protector was longer and reached down to the chin, while iron wires formed a cage which hid the eyes from view.

"I'm speaking to you!" the king said severely and he pulled down the cloth over the lower parts of the face. Horrified, he took a step back. For the first time in his life he saw an adult dwarf without a beard. The black curls that had showed at the edges of the cloth were just stuck on as a disguise. The deception had worked up to now. "By Vraccas, what the . . ." His hand fastened tightly on the handle of his club.

Without warning, the dwarf struck him on the head with the flat of his shovel, sending Malbalor flying back against the wall half senseless.

"Treachery!" he shouted as loud as he could, but then his heavy eyelids closed.

When he opened his eyes again soon after he saw

Ginsgar's concerned face with its red beard floating into his field of vision. To his surprise he was no longer lying in the corridor but on his own bed. He must have been unconscious for some time.

"He's coming round," Ginsgar called over his shoulder, "So, king. We have news for you that will make you doubt the honor of your own people," he said, enjoying his words. Then he stood back to make way for another dwarf.

Malbalor knew this one: Diemo Deathblade from the clan of the Death Blades commanded the troops in charge of protecting the passage to Girdlegard and the way to the treasure house. Seeing this dwarf and being told there was news made the king very uneasy.

"King Malbalor—there's been an attack," he admitted reluctantly. "We are the victims of a malicious ambush from within our own forces."

Malbalor sat up and got to his feet. "You don't have to tell me: There were about twenty of them—they looked like laborers," he guessed calmly. "One of them laid me low just now."

"Yes, the guards at the treasure house saw them and thought they had taken a wrong turning. By the time they noticed it was all a trick it was too late. They were attacked with shovels and overcome . . ."

"Overcome or killed?"

"Overcome. Slight injuries and cuts and bruises mostly, and hit over the head like yourself, Your Majesty."

Malbalor was pleased to be alive, of course, but he was surprised at the sudden restraint the thirdlings were showing with dwarves not of their own kind. "They weren't thirdlings," he said firmly and directly to Ginsgar. "I pulled the face cloth off one of them. None of us would willingly forgo a beard."

"A dwarf *without a beard*?" Ginsgar said incredulously. "Then maybe they are outcasts. We always treated outlaws like that in the firstlings; if you break the law your beard is shaved off and you have to leave until a new one has grown." He put his hand to his belt. "A malicious thirdling or robbers from the freeling cities?"

"What would the freelings want . . . ?" Malbalor looked over at Diemo. "What did they take?"

The warrior ground his teeth angrily. "Only the diamond, king."

"What diamond? We . . ." His voice died away as he understood the significance of the words. "That diamond? Gandogar's gift?" The furrows on his brow grew deeper; he could feel them cutting right into his flesh.

Ginsgar stepped forward. "What you told us is very useful. I suggest we send a message to the high king. I stick by the view it was the thirdlings or the freelings."

"What makes you so sure, Ginsgar?" Malbalor's question was harsh; he was removing this firstling from his mental list of those who might deputize for him. "What use is a diamond to them if they do not have a magus?"

"The freelings could be envious because they were not given one. They are outcasts—outlaws: criminals. We must not lose sight of that."

"You never lose sight of anything, Ginsgar. You never forget the past of the thirdlings or that of the freelings," the king answered sharply.

"As opposed to many others," he replied determinedly.

"Thirdlings steal, to bring us trouble. First they construct these machines, then they rob us to get the better of us: to make us look stupid. They take the most valuable thing in Girdlegard."

Malbalor strode past him. "The most valuable thing in Girdlegard is the common resolve of those who live here. *Our* common resolve." He looked at Ginsgar: "You, Ginsgar Unforce of the Nail Smiths of the firstlings, shall leave the Black Range tomorrow with your clan. You may cause trouble in your own land but not here where I rule." He left him standing and walked out.

He could not accept the interpretation of events this dwarf had given him, even if it would have been simpler to do just that.

Girdlegard,
Elf Land of Âlandur,
Late Spring, 6241st Solar Cycle

Looking at the forest they were passing through, Tungdil found it had changed a good deal since his last visit to see Liútasil. Trees in Âlandur obviously flourished and grew faster than anywhere else.

Ireheart, likewise walking along beside his pony, followed his friend's glance. "I thought I was imagining it," he said. "These shrubby things have shot up like weeds." He pulled his crow's beak out of the pack horse's saddlebag and weighed it lightly in his left hand. "Same as ever—I always feel naked here," he explained to Tungdil. "I may have lost my fighting fury but I'm still a warrior through and through. If one of these tendrils tries to grab me, I'll be ready for it."

"I trust the elves."

"So do I, Scholar." Ireheart shouldered his weapon. "But I don't trust their vegetation."

Two elves stepped suddenly out of the shelter of the trees. They wore robes of delicate textiles and had precious silver and gold clips in their long blond hair; the elegant clothing fell loosely about their tall, slim figures.

"Welcome to Âlandur, Tungdil Goldhand and Boïndil Doubleblade." The right-hand elf sang, rather than spoke, the words. Both elves bowed to the dwarves.

"By Vraccas, their faces look more fragile than ever," muttered Ireheart. "Or is it their clothes that give that impression?"

Tungdil grinned. "You're the one leading the mission. You must answer them," he whispered back.

"Me?"

"Of course, who else?"

"But you're the scholar."

"Gandogar entrusted this to *you*. I'm just here because you kidnapped me." Tungdil was greatly enjoying the warrior's discomfiture.

Boïndil sighed and gave a bow in his turn, even if his was not as low and gracious as that with which the elves had greeted him. "May Vraccas be with you," was his faltering salutation. "We are emissaries of our high king, and come to pay our respects." He pointed to the bundles on the back of the mule. "That is for Liútasil, and . . ." He went through his pockets slowly until he had unearthed the note from Eldrur. "And this is our letter from your own delegate." He held it out to the elves. "We . . . come in peace." Then he looked over to Tungdil and rolled his eyes. "I can't do it," he whispered helplessly. "Help me out here, or I'll end up starting a war."

The elves were studying the letter closely and smiling again. "We are pleased that the children of the Smith are warming to our culture. We shall be happy to take you through our realm and show you how we live," said the spokesman, standing aside and indicating the path. "Come. We have prepared quarters for you."

"I only hope it's not up in the tree-tops," Ireheart couldn't help remarking as he held his hand out for the letter. There was a moment's hesitation before it was returned. "The nesting places I'd rather leave to the birds."

"We know what your preferences are," the elf answered amicably, leading the way.

"Very considerate of you," Tungdil thanked them, aware that he should do the talking now after the mid-level insults his friend had offered their hosts. Boïndil sighed with relief. "We bring gifts for your Prince Liútasil."

"Our prince will be delighted about the donkey." One of the elves laughed, clear as glass; so high and pure a sound was almost painful to dwarf ears.

"No, of course it's not the donkey that's the gift," said Tungdil, joining in with their merriment—anything to drown out those high tinkling tones. "The donkey is carrying the treasures."

"As I thought. But nobody has ever given him a donkey before. It would be a novelty for him." He bowed once more, introducing himself. "I am Tiwalún, and this is Vilanoîl. We have been sent to escort you through Âlandur.

Please ask us anything you want to know. We will be glad to satisfy your curiosity."

"My thanks, Tiwalún." Tungdil recognized the path. It would lead to the clearing where he had first met the elf lord Liútasil and had spoken with him about the eoîl. He enquired courteously about the ruler's health.

"Our prince is well, but at the moment he is in the southwest of the realm dealing with important matters," explained Tiwalún, stepping into a clearing where a tent stood. "As soon as he has settled affairs there he will come to speak to you. Now I wish you both a good night."

Tungdil saw the walls of green velvet. "It is Liútasil's tent," he told Ireheart. "Thank you for the honor you show us," he said to Tiwalún, adding an dwarf-saying in their own elf language: "We know our friends by the hospitality they accord us."

Vilanoîl was startled and Tiwalún's countenance for a moment registered alarm. "Liútasil mentioned that you are known as the Scholar, but he did not tell us you had learned our language," said Tiwalún in acknowledgment, as he bowed, turning to leave. Then he stopped. "Might I please have that letter, Boïndil Doubleblade? I should like to send it to our prince so that he may read with his own eyes what good things Eldrur has written about you."

"Of course, Friend Elf," grinned Ireheart, groping at his belt. "A thousand dead beasts! I seem to have lost it!" he exclaimed. "I must have dropped it on the way here."

He made as if to turn round and go and look for it, but the elf lifted a hand. "That won't be necessary, Boïndil Doubleblade. Nothing in our forests ever gets lost, any more than a gold coin could go astray in your mountains.

We will find it, never fear." He made another bow. "We shall see you in the morning. May Sitalia send you pleasant dreams from the skies." With these words the two elves disappeared into the shadows cast by the trees.

"Well, I'll be struck down by the hammer of Vraccas! Hearing you talk like that!" gasped Boïndil. "Made me come over all funny. How long have you been able to do that?"

"I came across some old books in Lot-Ionan's vaults. There was a partly damaged work I found all about the lost realm of the northern elf, Lesinteïl. The author included some notes about the language. I only know a few of their sayings, that's all. It's awfully complicated." Tungdil held back the draped material at the tent door. "Let's get some rest."

"You cook us something delicious. I'll see to the ponies and be with you in a tick," answered Boïndil as he went over to where the animals were enjoying the juicy grasses on the forest's ferny floor.

Tungdil went into the tent, remembering exactly how the last meeting with the elf prince had gone. The carved wooden posts holding up the roof were the same, the pleasing fragrance, the gentle light from the oil lamps hanging from the supports and the warmth given out by the two stoves—it all created a relaxing atmosphere. He let the hardships of the journey slide from him.

Shedding his mail shirt, he threw it over a stool and went over to wash his face. In the middle of the tent he saw there was a table set with warm food. He would not have to cook anything.

Boïndil hurried in, wrinkled his nose because his friend

had taken off his armor, and took a seat at the ready-laid table. "This is the life," he said. "No worries about the mission if this is what it's going to be like!" He pulled the first of the dishes over. "There's a strong smell of flowers about this but it doesn't look too bad." He heaped his silver plate with portions of the various different foods, tried a bit of everything then hesitated with his fork above a yellowy ball-shaped thing. "Oh no, I remember this from last time. Didn't like it at all." Pulling a face, he moved it to the edge of his plate. "Come on, Scholar, dig in. You've lost some weight with all that walking, so you can afford to tuck in."

Tungdil laughed. "You were right to be so severe with me." He left the dark malt beer standing and poured out some water. He knew if he touched even a drop of the barley he'd be lost to it. The vice had held him in its grip far too long.

Their meal was delicious. When Tungdil afterwards discovered a curtained off section of the tent containing a tub and a large container of water which was heating on a stove there was no stopping him. He prepared a bath for himself, took a handful of the red crystals he found in a shallow dish next to the tub, strewed them into the water and lay back, eyes closed, in the warm water, his muscles relaxing from the journey.

His friend's voice called him out of his reverie. "I've got it!"

"Do you think you could get it slightly more quietly?" he complained, opening one eye to look at Ireheart who was standing next to the tub with only a cloth round his nether regions. He was waving a piece of paper excitedly. "I've found the letter again. I'd put it in my pocket. It fell out when I took my breeches off just now. Those elves will be angry when I let them know tomorrow they've spent a whole night searching through the bushes in vain," he grinned. "But let's not tell them just yet."

Tungdil remembered Tiwalún saying he wanted to send the letter on to Liútasil, and his curiosity was aroused. "Show me," he said, stretching out his hand for it. "I'd like to see the praises they heaped upon us."

It happened as the letter was being passed over. Either Ireheart let go too soon or Tungdil failed to take it in time—the page fluttered down into the bathwater. Both of them made a grab for it and it tore straight down the middle.

"That was the curse of Elria," said Boïndil knowingly, and looked down sadly at his half. "She destroys all our folk-knowledge with her water."

"Perhaps it was just us being clumsy," suggested Tungdil, getting out of the tub and wrapping a towel round himself. "The water's still hot if you want to get in."

"Me? Get in there? When the letter just drowned in it as a warning of how full of malice water is?" The warrior refused the offer of a bath.

"It'd do you good. You smell. And that's putting it mildly." He took both halves of the letter and placed them on one of the stoves to dry.

The elf runes were smudged and partially illegible, and only a few of them were similar to those used by the northern elves of Lesinteïl. Either their speech and script had always been different from that of their relatives or else their language had undergone changes in the course of past cycles.

As the paper dried, new pale blue runes started to appear between the lines.

"A secret message," said Tungdil in surprise. Why had Eldrur used invisible ink in the letter of introduction? Perhaps he had been afraid that one of the dwarves might decipher the runes and so he had not dared write his words openly.

Perhaps the delegates are spies, after all? wondered Tungdil, taking the letter and sitting down with it at the table to examine its contents in the light of the oil lamps. There had been some water damage to the script, which did not make the translation easier.

"Boïndil, come and look at this!" he called his friend over.

"Just a . . ." There was a loud splash and water ran out from under the curtain screening the tub from view; then came some spluttering and a volley of dwarf curses.

Tungdil grinned. "Are you all right?"

"Bloody water!" Boïndil raged, pushing the curtain aside and toweling himself. "Now I'll have to grease my beard all over again." He lifted the damp black mass of beard that hung sodden on his chest. "It's taken me a whole cycle to get it just right, with a proper shine." He turned round and gave the tub a hefty kick. "It's nothing but one of Elria's special tricks—a trap for dwarves. It shouldn't be allowed." He wrapped himself up. "It's enough to turn me mad again. I can feel the old anger welling up. It's too bad."

"Calm down. What happened?"

"I slipped, didn't I?" he complained. "Slipped on a piece of soap. And before I knew it I was underwater." He made a face. "Bah, it tastes dreadful!"

"If you're thirsty, why not try water on its own? But now you'll smell good inside and out." Tungdil joked, then pointed to the letter and grew deadly serious. "I've made a discovery."

Ireheart noted the differing colors of ink. "So they are spies, after all," he remarked with satisfaction. "I did not entirely mean it before, but it seems to be true."

"Don't let's jump to conclusions," warned Tungdil. He lifted the silver pot from the stove and poured himself a beaker of tea. "I'm going to see what I can translate. Perhaps it's an instruction not to show us every single secret in Âlandur."

"Spies," repeated Ireheart grimly. "There's no doubt in my mind now." He walked over to one of the guest beds and lay on it. After tossing and turning for a while, he grabbed a blanket off the bed and went to lie down on the floor. "Too soft," he said, closing his eyes. "You're on watch first. Wake me when you need me to take over."

"On watch? What do you mean?"

"I don't trust the pointy-ears anymore."

"But it may just be a harmless instruction . . ."

". . . then they wouldn't have needed to write in secret ink." He remained stubborn. "They could have written it out in the body of the letter."

". . . and we'd have thought that very discourteous, wouldn't we?" Tungdil was reluctant to pre-judge the elves, even if their behavior struck him as odd. A bit more than odd.

A loud snore showed him that Boïndil was not intending to pursue the argument. He turned up the wick in order to be able to see better. It was going to be a long night.

V

Girdlegard,
Pendleburg, Capital of the Kingdom of Urgon,
Late Spring, 6241st Solar Cycle

"Is it warmer in Gauragar than it is here?" asked King Ortger. A man of nearly twenty cycles, he was built much like any other and had regrettably protruding eyes; if it were not for the frog eyes one might have described him as dapper. He adjusted his gold-plated leather armor and took off his helmet to reveal short black hair already thinning at the back. But he did sport a thick black beard, thinking it made him appear older.

"Majesty, your journey takes you to Porista. I have heard that it is a very attractive region," his manservant answered.

Ortger looked over at the ten chests containing his robes for the journey. "I asked whether it would be warmer there. If so, I could manage with just the one chest."

"Only *one* chest?" asked his servant incredulously.

"Definitely. I want to travel fast and that will be impossible if we're weighed down like a cloth merchant's baggage train. I'll take this one. The rest stay here."

"Of course, sire." The servant bowed and gestured to four serving women, who began the task of placing the unwanted garments back in the cupboards.

Ortger watched them, then went over to the window to gaze at the seemingly endless mountain chains that stretched out as far as the eye could see.

The palace stood on the largest of the three hills on which the capital city was built. Below, he could see the settlement with its brightly colored stone houses. There was little wood to be had in the mountains, so they used stone for construction as far as possible. Employing different types of rock gave a range of shades, so in spite of the dull squat shapes of the houses, the town was bright and colorful.

It had been something of a surprise to Ortger to accede to the throne in Urgon. When the mad Belletain had threatened, in his deluded state, to launch a further attack following the foray into the Black Mountains and the deaths of thousands of innocent dwarves, courageous officers in his army had mutinied and ousted him. Ortger was a distant relative of Lothaire, the well-loved predecessor of Belletain, and had been leading a contemplative life far away from Pendleburg, up near the border with the troll country Borwôl, when the news reached him that he was to be the next ruler in the mountains of Urgon. He had not taken long to reach his decision. And he had never regretted it in all the five cycles of his reign.

There was a knock at the door and a guard came in. "The escort awaits, Your Majesty."

"Only the swiftest horses, as I requested?" Ortger wanted to know.

"Just as you ordered, sire. The five hundred miles to Porista will be covered very quickly."

Ortger fitted his helmet on and had the clothes chest carried downstairs. "Speed is indeed of the essence." He called to mind again the message that had come from Prince Mallen describing the raid. The news had given him a nightmare: how violently the frightful creature had attacked the guards in its quest for the diamond! The dream had been so real that he had awoken with a start, his heart racing. The beast had been chasing him through the palace and with its bare hands tore any man to pieces that stepped in its path. He had heard the shrieks and roars as clearly as if they had come from right by his bed.

He was terrified. Ortger did not want to think about the pictures conjured up in the past night, so he let his eyes wander over the landscape: the peaceful mountains of Urgon, and his own city.

This robbery brought back thoughts of the way the first of the diamonds had been stolen, in Rân Ribastur. "Is our diamond held secure?"

"We put it where you showed us, Your Majesty."

"How many men to guard it?"

"We have thirty men on duty, day and night. There are four spear slings ready to fire. We load and unload them in turn, so that the strings don't get overstretched and snap."

Urgon's ruler was pleased with this answer. He could not provide better protection than was already being given. Anyone forcing their way through the ranks of his soldiers would be met by the stone door of the vault, deep in the heart of the palace. The door was so strong and so massive that it had had to be chiseled out of the rock right there, and afterwards hinges had been attached. Only then had they tunneled out the chamber behind it. You needed the strength of four oxen to move it with the special equipment of pulleys and rope. Not even a troll would be strong enough to shift it.

Nevertheless it was with a feeling of unease that Ortger strode through his simple palace, more a fortress than a royal residence in appearance. He reached the courtyard, swung himself up into the saddle and rode up next to Meinart, the captain of the guard. "Off to Porista at full gallop!" he ordered. The horses thundered out through the gate and down through the streets of Pendleburg toward the southwest.

They raced along roads so narrow only two could travel abreast. To their right the walls rose sheer to the skies, while to their left loomed the dark abyss, the edge of a precipice, and long rocky slopes. Ahead, the sun shone on the far peaks and mountain pastures in an interplay of light and shadow. If you were to forget for a moment where you were riding, bewitched by the beauty of the view, you would be lost: sudden death awaited the unwary.

Their swift progress made constant vigilance essential. The captain sent an advance guard to ensure they met no other vehicles or riders coming suddenly round a bend on this treacherous path. They could lose some of their number to injury or death. If you fell from the saddle or from a wagon, the chasms of Urgon's mountains knew no pity.

They crossed a narrow pass.

Ortger remembered his dream and looked back, prompted by some vague feeling. From here there was a good view back to Pendleburg, which lay bathed in picturesque light. In one of the rays of sunlight breaking though the white clouds he caught sight of a metallic flash directly below the entrance to the palace.

"Halt!" Ortger ordered, reining his horse to a standstill and turning to get a clearer look.

Again there was a dazzling spark, this time too bright to be coming from a helmet or reflected off a shield. Immediately he saw there was smoke rising from the palace.

"We're going back!" The king's thoughts were with his capital city. "They're under attack. Our diamond is in danger. We'll take the enemy by surprise from behind."

"Your Majesty, is it wise to return now in the thick of the attack?" objected Meinart. "Think of Prince Mallen's message. If magic is being used you should stay well away from the fighting. Send a scout to find out . . ."

Ortger would gladly have followed this suggestion, but was reluctant to show any weakness. In his dream the creature had pursued him. Now it was time to turn the tables. "It's only a creature, Meinart. It took the men of Goldensheaf by surprise, but my soldiers are forewarned and ready. We will destroy it." Ortger thrust his spurs into his horse's flanks and raced back the way they had come.

The place was in uproar. The townspeople were running around in the streets, pointing up to the palace where smoke was pouring out of the windows. Many had armed themselves with buckets to help with the firefighting; others carried swords and spears to go to the aid of the soldiers. News of the attack had swiftly made the rounds.

With Ortger at their head the band galloped through the ruins of the main gate. The portcullis had melted out of shape as if giant red-hot fingers had played with it. Smoldering torn-off limbs, charred spear shafts and melted sword blades lay scattered in the courtyard. In places, blackened flagstones had crackled and split asunder in the intense heat.

"Our defenses won't have been able to stand up to this," Ortger said to Meinart, horror in his voice. He could not take his eyes off the blood-covered bodies. At dawn that very morning he had talked and even laughed with some of these his subjects who now were reduced to mutilated corpses. Ortger stifled a choke and trembled all over. Whatever it was that had done the killing had strength far beyond anything known in Girdlegard in recent history. Far beyond anything he himself had ever experienced.

They followed a trail of destruction through the devastated central tract of the palace; fire had broken out in several places. Ignoring the injured men lying moaning in agony, they raced straight down the steps to the cellar. The safety of the diamond was paramount.

As the soldiers ran down the last steps to reach the lobby to the treasure vault they heard a loud hissing sound and saw light flickering over the walls and the stairs. At the same time there came a beast-like roar and the cries of men in agony. A cloud of acrid smoke tumbled out of the vault toward them, so it was clear to every last man of them what was ablaze in the chamber.

Ortger stopped. The trembling that had seized him was worse now; his body refused to move toward the ghastly scene where death was raging ferociously, taking its victims at will. Even if his spirit knew clearly what power and what value were inherent in the diamond they had kept watch over so well, nothing could have made the young king move a muscle now in its defense. The being that had visited him in his nightmare was now reality.

With a loud crash the rock burst apart, great boulders breaking off and tumbling down off the walls, landing at the king's feet. They heard triumphant laughter. There came the clank of iron, then two heads rolled over to the bottom of the stairway.

"It's broken open the door of the treasure chamber! Palandiell save us!" whispered Ortger in terror as he stepped backwards. "The stone . . . is lost."

There was a dull thudding sound approaching the stairs, repeated at regular intervals like the footsteps of a giant. The light of the fire threw a long broad shadow, which advanced toward them, growing in size and coming nearer and nearer until their own shadows were overwhelmed and swallowed up. The creature causing the monstrous silhouette soon followed, bent double because it was too large to fit into the passage.

But this was not the figure he had seen in his dreams. This was something far, far worse.

It was made of tionium, completely of black tionium! Arms and legs were two paces in length, the rump no less tall and as wide as three barrels of beer. The demonic metal head, shaped like a bull's, displayed fiery red eyes, and clouds of white and black steam rose from behind the visor.

There was a mesh with indecipherable symbols covering the whole construction; these signs gave off an eerie pale green light as if lowering in wait for an opportunity to blaze out. Arrayed all round the structure were shining blades with spikes dripping with poisonous liquid. The blood of the fallen soldiers could be seen adhering to nearly all parts of this hideous form. Ortger saw scraps of clothing and bunches of hair on the spikes.

Meinart grabbed Ortger's arm. "May Palandiell protect us! Look at that, by its neck—isn't that an elf rune?"

Ortger's eyes were not able to locate the spot. His terrified gaze surveyed the surface of the whole monster but his mind refused to register the horror in its entirety.

Whenever the creature set a limb in motion, it gave out a hiss and somewhere in the center of the colossal black armor-plating a mechanical whirring, rattling and clanking could be heard. Just one of the metal claws would have been able to encompass the heads of three men at once. Underneath the neck there was a porthole of thick glass, through which a terrible but compelling visage could be espied, with fangs bared threateningly.

For Ortger this sight was more than enough. His quivering fingers opened of their own accord and his sword clanked as it dropped out of his grasp to the floor, smashing onto the stone and sliding down the stairs.

"Away from here, we must get away," he stammered, turning in retreat.

Suddenly the runes flared up and blazed with light. On one side of the metal figure five holes opened in a horizontal line, horribly reminiscent of muzzles.

Steam issued from these openings and the soldiers standing near Ortger fell screaming to the ground; he himself felt only a sharp breath of wind shooting past his left ear. The bodies of the fallen had the feathered shafts of steel-reinforced crossbow darts sticking out of them. The vicious arrows had pierced the trunks of the guards standing at the front, and had been traveling with enough force to injure those standing in the second row. Meinart, the captain, was among those slain.

Now there was no holding them.

The soldiers fled up the stairs, with Ortger racing ahead

of them all, pissing himself with fear. An experienced warrior would surely have given the order to man the battlements and dismantle the stonework to get missiles to hurl down at this creature. But the young king did not have the steady nerves needed for such leadership. Not after that dream. Not after this sight.

He was more than willing to allow himself to be led to a horse and then to flee Pendleburg—to flee for dear life. There was nothing left of the earlier eagerness for battle he had displayed when they had been climbing the pass. Not until he was a safe distance away did he call his retinue to a halt and send two men back to the city to find out what had happened after they left.

The reports they brought back were devastating.

"The diamond is taken, Your Majesty," one of them confirmed what they had all feared. "That creature just tore down the door and smashed its way in. It didn't take anything else. Your crown jewels are still . . ."

Ortger silenced the man with a gesture and looked at the second of the scouts. "They are saying different things about which way the monster went. Some say it went through the town streets and made its way to the mountains—the others say it vanished into thin air, Your Majesty. The fires in the palace have been put out now and the injured are being cared for."

The king could smell the drying urine on his clothes. It brought back to him the sense of shame and reminded him of the cowardice he had shown. It had been all too human and understandable a reaction. This enemy did not look like the opponent Mallen had described in his letter— apart from two details. Ortger conjured up again the sight of that terrible face behind the glass and he knew now what the illuminated symbols on the armor plates signified: sorcery.

"We'll head out for Porista again," he decided. "The rulers must be told that another of the stones has been stolen. It's vital the remaining jewels are put under much stronger guard." He spurred his horse onwards. "There is no time to be lost. It seems that there's someone in Girdlegard who's adept at magic and crazy for power. Onwards!"

The troop started off at a gallop and raced along the same road for the second time that day.

Ortger did not allow himself another glance back toward his city of Pendleburg. He was too afraid of having disaster stare him in the face.

Girdlegard,
Elf Realm of Âlandur,
Late Spring, 6241st Solar Cycle

"You are up already, Tungdil Goldhand! I hope I am not late with your breakfast?"

The dwarf jumped, although the friendly tones gave no cause for alarm. The greeting did not sound in any way threatening, only surprised and a little hurt. The elf must have seen the letter that he had been working on all night. There was nothing for it but to seize the initiative.

"I'm used to getting up with the birds," replied Tungdil and turned to face Tiwalún, who had come in silently and was standing right behind him. "I know knocking on a tent is difficult but you might at least have tried."

"My apologies. The breakfast was intended as a surprise," said the elf, bowing, but never taking his eyes off the piece of paper. "So you found it?"

Tungdil was not sure what Tiwalún meant: did he mean the letter itself or the secret message it contained? "Yes. My friend had put it somewhere silly." He decided to employ some of the truth. "It got wet and then these lines started appearing." He pointed to the pale blue symbols. "I insist on an honest answer: What is the meaning of all this cobold-like secrecy? Your delegations all over Girdlegard—are they spies? They seem to be. Don't try to lie, because I shall be asking Prince Liútasil."

Tiwalún looked at him intently, trying to see just how much he did or did not know. "I could never lie to a hero who saved Âlandur from destruction," he said earnestly. "The writing that becomes visible on application of heat has nothing to do with the dwarf people. I swear it by Sitalia."

"Then tell me what it says."

"I can't do that. Ask our prince. It's by his orders." He held out his hand for the paper. "May I have it?"

Tungdil folded it and slipped it under his leather robe. "I'd prefer to give it to Liútasil myself," he said amicably. That way he could be sure that the elf prince would actually grant him an audience; then he could ask him in person about all these goings-on.

Tiwalún made the face he might have made if an orc had asked for his hand in marriage. "As you wish, Tungdil Goldhand. He will be glad to speak to you." The smell of fresh bread pervaded the tent. "Have some food, then I'll take you and your friend on a tour of our land." He bowed and went out and some elves in less extravagant attire laid the table and served refreshments.

Boïndil appeared in his mail shirt as usual; nose in the air, he sniffed noisily. "Doesn't that smell good?" he called enthusiastically. He was looking forward to his food and watched as the elves completed their preparations at the table before retiring. "Did you stay up all night on watch?" he asked, once he was sure they would not be overheard.

"I was translating," Tungdil said and went over to the table.

"And?" urged Ireheart. "What had the elves written?"

Tungdil told him about his short exchange with Tiwalún. "What he doesn't know is that I've translated part of the letter. But it doesn't help us with the secret. The rest is illegible, either because of the bathwater or else written in symbols I'm not familiar with." He helped himself to a piece of bread, poured out some tea and put honey in it. The scent of cloves and cinnamon and two varieties of cardamom rose to his nostrils. The infused ingredients in combination with the herbs and the milk made an excellent spiced drink, he realized, after taking the first sip. Even though his whole body was crying out for beer, brandy or any other alcoholic beverage, he did not give in to the craving: he stuck with the tea.

Boïndil watched him crossly. "Are you doing this on purpose, Scholar? Keeping me on tenterhooks?"

"Oh, you mean the letter?" Tungdil grinned. "Sorry, I was miles away." With the slice of bread in his hand he looked round, as Ireheart was doing, for some juicy meat. It seemed that the elves didn't serve meat in the morning, so he helped himself to the boiled eggs. "What I could read was a recommendation, praising us as heroes and encouraging the greatest possible vigilance. The remaining words were *keep them from Liútasil* and *only show them the outsides* and then again *keep them away from our new buildings* and *not longer than four orbits; after that get rid of them with any old excuse. Say it's because of their bad manners*." He tasted one of the eggs and was surprised. Although he hadn't used condiments it tasted of salt and other aromas.

Boïndil had noticed the same thing. "Wonder what they feed their hens on?"

"Who says they're hens' eggs?"

The dwarf chewed more slowly. "I underestimated the dangers of this type of mission: foreign food," he sighed and swallowed noisily. He recalled the first meal he'd had with the freelings in Trovegold; there had been the oddest of ingredients like beetles and maggot beer. "I reckon the instructions mean that the elves are only to show us selected places, and not to let us meet up with Liútasil, and that we're to leave Âlandur very soon."

Tungdil nodded. "The mention of new buildings is bothering me. What is it about them that they want to keep hidden from us, and probably from the rest of Girdlegard, too?"

Ireheart was displaying his old fighting grin, even if he no longer had that fire-rage in his eyes like before. Apart from the sense of humor and the hair, he was exactly like his twin brother, the one who had died. "I get it. If they tell us to go right, we'll go left."

"Handing them a reason for getting rid of us even

sooner?" Tungdil took some more of the eggs, slicing them onto his bread and putting garlic sauce on top.

"But they haven't read the letter so they haven't got the instructions."

"Tiwalún came creeping in here as silent as a mountain lion. I don't know how long he'd been standing behind me. I think he must have been able to read quite a bit of it," he said. "We've got three orbits. During the days we'll do as they say and at night we'll go out snooping. Get ready to manage without sleep."

"Slinking around like a perfidious älf," complained Boïndil. "Never my strong point. I hope I don't muck things up."

"We'll have to fight them with their own weapons there," said Tungdil. "What choice do we have?"

They finished their breakfasts calmly and did not let themselves be hurried by Tiwalún when he came to collect them. Around midday they set off on the ponies again toward the interior. They rode through the peaceful lush-green woods, where dark thoughts had no chance. It was all simply too beautiful even if there weren't any mountains, much lamented by Ireheart.

The elf did not tire of eloquently listing the particular charms of the various trees they passed; it was as if he were trying to lull them into a sense of security with his long descriptions.

And if it had not been for that coded letter he might have succeeded.

As it was, Tungdil and Ireheart simply nodded, but they had a good look around, keeping an eye out for anything unusual. It didn't escape their notice that they never rode through mountain territory, always remaining in the forest, where you could only see about as far as an arrow might fly.

Of course they knew the reason. When Tungdil asked Vilanôil about mountain ranges or perhaps less wooded hills, the elf looked mortified that the guests were tired of the unique marvels of the quiet forest glades of Âlandur. He promised them an outing with a view for the following day.

As darkness fell they rode up to a brightly lit building that Tungdil and Boïndil were already familiar with. They had been here before when they came with Andôkai to ask the ruler of the elves for help in resisting the forces of Nôd'onn. Mighty trees formed living pillars holding up the thickly woven roof of treetops, two hundred paces overhead.

But the forest halls had changed radically since that first visit.

The artistically fashioned mosaics of wafer-thin gold and palladium sheets that used to sparkle suspended between the tree trunks were missing. In their place now you saw giant paintings, compositions in various shades of white; here and there a randomly placed diamond shimmered in the torchlight. Where once there had been showiness and skilled craftsmanship now there was a strange clarity in the work that impressed the dwarves just as much as its monumental nature.

"What have you done with all that other stuff?" Boïndil found himself asking.

"Is one constrained to seek artistic expression only in one single vein for all eternity?" responded Tiwalún. "We have hardly any visitors in our forests to see how often our tastes change, seeking subtle nuances and variety. Let us tell you, Boïndil Doubleblade, that we have experimented with many different art forms over the cycles. As with your own people, one or two hundred cycles are as nothing to us."

He took a left turning and was attempting to lead them out of the tree-hall when Ireheart pointed to a triangular white monolith standing where once they had seen Liútasil's throne. Guessing from this distance, the object must be at least fifteen paces high and seven in circumference. "May I have a closer look, Friend Elf?"

"It is nothing of significance," said Tiwalún, in an attempt to downplay the importance of what they had seen. "The meal will be waiting for us . . ."

Boïndil had forgotten Tungdil's advice that they should pretend to follow the elves' suggestions in all things during the daylight hours. Boldly he marched straight past Tiwalún to inspect the three-cornered monolith. "The eye of a stone-expert is called for here," he announced. "My people are renowned as excellent stonemasons."

The elf swiftly overtook him and walked backwards in his path, shielding the object from his view. "No, Boïndil Doubleblade. I would ask you not to do that. It is a holy and revered object that may only be touched by us elves. You should not have been permitted to see it even!"

Ireheart looked up the length of the elf's legs, slowly up along his body, till his gaze reached Tiwalún's face. "That seems very discourteous," he complained. "Your delegation is shown every inch of our land, but here I am not allowed to cast eyes on a stone?"

"It is a holy relic: didn't you hear, Boïndil?" Tungdil interjected to save the day.

"So why did he say it wasn't of any great significance?"

"Not of any significance *for you*," said Tiwalún with a smile. A drop of sweat rolled down his forehead, over that smooth unblemished skin that would surely remain wrinkle-free and youthful for at least a hundred cycles. "Please turn around."

"Elves revering stones?" grinned the warrior. "Our peoples have more in common than I had thought. Aside from the type of things you like to eat, of course." He turned around quite calmly and pointed to the passageway Tiwalún had previously indicated. "This way, is it?"

"This way," confirmed Tiwalún, sounding relieved. He strode off before the troublesome dwarf could change his mind. "Thank you for showing such understanding, Boïndil Doubleblade."

"But of course," grinned Ireheart, looking at Tungdil.

Late evening brought a surprise for elf and dwarf alike.

They were sitting with Vilanoîl and Tiwalún finishing the final course of a light but lavish supper when a messenger came in with a letter. On reading it the elf looked at the dwarves.

"Very worrying news," he said. "Three of the diamonds have been stolen—King Nate's has gone and so have King Ortger's and King Malbalor's. They're talking about dreadful creatures and dwarves, too, launching these raids." He read out the lines that described just how these terrible deeds had been committed in each of the three kingdoms. The guests listened in horror: the attacks by the awful machines in the Red Mountain Range were mentioned. "Evil has taken hold and is stretching out its claws to grasp total domination," Tiwalún finished.

"We'll leave first thing," said Tungdil, extremely concerned. In such circumstances he would have to ensure that the stone Gandogar had entrusted him with, hidden away safely in the vault, was being properly guarded. He was frightened for Balyndis, his wife, who wouldn't have heard the news. If these unknown raiding parties had found the stones in all these kingdoms and dwarf realms, then they would have no difficulty locating his own, deposited simply in mine galleries that were comparatively easy to enter. The only soldier left in charge was Balyndis herself, and she would be hopelessly outnumbered.

"But our mission . . ." objected Boïndil, until he remembered that his friend had one of the diamonds in his possession. "Forget it, Scholar. The ponies will carry us to your home like the wind."

Tungdil stood up from the table. "We don't wish to be rude, Tiwalún and Vilanoîl. We need to get some rest. The next orbits will be hard for us. Please give Prince Liútasil our warmest greetings. I assume we will see him very soon at the rulers' assembly."

Tiwalún looked distinctly relieved to hear of their departure. "Of course. He will understand why you have to leave. I shall get provisions brought for you so that you can set off as soon as you want." He got up and bowed to them. "I would have wished for a calmer conclusion to your visit here in Âlandur, but the gods are testing us." He smiled. "You will have an important role to perform, will you not?"

"I could do without tests like this," replied Tungdil. "But if my people and Girdlegard need me I shall be there." He strode to the door. Ireheart followed, a laden plate in his hand.

Vilanoîl and Tiwalún watched them go. When the door had closed behind them, Tiwalún reached for the wine and poured himself a glass full to the very brim. He had seen the hidden instructions in the letter; that morning, the dwarf hadn't noticed he had been reading over his shoulder, until alerted by the sound of his voice. This bad news could not have come at a better time, since it meant the unwelcome guests were leaving Âlandur of their own accord.

It had been a serious error letting the dwarves anywhere near the monolith. Any moment things could have got much worse.

Tiwalún raised his drinking cup. "Here's to you, Sitalia. I drink to you and in honor of your purest of creatures." Ceremoniously he lifted the vessel to his mouth, took three sips and then poured the rest on the ground as a libation. "May the eoîl one day return and take power."

Vilanoîl smiled.

But there was something afoot that night.

In spite of extreme tiredness Boïndil could not help going out on his own to inspect the white stone Tiwalún had so adamantly insisted he should not approach. They would be leaving Âlandur the following orbit anyway so it would not matter if he was observed. What else could happen to him? They surely wouldn't cut off his head for it?

Stealth didn't come easily to him: he wasn't good at it and didn't like it. He'd taken off his leather-soled boots and left off his chain-mail shirt. Completely naked—that's how it felt—he'd made his way through the tree palace as if stalking a deer; it seemed not a soul was around. He had thought he would remember how to get to the hall but he had soon lost his sense of direction. This would never have happened to him underground. "Wretched bloody trees. They all look alike," he'd grumbled, taking the next corridor to the left.

At first he had been delighted that there were no elf guards about, but now he was getting worried about it. This was the prince's residence after all and there should be servants all over the place. He bravely opened the nearest door and found an empty room; starlight fell into the deserted chamber and there were a few leaves on the floor. That was all: no clothes, no chests, no bed.

Boïndil continued through the palace trying a few more doors. He did not find a single room with any sign of occupation. It was nothing but a refuge for ghosts.

By chance he happened on the great hall with the tall white monolith dominating the space.

Although no torches were burning, the stone itself gave off a glow, as if it had stored up light during the day to release in darkness.

"So there you are." He grinned and stepped closer, circling the stone, to give it a thorough inspection. There was not a single join on it, not a scratch, not at least as far up as the dwarf could actually see. The white surface shimmered smooth as glass. Boïndil stretched out a hand.

When his skin came into contact with the stone he was

amazed how warm it felt. So it wasn't just storing up light
but also energy from the sun. This was new to him. Well,
he was a fighting man and never much good as a mason,
but he'd never come across anything at all like this. It
meant that they were mining new minerals here in Âlandur,
a completely different type of stone.

Boïndil was turning to leave when he saw that where
he had touched the stone there was now the mark of five
black fingers.

"Bloody orc bloody shit!" He looked at his hand: it
was clean. He tried wiping the stone with his beard at
first and then with a kerchief, but the marks on the stone
would not shift. They stared out accusingly from the otherwise immaculate surface of the monolith. The size of the
handprint desecrating the holy monument made it obvious
that only a small-handed dwarf could have done this.
There would be an outcry.

With Tiwalún's words ringing in his ears about non-
elves touching the stone, he went hot and cold all at once.

He ran back, shook Tungdil awake and grabbed his things.
"We've got to get out of here," he whispered. "Something's
up." He slipped into his boots and put on his mail shirt.

His friend struggled up, "What's happened?"

"I went off to look at the monolith and there are no
signs of life in the palace at all. They've only opened it
up because of us." He quickly related what he had seen
in the empty rooms. "And the stone is not normal. It
shows marks when you touch it," he murmured.

"Marks? You mean you did touch it?" Tungdil was
fully awake and alert. "But you heard what he said . . ."

"Yes, I know, it's holy. But I'm in charge of this mission

and if the dwarves are keeping things secret I want to find out why," he said defensively, crossing his arms.

Tungdil uttered an oath and got out of bed. The elves had at least one secret they were keeping. And this three-cornered white stone seemed to be tremendously important. "Come on. Let's see if I can clean off the marks somehow." He collected his armor to be on the safe side and took a bowl of water, a cloth, some soap and some of the perfumed toilet water that had been provided. Perhaps they could sort something out.

Boïndil showed him how empty the tree palace was; the scholar looked at the deserted rooms. He agreed: nobody had been living here in ages.

There were more and more puzzles.

As they made their way it seemed as if the wooden passage walls were shifting to prevent them finding the monolith. The corridors had turned into a maze and they were lost until Tungdil thought to cut tiny notches on the wall with his knife. No longer wandering around aimlessly, they soon found the great hall.

The handprint had got darker still, or so it seemed to Ireheart: the marks would be on that stone for all eternity. Nothing worked: they tried soap, they tried rubbing, they tried the perfumed water.

"It's no good," said Tungdil, throwing the cloth back into the bowl with a splash. "The stone is insulted because it has been touched by somebody that is not an elf."

"What do you think? Shall we tell Tiwalún and own up or shall we make a run for it?"

Tungdil thought about it. If the elves had been a bit friendlier and more open then he certainly would have

chosen the honest course: to speak to Tiwalún and ask for clemency for Boïndil. But their hosts had been behaving strangely. And anyway, he had to get back to protect his diamond. Speed was called for.

He dipped the soap in the water again and rubbed it between his hands until there was a good lather. Carefully he lifted off the top layer of soft soap with the blade of his dagger, and pressed it onto the dark stains.

It worked. "You're the cleverest damned dwarf I know," whooped Ireheart.

After Tungdil had applied three thin layers, the ugly marks had been covered over. An innocent superficial glance would not reveal anything suspicious.

"Right, that should do." Tungdil sighed with relief. "As soon as we have left Âlandur I'll send Prince Liútasil a letter apologizing. You will seek an audience and ask for clemency," he decided. His friend nodded. "So it's off to the ponies."

The two dwarves found their way back to their quarters. Then they went to the stables and were off as fast as they could go toward the mines. Not until they crossed the border at dawn, when the ponies' hooves touched Gauragar, could they relax.

Nobody had pursued them.

Girdlegard,
Queendom of Weyurn, Mifurdania,
6241st Solar Cycle, Late Spring

When Rodario and Tassia had finished asking around in the town after Furgas, they went back to the rest of the troupe. A distraught Gesa rushed straight into their arms like a startled hen. Her plump body was bouncing all over the place, doing its best to escape from her dress: the tight bodice was unable to hold it all back.

"Master Rodario! At last you're back!" She took him by the hand. "Come quick! Some men came—your caravan's been smashed to pieces and poor Reimar's been beaten up. Then we set the dogs on them and chased them off."

"All right, Gesa. Calm down." He stroked her cheek. Rodario had been expecting something like this and so could react sensibly.

Nevertheless, it was upsetting to see how his home had been destroyed. The little house on wheels had suffered considerable damage in being ransacked for the necklace. If he set eyes on them, those heavies Nolik's father had sent, he'd skin them for all they were worth. He'd have the pants off them, underpants too, just to pay them back in humiliation.

"O Palandiell!" moaned Gesa in distress, staring at the mess from the doorway. "How awful!"

Giving a sigh, Rodario sat down on the ripped-up mattress. "Thank you, Gesa. It's all right, I'll tidy up later." She nodded and left.

Tassia closed the door and retrieved the necklace from under the floorboards. "They're too stupid to do a decent search," she said, laughing with relief and putting the necklace on.

"And they think we've flogged the jewel in Mifurdania," he added, holding out his arms to her. "Come here, Queen of the Stage, and grant the emperor your favors. Display yourself in all your glory, with gold and jewels hung about your neck."

The dress she had pinched from someone's washing-line slipped to the ground and she lay down next to him, stroking his face. "So, Emperor of Lust. Shall we start work on your dramatic production?"

"Oh, that's daring! You'd like to make love on stage?" His grin was dirty, and his aristocratic face took on a vulgar leer. "We'd be thrown in jail and no mistake. For indecency."

She smiled and tickled him with a lock of her blond hair. "Let's do it anyway. Right now. And just for ourselves."

He kissed the nape of her neck and soon they were deep into their drama until they sank back exhausted into what had been a mattress and covered themselves with what had been a blanket.

After this delightful distraction Rodario found his thoughts drifting back to his missing friend and to their current adventures. "Someone has tried to kill us, good people have been lost and a man has been carried off," he mused. "And somehow it's all connected with Furgas."

Tassia picked up the dark yellow dress and slipped it on. "Why? And what does anyone want with the black-smith?"

"Lambus is a highly skilled craftsman. Others will be jealous of him." He put his own clothes back on, regretting that the girl was no longer visible in her exquisite entirety. "What if Furgas himself is behind it all?" he wondered. "Lambus told us he didn't want to leave town. What can have been so urgent that Furgas would have kidnapped him?" He dismissed the idea. That was not the way his friend would act.

"Didn't you say he'd lost his partner and his children?" she asked, standing up and leaning against the door. "Perhaps he's found someone new."

"You mean the child he had with him?" Rodario started tidying the mess. "I don't understand. He loved Narmora more than anything."

"People's feelings change."

"Sure, anyone else's," he agreed. "Not with Furgas. You don't know him or you wouldn't say that. Only if he'd changed completely."

"Mm." She had her hand on the door handle. "And what if it's not his kid? Perhaps he's just taken it in?" Tassia smiled at him. "I'd better leave you in peace to finish your sorting and your thinking."

"Great. Off you go."

She laughed winningly. "The queen knows when she is not wanted." And she stepped out.

"Tassia!"

"Yes?"

Rodario pointed at her throat. "The necklace."

"Oh." She ran her hand over the necklace that was catching the light so brilliantly. "It feels so nice against my skin."

"Don't wear it while we're here in Mifurdania," he told her. She took it off, ready to put it back in the hiding place. "But later we'll use it on stage a lot as a prop."

She blew him a kiss and ran out. He was left with the unwelcome task of restoring order in his domestic realm.

That done, he sat down on the caravan steps with a lamp and wrote some more of the play.

It came easily; Tassia and the events of the day were inspiring him. Everything they had been through found a place in the drama—it was full of passion, adventure and secrets.

How it was going to end wasn't yet clear. For that he'd have to find Furgas first.

He was pouring himself some wine from the only bottle to have survived when he heard Tassia's laugh. It was a very particular laugh.

Jealousy flared up. He put the glass down and went over to Reimar's quarters. He stood on tiptoe outside the window and peeped through. Hearing that laugh had aroused his suspicions and now he was sure. His Queen of the Stage was cheating on him. So, she was seeking entertainment elsewhere. And Reimar, that bear of a man, was assisting her, not completely selflessly, in her quest.

Rodario returned to his narrow steps and picked up the glass. He laughed. He laughed and laughed until he was out of breath and inquisitive heads popped out of neighboring caravans. Even Reimar came out, a towel round his middle, to see what was up. The actor pointed at him and started laughing again, tipped over backwards, gasping for air.

"All right, folks," he waved the observers away. "It's only my normal attack of evening madness. It gets me whenever I hear another man making love to my woman."

Reimar blushed and whizzed back inside his caravan. Rodario had hysterics again.

He looked up at the stars, veiled now by a thin screen

of clouds that had covered them in milk. "O ye gods! That's some girl you've sent me!" He grinned. "She's paying me back for what I used to get up to with other women." He emptied his glass. "I'm wise to your game. Was it your idea, Samusin, god of justice?" he called out, raising his glass and saluting the stars. "I thank you! I've not been this inspired for ages." Cool dark wine ran down his throat. He put the vessel down and started writing.

Time sped by, but he was on fire. He cut bits out, wrote anew and changed the wording of act after act, scene after scene. It was thirsty work. Without looking, he stretched out his hand for the bottle; there was a tinkle of broken glass and the lamp he'd been using went out.

He looked up in surprise. He couldn't have knocked it over, his hand had been lower.

A mistake, it seemed. The lamp was still in the same place, just behind him to one side on the top step. Rodario stared at the arrow that had shattered it and then buried itself in the wood. Half an ell to the left and it would have got him straight in the eye!

The archer-woman from Mifurdania! he realized in a flash as he dived to one side, crawling under the wagon. He listened out.

There were insects humming, the odd cricket chirping, the horses were dozing quietly in their temporary paddock, and Hui the gray and black hunting dog lay snoring in the grass, head on its paws.

Altogether it sounded like a perfectly normal night— apart from Tassia's faint moans, Reimar's loud groans and the complaints from the overworked caravan springs.

Amazing! They are bonking their brains out while I'm

the victim of an assassin. So ran his gallows humor as he looked at the wagon where the girl and the workman were enjoying themselves so violently that the lamps swung to and fro. This had nothing in common with what he and Tassia had shared earlier. But what had she said? Sometimes a woman just needs a man with muscles.

Flock. A second arrow landed close to him, hitting the wood. Then a third clanged onto the metal wheel hub and broke. He threw himself flatter still and stared out at the darkness being used for cover. He didn't want to wake the others. There was too high a risk that one of his troupe would be injured, or even killed, whether by accident or design. "Pssht, you so-called watchdog," he hissed, "psssht. Get up, hound." The dog opened one eye and wagged its tail. "No! No wagging. Be a bad dog. Find, go get it! Fetch! Bite!"

The hound got up and took a leisurely stretch, then trotted over to where Rodario lay under the caravan and licked his face.

"Stop that!" The actor fended off these wet offerings of affection. "Kill!" He pointed over at the other side. "Fetch!"

Hui had finally got it. He lifted his nose and sniffed, then, nose to the ground and tail straight out behind, he sloped off in the direction Rodario had indicated.

The showman felt bad about sending the dog out. He peered out again and soon could see neither the dog nor the assassin. And Reimar's wagon wasn't swaying anymore. They'd had enough, then.

A cold blade touched his throat. "Disappear, you!" said a rough voice. The smells of cold smoke, rust and heated metal met his nose. "First thing in the morning. Pack your stuff and scram. Take your painted wagon and be off! Out of here!"

"May I ask . . . ?"

He felt a sharp pain at the base of his throat where the blade had cut into his skin. "Get out of here and stop asking questions about the magister, got it?" the voice whispered in his ear. "We're watching you, showman."

Reimar's door opened a fraction and Tassia looked out to see whether he was still sitting on his steps. Seeing him gone and the lamp extinguished she flitted out of the caravan.

"Look at your fine mistress, showman. If you keep on trying to find Furgas, she will die," the man threatened. His hair was grabbed and his head forced up and back until his forehead touched the underside of the caravan. "And then you. Then the rest of your troupe. Then the magister."

There was a further jab to his neck, this time a deeper cut. Something warm dripped down over his Adam's apple, and Rodario felt sick. He couldn't think of how to extricate himself. He was at the mercy of whoever it was crouched behind him, ready to kill with a movement of his hand.

"Yes," he croaked: fear and the unnatural position made speech difficult.

"Very good," laughed the stranger. "Think about it. We're watching, right?" The hand let go of his hair and he received a mighty blow to the back of his head, probably with the handle of the knife. It was enough to disturb his vision for a moment. He could hear the man crawl off, get up and run. The danger was over.

Groaning, Rodario struggled out from under the wagon, stumbled up the steps to his caravan and then inspected the damage in a mirror.

There was a red line all along the front of his throat; the cut was bleeding badly and it was deep. It would be difficult to apply much pressure to the wound, but he made a linen pad and tied a scarf round to hold it in place. He'd go to some healer-woman in the morning. After they'd struck camp and got away.

"The adventure side is getting out of hand. Too much even for my taste," he murmured, checking the bandage. Looking down at his fingers, sticky with his own blood, he started to feel giddy and sat down suddenly. "Much too much."

He dealt with the pain by drinking the rest of the wine from the half-full bottle. It was a good thing the archer-woman had hit the lamp and not the bottle.

VI

Girdlegard,
Kingdom of Idoslane,
Early Summer, 6241st Solar Cycle

Galloping ponies were seldom observed in Girdlegard. The thundering of small hooves did not really sound threatening, but, together with the sight of the grim-faced dwarves in the saddles and the clattering of weapons and armor, it ensured that any pedestrian on the roads would rapidly make way.

"Is it far now?" Boïndil regretted they weren't using the tunnels—the easiest and quickest way to travel through Girdlegard. He was not particularly good on horseback and he was feeling stiff; his back hurt with each jolt the pony made. And he seemed to have swallowed several flies.

"You'll manage." Tungdil showed mercy neither to himself, nor to the ponies, nor to his friend. It was obvious why he was in such a hurry. Apart from the life of his partner Balyndis being at stake there was a diamond that had to be saved. He knew that the stone was far more valuable than it appeared, rough-cut as it was. "Only half an orbit still to go."

They heard hoof-beats from behind getting closer. A horse came up level with their mounts—but in the saddle sat not a human but a solidly built dwarf! Ax-handles jutted out of the saddle-bags Tungdil could see bouncing up and down, and he could hear metal clanking.

The dwarf was dressed in black and wore dark brown leather armor and heavy boots. The shape of his beard was eccentric and there was blond hair round his mouth and chin but the rest of his face was shaved. Long light blond braids flew back with the wind; there was a black scarf covering his head.

Tungdil recognized him at once. "Bramdal Masterstroke!"

The other dwarf, considerably older, turned to him. "I know you," he said loudly enough to be heard over the noise of the hooves. "Hillchester, wasn't it? They mistook you for me." He pulled hard on the reins to slow his horse down. "And you were off to the freelings. From what I hear, you made it." They trotted along, side by side. "Who'd have thought you'd turn out a hero?" He smiled and reached down a broad hand. "Good to meet you again, Tungdil."

Tungdil wasn't sure how he felt about seeing him again. It had been thanks to Bramdal that he had found the way to the freelings and the city of Trovegold, Bramdal having given him the tip about the pond and the hidden entrance. But at the same time Tungdil despised his trade.

"Bramdal? The executioner? Selling body parts to the long-uns?" asked Ireheart. He sat up in the saddle. "Revolting. And thanks—it was your fault I ended up in that stinking water."

"You must be Boïndil Doubleblade, then," Bramdal grinned. "Two heroes off on their next adventure?"

"And you'll be on your way to the next execution?" replied Tungdil. He did not want to give out any information.

"I'm riding to Porista. King Bruron pays well for my

services. I'm training up his executioners." He shrugged apologetically. "Afraid I can't stop for a drink and a chat—got to hurry."

"That means you'll be doing yourself out of work," grinned Ireheart.

"Yes. But I don't care. I'm looking for a new line of work." Bramdal seemed to have changed his mind about Vraccas's injunction to protect humans from evil. In Hillchester he had told Tungdil that he was carrying out the dwarf-creator's wishes by executing human criminals. He considered them malignant, just as other dwarves held orcs to be evil.

"In Trovegold?" Tungdil remembered the freelings' city, which lay in a high-vaulted mile-long cavern. He heard again how the mighty waterfalls thundered and saw the gardens and the fortress where King Gemmil lived; he saw the dwarf priests praying and heard the hymns they sang echoing away. It had been wonderful, the time he had spent there.

"Going into trade," said Bramdal. "If anyone knows how to make the equipment an executioner needs, it's me. Why shouldn't I use what I know? The kingdoms always need it and we've always got the craftsmen."

"Has anything changed in Trovegold?" asked Tungdil, rather sadly.

"How long since you left?"

"It'll be quite a few cycles; I'm not quite sure." But that was a lie. Tungdil knew exactly when he'd last seen Gemmil. It was five cycles ago.

"Oh, a lot has changed. You'd hardly recognize the town. We've had to dig up the gardens to build workshops. The cave's been extended by a mile to make room for everyone."

"So many children?"

"Not just that: The Five Free Towns have grown in population. Trade with the dwarf realms has made the dwarf folk curious. It's not just the outcasts who come to us; plenty turn up who want to get away from the clutches of their clans and their families." Bramdal swiped at a bee that was buzzing around and investigating his jacket. "It's obvious why the advantages of our community appeal."

"Not sure about 'advantages'," grumbled Ireheart. "A dwarf needs stability." He fell silent.

"May they all achieve happiness: some in the mountains, some below the ground. It's a good way of life we have. Trade has brought prosperity." Bramdal saw a crossroads. "Our paths split here. Did you know that Gemmil is dead?"

"No." The news of the king's death affected Tungdil, and Boïndil shook his head sadly, too. "How?"

"Murdered. We think it was one of the thirdlings. We caught a dwarf sneaking out of Trovegold, his clothes all covered in blood. He fought the guards like a berserker and killed seven of them before they shot him down. We still have no idea why he did it."

"To make trouble," Tungdil guessed. "If he was one of the dwarf-haters he'll only have wanted to cause strife. It's a terrible shame that the king who made me and my friends so welcome should die in that way. Who succeeded him?"

"Gordislan Hammerfist."

"Hammerfist?" Ireheart pricked up his ears. "Did he give himself that name or is he an exile from the clan?

"Do you think it could be a relative of Bavragor Hammerfist?" Tungdil conjured up the picture of the secondling's best stonemason, a barrel of a dwarf, strongly built, with huge, callused hands. He always wore an eye patch and they called him "the singing drunkard." He had shown his courage in countless battles at Tungdil's side and had died for the sake of the group fighting off the orcs at the Dragon's Breath forge. Without his sacrifice they would never have escaped with the ax Keenfire.

Bramdal shook his head. "I don't know. If members of the Hammer Fist clan tend to have dark brown eyes with a bit of red in them, then it could be he's related. At any event, he has quite a tolerance for brandy when there's a party on."

Ireheart grinned. "No doubt about it. He's related to Bavragor." He grew serious. "What could have made him leave his own clan? I've not heard anything."

"He's been with us in Trovegold for some time." They'd reached the crossing now and the time for parting was at hand. "A safe onward journey to you both and success in your endeavors," said the executioner, turning his mount toward Porista. He lifted his hand to urge the horse to a gallop and soon disappeared in a cloud of dust.

"Strange kind of saddle he was using," Tungdil said. It was a shame he'd not had time to ask about it.

"I'm glad he was going the other way," said Ireheart, sounding relieved. "Or he'd have started to try and flog us something from his saddlebags. I can do without a

thief's desiccated finger or an adulterer's pickled eyeball."
He spat. "It's disgusting, what he does."

Tungdil didn't reply. Those few words with Bramdal
had reminded him of a happier time in his life.
"Trovegold," he murmured. "I should go there again."

"Better not," was Ireheart's ambiguous recommendation.

At last they reached the lush and luxuriantly blossoming
land near the vaults where once Lot-Ionan had resided,
one of the mightiest magi of Girdlegard.

Tungdil was pleased to be back, even though he had
not been away very long. There was much he needed to
tell Balyndis. If she saw how much weight he'd lost since
leaving the Gray Range she'd know at once that he had
changed.

"There we are," he called out to Ireheart, pointing to
a narrow path. "Relief is at hand for those saddle sores."

They approached the large gate behind which his own
small dwarf world lay hidden. Tungdil's foster-father Lot-
Ionan had spent all his time thinking up new spells,
studying old rolls of parchment or training up his famuli.
Until, that is, he had crossed magic swords with the traitor
Nôd'onn. And lost.

Since that day the magus was nothing but a statue
made of stone, lying somewhere in the ruins of Nudin's
palace in Porista. In these current times there was no one
with sufficient magic powers to follow in his footsteps.
Nor could any provide a replacement for the magic wellspring that had now dried up. That was what everyone
had thought, at least. But now, with the news from
Âlandur of the mysterious diamond thief and their even

more mysterious suit of armor. Someone must be using magic suddenly.

Tungdil stopped, dismounted and stood at the gate, lifting his hand to knock. Then he hesitated.

"Scared, Scholar?" Boïndil slipped out of the saddle and stretched, both hands in the small of his back. "I always knew that Elria was trying to drown us but who is the goddess responsible for creating ponies to torment us with?" He tapped his friend on the shoulder. "You can do it. You are coming home to her as the same Tungdil Goldhand she loved far more than the other one, the one I met a few orbits back in the Gray Range." With the handle of his crow's beak he gave three hard blows on the wooden gate.

"That's all your doing." Tungdil thanked him once more. "If you hadn't made me face up to things . . ."

From the other side of the gate there was the sound of a bolt being drawn back. Then the gate was opened to admit them.

A surprise awaited.

On the threshold stood a female dwarf with long dark blond hair jutting out from under her impressive-looking helmet. Over the black leather raiment there hung a chain shirt hung with metal plates. She also had a protective skirt-like armor covering that reached down to her ankles; her shoes were reinforced with metal.

In her right hand she bore a shield, and in her left a studded flail, a type of morning star. Instead of one spiked iron globe there were three smaller metal balls, which had blades arranged in a circle round each of them. Weight, impetus and those blades, combined, would inflict terrible wounds.

And it was not Balyndis who had the weapon in her hand.

Nevertheless, Tungdil thought he recognized her. "Sanda?" The name slipped out, his voice incredulous. "Sanda Flameheart?"

"By Vraccas! The dead are come to life!" mouthed Ireheart, taking hold of his weapon.

The dwarf-woman smiled and hung the morning star back in its harness. "You are Tungdil Goldhand and Boïndil Doubleblade. Your words make that clear. It is an honor to greet you both."

Tungdil stepped forward. "You have the advantage of us." Then he saw that although she looked like Sanda Flameheart, one-time wife to King Gemmil, she was much younger. The down on her face had not turned silver and he'd be surprised if she were more than forty cycles old. Half a child still, but broad and strong as a warrior. Her thirdling ancestry could not be denied. "But *who* are *you*?"

She took off her helmet and showed them a friendly, and not quite so round a face. "I am Goda Flameheart from the Steadfasts clan of the thirdlings." She gave Boïndil a direct, brown-eyed stare. "Sanda Flameheart, who died at your hand, was my great-grandmother." Ireheart's face grew pale, in striking contrast to his black beard. "I demand vengeance," she demanded harshly. "Because you . . ."

"Where is Balyndis and how did you get in here?" interrupted Tungdil, finding it very strange that his wife had not appeared. He was afraid that Goda in her anger might have harmed her.

"She's sleeping," was the answer. "She's not been well

of late." She stared at Ireheart again. "As I said, I want satisfaction from you, Boïndil Doubleblade."

Ireheart looked her up and down. Now it occurred to him that running into Bramdal had been no accident. He should have known. "I understand what you want. I shall not fight with you, Goda. You are too young and inexperienced to have a chance against me. Let your clan send one of their warriors, or go and study and come back in fifty cycles and we will fight and you shall have your revenge, if Vraccas has no other plans for me and if he lets the fires in my life-forge continue to blaze."

The dwarf-woman gathered her long hair into a pony-tail, tying it with a leather thong. The muscles twitched as she lifted her arms. She shook her head defiantly. "There are no others in my clan." She certainly had the air of a warrior. "I insist."

"No, by Vraccas. I don't kill children!"

"So you refuse me? I'll go through the dwarf-realms from land to land and I'll blacken your name and say that Boïndil Doubleblade would not give satisfaction. You'll bring shame on yourself and on the shade of your brother. You'll be spat on, you and your clan. And they'll spit on the memory of your brother, the hero."

Quick as a flash the old rage flared up in the dwarf. The mad spark was back in his eyes, a light that had died five cycles before. He took two swift steps forward. And grabbed Goda by the leather dress she wore.

"No, Boïndil!" warned Tungdil.

"You shall have satisfaction," he growled furiously to Goda, who stared at him with triumph and fear in her eyes. "Right now?"

"Right now," she nodded. "Under my conditions?"

"Yes."

"Swear by Vraccas and on your dead brother."

Ireheart let go of her, stepped back and took hold of his crow's beak. "I swear by Vraccas and by Boëndal. "He spat out the words before his friend could stop him. "Whatever happens to you now is your own fault."

Goda nodded. "You took my great-grandmother away from me and she was forced into exile to live with the freelings. You killed my last living relative." She drew her weapon. "Now it is your duty to train me." She bowed her head.

Boïndil had been expecting an attack. It took a while before he realized what she was demanding of him. "Train you? In what, for Vraccas's sake? Child, I thought . . ."

"I demanded recompense and you have promised it."

"*That* is the satisfaction you are asking for?" The words tumbled out. "I can't do that. How could I . . . ?"

"Because of you a magnificent female warrior was sent to the forge of the eternal smith. You have stolen any possibility I might have had to take over from her and so it is only right that the one who subjugated Sanda should teach me." Goda stayed resolute: "I take you at your words—at the words of your oath." She went up to him and held out her weapon. "We call it the night star and I'm pretty good at it. What I need is an experienced teacher to show me the tricks to use in battle."

Tungdil grinned at Ireheart. "Now see what it was like for me with Bavragor. He tricked me just like that," he said. "I'll see you inside." He disappeared into the vaults to look for Balyndis. He wanted to greet her, take her in his arms and surprise her with how he looked now. There would be plenty of time later on for long talks with Goda.

Boïndil stared at the dwarf-woman and felt completely at a loss. It was true, he had sworn an oath. "Right," he sighed. "I'll quickly show you a few . . ."

"No," said Goda. "You'll teach me properly and you won't stop until I'm at least as good as you. Same as my great-granny. And then we'll fight to decide just how good your training has been." She raised the night star and the blades grated against each other. "A proper fight, master."

He rolled his eyes, put the crow's beak on the ground and leaned his weight on the head of the weapon. "Goda, I may have been a good warrior, but I'm out of practice. And just because I'm a good warrior doesn't mean I'm any good as a teacher."

"You can say whatever you want, master; I'm not leaving your side until my training is complete." The face of the dwarf-woman showed the familiar stubbornness of her people, coupled with the determination of all womankind. "Wherever you go, I'll be there."

And she stuck to his heels, as he attempted to enter the vaults, following him at half a pace. "You're going to leave me in peace some of the time, though?" he asked over his shoulder.

"If you need to relieve yourself, master," she answered, cockahoop that her trick had worked. "When shall we start the training sessions?"

Boïndil stared straight ahead, and a broad grin spread across his weathered face. He would be so tough with her that she'd leave of her own accord. And then he wouldn't be breaking his oath. "The training starts now without a break." He found a pile of old beams that Tungdil had placed tidily against a wall. "Carry those out, one by one and pile them up outside by the gate," he ordered bad-temperedly.

"Yes, master." Goda did not even ask the reason for the order. She put down her weapon and shield and got ready for the task.

Ireheart picked them both up. "Who said you were to put those down?" he said bitingly. "A dwarf never leaves weapons lying about. And certainly never puts down his weapon if he's only got the one." He nodded at her. "Carry the wood, then you can start the search of the vaults."

She wrinkled her brow. "What search?"

Boïndil rattled the metal balls of the night star and started to swing it. "Later. I'm going to hide it and you can't go to bed till you find it." He stepped round the corner. He was only just out of sight and chuckled to himself. He heard her give a big sigh as she tried to lift the first of the beams onto her shoulder. He was thrilled to bits with his plan. He'd think up some more good ideas soon. He'd be rid of the child within a few orbits, he was sure.

Tungdil stepped quietly into the bedroom.

Balyndis lay under a thick blanket. Her eyes were closed and her face was half hidden in the pillow. The long dark hair made her face look chalk white in contrast: she really did look weak and sick. Cautiously he sat down next to her, thinking through what he had prepared to say; he stretched out a hand to touch her gently on the shoulder.

"If I didn't know better, I would think I was dreaming," she whispered. "A fine-looking dwarf has entered my chamber." She opened her brown eyes and reached for his left hand with her right. "You're looking good, Tungdil Goldhand. It's been a long time since I saw you looking like that. What does this change in appearance signify?"

"It's not just an outward change." He kissed her fingers. "I've been a fool. Boïndil forced me to see the error of my ways. I've stopped drinking," he said quietly, looking her straight in the eyes. "I was making you suffer for the pain and the guilt that I was feeling and I behaved like a . . ." He swallowed.

". . . like a stubborn, blind drunkard, self-obsessed and tortured by his conscience," she completed for him without mercy. "You mean to say you've been off on a trip, had a chat with Ireheart and now you're completely transformed?" Her surprise was obvious and her voice incredulous. "You've changed, just like that, in a few orbits?"

Tungdil nodded.

"How? Tell me everything, so that I can believe you."

He told her what had happened at the edge of the precipice and how his warrior friend had forced him to choose between life and death. "The wall round my mind broke down and I saw things clearly for the first time in many cycles. I can only beg for forgiveness," he said quietly. "Will you believe that I have changed?"

When she put her arms around him, Tungdil started to cry. He embraced her in return, pressing her to him; he closed his eyes. He smelt her hair, felt the soft down on her cheeks and her warmth against his skin.

They sat like that for a long time, holding each other tightly, each enjoying the nearness of the other—a closeness shared once more. Shared wholeheartedly.

"It's not just your fault that we grew apart. I withdrew and left you on your own," she confessed. "It won't happen again."

"Never again."

She hugged him and took a long look at his face. "Give me time to get used to the new old Tungdil. This seems too good to be true."

"It is true, Balyndis," he smiled, but then a shadow fell across his face. "You look ill," he said, his voice full of concern.

"It's just the remains of a chill," she answered. "I'm feeling much better now." She kissed him on the brow. "You've met Goda?"

"She was quite a surprise. Especially for Ireheart."

She grinned. "It will do him no harm if he has to contend with a dwarf-woman."

Tungdil looked surprised. "You knew about her plan?"

"It was my idea."

"What?"

Balyndis chuckled and sat back against the pillows. "When she turned up and asked if she could stay, I had no idea who she was. We talked a lot that first evening and I learned that she had been to the Blue Mountains. She had hoped to find you here to ask you where Boïndil was. The secondlings refused to tell her."

"You have set a young child on him, not a dwarf-woman."

"She's four and forty cycles old. You can see by her stature that she's no longer a child," Balyndis contradicted with amusement. "Ireheart will soon discover her female charms."

"She's related to the dwarf-woman he killed. There's not likely to be any romance blossoming between those two," he countered. "What was her original plan before you suggested this approach?"

"She wanted to kill him."

Tungdil stood up, opened the buckles on his chain shirt and let it fall to the ground. Then he hung it carefully on the stand by the door. "She would never have been able to. But by the time her training is over, things might be different." He slipped off his leather over-garment and stood before her in his shirt, breeches and boots. "She's a thirdling, Balyndis. She'll have picked up all the fighting skills and soon be better at it than him. Do you want her to kill him?"

She folded her hands and laid them on the blanket. "It won't go that far."

"What makes you so sure?"

Balyndis shrugged her shoulders and kissed him again, this time on the tip of his nose. "I can't really say," she admitted. "Call it intuition."

"You women and your intuition," he murmured and gave in. "Let us pray to Vraccas that you're right about this." He looked at his armor. "Have you heard what's happening in Girdlegard?" When she shook her head, he summed up all the recent events he and Ireheart had experienced or heard about. "You're sure that Goda isn't after the diamond? What does your intuition say on that score?"

"It was good in the past when you could meet a child of the Smith and not have to worry about whether they were telling the truth," she groaned. "I can't be absolutely sure, of course, but in all the orbits she's been here there hasn't been anything suspicious about her." She stroked his bearded chin. "The stone is exactly where we hid it."

"I'll go and tell it I'm home."

"I'll make us something to eat. If I know you and Boïndil, you'll both be ravenous." Balyndis got up and quickly threw on a simple woolen dress over her linen nightgown, then put on her boots. "The meal will be ready soon, so don't spend too long talking to your precious one."

"My precious," he hissed, imitating the stance of the greedy rock gnome that grabbed and kept anything that looked valuable. Then he laughed and walked out of the chamber hand in hand with his wife. Soon their ways parted and he took a different corridor, using an oil lamp to light his path into the other gallery where once Lot-Ionan's apprenticed famuli had had their quarters. Most of the iron doors were still in place. Behind them the student initiates had followed their studies of magic and had dreamed of one day inheriting Lot-Ionan's enchanted realm.

Now nothing was left. No magic, no enchanted realms. No Lot-Ionan.

Tungdil entered the laboratorium.

It was in this very room that a trick had once been played on him that had resulted in most of the fittings and equipment going up in flames; it had not been his fault. The flasks full of elixirs, the pots of ointments, the glass tubes containing extracts and essences, all that priceless experimentation had melted into one dangerous mass. A powerful explosion had ensued and little had survived of the benches, shelves, tables and apparatus.

And that was still how it looked. He stepped over the splintered glass and the broken pottery, walking over to where a pile of glass was all that remained of what had been complicated distillation equipment. Before the explosion.

The dwarf bent down and rummaged around. He didn't locate the diamond immediately. There was so much broken glass that it was practically invisible. Nobody would ever find it if they didn't suspect it was hidden in the rubbish.

Tungdil took delight in the cold fire shining from the stone's facets. His heart leaped. He turned it this way and that, so that it could blaze at its best, returning the lamplight, and throwing reflections onto the dark and somber walls.

Whenever he took the stone in his hand he waited for the jewel to show him somehow whether it was just a diamond or the most powerful, magic artifact in all Girdlegard.

And, as always, he waited in vain. He put the stone back in its mound of glass fragments and pushed it down to the bottom of the pile.

Girdlegard,
Kingdom of the Fourthlings,
Brown Mountains,
Early Summer, 6241st Solar Cycle

A shrill whistle sounded up through the broad shaft and straightaway the bell rang in the winch room. Apart from one alcove, the entire room was filled with a strictly logical system of pulleys, winches, winding gear, cogwheels and levers, weights and counterweights in every conceivable size, all carefully proportioned. The alcove was the lift master's post.

Ingbar Onyxeye of the clan of the Stone Turners, faithfully carrying out his important duties, had recognized the signal. "Here it comes!" he shouted back down.

His hands worked the various iron levers in turn, each as big as a dwarf; these released the brake blocks from the rollers and the wheels. Machinery whirred loudly into action.

The rotating parts set up a draught that smelled of oil and lubricating grease; the sheer mass of weights on the end of their chains pulled the lift upwards without a single dwarf wasting his muscle power. By this means, forty hundredweight could be heaved up easily.

Ingbar closed his eyes to listen better. Responding to the sounds, he took his oil can and applied lubrication where the machinery needed it to run more smoothly. It was intolerable to know metal was rubbing against metal, causing lasting damage. Oil would prevent unnecessary wear.

Suddenly there was a sound the lift master had never heard before, and the whole winding gear came to a halt.

"What's wrong?" he muttered, swiftly checking all the most vulnerable parts of the equipment. He couldn't find anything untoward. The cogwheels were intact, as were the chains, and the pulley belts had not come out of their runners.

Ingbar went over to the shaft. Right at the bottom he

could see a pale shimmer of light coming from the lift cage. It had to be at least fifty paces down. "Oi, you down there! Has the pulley jammed?" he yelled.

In reply the little bell rang wildly, somersaulting and ringing fit to bust, so loud that it hurt his ears. Then its cord broke and the bell fell silent. "What are you doing down there?" he called, worried now.

The chain jerked, started and stopped, the metal screeching as the load increased.

"Have you gone mad? What are you doing? Are you dancing down there in the cage?" Ingbar stared at the winding gear. The whole system was running in reverse and the lift was dropping down. He ran back over to the levers and applied the brakes. "You're overloaded. Unload something quickly, otherwise . . ."

With a scream of grinding metal the first brake gave way. A high-pitched metallic clang resounded as the other holding devices failed one after another. The bolts shot out like bullets. One of them, sharp-edged, flew through the chains and pierced the lift master's leg. Slowly the chains unwound, sending lift and cargo down toward the bottom.

"What the hell?" Ingbar clamped a hand over the gaping wound. There was no time to bandage it now. He had to save the workers in the cage and stop them crashing to their deaths.

He limped over to the ramps where the extra counter-weights were stored. They used these when particularly heavy loads were being transported; they would be applied to the winches, but nobody had ever tried to do that while the lift was already running.

Ingbar knew the winding gear very well indeed; he knew the ins and outs of the system and its peculiarities and foibles. He fixed new weights to a long chain, attached a huge hook and thrust it into the emergency slot on one of the winches that was still moving.

The hook sat firm. The chain came taut with a clank and pulled the new weights down towards itself. Because of the tons of extra ballast the chain was prevented from unwinding, so the lift came to a standstill.

"Are you all right down there?" he called down the shaft. The cage with the workers must be a hundred paces down, he reckoned, judging by the chain length. They'd stopped by one of the secondary galleries. "Good," he shouted. "Now unload the shale-tailings or some of you will have to get out. Otherwise it'll never move."

He waited a while to be sure they had followed instructions, then removed the counterweights and set the winding-gear into action, to get the lift up at last. For brake power he took a long iron bar and inserted it into one of the smallest cogwheels; as soon as the cage arrived he jammed the bar all the way in to block the cog. The cage had come up.

"That was a near thing." Ingbar wondered why the lights had gone out. The faint glow given by the lamps in the engine room was not strong enough to show what was inside the cage. The iron door rattled open. "I'll have to close the shaft down till we've renewed the brakes. What were you . . . ?" What he saw robbed him of the power of speech.

Huge figures stepped out of the lift cage. They were

armed to the teeth, carrying cudgels and shields with unfamiliar writing. But one glance at the brutal faces with the jutting tusks was enough to tell the dwarf what he had here: Orcs!

"To arms!" he screamed, drawing out his ax. "Greenskins!" Before he knew it, a missile flew toward him and hit him on the brow. It knocked him flying and he collapsed. Half conscious, he imagined he saw a pink-eyed orc bending over him, fingering his skull, then disappearing . . .

When Ingbar came round later he was still lying in the engine room. He could hear the rattle of chains. Groaning, he struggled upright and felt for the lump on his head. Next to him a stone lay on the ground. The orcs must have thought he was dead, no two ways about it. They would never leave a dwarf alive.

Footsteps were approaching and in the torchlight he could see a band of warriors coming up. "Ingbar! Did the greenskins come this way?" one of them asked him urgently.

"They came up here, but whether . . ." He looked for the lift cage. It was gone! "No . . . Look! They're on their way down."

The warrior stared grimly and helped him to his feet. "Then bring them up again!"

Ingbar limped over to the machinery, adjusted some of the cogwheels and attached extra weights again. The orcs had collected a lot of booty during their raid on the Brown Mountains, it seemed. The cage was overloaded. "What happened?"

"We hoped you could tell us that," replied the dwarf.

His companions arrayed themselves in a semicircle round the shaft, crossbows at the ready; the enemy would be met with a hail of bolts. "The orcs appeared from nowhere, overcame the guards and stole the diamond."

"*The* diamond?" Ingbar was horrified. "What are the monsters planning to do?"

One of the warriors took a look down the shaft. "Another twenty paces, and they're up," he reported, moving into place.

"We don't know. Notice anything unusual about them?" asked the dwarf.

"No, not . . ." Ingbar hesitated. "Yes! One of them had pink eyes." He gave a brief description of events. "And when I came round, you arrived." He stopped speaking, for the cage had arrived. The door stayed shut. So maybe the orcs were afraid to come out.

"Come out and face us, you cowards!" called the warrior. "You can't escape!" Nothing happened, so he sent one of his men over to open the iron door.

That was when Ingbar realized what had been bothering him: the cage was too heavy! Whatever was in there it couldn't be the orcs; because before he'd pulled them up with the conventional forty hundredweight. Now he'd applied the forty plus the extra counterweights. No diamond in the whole of Girdlegard was that heavy!

The soldier who'd been sent forward to the lift freed the catch and pulled the door open a little way.

A steel arm shot out through the narrow gap and forced the doors wide. A cloud of steam hissed from the cage, enveloping the astonished dwarves. They staggered, fighting for air; the scorching fumes hurt their lungs and stung their eyes; water droplets formed on their cold armor.

Clicks, clanks and rattles; a rain of crossbow bolts shot through the air randomly, mowing down several of the soldiers. They fell to the stone floor, dead or injured.

"Get back!" cried Ingbar. He knew what it was that had got itself transported up in the lift. All the dwarf regions had by now received the warnings of the death machines wreaking havoc in the mines of the children of the Smith. There were at least a dozen of these machines now, that was for sure. And he knew there was little chance of combating them.

The mist cleared enough for him to see his immediate surroundings. "I'll send it back down before it can get out of the cage," he coughed into the vapor cloud. He unhooked the weights from the winch-pulleys and stretched out his arm for the iron rod blocking the vital cogwheel.

At that point a monstrous shadow appeared out of the fog next to him. An iron vice-grip snapped at him, biting down on his left arm.

Ingbar was lifted up and whirled against the roof as if he were a doll. It felt like being in the mouth of a dragon. From up here he could see the back of the devilish machine, as strongly armored as the front. Dwarf-warriors were courageously attacking, but the machine rolled steadily forwards over the bodies of the dead and wounded.

He could see how the rod was slipping under the cogwheel. It was being forced out of true. The winch gave way under the sheer weight, having no ballast, and the cage shot down to the depths.

Pulleys, cogwheels and rollers worked faster and faster,

chains unwound at great speed. But Ingbar's plan had failed. The devil machine had already left the cage.

The metal grab-hand gave him another mighty shake, a sharp pain shot through his shoulder, then he was thrown to one side.

The death machine had aimed well. Ingbar was hurled straight into the mess of whirring cables and winches. He crashed against a speeding chain, landed under a huge rotating cogwheel and he and his chain mail armor were crushed to pieces.

Girdlegard,
Kingdom of Gauragar,
Porista,
Early Summer, 6241st Solar Cycle

Prince Mallen sat in his room on the top floor of the house he and his companions had been assigned. Through the window he observed the cranes on the site of the new palace, constantly in motion, turning, lifting, lowering. A continuous stream of carts loaded with stone rolled through the streets, and the army of laborers grew from orbit to orbit. The breeze brought the sounds of a new beginning to Mallen's ears: banging, clattering, sawing, hammering—and there was singing and the workmen's shouts.

King Bruron was losing no time. The empty space in the middle of Porista was to be filled with a splendid building which promised to outshine Nudin's palace in opulence. Five towers and three keeps were planned, arranged stepwise and connected by smaller transept buildings. The architects had estimated the work would take five cycles, and the foundation stone was already in place.

Mallen stood up, and now he could see the tips of the tent poles emerging from the top of the huge white canvas marquee erected in the center of the cleared site. This was where the kings and queens were meeting this afternoon. Bruron wanted the great monarchs assembled on the spot whence in former times the mightiest power of Girdlegard had issued. In the place of the magic wellspring they now had unity and harmony among the rulers—this was the sign for all of their peoples.

Mallen chose a light fabric coat to throw over the bright red robe. He strode out of the room. The bodyguard waiting outside fell in beside him. On horseback he moved through the busiest streets of the town, where the crowds drew back respectfully, proud to be providing hospitality to such visiting dignitaries.

In silence the prince rode on, not responding to the occasional cheer. As so often, he was preoccupied with thoughts of the terrible raid on Goldensheaf; he was missing his trusted comrade in arms, Alvaro, whose dead body he had examined in minute detail. It had been the slash to the throat that had robbed him of his lifeblood and he knew it had not been the terrible creature that had inflicted this wound. Of that he was convinced. Since that day he had never turned his back for a second on Rejalin or any other elf. The matter of the elf runes he had kept from the other rulers when he described the events of that day. He could not have said why this was. He wanted to speak to Liútasil in private about it.

His troop reached the marquee. Young pages hastened to take hold of the guests' horses.

The prince stepped inside the airy enclosure; the tent was lined with colorful silks and decorated with ribbons and painted banners. It must have taken several orbits to bring in all the furnishings—the long table, the heavy chairs and cupboards—so that the meeting hall looked dignified and stately in spite of being under canvas.

Apart from himself only one other was present: a man in dark attire. The frog-like eyes and short black hair identified him as King Ortger of Urgon. Mallen went up and shook hands. "It is good to see you again," he greeted the young ruler.

"The last time we met it was at the celebrations for the third cycle of my reign," Ortger nodded. He was obviously pleased to meet the blond-haired Idoslane prince again, having found him from the start to be someone he trusted. "The occasion for our present meeting is far more serious."

"I heard that you too have suffered under an attack from one of these monstrous beings." Mallen let go of his hand and sat down opposite Ortger. Servants brought wine and water, and then withdrew discreetly. "I don't want to jump ahead of the plenary discussion, but can you tell me what happened?"

"It was quite a different type of creature from the one you had warned me about in your letter," sighed the young king as he took a mouthful of wine to give him courage. "A monster made of tionium, black as evil itself and as strong as ten oxen, but more cunning than a nest full of malicious vipers. And inside it there was something alive, staring out at us from behind a glass window." He took a drawing out of the bag that lay next to him. "Some say it had wings of iron, others that it flew up to the heavens on flames and transformed itself by magic into a black cloud. Here, that's what it looked like."

King Nate entered the tent, dressed in dark green ceremonial robes embroidered with stylized depictions of ears of corn. "My greetings. You are at work already?" He made a perfunctory bow to the two men and joined Ortger to study the picture. "No, it's not in the slightest like the creature that robbed me of my diamond and of three of my fingers," he said after a preliminary look. He was about to add something but stopped because all the other kings and queens from the human realms were now entering the tent. The ceremony of welcome took some time. Mallen would have liked to ask them all to get straight to business.

His mood did not improve when two elves simply attired in white joined their circle and introduced themselves as Vilanoîl and Tiwalún. They had travelled to Porista from Âlandur on the orders of their elf lord to give his excuses and to represent him in the talks.

This gave Mallen a valid reason for his ill-feelings. "Why would Liútasil stay away from this conference?" he enquired, although it would have rightly been the office of their host, King Bruron, to ask this. "We're not here for fun. There are vital issues to discuss. The presence of the prince of the elves could have been expected."

The kings and queens threw him looks that ranged between surprise and displeasure. To use such a sharp tone with the elven envoys was not, in their view, justified.

Mallen thought they were acting in their own interests. He considered they were afraid that if he were brusque with the elves their promised knowledge-sharing would be jeopardized.

"And where are the dwarves, then?" asked King Nate, jumping to the defense of the elves.

"I can explain." Bruron lifted his hand. "High King Gandogar told me that they have themselves called a gathering of their clans to discuss events that have occurred recently in their tunnels. When that meeting is over, he writes, they will come here to Porista. But one of their representatives is on his way to us."

"It is a similar circumstance that makes it impossible for my own lord to be with you," said Tiwalún, following this with a smile. "We too are holding an emergency meeting about occurrences in Âlandur." He bowed again, as did Vilanoîl. "I offer our apologies once more."

"You must forgive Prince Mallen's way," King Nate requested, taking a sideways glance over to the fair-haired Ido, "but in the attack on my castle he lost a close friend. It will be his grief that overwhelms him and lets him speak out of turn and unfairly."

"It is kind of you to speak for me, but it has nothing to do with the unfairness you accuse me of," objected Mallen. "I was speaking about the status of this meeting, the vital importance of our assembly."

"And since that attack he tends to view the peoples of Âlandur with the same mistrust his fallen comrade had harbored," continued Nate.

"I understand," said Tiwalún with regret. "My commiserations, prince."

A messenger entered with a message for King Bruron. He gestured over to the entrance. "How good to see that you, Glaïmbli Sparkeyc from the clan of the Spark Eyes in the kingdom of the fourthlings, have been able to make the journey so swiftly," he greeted the dwarf at the door. "You are welcome. Please take your place at our table. We are about to tackle the real reason for calling this assembly," he added quickly, before Mallen had a chance to challenge the elves on anything.

"My thanks, King Bruron." The dwarf bowed to Bruron and to all the others gathered there. His plated armor glinted immaculately, as polished as a silver salver; his dark hair and beard were well groomed. He must have changed and washed before appearing.

Mallen, who knew his dwarves, recognized immediately that this was a fourthling. A slighter figure and slimmer build told of his race, and the gemstones worked into his armor gave another indisputable clue.

"I bring you greetings from the high king and his regret that he and the other delegates of the dwarf folks, and also those from the Five Free Towns, will not be arriving in Porista for a few orbits. Until they come I am to represent them." He took his seat and was acknowledged by all with nods of welcome.

"Let us begin." Bruron looked at the assembled participants. "The events are extremely worrying. In the meantime five diamonds have either been stolen or have simply disappeared." In response to Bruron's gesture, servants brought out and displayed a large map of Girdlegard. "Tabaîn, Rân Ribastur, Urgon, and the dwarf kingdoms of the thirdlings and fourthlings have all been robbed of their jewels. As far as Tabaîn and Urgon are concerned, we know that the raids were carried out by creatures, the like of which have never been seen before. Not even when the Perished Land had everything under its influence in our realms. Furthermore I have been brought the news that it was orcs who stole the fourthlings' diamond." He hit the map. "*Orcs!* These beasts have not appeared for over five cycles, not since the Star of Judgment fell. What is behind this? Does anyone have an idea?"

"The beings Ortger and I were faced with look like a cross between several monsters. They use magic and bear runes on their armor, runes like the ones the älfar are described as having," said Nate. "It all points to unknown creatures from the Outer Lands suddenly invading our realms."

"The passes are guarded and defended," Mallen pointed out. "They could never have got past the axes of the dwarves." Glaïmbli nodded in agreement.

"Perhaps not past them." Tiwalún smiled him down. "If you can't get past an obstacle you can sometimes go under it."

Ortger nodded. "The same thought had occurred to me. There's none of the evil left in Girdlegard, if we discount the malice of some of the thirdlings that I've heard about." With his protruding eyes, he gazed directly at Glaïmbli, awaiting an answer.

The dwarf opened his mouth, then hesitated. "I don't know if I should speak for my high king on that matter."

"Oh, then I misunderstood you. I thought you said you were his representative, Glaïmbli Sparkeye," interjected Tiwalún.

"I certainly am. But it is not my place to reveal every-thing. There are some issues about which only the high king himself should speak." He crossed his arms over his chest in an unambiguous gesture of refusal; he was like a defensive wall of muscle and bone: the embodiment of the innate stubbornness of dwarves.

Queen Isika, a woman of middle age, pale-faced, with long black hair and with a penchant for luxurious clothing, turned to Mallen. "Prince, be good enough to explain to our friend here how unfortunate the whole situation is. You get on better with dwarves than I do."

Mallen leaned forward, his arms on the table. "Look, Glaïmbli, we're just trying to explore the connection between the horrific incidents of the last few orbits. If you've got something to contribute, please let us know. Then your high king can fill us in later on the details." He looked the dwarf directly in the eyes. "I'm asking you, please, to tell us what you have learned."

Glaïmbli fidgeted uneasily on his chair. He disliked having so many people staring at him. He dropped his head down between his shoulders—the age-old reaction of a dwarf in trouble. Only when he spotted the haughty smiles of the elves did he let himself be moved to comment. "The thirdlings have declared war on us again. They are making war with machines."

"Machines?" echoed Nate in surprise. "It's the first I've heard of this. What sort of machines?"

"A device that can travel through our tunnels and attack our people. More I cannot say. You must wait till our high king arrives." Glaïmbli's head sank even lower and his eyes sparkled defiantly; he'd not tell them anymore now.

"This is news to me as well," said Queen Isika sharply. "If you put this information together with what we had already heard one could surmise that the thirdlings have formed a united front with these malformed nightmare progeny of Evil."

Bruron turned to her. "What makes you say that?" Her light blue gaze was directed first to the obstinately silent dwarf, then to Mallen. Receiving no indication from him she went on, "You know the thirdlings well, prince, because you made use of their services against the orcs. How great a thirst for revenge might they be harboring?"

"They always hated the other dwarf folks, but the need to sustain Girdlegard must rank higher for them," he replied. "You remember, King Lorimbas wanted to eradicate them all and to take on the task of protecting the passes himself?"

"I am not speaking of hatred for other dwarves." She looked round the circle. "I am speaking of hatred toward us, the humans." She turned her pale, stern face to Ortger. "The thirdlings were almost completely annihilated in the course of mad king Belletain's attack on the Black Mountains." Her gaze fell on Mallen once more. "Do you think them capable of breaking a new tunnel through to the Outer Lands for monsters to come through, bringing disaster and destruction to our homeland, prince?"

"If that were the case there'd be armies of orcs in one of the kingdoms by now," ventured Mallen.

Tiwalún had not taken his eyes off Glaïmbli and had seen the bearded face of the dwarf twitch briefly as Queen Isika spoke these words. "Even if you vowed just now that you would say no more, Glaïmbli Sparkeye, I must insist you let out some more of the truth that you are holding back between clamped teeth," he said quietly, but clearly enough for all to hear. "I ask you to tell us, so that our suspicions, vague as yet, may give us more insight into how we can stave off the threat of Evil and protect Girdlegard."

"No!" returned the obdurate Glaïmbli.

There was a sharp intake of breath from Bruron. "You may be here as the high king's representative, but you bear responsibility for the fates of humans and elves. I implore you in the names of Vraccas, Palandiell and Sitalia. Speak!"

Again, at first, the dwarf was silent. Not until he had exchanged glances with Prince Mallen did he open his mouth. "After the orc raid there was another attack by a thirdling machine," he reported reluctantly. "The orcs pushed it into the lift to cover their escape." Glaïmbli's mouth was distorted. "High King Gandogar thinks the orcs and the thirdlings are working hand in glove. They have set up their encampment on the far side of the Stone Gateway up on the Northern Pass to the Outer Lands. It's from there that they are launching their attacks. We've seen nothing yet of the creatures that bear the älfar runes on their armor."

"So the thirdlings are against all of us and not just at war with the other dwarf folks." Tiwalún's face was full of concern and Vilanoîl looked downcast. "What is Gandogar undertaking against the traitors in his midst?"

"They are outside Girdlegard," reiterated the dwarf, throwing him a hostile glance.

"I beg to differ on that point," said the elf courteously. "The thirdlings used to have spies in all the dwarf realms and why should these spies no longer exist? Admittedly, in the past five cycles things have been more or less peaceful between the tribes. I agree with Queen Isika. Who is to say that the thirdlings are not plotting to open up all five gateways at once, to flood Girdlegard with Tion's monsters?"

"The Revenge of the Dwarves," murmured Ortger.

"If it were revenge, it would be revenge of the misguided thirdlings, not of all the dwarves," corrected Mallen, turning to the elves. "And you are exaggerating with your fears, Tiwalún," he warned. "Anyone would think you had persecution mania."

"Am I exaggerating?" The elf smiled persuasively. "A degree of persecution mania, as you choose to call it, Prince Mallen, would well become us all. Personally, I fear the worst when I hear that the thirdlings have formed a pact with orcs from the Outer Lands in order to steal the diamonds."

"He is right. Gandogar must sift out and reject the poisoned corn in his peoples." With a smile, Queen Isika added: "Or, to phrase it better, he must sort the false gold from the genuine article. Only if he roots out the concealed thirdlings in the dwarf tribes can we have any security."

"And just how is that to be done?" objected Glaîmbli.

"Interrogations? Investigations? Torture?" suggested Vilanoîl helpfully. "The sooner we find and eradicate the spies, the better it will be for humans, elves and dwarves."

Mallen held his breath, seeing Isika, Nate and Ortger nodding in approval, and then the face of the dwarf, suffused and dark red with anger.

"You're seriously suggesting we arrest and torture

dwarves who may be completely innocent?" Glaïmbli growled at the elves. "It may be that your folk do things like that but it's certainly not our way—it's not the way of the children of the Smith."

"Leave the decision to your high king," came the reproof from Isika. "You said yourself that you only represent him. Let us deal with the question of what the orcs and the thirdlings can possibly want with the diamonds." She took a sip of her wine and ignored the vicious looks winging her way from the dwarf.

Mallen was getting the impression more and more that the elves were trying to drive a wedge between the participants, endangering the harmonious community of the different peoples and various dwarf folks. With Nate, Isika and the inexperienced Ortger they had already achieved a measure of success. Alvaro's distrust of the proud elf race seemed increasingly justified.

"They are aware that one of the stones has particular properties. But there have never been any dwarves with the slightest desire to learn or use the magic arts," said Tiwalún. "Correct me if I'm wrong, Glaïmbli. The thirdlings wouldn't know what to do with the power latent in that stone. And the stupidity of the orcs is well known."

"And we have these appalling creatures in their tionium armor," Nate reminded the assembly. "By Palandiell, if there's not magic involved *there* where on earth else do they get their powers?"

"So they're out looking for the diamonds independently of the thirdlings and the orcs . . . in order to take over control?" Ortger gestured to the map. "There are no magic force fields any longer, so these beasts must be from the

Outer Lands. How did they get in and how did they find out about the stones? Are they capable of sensing magic?"

"No. Otherwise they would not be wasting their time stealing the false stones." Mallen tasted his wine, hoping that the effects of the alcohol would calm him. "That's obvious. None of the three groups has yet found the real diamond that the eoîl invested power in."

A servant bearing the insignia of Idoslane entered the council tent, bringing a message, and waiting for the ruler to read its contents.

Mallen's eyes flew over the page and, when he had finished reading, he drained the wine in his cup. "It seems that evil does not merely have the diamonds in its sights," he said out loud, laying the letter on the table. "One of my villages, Calmstead, has been razed to the ground. There are no survivors. People were burned to death in their houses. Why the village was singled out I have no idea. The commander of the neighboring castle reports there are signs that orcs were responsible. He has sent scouts into the caves of Toboribor."

"I thought the caves were empty," said Nate. "Didn't you have all the passages searched that time?"

"That was five cycles ago. If orcs have found a new entry into Girdlegard they may have reactivated their old breeding grounds." Mallen rose. "You must excuse me. I must issue orders for the soldiers."

"We ought to defer the rest of our talks in the circumstances, until High King Gandogar can be with us," suggested Bruron. "In the meantime we can ponder further on these issues. If anyone would be interested in inspecting the site for my new palace . . . ?"

"I move that the remaining diamonds be collected together in one place and guarded with the greatest force we can muster between us in Girdlegard." Queen Wey, a woman around fifty cycles of age, wearing a floor-length dark dress studded with numberless diamonds, raised her voice and surprised everybody with her proposal. She did not belong to the circle of those known for their military prowess. "Apparently the individual races are not in a position to keep their stones safe from these robbers. Why shouldn't all of us help? Let's have them behind the walls of the strongest castle, surrounded with all the engines of war at our disposal, and have thousands of soldiers guarding them. Then no one would be able to steal them. Kept separately they are much more vulnerable."

Nate nodded assent at once. "Excellent idea, Queen Wey."

"Indeed," Isika spoke warmly. "We might all have come to that conclusion, dear sister." This form of words surprised no one. The two queens, so different in appearance, addressed each other as siblings in order to stress their unity of purpose. She raised her hand. "I am in favor."

All the assembled monarchs followed her example.

Glaïmbli and the two elves, however, did not stir. "Wait for Gandogar," was the only response from the unwilling dwarf.

Tiwalún and Vilanoîl promised to inform their prince and to tell the assembly of his decision. "By the time Gandogar arrives we shall have Liútasil's view on this," said Tiwalún. "Now, I should be delighted to see the progress on your new building. Were your builders able to make use of the advice we gave you, King Bruron?"

Mallen went past them and hurried over to find his horse, puzzling as he walked. So far no elf delegation had appeared in his own kingdom to negotiate any exchange of skills. Bruron, on the other hand, seemed to be enjoying the privilege of benefitting from Âlandur knowledge already.

He doubted whether Idoslane was still a candidate after the quarrel with Rejalin. So he was more than amazed on returning to his accommodation to find waiting for him a letter from Liútasil announcing the arrival of a deputation.

Mallen was not at all sure he wanted them in his kingdom.

VII

Tungdil lay next to Balyndis staring at the ceiling. Then he stared into the darkness just underneath the ceiling. It didn't make a whole lot of difference. He might just as well have stared into the fire, at the sun or into the abyss.

He thought hard. He thought so hard and so long that in spite of physical exhaustion he was unable to sleep.

Something was wrong.

The joy at being back again with Balyndis had not ebbed; in the same way, their mutual avowals of affection, and the tender gestures which they had exchanged for the first time in ages—it all felt genuine.

But still, everything he did and said had a touch of emptiness. It was like spring with no blossom. Things were growing, but colors and fragrance were missing.

And because he felt so absurdly discontented and unfulfilled, he hated himself. He was starting to destroy their newfound happiness—and totally without reason. In past cycles he had attributed this feeling to his guilt about the death of their son. But that wasn't it.

Carefully, so as not to risk waking the dwarf-woman by his side, he got up, put on his nightshirt and left the bedroom.

He strolled through the vaults but even there he didn't have the feeling that he was at home.

Tungdil went into the kitchen, prepared some herbal tea with yarrow, hellebore and fennel, sipped it slowly and waited for the calming effect that would stop his brain spinning.

Just when his eyelids were growing heavy and his head was sinking slowly onto the table he heard a dull thud somewhere near the front of the vaults. A rotten beam giving way would have sounded different. Someone was busying themselves at the entrance door, trying to break in. Tungdil feared the worst.

Calm was out of the window; all his senses were on alert. He ran back into the bedroom, threw on his chain mail shirt, thrust his feet into his boots, and grabbed Keenfire.

"What's happening?" Balyndis sat up.

"We've got visitors," he replied swiftly. "Ireheart!" he bellowed. "Get up! There's work for your crow's beak." He buckled his weapon belt on and turned to her. "Do you think you can help us?"

She grinned. "What impression did I make on you just now in bed?" Balyndis was on her feet, already putting on a chain mail shirt. After a second's hesitation she made her choice and picked up a hatchet and a shield from the weapon-rack.

"Where's the fight?" Boïndil had not bothered to put on armor. He stood bare-chested, his hair unbraided, his beard flowing free. At least he had on his leather breeches and boots, and his crow's beak weapon shone in his fists. Next to him Goda appeared, having taken a little longer to get armed. "What do you mean . . ."

Another crash came from the entrance and they heard the splintering of wood.

"Right, I get it," Boïndil said grimly. "Someone's hoping to pick up a stone that doesn't belong to him."

Either that or the elves had taken the dirty fingerprints on the monolith more seriously than they could have dreamed. But Tungdil had not wanted to tell the women-folk anything about their less-than-heroic adventures in Âlandur. "Let's take a look," he commanded, and crept along the passageway.

The evening air reached them and the flames of the oil lamps flickered in the breeze. There was a smell of dew-laden grass and damp warm earth . . .

That shouldn't be so! It would mean the gate was open and their uninvited guest already inside the vaults!

They turned round a corner and saw that the double gate had been destroyed; it lay in pieces on the ground.

"Has he got a battering ram?" whispered Boïndil, looking around. There were any number of openings in the tunnel they were in. The enemy might jump out at them from any of these.

"If it's one of those monsters, it won't need a battering ram," replied Tungdil. He listened intently. There was another sound. It came from the back of the section where Lot-Ionan's old magic school had been. "Quick!" he called out, sprinting along to the laboratorium. "It's looking for the diamond in exactly the right place."

Balyndis dropped back behind the others. She was still grappling with the after-effects of her illness. The others mustn't be held back because of her. They hurried on, even though now their numbers were reduced.

"I wonder which of the beasts we're fighting this time," said Ireheart as they ran. "The one in armor or the device that rolled into the throne room?" His eyes sparkled with life and fighting spirit. Goda and the new tasks had re-kindled the warrior's vital life-forge. "Ha! We'll thrash it out of its metal and hack it into tiny pieces, if . . ."

In a flash the fiend stood before them.

It seemed to emerge from the shadows, with no warning and no sound. The sight was enough for the dwarves to know that it was neither of the beings they had already heard described. They had a third variety of monster facing them.

It was twice their size in height and breadth. Its body was covered in gray and green blotches, like an orc's; it consisted entirely of muscles without a hint of fat. Long black hair hung in strands from its head, where two pointed ears stuck up.

The face reminded them in a terrible way of an elf, but instead of their refined beauty, there were dead eyes and sharp incisors, which the creature was baring viciously.

It wore only a leather loin cloth and carried a ruck-sack. No iron in its body, no tionium here, no machine this time. Round its forearms were slung white chains and under them iron bands to which the last link in the chain was fastened.

"Out of the way, groundlings," it said in an elf-high voice, its dark eyes flashing green.

"You won't get past us, monster," said Ireheart, full of confidence, crashing the blunt end of his crow's beak weapon against the passage wall. "What shall I call you? You don't look like one of the snout-faces."

Goda watched her master in confusion; why in the face of this terrible being was he quibbling about nomenclature? She had heard strange tales about Boïndil and she was starting to fear they were all true.

"Do you have the stone?" Tungdil demanded, as he brandished his famous Keenfire ax in the creature's direction. "Give it back. You know how things will end for you otherwise."

"But it'll end badly whatever happens, won't it?" Worried now, Ireheart mouthed at his friend.

The monster shook its dreadful head. "Get away," it repeated, taking a step forward.

Boïndil bared his teeth and lowered his head; his hair fell down over his forehead. "The old way, Scholar?"

"The old way, Ireheart." Tungdil attacked the right hip, giving no warning, and turned in toward the enemy, his friend following through at his back.

A split second before Tungdil's blow hit home Boïndil crouched down and sliced at the creature's right shin. It wouldn't be able to parry both strikes at the same time, and, more importantly, what could it defend itself with?

The movement with which their opponent evaded their blades came too fast and too unexpectedly for the dwarves.

The creature launched itself off the ground, sprang diagonally against the passage wall and ricocheted over Goda's head. Her attempt to hit at it failed, and the robber escaped into one of the side tunnels.

"Hey! It can hop like a frog!" Boïndil was furious. "Come back here, froggy!" He raced past Goda, reproving her for her badly aimed blow. "You'll be dragging beams again for that." She hurried after him, her eyes downcast in shame.

They took on the pursuit together.

The monster had lost its sense of direction in the maze of tunnels, as Tungdil soon realized, because it was running off toward the kitchen. There was no way out from there.

They stormed into the room and confronted it just as it was trying to force its way up into the flue. Its shoulders were too broad for it to escape up through the chimney.

When it heard its enemies approach it came back out of the fireplace and stared at them. A brief shake of the arms was enough to free up the chains it bore; the runes glowed on the wrist bands. Its fists closed in a grip at the ends of the chains.

"Look out. It will use the chains like a whip," guessed Tungdil, speaking tensely. "Boïndil and I will attack simultaneously. Goda, watch the door."

The dwarves went for the monster from both sides, but saw that in spite of its huge size they had a cunning and damnably agile adversary.

Ireheart ducked under the flying chains, but was kicked in the chest and crashed back against the place where the pots and pans were stored. The wooden door gave way under the impact, shelves fell out and buried Boïndil under the contents of the cupboard.

At first Tungdil had better luck. He too lowered his head, avoided the whirling chain, and heaved Keenfire up with both hands in an attempt to whack it into the belly of the monster; but the creature's other claw shot forward and grabbed the haft.

Something extraordinary happened.

The ax head started glowing, the inlay flamed up and the diamonds blazed like tiny suns, so that Tungdil closed his eyes against the glare.

The monster shrieked in anger and shock. It had let go of Keenfire and was stumbling backwards, as the dwarf could hear. There was the smell of burning flesh.

Hardly had Tungdil caught sight of his opponent as a shadowy form than he hacked at it. The ax Keenfire, dragging a comet-like fire behind it, stopped short at the monster's hip and was jerked aside. Tungdil nearly lost hold of it.

Glowing chain links wrapped themselves around the head of the ax, stopping its impetus. With a great hiss the magical power of both weapons collided and red and green sparks flew through the kitchen, scorching wood and stone alike. And what was worse: the sparks fizzled in Tungdil's beard, burning holes. Slowly but surely the handle was growing hot.

"What the hell is happening here?" yelled Boïndil, struggling out of the mound of frying pans. He'd lost his crow's beak in the heap of broken pots. "Magic?" He picked up a particularly sturdy casserole dish and hurled it at the creature. "Stop that now, frog! Fight like a proper monster!"

The casserole smashed into its broad chest.

With a grunt the creature spun round and looked at the warrior, who had just found the handle of his weapon and was extracting it from the debris, ready to use. It swung its left arm, allowing the second chain to surge forward suddenly with a snake-like movement. This time the chain glowed dark green and made no bones about concealing its magic powers.

Boïndil swerved to avoid it, but the creature knew full well how to use its unusual weapons to best advantage. A short jerk and the chain changed direction in mid-flight, wrapping itself around the dwarf's neck.

Ireheart gave a sharp, strangled cry, dropped his crow's beak and fell to the ground.

Tungdil pulled the ax free with a shout, and the chain rattled to the floor.

"Get back or the groundling dies," commanded the fiendish creature. As if to back up his claims the älfar engravings on the left wrist band lit up, and the chain tethering Ireheart glowed more intensively. He began to make convulsive movements and gurgling noises escaped his throat as he collapsed.

Suddenly Goda was standing at Tungdil's side. "What shall we do?"

"Let it go!" he hissed through clenched teeth as he stepped to one side. He did not want to lose Boïndil. "We can get the diamond back when it thinks it is safe and has let Ireheart go."

The green glow faded. The monster pulled the captive dwarf over toward it, winding the chain back round its wrist until it showed only half an arm's length. Ireheart was being forced to his feet. He stood swaying on his tiptoes so as not to throttle himself. The chain was hot and had scorched his lovely black beard and long hair. "Don't follow!" the creature ordered as it went past Goda and Tungdil.

It went backwards through the tunnel, keeping one eye

on the dwarves. It sniffed loudly, getting its bearings from the smells to locate an exit from the vaults; its nostrils were flared wide. It continued on its way, dragging Ireheart in its tracks, panting and choking.

"When do we free him?" asked Goda in a hostile whisper. "He can't breathe!"

"As long as he's still making some kind of noise he's all right," answered Tungdil, racking his brains for some ploy to use against the enemy. It seemed Goda was completely ignoring the intruder's magic, which probably had not yet been used to its full potential. Keenfire would protect him from sorcery, as it had done at the Blacksaddle when he fought the Mist Demons. But a well-aimed strike on the head with the heavy chains would certainly cause a very serious injury.

The creature had found the passageway leading to the gate and was increasing its pace. With a swift movement it loosened the throttle-hold on Ireheart's neck and he collapsed on the ground, gasping for air. Horrified, he groped the singed beard and hair ends: "I'm crippled! For that I'm going to strip the skin off you and slice it into pieces, frog," he grated, as he pushed himself up onto his feet. "Your weapon, Goda!"

"No, master. You said yourself a warrior never lets his weapon out of his hand."

"Goda, this is not another silly test! Give me your weapon." It was an indistinct cough rather than speech. A quiet but horrified exclamation from Tungdil made him look. Balyndis was standing directly in front of the creature, blocking its way to the exit.

"Get out of the way," yelled Tungdil," Otherwise . . ."

The warning came too late. Boldly Balyndis was attacking with her hatchet, fending off the spiraling chains with her shield. She was in range for a hit.

The monster used its chain-wrapped left forearm as a decoy. Hardly had the blade touched the links of the chain before magic was released.

A green lightning bolt struck the weapon, which burst into pieces, showering the dwarf-woman with a hail of shrapnel. The shield was penetrated in several places. Balyndis staggered and fell first against the tunnel wall, then slowly to the ground.

"Balyndis!" Tungdil rushed to her aid. Ireheart and Goda followed him.

The creature turned around with a roar, lifted up a wooden spar from the broken gate and hurled it in their direction.

The aim was true and swept all three of them to the ground; they were helpless against the force of the blow. By the time they were on their feet again, the monster had disappeared.

"After him!" Tungdil commanded Boïndil and looked at Goda. "You, see to Balyndis." She nodded, wordlessly passing her night star flail to her master.

The dwarves ran out of the vaults and pricked up their ears. Moon and stars were shining brightly down on Idoslane. The excellent night vision they both possessed showed them a still and sleeping silver landscape, peaceful and calm.

"Where did it go?" whispered Ireheart, observing the ground for tracks. "It ought to have left some marks big enough for a child to hide in. There's nothing here. Froggy must have hopped away."

Tungdil could make out a movement in the distance. "It has indeed." He sighed, pointing toward the west. "There it goes."

Where he was indicating a figure crossed the rough terrain by leaps and bounds, eschewing the roads and pathways. It jumped over bushes and small fruit trees as if on an athletics training run.

"It's taking the shortest route home," Tungdil ventured.

"Wretched devil-creature!" Boïndil stamped on the earth in anger. "Why the west?"

"Why not the west?" countered Tungdil. "We know nothing about it or its two siblings. West is as good as east."

"Yes. But I thought it would head for Toboribor. The caves of the old realm of the snout-faced orcs would make an excellent hiding place."

"Maybe it's trying to trick us." He couldn't make the figure out anymore. The dark edge of the forest had swallowed it up and was providing all the cover it might want.

Ireheart shouldered the weapon he had taken from Goda. "Shall we get after it?"

"There's no point. Did you see how fast it was traveling? No rider could overtake it." They returned to the vaults. "We'll look for tracks in the morning. Perhaps they'll lead us somewhere we can find out more about these monsters. I will let Prince Mallen know what has happened, so that he can send us a squad of soldiers."

Goda had levered Balyndis up into a sitting position. There was blood streaming down from her many wounds. One long thin metal fragment had narrowly missed her right eye, and now jutted out of her skull. She was biting her lips so as not to scream with the pain. She grabbed Tungdil's hand, desperate for his help.

"You'll be fine," he said to her cheerily.

Ireheart pointed out a large red stain under the chain mail. "That looks bad. We need a healer right away to look at these wounds and remove all the splinters." He spoke in a hushed voice so that Balyndis wouldn't hear.

She pulled her husband nearer. "I'm going to pass out, Tungdil," she managed to say. "Only Vraccas knows whether I shall wake again, so you must listen to me." The grip of her hand was so tight that it hurt him. She was racked with a wave of pain and then her eyelids fluttered. "Djerůn . . ." she groaned, then her body went limp.

Horrified, Tungdil listened for her heartbeat. "It's still beating," he said in relief. "Quick, Ireheart. We'll carry her to her bed. Goda, run to the settlement and fetch a healer. No matter what he's in the middle of. Just bring him here."

"Yes." She nodded eagerly, but smiled when she saw Boïndil's mistake. To pick up Balyndis by the feet he had leaned the night star against the passage wall. She grabbed her weapon. "Now, master, it'll be your turn to drag the beam today. You know where I've left it," she called out cheekily and raced away.

He watched her go. "What a . . ." He spared himself the rest.

With Balyndis resting on her bed, and with most of the sharp-edged iron splinters removed carefully by Tungdil, the healer arrived to look after her and calm was restored.

Tungdil made use of the time to search the laboratorium to ascertain the unwelcome truth. Like many of the rooms he passed, it had been totally ransacked. Not a shelf was left in place.

He soon came to the conclusion that the creature had found the diamond by chance. There was a huge bloodied footprint by the pile of glass. It must have stepped on the shards, injuring its foot, and then must have noticed the diamond amongst the shattered fragments.

"Damnation!" he shouted in anger. He went into Lot-Ionan's old study, where there was an immense collection of books. He sat at the desk and started a letter to Prince Mallen, telling him what had happened. He found himself occasionally picking his nose with the end of the quill pen—a bad habit from the old days, the not-so-very-old days. He rapped himself on the knuckles, took a new nib and started again.

There was a knock on the door and the healer stepped into the room. He was wearing a dark gray robe over his white nightshirt; his boots were still undone. Goda really had dragged him from his bed. "Excuse me, Master Goldhand." He ran his hands through his medium-length gray hair, which was standing up around his head. "I'm done here. I've stitched the wounds and treated them with salves. She will recover. The tincture I have given her will let her sleep for two orbits."

Tungdil nodded to him, reached into the drawer of the desk and took out a gold coin. "This is for your trouble," he said. "In the morning, please bring me anything else she may need."

"Thank you, Master Goldhand." The healer took the money, then looked at the dwarf. "What happened? If I may ask? It looks as if a horde of orcs had broken in."

"You may ask," replied Tungdil shortly. But he preferred to keep the truth to himself. There were already too many rumors circulating in Girdlegard. "Thieves. We chased them off. I'd prefer it if you'd keep this to yourself. If anyone asks, say it was an accident." He threw him a second coin.

"Of course, Master Goldhand. You may rest assured on that count. I wish your lady wife a speedy recovery." The healer bowed, and as he did so the sides of his robe swung gently under him. "Make sure she has bed-rest for at least forty orbits."

"Why?"

He indicated his right side. "One of the largest fragments has damaged an internal organ, as far as I can see, but I specialize in healing humans and not dwarves. It looks all right, but as I said . . ."

"She will remain in bed," Tungdil nodded for him to go. "Thank you." The man turned and left the room.

Tungdil was finishing his letter to Mallen when Ireheart came in. He had put on his leather jacket and chain mail now. "Balyndis is fast asleep," he reported, settling into the armchair by the fireside. With his short hair and ruined beard he looked very odd. "What next?"

"We'll see at sun-up," Tungdil replied as he signed the letter and placed his seal on it. He did not hold out much hope that they would find the creature, but said nothing.

"Look what froggy has done to me. I'm like a plucked chicken," Ireheart complained, tugging at the remains of his beard. He had trimmed its ragged edges so that, although very short, it still looked reasonably tidy; it would be many cycles before it was back in all its long glory.

And his hair was only shoulder length now. "I'll be laughed at. If for nothing else it deserves to die for doing that." He put his feet up. "Do you think it's maybe always the same creature but appearing in a different guise each time?"

"Hard to say. I don't think so." Tungdil was chewing over his wife's last word before she fell unconscious. He told his friend about it.

"Djerûn? Old Tin Man?" Ireheart thought back to Andôkai's huge bodyguard. "Did she mean froggy was one of those? It was the right size. And that was from the Outer Lands, too."

"No, I don't think they're related. This creature bled like an orc. Djerûn's blood was bright yellow."

"Mm," said the warrior, at a loss. "Then I've no idea what she could have meant . . ."

"Of course!" Tungdil clapped himself on the forehead with the flat of his hand. "Djerûn's armor!"

"But it wasn't wearing any armor," retorted Ireheart.

"No, but those wrist bands, and the chains." Tungdil frowned into the flames. "I think Balyndis was trying to tell me that they were made of the same metal as Djerûn's armor. Do you remember? It carried the magic." He stood up and came over to join his friend at the fireside.

"That must mean that others have got the formula?"

"More than that, Boïndil. It means they've found a way to store magic power to use when they need it. It is more than protection. It is a reservoir that they can have recourse to for stocking up on magic now that Girdlegard has lost its magic source." In a frenzy he racked his brain.

"And what if it's the other way around?"

Tungdil stared at Ireheart's wrinkled face in irritation. "What do you mean?"

"Perhaps froggy itself is magic?" He stroked the remains of his beard ruefully. "Like the wire the eoîl put leading up to the roof of the building from the magic source. That siphoned the energy up so it could be used at will."

"An upside-down storm-milker?"

"A what?"

"A storm-milker. In one of the ancient alchemy tomes I read that you can do certain experiments when there's a thunderstorm. Copper and iron attract the lightning bolts, it said." Tungdil hurried over to the bookshelves and climbed the ladder to look for the book in question. "Here it is!" He opened the pages. "'Place the ingredients in an iron bath when a thunderstorm is nigh. Let the bath be carried to the top of a mountain and stick a lance upright in the tub. Lightning will enter the tub and the energy released will effect the transformation.'" He slammed the book shut again. "With these creatures it's the other way about: they are the thunderstorm and the energy shoots out through the metal."

"There you are," joked Ireheart. "That's a scholar for you."

"Yes," sighed Tungdil, his enthusiasm failing. "Of course it's only a theory," he said with regret. "We don't have anyone who knows enough about magic to advise us."

"Makes sense all right to me," Boïndil consoled him. "Why not tell Mallen what you think?"

Tungdil hesitated. "No."

"Why not?"

He returned to his seat by the fire. "Who knows the formula, Ireheart?"

"The special metal? Well, Balyndis and Andôkai. And the eoîl, I think, but it's dead." Boïndil studied Tungdil, not knowing what he was getting at.

"I wonder how likely it is that one of the Outer Land races knows magic and is in possession of the formula for this alloy."

Now Boïndil was following. "You think the beasts *don't* come from the Outer Land?"

"There are lots of possibilities, I admit," nodded Tungdil. "But where have the indestructible siblings got to? Rodario and I couldn't find a trace of the unslayables on the tower. Of course, that was *after* the Star of Judgment fell. There was neither armor nor ash like with the älfar and the orcs that were wiped out by the Star's force." He leaned back. "Balyndis told some of our people the details of the special alloy before she left the Gray Range. And thirdlings have spies all over the place."

"You're not saying the embittered thirdlings and the unslayables have made common cause?"

"I don't know." Tungdil lowered his head, massaging his temples. "Damn it all. We're completely in the dark here, Ireheart. We'll have to step carefully through the pitch blackness, throwing light on the individual secrets as we go."

Ireheart stood up. "Then let's make a start in the morning, as we'd planned. We'll find froggy." He made for the door. "I'll send Goda to the gate to take first watch."

"Have you dragged your beam yet?" Tungdil baited him about his mistake.

"No," Boïndil growled.

"But you'll be wanting to set a good example, won't you?"

Ireheart turned round and stepped out into the passage. "Fine friend you are," he said, quite offended. "Go on, take my pupil's side. You thirdlings are bound to stick together." His footsteps died away.

"Mmm. The thirdlings stick together," repeated Tungdil to himself, and he cast an eye on the bottle of mead that stood next to the desk, calling to him with its sweet dark contents.

But alcohol didn't attract him. Not tonight. Tonight he needed a clear head.

A symbol on the wrist protectors worn by the creature had caught Tungdil's eye. To be sure he'd understood carefully, he looked for the small book he had in the past spent long evenings poring over, so as not to have to spend time near Balyndis. He turned the pages. It turned out he was not mistaken. It was the sign for the elf word meaning *to have*.

He closed the small volume and replaced it on the shelf. *So what did that signify?* He would have to ask Mallen and Ortger whether the other monsters had borne elf runes on their armor.

He got up and went back into the bed chamber. Dressed as he was he lay down next to Balyndis as she rested on the sheet. He laid his head on his hand and watched her face, examining the feelings that were going through him.

He stayed like that until dawn.

When Goda knocked to tell him a messenger had arrived with a letter from Gandogar, he was still debating with himself, and wrestling with his emotions. The night had made him no wiser.

Girdlegard,
Queendom of Weyurn,
Early Summer, 6241st Solar Cycle

The *Curiosum* had struck camp overnight. The brightly coloured wagons had left Mifurdania at dawn without having put on a single performance. Now they were making their way westwards.

A ragged hunchbacked beggar in a big floppy hat on his greasy hair was searching for something to eat amongst the remains of the cooking fire and the rubbish left behind.

Not finding anything to his taste, he headed toward the town and the fish market. He sat himself on a barrel with a good view of the newly laid-out port and stretched out a hopeful hand whenever anyone passed by. "Please can you spare a coin for a starving man," he coughed plaintively.

Nobody knowing Rodario would have suspected that the impresario's refined features were concealed under the filth covering the beggar's face. The actor had delved deep into his stage make-up box for the wherewithal of disfigurement. This included putting an ugly scar on the left cheek, applying stains to his teeth and giving himself a full shave. His beard had gone, much admired though it had always been: a painful sacrifice for the sake of his mission.

Tassia and the others had been taken aback when he

summoned them in the middle of the night to tell them what he intended to do: there was a sensitive and dangerous task to be carried out, investigating the recent occurrences in Mifurdania. He placed the running of the *Curiosum* into the hands of his blond muse, not knowing how long he would need to fathom out the Furgas mystery. Tassia had accepted the promotion with a charming smile and had gone on in the intervening hours to make it almost impossible for him to leave.

"Give me a little something," Rodario begged a rich merchant, who spat at him and went on his way. "No, that's not what I meant. Your snot will buy me nothing. Give me a coin," he called out after the man, earning a few laughs in the process.

The morning passed by. The sun rose high overhead and then sank toward the horizon.

Rodario stuck it out bravely in his chosen place of duty. He warded off importunate flies, annoying urchins and a tradesman who disputed his right to the barrel. Altogether his modest takings for the day were enough to get him a piece of bread and a cup of plonk. You could put up with poverty better like that.

The waiting continued.

Twilight arrived. Then he noticed the barge the archer-woman had used. The load line on its hull was now well above the surface of the water. So it was traveling to town empty.

Rodario made for the port and lay down between a couple of heaps of coiled rope opposite the freight quay. He looked like a beggar who had found a corner for the night. Nobody would be suspicious.

It wasn't until darkness fell that the brown-haired woman appeared, wearing a black mantle over her shoulders. Beneath it Rodario espied a dark, tight-laced dress and a dagger as long as a man's forearm hanging from her belt She looked familiar, but he couldn't place her.

She walked over the deck, jumped elegantly onto the quayside, put finger and thumb into her mouth and issued a deafeningly shrill whistle.

Near to where Rodario lay a warehouse gate opened; light cascaded onto the cobblestones and a man dressed in a brownish robe came out. He wore a hat, and the chain around his neck marked him out as a member of the merchant's guild. "Kea! Back so soon?" He was about to go over to her when he caught sight of the apparently sleeping form of the beggar. "Oi! Scum!"

Rodario did not move, hoping to be left in peace, but he was kicked in the side, and cowered in a heap, groaning.

"Up with you, you tramp. Sleep it off somewhere else." The man leaned down and punched him on the back of the neck. "Can't you hear? I'll get a knife to help you."

Rodario could hardly not react to that threat. He struggled up, drunkenly protesting and slouched off along the warehouse wall to turn into the narrow space between this building and its neighbor. He had to force himself into the gap.

"You may have driven me off but you haven't got rid of me," he murmured. Making use of the slits between the wooden boards he climbed up onto the roof, hoping to overhear their exchange from above.

He worked his way forward to a ventilation cover, which he managed to open and then slip quietly inside.

He landed in the dark on something soft that gave a bit under his weight. The smell and slight crunch told him it must be sacks of corn. The store was stuffed up to the roof with it, as if Mifurdania were planning for a famine or a siege.

Rodario wormed his way across and stopped where he could see a shimmer of light, pressing his face to the slight gap to see what was happening. He had missed the beginning of their conversation.

"And how much would that be, Deifrich?" the woman called Kea was asking, as she leaned against one of the roof posts.

The man pointed round the warehouse, which was bare except for a few loose grains of corn and some dirt. "One hundred sacks? Look around you, Kea. There's hardly any grain in the whole town."

She gave a false smile—gain Rodario felt he knew her from somewhere. "Only because you have bought it all up, Deifrich. To force the price up."

"Me?" he said indignantly. Even a fool would have seen through the exaggeration.

Kea looked up, taking out her dagger and holding it point upwards. "Suppose I were to go up there, what do you think I would find?"

"Not much," Deifrich lied with a grin, not attempting to look particularly convincing. "Let's say ten Weyurn coins. For each sack."

Kea gave an ugly laugh. "You despicable cut-throat," she said with a threatening undertone, lifting her index finger. "I'll give you *one* coin."

Deifrich wiped his chin with his sleeve. "No, Kea. I

know you have enough. So you will pay." To be on the safe side he put his hand on the handle of the short sword that he carried at his back on a belt.

Perhaps this was an agreed signal. Rodario heard footsteps. Two men approached Deifrich from left and right wearing leather armor and carrying long swords. They had the air of mercenaries or at least former soldiers. Kea did not even look at them.

"All right. Let's say nine coins per sack," said Deifrich haughtily. "I can get you the grain by daybreak." He held his hand out. "But only if I get the gold now. And I won't mention the other things you buy from me."

Kea put down her finger. "You have become greedy," she said quietly. "You are abusing my trust."

Deifrich shrugged his shoulders. "I am a trader. Where there is a business opportunity I take advantage of it. Nobody gives me anything for free."

"I understand you all too well. You would never get anything from me, either, without paying for it." She gave a cautious movement, so as not to give the soldiers cause to step in, fetching a small bag out from under her mantle. She opened the cord tie, put her hand in, fished around and pulled out a coin to give to Deifrich. "One of fifty gold pieces. I do not have any more on me."

He took the bag, then the proffered coin. "So you will receive five . . . let's say six sacks," he said, biting on the gold to test its worth. A splintering noise was audible. Deifrich yelled out in surprise, spat and collapsed to the ground. He lay convulsed, throwing himself from one side to the other, then finally remained still.

One of his hired soldiers bent over him. "Nothing to

be done," he said calmly and regarded the imitation coin. It had a thin center of lead, surrounded by glass and covered in gold leaf. A clear liquid dripped out of the remains. At first glance it was no different from any real coin. "What sort of poison is that?"

She lifted the bag. "Wouldn't you like to know?" she answered, pointing her dagger at the soldier. "The same poison is on the blade of this knife. Be off with you and keep quiet about what you've seen. You've been paid by Deifrich and didn't have to work for it. Be content with that."

The men looked at each other. Rodario thought they might try to jump Kea and take the rest of the gold.

The woman's cold-blooded attitude warned them off taking any such rash action. Hesitatingly and being careful not to turn their backs on her they inched out of the warehouse.

She laughed quietly and gave a second whistle. Five men hurried up to her. "Get up there and see how much corn the bastard was hiding. Get the sacks onto the barge as quickly as you can. And then let's get out of Mifurdania." She prodded the dead body with her foot. "Find something heavy to weigh him down with, then chuck him in the water."

Her people nodded and swarmed out while Kea disappeared to the left out of Rodario's line of sight. The noise of boots on the steps announced the arrival upstairs of at least two of the men.

Now things were getting uncomfortable for Rodario.

He was just crawling in deeper between the sacks when there was a crackling and a rattling in the dark above him with a winch being set to work. The floor he was lying on descended rapidly. Somehow he'd got himself onto the loading base, while the mechanism was activated, taking himself and ten sacks down to the ground floor.

Though he tried to hide between the sacks it was a lost cause. At the other end of the building he saw four long boxes. Kea was standing in front of one of them. She had opened the lid and was looking at some blocks of iron. To Rodario's eyes it looked like a mass of casting molds.

"Hey, watch it. There's a tramp," yelled one of the men up at the hoist.

"I'm on my way, don't worry. Just needed a place to sleep." Rodario coughed and crawled over toward the door. He didn't want to give up his disguise. Perhaps he would need the element of surprise more urgently.

Kea closed the boxes and stood herself calmly in his path, keeping the dead body of the tradesman from his view. "Not so fast, old man," she addressed him, not harshly.

Rodario read it as a good sign that she wasn't brandishing her dagger and that no one was manhandling him. His masquerade seemed to be holding up. "Oh mistress, forgive me. Don't call the Watch, please don't," he begged, dribbling and slobbering to make himself even more unsavory. He didn't want her to expend any time on him. "They hate me."

She measured him with a glance. "You know Deifrich?"

Rodario gave it some thought. "No. Does he belong to the Watch?"

One of Kea's people came over and grabbed him by the arm. "Kea, you know what has to be done! He's seen us now."

"I see a lot of people in Mifurdania," said Rodario in an old man's falsetto. He laid his hand on the man's arm. "It's not a crime, young man," he announced argumentatively.

"No." Kea fingered the handle of her dagger. "Seeing us, old fellow, is certainly not a crime. But it is bad luck." She drew her weapon and stabbed quick as lightning.

Rodario had been expecting the blow, so moved quickly to the side, grabbing the other man and using him as a shield. He hadn't counted on the old tramp being so strong. He it was that received the stab in his ribs. The dagger did not go through to the internal organs—it did not need to. The poison brought the man down. "Surprised, huh?" Rodario walloped Kea on the nose and she fell back with a scream. He ran off to the nearby door, pursued by shouts from the men and curses from the woman.

Even if it had been a long time since he had been in Mifurdania, he still knew his way about. He shook off his two pursuers in the confusion of the port. But then he made a bee-line for the warehouse again, after first making a wide circle to throw them off the scent. He wanted to see what had been happening following his bold escape. He watched from behind a fishing boat on the other side of the quay.

Swiftly the men loaded the sacks onto the barge, even Kea helping with the task. They must have needed the corn so badly they could not leave it behind despite the incidents with the tradesman and the mercenaries.

One hundred sacks was a lot of corn. You could feed a small army with that. But where could an army be encamped in a land like Weyurn that was mostly water?

And what would be the point? Soldiers who had deserted and were trying their hand at piracy and making sure of provisions before setting off? Where did they get so much gold? What was Furgas up to with them?

Questions on top of questions and nobody to give him any answers, of course.

Once the boxes with the iron molds were loaded the barge pushed off, not using any lights. Rodario decided to carry on following them. Water; the goddess Elria's element, was not going to deter him.

He found a little dinghy tied up at the quayside. Borrowing it, he hopped in and found to his delight it obeyed even his landlubber efforts. Luckily the barge was not moving fast, so it was easy to keep up.

It was heading for the center of the huge body of water that now made up Weyurn. The waves glittered in the light of the stars as if enchanted. Rodario kept his distance and tried to hoist the sail on the small mast. It was difficult but he managed it. Not having a seaman's training, he was not doing very well about holding to a course.

The barge disappeared behind the cliffs of an island and it took him some time to get his borrowed boat to go in the same direction.

Before rounding the rocks he heard a splashing, hissing, gurgling noise, as if a red-hot shooting-star had fallen from heaven into the waters. The surface of the lake was very rough; small waves rolled over the bow of the boat, threatening to swamp the dinghy.

Rodario rounded the cliffs. He did not have long to wait.

"For heaven's sake! What in the name of all the bad

actors in Girdlegard ... where the hell is it?" Rodario stood up, his hands on his hips and stared at the lake before him. Stared at the empty lake.

There was nothing to see and nothing to pursue. The barge had disappeared from one moment to the next.

"How can that be, Palandiell?" he said, trying to keep his balance in the rocking boat. The moonlight showed him that there was nothing but the islands, and they lay over a mile away to his left. "Has Elria drawn them down to the depths because of their dreadful deeds?"

A new shuddering movement disturbed the surface and a mighty wave rolled toward him in the form of a foaming black wall, blotting out the moon and stars.

"O merciful Elria! What have I done to enrage you?" he murmured, motionless with terror, clinging to the mast of his small boat before the craft was seized by several tons of water and he was dragged under.

Girdlegard,
Red Mountain Range,
Kingdom of the Firstlings,
Early Summer, 6241st Solar Cycle

In these times, when the children of the Smith had to be more watchful than ever as they stood guard at the entrances to Girdlegard, it was harder for wanderers and merchants alike to overcome the suspicion that met them at any of the five gates. That was if anyone dared to turn up at the gates at all. It was not always going to be the evil that wished to come in.

And so it was in the Red Range.

The nine imposing towers and the two mighty ramparts of West Ironhald presented an almost insuperable obstacle even for peaceful visitors. In the area between the defending walls in the chasm that led to the Ironhald gateway and thus to the kingdom of the firstlings, around two hundred people were encamped, waiting for the dwarves to admit them.

For the most part they were traders, but there were also refugees from regions that had been devastated five cycles beforehand by the so-called avatars and their army. Their homelands were still not habitable.

Queen Xamtys had instructed the guards to let the groups progress forward one section at a time every two orbits. In the whole ten orbits they were waiting, the guards had them under observation and could examine the people, their baggage and wagons and animals, in minute detail, watching out for unusual behavior. Only the ones who conducted themselves well and passed the final interrogation examination at West Ironhald were allowed to enter. They were let into the halls and allowed over the pass.

The guards became increasingly restless. Sometimes there would be the faintest trace of orc in the air, as if maybe a small band of them were in hiding away off in the distance, waiting for the chance to storm the fortress. Maybe one of their spies was inspecting the fortifications.

Amongst the applicants who had got as far as the first gate was a strapping, rough-hewn tradesman who made a great thing of secrecy about his cargo. On his big four-spanned cart he had square blocks, it seemed, that were covered in leather and canvas to shield them from prying eyes and to protect them from the weather.

The wagon jolted its way toward the sentry post, and the man, dressed in light leather from head to foot, halted his oxen. He came over to Bendelbar Ironglow of the clan of the Glowing Irons, superintendent of the guards, and bowed. "My greetings. My name is Kartev and I've come all the way from Ajula to speak to your ruler."

"Why would Queen Xamtys want you to?" responded Bendelbar, a sturdy dwarf sporting long blond hair, a colorful plaited beard and a military abruptness of manner that combined unfriendliness with surprise. Some self-important merchant. That was all they needed.

Kartev walked back, loosened a few of the ropes securing the tarpaulin, then lifted the cover, behind which cage bars were visible. Then he motioned to the dwarf to come over. "See for yourself."

Bendelbar approached and took a look. Inside there were three small figures, chained by the ankles and in a miserable state. They were beardless, one and all, and looked, apart from that strange feature, exactly like Girdlegard dwarves. The guard knew at once who it was he had here. The news from the Black Mountains had traveled swiftly: the diamond thieves. "By Vraccas!"

"I call them Ancient Children. I thought your people would be interested. They must be related to you, don't you think?"

"And why did you take them prisoner?"

"I didn't capture them, I bought them. I bought them off a judge in Ajula. He had them arrested for robbery," he explained hastily, so that no one would start to reproach him. "They were very expensive," he added.

Bendelbar watched the wrinkled naked faces; the sight was new to him. He saw that two of the captives were women, but there wasn't a single hair on their cheeks. "Let me guess. They were looking for diamonds?"

Kartev looked surprised. "Yes. You're absolutely right." His eyes narrowed. "So they've already tried it here, too?" He stood up straight. "Pleased to be able to help you. I'll hand them over to you. Just need my expenses met." He dropped the heavy canvas again and the strange dwarflings were back in the dark. "Take me and my captives to your queen, so we can sort out a price."

Bendelbar wrapped one beard strand round his index finger thoughtfully. He finally agreed. He couldn't let slip this opportunity to cross-examine the thieves. History would show him no mercy if through his fault a chance to avert disaster were to be missed. He gave the order to open the gate for the man and his laden cart.

Escorted by ten guards they started on their long way, taking several breaks, through the long passageways and halls of the eastern part of the Red Mountains, until the troop finally stopped in a cavern used by the firstlings as a quarry.

"Wait here," ordered Bendelbar. "I'll have Xamtys sent for." He called one of the guards over and gave the instruction. The dwarf-guard trotted off. Bendelbar thought he could sniff orc-ness in the air again, but that was impossible. Not in here. He dismissed it as imagination.

"So, what's new in Girdlegard?" Kartev was feeling chatty. He undid the buckles to pull the tarpaulins and the leather covers off the cages. "I haven't been back here for ages. Are the orcs still hanging out in Toboribor?"

Bendelbar got the other soldiers to help. The crates containing these strange dwarves, known in Girdlegard only as undergroundlings, were revealed bit by bit. The trader had two dozen of them. They were huddled together in the middle of their prisons and were staring at their distant relations mistrustfully and in silence.

"In Toboribor? Nothing happening there anymore." Bendelbar shook his head, unable to take his eyes off the captives. "After the Star of Judgment struck, all the evil went away."

"That's not what I hear," replied Kartev, jumping up to the front of the wagon, where there were five barrels. He opened the left-hand one, took out a few hardened loaves and chucked them into the cages. The undergroundlings grabbed the bread greedily. "There are said to be strange creatures about the place, murdering and pillaging."

Now Bendelbar did turn his attention to the man. "Rumors spread quickly in the Outer Lands."

The tradesman smiled at the dwarf. "Don't forget I'm a merchant. Merchants are quick to panic when their wares might be in danger." With a powerful leap that Bendelbar wouldn't have thought him capable of, the trader landed at his feet. "Do these creatures exist or not?"

"They do exist," he sighed. "But we're close to catching them." He placed his hand on the handle of the ax he carried stuck in his belt. "You can set your mind at ease . . ."

There was a loud crash behind them.

The base of the cage had broken and a dozen of the

undergroundlings dropped through onto the stone floor. Initially Bendelbar thought the cart must have given way under the weight, having suffered damage on the long journey, but when he saw the undergroundlings were making off, left and right, unrestrained, he realized they had unchained themselves.

"Stop them," yelled Kartev, catching the arm of a guard who was about to fell one with a spear-thrust. "Don't hurt them! They're my property, got it? I want them back safe and sound. There'll be hell to pay if you kill one."

Bendelbar pushed him to one side. "After them!" he commanded, reaching for his long horn.

Then a whole side fell out on the second cage; loose bolts clattered and rolled away. The dwarf was caught on the head and shoulders by the iron bars of the cage as the remaining dozen undergroundlings made a bid for freedom, rushing the guards. Grabbing the sentries' weapons and armor they raced to the exits.

Bendelbar could not move. The heavy iron grating kept him pinned to the ground; he couldn't even move his arms, let alone sound the alarm with a blast on his horn.

"I'll get help," said Kartev, taking the dwarf's ax. "Just in case they attack me on the way," he explained. "You'll get it back. Which way do I go?"

"My bugle," groaned Bendelbar. "Blow the alarm." But however hard the tradesman tried to sound the horn he couldn't produce anything more convincing than a damp fart. "They'll be after our diamond," grunted the dwarf, nodding to the left-hand passageway. "Run and warn the queen!"

Kartev nodded to him. "Right." He stood up and ran

off, faster than Bendelbar had ever seen a man run before. He could do nothing but wait for help.

It was a long time coming. He heard alarm horns sounding, excited voices, weapons clashing, and now and then the sound of a dwarf in pain and furious. Every fibre in Bendelbar's being demanded he join the hunt for the intruders, but he was helpless under the iron grating.

At last, steps came near.

Kartev's coarse face appeared above him. "I'm back," he said. Many hands helped to move the heavy grid. His shoulder painful and his skull throbbing, Bendelbar slid out from under the metal bars. Someone helped him to his feet. Before him stood the trader and Queen Xamtys. And maybe sixty warriors with blood on their weapons. "What happened?" he asked, bowing to his queen.

"We had to kill most of them, they were so wild," she said. "They even got as far as the treasure chamber, but I don't know what the outcome was. Terrible confusion." Xamtys looked at Kartev. "Two of them fled, but you won't get them back alive." She handed him a bag that clinked in the familiar way: gold coins. "Take this as compensation and as my thanks for your attempt to aid us in our fight against the undergroundlings in the treasure chamber."

The man bowed. "Thank you, noble lady. I am sorry that our commerce should take this form. I would have preferred to hand the captives into your keeping alive." He pointed to the broken base of the cage. "I would never have thought them capable of breaking it open with a few pieces of iron. And they freed themselves from their chains, too."

"It is not your fault. My guards should have checked the wagon more thoroughly," she said, looking at Bendelbar. "From now on I shall expect my gate guards to be three times as watchful." She spoke the words c·-mingly. "Return to your post and let this be a lesson to you. This raid could easily have been successful." She turned and moved off, followed by her retinue and surrounded by her bodyguards.

Bendelbar grimaced. He was in pain and was in disgrace with the queen. The last piece of news in particular would not be popular with the chief of his clan. He'd get another dressing-down there, for sure. He looked angrily at Kartev, who was loading the first bits of ruined cage on to his cart. "Leave it." He gave the order for the rest of the guards to take over.

Not long afterwards Kartev was on his way back to the Outer Lands, accompanied by Bendelbar with what remained of his vehicle. It was a long journey for them both: three sun orbits on the broadest of roads in the dwarf realm, past many wonders, large and small, constructed out of stone, steel and iron. The sight of statues, bridges and murals raised the dwarf's spirits.

Although the tradesman had received adequate recompense for his trouble, he was not happy about the outcome of his journey. It seemed to Bendelbar the man was mourning the loss of the undergroundlings. At any rate, he wasn't appreciating the wonders they passed.

Seeing as he did not have the slightest wish to communicate, they were both silent when they went back through the gates of Ironhald. More than a mere "Vraccas keep you" did not cross their lips.

Bendelbar stopped. He ordered the outer gate to be closed and the wall gate to be opened for the trader, then he rushed up to the battlements to follow the progress of the ox-cart with his eyes.

Just as he was wondering why Kartev, after all that long waiting period at the gates, had not gone into Girdlegard with his gold to buy goods to sell on his way home, the man was doing something even stranger.

When he had left the last ramparts behind him, Kartev stopped to chat to a new arrival who was heading for West Ironhald: he pressed the reins of his oxen into the man's hand and continued on his way without his cart or belongings.

"Vraccas, what is it with this fellow?" wondered Bendelbar, coming down from his vantage point. He wanted to find out.

He had just commandeered a pony and ordered five mounted guards to accompany him, when a messenger hurried past, storming into the quarters of Gondagar Bitterfist of the clan of the Bitter Fists, the commander of West Ironhald.

"Wait," said Bendelbar to his companions, guessing that this agitation had something to do with the trader.

It took just about as long as a dwarf needs to draw an ax, take aim and hurl it at an enemy—that's if you had a second one on you—before the threatening thunderous voice of the stronghold's main alarm horn sounded. It was powered by huge bellows and activated from inside the commander's quarters. It sent out its continuous message along the ramparts, up the slopes of the mountain, and all along the ravine.

The door flew open. Gondagar appeared, pulling his helmet on over his black curls, and gesturing at the dwarf next to Bendelbar. "You there, dismount. Let me on," he ordered, swinging himself up into the saddle. "Let's go. Stop that trader!" he yelled, spurring the horse so that it reared up at the pain and galloped off. "In all that confusion he's replaced the diamond with a false one made of glass."

Bendelbar ran hot and cold. His guilt was growing by the minute.

The dwarves on their ponies chased along the twists and turns of the ravine, and the gates opened before them in the nick of time.

Every hoofbeat brought them deeper into the Outer Lands. They followed the broad but uneven road; however hard they pushed their mounts they did not catch up with the trader.

Round each corner they expected to see him but were disappointed. There was nowhere he could have hidden. The walls of the chasm either went vertically upwards or there was a precipice down on the other side. The stone was too smooth to give any hand- or foothold.

Not until the sun was sinking over the Red Mountains and darkness was falling over the area like a black cloth, did they come to a halt.

Gondagar cursed roundly. "Where the hell has the bastard got to?" he called out furiously to the echoing mountain walls. "He must be in league with Tion, or how else have we not overtaken him? May Vraccas strike him down with his hammer!"

Bendelbar's pony snorted in alarm and skidded round

a harmless piece of rock on the roadside. The other mounts blew sharply through their nostrils and pricked up their ears, dancing on the spot and only kept from bolting by the riders pulling hard on the reins.

Then Bendelbar smelt it, too: orcs. The smell of their sweat carried on the evening air, polluting it. He slid out of the saddle and took his ax in his hand.

Gondagar followed suit. "I can smell them but I can't see them," he growled. "What devilry is this?"

Bendelbar approached the rock the pony had shied from, and held his weapon at the ready. "Perhaps there's a secret under the stone—"

Suddenly the rock turned into Kartev. The trader threw himself forward with a huge cudgel in his right hand, hitting the dwarf on his injured shoulder.

The blow was hard, too powerful to have come from a normal man, who would not have been strong enough to wield a large club like that with one hand. Equally, it was impossible for a normal man to take on the shape of a rock. Something was not right here.

Bendelbar fell against the pony and under the whirling hooves of the terrified animal. Before he could protect himself from the kicks and get upright again, clenching his teeth against the pain, the fight with Kartev was decided.

But not in the way Bendelbar had expected.

His dwarf friends lay moaning or silent on the path, the man standing over them, taking deep breaths. He looked down at Bendelbar. "Stay where you are. I've got what I wanted," he said, his voice sounding more guttural now, more like—an orc. "I don't want to hurt you."

"But I want to fight!" yelled Bendelbar, lifting his ax

and leaping forward. "Vraccas, come to my aid against the accursed greenskin."

His ax blow was parried, and the cudgel jabbed him on the cheek and pushed him over.

To the dwarf it felt like being kicked by a pony. Half stunned, but determined not to submit to the enemy, he got to his feet and brandished his ax to keep the attacker at arm's length. He could see the hazy outline of an orc in front of him. "You won't get away," he threatened, his words slurred.

The broad shadow rushed past him and his blade met empty air.

"But I've already got away," the being called from afar. "Go back to West Ironhald and have your wounds treated." The sound of speeding hooves was heard.

Bendelbar shook his head, trying to clear it. It was no good. He would have to wait until his head stopped spinning and his vision was no longer blurred.

When he stood up, Gondagar was just coming round. The cudgel had made a substantial dent in his helmet and blood was trickling through his black hair, down his chin, his beard and his neck.

"What a ghastly country," he groaned. "You can't tell the difference between the orcs and the people. Apart from the smell, that is." He took in his surroundings. "He's stolen our pony."

The dwarves slowly got to their feet. Bruises, one broken arm, painful cuts but no fatalities. Bendelbar was not the only one to express surprise at that. The orc had spared them. This incident would surely give rise to intensive debate at the dwarf folks' assembly.

They gave up their pursuit and returned to West Ironhald. Halfway there, support troops from the firstling kingdom came out to meet them. A band of about fifty male and female dwarves were approaching on horseback.

As quickly as possible Gondagar related their encounter and spoke of the peculiar abilities displayed by their adversary. "Beware of his magic. It seems he can transform himself into anything he likes. But he still smells of orc," he told them. "Pay heed to your noses and your ponies. They are less likely to be fooled than your eyes."

The leader of the troop nodded. "And you be careful, back in the stronghold, what you drink. Several wells have been poisoned. The experts are testing them, one by one."

"What?" Bendelbar stopped short in the act of opening his own flask.

"A hundred dead have been discovered to the south of the Red Range. They must have died several orbits ago. They all showed signs of bleeding from their mouths, eyes, noses and ears. The clan of the Hard Hammers has been completely wiped out. The queen thinks the thirdlings are behind it." He nodded at them grimly. "They'll tell you more back at the fortress. We must push on." The troop surged forward, leaving the five dwarves behind in a cloud of dust.

Yet more deaths among his kind. But this time Bendelbar was certain that the raid did not stem from the undergroundlings. If it *had* been the undergroundlings, the weight of his own responsibility would have been incalculable.

VIII

Girdlegard,
Kingdom of Gauragar,
Porista
Early Summer, 6241st Solar Cycle

"Do you think the elves are going to cause trouble about the Âlandur thing, Scholar?" Ireheart was growing increasingly uneasy, the nearer they got to Porista. On the horizon now, the city—the future seat of Gauragar's administration—promised reunions with old friends and probably with old enemies. The dwarf had not forgotten the incriminating finger marks he had left on the elves' holy stone. Nor had Tungdil.

"We won't let it get that far," said his companion, scratching his pony behind the ear. "The good thing about this assembly is that we can tell Liútasil what you did face to face." He glance at Goda; they had spoken to her about her master's elf-land mishap. The dwarf-girl kept out of the exchange, but followed every word with silent glee.

"Right." Ireheart resigned himself to his fate. It was difficult to predict what consequences might result from his having touched the monument. "It didn't break and it didn't crack," he said, eliminating the worst-case scenario. "It left a stain, that's all. I bet it'll go away when it's polished up." He clapped his thigh. "It'll be fine. Bit of elbow grease and it'll be good as new. If there's still a problem we can send one of our master masons to show the elves how to treat a decent piece of stone so that a perfectly clean hand won't leave marks."

"Your words flow like molten gold. Could it be that you are trying to reassure yourself?" grinned Tungdil.

"Me? Am I bothered? Who would I have to be worried about?"

"Liútasil, perhaps?"

"Rubbish! Not scared of elves." The warrior fell into a sulk and urged his pony on ahead. The sooner he met the lord of the elves and could explain what had happened—he might need his friend's help there—the sooner the punishment would be over with.

"Sounds like it, though," whispered Goda to her pony.

Ireheart looked back over his shoulder. "Goda, get down. You're going to walk."

"What?" She sounded incensed.

"It's not your place to question me, girl. Carry your baggage while you're about it." He turned his face away quickly to hide his grin. He really enjoyed tormenting her.

Obedient but furious, Goda slipped from the saddle, threw the bags over her shoulder and stomped along next to her pony. "What on earth's the point? I wanted combat training, not to learn how to be a porter."

"Listen. A woman fighter needs strong legs to stand firm," he answered swiftly. "Imagine you're marching along reckoning any second with a snout-face attack. Have you heard the one about the orc that asks the dwarf the way?"

Goda snorted. Tungdil laughed, hearing a curse in the sound. But his levity was a little forced. His thoughts were with his injured Balyndis, back in Lot-Ionan's vaults. He had been puzzled by his own mixed feelings on leaving her behind.

On the one side he was extremely worried about his wife, on the other he was pleased to be away from her again. He could not fathom this discontent. It had looked, that first night, as if they had a new chance together, but the longer he played with that idea, imagining a long life with Balyndis, the more frightening it seemed. He could not understand why. He was still fond of her.

Tungdil shifted in the saddle and gazed at Porista's city walls. The city was a masterpiece designed by Furgas. Perhaps that's what it was. He was still *fond* of her, but there was nothing deeper behind it. They were like brother and sister. Like comrades in arms.

". . . and then the dwarf laughed and went on his way." Tungdil caught the closing words of Ireheart's joke.

Goda was having trouble suppressing a grin. The corners of her mouth would not obey her. Dimples were forming, in spite of her efforts to remain deadly serious. You couldn't be furious and want to smile at the same time. It was a very good joke.

Boïndil's attempts to lift the mood were met with merry laughter. All of them joined in. They could not help it.

They rode into the city and as soon as they had announced themselves were taken to the assembly tent. A few smaller tents had been put up, to serve for more private discussions.

"Let's go to Gandogar and explain what's happened, then we'll see Liútasil," Tungdil suggested. Ireheart nodded his agreement.

Goda's face was shiny with sweat; she emptied her

drinking flask in one go and looked round for a fountain where she could refill it.

"Don't worry, apprentice. You'll get something soon enough," Ireheart grinned at her. "How are the old legs?"

She lifted first the left foot, then the right. "Both still there," she retorted, wiping the perspiration off her forehead. A dark blond lock of hair clung to her cheek. "And both of them quite keen to kick someone's backside, master." She grinned. "An orc backside, of course."

Perhaps it was the light here in Porista, perhaps it was their surroundings or perhaps it was the dwarf-girl's sparkling eyes that suddenly made Ireheart quite enjoy looking at her. From one second to the next his feelings changed. He became unsure of himself. "Let's see what there is," he stammered and averted his eyes quickly. Something that shouldn't happen was happening. Not with her.

They made their way over to the tent flying the fourthling banner. The sentries announced their arrival at once. Goda stayed outside, but Tungdil had someone take her a drink.

Gandogar received them, stretching out a hand to each dwarf. "Events are threatening to overwhelm us," he said, noting with pleasure the change in Tungdil's appearance. He sensed the new vitality. "I was just about to address the clan leaders about a campaign to the Outer Lands, but now I've had to come to Porista with the assembly to deal with the newest outrage." Tungdil thought the high king's face was far more deeply lined than before. Worry was taking its toll. "How did you get on with the elves?" Gandogar's eyes strayed to Ireheart's shorn head. "Is this a new fashion?"

"A fight. Tungdil can explain." Boïndil preferred not to have to say much, or he'd find himself confessing the truth to his sovereign.

Tungdil bowed his head. "To be honest, sire, it was quite boring. We didn't get to see Liútasil. They fed us. They showed us only places of no significance." He lowered his voice. "I think they were trying to keep something from us. There are new holy objects in the clearing, and we learned by chance of new buildings they kept secret from us. Yet we have let their people see everything. It is not fair. With your permission I should like to address these issues with Prince Liútasil. He is here, isn't he?"

"No." Gandogar poured some water and they took the polished gold cups he proffered. "He has sent representatives: Vilanoîl and Tiwalún. They said he'd be coming along later because something important needed discussing first."

Boïndil frowned. "That's what they told us, too. It must be something really huge if it's taking this long to debate." He glanced at Tungdil. Now life was going to get difficult for him. The last people he wanted to meet here in Porista were their Âlandur elf guides, who were very likely to know all about what he'd done.

Tungdil was silent, looking at the contents of his beaker. "Strange things are happening in Âlandur."

"What do you mean?" asked Gandogar in concern.

"I mean just that: something strange is happening in Âlandur." His old gruffness broke out. He pulled himself together. "I hope there will prove to be an innocent explanation." He emptied his drink, bowed and put down the cup. "When does the session begin, Your Majesty?"

"We should already have reconvened. They will sound a bugle."

Tungdil looked at Gandogar. "I have bad news. My diamond has been stolen. A new monster invaded Lot-Ionan's vaults and attacked us. Balyndis was injured." He summarized the events. "We lost track of the monster; it escaped off through the rocks where it left no prints. Then we got your order to come straight to Porista."

"So you've lost your stone as well? The same as happened to the firstlings. A shape-shifting orc and a handful of beardless undergroundlings robbed the firstling queen." Gandogar let out a long breath, clenching his fists. "And there's more bad news. Xamtys suspects the thirdlings have poisoned their wells in the Red Mountains. Countless dwarves had died, men, women and children, before anyone noticed the water was poisoned. The experts have found that the fatal effects don't develop until you've drunk a certain amount. Boiling the water doesn't help at all. They have to bring their drinking water from a long distance away. In the Red Range no one trusts anyone now."

"This suspicion will spread when the dwarf realms learn about the poisoned cisterns," Tungdil reflected. His hope that the thirdlings might ever assimilate peaceably had died.

The age-old deep-seated hatred amongst some of the dwarves was still fermenting. The insidious lust for revenge was hitting the other dwarf folks more cruelly than ever. And those thirdlings loyal to their origins would soon become disaffected. Things would get worse.

"Perhaps it is better to rally the thirdlings who are living dispersed in other communities, and put them all together as a tribe somewhere away from the dwarflands," Tungdil said thoughtfully.

The bugle sounded, summoning Girdlegard's great and good back to the conference table. Their discussion must end for now.

"With you, then, as their king?" Gandogar picked up the idea quickly. He put his helmet under his arm. "I was thinking as much. We ought to discuss it with the clans and with the freelings as soon as we've dealt with the matter of the diamonds. Maybe there's a place for the thirdlings amongst the Free Towns."

"What . . ." Tungdil bit his tongue, suppressing the words "What rubbish!" He laid his hand on Keenfire's ax head. "Would it be a good idea to exile them again? I am not sure if the freelings would want so many thirdlings in their towns. If I were their king I'd be afraid of armed insurrection. Who would stop them?"

"Oh, this is all so ghastly," cursed Ireheart. "Anyone would think Vraccas had granted us five cycles of peace purely to thrust us straight into the furnace now. The diamonds are being stolen, orcs and monsters stalk our lands, the wells are poisoned and the elves are cooking up Vraccas knows what devilry."

"Did you say a *shape-shifting* orc just now?" Tungdil broke in, stepping alongside Gandogar. They walked over to the assembly together.

"Reports were vague," the high king answered. "But magic was involved."

"What? The snout-faces and magic now?" murmured Ireheart. "Have Tion and Samusin completely lost their godly senses, sending them after us? They can't be

Girdlegard orcs. Damned sorcery! Never could stand magic."

Goda tagged along at a discreet distance. She was exhausted by the enforced march, and Ireheart was regretting his instructions to her. He might have overdone it, he thought. But he did not let it show. "Wait outside again," he said, adding a mumbled "Have a bit of a rest."

Tungdil entered the tent and watched the sovereign rulers of Girdlegard take their places. He knew most of them; the human faces had aged quicker than the dwarves and elves, of course, in the last five cycles. The thorn of mortality was lodged deep in their flesh.

He observed Ortger with curiosity. Urgon's young ruler was talking quietly to his neighbor at the council table, Queen Isika, nodding repeatedly. Then he stood up with a respectful bow.

Vilanoîl and Tiwalún did not accord the dwarves a single glance. Their unfriendly demeanor warned Tungdil and Ireheart that the black finger marks must indeed have come to their notice.

King Bruron stood up and tapped his ring against his drinking vessel, the melodic ping cutting short the assorted rulers' conversations. All their attention was on him. "Let us get back to business, Your Majesties." He indicated Tungdil. "As you see, we have a trusted guest and old friend among us. One of Girdlegard's famous heroes—Tungdil Goldhand—has come to be with us in our dark hour. He will help us with our deliberations, I am sure."

Gandogar leaned over toward Tungdil. "His gold cup is an inferior alloy. The sound it made wasn't good at all.

Either the goldsmith has taken him for a ride or he's having to cut costs but wants to keep up appearances."

"And of course we are delighted to welcome Boïndil Doubleblade, whose services to our homeland are no less significant," continued Bruron with a smile. "We need heroes like these if we are to avert the coming dangers."

The rulers inclined their heads in acknowledgment. It seemed the elves had neck problems, but only the dwarves noticed that.

The king surveyed the room. "As usual when we meet I have to start with unpleasant news: The statue of Lot-Ionan has been removed from the rubble and stolen. Despite our best efforts there is no trace of it."

Tungdil swallowed hard. He remembered clearly having seen the statue, which was his very own foster-father, in Andôkai's palace. Nudin, or rather Nôd'onn, had turned him irrevocably to stone in the course of a battle many cycles ago. Secretly the dwarf had hoped to bring the petrified figure back to the vaults so that at least he could stand where once he had lived.

"What could anyone want with his statue?" Mallen looked at Tungdil.

"How should I know?" he retorted sharply. None of the other famuli were still alive. Otherwise he might have thought them capable of carrying off their mentor's statue, in order to honor it in some secret location. But the magus had been so revered they could have honored his statue in full public view.

Tungdil felt the robbers had betrayed him somehow. The magus had been a father to him. It was a personal attack.

"I can't understand it, either," said Bruron. "But I shall have my soldiers continue the search." He turned to Ortger. "You have news for us, you said, King Ortger?"

"Yes. A large town near Borwôl has been destroyed. Annihilated. Not a single inhabitant has survived. All the signs point to it having been orcs or some other of Tion's monsters." He noted the concern on their faces. "There is no longer any doubt: the beasts are back in Girdlegard."

Gandogar raised his hand. "I, too, have terrible news to report." He told them of the theft of the diamond and the poisoning of the dwarves, then handed over to Tungdil, who recounted how yet a further stone had been lost and how a new version of Tion's creatures had appeared.

Like all the others, Bruron sat thunderstruck. "Undergroundlings? Dwarves from the Outer Lands in alliance with magic orcs to get the diamonds? Am I hearing right?"

"They're all in it together," Queen Isika said with conviction. "The orcs, the undergroundlings and these magic hybrids." She addressed Gandogar. "You will have to face up to the question, high king of the dwarves, of how these beings have been able to enter whenever they want, through the gates and over the passes." The woman's voice was sharp enough to cut glass. She made no attempt to hide the fact that she had no faith in the dwarves' defense provision.

"Against magic we are powerless," admitted Gandogar. "You are forgetting that the orc we have heard about was able to change its shape. If there are more of them, then they have probably been able to walk right into Girdlegard unimpeded."

"That would explain the finds in Toboribor." It was Mallen's turn. "The search party I sent out after the village was destroyed found evidence of recent habitation in the old orc caves."

"It's all coming together. So it was orcs, magic orcs, that stole Lot-Ionan's statue," Queen Isika suggested. "They took the last of our magic so we would have nothing to fight them with." She leaned back. "We need a new magus for Girdlegard." She faced Tiwalún. "Perhaps one of the elves can weave magic?"

The elf bit his lips. "Even if this were the case, there are no more magic force fields where we could source the powers." He exchanged glances with Vilanoîl. "I did not want to mention it. Not yet. But in the circumstances we cannot keep the truth from you." He took a deep breath. "Lord Liútasil is dead. He lost his life trying to defend our diamond."

"Ye gods, protect us," whispered Queen Umilante in horror. "If even the elves are not safe from the beasts, who can help us then?"

Total silence reigned.

Nobody moved, no one spoke. They were able to pick up the sounds of the canvas flapping gently in the breeze and the guy-ropes easing or taking the strain as the wind made the tent walls move.

"We can," Tungdil called out, determination in his voice. He was sick of seeing these powerful rulers behaving like frightened animals herded into a corner by cattle-rustlers. "The children of the Smith! And all of you! We overcame Nôd'onn together, and together we drove out the avatars." He placed Keenfire on the table before the high king. "This weapon was able to inflict injury on that creature and it will protect me from all magic attacks."

Wey regarded the impressive ax, and encouraging memories of past victories over evil returned. "He is right. But he can't be everywhere all at once. As I said before. Let us take all the remaining diamonds to the safest of our fortresses and let us give Tungdil Goldhand our best warriors. In this way we can protect the stones and perhaps recover the ones that have been stolen."

Mallen applauded. "Let us cease talking up our fears. We sit back waiting for the next onslaught. We need to act!" He stood up and went over to the map of Girdlegard. "I suggest we take the diamonds to Immengau." He drew his dagger and placed its point at a spot immediately below Porista. "King Bruron suggested the old fortress in Paland from cycles long past, when trolls and ogres battled for possession of Gauragar. It was never taken by the trolls— the walls were too high, too strong. It's been abandoned for ages. Farmers keep their cattle there. Let's restore it to its former glory."

"I've already sent a workforce to Paland to start clearing the site," said Bruron, turning to Gandogar. "Be good enough to send us your best masons to have a look at the state of the walls."

"At once," agreed the dwarf.

"And the rest of you," Mallen addressed them with authority. "Send your best archers and warriors to Paland to occupy the battlements and to show a determined front to any who would rob us of our diamonds. Meanwhile, let the most knowledgeable scouts be sent through the caves of Toboribor to find those orcs." He slammed his fist onto the table. "Long enough have we conducted ourselves like mice terrified by a cat. From the present orbit onwards we shall be like wolves!"

Isika rose. "One condition: no dwarves in Paland. Apart from Tungdil Goldhand and Boïndil Doubleblade."

Gandogar lowered his head "What is the meaning of imposing such a condition, Majesty?"

"You said yourself that you are fighting the thirdlings in your own ranks. If *you* cannot recognize them, how should *we* be able to? After everything that has happened, they might see fit to ally themselves with the orcs and the undergroundlings rather than fight on our side." She did not avoid his stare but answered him with all the sovereign dignity at her disposal. "I do not propose this to diminish you and your people. My only concern is to preserve the security of the fortress. No more, no less."

"She is right." Tiwalún rushed to defend her. "The children of the Smith must sort out their own house first. Send an army to the Outer Lands to find the camp of the thirdlings who are pursuing you with death machines. Find them and destroy them. Sift out the traitors from your own ranks and make sure the gates to Girdlegard are protected." He bowed to Gandogar. "Twice the dwarves have been instrumental in saving our homeland. Now it is the turn of the elves. We shall come to Paland with all the warriors we have. That was Liútasil's dying wish."

Isika was the first to start clapping, and the others all joined in. The elves were nurturing that tiny seedling of hope sown by the dwarves, giving it water.

Gandogar agreed.

Then the wholescale planning began: when and how to

take the diamonds to the fortress Immengau, along which secret routes and under what security measures. Not until late that night had they managed to settle all the open questions.

"Let's lose no more time." King Bruron gave the signal to dissolve the assembly. "Is there anything more to discuss?"

"In all our concern about protecting the diamonds there's something we mustn't forget. I extend my sympathies to you both, Tiwalún and Vilanoîl, on the death of your sovereign lord." Mallen's voice was heard. "His death, and that of all who have died in defense of the diamonds, shall not have been in vain. But before we part, to meet again in Paland, tell us: Who is to succeed Liútasil?"

Vilanoîl smiled. "My thanks to you and all who mourn with us in our loss. In ten orbits I shall be able to answer your question, Prince Mallen of Idoslane. We are presently deliberating. Liútasil named no successor. We shall inform the realms of humans and the kingdoms of dwarves when joy replaces sorrow in our hearts."

The elves left the tent and the leaders made their way back to their quarters.

Mallen and the dwarves remained there under the canvas roof, drinking up and thinking back on what had happened and on the plans that had been forged.

Tungdil went over to the map to look at the locations of the village that had been destroyed and the town that had been wiped out. "It doesn't make any sense," he muttered. "They are much too far apart to have been attacked by the same group of orcs in such a short space of time. And why attack them but leave villages and farm-steads round about untouched? Orcs will always destroy everything in their path."

"Maybe these orcs are different?" interjected Mallen. "Gandogar, didn't you say that there wasn't a single death amongst the dwarves when the orcs stole the fourthlings' stone? Odd, isn't it?"

The very moment the blond prince spoke, Tungdil remembered what had struck him as strange in the descriptions of the attacks. Neither the undergroundlings nor the mysterious orcs with the pink eyes had done any *killing*. The indiscriminate slaughter had only begun when the machine arrived in the lift-hoist before retreating into the galleries and disappearing.

"Cudgels," he breathed. "The orcs attacked with cudgels. And the undergroundlings creating that diversion in the Red Range—they injured people but killed no one." And that was in spite of none of them surviving the battle. Two had previously evaded the queen's guard and gone off through the body of the mountain. They had all sacrificed themselves for the sake of this robbery. He put his suspicions into words. "Gandogar, we have to find those undergroundlings, alive, to interrogate them."

Ireheart saw it the same way. "They are giving their lives to recover their property."

"Their property?" chorused Gandogar and Mallen.

"My word, Ireheart!" Tungdil ran to his friend and grabbed him by the shoulders. "Of course! How could I miss that?" He hit himself on the forehead. "And they call me the Scholar!" he cried. "It should be *your* name!"

"You never know!" Ireheart was immensely proud and

felt the need to stroke his long black beard but his hand met empty air. He had managed for a time to forget about that loss.

"They're after the diamond, *because it's theirs*!" Tungdil turned to the prince and to the high king. "Do you remember how we always thought a diamond with all those wonderful facets could only have been cut by dwarf craftsmen?"

"By Vraccas, we must have been blind!" exclaimed Gandogar, conjuring up the exact image of the diamond in his imagination. His tribe had fashioned the imitation stones and they had needed to apply every ounce of skill to come near to the original. "The eoîl had stolen it from the undergroundlings!"

"And when they found out how powerful an artifact it has become, they wasted no time in trying to get it back. They know very well we're not likely to surrender it voluntarily," Tungdil deduced.

"But what have the orcs got to do with the diamond? Why are they helping the undergroundlings to recover it?"

"That's what I was wondering," grunted Boïndil. "There can't be a pact of any kind between our kind and these beasts."

"The undergroundlings must think differently on that score," Tungdil reminded him. The word *pact* gave him an idea. "This town and the other place that have been destroyed—do they have anything in common?"

"Apart from being located near the realms of monsters?" Mallen studied the map. "King Ortger didn't mention any alliance. I think that many cycles ago, when the trolls ruled Borwôl, the town wanted to send out a troop to negotiate with the monsters. It was about mining rights."

Tungdil looked at the lines delineating Toboribor. "This village will have paid tribute to the orcs in the old days, surely?"

"I expect so." Mallen suppressed a yawn. "Excuse me. I'm really tired and would like to go to bed."

"Just one more question," said Tungdil. "When you faced the monster in Goldensheaf, did you see any elf runes on its armor?"

"So I'm not the only one with sharp eyes," said Mallen. He nodded. "I didn't want to tell anyone before I'd had a chance to speak to Liútasil about it."

"Describe them." Mallen sketched them out for Tungdil on a piece of paper. "I think it means YOUR," Tungdil said, considering. "Our attackers had HAVE on their wrist protectors."

"Perhaps it's a message that won't make sense until all the monsters have appeared?" the Idoslane prince mused.

". . . to the elves." Tungdil was more specific. "The monsters are carrying a message to the elves. Whatever the purpose might be, they want the elves to piece it together bit by bit."

"So they see themselves as unstoppable." Mallen pointed to the doorway. "I'll ask Ortger if he saw anything. Perhaps we can solve the puzzle, even if it's not intended for us." He shook hands with the dwarves, wishing them good-night, then left the tent.

"It's time for me as well," said Gandogar. "Tungdil, I want you to guard the fifthlings' stone on its way to the

Gray Mountains and Paland. I don't want to take any more risks. Keenfire will be up to contending with any threats. There's none better than yourself to be entrusted with the task."

Goda and the two male dwarves walked away from the square and were shown to their quarters by one of Bruron's servants. Ireheart told Goda briefly about what had happened, and instructed her to take the first watch.

"Master, I am tired . . ."

"Yes, I know. You walked, in the sun, carrying baggage." He dismissed her complaints. "But a warrior girl such as yourself must be ready to ward off an attack after a long march. Your enemies won't care whether you've had a rest or not. They'll be waiting, come what may." With a sigh he slipped off his boots and his chain mail shirt, opened the fastenings on his leather jerkin and collapsed on his bed. "That's your next lesson."

"Thank you, master." She sat down on a chair by the entrance to be able to watch the door and the window at the same time.

Tungdil lay down under his blanket and thought about the evening's long discussions. A thousand things went through his head as he searched for explanations more convincing than Isika's.

The undergroundlings and the orcs held one key to the events in Girdlegard and the new beasts held the second one. Those keys would shed light on the secrets. Probably they would reveal even greater challenges in store for the homeland.

"Why did Tiwalún not say anything?" Boïndil asked.

"About the stone?" Tungdil turned to his friend, who

was sitting on his own bed and also seemed to be thinking hard; he was watching Goda. "Would it have been better if he had?"

"Why am I having to keep watch if neither of you is even asleep?" asked Goda in a resentful huff.

"Don't worry, Goda. We'll be quiet soon," grinned Tungdil. "And as for you, Ireheart, I expect the new elf lord will summon you soon enough." He turned to face the wall and closed his eyes.

And then, just before he nodded off, he realized what the connection was between the two ravaged settlements. But by the next morning the recollection had gone.

Girdlegard,
Queendom of Weyurn,
Early Summer, 6241st Solar Cycle

Rodario was woken by a strange noise and was astonished to realize that it was him making the clicking sound himself—faster than a rabbit mating, his teeth were clattering against each other. They could have shredded his tongue to ribbons.

He opened his eyes. Shaking all over, he threw himself onto his back and struggled up. There was thick fog all around, but bright, as if the sun were about to come up over the horizon.

He found himself lying on a shingle beach, with waves lapping around his legs and hips, pulling and sucking at him on the gravel, coaxing him back into their waters.

"Elria, I give you thanks for sparing my life. So you

decided you didn't want an actor in your realm," Rodario stammered. He got to his feet to walk along the beach and look for help. He assumed he must be on one of the islands he had sailed past the previous night.

Soon he came across a fisherman's hut with nets hung out to dry.

"Anyone awake?" he called out, knocking at the door. "Please let me in. I'm catching my death."

The door opened a little way. Two sets of curious young eyes peered out at him from the dark interior. Then the smaller girl disappeared. The older sister, maybe eleven cycles, studied him. She was wearing a worn old dress and two aprons. She had greasy short brown hair sticking to her head. "Who are you?"

"My name is Rodario. My boat capsized." He could not stop shivering. He was shaking like aspen leaves. "Please, let me come in and dry my clothes by the fire."

"Father is out fishing and Mother said we mustn't let anyone in when she's off looking for herbs." The girl considered him. "You're not a pirate. You're much too thin." She opened the door and let him in. "Over there," she said, pointing to the open fire they cooked on. "I'll put some more blocks on, but you'll have to pay—they're expensive."

"Thank you . . . What's your name, little one?" he walked past her, striding to the fire in the middle of the hut, relishing its warmth. There was a smell of fish, of smoke and of fat from a cauldron bubbling gently further along. Either they were rendering blubber or making soap. It was a miracle, he thought, wrinkling his sensitive nose, that they could put up with the smell.

"Flira." She introduced five siblings and then clambered up a ladder to get blocks of compressed seaweed for the fire. She threw them down to him. "One coin each."

Rodario felt on his belt for his day's takings. He unfastened the purse and threw it over to the girl. "Keep it. You need it more than me." He piled the seaweed blocks on and enjoyed the heat they gave.

With a suspicious look she opened the purse and counted. "That's seven! Thank you. May Elria bless you."

"She already has," he grinned, stretching out his hands to the flames. "I survived that huge damn wave. But my boat didn't."

Flira's eyes widened. "Another one? When?"

He shrugged his shoulders. "Some time ago." Then he understood why she was asking: she would be scared for her father. "Do these waves happen often?" He pulled off his shirt and flapped the legs of his breeches about to dry better. He did not want to take them off in front of the children.

"Father says they never used to. Not till the earthquake and the flood, that's when he says the lake got so treacherous—as dangerous as any monster in Tion's dreams, he calls it." Flira sat down and passed him a cup of hot tea. "They keep coming, and out of nowhere. Seven fishing boats have been lost just from here. He says other islands have fared even worse."

Her brother, called Ormardin, came over. The light in his eyes told the impresario that the young boy was fascinated by the occurrences on the lake. "Tell him about the älfar Nightmare Island."

Flira cuffed the back of his head. "Who said you could come and talk with the grown-ups? Tell him yourself."

"A nightmare island? Sounds intriguing!" laughed Rodario. "I'm all ears, Ormardin." He sipped his tea and waited to hear what fairy story the boy would serve up.

Ormardin grinned and began.

"Five cycles ago, just before the Judgment Star rose in the sky, a band of älfar was abroad in Girdlegard, sent out by the unslayable siblings to look for a new and safer base.

They came to Weyurn and travelled through our homeland on a ship they'd made out of the skeletons and skins of humans and elves.

They looked at island after island—solid ones and floating ones. Nobody saw what they were up to and any unfortunate fishermen they met on the high seas got killed. And eaten.

One night the älfar landed on a wonderful island that awoke their curiosity. They saw it had mountains and caves where they could hide.

They slaughtered all the inhabitants and took the island over, dragging the corpses to the caves, where they skinned them and removed the bones.

They were about to set up a spit to roast their kill, when one of them stuck his lance in the ground. It penetrated the island's crust. Water shot up and flooded the caves.

The island sank down into the depths, together with the älfar. That's how it escaped the effect of the

Star of Judgment, whose power could not reach the bottom of Weyurn's lakes.

But Elria did not let them die. They were to do penance for the evil they had wreaked on the people of Weyurn. She granted the älfar everlasting life and condemned them to eternal exile on the island.

Sometimes, when the stars are favorable, the älfar are allowed up to the surface with their island, so that they may see the night. It's said they will not die until they have covered the walls of every cave and grotto with paintings.

Anyone surviving the huge wave they bring and unwise enough to set foot on their island, gets eaten by the starving älfar, their skin is torn off and their blood used for cave-paintings."

Ormardin fell silent and looked at Rodario, his cheeks scarlet. "Did you like my story?"

The showman applauded. "Young friend, I bow to your talent. If your parents don't have another trade in mind, you'll be the best storyteller in Weyurn one day. I would bet my daily theater takings on that."

"You're an actor?" The boy couldn't believe his luck.

"Oh yes, I'm the Incredible Rodario, the Emperor of Actors and Showmen in all of Girdlegard," he boasted in his normal patter. "I have the good fortune to lead my own company, the *Curiosum*, the best in the world. If it were nearer, I would invite you to see it, young man." He ruffled the boy's short brown hair.

Ormardin stood tall. Praise from the mouth of such a master meant a great deal to him.

The door opened and, silhouetted against the light, Rodario saw the figure of a long-haired woman carrying a basket. "Who are you?" she asked, in obvious agitation. "Get away from the children!"

Rodario took her point. "Don't be afraid, good woman."

"It's the Incredible Rodario. He's an actor. And he's washed up," said Ormardin at once, jumping up and embracing his mother, full of delight. "I told him the Nightmare Island story and he said I've got talent!"

"Has he been giving you big ideas?" She came in, shutting the door behind her.

Rodario saw a woman slightly older than himself, in simple linen clothing. Fishermen, it seemed, weren't doing too well in Weyurn. "My greetings," he said, then remembered he was not wearing a shirt. "Forgive my appearance, but my clothes were wet."

She soon calmed down, realizing he presented no danger to the children, herself, or what they owned. A nearly naked body couldn't conceal anything, neither a weapon, nor stolen goods.

"I am Talena." She placed her basket on the table. "I'm sorry I was unfriendly."

He waved away her apology. "But of course. I quite understand."

"He gave me money!" said Flira, handing the purse to her mother.

"That was for the fuel for the fire." Rodario smiled at her. "Can you tell me how I get off this island? I have to go to Mifurdania."

"If you go over the dunes and follow the path to the

right you'll get to Stillwater, a little fishing village. You'll find someone there to take you." Talena took the herbs out of her basket and rinsed them in a bowl of water. "Did you really enjoy my son's story?"

"Very much," Rodario confirmed, giving Ormardin a wink. "And I was quite serious about his talent. I know a few storytellers who might be glad to have a gifted pupil like him."

"Oh please, mother. Flira will do the fishing when she grows up," begged the boy.

"No, I shan't," came the answer, quick as a flash.

Talena turned round. "Quiet, you two. See what your father says." She looked at Rodario. "You'd better get on your way now. Mendar will be taking his sloop over to Mifurdania around midday. He takes seliti-oysters over to the market. Tell Mendar I sent you and he won't charge."

"Talena, thank you." He pulled his shirt down from the rack and put it on. "Perhaps we will meet again," he said to Ormardin, crouching down in front of the young boy. "Have you got something to write with? I'll give you the names of some famous storytellers."

The boy nodded and went off to find a piece of slate and some chalk. Rodario wrote the names of two celebrated narrators and the kingdoms they lived in. "But you'll have to ask around because they're usually touring. You'll find them all right."

He ruffled the boy's hair again. "Palandiell will help you, Ormardin."

Talena gave him some bread and dried fish. "For the journey," she said. In her eyes he could read that her son would never have the opportunity to leave the island. It was his lot in life to become a fisherman like his father, and his father and grandfather before him. "Elria be with you."

She went with him to the door and pointed to the fog-bound dunes. He had only gone three paces before he heard the door close again.

The white veils of mist that enveloped him tasted sweetly of salt and sand. Rodario strode up the sand dunes and found the path Talena had described. On the way he ate some of the food she had given him; the fish had a fine aroma of smoke and salty herbs.

As the mist lifted, Rodario saw a flat, bare island with scarcely any trees, but plenty of small shrubs and grass-land where sheep were grazing. The summer sun began to dry even his shoes.

He was taken with that saga of the island. What if it were true? Had that been how his barge had capsized? Or had the vessel run aground and then been dragged down, her back broken from the rocks?

At least, thanks to Ormardin, he had a possible explanation for the loss of the barge, even if the idea was worrying. A lost colony of älfar that could not be pursued. It could become a breeding ground for terrible dangers for Girdlegard.

Rodario found the village easily and the fisherman was soon located. He was told to squat in the bow with the extra sails, where a sailor sat mending holes in the canvas.

The craft set sail, cutting swiftly through the water toward the port.

Rodario dozed a little, then sat watching the sailors at work. His thoughts were wandering, and instead of the men on deck he saw Ormardin in his mind's eye. How sad that this talented child would not enjoy a better life.

"What are you staring at me for?"

The unfriendly question dragged Rodario out of his reverie. "Forgive me. I was lost in thought." He smiled. Maybe this man could tell him more about the mysterious island. "I was wondering if you had any ideas as to what caused the giant wave? Last night I . . ."

The sailor put down his needle and stared at him. "Are you mad?" He spat over the side of the boat and called Elria's name quickly, three times. "You'll call up Nightmare Island and kill us all."

Rodario was astonished to find a grown man so in thrall to a myth. "So it's true?"

"As true as the sun overhead," the sailor spoke quietly in reply, his eyes on the waters that shone mirror-like in the light. "Keep quiet about it, right?"

Rodario did not think for a moment of keeping quiet. An idea occurred. "I've got to know whether anyone has ever stepped onto the island and survived."

The sailor grabbed him by the collar and shook him hard. "If you don't stop at once . . ."

The lake began to seethe around them. Bubbles rose to the surface and a bestial stink reached their noses, making Rodario cough and retch.

A bell clanged on deck, the crew scuttled to and fro to hoist full rig. They had to get out of the danger zone as fast as possible.

"You damned idiot," screamed the sailor, hitting

Rodario on the chin. "It's your fault!" He clambered up, dragging the actor to his feet. "He did it!" he yelled, drawing back his arm to hit out again. "He talked it up!"

"What do you mean?" demanded Rodario, ducking the next blow and tripping over a folded sail; he stumbled against the railing and lost his balance.

Instead of helping him the sailor gave him a shove backwards, overboard. "Take him, Elria! Take him, you älfar!" he shouted after him. "Spare us. Only spare us!"

Rodario was submerged anew in Weyurn's predominating element. The water was as cold as ever; he swallowed mouthfuls that this time tasted unpalatably bitter and smelt strongly of sulphur. Bubbles of varying shapes and sized floated up past him. Some were filled with greenish gas, some were bluish or yellow. Refracted sunlight piercing the water gave them a strange beauty and diverted attention from the peril they implied.

He bobbed round the gas bubbles and struggled back up to the surface. Spluttering, he gasped for air, but the fumes made him choke. Bursting bubbles made the lake look as if it were boiling, though luckily for him this was not the case.

The boat slipped past him; he had no chance of catching up. "You can't do that!" he called out in horror. "I'm really not a good swimmer! Help me back on board!"

At that moment a rocky formation broke through the frothing surface and continued to rise inexorably, sharp rock following rock, as the waters heaved and sloshed.

The higher the rocks grew the broader they became until they had formed a massive unscaleable cliff. Water poured back off in great torrents.

The lapping of small waves had turned into the heaving mass of great rollers that rose and fell in a terrifying fashion.

The sloop provided a welcome victim. She spun round and round as her planks creaked and loosened, some falling on deck and some in the lake. She lost her mast, then listed badly to one side.

The mountain continued to rise from the depths, exuding hissing clouds of air and gas through cracks and crannies in the rock.

Rodario grabbed one of the wooden beams that had crashed down into the water from the stricken vessel; then, holding fast with all his might, he gave his attention once more to the horrifying spectacle before him. The sloop collided with the cliff face, shattering as the sharp rocks sliced through her wooden hull, splintering the planks. Her sails and rigging caught fast and were heaved upwards as the island rose. The boat broke up and her crew fell or jumped overboard.

The mountain was still surging up out of the water. Rodario reckoned its peak was about two hundred paces high, and still it was rising.

With a final horrific gurgle the process finished. Lake water cascaded off the rock, streaming and splattering down, with the sunlight setting magnificent rainbows in the spray. The sight was unforgettable.

"Ormardin was not making it up," he whispered in awe, staring at the impossible cliffs towering in front of him. "Nightmare Island really does exist." The island by now must have been about one hundred paces wide and four hundred high. It consisted of dark blue, nearly black stone glittering with minerals. It seemed to resemble a piece of the night sky that had broken off and fallen to earth.

A petrified sheet of cooled lava had formed a flat beach on the side of the island nearest to him. Tall, thin figures emerged from caves, to launch boats. The älfar were about to bring in their harvest.

Rodario concealed himself under a floating scrap of canvas. The current was bringing him closer inland than he wanted to be. It was not his intention to explore the island, but Samusin seemed to like the idea of feeding him to the älfar.

Peering out from under the canvas he observed how the älfar went about picking up the dead and any survivors clinging to the pieces of the wrecked vessel. The injured they left. They only wanted the dead or the whole.

It reminded Rodario of a seal hunt he had once watched. As soon as one of the sailors surfaced to grab some air and they sensed he was injured, the iron point of a spear or whirr of an arrow brought instant death.

The älfar took their time and went about their task assiduously. The rowed past Rodario's hiding place, piercing it several times with their spears without touching him. The random piece of canvas was then ignored as it drifted nearer the shore.

A gong sounded and the boats returned to the shore. The älfar pulled them up to the caves and the island emitted more clouds of stinking gas. Then the shoreline dipped under the surface and the island started to dive.

"Ye gods, protect me," prayed Rodario fervently, before emerging from his hiding place, struggling out of the water and running for the dark entrance into which the älfar had just disappeared.

Girdlegard,
Kingdom of Idoslane,
One-time Orc Realm of Toboribor,
Early Summer, 6241st Solar Cycle

The spear-leader Hakulana observed the sparsely vegetated hillside in the midst of Idoslane's green landscape. It marked one of the many entrances to Toboribor's underground caves. She recognized the ruins of the old orc fortifications standing like ancient gravestones uneven against the sky.

"It looks quiet," she said to her companion Torant, an aspiring young equerry who rode at her side. She liked his calm nature and the care he took over any task assigned to him. "Did you find any tracks?"

"No, spear-leader. Nothing."

Hakulana watched the sky, where a summer storm was brewing. Dark clouds were gathering in front of the blue; her lance-pennant fluttered in the growing breeze.

Together with the twenty mounted scouts she led, they were now half a mile from the area to be traversed to reach the realm of the orc prince once known as Ushnotz.

Hakulana was too young to be able to remember the monster, but some of the veterans in Prince Mallen's army told tales of the creature and its voracious cruelty. It had attempted to move north to found a new kingdom after the lost battle of the Blacksaddle. It was thanks to the dwarves that this terrible plan had been thwarted.

Torant glanced up at the movement of the clouds. "Should we put up the tents, spear-leader?"

Hakulana shook her head. "No." She pointed to the hill with the tip of her lance. "We'll camp over there at the cave entrance; that will save us the trouble."

"As you command, spear-leader." Torant called out the order and the troop of riders made off at a smart pace.

Hakulana followed them at a slight distance, never taking her eyes off the hill whose defenses had been demolished by Prince Mallen's soldiers shortly after the battle of the Blacksaddle. There was no sign now of the orcs' reign or the ugly constructions of rough-hewn stone blocks that they'd forced their human serfs to build for them.

She was here with her scouts to make sure that it stayed that way. The slightest hint of any orc activity in the area they would report immediately and the army would march in. She had a feeling that there was something hiding in that hill.

As the first raindrops started to fall they rode through the broken walls, past the ruined gates, and into the darkness of the cave.

Her people, including the women, lit torches and set up camp. Each had a specific task to carry out, be it caring for the horses, preparing a meal or keeping guard.

"Spear-leader," Torant's voice echoed through the cave. "I found orc bones at the back there." He handed her an orc thigh bone. "It's not been there more than one cycle."

"You're sure about that?" Hakulana got out of the saddle and looked over at the cave mouth. The clouds were racing past low over the landscape, bellies against the hillsides; vast amounts of water cascaded down in front of the entrance in great streams, splattering onto the ground and carrying off the loose earth.

"Absolutely sure. There are lots of them."

A first lightning bolt hit the hill opposite; almost immediately the rolling peal of thunder sounded. The horses whinnied in fear. Hakulana heard their panicky steps as they pawed the ground.

"So we've got proof. I'd rather we hadn't." She turned to her troop. "It's a good thing we didn't put the tents up," she said to Torant. "Go and help the others calm the horses down, or they'll break away and trample everything. I'll go and inspect the place straightaway."

But then, in the dazzle of a second lightning bolt she saw the monster approaching the camp. Fleeting though the glimpse was, Hakulana was able to take in every terrible detail of its appearance.

It was huge, at least three and a half paces high and extremely broad. On its head a solid tionium helmet in the shape of a skull bore polished silver insignia arranged to increase the intimidating impression. The helmet had an opening for the mouth. The creature's lips had been removed so its fangs and incisors were visible in a permanent grin. The helmet itself had long spikes bolting metal and skull together.

Hakulana drew back and in her fear did not even realize she had left her shelter and was being soaked to the skin by the downpour. She could neither speak nor tear her eyes away.

The creature's body was covered with scale-like plates

of tionium, nailed or wired through its flesh. The forearms had been removed between elbow and wrist and
replaced by a metal pole that enclosed a core of shimmering glass. The hands were in the right place and wielded
two axes decorated with runes.

Another thunderclap sounded and the creature disappeared back into the dark, except for its huge eyes which
had been lit up dark green. But for those, Hakaluna might
have thought she had imagined it all.

"Palandiell, be with us" she mouthed, slowly regaining
the power of movement. "Retreat!" she screamed, drawing
her sword, "Everyone out of the cave, now!"

At once all the torches went out.

The unexpected pitch blackness, together with their
leader's surprise command, resulted in total confusion.
The horses were terrified by now and pulled themselves
free, racing out past Hakulana to her right and left.

Immediately there came the sound of dull impacts and
tearing metal, and the ugly noise of twisting limbs and
breaking bones. A shrill cry, hardly to be recognized as
issuing from a grown man, indicated the first death
amongst the soldier-scouts.

But for Hakulana this was only the beginning.

The lightning bolts came thick and fast as the thunderstorm reached its peak, allowing her a clear view of the
ghastly events in the cave. It was a vision of horrific
brutality. The monster was hacking men to pieces with its
axes; then it bit through the neck of one of her young
lieutenants and crushed another man's skull with a blow
from its foot. The resulting noise made Hakulana gag.

Her legs refused to let her re-enter the cave, however

her brain might command it, to stand by her troops. She remained in the rain, shaking all over, and watched her people die.

A shadow raced up to her out of the blackness. With a scream she stepped aside and dealt a wild blow. Too late she saw her mistake. She had slain Torant.

A deep slash in his throat, he fell at her feet in the mud. He turned his unbelieving gaze to his leader as he breathed his last.

"No," she whispered, taking two strides backwards, away from the accursed caves which housed evil. The dying breaths of the young man would haunt her for the rest of her days.

Two more soldiers stumbled out into the air; one was missing an arm and his comrade was bleeding profusely from a wound on the chest, though it looked possible he could survive it.

Now at last Hakulana shook off the paralyzing fear. She supported the less severely wounded man and left the amputee to his fate. The loss of blood would do for him and nothing could alter that.

"We must get away from here!" she shouted above the noise of the storm. "We have to report to the prince. There's nothing we can do against the monster."

"What was that thing?" whimpered the man, his legs collapsing under him.

She grabbed him under the arm and dragged him back down the hillside to where some of their horses still stood, having found shelter under a tree. "A new misbegotten monster of Tion's." She gasped. The man was heavy and she was bearing most of his weight and that of his armor.

Something hit him on the chest. Hakulana felt the force of the blow. At once he went limp. She stared at the long black shaft of an älfar arrow sticking out of his body.

When she looked up she saw the monster at the entrance to the cave. Right next to it there was a tall slim figure wearing fantastical black tionium armor in the style favored by the älfar. The head was concealed behind an elaborate helmet; two swords hung from its belt. It seemed almost like a monument, erected to remind people of the danger presented by the cruel race from Dsôn Balsur.

The figure notched a second arrow to its curved bow and aimed straight at Hakulana.

Dropping the corpse in her arms, the girl vaulted swiftly to one side, but felt a burning sensation in her left shoulder. She had been hit.

With a curse she broke the arrow's shaft, leaving the tip embedded in her arm for now. Keeping in the shelter of the ruins and rubble, she slid down to the nervous horses and tried to mount one.

Just as she managed to grab the mane to swing herself up onto its saddleless back, it collapsed in a heap, struck in the right eye by an arrow.

Showing great presence of mind, she quickly transferred herself to the next animal, clambering on it just before it raced off in terror. The next missile missed her by the breadth of a hand, but buried itself in the horse's neck, spurring it to double its speed.

Lightning struck all around. The troop leader had never experienced a worse storm. But in spite of the thunder she could hear something else. Rhythmical pounding. She looked back over her shoulder.

The monster was pursuing her! Pursuing her with huge strides and in all its terrifying ugliness, its lipless mouth gaping wide, and issuing loud snorts. Its boots left dents in the soft earth, from which water spurted up as it bounded along.

"Faster, faster," she urged her horse, forcing the arrow deeper into its flesh to spur it on.

The monster took aim with one of its axes and was about to hurl it at the fleeing girl when Hakulana received truly divine help.

The next lightning bolt shot down from the black clouds to meet the tip of the raised ax blade. All the rune signs on the armor and weapons flashed bright green. The eyes, too, behind the helmet mask, sent out a light brighter than that of any lantern.

The power of the lightning was too much even for a creature of Tion's. It crashed down at speed, dropping its weapons, to lie motionless on the ground, steam rising from it.

Hakulana did not fall into the error of stopping. She rode on through the storm to find the nearest garrison. If she did not reach the safety of its walls alive there would be no one to carry the news to Girdlegard of the unslayable she had seen.

IX

Rodario ran for all he was worth. The cave was long and narrow, and at the far end a path led steeply upwards to an iron gateway. The water was already lapping round his ankles, so he raced to reach the opening.

Realizing it was unlikely to open for him he rushed past and tried to find somewhere further up where he might get inside the mountain without being seen.

As the water mounted so did the fear that he might not survive this unexpected adventure. Finally, well hidden between the rocks he found an iron grating emitting foul gases. Before common sense could prevent him, he had opened the grating and forced himself inside, climbing up the chimney-like shaft.

Up and up, as if the flue would open at the very top of the mountain. The all-pervasive smell of rotten eggs made Rodario gag, cough and splutter, but, using hands and feet, he continued to work his way upwards, until finally he slipped through an opening into a large chamber.

Water was bubbling into a huge pool below him, filling more and more of the hollow space. If the iron door ten paces in front of him stayed shut he would be done for.

Rodario hurried to the door and prayed that no sentry would be standing guard. Pushing on the bolt, which miraculously moved in his hands, he found and turned a small wheel above it. It clicked several times in succession as he continued to turn it; then the door opened and he was able to escape to safety.

No one was expecting him, spear at the ready.

He found himself at the end of a twisting passage with rounded walls polished like marble. Moss glimmered and spread a faint brownish light.

Carefully he moved forwards, listening out for suspicious noises that might warn of a possible encounter with an älf. He remembered how silently Narmora, the partner of his friend Furgas, had moved. She was part älf. Presumably, then, he wouldn't notice an älf coming until after it had cut his throat.

Soon he found himself in front of a door similar to the last; this one was secured with several bolts and a wheellock. Rodario opened it a little way, halting when he felt heat from the other side, and heard noises—dull thuds at regular intervals: the stamp and hiss of machinery, the clunk of forge hammers, the sounds of workmen calling to each other. The air smelled of hot metal, of slack, of coal fire and of oil. Going by his ears and nostrils alone he would have said he was in a forge in the fifthling realm.

To avoid immediate discovery, he crouched down on all fours, pulled the door open and crawled inside. Underneath him was an iron platform attached to a metal ladder.

Rodario's heart stood still. On the ladder were two älfar! They wore black armor, held spears in their hands and were looking down.

"That was worth the wait," said the blond one. "A

nice fat sailing boat with lots of crew and passengers to set to work for the master."

"Then we can stop work at last," laughed his friend, scratching his ear; the tip had come away in his hand. "Oh, damn, the resin's gone soft again. Wretched heat!"

Rodario had already started to wonder why the älfar were talking in human language. Now he understood. They were acting. These "älfar" were just men, dressed up as älfar; they gained their height from special shoes they were wearing. The disguise might have deceived a simple peasant or a fisherman, but not him.

"It's a shame we had to kill so many of the injured," said the blond one, helping the other to mend his ear.

"Looking after them just takes too much time." He laughed. "And the prisoners enjoyed the goulash."

Rodario peered over the edge of the platform. Below was a workshop two hundred paces in size, with machine floors on several levels. Forges had been set up in niches in the rock face, and platforms like the one he was on had been fastened together and fixed into the stone with strengthening beams. These too served as smithies.

Humans, chained hand and foot, were working to produce various metal shapes, including wheels and iron rods. Each worker had a set number of repeated movements to carry out, and finished items were thrown into the wire cages that travelled up and down at speed on a chain. At the bottom of the workstation these were unloaded and carried out by yet more prisoners.

Several machines were as big as a house, moving by means of cog wheels, pulleys and pistons, with belts and chains traveling over the cogs toward other devices that they powered. In places, some of the belts passed through the walls to other chambers.

The machines emitted hissing clouds of steam. People ran around, shoveling coal or pouring water into huge containers for the boilers. The noise close to them must have been unbearable.

Rodario had no idea what was going on. But this island had nothing to do with älfar, that much was clear. It was what the inhabitants of Weyurn were expected to believe, however, meaning that they would stay away at all costs and never talk about it. The best form of concealment.

Feet came stomping up the stairway. "Hey, you two! You're supposed to be standing guard, not playing with your ears!" Next to the men there appeared a dark-haired dwarf in leather breeches, boots and a leather apron. His naked torso, decorated with tattoos, shone with sweat. In his hand he swung a smith's hammer as if it were made of tin and balsa wood.

From his voice Rodario recognized him as the man who had attacked him outside his caravan. He was sure now that the barge he'd been following had not broken up on the island, but it had disappeared inside it. The island must have sunk down again causing Rodario's nutshell-boat to capsize.

"It's the heat, Master Bandilor," protested the one who'd been told off. "It makes the resin go soft."

"Then sew it on properly," growled the dwarf. "I don't want to see this sort of thing again, you fingering each other's ears, right? If one of the prisoners sees it, the masquerade is over." He turned his head and Rodario saw the thick beard, dyed blood red. "Did either of you leave that bulkhead open?"

"No," said the blond one. "I've no desire to burn up."

Bandilor's eyebrows crinkled. "Did Mistress Veltaga come past you on her way to check the second chamber?" He walked past them, his hammer held at the ready.

"No, Master Bandilor. Nobody."

From what he had heard and seen Rodario worked out that he had found a secret headquarters of the thirdlings. No one would ever think of dwarves voluntarily living on an island, let alone one that could sink down to the bottom of Weyurn's lake. And their captives had no chance to escape.

To Rodario's horror, Bandilor started up the steps. No matter where he looked, he could see no way to avoid being seen. He got half upright, ready to crawl back into the passage, but Bandilor spotted him.

"Unbelievable! It's that crummy actor, isn't it?" The dwarf took a step forward and made to grab him by the leg.

Rodario launched himself off the platform, holding fast to its edge so that he could do a forward roll. His lower body swung freely over the abyss, but he landed with his feet on the solid iron steps, quite near to the two false älfar. He opened his fingers, his heart beating wildly.

"More respect, please, for my art," he called up to the dwarf, who had flung his hammer at him in fury, but missed. The metal tool clunked down the stairs into the depths.

The guards lowered their spears and attacked.

"Forgive me, I don't feel like fighting you." Rodario

certainly was not going to involve himself in combat. Without a second's hesitation he leaped into a passing wire basket and let himself be carried down in it. "I'm looking for a happy ending!" he called, waving up. "We'll meet again, Master Bandilor. And I'll be back with an armada of Weyurn's warships."

He went past the astonished prisoners, who were not daring to move a muscle. They didn't help him, or join him. Their fear of the älfar and the punishment they could expect should they do so held them back. He couldn't hold it against them. After all, he had no idea whether it was possible to escape.

A spear missed him narrowly and got stuck in the grating. "Thank you for the weapon, älf," he called, only to see a second missile on its way. This missed him, too, the angle for the throw being a difficult one, but now archers were dispersing round the upper galleries; they would have no trouble hitting him.

Rodario jumped up out of the cage at an intersecting passage and ran through the corridor bent double. Somewhere in the middle of the mountain he suspected he would find his friend Furgas, held in chains. Tungdil and all the rulers had underestimated the malice of the thirdlings. Perhaps he could find out what their intentions were. They had to be doing more than simply forging strange devices. They would surely have a grand plan.

He arrived in a second cavern, which was somewhat smaller than the first but similar in its arrangement. Here it was hotter still, because of the many furnaces at work on the platforms, with molten metal streaming out of them.

There was a dwarf-woman standing among the workers on the cavern floor. She was issuing instructions while sparks flew about her. Close by, white-hot metal was just being released; molten streams of alloy ran along the sand channels to the molds, where they would cool into shape.

That was all Rodario could see. He reached a door and found himself in one of the twisting polished stone corridors again, worming its way through the center of the mountain.

He met another guard keeping watch at one of the side doors, a false älf who attacked him with a ridiculous hiss.

"No grasp of character or motivation, but you want to be center stage," laughed Rodario critically. He wasn't afraid of a human in disguise. If it had been a real älf his reaction would have been different, no doubt. As it was, he could rely on considerable experience in fighting, even if he were a trifle rusty.

He walloped the guard's spear aside and thrust the blunt end of his own weapon into his assailant's groin, making him fall back in agony, "The älfar, you know, don't hiss when they attack. Get it right next time. They are as silent as the night and as deadly as . . ." He searched for an appropriate simile. " . . . as . . . Oh what the hell." He hit the man on the forehead with the blade of his spear and sent him unconscious to the floor of the passage.

"If you were standing guard in front of a door, there's probably something valuable on the other side," he addressed the man lying on the ground. He put one hand on the handle. "Let's have a look."

He pushed the handle down and rammed his shoulder against the wood, whirling into the room.

Clothes were strewn all over the place, the air was stuffy, smelling of stale food and there were papers everywhere, covering any flat surface and stuck up on the walls, each bearing sketches of eccentric-looking machines and strange apparatus.

Furgas was sitting on the bed, his legs crossed. His gray-green eyes stared straight through his old friend. He looked neglected, with a long beard, filthy clothes, and badly matted hair that reached down to his chest.

"Furgas! My dear Furgas!" called Rodario, hurrying over to him. "It's me, the Incredible One." He shook him by the shoulder, keeping on eye out for any more älfar approaching. "Get up. On your feet. This is the dramatic escape scene where the hero gets away and finally vanquishes evil forever. Well, that would be neat, anyway." He dragged the lethargic figure of his friend to his feet. "Come on, we're getting out of here."

Furgas followed him like a reluctant child. "Rodario? What are you doing here? How did you find the island?" he murmured in a daze.

"It's a long story," Rodario answered as they stepped out into the corridor. "Prologue, then three or four acts, I reckon. It's got the makings of a terrific series. Any idea how we get out of here?"

Furgas started to come round. "Depends whether we've dived yet."

"Yes, we have." The smell from Furgas took Rodario's breath away. Sixty orbits without a bath was the minimum he must have had to produce body odor like that.

"Then there is no way out."

"Furgas! Pull yourself together." Rodario stared intently

into his friend's eyes. "If I managed to get onto this damned island, we will find a way to get off it."

"But there are guards everywhere . . ."

"Nôd'onn had orcs everywhere, the avatars had soldiers," he retorted, playing down the dangers. "We beat them. It is our duty to return to Tungdil and the others to tell them about the thirdlings. Come along, for goodness' sake!"

Now Furgas looked at him properly. "Rodario," he smiled. "The Incredible Rodario. You've earned your name again." He pointed to the left. "And you're right. There's a shaft that the hover-gas goes out through. We could escape through there and swim up to the surface. If we survive."

"Are you sure?"

Furgas grinned at him, showing corn-yellow teeth that had not received any attention from a cleaning-root for a very long time. "I built the island. I should know its weaknesses."

The door on their right flew open and five älfar stormed in; two of them carried bows. Bandilor pushed his way to the front with a two-handed ax at the ready.

"There he is, the play-actor," he roared.

"Threaten me," whispered Furgas to his friend, standing in front of him. "I'm too valuable to them—they won't hurt me."

Rodario couldn't come up with a better solution, so he broke a spear from the wall in half and pushed the blade against his friend's throat. "Get back, you rejects from a third-rate theater," he called with disdain. "If you try and follow us I'll kill him and you'll have no one who can work your accursed island."

And Bandilor actually stopped in his tracks. "Halt," he ordered the guards. "We'll get them later."

"Get the island back up to the surface," demanded Rodario.

But the thirdling shook his head. "We can't do that. We'd have to collect enough hover-gas again. The ballast chambers are full." He grinned maliciously. "You'll have to give up."

"We'll do it the way I said," Furgas mouthed to Rodario and started to walk backwards. "Through the bulkhead door, then we'll bolt it from inside and disappear."

It seemed like a mile to Rodario before they reached the opening. At last they got through to the next passage, closing the heavy iron door behind them and wedging the catch shut.

Furgas took the lead and steered them through the narrow tubes, climbing natural and artificial ladders until he forced himself through an opening. There he waited and held out his hand to Rodario. "Thank you for never giving up on me," he said, emotion in his voice. "Without you I'd never have had the courage to escape. I'd lost the spirit ages ago."

"What are friends for?" beamed Rodario. "And between ourselves, you're the best props man any theater could have. The *Curiosum* can't function without you." He stepped into the shaft. "After you."

Furgas moved aside. "No, you first. I've forgotten to release the flood-hatch safety mechanism."

He crawled out again while Rodario started the ascent. It was quite a while before Furgas followed—but it was less of an effort for him to do so. Rodario was horrified to see how water rushed up in the tube, with Furgas on top, bobbing like a cork.

"There we are, that's the easy way," he said, spluttering proudly.

"Do you want to drown us?" Rodario exclaimed.

"No." Furgas pointed up. "I can't open the hatch until the passage is flooded. Otherwise the body of water surging in would hurl us back down again." He smiled at the actor. "You still have no idea about technical matters, do you?"

"I always had you for the technical stuff," laughed the showman, high on excitement. He was about to do the impossible: he had found his friend and was going to rescue him. "What are the thirdlings up to here?"

"They're making machines. Death machines." Furgas's countenance grew dark. "Tell you later, Rodario. We need to save our breath."

They reached the hatch, and as soon as the rest of the cavity was full of water, Furgas opened it to make the connection between the shaft and the waters of the lake.

Far above them the sunlight glittered with promise. They struggled to the surface with vigorous arm movements, but it was a tortuously slow process.

Rodario was running out of air. He took a breath against his will and swallowed water, but at that moment broke through above the waves and paddled around, coughing his lungs free. Furgas was also coughing up water. When they had got their breath back they looked around.

They were drifting in the middle of Weyurn's lake and there was no sight of land.

"Some great escape that was," Rodario said, blinking at the sun. He reckoned the island would shoot up next to them at any moment. But then to his relief he remembered what Bandilor had said: even if they wanted to, they couldn't surface. Not yet.

"Well, we won't die of thirst. There's plenty to drink."

"The gods are with us." Furgas pointed over to the horizon. "There's a boat!" He lifted his arms to wave, shouting and calling to get their attention. Rodario helped out to the best of his ability and soon the barge was heading over their way.

They were heaved on board and after Rodario told the mariners the story of Nightmare Island and how the sloop had foundered, the terrified captain steered an urgent course to Mifurdania, all sails set.

The two friends sat on deck exhausted, wrapped in the blankets the sailors had supplied.

"There's a lot to tell," said Furgas, his face serious. "I pray to Vraccas that the dwarf tribes can forgive me for my part in what has happened to them."

"You? What do you mean . . . ?"

He lowered his head. "Bandilor forced me to make vehicles. Vehicles to be run on the tunnel rails to bring death and destruction to the dwarf realms." He wiped the water from his face and Rodario wasn't sure whether there were tears there, too. "He's planning something worse than that. The apparatus is ready," he said quietly. "It will cost the lives of hundreds of dwarves."

Rodario slapped him on the shoulder. "Only if we can't prevent it, my friend. And we shall prevent it." He smiled. "This diving, by the way, has one big advantage—apart from freedom, of course. Do you know what?" His smile became a wide grin. "You don't stink anymore."

Girdlegard,
Kingdom of Idoslane,
Former Orc Territory of Toboribor
Early Summer, 6241st Solar Cycle

"Do you know what torture it is to live without your voice?"

This quiet sentence, spoken in the deepest mourning and despair, floated up to the roof of the cave, shattered against the rock and drifted back down again to the sintoì. He was wearing close-fitting clothing in black silk embroidered in dark green and was kneeling in front of a simple bed on which a sleeping female sintoì rested. A cloak the color of night lay over his shoulders; he held her pale left hand in his own, gloved in black velvet. The sintoì herself was similarly dressed.

"I see your wonderful face, I can touch your black hair and I cannot believe what has happened to us. Not even after five long cycles." His graceful features, which would have entranced any human, grew dark. None was more beautiful than he. Apart, that is, from his sister, his beloved sister Nagsar Inàste.

"Inàste and Samusin have deserted us, dear sister. We are our own gods." The deep-shadowed eye sockets turned disdainfully toward the rough-hewn ceiling of their meager accommodation. Nothing was properly finished, not even the walls. Those wretched orcs were good for nothing.

"This was never a place for us. Forgive me for having brought you here. It was not what I intended, but I had been too unwell." He touched her forehead with his right hand and adjusted her hair. Even in this condition her beauty was greater than that of any elf. Weak creatures might expire at the mere sight of her, strong ones lose their wits. "When you wake, we will go to the Outer Lands and seek ourselves a new realm. Dsôn Balsur will be small and insignificant in comparison." He smiled at her, and even the rock face seemed to admire the creature.

"Do you remember? I promised you I would find you a new home. It is now ready." Carefully he lifted her up and carried her through the dark passageways of the empty orc realm. He was slim but anything but weak. A thousand opponents had lost their lives through that misconception. "I will show you."

The unslayable one did not make the slightest of sounds as he walked; only his mantle rustled quietly as it brushed the stone. "You will like it, my sister. It is the only room in this plagued earth that I can ask you to endure in the coming orbits while you lie thus unwaking." He walked past countless gallery openings but knew exactly where he was heading.

His path ended at the transept of a vaulted cave that he had prepared for her. The air was cool and pure and no longer heavy with heat and the foul smell of orcs. "We are here," he said, softly.

The cavern measured fifty by fifty paces, and its highest point was forty paces up. From there a mighty dark stalactite hung, as if it were the tip of a titanic sword that some giant had rammed into the mountain. Its sharp end pointed to an altar of black basalt at the top of four steps. Älfar runes decorated it, and they told of the immortal beauty of Nagsar Inàste.

"I have polished the walls so that the paint holds better," he said to the sleeper, as he studied the elaborate paintings rising all the way up to the stalactite. They showed Dsôn as it had been before the fire, in all its glory and crowned with a tower made of ivory. The capital of their realm might have been lost, but it lived on in pictorial form on these walls.

The unslayable one went up to the altar and strode over the countless crushed skeletons of orcs covering the floor. The bones hardly moved under the soles of his feet, but gave off wooden-sounding clicks.

"Do you hear, sister? I killed them all. Their inferior blood I used to paint the walls. They have paid for what they did to you," he said to her. "I wish I had awakened earlier from my sleep to prevent the outrage they perpetrated on you." He mounted the steps to the altar, and laid her carefully on it. With loving gestures he folded her hands in her lap, adjusted her dress and moved to her feet. "I will never forgive myself that they touched you and defiled your body," he whispered, making a deep bow before her, and planting a kiss on the tips of her boots.

As always, not the slightest reaction showed on her countenance. There was not even a hint that she might be able to hear his words.

"It won't be long now, beloved sister," promised the unslayable. "I have shown myself to the humans. They will send their warriors here as I have planned. That gives us at last the opportunity to regain the diamond with which I can bring you back to life. For I know where they are going to take the remaining stones." He laid his hands on her ankles. "Patience, Nagsar Inàste. What are a few more orbits for such as us, who have seen a thousand cycles come and go?"

Her face remained still.

"You want to know what has happened to the dregs of deformity that crawled out of your body?" He withdrew his hands and placed them on the hilts of his swords. "They serve us well. But I shall kill them so that nothing remains to remind us of your shame. Only our own true son may live." His features produced a smile. "He is perfect, beloved sister. The purest blood and, thanks to the magic source, he has greater strength than any previous sintoìt before him. Your eyes will find pleasure in him. You may be proud of what issued at last from our union. He appeared at the right time." Again he kissed her feet, bowed and moved next to her to stroke her hand. "I shall leave you now. But do not worry. I shall return soon. With the diamond."

The unslayable one went down the altar steps backwards, then turned and left the cool cave.

He had not wanted to say that he had doubts, that their true son had turned against him . . . and that he was still very weak.

I need that accursed stone. What took away my power shall restore it. He clenched his fists. *Eternal damnation to the eoîl.*

It was the eoîl who had thwarted the magic charm that was intended to save him and his sister from destruction.

He remembered.

He remembered everything.

He remembered how he had hung imprisoned in suspended animation, remembered the physical paralysis, the work of immense effort on the magic journey and the effect of the eoîl's interference.

Never before had he applied such a powerful spell or undertaken such a great risk. He and his sister had been protected from destruction in the caves but the price had been high.

He had been hurled into an abyss, separated from his sister and immobilized. His mind, however, had been constantly at work trying to work out where he was.

When evil orc fumes reached his nose he had started to realize that some of these low creatures had survived the unspeakable blast of light.

Captive in the remote tunnels, he remembered the warning lines in the old writings of his kingdom Dsôn, which had spoken of the eoîl.

The eternal eoîl. Apart from immortality and mutual hatred there was nothing to connect him to the age-old elf woman. The writings told only of the incredible power which the eoîl was able to harness. And how to make it your own.

He needed this power urgently and thanks to those writings he knew the formula for acquiring it. When he had first heard of the avatars, he had sought out the verses, and learned them by heart, making them as much a part of himself as was with his love of Nagsar Inàste. The verses meant sovereignty and signified victory over the elves and their allies.

He could not have known what the eoîl was intending to do in Porista. They had almost managed to avert it— but the eoîl was too strong and had nearly annihilated him.

So he lay and waited until his body belonged to him, cycle after cycle he waited. He could do nothing.

Eventually the feeling had returned to his limbs and he had risen up. Furious and mad with concern about Nagsar he had searched all the passages until he found her.

She was lying half covered with a dirty cloth on a shabby table standing away from the wall; someone had placed a second cloth over her face to hide her terrible beauty. Her thighs had been forced wide apart and bruises and bloody marks betrayed the shameful acts wrought upon her.

Eight orcs had been sitting nearby playing cards and did not notice him. The orc with the winning hand had stood up to the jeers and complaints of the other players. His hand was at the buckle of his belt as he made his way to the table where Nagsar Inàste lay . . .

The unslayable one stopped in his tracks as he recalled the moment. Memories of that sight of his humiliated sister overcame him and forced him to seek support from the wall.

The first eight orcs he had killed more quickly than an arrow singing from the bow to its target. Then he had continued the carnage until the last of the beasts lay destroyed at his feet; dark green blood had flowed like water.

The countless acts of violation committed by the orcs against his sister in past cycles had left five hideous fruits. When he discovered the bastards in a neighboring cave he had nearly beheaded them all, but then a groundling had appeared and suggested a pact. A good pact, which he had agreed to. The creatures could be made use of, though he would not spare them once they had fulfilled their role.

The unslayable one struggled for breath and forced himself to walk on. He entered the chamber where his armor was kept. Piece by piece he took it down off the stand and put it on. His thoughts moved to his son, a pure-bred sintoìt.

In order to show his paralyzed sister that he was with her once more he had made love to her devotedly after he had killed the orcs, giving her the kind of pain and passion that a sintoì desires. To compensate for the five ugly beings that had crawled out of her body, she had then borne him a son. Hundreds of cycles they had waited for such a one, and finally in the midst of all this horror the longed-for event had occurred.

But on returning from the magic wellspring, disappointment had followed. The son had turned against him; he did not understand his task and refused to take it on. *I hope I can change his mind. Nagsar Inàste must not be disappointed in him.* He tightened the final chain; his armor was ready.

Now he would have to be watchful and guard the entrances. The scout girl that had escaped would bring the army. But until he had completed his preparations, no soldier should enter the depths of Toboribor. Not until the helpless Nagsar Inàste had opened her eyes.

He drew his swords out of their sheaths, studying them in the lamplight. He was pleased to see how immaculate the blades were. In spite of the intense use they had been put to they showed neither scratches nor notches.

It doesn't matter to them whether they slice through

tough flesh or thick iron, he thought, and gave a vicious smile thinking back to the orcs he had slaughtered. He had sprung among them, his swords taking three or four lives with one swipe, while they had writhed and yelled. *They are simply too slow; they cannot stand up to risen gods. I have never understood why the humans fear them.*

Those three hundred orcs had been the beginning.

He put the swords back again in their sheaths. *Only serve me as you have done, my good friends. Let us bring such fear to the humans that they are too dazzled to see our true intentions.*

The unslayable one fastened his long black hair back under a black cloth and put his helmet on his head. The beauty of his face, not to be revealed to any other than Nagsar Inàste, disappeared behind the visor.

It would be wasted on others.

Girdlegard,
The north of the Kingdom of Gauragar,
Summer, 6241st Solar Cycle

Even at the beginning now of the cycle's best season, Girdlegard was wreathed in a sense of depression. Although Nature was at its most bountiful, the sun warm, the first harvests in and delicious fruits ripening, promising variety for jaded palates, it was not enough to lighten the mood.

In the interim, the human kingdoms had learned of uncanny and terrible events. The rumors did not merely furnish descriptions of the monsters. Each tale spoke of threats and dangers, made greater by a hundredfold every time it was retold.

"Have you heard? Now it's said they can fly, become invisible or transform themselves into a mountain." Goda rode along a little ahead and to the side of Ireheart and Tungdil. Behind them there followed a troop of dwarf warriors, male and female; they were escorting the diamond from the Gray Range to Immengau. They had ten small armored wagons with them and in each was a newly made imitation of the diamond they were taking to Paland.

It had been Tungdil's idea to increase the number of stones in the hope of complicating things for would-be thieves, be they undergroundlings, pink-eyed orcs, monsters or the immortal unslayables. The fourthlings were busy producing yet more copies.

"You forgot to add that one glance is enough to kill a grown man and that they spit fire," sighed Tungdil. They heard these stories everywhere. The latest rumor of the return of an unslayable sovereign, one of the mightiest of the älfar, had brought deep and widespread fear. "I can understand the long-uns being worried," he mused. "If one of the immortal alfar has managed to survive the effect of the Star of Judgment, then I would think, if I were a human, that maybe more of them survived."

"That was rumor number seventy-three," said Goda flatly. "There's an army collecting in Toboribor ready to send out raiding parties."

Ireheart turned to her in surprise. "You're really keeping score?"

She grinned. "Of course. It's helpful to see how quickly

a handful of enemies can become an undefeatable army. The monsters got bigger, more terrible and impossible to vanquish, as we moved through the villages. We didn't beat that thing in the vaults but we could have done."

Tungdil looked back at their troop. All was in order.

"And in the last town there were the first rumors of a powerful artifact in Paland." Goda looked at Tungdil. "People have noticed that soldiers from all the different kingdoms are gathering in the old fortress."

"But no dwarves," muttered Ireheart.

Tungdil knew that this fact, widely known, was fomenting talk about quarrels between dwarves and elves, dwarves and humans, the high king of the dwarves and the kings of the human realms.

"Have you heard number seventy-four?" Goda loved being able to tease her master with news. "These monsters can steal a maidenhead with a single word."

"If I have to listen to this nonsense a moment longer I shall put wax in my ears," said Boïndil bad-temperedly. "You'd almost think people prefer the bad news to the good."

"You may be right there," nodded Goda. "It is a thing the humans do, seeing the bad side rather than praising the good."

"They aren't all like that." Tungdil softened the reproof, knowing that what the dwarf-girl was saying was largely true. He found it worrying since she had only recently come into contact much with humans. "We can hardly tell them the truth, can we? We're lucky the ordinary folk have no idea what the monsters are really after. The secret of the diamond's power has been kept so far."

"Yes, you're right again there." Boïndil slipped from the saddle, preferring to walk beside his small horse. His buttocks were too sore. "I'll never really get used to this way of traveling. It may be quicker, but your bottom gets as broad as the pony you ride on."

Without saying a word Goda also dismounted. She was persevering with Ireheart's instructions, and was capable now of physical feats that surprised both of the dwarves.

If Tungdil were not mistaken there had been a slight change in his friend's attitude toward the girl: he looked at her more often than before, and did so not with the eyes of a master observing an apprentice but with the eyes of dwarf attracted to dwarf-woman. Like now.

"Does she please you?" he asked with a smile.

"What?" Boïndil jerked upright and even blushed a little. He immediately turned his gaze to the road.

"In the progress she's making?" said Tungdil, making the question more objective.

"Oh yes, of course," answered Boïndil in relief. He looked at his friend. "But that's not what you meant, is it?"

Tungdil only grinned and pointed to the wood on their left. It had to be the easternmost point of Âlandur, or at least it was composed of the same trees that grew in the elf groves. "It's time for a break."

He had the troop stop in the cool shade and rest a while. Even if the children of the Smith regularly did guard duty on the surface, a long march such as this was unusual for most of them.

Ireheart left Goda to keep watch. When they had moved away from her, he took up the thread once more. "You are right, Scholar," he sighed. "It makes me happy to see her. And I am dreading the day when she leaves."

"You will have her with you for a long time yet. It will take cycles for a good warrior-girl to be trained." Tungdil winked, but then he grew serious. "You've really fallen for her."

Boïndil sat down, one hand on his weapon. "It's crazy, isn't it? My heart is on fire. It was her that re-awoke my lust for fighting. And I know that it can't go anywhere. I killed a relative of hers. Goda will never see me any other way. She will hate me. I can sense it, even though she hides her true feelings."

Tungdil thought back to the conversation with Balyndis. He did not tell his friend that Goda had originally arrived with the intention of killing him. Now would not be a good time to tell him that. Instead he said, "I wouldn't be so sure."

"Oh, do you think she *likes* me? After I murdered her grandma?"

"You'll have to find out."

"Do you know how long it's been since I courted a dwarf-girl, Scholar?" Ireheart gave a helpless sigh.

"Somebody told me that you have to rub them with their favorite cheese and then spin them round four times to win their heart," laughed Tungdil, citing the not entirely serious advice the twin-dwarf had once given him. "But really—just be yourself." Those had been Boëndal's words of wisdom. "She's a thirdling. She has no clan, no family. That should make it easier for you. You don't have to impress or convince anybody else."

He thought back ruefully to when he had first spoken

to the father of Balyndis. He had been rejected out of hand, but in the end she had remained resolute and had left husband and clan for his sake and for their love. Now the bond between them was breaking, and the recriminations that he leveled at himself could not be dismissed. He felt he had betrayed her, but knew they could no longer live as man and wife.

"Oh, Vraccas," said Ireheart despairingly. "It's all too much. An honest fight and you know where you are. But this love stuff . . . it's complicated."

Tungdil did not envy his friend's state of mind and hoped that things would work out for him. "Stick with it and wait for the right moment." He clapped him on the shoulder. "And whatever you do, don't listen to what others in your clan have to say about it."

Ireheart grinned. "Oh, I have no reputation left to lose. You forget—I'm a friend of yours, Scholar."

A rider was approaching them from the south. At first, given the rider's size, they took it to be a child on horseback but they soon saw they were mistaken. Dark clothing, a scarf round the head, full saddlebags clanking.

"The executioner again?" Boïndil was surprised. "Can't just be coincidence."

"It won't be coincidence."

"Then send him packing if he tries to join us here. I don't trust him."

"Wait and see."

Bramdal pulled up his horse where Tungdil and Boïndil were resting. "Greetings," he laughed down at them. "Mind if I join you for a breather?"

"So, have you finished your business in Porista?" To

Boïndil's surprise, Tungdil gestured for him to sit with them. "We've got some tea if you want."

"Great." Bramdal reached behind and pulled out a kind of rope ladder. He stepped onto it out of the stirrup, and from there down onto the grass. "Neat, eh?" he grinned. "I thought, why should a dwarf go slowly on a pony when he can go fast on a horse? So I came up with this contraption and got the saddle made."

Ireheart shook his head and looked up. The executioner had chosen a particularly tall mount. "You won't get me up on one of those."

"But there's a very good view." Bramdal followed Tungdil over to where the tea was brewing. "Thanks."

"Don't mention it. What brings you to the north?" asked Tungdil.

"I'm heading back to Hillchester." Bramdal blew gently on his hot tea. "King Bruron wants me to start a school."

"For executioners, I assume."

"Absolutely. He didn't want it to be in Porista, for fear of tarnishing his new capital city's reputation," grinned the dwarf. "Although I only carry out the letter of the law. Odd, isn't it? The humans set the death penalty and then want nothing to do with it."

Tungdil smiled. "We didn't come across each other in Porista."

"No, I'll have been too busy." Bramdal winked. "You don't believe me. What do you think then? That I'm a spy for the dwarf-haters?"

"Yes," Ireheart jumped in, his hands on the crow's beak handle.

Bramdal laughed out loud, sounding genuinely amused.

His gaze went past the warrior over to Goda, and his curiosity was aroused. "A fine-looking dwarf-girl. She looks nice and strong. I bet she wields her weapon with a strong hand. Excellent material for an executioner."

"Leave her alone," was Boïndil's immediate response. "She is *my* pupil," he added quickly. "If she's going to be doing any beheading then it'll be orc heads that roll." He was getting hot and bothered, the blood surging in his ears. Was it jealousy?

"I understand. Your *pupil*," said Bramdal with a grin, leaving his true meaning unspoken. He sipped his tea. "I was talking to Gordislan Hammerfist in Porista. He's worried about Trovegold: it's been attacked."

Tungdil let out his breath. "Thirdling machines?"

"No, it was sabotage." Bramdal looked serious. "The sluice on the dam was jammed full open and a third of Trovegold left under water. The townspeople eventually managed to repair the damaged sluice, otherwise even more of the freelings would have drowned."

"How many were lost?" Ireheart wanted to know.

"Two hundred and eleven. More than thirty houses will have to be rebuilt." He lowered his eyes despondently. "No, it wasn't the dwarf-haters' machines; they can't reach us through the cave network. They're using other methods of attack." He poured himself some more tea. "The worst thing is there's no one to actually blame. The guards out at the sluice were all killed. Nobody saw the murderers."

"That's terrible." Tungdil was moved.

"The flood means Trovegold is a hotbed of suspicion now. There are accusations it was the clan-dwarves and not the thirdlings at all. They think wealth is causing envy amongst the dwarf folks—they all want our vraccasium and gold. One of the dwarves in the fourthling clan assembly is supposed to have said we were trying to curry favor with Vraccas with all these sacrifices and donations, and that it's unfair and has got to be stopped. Others suggested the leaders want to force the dwarves back into the dwarf realms again." Bramdal was silent, waiting for a reaction.

"Rubbish," thundered Ireheart. "The mountains have enough gold to fill that town's entire cave. Why would the secondlings or whoever want the outcasts' gold?"

Tungdil leaned back against a tree, closing his eyes. "Soon the thirdlings will be getting the blame whenever anything happens. Suspicion will be rampant and no one will trust anyone anymore. That's just what the dwarf-haters wanted, of course." He looked up. "Bramdal, wherever you hear talk like that, tell them to pay no attention. The more discord there is, the quicker the dwarf-haters will have achieved their goal."

The executioner nodded. "That's what Gordislan Hammerfist said. I'm sure you know how hard it is to put such rumors down." He placed his empty cup on the grass. "I'll be off. Perhaps we'll meet again. If we do, you mustn't think straightaway I'm one of the bad ones," he said to Ireheart. He got up and climbed onto his horse again. With his boot he fished for the patent ladder, pulling it up behind him. "May Vraccas bless you." He lifted his hand in farewell and rode off.

Tungdil and Boïndil watched him go. "Do you know what gets me?" Tungdil asked his friend. "He never wanted to know what we've got in the wagons."

"I was right. He's definitely a spy." Boïndil stood determined, hands on his hips.

Tungdil smiled. "Because he fancied Goda?"

"No," said the twin. "Well, yes, because of that, too." He sighed.

"Master! Tungdil!" called Goda. "Over here! I've found something!"

"Perhaps it's your heart?" Tungdil teased Ireheart, who jabbed him in the ribs.

"Let's hear no more of this sentimental nonsense," he growled, getting up and running over. Tungdil followed him. It was still strange to see his friend without his long black braided plait.

Goda was kneeling by a bush, and she pushed the branches apart when the two dwarves came over. "Look!"

Amongst the foliage and purple flowers elf features were visible. The elf lay as if dead, with eyes closed and a few withered leaves on his face.

There were three arrows sticking out from the elf's chest. The arrows had penetrated the leather armor and earth-colored clothing under it. Judging by the splendor of the finely embroidered garments this must be a high-status elf. The fact he wore only a limited amount of armor suggested he had been hunting. His camp was probably not be far away.

"He's breathing!" said Ireheart, astonished, as he saw the chest move almost imperceptibly. "Well, these pointy . . . I mean, these elves, are tougher than they look!"

"Give me a hand." Tungdil was sitting the injured elf up carefully so he could inspect the arrows. Two broke off, the third was still in the body. "By Vraccas! Those are elf arrows!"

"If it were *one* arrow, I'd think it was an accident," said Ireheart. He studied the elf's bloodstained back. "But with three I'd say it's out of the question. Unless they choose to hunt their own kind."

"Why would elves be killing each other?" Tungdil looked at the face. "Or perhaps we should be asking, why did they want to kill *him*?"

"The arrows could be a trick—forgeries," suggested Goda. "The thirdlings, perhaps?"

"No. They'd have used crossbows to put the blame on us. And they'd have dragged the body somewhere more public. And they wouldn't have left the poor devil alive," replied Tungdil. "No. This elf has been shot by his own kind. Either they've left him for dead, or he ran away and they lost him."

Boïndil regarded their unusual find. "What shall we do with him? Those wounds are deep. He's not going to last long."

Tungdil glanced at the wagons. "We'll take him with us. If the elves wanted him dead, I want to know the reason." He couldn't remember reading about any internal strife in Âlandur, but the strange conduct of the elf delegates, their secret message in invisible ink, the stone, those new buildings that had been kept hidden—they could all have some connection to this injured elf.

Perhaps it was a question of a personal vendetta or a high-ranking criminal who'd been challenged and pursued. No one knew how the elf folk managed their own affairs in the forests and groves. Anything was possible.

"Let's make sure he stays alive and can open his eyes soon." Tungdil called some of the other soldiers over so they could help carry the elf. They put him in one of the wagons, cushioning him on furs and skins. One of their healers saw to his wounds.

Tungdil gave the troop the order to move on. He wanted to make good use of the rest of the orbit's sunlight to get as far as possible away from Âlandur's borders. It was not forbidden to transport injured elves in wagons, but it wasn't the normal thing for a dwarf to be doing. If the worst came to the worst the dwarves might be accused of kidnapping.

So the troop trundled off toward the south with what now was a doubly sensitive cargo.

Whether he wanted to or not, Ireheart had to get back in the saddle again. Otherwise he'd be slowing everyone down. And as Goda did not seem to mind riding, he kept quiet himself. It would not make a good impression for the master to be making a fuss if the pupil was not complaining.

"Who was the dwarf you were talking to?" she enquired.

"No one you need to know about," Ireheart replied rudely.

Goda raised her eyebrows. "A child of the Smith, riding on a full-size horse—unusual."

"He's not unusual. He's an executioner." Boïndil was unsettled by her curiosity. "He kills criminals for the long-uns. For money."

"Is his name Bramdal Masterstroke?" she asked excitedly.

Ireheart growled, "Yes. Why?"

"I've heard a lot about him. He fought at Blacksaddle and in Porista, they say. He killed ninety orcs all by himself. And a hundred avatars," she enthused. "I'd love to meet him."

"Pah, that's nothing compared to what Tungdil and I have done. Or compared with the number of snout-faced orcs we two've split down the middle." He turned round in the saddle to face her. "Forget about Bramdal. He may be a legend in his time but not in my eyes. Don't trust him. Now, no more talk of him."

She stared at him in surprise. "Yes, master." She looked helplessly over to Tungdil, who shrugged his shoulders to say it was none of his business.

When the sun gave way to the night, Tungdil led his troop to the bank of a swift-flowing river, so that they could not be attacked from all sides at once. He wasn't happy near water, because it brought back too many disturbing personal memories, but the security of their mission was paramount.

The team were lifting down the injured elf and starting to release the ponies from their traces. That's when it happened.

The ponies whinnied and one after another reared up, kicking, and pulling away. With nothing to restrain them now, they made off along the river bank as if pursued by invisible spirits.

Tungdil knew why they had suddenly panicked and bolted. He had seen tiny bunches of feathers in the animals' flanks. Blow-pipe arrows. And arrows did not just happen. Enemies had been following unseen hard on their heels, waiting for an opportunity to strike.

"To arms!" he called. "Undergroundlings!"

Ireheart and Goda hurried over while the other dwarves raced after the runaway wagons. "Why d'you say undergroundlings?" Boïndil asked his friend. He looked around but saw nothing. Thirty dwarves were at their side now, axes and shields at the ready, but there was nobody to fight yet. "It might have been Bramdal."

"No. The ponies were shot at with blow-pipes to make them bolt," he said. "We didn't see the attackers. That means they could just as easily have killed the lot of us. But they didn't."

Shouts and frenzied whinnying caught their attention. The entire mounted unit had crashed to the ground, ponies struggling in the dust. A rope had been spanned across their path at knee height, abruptly stopping their pursuit. Some were stunned, or unable to rise, but the others jumped bravely back into the saddle despite their cuts and bruises and took off after the wagons.

"It was a trap," growled Ireheart, his head down between his shoulders. "Come out here, you bare-faced cowards!" he yelled, stepping forward in challenge. "That's not how a dwarf fights! If you've a proper dwarf amongst you, come out, instead of skulking in the undergrowth like some scurvy gnome!"

There was a rustling and cracking in the reeds twenty paces off.

Ireheart's eyes flashed. "We're off to mow a meadow, Goda!" He stormed off, the dwarf-girl following boldly.

In Tungdil's imagination there rose the image of the dead twin Boëndal at his friend's side in the place of the young thirdling girl. With Goda trained to the peak of perfection, these two would make as good a fighting partnership as the brothers had always done. "After them!" he commanded. "Try not to kill any undergroundlings. They have spared us harm where they could."

A posse fanned out into the mass of thin grasses that stood four times as high as their heads.

Tungdil hoped they would find one of the strange dwarves. Otherwise there was no chance of regaining the diamonds they had already lost to the undergroundlings.

The further they moved in amongst the tall grasses the paler that hope became. They had reached the far side of the reeds without coming across a soul.

"Over there!" called Goda, pointing to a figure heading for an incline to the side of the grass stalks. Taller than a dwarf, but too small to be a human.

Tungdil swung round and chased after the undergroundling, Goda and Ireheart at his side. The other dwarves were too far away to overtake their quarry.

The fugitive disappeared over the brow of the hill, the three dwarves in hot pursuit, not losing or gaining any ground all the while.

"This isn't working," muttered Boïndil, raising his crow's beak hammer and hurling it as he ran. "Fly, hammer, and stop him!" he called after it.

Whirling round in circles during flight, the heavy weapon covered the intervening distance with ease. The blunt end hit the undergroundling on the thigh, bringing him to the ground. He slid downhill on the slippery wet grass, and lay there groaning.

"A masterly throw," Tungdil complimented him. He

had been afraid the weapon's mighty spur, as long as a forearm, would bury itself in the undergroundling's back and kill him stone dead. Ever since Ireheart had regained his love of fighting there was no holding him back.

"Never throw your weapon unless you have a spare one with you." Goda mocked. "Master, you—"

"Ho, not so fast." Boïndil raised his broad fist. "I've still got these two weapons, pupil mine. They're quite sufficient for an opponent like this one. If it was orcs I'd have had to think of something else."

"You're making excuses," she complained. "If I'd done that you'd have made me drag heavy beams about or do some other useless task."

"Yes," he admitted with a laugh. "But that's because I'm the master."

They reached the injured undergroundling, who was trying to sit up. Tungdil knelt by him and laid him back down. "Take it easy," he said reassuringly. "We don't mean you any harm."

It was a dwarf, definitely, even if there was no beard, even if the facial features were much harder, the stature somewhat taller and the skin darker than usual. The hair was braided and dyed dark green, dark blue and black. It grew back from the middle of the skull, with the hairless brow displaying tattooed designs.

He wore no armor. The only protection against weather and weapons alike was thick leather clothing. On his feet were thin-soled leather boots. And one of those very boots delivered a sharp kick to Tungdil's chin, sending him flying.

As he fell backwards he heard Ireheart shout out, then

his friend landed in a heap on top of him, his nose streaming blood.

"He kicked me!" said Ireheart, amazed, wiping the blood away. "The scoundrel kicked me like a dog!" He sprang up in a fury. "I'll tear him apart with my bare hands, the baldy-patch!"

Tungdil stood up and saw the undergroundling was escaping with practiced ease from the wrestling holds Goda was attempting. In a swift counter-move he gripped her forearm and shoulder and used her own body weight to throw her. She crashed to the ground.

"Don't kill him, Boïndil!" he shouted.

Ireheart's wild attack would not go well, at least not for the warrior twin.

In fact the undergroundling moved neatly and fast as if dancing with his opponent. As soon as an opportunity presented itself he would grab a handhold on a belt or the mail shirt and use the leverage it gave him.

This time it was the weapon belt. Ireheart was lifted up again, crashing down onto his front, cursing so viciously that the setting sun had to seek the shelter of the nearby clouds.

"He's cracked my bones!" he shouted, pounding the grass with his fist. "By Vraccas, what a bastard! That's not fighting! That's cobold tricks!"

The undergroundling limped off at a run.

Tungdil chased him, glad he had got back his old stamina. Forty orbits ago he would not have been able to run like this and would have collapsed in a gasping heap. "Stop! We need to talk about the diamonds!" he called. "They're important for us."

The undergroundling certainly wasn't paying any attention to his words but Boïndil's hammer-throw had taken its toll.

After two hundred paces on the open plain Tungdil got close enough to launch himself on his opponent, bringing him down, but even as they fell the undergroundling, with remarkable agility and slippery as an eel, turned and twisted under him and would have escaped if Goda had not whacked him over the head with the handle of her night star flail. He sank down unconscious.

"Thanks, Goda," gasped Tungdil, sitting on top of their captive to tie him up, hand and foot, using their belts. He wouldn't get away now.

When he searched the undergroundling's pockets he found a number of the red-feathered blow-pipe arrows. And a little bottle with an evil-smelling liquid, which he assumed was a poison for the arrow tips.

Ireheart lumbered up. "Next time he'll have to use a proper weapon for a proper dwarf," he said crossly, holding his left hand pressed against his chest. He examined the captive with his eyes. "What? Only a dagger?"

The undergroundling's eyelids fluttered and opened. He did not struggle anymore, knowing that escape was impossible now. He studied the faces of his captors. "Let me go," he said in a striking low voice with a harsh accent. It sounded aristocratic—like the tones Rodario sometimes adopted to make fun of people. "I've done nothing to you."

"Done nothing?" Ireheart pointed to his right shoulder. "You've dislocated my shoulder with your damned wrestling throws."

"You tried to kill me. If I had wanted to kill you I would have done so," was the reply. "So don't complain."

Ireheart laughed in disbelief. "Hark at that! By Vraccas, have you been chewing on the old hulto-herb?"

Tungdil signaled to him not to go overboard. Goda stepped up to her master's side and was granted a look of grateful praise, because it was down to her that they even had a captive to interrogate. Her proud smile calmed him in a trice.

"I am Tungdil Goldhand. This is Boïndil Doubleblade and this, Goda Flameheart. Many of our people have lost friends and family in trying to protect the diamond that you want to steal from us. What is it about?"

Some of the other dwarves had come up to join them now. Someone told Tungdil in a whisper that the wagons had been found. The chests containing the stones had all been broken open and the stones had gone.

"We don't steal. We take back what is rightfully ours," said the undergroundling. "It was a broka that took them and carried them off. We had been searching for many star-courses before the ubariu told us where they were."

"What's a broka?"

He thought for a while before replying. "You'd say elf-woman."

Tungdil nodded to Ireheart. "As I thought. We called her eoîl and she brought terror to Girdlegard. But she gave the stone amazing power."

"It always was a powerful artifact," the undergroundling responded. "And it doesn't alter the fact that the diamond's ours."

"Can you take us to your leader?" Tungdil untied the

belt on the captive's hands, and then the bonds round his feet and stood back up. "Your attacks must stop. We all need a solution." He held out his hand to help him up.

"Scholar, they're in league with the orcs," Ireheart warned. "I don't think we can trust them."

The undergroundling pretended not to hear the objection, and stood up without taking the proffered hand. "I'll take you where you can wait for Sûndalon. That's all." He brushed the grass off his clothing.

"The three of us will come with you. You take the lead." Tungdil gave orders for the other dwarves to wait back at camp. "Do you have a name?"

"Yes. I do." He nodded and limped off. Boïndil was pleased about the limp. It made up for the appalling pain in his arm.

Suddenly he felt Goda's hand on his right shoulder. Her other hand grasped his arm, forcing it backwards. He gritted his teeth as the bone slotted back into its socket. For one moment their faces were very close. He could feel her breath on his skin.

"Forgive me, master. The less time you have to tense up, the easier it is to deal with the dislocation."

"It's fine," he said and smiled at her. Not as her master, but as a dwarf. A dwarf in love. Then he cleared his throat, moved swiftly to the side and stepped past her. "Come on, let's catch up. We don't want to abandon the scholar."

Goda had noticed the difference in the smile. That would explain his over-reaction when she had gone on about Bramdal. "Oh, Vraccas." She gave a deep sigh and followed.

Girdlegard,
Kingdom of Gauragar,
Thirty-eight Miles West of Porista,
Summer, 6241st Solar Cycle

The wagons hurtled through the landscape. The *Curiosum* had seldom been in such a tearing hurry to get to the next venue.

The reason was obvious. Furgas must inform the rulers what had happened on the thirdling island. But there was going to be a real problem with that.

"And he still hasn't spoken a word?" Tassia asked again as she sat next to her lover on the driving seat of the first wagon, tossed about as the vehicle rattled along. "So he's just sitting around mending props and his theatre gadgets from the old days?"

"Yup. His mind is busy trying to forget what he's gone through these past five cycles." Rodario slowed the wagon; he had seen a place off the road where they could camp for the night. It was important none of the vehicles damaged an axle now when the end of the journey was practically in sight.

They made a circle with the caravans. Rodario helped Tassia down and tried—though not very hard—to avoid looking down her cleavage. "Oh, now I know what I've been missing." He grinned and then kissed her.

She laughed and tapped him with a pile of papers she had been sitting on. "And how many women did you gladden in Mifurdania while I was busy taking my troupe north?"

"Your troupe, eh?" he said with emphasis, crossing his

arms over his chest. "I'm back now, my girl, and I'll have you know that I am in charge of the *Curiosum* again. Or have you been inciting the troupe to revolution with your pretty eyes and your charming mouth?"

She placed a forefinger under his chin. "That is the way of it, my love. I've slept with every man in the theater company and made them all my slaves. The women never liked me in the first place. You may be the emperor of the acting fraternity, but there's a new queen in the realm." Tassia was only half speaking in jest.

Rodario had certainly noticed that his instructions were only carried out when Tassia gave the nod. He thought it was a joke at first. "No, you don't mean it," he said uncertainly.

"Have another look at your play. I've changed it a bit. It's better now." She spoke confidently and pressed the papers into his hand, grinning at him. She planted a passionate kiss on his lips, then hurried off to help Gesa with the meal.

Rodario watched her go and scratched his head. "That woman has a demon in her blood," he muttered. "If I'd known that before, I'd never have agreed to the deal back in Storm Valley." He went round to the back door of the caravan and let down the ladder to sit on, while the crew took the horses out of the shafts and led them off to be fed and watered.

In the light of the setting sun he skimmed through what Tassia had changed on his playscript.

He was annoyed to find himself laughing out loud at several of the new ideas she had added. She had certainly shown her talents here. Rodario had come across many works by experienced playwrights that were nowhere as good as this.

He surfaced eventually as thirst and concern for Furgas made themselves felt. He got up and went up the narrow steps. "Furgas?"

While he waited for an answer he turned his head to watch Tassia. She was laughing with Gesa. The women were having a potato-peeling race. Anyone in the troupe who was not busy with other work had gathered at the fireside to be near the warmth of this delightful girl. Rodario realized that she had been telling the truth. The *Curiosum* was now securely in Tassia's strong and capable hands. He had trained her. She had been his muse.

"By Palandiell, I can't have that!" murmured the dethroned emperor. "I must have a quiet word with the young lady."

He was starting back down the steps when he heard a moan coming from the caravan.

"Furgas?" He opened the door without further ado. His friend was lying on the floor covered in blood. Furgas had slashed his own wrists with deep lengthwise cuts and had fainted from the blood loss.

"What the . . . ?" Rodario rushed in, grabbed a sheet and tore it into strips to bind the gashes. "What were you thinking of?" he yelled at Furgas, pulling him upright. "I didn't rescue you just so's you could kill yourself."

"It's the guilt," whispered Furgas. "I built machines designed to bring death to the dwarves." He was struggling to regain control. He swayed again, but Rodario had him fast.

"Go easy on yourself, my friend. They forced you to do it . . ."

"I could have killed myself instead of doing what they demanded, but . . ." He looked the actor in the eyes. "First they sent drilling rigs through the old blocked mine galleries trying to get through. Then the death machines followed." He wiped his eyes. "The machines . . ."

Rodario gave him a cup of water. "Take it easy."

"I *can't* take it easy. Have you heard what the people are saying? Those monsters of flesh and steel?" He swallowed, his hands gripping the cup convulsively. "They are all my work. The thirdlings are in league with the immortal siblings," he said, trying to keep his voice level.

Rodario felt icy fingers up and down his spine. "No." He saw Tassia's face at the door, not moving lest she intrude. She stood in the doorway listening.

"Yes." Furgas gave a bitter laugh. "Bandilor came to me and showed me some weird sketches of disgusting hybrid creatures to be made partly of iron. He had the formula for the alloy that can conduct magic, and had stolen some of the embers from the fifthlings' dragon-forge. He used that to make the alloy and I made the machines from it following his instructions. I built them, not knowing what he wanted to do with them." He turned pale.

"Then they came. I remember exactly . . . We came to the surface and they were brought to us. Ugly little bastard-hybrids of orc and älf—the biggest no older than four cycles. Bandilor took the island to a secret location somewhere in the lake and sank it to the bottom. Then we put the bastards in the machines, screwed and hammered them all up tight, cut off their limbs and attached in their place the things Bandilor brought. Glass or crystals, I don't know which. He pushed the rods of magic-conducting metal through the small bodies and threw the little bastards into a hole he had dug. They screamed. Oh, how they screamed."

He shuddered with the horror of the images he was bringing to mind. "Green lightning shot up out of the hole and into the iron. Älfar runes flamed and flared and these hybrids . . . they grew and they screeched. Their bodies became fused with the contraptions. With my contraptions." He emptied the cup. "I don't know how long it took. Then Bandilor had the island brought up to the surface and I never saw the creatures again. Till we heard about them on the journey."

He fell silent. All about them was quiet for some time.

Tassia had goosebumps all over as her imagination conjured up these horrific beings, filling her with terror. "Ye gods!" she breathed. "How awful!"

Rodario, too, needed some time to recover from what he had heard. His own technical theater-genius had created his masterpieces. Masterpieces of destruction and cruelty, driven by evil and suffused with the will to wreak havoc and death. "You are not the guilty one," he breathed finally, helping Furgas over to the bed to sit down. He poured out wine, which his friend gulped down.

Furgas was shaking all over. "I don't deserve to live, Rodario," he said, despairingly. "Of course the thirdlings forced me to do these things but I carried out my tasks with precision. I did my work only too well." He clenched his fists. "All the time I was thinking about Narmora and my children. I served the thirdlings well in order to avenge myself on the dwarves and on Girdlegard for what happened when they took my family. Only toward the end did I realize what harm I was causing to humans, elves and dwarves." He emptied the wineglass and closed his eyes. "I . . . feel giddy," he whispered and fell sideways onto the pillows. Wine and blood loss were taking their toll.

"Sleep as long as you can," Rodario told his friend kindly. He covered him with a blanket and wiped the blood from the floor. He would scrub the floorboards later. "And don't touch the knives." He left the caravan, pulling the door to behind him.

He sat himself on the steps with the bottle of wine and watched the last rays of the setting sun. He took a swig of wine and passed the bottle to Tassia.

"What did he mean about his family being taken?" she asked hesitatingly. "I thought it had happened at the battle of Porista?"

He put his arm around her and pulled her to him, looking her deep in the eyes; imagining all of a sudden what it would be like to lose her forever, he felt a wave of fear surge through his being. He kissed her tenderly.

Tassia was aware of the difference between this and his usual passionate embraces: a kiss now not of desire but of such deep emotion that not even a poet would have been able to describe it. She smiled at him and put a hand to his face. "What was that for?"

Rodario sighed. "His life's companion, Narmora, was a half-älf. She fought with us on the side of good against Nôd'onn and then was apprenticed to the last of the magae, Andôkai the Tempestuous. She took the maga's place and protected Girdlegard from avatars and the eoîl. But in return for her efforts, the älf part of her was burnt to ashes. The Star of Judgment knew no mercy. Not for her . . ."

". . . or her children?" Tassia continued, shocked and saddened. "How terrible. Poor Furgas."

"After the battle he blamed dwarves and humans alike for their deaths. If they had let the avatars have their way, he used to say in his utter despair, there would have been fewer victims in Girdlegard. They would have destroyed the evil in the form of the älfar and then they would have withdrawn. Without letting the Star of Judgment rise. And he could have been a contented father." He looked past her to the red of the dying sun. "Sometimes I wonder if perhaps he was right."

She was silent, took a mouthful of wine and passed the bottle back to him.

"I'd be lying if I said I'd understood him at the time. Now I'm able to imagine what it must have been like for him." He stretched out a hand to stroke her hair. "I pray to the gods I'll never be put in that situation. Like him I should hate—hate and hunt down—to the end of my days, anyone who caused me such pain."

She took his hand and laid it on her cheek.

So they sat until darkness fell. Rodario looked in on the patient, now sleeping soundly, then he and Tassia moved over to the campfire to join the rest of the troupe, where they sat, arms around each other, listening to Gesa sing.

Girdlegard,
Kingdom of Gauragar,
Fortress Cowburg,
Summer, 6241st Solar Cycle

Balba Chiselstrike from the secondling clan of the Stone Teasers was feeling a little out of place amongst all these humans.

Queen Isaka's direction that no dwarf be allowed inside the walls of the castle she found ridiculous. She could not understand the ruler's fear. The humans, it was clear to Balba, would be completely lost without the fighting power of the dwarf peoples.

In spite of her resentment she intended to carry out her task conscientiously. Supervising the completion of defense works with the foreman, she was checking every stone in Paland's bastion walls.

"It's a wonderful fort, isn't it?" the man said admiringly.

"No, it isn't," Balba smashed his complacency. "It's ugly. The whole construction lacks grace and has been thrown uncaringly at the landscape. The old builders always planned meticulously but they never considered aesthetics."

Her condemnation wiped the foreman's good mood straight off his face. As a descendant of Paland's original builders he felt this was a personal attack. "You dwarves all think you can do everything better."

"I never said we would have done it better." Balba knew her people would indeed have done it better but refrained from saying so. "I miss here the soul that every dwarf building has. The humans who built Paland hewed the stones into shape without paying attention to the strata and structure of the rock. Instead of listening to the grain and fitting the stones so that they last forever, an artificial mountain, the builders have forced the stone, violated it. That is why our buildings last longer than yours." Balba and all dwarf masons knew the characteristics of every type of rock, from granite to slate, from basalt to marble or sandstone.

By the light of the setting sun she promptly discovered a damaged stone. "Hey, you there!" She called over one of the workmen the king had supplied her with. She pointed out a finial on the passageway arch to the main building. "I told you to take that one out and replace it."

"We haven't had time, Balba. We had to—"

"Right, I'll explain to King Bruron when that stone starts to shake and the arch falls around his ears at the first fanfare."

She put her hands on her hips—she was not going to be changing her mind.

The foreman sprang to the defense of his worker. "I'll get a couple of people over and start work at once, Balba," he said, lowering his head so she would not see the scowl. He hurried off, glad to escape her harsh tongue.

The dwarf-woman shook her brown hair back and adjusted her leather apron. "Humans," she muttered and walked off.

When she thought how many cycles the fortress had stood, and the neglect it had been subject to—the dilapidated condition she and King Bruron had found it in— then she could really be quite pleased with the work they had done here. The outer walls, laid out in a star shape, were twenty paces high and had been repaired and topped out with sturdy new battlements. It had been a master-work to replace the crumbling stones without any walls collapsing. The humans had not thought it would be possible. She, the dwarf, had shown them what was what.

She had decided to pull down the ruined towers, with the weathered stone broken up for use as missiles, piled now on the top walkways and in heaps next to the cata-pults. The walls were high enough to serve without towers, but she had put up ramps to use for the spear-throwers.

She was surprised how easily the humans were satis-fied with the work. The critical eye of a dwarf would have been much more demanding about standards. She was determined to get Paland into a state that made even the elves praise the speed at which the work had been completed. Not its beauty but the speed and thorough-ness of the work.

So far only one of the remaining diamonds had arrived safely in the fortress. Queen Wey and her soldiers were already here. The messengers sent out from the other groups heading for the fortress were keeping the commanders informed of their progress.

It looked as if Sangpûr's jewel would be the next to arrive. It would be placed in a room with walls many paces thick. Balba had had the roof reinforced and had put in extra supporting pillars.

Even the comet that had once hit the Outer Lands would not destroy this granite armor.

The dwarf directed her steps to the walkway that faced south. She wanted to see the size of Queen Umilante's force approaching from the hot desert lands, the army protecting her diamond.

As she stood on the battlement walkway taking a drink of water from her flask, an armored elf came up to her. "Greetings," he said.

"Greetings." She knew that he had arrived with the two-hundred-strong contingent sent as an advance party from Âlandur; other soldiers would follow.

Apart from them there were a thousand fighting men from Weyurn in the fortress. The rest, a further fifteen thousand infantry and two thousand mounted troops led by Prince Mallen, were advancing swiftly toward Idoslane to storm Toboribor and to destroy the unslayables and the monsters in those caves. Now that they had shown themselves, there was finally something to attack.

"Sitalia has sent us a fine day," the elf addressed the air as he looked down toward the wall beneath them. "The goddess looks after her own." He took off his helmet, letting his pale gold hair shine on his shoulders.

Balba took another gulp of water and put the flask down. "Sitalia looks after the elves, so she'll only send the fine day for you guys. The humans are giving thanks to Palandiell and we praise Vraccas. That's the way of it," she said amicably. She pointed over to the right where the sun was going down. "The day's not over yet." She looked at the white metal armor. She had never seen it before. The elves were all in new clothing, all two hundred of them, in white and pale colors, a dazzling sight in the sunshine. Their new appearance reminded her of something, but she couldn't think what.

"You are right there, Balba Chiselstrike of the Stone

Teasers," responded the elf apologetically. "I wanted to praise the work you have done here. It is excellent. The diamonds will be safe here."

She nodded in acknowledgment and gave a shy smile. "Would you like some?" She offered her flask.

The elf stretched out his armored hand and took the bottle. "Thank you." He sniffed at the contents first to find out what he would be drinking, then placed the opening to his lips—and froze. "By Sitalia!" he whispered, pointing south. "Do you see what I see?"

Balba looked where he was pointing.

The escort force for the diamond had appeared between two hills and was passing a wood whence an attack was being launched. The girl saw a huge black monster capering around amongst the tiny forms of the soldiers, swinging a scythe-like weapon; from time to time green lightning bolts shot out, and where they hit home men fizzled to steam where they lay.

"The unslayables have tricked us! They aren't in Toboribor. They have sent their evil misshapen devils here to steal the diamonds before we can place them in safety." The elf dropped the flask, ran down the steps and put on his helmet as he went, calling out in a language Balba did not understand.

The elf troops rushed to their white horses and thundered out through the southern gate to support Umilante's soldiers. A handful of their messengers were setting off in other directions to warn approaching groups of dwarves and humans of the acute danger.

The fortress commander had the gates shut and called everyone to arms.

"I said the day wasn't over yet." Balba was faced with the prospect of a battle. She was not bad with a cudgel, but didn't really consider herself a fighting champion. Now, under cover of the uproar, she left the battlements and went off to hurry her workforce through the remaining tasks while there was still light.

Unexpectedly there was a commotion at the eastern side of the fortress but Balba remained at the construction site until the humans had completed their work to her satisfaction. Any faulty workmanship would reflect badly on her family and her clan. When all was done she hurried back up to the battlements, shield in hand.

A cloud of dust was making for the eastern gate.

And whatever was creating the dust was moving extremely fast. Too fast to be a human, an elf, a dwarf, a beast or an animal.

"What happened to Umilante's troops?" she asked a soldier nearby.

The man had gone pale and was clinging to the shaft of his spear. "They're all lying out there by the hills and they're not moving."

"And the elves?"

"Gone. Swallowed by the monster," he whispered and gulped with horror.

The sun had gone down and Gauragar was plunged into the half light preceding the dark of true night with its stars.

Torches blazed all round the fortress, chasing away the frightening shadows. Men ran out to bring up the wooden drawbridges and to set alight tar and brushwood piled in the moats. The first line of defense was in place.

Balba heaved one of the rocks onto the battlement wall, ready to cast it down on the attacker. She quickly scratched her initials into the stone, grinning with excitement.

Fifty paces in front of the gates the thing halted in the middle of the roadway, having advanced with such speed. It showed itself to the defenders of the castle. The surrounding veil of dust was carried off by the heat rising from the blazing moat. The image that appeared was a mixture of monster and machine.

From the hips up it was like the other monsters, a bastard hybrid of orc and älf or worse, and covered with a solid armor plating of tionium. There was not a single glimpse of bare skin to be had. Everything was protected by the plates of resistant material from any attack with arrow or missile. Only the face within the open visor showed the armor contained life.

But where legs would normally be there was a large black block, two paces high, two paces wide, and three paces long.

The sides of the block were rounded and the shiny black surface was sloped so that liquids—blood, water or whatever—would run off quickly. Balba saw the surface had openings and flaps hiding any manner of deathly surprises. Round about there were sharp spikes of tionium as long as your forearm. On the bottom of the block were the large wheels used to propel the hybrid along so swiftly using some invisible power-source inside the block.

"A fighting chariot without any horses," judged one of the soldiers. "What the hell have they thought up here?"

"Nothing good," replied Balba. The sight of the thing was making the hairs stand up on the back of her neck.

"Give me the diamond and you shall live," it called out in a clear voice. "My brothers and sisters will soon be here. These walls will not hold us back."

"You shall have your answer," the commander called down, lifting his hand and dropping it sharply as a signal.

Four spear-throwing war-machines hurled their death-bringing loads toward the creature; clouds of black weaponry swished through the evening air.

The missiles would certainly have hit their target, had the creature not suddenly rolled backwards. The thick covering on the front opened up to form a shield against the spears that reached it. The wooden shafts broke and the tips splintered, bent out of shape on the rigid tionium. They made not the slightest indentation in the armor. The archers hurriedly reloaded.

"Aim for the wheels. We'll get it this time round." The commander turned to the stone catapults. "Ready to fire!" he called. "When I . . ."

Then all the lights in Paland went out. Candles, torches, the fire in the moat—it was all extinguished in a trice. Blackness swallowed the twilight. Everything lay in total darkness, with not even a star daring to show its face.

"Fire!" called the commander. The sounds of the mechanism being released and the ropes unwinding could be heard. And soon there was the rumble of the missiles hitting home.

Balba was not convinced she would ever hear this creature's death cry.

Bright green runes blazed out in front of the gate, then there was a powerful bolt of lightning and the gates themselves were blown open, blasted off their hinges with such force that shards cascaded against the far wall of the fortress.

At least now the torches were not refusing their light. So the defenders in the courtyard could see exactly what death looked like, just before it struck.

The huge block had travelled over the moat and now raced through the courtyard. To the right and the left blades of tionium shot out, two paces long, slicing the armored soldiers in half. The sight of these truncated soldiers so appalled their comrades that they stood rooted to the spot.

At the front an iron protective apron had opened up and anyone standing in the way of the machine was forced into the blades or was caught under the jagged edges of the wheels. None survived. Conventional arrows raining down on the vehicle and on the creature itself had no effect.

Balba shook off the paralyzing fear. "Your commander is right: the wheels are the weak point," she called, racing down the steps. "Do you hear me? Shove iron rods in through the wheels and it'll be forced to stop. Get chains. We can overturn it."

In all the noise and shouting only a few of the soldiers could hear the brave dwarf-woman's advice, but they tried their best to follow her commands.

Just before the entrance to the diamond vault, they overtook the vehicle, which was emitting strange noises. It was clicking and ticking, hissing and steaming behind its tionium plating.

"Bring the chains," called Balba to the men. The soldiers

did not hesitate to obey her orders. They had grasped her meaning. Balba grabbed hold as well, dragging a hook and getting ready to sling it. "Hook it in the . . ."

A loud rumbling sound made her turn her head to look back at the blasted gateway.

A second monster was forcing its way through. Its creator had placed a huge armor contraption round it. Fists of tionium were battering against the walls, tearing out great parts of the fabric and hurling the rocks at the castle's defenders. The brave soldiers from Weyurn were losing their lives in scores against the superior power of this attacker that was kicking at them as if they were vermin. A cage-like globe rolled through their open ranks, coming to the aid of the monster at the entrance to the vault.

Balba stopped, her heart in her mouth and her courage melting like lead in a furnace. A third of Tion's creatures, this time with forearms of metal and glass, was climbing up the southern battlements. It swung its hands round and sent bolts of green lightning toward the soldiers. Their protective iron armor glowed and the men vaporized to nothing in the deadly light-beams. The commander himself was among the fallen. The rest gave up and ran off screaming. From one thousand maybe four hundred men were still alive.

Balba understood that without a magus there was no hope of combating these hybrid monsters. The combination of superior machinery, the strength of the creatures and the unrestrained power of magic could not be matched by any force they could offer.

She let the hook fall and ran off, in contrast to the

fleeing humans, out through the northern gate. Later she was to learn that all Weyurn's soldiers had been annihilated.

X

Boïndil stomped off after the undergroundling and made no attempt to conceal his displeasure. "We're putting ourselves voluntarily into their hands. They attacked our people! It's not good."

"They will give us a hearing. If we can reach an agreement, that's always going to be better than more attacks," said Tungdil.

"And he still hasn't told us what his name is." Boïndil found another reason for his bad mood. "Oh yes, and they're friends with the snout-faces."

"Just wait and see," advised Tungdil, who had by now had enough of these complaints. Goda was walking next to her master and not getting involved, but judging by her face he reckoned she would have preferred Boïndil to be less argumentative.

All three were tense as they followed the dwarf-stranger. No one knew what to expect from the coming meeting with their distant relatives from the Outer Lands.

Tungdil watched how the undergroundling moved. His walk was smoother than a Girdlegard dwarf's rolling gait: he set his feet down in a straight line, not a little way apart like them. He kept his upper body straight and hardly made a sound as his boots touched the ground. In contrast to Ireheart. The undergroundling was so good at moving silently that he might have learned his skill from the älfar.

They marched till sundown, when they found themselves at the foot of three hills in a gentle wooded valley, in the middle of which a bubbling stream arose.

The undergroundling led them straight over to the water, called out some incomprehensible words and sat down at the edge of the spring. He drank from his hand. "Sûndalon will be here soon," he said.

Ireheart rammed the head of his crow's beak into the soft moss-covered earth and listened. "How peaceful it is," he murmured. "Might just as well be one of the elves' sacred places. The only thing missing is the big white stone."

The undergroundling looked up. "A white stone? With the broka?"

Tungdil remembered that this was the undergroundling's word for elves. It seemed he and his folk were already acquainted with them. "Yes." He described the stone, its appearance and the secrecy the elves had tried to maintain. "Does that sound familiar?"

"Yes," nodded the undergroundling, giving him a sympathetic look. "We had broka and their stones in our land, too." He drank some more water and washed his face, without smudging the sign on his forehead.

"What does that mean?" grunted Boïndil impatiently.

"What do you think?" The undergroundling looked annoyed now. "That we had to destroy them before they destroyed us."

Ireheart looked at Tungdil and gulped. "Did you hear that, Scholar?"

"Loud and clear." Tungdil sat down on the moss and leaned back against a tree. It was high time they met up with the leader of the undergroundlings. His friend and Goda both sat down next to him.

"What do you reckon? Think they like jokes?" Ireheart considered the undergroundling. "Perhaps that will lighten the atmosphere a bit."

"But not the asking-the-way joke," Goda rolled her eyes. "If you must, then try the one about the elf and the dwarf and the forest."

"Yes, you're right. The asking-the-way they might not appreciate." He placed his fingers round the handle of his weapon. "They're so difficult."

"Just because they won't laugh at your jokes? Well, that's certainly a good reason for mistrusting a whole people," said Tungdil lightly. "That can be your new motto: Laugh, or I'll thump you. You could get it engraved on the side of your crow's beak."

Goda laughed out loud.

"Forty push-ups for you, apprentice." Boïndil's pride was hurt.

"No sense of humor, master?"

He pretended to be offended. "Not when the joke's on me." He pointed to the ground. "Forty, if you please. And right down. I want to see moss on your nose."

Protesting, Goda stood up and did what he had ordered.

Tungdil shook his head in disapproval, but Ireheart showed his teeth.

"Get your face right down into the moss," he reminded her after the first thirty push-ups. He was enjoying watching the play of her muscles in the upper arms.

Nowadays this was a sight he was finding altogether more attractive.

The undergroundling had kindled a large fire and took no notice of the three dwarves. Flames shot up high into the night sky, sending out a clear signal.

As if from nowhere there they were: two dozen silent figures standing between the trees, in light brown and black leather armor, leather breeches and boots. Their heads were protected by helmets, none quite like the next. The faces were all hidden. Each shut visor bore a demon visage engraved on the surface. The effect was uncanny and intimidating.

In their hands or on their belts Tungdil caught sight of short blackened iron batons one pace in length. At the end of each baton flashed a slim blade and a hook. It seemed the undergroundlings did not share the dwarves' preference for heavy weaponry.

"Show yourselves," said the dwarf who had led them to the valley. They all opened their visors.

Tungdil watched the beardless serious faces and noted that some of them were women. This aroused his curiosity. They did not seem to have the plumpness of dwarf-women that he knew; their form was taller and slimmer—more like human females.

One of the undergroundlings, at first sight just the same as the others, stepped forward. "I am Sûndalon. You want something from me?" He rammed his staff into the mossy woodland floor, lifted the helmet from off his short light blond hair and waited.

Tungdil and his companions stood up and he introduced them all. "We must talk about the diamond," he said, speaking freely. "We know now that it belongs to you, but through broka magic it has become much more powerful. We can't just simply hand it over."

Sûndalon reached to his belt and took out a pouch. He opened it and tipped the contents out: glittering fragments and scintillating dust spilled onto the moss. "That is all that is left of the stones that we and the ubariu have captured. They were all forgeries."

This did not make Tungdil feel more at ease. Now it was even more likely the genuine stone would fall into the hands of the unslayable siblings. And what they might be capable of doing with its magic power did not bear thinking about.

"We demand the return of our property," said Sûndalon. "It was stolen from us by a broka. It has taken five star courses for us to complete our preparations and to have the opportunity to regain it at last."

"Why don't you just cut yourselves a new one and leave us in peace?" Ireheart suggested, holding his crow's beak weapon lightly in his hands. Lightly, but ready for use. Goda held her night star ready as well.

"Because only that diamond has the quality we need," was Sûndalon's sharp reply. "It would be like having a key that fits but won't turn in its lock." He looked at Tungdil. "If the news we've gathered is true there are still three in the hands of your people and one has disappeared? Give us those three and we swear we'll protect them against all threats."

"You didn't manage to keep yours safe the first time," Boïndil rubbed it in.

"And you can't do it at all," Sûndalon retorted. "You

can't protect them from us or from the ubariu or from these monsters."

"If you could explain why it's so important, perhaps we could be persuaded to let you have it." Tungdil attempted enticement.

To his disappointment the undergroundling shook his head. "If we could explain it freely we wouldn't have kept ourselves hidden in your homeland for so long. Our land and our town are helpless without the diamond. Our enemies are strong and would attack us at once if they were aware of our weakness."

Tungdil took a careful step forward. "We are dwarves, as you are. We would never betray you to your foes." He knew that his statement contained a trace of untruth. He suspected that some of the thirdlings were certainly capable of malice and deceit, but Sûndalon did not have to know this. "And anyway, the kings and queens know that it's the undergroundlings, together with the orcs, trying to get the diamonds. You might as well talk about it. Your raids are no secret, Sûndalon."

"He is right," said the undergroundling who had brought them to the valley. "Tell him about the trouble we are in and then let's talk to the kings and queens."

"No," said Sûndalon harshly. "What happens in this land is not our concern."

"But they don't understand the danger they're in. The broka have put up white stones," continued the undergroundling. "It's starting here like it did with us, Sûndalon. We could help avert the worst if we warn the dwarves and the humans."

Sûndalon fell silent and thought hard.

"I don't know how you feel about it but baldy-patch is starting to worry me," whispered Boïndil. "What's all this about the white stones? Does he mean what we saw when we were with the pointy-ears?"

"Saw? You touched it, remember?" Tungdil said quietly. "Who knows what it's done to you."

Ireheart went pale.

The nameless undergroundling turned to them. "Don't trust the broka now, neither their words, nor their deeds, nor their smiles. They have been staring too long at the sun and aspire to become like it. They have become blind to everything else." His tone was insistent. "It will start with deaths and nobody will know by whose hand the victims died. Then towns and villages will burn and there will be no survivors. Your people will suffer losses and will lie dead in the tunnels because the water is poisoned . . ."

"By Vraccas!" Ireheart exclaimed, horrified. "Do you hear that? They're describing what's happening in Girdlegard . . ." He stopped, lifting up his crow's beak. "Was it you that did that and now you're all for peace because it'll make it easier for you to get the diamond?" He lowered his head aggressively between his hunched shoulders. "I swear by the dwarves that have died that I shall take revenge on you if it was you that did this!"

"No, it was not us," said Sûndalon. "Agreed. You shall learn the history of the diamond. Perhaps then you will believe us." He sat down and started to relate . . .

"The stone originated in the deepest mine of Drestadon. The finder paid for it with his eyesight

because it was so dazzlingly bright. It was only possible to view and to cut the diamond when it was covered with a thick black cloth.

The gemstone-cutter needed seven star-courses to give the diamond its true form. The work took the flesh from his fingertips; his back became permanently bent and his eyes as weak as those of an old, old man. Finally he finished cutting and polishing the stone.

We took it to the ubariu rune master and he realized why the god Ubar had sent us the diamond.

The rune master prepared for war. He gathered an army and marched with it to the Black Abyss. Arising from the lightless depths and dark crannies evil had issued unceasingly to plague us. Ever since the stars started running, evil's progeny had surged out from thence to attack us.

But there was also an age-old iron artifact, of no apparent use. It had long lost any power it once had wielded.

The runes it bore promised to close the Black Abyss for ever—if the Star of the Mountains ever returned to it.

The rune master led us and the ubariu into the midst of our enemies. There ensued a terrible battle waged against creatures more bestial than any you may have known in Girdlegard, but yet blessed with a form of outstanding beauty. Some found their way here: creatures you know as älfar. We call them sintoìtar—they crawled out of the Black Valley over the mountains and came here.

Together with the ubariu we fought tirelessly and forced a path for the rune master through the black army to reach the artifact. That day many friends and relatives lost their lives and whole generations were wiped out.

Then the beasts realized that a greater danger was threatening them than they had ever known. If you had not seen it with your own eyes you could never imagine the merciless killing and slaughter.

The rune master floated up to the artifact. He placed the stone in its setting. It fitted! The stone awoke with dazzling beauty. Splendid and terrible beams of light transformed the ancient machine and brought it to life.

Evil's creatures were driven back into the Black Abyss; most of them had met their deaths at our hands. Only a few of the more harmless ones managed to escape. They no longer presented any danger to us.

The artifact wove a veil of impenetrable magic, under which the abyss lay captive.

Until the day the broka arrived, overpowered our guards and stole the Star of the Mountains.

Sûndalon dipped his hand into the spring and drank. "So far the creatures in the ravine have not yet noticed that their prison has been opened. They had sought new escape routes, but the gaps they discovered were always dangerous and difficult to use. Again and again some of them managed to get out." He lowered his voice. "If one of them should realize in the course of a sortie that the main exit path is now open, and if it returned to summon the others, they would storm out of the abyss fueled by hatred and fury. They would destroy everything they came across." He pulled his staff out of the mossy floor and indicated himself. "Us first." The sharp end now pointed at Tungdil. "Then you. The älfar are the least dangerous of them."

"So do these hybrid monsters made of beast and metal perhaps come from the Outer Lands?" Tungdil wondered aloud.

Sûndalon shook his head. "We know of none such. They must have been born here."

"That can't be so. The älfar and all the dark creatures were destroyed by the Judgment Star. Most of them, at any rate," said Goda, who had listened to the story as intently as the two other dwarves.

Sûndalon considered this. "Was this Judgment Star a wall of white light that swept over the land?" She nodded. He drew his dagger, plunged it into the water and held it out with the broad side facing up. "If that is your land and my finger is the wall of light," he ran his finger along the metal, wiping off the water, "what remains under the earth?" Large drops collected on the underside of the blade.

"You mean the magic won't have penetrated the mountains and the deep ravines?"

"That is so. We have been to regions where this had been attempted before. There were always some beasts that survived." Sûndalon gazed at the dagger's blade, wrapped in thought. "It didn't work with us. The broka came and stole the stone and waited for the monsters to show themselves, to destroy them by magic so as to gain sole power. But they didn't do her that favor, so the broka left with her retinue. Afterwards all the broka behaved strangely and we had to kill them before they destroyed us all." He put away his dagger. "It wasn't easy to eradicate them, but it had to be done." He gazed at the dwarves' thoughtful countenances. "They had lost their minds."

"You won't deny that our elves are behaving strangely, will you?" Boïndil asked Tungdil. "I mean more strangely than usual."

"We must nurse the injured elf back to health as soon as possible. He is certain to be able to tell us more. It won't be for nothing they shot at him." Tungdil nodded to Sûndalon. "Come with me to Paland and tell the kings and queens what you have told us. Convince them! There's no other way for you to get the true diamond because you won't ever get inside the fortress walls. I give you my word that no one will take you prisoner, injure or kill you." He lifted his ax.

"I swear this on the blade of Keenfire."

The undergroundling with no name nodded to his leader encouragingly and finally Sûndalon agreed. "We shall accompany you, Tungdil Goldhand." He stood up. "But we would have got into the fortress," he said with a smile of utter conviction.

Girdlegard,
Kingdom of Gauragar,
Porista,
Summer, 6241st Solar Cycle

Tungdil, Boïndil, Goda, the fifthling contingent and the undergroundlings did not have to go all the way to Paland.

In Porista the royal banners of the human realms stirred in the breeze above the city walls indicating that the mighty rulers of Girdlegard were once more assembled. And the banners were flying at half mast.

The dwarves marched through a town that was eerily quiet. The atmosphere in the streets was muted from oppression and fear, with any pleasures or delights smothered. On the way to the assembly tent they heard what had happened in Paland and how the defense force had been destroyed.

When Tungdil, Ireheart and Sûndalon entered the royal marquee in the early part of the afternoon, humans, dwarves and elves were debating what they should do next. Goda waited outside, as always.

Prince Mallen's seat was empty and on the throne-like chair that had once been Liútasil's Tungdil saw an elf-woman in white robes and bearing the insignia of a sovereign. In her long pale hair costly gems were set; the bright gaze of her blue-green eyes scanned the newcomers. A successor to Liútasil had been found and she surpassed all others here in her beauty and her presence. She was introduced to him as Princess Rejalin. Tungdil immediately thought of the eoîl.

King Bruron received the dwarves with a half-hearted smile and looked in surprise at the beardless dwarf who was taller than Tungdil by a hand's breadth. "You will have heard about Paland?"

Tungdil nodded and bowed to the other rulers. "I was shocked to hear the news. So now there is only one diamond in Girdlegard. And nobody knows where it is."

"One?" said Isika, deep foreboding in her voice. With

her black hair and lined face she presented a dark contrast to Rejalin. The robe of the elf princess made her own sumptuous attire seem inferior. "Were you routed by these beasts as well?"

"No, I was defeated by Sûndalon." Rejalin stepped to one side to let the undergroundling be seen. "He comes from the Outer Lands, from a town at the foot of the mountain range. And he is on a quest to regain what belongs to them. Listen to his story."

And Sûndalon told them, as previously agreed with Tungdil, about the artifact whose power had stopped up the evil chasm. He told them how the eoîl had stolen it, without mentioning that this eoîl was a broka—an elf-woman. "We couldn't tell anyone. We feared there would be long-drawn-out negotiations, even though it rightfully belongs to us. We also feared the monsters would hear about the missing artifact." He stepped up to the table and spread out the fragments of the gemstone copies. The rulers looked despondently at the shimmering pile of crystalline remains.

"Either the beasts already have the real diamond or the one that's got lost is the one with the incomparable magic power." Tungdil's voice broke the silence. "I think the beasts have long been in possession of the one that's disappeared." He turned to address the kings and queens. "We must put all our efforts now into getting it back. Two reasons: It must not be allowed to serve the sinister purposes of the unslayables and its power must be used to permanently seal up the evil ravine. Otherwise Girdlegard will not be safe."

Rejalin turned her head to one side and observed

Sûndalon. "You formed an alliance with the orcs to get the stone back. Is that correct?"

Sûndalon wrinkled his face in distaste. "I would never fight side by side with those creatures. The ubariu are honorable and are sworn enemies of the orcs. They are our brothers; our races were both created by the god Ubar."

"They are like the orcs apart from the tusks, aren't they?" Rejalin smiled. For that smile men would worship her as a goddess.

It had no effect on Sûndalon. "They are taller in stature than orcs. Their eyes are the red of the rising sun and their philosophy is a thousand times better than that of a broka," he retorted sharply. "If you regard them as your enemy you must take us as enemies also."

"Strange," said the elf-woman thoughtfully. "And what are . . . broka?"

"They are like you, but corrupt and false. They pretend to be benign and wise and keen to befriend all other folk. In reality they are trying to spread their own ideas. With no thought for others. They must be eliminated."

Sûndalon had spoken in dark tones. He was finding it hard to restrain himself.

"He means the älfar," Tungdil came to his aid. "We cannot judge by appearances, Princess Rejalin. Your people know that only too well."

She dropped her penetrating gaze. "I ask your pardon, Sûndalon. I did not want to offend."

"This is not good news that you bring us, Tungdil Goldhand," sighed King Bruron. "It will be best if you set off for Idoslane straightaway with Keenfire in your hand. Prince Mallen is laying siege to the caves of

Toboribor. We think the monsters are hiding their prize there. It will be extremely dangerous to fight these monsters without a magus at your side. We have been shown that superior numbers are no threat for them." He contemplated the wonderful engravings on the head of Tungdil's ax. "Only Keenfire will be able to withstand attacks from the sorcery of the unslayables and their allies."

"As soon as the sun rises, I'll be on my way," nodded Tungdil.

A messenger hurried into the marquee, stepped up to Bruron and whispered to him. Tungdil feared that their planned daybreak departure would already be too late.

"We have a delegation wishing to bring us news," said the king, turning to the doorway. "Send them both in."

The curtains parted with a theatrical flourish and in stepped Rodario, in flamboyant robes as magnificent as any worn by the assembled monarchs. "My respects to you all, mighty sovereigns of Girdlegard, you humans, dwarves and elves, one and all." He made a deep bow.

Tungdil was delighted to see his friend. This type of grand entrance was typical. For Rodario it was in fact quite restrained. No drums, no fanfare, no herald?

The kings and queens watched the dramatic approach of the new arrival with amazement, but limited their reactions to an amused raised eyebrow here, an expression of slight disapproval there.

"Wherever heroes are gathered and history is written, I must also be to hand. For who else would take true note and show events on the stage to future generations, if not myself?" Rodario granted the company the benefit of his dazzling smile.

"What ho! Lock up your women! The Fabulous Rodario has returned!" grinned Boïndil.

Rodario smiled and stroked his elegant beard—shorter now than Tungdil recalled. "I have not come on my own, Your Gracious Majesties. I bring you a man who is able to answer many of the open questions puzzling Girdlegard." He gestured to the door with his cane.

A moment later a man appeared. His short black hair and his thin moustache gave him a fleeting resemblance to Furgas, except for how old he looked. He was wearing a simple pair of breeches, a shirt over them, boots and a cloak. His clothing all seemed too big for him and flapped around his shrunken body.

"I have come to . . ." he whispered and threw Rodario an uncertain look. "I have come to atone for my deeds. I cannot ask forgiveness for what I have done."

"By Vraccas! It really is Furgas," Boïndil said, horrified. He had recognized the magister technicus only by his voice. "Rodario the Incredible has incredibly managed to dig him out."

"No, I did not dig him out, but freed him, good friend Boïndil Doubleblade. On my own. Freed him from the clutches of thirdlings known as Bandilor and Veltaga, who have made their home on an island that they can submerge or bring up to the surface as they choose. In the middle of Weyurn's waters." The actor used every rhetorical trick in his repertoire as he described the meeting with Furgas. His narrative arts were such that the entire audience hung on his every word. "Finally we swam the five miles through the wild waters and arrived at Mifurdania. From thence we journeyed with the traveling *Curiosum* outfit to reach

Porista," he told them, concluding his tale. "So we have found the culprits who send out death devices to hound the dwarf peoples."

"Masterly, indeed, Rodario," said Isika graciously. "Magister Furgas. What deeds were you speaking of? Why did you say forgiveness could not be sought?"

"Because not only did I construct the island for Bandilor and Veltaga. I built the machines as well," he whispered. He repeated the account he had given to Rodario. "Through my actions countless dwarves have lost their lives. It is my fault. More will die. The next device is on its way." He asked for a glass of water. "You must pronounce sentence on me. I will accept any punishment."

The marquee buzzed.

Tungdil went over to Gandogar to ask for clemency for Furgas.

The high king bent forward. "Do not worry. I am not seeking his life," he said quietly. Then, raising his voice: "We shall not hold you responsible, magister technicus. Your genius and your injured soul were both abused by the dwarf-haters. Our revenge shall be against *them*, not you. You were their tool; they used you for their malign plans. But we shall never forget the countless victims. We demand of you that you do everything in your power to stop further dread events. For now you have our understanding. Do not disappoint us."

"You see? Like I said: they can tell the difference. Now be brave and tell them everything," Rodario said gently, brushing over Gandogar's threat. "They won't hurt you."

Furgas sobbed. "I . . . built the machines," he repeated, in despair.

"We have pardoned you," repeated Gandogar.

"No, there are *more machines*, though." He told the story through his tears of the malformed hybrid creatures he had adapted, constructed with his own hands. The kings and queens sat thunderstruck. They listened, horrified and enthralled at one and the same time. It defied imagination. "I am to blame that they are rampaging through Girdlegard, killing, maiming and bringing destruction."

Tungdil watched the elf princess. Apart from himself she was the only one whose countenance was not a mask of disgust and fascination. On the contrary, she seemed glad. She was assuming, as was he, that she now understood the significance of the pit at the bottom of Weyurn's lake. She turned her head abruptly and looked him in the eyes. He felt she could read his thoughts. "Let us look on the bright side of Master Furgas's report: it means there is a new magic source in Girdlegard." Rejalin's voice rang out clear and true. "And it seems the unslayables do not know where it is. Those two thirdlings will be clever enough to keep it hidden from them, so that they can hold sway over them and keep them dependent."

"Of course." Tungdil understood at once what she meant. "The magi of Girdlegard left nothing to chance when selecting their own prime locations. They chose to be within the magic force fields: their power source. When the magi left the fields they would find their magic diminished after a few spells," he explained. "Andôkai the Tempestuous and my own foster-father Lot-Ionan once told me how it all worked. Only by using the power of the magic source were they able to perform their incredible feats with words, gestures and immense concentration." He stopped to catch his breath. "I assume these machine monsters function by the same principle. They will have to reload with the magic, never mind what complicated mechanics they employ."

Gandogar slammed his fist down on the table. "At last! A weak point!" he exclaimed with relief. "Magister Furgas! Where exactly is this source?"

Furgas shrugged his shoulders. "I don't know. Somewhere at the bottom of Weyurn's lake."

"You've no idea? A clue? Some island in the vicinity?" Isika gave an agonized groan. "By Palandiell, get thinking, man! It's you we have to thank for this whole ghastly plague!"

"Most of my islands float, Queen Isika," Queen Wey came to his rescue. "Even if he had noted one of them it wouldn't help us."

"Then," said Tungdil Goldhand slowly, "we must bring up the island together with its thirdlings and just ask them."

"We'll be with you there." Gandogar grinned. "For a cause such as this even dwarves shall take to water and defy the curse of Elria." He looked at Queen Wey. "This is a matter for our folk, Your Majesty. I shall send you a contingent of my best warriors, dwarves of untarnished reputation without the slightest shred of a thirdling connection. They will be glad to fill the gaps in the ranks of your own army to make good the losses sustained in the Paland massacre. The island of the thirdlings will be taken by storm. And the magic source will be protected."

Queen Wey inclined her head in agreement.

"I suggest we retire now and convene again in the morning for the last time. Then the groups will leave and do what has to be done," announced King Bruron. "At long last we have an opportunity to do something about the dire threats that paralyze our native land. Palandiell will protect us."

"May I help alleviate the shock and worry?" offered Rodario, bowing deeply. "I invite the mighty rulers this evening to attend an exclusive premiere performance in the *Curiosum*. The production is an exquisite comedy which should restore some laughter into these serious times. If we lose the ability to laugh, we have lost everything."

Tungdil turned to Ireheart. "Your brother in spirit. Another who enjoys a joke."

"Nobody tells them like I do," the warrior replied quietly.

Rodario grinned. "Entrance will of course be free of charge. I shall not discourage you, however, from making a small donation to reward the troupe for their skill and artistry."

To his surprise the monarchs promised to attend. It would be the most important performance of his entire life.

Tungdil, Ireheart and Goda had found a big room near the square where Bruron's new palace was being built and the assembly marquees stood. The undergroundlings were staying in the same house. The landlord was a little more puzzled by them than by the dwarves, now a familiar sight.

They were brought a decent meal and a large jug of beer.

Goda was getting a lesson from the warrior twin about standing firm in battle. Boïndil was showing her the various methods of sweeping an opponent off his feet with the edge of a shield.

"You have to make yourself heavy," he explained, ramming his own shield against hers. There was a loud crash and the dwarf-woman retreated two paces. "Make yourself heavy, I said!" he scolded.

"But I had my whole weight on the floorboards," she protested.

"Standing firm is a skill." He waved her back into position. "But it's more than just having broad feet and sturdy thighs. Stand so that your center of gravity is between your two feet, then bend your knees slightly and bring your head in and down." He demonstrated. "Now try to push me over."

Goda lifted her shield, took a run-up and slammed against her instructor. The noise was ear-splitting.

Boïndil didn't budge. "That's what I meant by making yourself heavy. It's important to be able to withstand an opponent's attack—an orc in a fury, if need be." He rubbed his belly. "And they're twice as heavy as me." He tapped her shield. "Try again. We'll practice all night if we have to."

"Ho, stop there," called Tungdil, who was writing notes on the discussion in the assembly. There were still some puzzles. Speaking to Balba Chiselstrike, the only one to escape from Paland, had not thrown up any clues. She couldn't recall any of the elf runes on the wheeled monster.

Even Furgas could not remember any elaborate runic designs. But Tungdil knew the rune was there. Each of the creatures had been carrying one. Now he was annoyed not to have peace and quiet to work things out. "I'm trying to think. How can I when you two are carrying on like a couple of Vangas?"

"What are you trying to work out? It's time for fighting now, not thinking, Scholar." Ireheart's eyes were blazing. "We haven't found any orcs yet but these machines are quite something." He whirled his shield around. "Ha! I'm itching to measure my skills against one of the under-groundlings!"

"Haven't you already done that?" Tungdil remarked. "You lost, didn't you?"

"That wasn't a proper fight, for Vraccas's sake. That was like trying to catch an eel." He gave himself a shake. "When I say fight I mean axes and blades and heavy weapons. Crashing and clattering. I don't really think they're related to us."

The way he said it, he'd already made up his mind: dismissive of them. Tungdil looked up. "They are dwarves. Nothing can change that."

"Well, they see themselves as brothers to those orcs." Goda's answer was too swift. It seemed the two of them had already been discussing this during their combat exercises. "Their god created them at the same time. What was it they call him?"

"Ubar," Tungdil supplied. He put his arm on the back of the chair, his expression reproachful. "I'm glad you two agree about something for once. But you sound just like the elf princess."

Ireheart made a face. "Scholar. We can't make common cause with the undergroundlings. They're taller than us, they fight differently and they don't even use axes. Only this . . ." He made the shape with his hands. ". . . this toothpick thing. No, we weren't made from the same stuff as them." He nodded at Goda, who charged at him again. Another mighty crash.

"You are being unfair," said Tungdil, shaking his head.

"And you are obsessed," the dwarf countered. "I saw how you were constantly watching them. It was obvious you wanted to talk to them to find out more. It stops you being objective. That's science for you."

"On the contrary. My judgment is extremely objective." Tungdil wasn't taking this lying down. "I'm probably the only one in all the five dwarf folks who *is* looking at them clearly. From everything you say it's obvious how blinkered your viewpoint is. And you're one of the few who are more open to new ideas . . ."

"And you have the right to judge others?" Ireheart charged Goda, who was steadier on her feet this time. This earned her a nod of respect. And a long gaze right into her eyes. Perhaps overlong.

She lifted her shield to cut his stare short.

"I'm not judging anyone." Tungdil sat sighing over his notes. He was regretting this conversation. He knew it was no use talking to a stubborn dwarf like Ireheart. Every word would be misunderstood. "I'll speak to Furgas later, to see if I can find out anything else about these creatures' weak points. We won't stand much of a chance without that knowledge. None of us—not even you."

"We'll see. My crow's beak always finds a crevice to

latch onto." Ireheart was offended. "Come on, Goda. We'll go and practice outside." She rolled her eyes and followed him.

But once the others had left the room Tungdil was not able to regain his train of thought. Instead he mulled over Boïndil's words.

His friend was right. He was indeed fascinated by the undergroundlings. He knew hardly anything about them apart from their appearance being different from his own. He didn't know how they lived in the Outer Lands, nor what the values and philosophy of their community might be.

He stood up and went over to the window to look down onto Porista. Its roofs, smoking chimneys, laundry fluttering on washing-lines all gave an impression of settled permanence. People had found the place they wanted to remain, they had started their families there.

This all ran contrary to his own feelings. He did not feel at home either with the dwarf folk or with the exiles, or with the humans. Even Balyndis could no longer give him that feeling of belonging; he was a loner, a fighting scholar.

Or perhaps, deep down, he did not really want that safety, that sense of belonging?

"Am I destined to be an eternal wanderer? Should I maybe go back to the Outer Lands with the under-groundlings? To help them restore the diamond to its rightful place?" He spoke quietly. "Will I find happiness, Vraccas?"

He looked at the jug of beer. The alcohol was calling to him, its smell reminding him of nights he had spent under its influence. When drunk he had ceased to quibble and worry.

Tungdil tried to resist the temptation but still he moved over toward the table. Just as he stretched out his hand to the handle of the jug there came a knock.

He dropped his hand at once and went over to open the door.

In the doorway there stood an undergroundling. A woman.

He had noticed her on the journey. Her skin was as dark brown as a nomad's and she had kept near him on the march. She wore a beige tunic embroidered with thorny branches, fastened at the front with lacing, but showing part of her breasts. Now he could see her for the first time without the rather intimidating helmet. He stared at her shaven head. He had not been prepared for that. A woman without her crowning glory!

"May I come in?" she asked him with a smile. Her speech had the attractive lilt of a foreigner's.

"Of course," he said quickly, stepping aside to let her in. She was a hand's breadth taller than he was. "What message does Sûndalon send?"

She strolled around the room, stopping to examine the sketches in his little notebook. Her clear blue gaze alighted on the helmet he had drawn. "You've drawn mine!"

"Yes. Should I not have done that?"

"It doesn't worry me." She held out her hand and he noticed a wide scar on it. "I am Sirka."

He shook hands with her. "Pleased to meet you. My name you already know, I think." He waited in vain for her to tell him Sûndalon's message.

"It would be strange if I didn't," she replied with another smile.

He cleared his throat. "Forgive me if I was staring just now. The dwarf-women of Girdlegard have a different skin color and they don't shave their heads. They wear their hair long." He was feeling awkward.

"I don't suppose we have very much in common," said Sirka. "Sûndalon tells me you're a scholar." She took up the little notebook and turned the pages. "You are interested in everything that's new?"

"I am." Tungdil was caught unawares by the dwarf-woman's behavior—she suddenly stepped toward him, tossing the notebook onto the table.

She put her hands to his face, and pressed a kiss onto his lips. He did not try to push her away. "I like you very much, Tungdil," she confessed, running her fingers over his chest. "I would love to show you something new, if you'd let me do that?" There was no doubt what the offer entailed.

"You undergroundlings indeed have little in common with our dwarf-girls," Tungdil stated, with the touch of her lips still felt on his own. He had enjoyed the kiss. A great deal.

So much that this time it was Tungdil who kissed her. His placed his hands on Sirka's slim hips and pulled her to him. He could smell the intense perfume on her neck, could feel the warmth of her body through the thin tunic. His hands wandered up to the laces of her gown . . . Then his conscience flared up.

"No," he said hoarsely and quickly stepped away. "I belong to another."

But Sirka followed him and embraced him. "What does that mean, '*belong*'?"

He avoided her and put a chair between the two of them. "Sirka, you flatter me," he said, trying hard to control his feelings and not give in to her urging. "But I am tied to Balyndis and as long as that is so I cannot allow myself to indulge in an adventure like this."

She laughed. "Oh, I understand. You people go in for lasting relationships."

"Don't you?"

"No, we love for as long as we like. When feelings change, we part. Perhaps for a while, perhaps for ever. It makes life easier, Tungdil. Life is short enough." Sirka gazed at him. "You're looking for something new? How would this be: Accompany us to Letèfora. On the way I'll tell you everything you need to know about our people."

"Letèfora is . . . ?"

"A town. One of many in my homeland. And very different from towns in Girdlegard."

"Yes," he said, without a moment's hesitation. "That would be delightful," he added more thoughtfully.

She laughed and gave him another kiss, running her fingers through his hair and stroking his beard. "That would be delightful," she repeated as she went to the door. "We shall be seeing a lot of each other, Tungdil. I shall teach you well. The lesson you missed today we can take up again at leisure." She opened the door and left the room.

Tungdil sat down. He was aflame, with her scent still in his nostrils and the taste of her mouth in his own. Sirka had captured him with her open unaffected manner. It was not only her physical charms he was thinking of. He was looking forward to the lessons she had promised him.

But first he would send a letter to Glaïmbar and talk to Balyndis. Or, better still, he would write her a long letter.

He took a sheet of paper and wrote a few lines to Glaïmbar first, sealing the note and laying it on the table in front of him.

Then he started the letter to his consort Balyndis, ending his relationship with her. Not an easy task, even for a scholar like himself.

The words would not flow smoothly from the pen. He was struggling. He wrote that he would never be able to make her happy. Not in the long term. Not how she would wish it. And the long term, for his people, was a very long time. He did not want to do this to her.

Meeting the undergroundling woman was only a prompt for this parting. He had long been aware in himself that things were not as they should be, but he had always sought the reason elsewhere. He had never been more certain than now that Balyndis deserved better than this.

In his choice of phrasing he was scrupulous to take the blame on himself and not to give her the impression that she bore any responsibility for the failure of their partnership. His lines would affect her harshly, all the same.

This letter, too, he sealed and laid on top of the note to Glaïmbar.

There was no going back. The meeting with Sirka brought home to him what was missing in his life: passion. Something new. Scholarship and the spirit of enquiry were his curse. He did not want safety and shelter.

"Vraccas, what malleable stone did you take when you formed me?" he sighed. He had absolutely no desire to attend the theater performance.

Girdlegard,
Kingdom of Gauragar,
Porista,
Summer, 6241st Solar Cycle

Tungdil woke with a start. He must have dropped off over his notes and in the meantime night had fallen in Porista.

Standing up and stretching his aching back, he heard the vertebrae click back into place.

Sleep had brought no brilliant ideas about how to catch the elves out and expose their malice. He had no evidence—only the undergroundlings' warnings and his own observations back in Âlandur. The elf they had found in the forest was still lying unconscious in the guesthouse on the edge of town, where they had left him guarded by ten soldiers. They had managed to keep his presence quiet.

"If only he'd come round." Tungdil shook his head. He picked up the tankard of beer. This particular temptation must be removed before he went to bed. He opened the window and chucked the contents out. It splashed onto the cobbles. The danger was past. "Why isn't everything that simple?"

A shadow swung down from the roof and in through the window, striking him on the chest.

Tungdil crashed back and hit his head on the edge of the table. He saw stars.

Three black-garbed figures leapt in. Their faces were masked and they carried short swords. One secured the door, and the other two pinioned Tungdil's arms. A blade was pressed against his throat.

"Where is it?" whispered a female voice.

"Where's what?"

"Keenfire!" she hissed.

"Hey, thickheads," said the man at the door, pointing to where the ax hung in its case from a protruding beam against the wall.

"Samusin is with us. It's going to be easier than I thought," she laughed. "I was afraid we'd have to deal with that mad fighting dwarf and his apprentice as well." The man next to her stood up and reached for the ax.

This galvanized Tungdil into action. He jerked his head to one side and thrust the blade away, forcing it into the woman's unprotected thigh. He reaped a small cut on his hand but she received a deep slash on her leg.

"It's mine," he yelled, drawing his knife. He had soon realized that these intruders were not trained assassins or experienced thieves. They were mere beginners and he was eager to find out why they had set their sights on the most important weapon in Girdlegard.

The woman yelped with pain and he whacked her on the forehead with the handle of his dagger so that she collapsed on the floor. He set after the man who had just grabbed the ax, stabbing him from behind in the leg.

The man roared and spun round, swinging Keenfire to

attack him. Tungdil ducked and the tip of the ax buried itself in a wooden post.

"Let go," growled Tungdil threateningly, leaping forward knife in hand to force his adversary to retreat.

The man crashed against a chest of drawers and the blade struck him in the side; he broke off cursing and pressed his hands over the spurting wound.

Tungdil wrenched the ax out of the wooden beam and whirled it in his hands. Watchfully he approached the last of the three masked intruders. "Now tell me who you are and how you got the crazy idea to steal Keenfire from me."

The man brandished his short sword, the blade quivering. "Get back!"

"On the contrary." Tungdil feigned an ax-blow, and while the other was trying to dodge it, he kicked him in the groin so he sank groaning to his knees. Tungdil placed the heavy blade at his neck to let him feel its deadly pressure. "Well?"

"Kill us and you will never see Lot-Ionan again," the woman spoke, pulling herself upright on the post. She let herself fall, groaning, onto a chair and examined the wound in her thigh.

"So you're the ones who stole him?"

"I said right at the start that it was a stupid idea to steal the dwarf's ax," moaned the man who had been stabbed in the side. "Get a medicus. I'm bleeding to death here."

"No one leaves this room till I know who you are." Tungdil stood threateningly at the door.

The woman pulled off her face-mask and used the cloth

to bind her wound. She was no older than eighteen cycles. A hank of light brown hair had escaped from her head-scarf. "I'm Risava of Panok. That's Dergard, and he's Lomostin. We were Nôd'onn's famuli and ever since his death when the force fields were lost we've been trying to find a way to bring magic back to Girdlegard," she revealed to the astonished dwarf. She stood up and limped over to where the injured man lay.

"What do you want with Lot-Ionan's statue if you were followers of Nôd'onn?"

Risava looked at the men, who both took off their masks. "We were going to try to free him from the spell. He can help us. Our land needs the skills of magic so that we can stop the creatures who are hunting down the diamond." Her face darkened. "If you had only listened to Nôd'onn this would never have happened."

Tungdil thought she must be joking. "Andôkai said the petrification spell was irreversible."

"Perhaps for Andôkai it was," Risava spoke with disdain.

"Have a care," warned Lomostin. "Don't tell him too much."

"Wrong." Tungdil stroked his ax. "Tell him everything. It is better for your health. You can still cast spells if need be without your foot."

Risava moved back and spoke to her companions. Tungdil did not take his eyes off them and readied himself to prevent them escaping.

At last she turned back to him. "Right, I'll explain. Andôkai did not have the knowledge that we have. We have spent the last few cycles studying Nudin's secret library and learning magic spells. In theory. But we do not have the magic energy to give life to the formulae." Risava indicated the ax. "We thought we'd be able to get enough magic force from Keenfire to free Lot-Ionan. He would know what to do."

"He would never teach you." Tungdil did not dare to believe what she was saying. He could not tell whether she was speaking the truth or not.

"Nôd'onn or Nudin, no matter now. He is dead," said Dergard, still holding his privates in agony. "We mourned him for long enough to know his views had been corrupted by the daemon within. He had no free will anymore." He looked at Risava. "She'll understand. In our hearts we renounced Nôd'onn long ago. As she said: we have Nudin's knowledge and want to continue his works—*his* works, not Nôd'onn the traitor's. Lot-Ionan *would* have taken us on, I'm sure of it."

"Stealing the statue wasn't a good start." Tungdil took the ax away from the neck of the famulus. "You should have told me and King Bruron."

"He'd not have believed us any more than the people of Girdlegard, or you." Risava stood up carefully leaning on a chair. "We want to bring Lot-Ionan back to life. The humans, the elves, the dwarves—they all have faith in him. He would have found a way to present us as his new initiate pupils without our reputation going before us."

Tungdil stepped past her to check the injured man's wounds.

"The wound in the leg isn't bad and the left side will heal quickly," he said after a swift inspection. "We'll clean it up and get you stitched up. Then you should have bed-rest for a few orbits until it has all healed over." He looked at Risava. "You will take me and my friends to the statue. You may have Keenfire and you can try to revive Lot-Ionan with it." His eyes took on a threatening glint. "But if you try any treachery, you and your friends will be killed. At the moment you are no use to Girdlegard, so it makes no difference whether you're around or not."

"It's a waste of time," said Lomostin through clenched teeth. "I was holding the ax in my hands and there's not enough magic in it. It won't be any use for our plan. The magic source . . ."

Risava bent down and touched his wound as if by mistake; the rest of his sentence disappeared in a howl of pain.

For Tungdil the hint was enough. He grabbed her arm and twisted it. "You know about the source?"

Risava stared at him stubbornly and remained silent.

"Tell him," said Dergard. He took a deep breath to relieve the pain in his side. "Perhaps he knows what we can do. The fate of Girdlegard is at stake now, not just our own futures as famuli."

"So what are you supposed to tell me?" Tungdil increased the pressure on her arm. Her wrist would soon snap. "It'll be difficult to do magic without your arm."

She clenched her teeth, tears streaming down her face. "I'll turn you to ashes with a single spell," she grunted.

"But you can't," he replied, twisting further. There was a grating sound. "Speak now or watch your bones stick out through the skin."

Risava moaned. "A new magic source," she stuttered. He let go of her arm. She curled up in pain, her forearm against her chest. "We have found a new source, but it's in Weyurn. Under the lake. It's too deep to get to."

Tungdil felt enormous relief. He felt elated for the first time. There was going to be an answer to the threat from the unslayables. Lot-Ionan, the submerging island and the famuli—together they gave him the answer to the prayers he had sent up to Vraccas.

But he forced himself to conceal his feelings. If they really had Nudin's archive and had studied his spells they must not be allowed to learn that it might be possible to get down to the lakebed. Not until Lot-Ionan was restored to life and could decide for himself. "We shall see what we can come up with," he said calmly. "First take me and my friends to where the statue is. Lot-Ionan shall be in my care from now on."

"What are you going to come up with that hasn't already occurred to us?" objected Risava. "The water is many hundred paces deep according to the fishermen we've asked. No diver can get near. If you could get down you'd never get back up."

"My race has achieved many things," he smiled at her. "Now, let's get some of my friends and we'll bring the statue to safety." Tungdil opened the door, one hand still keeping Keenfast at the ready.

Dergard pointed to Lomostin. "What about him?"

Tungdil gave him an encouraging glance. "A medicus will come and see to him. As soon as we have the statue." He waved the others out, closed the door and blocked it from the outside using a flagstaff that he'd taken off the wall, jamming it under the door handle.

*   *   *

The performance was going very well.

The great and the good of Girdlegard were sitting in the *Curiosum* watching the action on stage with refined smiles. The script was from Tassia's pen. Those who were not so great and good were splitting their sides with laughter. The combination of Tassia's acting talent and her undoubted physical charms had enthralled the audience.

Rodario, not needed in this first act, was watching the spectators happily, if slightly enviously, through a hole in the scenery. Tassia was his creation but she was getting all the attention these days. She was overtaking him in the theater hierarchy here—in his own troupe and in front of his own audience.

"Look, Furgas," he whispered. "The men adore her and the women admire her."

"You've conjured your rival up yourself," the props man retorted quietly, as he checked the strings that controlled the smoke colors and the flames—anything to do with his special stage effects.

He had spent the preceding orbits sorting out any small hiccoughs in the various contraptions. Time had not left his inventions unscathed. But now everything ran like clockwork. The scenery changed by itself, with the sun rising and sinking automatically. Trees moved in the wind and Furgas had even introduced some artificial forest smells to make the illusion complete.

"Have I said how glad I am to have you back with us?" Rodario said seriously.

"Because I've repaired everything?" his friend grinned.

Rodario turned to face him. "Not only that," he smiled back, clapping him on the shoulder.

"I'm very glad to be out of the clutches of the thirdlings. I'm in your debt." When the cue came on stage, Furgas tugged the yellow string and the lamp above Tassia went dark. The light faded gradually, the sun set, and the night sky was revealed, to murmured appreciation from the audience.

The actor laughed out loud. "You're working off your debt to me splendidly."

A door flew open and Tungdil stepped into their narrow space backstage. "Oh, sorry. I thought it was the side entrance."

"It is. For the actors," hissed Rodario. "Quiet. You're much too late for the performance. We haven't got any more seats but you can watch from the gangway. I will give permission," he said graciously.

"There'll soon be a seat free. I need Ireheart." He pushed Rodario aside and looked through the spyhole to find his friend in the audience.

"What's happened?" asked Furgas tensely. "Have the monsters arrived?"

"No. Something good's happened at long last," he whispered happily. "Three famuli have turned up—they stole Lot-Ionan's statue and they tell me there's a way to bring him back to life. One of them's injured; up in my room. I'm going off with the other two to collect the statue."

"By Palandiell! Can it be true?" Rodario bent down. "Shall I stop the performance?"

"No, I want to be absolutely sure they've got the statue, and I want it in my hands before we tell anyone else." Tungdil beamed at him. "And they know where *the* source is."

"What source?" Furgas pulled the red string now, letting a cloud of fog rise onto the stage. "*The* source?"

"The magic source, exactly. The one the monsters get their power from." He hurried to the corridor that led to the auditorium. "I'll tell you more later," he said excitedly. "I've got to get on now." He nodded to them both. "There's hope. Great hope." Then he disappeared.

Watching through the spyhole, Rodario saw Tungdil go up to Ireheart and Goda. The three of them left the marquee at once. "What do you say to that?" he smiled. "It's just one momentous occasion after another. I've got more material than I can ever turn into plays." He stroked his beard. "I'll start up another *Curiosum*," he decided. "Tassia can run it. What do you think?"

"Smart idea, Rodario," said Furgas. "That's the way to sideline your rival—promote her."

Rodario nodded. "Exactly. And she'll be eternally grateful to me. Lovemaking right, left and center, nights of passion whenever I knock on her door." He heard his cue and adjusted his costume before he stepped out through the curtain on stage, winking at Furgas. "I'm terribly pleased with myself."

The scene was an adaptation of the time Nolik had stormed into his caravan. Here on stage the number of attackers had obviously been increased for the sake of the action; the fight for Tassia's affections and the struggle for the jewelry were even more dramatic. Soon the ruffians lay senseless on the floor or had taken flight.

"And thus love and a sword triumph over adversity." Rodario addressed the spectators.

Tassia joined him, holding up the necklace. "And the

necklace makes up for everything I had to endure." The thin gold shimmered and glowed; the rock crystal flashed in the lamplight from the stage and sent sparks dancing over the audience—over humans, dwarves and elves. Tassia threw herself into Rodario's embrace. "What are you going to give me to make up for what I shall have to endure with you?" she asked, fluttering her lashes.

"The diamond!" came a shout from the audience.

"No, not a diamond," Rodario picked up the cue. "Not a diamond—I shall give you my heart!"

Gandogar leaped onto the stage, his right hand closing over the pendant. "Lights!" he shouted.

"Your Royal Highness, Noble Majesty, high king of all the dwarf realms, sire. I know your people are awfully keen on gems and jewelry and that you get really passionate about them, but you are ruining my play!" said Rodario, politely but with impatience. He grabbed the necklace. "Go and sit down again, Your Majesty, and watch the final act. I rule here on this stage. You will be good enough to recognize my status."

Gandogar pulled the jewel out of his hands again. "This is one of the diamonds, you idiot thespian!" insisted the king. "Can't you understand?"

Rodario laughed. "Your connoisseur's eye has been deceived here, Your Noble Majesty." Faster than the dwarf could react, Rodario had taken possession of the necklace. "The pendant is made of polished rock crystal, not diamond." He swung it from his hands. "It is paste, Your Majesty. I would never use a genuine precious gem as a stage prop."

"I am the king of the fourthlings; my tribe is descended

from the best gemstone cutters amongst the children of the Smith and if anyone knows about jewels then it's going to be me, not some actor!" he retorted so angrily that his beard quivered. "Give me the diamond! At once!"

Tassia tried to mediate. But just then a huge creature mounted the stage. It was taller than dwarf or human and thick strings of twisting muscle showed under its gray-green skin. Apart from a leather loin cloth and boots it was naked. Round its forearms white chains hung.

Its contorted älfar gaze was focused on the pendant, the eyes glowing green. "Give me the necklace!"

Everyone in the auditorium stared in surprise.

King Bruron was the first to applaud. "What a magnificent performance!" he called. "The creature looks just like the one Tungdil and the soldiers described."

"Totally lacking in taste," complained Isika.

Rodario and Tassia stepped back; the actor held up his sword. "Run, Gandogar!" he said hoarsely, horror compressing his larynx. Hastily he thrust the jewel at him. "Save the last of the stones from Tion's creatures."

Then mayhem broke out in the theater marquee.

XI

Girdlegard,
Kingdom of Gauragar,
Porista,
Summer, 6241st Solar Cycle

Risava stopped outside an anonymous-looking house wedged in between properties that reflected the status of wealthier owners. "Here it is." She opened the door and went in.

Tungdil, Sirka, Boïndil, Goda and two dozen dwarves followed her in, prepared for action; the wagon lined with straw was ready in the street outside.

They saw at once that the building had not been occupied for some time. There was a layer of dust on the furniture. Only the tables and chairs showed frequent use. It all smelled of cold smoke.

"We come here because of the cellar," said Risava, who had come to a halt in the entrance. She touched a special place on the wall and steps appeared, leading down, when a stone slab moved aside. From the vaulted basement Tungdil caught the familiar smell of paper and parchment. "Is this Nudin's library?"

"No, it's mine," said the woman, lighting a lamp and leading the way.

Soon they were all crowded into the small cellar room with walls full of shelves and books. In the middle stood Lot-Ionan's petrified statue inside a circle drawn with magic symbols; several runes had been sketched on the surface of the statue itself.

"We've got everything ready," she explained. "All we need to revive him is the magic."

"How did you get him here?"

Risava indicated the steps. "Carried him down. It took nearly all night."

Ireheart walked round the statue. "There are a few bad scratches," he said, running his fingers over the grooves.

Tungdil examined the damage. It was a strange feeling. Was he looking at a statue or a person? Perhaps Lot-Ionan would soon be emerging from the stone, the magus he had lived with for many cycles, his own foster-father. They could not afford to make any mistakes. "Should we fill the marks in with mortar before trying to bring him to life? We can't have him bleeding." He saw a hole in the stone robe near the spine. "Or he might fall down dead."

"What do you think?" he passed his query to the famuli.

Dergard shook his head. "I wouldn't do that." He studied the hole, a finger's width. He seemed surprised. "I didn't see that before. Could have been rats or something else like that."

"I agree." Tungdil ordered the dwarves to get the carrying belts from the wagon. "It would be like a foreign body to introduce mortar into his flesh. If it wasn't part of him when he was turned to stone then it won't be changed back when he is restored to life."

Ireheart bent down, picking up some of the powder he saw on the floor. "Stone dust." He scratched around the opening. "It all fits. This hole has been drilled on purpose."

He turned to Risava and Dergard. "I don't know of any animal outside of the mountains that eats stone."

The two humans looked at each other helplessly. "I swear by Samusin it wasn't us," said Risava.

"Perhaps a fourth famulus, still loyal to Nôd'onn and who wants to see Lot-Ionan dead?" suggested Goda. "The hole was concealed. It was probably to serve as a fallback in case we managed to bring him back to life."

"Then they would have knocked his head off, apprentice," Ireheart said, looking at her crossly. "That should cost you fifty push-ups, but I'll be generous."

Tungdil tore an empty page out of a book, rolled the paper into a spill and pushed it into the hole to see how deep it went. "As deep as my little finger. A person should be able to survive that." He ran his hands over the statue. "And anyway, he'd be able to heal himself at once. We must just risk it."

The dwarves came back with the leather harness. With a combined effort they managed to load the stone figure of the magus onto the wagon, bedding it down on the straw.

"The diamond!" The monster's dark eyes shone green as it shook the chains free from its forearms. The älfar symbols glowed and transferred their light to the iron links. Then it swung the chains at Rodario and Gandogar; both were caught within the coils.

At the next moment and before any of the spectators could move, the creature launched itself into the air, catapulting straight through the stage scenery, dragging its captives after it as if they weighed nothing at all. Pieces of the stage flats broke off and fell down, one of them hitting Tassia and trapping her while dwarves and soldiers rushed off in pursuit. "Help!" she sobbed. Planks collapsed, bringing down sections of canvas from the tent. Smoke started to rise. Tassia could hear people stampeding past her to escape from the monster. There was no time to come to the aid of some actress.

At last Furgas came over to free her from her distress. She wept and threw herself at him, grabbing hold of his shoulder. He froze. Finally he put his arms hesitatingly around her and consoled her.

"Come along, let's get you out of here." He yelled orders to the theater group, most of whom were standing rooted to the spot in terror: they must put out the fires. He carried Tassia out and sat her on a makeshift bed. "You'll be safe here," he said. "I must go and save Rodario."

She nodded and calmed down but the pain, coupled with the shock of the monster's appearance, had hit her hard.

Furgas ran off, following the sounds of commotion. He could see from Porista's lighted windows that the towns-people had been aroused. It wasn't long before he found a crowd of soldiers and dwarves surrounding Rodario and Gandogar.

Whereas the actor had got away comparatively lightly, the monster had torn off Gandogar's forearm. The dwarf king lay unconscious on the cobbles, being attended to by a healer who was binding up the stump.

Rodario was bleeding from numerous cuts and grazes. Both he and the high king had burn marks on their clothing from the red-hot chains. He was holding his head. "Awful," he said indistinctly. "I was nearly dragged to my death. It has the strength of twenty horses." He looked over at Gandogar. "This courageous dwarf refused to give up the diamond and actually attacked the monster. It simply wrapped the chain around his arm and yanked . . ." He turned pale and covered his mouth with his hand. "I mustn't think of it."

"Where did it go?" one of the soldiers asked.

"I don't know." Rodario pointed up to the roofs. "It made one great leap and disappeared. It had no trouble getting right up to the rooftop and then jumped to the next one. You won't catch it now. It'll be over the city walls."

Bruron appeared, surrounded by his bodyguards. He saw he had arrived too late. "Summon the assembly," he commanded one of his servants. "And get Tungdil Goldhand. We need to make a new plan and must hurry if we are to save Girdlegard. There's no doubt now that the unslayables possess all the diamonds." Cursing, he turned and walked back to the tent.

Furgas gave Rodario a helping arm.

"How is Tassia?"

"She has a scratch on her shoulder," Furgas told the actor calmly. "Nothing serious."

"Amazing." Rodario looked up at the rooftops as if he could still see the monster. "I had the most powerful of the gems and had not noticed." He gave a wry laugh. "I am stupid enough not to be able to tell a crystal from a diamond."

Furgas patted his shoulder. "Don't fret. You didn't know what the stone looked like. It wouldn't have helped if you had known—it wouldn't have stopped this catastrophe."

Rodario nodded and fell silent.

"Hey! Take care, you clumsy idiots, or you'll have his nose off!" Ireheart called with a grin. "He'd turn you into a gnome for that."

The dwarves sweating with the effort of heaving up Lot-Ionan's statue laughed and renewed their endeavors to lower the magus gently down.

Then they heard the alarm boom out through the night. There was no more peace and quiet in Porista now.

"What does that mean?" growled Ireheart. "Are they hunting down the impresario?"

There was a clink and a green glowing iron chain shot down from the sky, coiling itself around Risava's neck.

She grabbed at it, gasping for breath, but at once skin, muscles and vertebrae were ripped apart as if made of paper and rotten wood. The torso remained upright for a moment then collapsed convulsing to the ground. Blood pumped out of the neck stump. The famula's head fell to the cobbles with a dull thud.

"Stand against the wall!" Tungdil ran to the side and pressed himself against the side of the house, to give the whipping chains no chance. He raised Keenfire and looked up.

"The damned froggy," growled Boïndil. "This time you won't get away. I'm going to pull off your fine legs and I'll have you crawling. You will pay for ruining my beard!"

The creature scurried over the roofs to right and left,

covering huge distances effortlessly. Every so often it would show itself to the dwarves to mock them.

"What does it want here?" Goda wondered, not taking her eyes off the roof-line.

Tungdil looked at Risava's corpse. "It must have felt that hope was emerging for Girdlegard." He turned to Dergard and signaled ten dwarves over to protect him. "Ireheart and Goda, you lead them. The rest go with me," he ordered, running off to the wagon on which Lot-Ionan lay. "Let's get him away from here."

The chains hissed close and tore both the dwarves nearest to Tungdil screaming into the air; they crashed down, ripped in two halves, as if a giant child had broken and dropped them.

Then the creature leaped on to the street to face Tungdil, bared its teeth triumphantly and let the chains sway and dance.

"I shall kill you all," it promised in a clear voice. A jerk with one arm was sufficient and the chain killed one of the undergroundlings as the tip smashed the dwarf's head.

Sirka appeared at Tungdil's side. "Let's get going. I'll distract it and you strike," she said earnestly, attacking the monster without waiting for Tungdil's reply.

While she was moving in on the creature the second chain came whipping out and wrapped itself around her weapon, making the iron glow red hot.

With a scream the undergroundling released her hold but she was not giving up. She drew a dagger and stabbed at the monster.

Tungdil swung Keenfire, swiveled on his heel and slashed

at the thigh of his huge opponent. The ax flamed up, diamonds blazing out a cold light and the weapon-head drawing a fiery circle after itself.

The creature saw the danger and swerved to the side, taking the relatively harmless dagger-blow to its belly and avoiding the swipe from Keenfire. The ax had missed by a hair's breadth.

But the long spur of a crow's beak smote it on the kneecap. "Ha, how do you like my brother's ax, froggy?" came Ireheart's malicious laugh, as he jerked the haft of his weapon to bring the monster down. "You didn't think that I would hold back when I can kill this beast, did you, Scholar?"

The creature yelled out. In the high elf-like tones the animal sounds of an orc-voice could be heard. Then it thrust its hand out and grabbed Ireheart by the shoulder. The älfar runes on its forearms started to glow.

The dwarf cried out, held stubbornly fast to the handle of his crow's beak and kept pulling.

"Mind out!" Tungdil swung Keenfire again. This time the blade bit home and the monster's forearm sheared off, together with the wrist guards and the chains.

The enemy stared at the severed arm and at its own gushing black blood, staggered backwards and launched itself howling from the floor. In spite of its injury and the crow's beak in its knee it managed to jump onto the next roof. Thatch and shingles tumbled down to the street. The monster had gone.

Goda ran off after it.

"Stop! Come back!" Ireheart crouched on the floor. A cloud of steam rose from his shoulder and there was a smell of burnt flesh, hot iron and scorched leather. "Look at that! Froggy's got me!" he spoke through clenched teeth. "We nearly did for it, though?"

Tungdil saved his remonstrations; the pain was punishment enough for his friend. The mail tunic had heated up with the effect of the magic and had burnt through all the layers of clothing, stencilling a black pattern. "You are mad, Boïndil," he said, helping him to his feet. "Let's find Goda."

The dwarf-girl was back already. In her hands she bore the bloodied crow's beak, its spur missing. "I heard it break and went off to see," she explained, handing the weapon to her master.

"That fine spur," he grumbled, examining the damage and running his hands over the jagged edge. "I'll have to get it repaired."

Goda slipped under his arm to support him and he used the remains of the crow's beak as a stick. "You must rest now and get that wound looked at."

"Oh that's nothing," he said, playing it down. "I've had worse than that, great gaping wounds with blood and guts spilling out. A bit of burnt skin is not tragic."

Tungdil looked at the group of dwarves round Dergard, then at Risava's body, already starting to grow cold. "So now we have only two magi," he murmured. "We'll have to protect them well. This won't be the last attack." He gave the signal to return to their quarters and was just about to send a messenger to call in the assembly when a soldier came running up.

"There you are, Tungdil Goldhand! King Bruron is looking for you everywhere. The monster has stolen the final diamond," gasped the man. "It happened during the performance. It surprised us all. We had no chance to stop it. We need you there so they can decide what to do next."

"Damn! The froggy had the stone. And we've let it escape," groaned Ireheart. "Oh Vraccas! How did that happen?"

Tungdil exhaled sharply and looked at Sirka. "The dwarves and the undergroundlings have one thing in common at least." He wanted to clap her on the shoulder in acknowledgment, but put his hand on her back instead and to his own surprise left it there. She held a strong attraction for him. He watched her face, thought about that kiss and would have gladly repeated it. Now, right now.

"Courage?" she said, laughing.

"Exactly," he agreed swiftly, because he had left far too long a pause and had been staring at her. His behavior had been noted by Ireheart and Goda. He swiftly took his hand away from Sirka's back. First he had to talk to Balyndis.

They hurried through Porista's lanes and narrow streets, now full of guards.

"One more thing, Tungdil Goldhand," the messenger addressed him. "We found a dead body in your room. It looks as if he had been stabbed and died as a result of his injuries."

"That can't be so," Tungdil replied at once, as they approached the assembly marquee. "He was an intruder I confronted. I wounded him on the leg and on his side. The injuries weren't dangerous."

"Very strange. I saw the dead man myself and I assure you, the body had been carefully slit right up the middle."

"The froggy! The monster got to him as well!" Ireheart exclaimed, looking at Dergard and the dwarf-guards who surrounded him. "Don't leave him for a second, even if he needs to have a shit, right?"

Tungdil and Sirka exchanged glances and he could read her thoughts: The monster might have ripped the man to pieces, chucked him off a roof, torn his throat out, but it would never have sliced him through with a clean sharp blade. He would know more when he had seen the body.

The undergroundling came to his side, her hand this time on his back. She put her face down to his ear. "I think you have a traitor in your midst, Tungdil," she whispered.

He shared her assumption. The thirdlings had a long arm and it reached all the way to Porista.

Girdlegard,
Kingdom of Gauragar,
Porista,
Summer, 6241st Solar Cycle

"Under the circumstances I don't think it would be advisable to split our forces," said Ortger. "Tungdil Goldhand must protect the magus with Keenfire until he is able to defend himself against the attacks from the unslayables and the monsters." He regarded the men and women in the assembly. "Besieging Toboribor seems pointless now. Soldiers cannot combat these powers. Not now the enemy holds the genuine diamond." He indicated Dergard, who was sitting between Gandogar and Tungdil. "Let us send him and the dwarves to Weyurn to seek out the island."

Tungdil rose. "Indeed. The sooner we take Dergard and Lot-Ionan to the source, the better." He moved over to the map of Girdlegard. "The unslayables will need to find a way to use the stone. The eoîl stole it from evil but transformed it into a power for good. I don't think the älfar will immediately work out how to use it." He circled Toboribor with his finger on the map. "And we should keep the siege going. We ought to send raiding parties into the caves to harass the unslayables. Have you considered why they never set out themselves to find the diamonds?" Tungdil paused. "I think they are too weak and so they sent out their creatures instead. We must not give them a moment's rest. Even if it means risking the lives of more of our troops. If they acquire the stone's power before we revive Lot-Ionan and before Dergard can cast any spells, we are lost." He sat down.

"Are any better suited to combat in caves than the children of the Smith?" Rejalin's question was friendly. "It would be madness to send such experienced fighters out to storm an island when they're invaluable underground, because they can see in the dark better than a human or an elf." She looked at Gandogar. "I trust the dwarves, Your Majesty. You should send your warriors to Toboribor, every man you can spare from duty on the gates."

Tungdil grew hot under the collar. He cursed the fact there had been no opportunity to give the high king Sûndalon's report about the broka. He sensed a trap in the elf princess's suggestion. He could not pin it down;

her words had seemed eminently sensible. Dwarves were indeed excellent at fighting in tunnels.

Sirka, standing behind Tungdil, now leaned forward. "That broka is up to something," she warned, reinforcing his unease.

Gandogar, however, was flattered by Rejalin's words and was ready to accept the proposal. "You are right, Your Highness. But I must insist it should be our people who take the thirdlings' island. If the other sovereigns are in agreement I shall send our warriors to Toboribor." Pain was audible in his voice; the sedative herbs were only a slight help in stilling the agony from his injured shoulder and mutilated arm. All those present in the assembly admired his stamina.

"It will take too long," Tungdil objected. "At least sixty orbits. We would be wasting precious time. The cave attacks must start much sooner than that."

Queen Isika had not yet—luckily for Tungdil—accepted Rejalin's idea. "We mustn't forget that there may still be traitors in the dwarf tribes looking to make common cause with our enemies."

"And if this were so, Queen Isika, we should be the ones exposed to them in the tunnels of Toboribor—not your people," Gandogar interjected. "Let that be our concern. If there are ten traitors among my five thousand warriors, what harm can they do?"

"I agree with Rejalin," said Ortger, smiling at the elf princess. "The dwarves know what they're doing and we can keep this area safe. My soldiers are used to moving in the mountains and can secure the peaks."

While the rulers gave their assent one by one, Tungdil

hurried to Gandogar's side. "The elves are not to be trusted," he whispered. He gave a quick summary of Sûndalon's story.

"If you ask me it looks as if the same thing is happening here as the undergroundlings suffered."

Gandogar had listened carefully, his eyes closed. Then he looked at Sirka. "How long have you known these undergroundlings?" he asked Tungdil.

"You know how long."

"And you think you can trust what they say?"

"Your Majesty, I . . ."

He raised his hand. "No, Tungdil. Our peoples have been living in harmony for many cycles now. Now they have sent envoys to impart their knowledge to us." His eyes sought Tungdil's. "Apart from the word of the under-groundling dwarves, whose origins are questionable, have you . . . ?"

"Gandogar, you . . ."

"Enough," came the unusually sharp command. Sweat was collecting on the king's brow; the effort of controlling the pain was too much. "Everyone knows their origins are in doubt. And until I've seen one of these supposedly harmless orcs they call ubariu and been given proof of their good intentions I shall stick to my opinion." His brown eyes were resolute. "Even if I believed you, the others here would not. Not without evidence." He lowered his head. "Do you have evidence?"

Tungdil clamped his jaws so tightly shut that they hurt.

"Do you have this proof, Tungdil Goldhand?" repeated Gandogar.

"No, I don't," he admitted reluctantly. He was near to

despair. If only the injured elf back at the inn would regain consciousness and could speak! "No."

"Then I must keep silent on this matter."

"Promise me at least that you'll warn our warriors about the elves," begged Tungdil.

"I shall." Gandogar turned his attention again to the assembly. The great and the good of Girdlegard were unanimous now; even Queen Isika had accepted Princess Rejalin's suggestion. "It is decided. The united fighting force of dwarves will set off for Toboribor. The thirdlings and secondlings will form the vanguard," he announced, wiping the perspiration from his forehead.

His words were greeted with applause.

Sûndalon could stand it no longer. His request had not been considered. He raised his hand and waited until the clapping ceased. "Do we get the stone back when you have defeated the unslayables?"

"No," answered the elf princess at once.

"I think we should let Lot-Ionan decide," said Tungdil, in an effort to avoid a dispute. "He will know best what the diamond's power is."

"In my opinion it would be too dangerous to give the diamond away before it has been minutely examined." Rejalin gave the undergroundling a gracious smile. "Don't misunderstand me. I trust you but I don't trust the Outer Lands. And you tell us that these supposedly mild-natured orcs have a . . . was it a rune master?" Sûndalon nodded. " . . . they have a rune master who is versed in magic. The last thing we want is an orc with limitless magic powers. Not even in the Outer Lands."

"Then you are condemning our land to destruction,

broka," snarled Sûndalon. "And if creatures from the Black Abyss find their way to Girdlegard, then think on this day and on these words of the broka."

"We have the children of the Smith guarding our gateways," she replied calmly. "So far they have failed only the once to defend us. It will not happen again. Is there an alliance stronger than this?"

Sûndalon grabbed hold of his weapons with both hands, as if needing them for support. Or perhaps it was the princess's throat he imagined in his grasp. "It is typical of your people to spread insults or poison. It is not for nothing we have eradicated them in our realm."

Rejalin raised her eyebrows smiling still. She had achieved her goal; she had the undergroundling breaking through the thin ice she had led him onto.

"You have done what?" whispered Queen Wey, grown suddenly pale.

"Then broka means *elf* and not *älfar*," said Isika, her voice toneless. "We are sharing a conference table with creatures from the same creator as the orcs who have wiped out all the elves in their land?"

"You misunderstand," Tungdil objected, trying to salvage what he could. "They had to do this! The eoîl stole their diamond and incited the elves to violence against them. They could not see clearly." He was gathering all his courage to speak his suspicions out loud, but Rejalin was ahead of him.

"Then there is no question of giving you the diamond, Sûndalon. My people will never let that happen." Her beautiful features displayed arrogance and ice-cold determination. "If you should ever get possession of the stone you will lose it again through our doing. Whether it be in Girdlegard or in the Outer Lands." Her bodyguard behind her put their hands on the pommels of their swords.

"It is better if you leave," said Gandogar to Sûndalon. "And you, Princess Rejalin, watch your words before they launch something that cannot be stopped."

The undergroundlings left the assembly tent.

After a brief hesitation Tungdil followed them out. When he was halfway through the lobby he turned on his heel. "We shall meet in Toboribor," he told the gathering. He made no bow to them. "May your gods stand by you and may they open your eyes, Your Majesties all, before it is too late." He left, Ireheart and Goda in his wake, together with Furgas and Rodario.

What remained was an uncomfortable oppressive silence.

Nobody spoke; Bruron closed the meeting. There were tasks enough before them and issues in the air that neither elves nor humans nor dwarves wished to discuss.

Girdlegard,
Queendom of Weyurn,
A Hundred Miles West of Gastinga,
Summer, 6241st Solar Cycle

They were taking far too long to get from Porista to the shores of the lake where their ship was waiting.

There were many reasons for the delay: unexpected rainfall meant the cart with Lot-Ionan's heavy statue was getting bogged down, then Dergard fell sick and they had to stop over at a farm until the fever passed. They could not take risks with his life, and at the same time they must not deplete their force by splitting into two groups. The ax Keenfire could not be wielded in two places at once.

Tungdil sat with Rodario and Furgas in the farmer's parlor studying a map. This was a rare document that actually showed the Weyurn territory now under flood-water. They were trying to guess the location of the disappearing island.

Ireheart and Goda were doing sentry rounds with the guards. They had a hundred secondling dwarves and a dozen undergroundlings led by Sirka, even if Boïndil did not approve. He was also far from approving of the apparent flirtation between Tungdil and Sirka. He had made his views clear to his friend after Sirka made no attempt to conceal her affections.

Rodario raised his head. "Is our esteemed Boïndil in a bad mood?" he asked Tungdil. "I just heard him yelling at the guards again."

"It's the weather. Dwarves can't stand rain. And he's hot-blooded and spoiling for a fight." Tungdil went on poring over the chart. They'd got a shortlist of five loca-tions. "Can the island travel along underwater?" he asked Furgas.

"So, it's his hot blood, is it?" Rodario stepped over to the window. "Or is it his pupil?" He watched them practicing in the barn. At first glance it all seemed straight-forward, but his dramatic training had sharpened his senses to signs of physical attraction. "I get the feeling there are sparks flying there." He turned to Tungdil. "Yes, definite sparks."

"Best stay well out of that," said Tungdil with a wry smile. He was keen to avoid discussion of feelings and attraction, for fear he and Sirka might be the actor's next target.

Furgas drank the tea the farmer's wife had brought them. Still underweight and pale, he would sometimes sit in the corner all day saying nothing. Other times he'd be completely normal. The effects of whole cycles in captivity would not be easy to get over.

"Yes, it can," he said, in answer to Tungdil's question. "I made a system of tubes and chambers that fill with water or steam. If the valves are opened, and the contents expelled, it propels itself slowly forward."

"Not good." Tungdil leaned back in his seat. "Then it could be absolutely anywhere."

"No. It can't move fast. It's a mountain we're talking about, creeping along under the water." He drew a ring round the place they presumed was its last sighting. "It would be roughly in this area. It has to come up every so often to take on air and to get food for the workforce."

"They can see it but nobody will talk because it's the nightmare älfar-island and everyone's terrified," Rodario added. "Ingenious, these thirdlings. The front-story of älfar was a neat idea to keep people quiet."

"We can only hope the queen's ships come across the island by chance and word gets round they're not really älfar and that there's a considerable reward for information about the island's whereabouts." Tungdil helped himself to tea and let his thoughts wander a little.

In his mind's eye he saw Balyndis and Sirka. Dwarves as different as it was possible to be.

He had been hoping his fascination with Sirka would be a passing infatuation, intrigued though he was by her appearance and behavior. She was the opposite of Girdlegard dwarves. But he still couldn't keep his eyes off her or his thoughts away. He recalled another time his loyalty to Balyndis had been tested. Myr.

She had been a thirdling spy, a scholar like him, and Balyndis, under pressure from the elders of her clan, had been advised to leave him. It was no wonder that Myr and he had got together—until her treachery was revealed. Then it had been easier not to be troubled by conscience.

"For a magus in training, Dergard's a bit on the vulnerable side, don't you think?" Rodario had discovered the cake the farmer's wife had left on the side. And then he spotted the daughter of the house running past the window in the rain to the barn to milk the cows. "What a delight," he murmured dreamily, cutting himself a slice.

"What would Tassia say?" Furgas said crossly. "You're the same as five cycles ago. It's not clever, just selfish."

"I've no idea what she'd say. She didn't ask me my opinion when she slept with other men," he retorted, taking a bite. "We're both grown up and have a taste for life. So what's the problem?" He would never admit to the jealousy he felt. "Don't you have eyes for womenfolk anymore?"

"There aren't any women in my life now. I swore to be faithful to Narmora. Just because her body no longer exists doesn't mean I don't stay true," he said, his voice unsteady. "I dream of her each night and she gave me the strength to survive the time on the island. I would never betray her by desiring another."

"An admirable attitude, Furgas. Keep away from women and you won't get hurt." He chewed the mouthful of cake, his eyes still on the farmer's daughter. "Imagine if *you* had fallen for Tassia. Oh Palandiell, what a disaster! She's my female equivalent."

Tungdil noticed Furgas was getting jumpy.

"The girl certainly understands the art of seduction, I can tell you. She's as faithful as a leaf in the breeze, blowing this way and that." Rodario rattled on, stuffing his face with cake. "It has cost me dear, finding that out. I can only warn everyone about her." He laughed quietly. "Little slut. But I can't stay away." Then he turned to face the dwarves. "Do you still need me? I'd like to help the farmer's girl with her churns."

"Leave her be," said Tungdil. "I don't want a row with her father. They've been so good to us."

"Don't you worry your head, hero. I'll be as discreet as anything." He winked at them and left the room.

The barn where Goda and Boïndil were working out was huge.

The farmer had put fleeces down in the old hay loft and new washed wool waiting to be spun. Two weaving looms behind had been clattering away the last couple of orbits.

Boïndil took a couple of ropes from the wall and was snaking them in turn toward Goda. "Imagine these are lots of opponents attacking you." The first one, with an iron ring at the end, was coming at her fast. She turned and avoided it.

"Excellent," he said, aiming the second at her left thigh.

Goda managed to swerve out of the way several times but the fifth rope hit home. The iron ring hit her on the breast.

Ireheart tutted impatiently. "That's you dead, Goda. That was a sword-thrust in the chest." He pointed to the floor. "Forty!"

"I'm not doing press-ups," she protested. "I would have warded off the blow."

"You wouldn't." He looked her full in the eyes and regretted it at once. His warrior heart was working overtime. "Fifty."

Goda picked up her flail. "Try it again, master. I'll show you what the night star can do."

"No, you won't. You're supposed to be taking avoiding action." He was angry that she was questioning his authority. "Sixty." Now he made a threatening move toward her.

She raised her weapon. "First you'll have to get me on the floor." She pulled in her head, and her eyes blazed. "I have had enough of being ordered about, master."

Previously Boïndil would have rejoiced at the prospect of being free of his young pupil. But now it was his worst nightmare. "You're confusing persistence with bullying. It's for your own good," he said to cover his embarrassment. "You asked me to teach you how to fight."

"Or else? Seventy?" she laughed with malice.

Ireheart grabbed the handle of the night star and rammed the top of it against her head. Goda started to topple and he placed his foot behind hers, pulling it from under her so that she fell. "One hundred," he said, twirling her weapon in his hands. "You let go of the night star.

You know only to do that if you have a second weapon on you."

She propped herself up on her elbows, ignoring a trickle of blood from her forehead.

Boïndil sighed and went over to crouch down beside her. "Goda, I'm trying to keep you safe and alive."

"With push-ups? Is it to impress the orcs? Perhaps I can challenge an opponent to a contest?" she hissed, sitting up.

Again their faces were very close.

Ireheart swallowed hard and swung back as if a Vanga had bitten him. "No. It's to motivate you to make more effort," he muttered. "If you don't make the mistakes you don't have to do the press-ups." He took a handful of the wool and tried to wipe the blood from her face.

"What do you think you're doing?" Goda thrust his hand away roughly.

"I wanted . . ."

"I know what you wanted, master." She flashed at him. "And I know what you *want*. Don't forget you killed Sanda. I feel nothing for you. I'd rather have Bramdal than you. Make me a warrior and then let's fight to see how good your teaching was. You can keep everything else. I don't care." Boïndil was thunderstruck. Her harsh tone had hit him to the quick; she had known exactly what he was thinking. "It . . ." He swallowed, searching for words. His spark of hope was dying. Then he pulled himself together. "It's not what you think. I am your instructor and I am concerned for you. That is all."

"So I should hope." Goda turned and pushed herself up from the floor. She began her press-ups. One hundred of them. Blood dripped from her forehead but that did not bother her.

Ireheart watched, vowing to himself that he would not give up.

When Rodario opened the door he found a soldier whose armor bore the insignia of King Bruron.

"A message for Tungdil Goldhand," he announced, looking past Rodario. "That'll be you?"

"Eyes as keen as an eagle's," joked the showman. "How many dwarves do you see sitting here?" The soldier went over to Tungdil, handing him several rolls and folded papers.

"I am to bring your answer straight back to His Majesty," he said, retreating. "I'll wait outside."

"Get yourself something to eat and have a rest," invited Tungdil. "It will take some time. Send Boïndil and Sirka in."

He waited silently until the messenger had left the room and the others had joined him, then he unrolled the parchment.

Goda came in as well. She seemed to have her mentor's complete confidence. Tungdil noticed she had dried blood on her face. Weapons practice must have been rougher than usual today.

"It's from Prince Mallen," Tungdil read out. "The initial attacks on the caves at Toboribor have been successful. The monster whose arm I severed has been killed." His face showed regret. "So far Mallen reports he has lost seven hundred and eleven men in the caves; most of them died through sorcery. There is no indication that the unslayables are using the diamond's power. Furthermore, the first contingents of thirdlings and firstlings have arrived. They will be taking over from his soldiers."

"May Vraccas keep them safe," murmured Ireheart.

Tungdil started to read Gandogar's missive. "In exchange the elves have sent warriors to the realms of the secondlings and thirdlings to undertake guard duties on the walls and gates. Everything is running smoothly, he writes."

"The broka will kick up soon." This was Sirka's dark interpretation of events. "They're just taking up their positions. They have all the monarchs in Porista at their mercy, and they're creeping into the mountains to get close to the dwarf rulers. It's like what they did to us." She clenched her fists. "The difference is that no one in Girdlegard is prepared to stop them."

"Not without proof." Tungdil repeated the words of the high king. "I tried my best in the assembly but Gandogar would not let me speak."

Ireheart looked at the undergroundling. "That is the way of it. No one would have believed you or Sûndalon. Not after he'd said that about exterminating elves."

"There's no reason to lie. They were the danger, not us," objected Sirka.

"You carry orc blood. I bet most of them see you and your kind as a threat," he grumbled, resting his hands on the head of his crow's beak. Since learning of their origins his attitude to the strangers had changed. He rejected them out of hand. He despised them.

"Ubar formed us out of mountain blood. We have the strength of the mountains within us." Sirka had had enough of being insulted in this way. She stood up and approached Ireheart, her eyes blazing with anger. "Ubar created the ubariu from that same blood, made them taller and stronger still and instilled in them a hatred of evil. That is what binds us and the ubariu, dwarf. They have never betrayed their land or the people who live there." She pointed to Goda with her weapon. "Look. She's a thirdling. Can she make that same claim? Which of us two is more trustworthy?"

"Your status is far below that of my pupil, undergroundling." The warrior twin was not impressed by her anger and was not going to tolerate her attack on Goda. "Hold your tongue."

Now it was Tungdil's task to settle this. Sirka was being attacked. "She is right, Ireheart. Goda could easily be a traitor. You know nothing about her except what she tells you. Has she given you any proof of where she's from or of the story she tells? Is there a thirdling who can back up her story? You know just how clever Myr was. I don't like you bringing her to a meeting where secrets are being discussed."

Ireheart looked up in amazement. He would never have expected his friend to criticize him in this way.

Goda stepped forward. "I will not take your insults, undergroundling."

Sirka smiled at her. "I have told no lies about your people. Not all of you enjoy the same good reputation as Tungdil Goldhand or Sanda Flameheart. We are on our way to seek out and bring two evil thirdlings to justice. They are *thirdlings*, Goda. Not undergroundlings. We have no malicious intent on Girdlegard. We wouldn't have spared dwarf lives as we did in our pursuit of the missing diamond."

Rodario insinuated himself between the warring parties and offered round the plate of cake. "Perhaps it's time we all calmed down and remembered who we are really here to fight, before you two scratch each other's eyes out. Have some cake. It's delicious."

Goda sat down and rested her hand on the night star, mirroring Ireheart's gesture with his crow's beak. Sirka went round the table to stare at the map. Nobody ate any cake.

"Well, it's all for me, then," mumbled Rodario between mouthfuls and he went back to the window to watch the farm-girl again.

"Rodario is right," Tungdil looked at Ireheart and his pupil, but there was no apology forthcoming. Instead he held up the letter. "Gandogar says that the secondlings have halted and destroyed a machine that was killing dwarves with gas. Inside it they found containers made of stone with substances in glass tubes which combined to make a poison that did for thirteen dwarves before the machine was tipped into a mineshaft and buried under rubble. They assume it was a similar machine that poisoned the firstling wells."

"So much for the elves being the guilty parties," Goda said to Sirka, who waved her hand dismissively.

Ireheart watched Furgas, who was weeping softly, his hands in front of his face. Once more it was an invention of his that was causing death and destruction.

They sensed it could have been much worse. Poison gas in a densely populated part of the Blue Mountain Range would have meant the number of victims would have been higher still. Hundreds, Furgas thought.

"We have to find the island quickly and capture it," he said, his tone subdued. He took his hands from his face, wiping away his tears and running his fingers through his hair. "The monsters will soon have to visit the source to recharge with magic. They need the island for that. It will be soon. There must be no more victims."

Tungdil agreed. "I'll ask Dergard if he thinks he can travel. Then we'll set off for the shore to embark in search of the island. We'll leave the injured elf on Windsport Island—it'll be the safest place for him." He tried not to look at Ireheart while he was dispensing further orders. "Prepare to move off. The meeting is over."

Boïndil and Goda left the room. Rodario went too, wanting to escape the uncomfortable atmosphere. Furgas finished drinking his tea and left Tungdil alone with Sirka.

"Your friends will blame me that you spoke up on my behalf," she said, coming over and stroking his beard.

He caught hold of her hand and pushed it gently away. "No, Sirka," he smiled. "Don't make it harder for me than it already is." He still had received no answer to his letter to Balyndis. "I'm finding it too hard to resist."

"Then give in," she whispered, raising her arm again to touch him. "There's no harm, Tungdil. We like each other and we will love each other. It is only a question of time. We can postpone it or go ahead and feel much better. Who knows what the morrow may bring?" She moved forward and kissed him.

This time he did not try to stop her. He relished the tenderness; his body was eager for more. He placed his arms round her. She was slim and wiry and at the same time immensely strong under his hands.

And yet he pushed her away. "Wait. I have to ask you something," he said breathlessly, blood surging through him like a river of fire. "What is Sûndalon going to do?"

"You want to know that right now?"

"I couldn't ask you when the others were here," he smiled. "I didn't know you wanted to kiss me. I just wanted to talk."

Sirka took a deep breath and clasped his hands. "He will prepare my homeland to avert the worst," she answered vaguely.

"That could mean anything."

She gazed into his eyes. "I will tell you a secret. Before we left to come to Girdlegard, Sûndalon called the ubar people and the acrontas together," she said slowly. "They will have gathered on the northern border by the gates."

So that was why the orcs were desperately attempting to break through the fourthlings' Brown Mountains. They had an army of orc-haters at their backs, driving them on. "An invasion? You want to conquer Girdlegard?"

"No. We want the stone back. We want to crush the seed of danger that threatens our land. Stone and seed—both are here in Girdlegard."

Tungdil swallowed. "Sirka, how big is the army?"

"They will be eighty thousand ubariu, four thousand acrontas and fifty thousand of my own people."

"Oh Vraccas," he groaned, seeing Girdlegard submerged in blood. "The fourthlings will fight you because they think you threaten them. They will launch everything they have against you to keep you away from the diamond."

"And fail. For the acrontas it will be easy to blast the gates open. We have reconnoitered and found your weak spots." Sirka seemed relieved to be able to tell him everything at last. "But they won't have to. Our scouts have found a way through the Brown Mountains."

"Never!"

"Yes. Ubar showed them a broad path that an army can use without being seen; they can go straight past the fourthling bastions."

"It's impossible," Tungdil contradicted her. "It can't be done! The peaks can't be climbed."

"You will soon see it is true."

"The monsters from the Outer Lands could have found it just as well!"

"They *did* find it, Tungdil. Several times. We stopped them ever carrying the discovery back to their own kind." Sirka paused for breath. "Sûndalon did not want us to tell you before we had recovered the diamond. But I think you need to know." She stroked the back of his hand. "Take it as a proof of my trustworthiness."

"So the peace we have had in Girdlegard is due not only to harmony between the dwarf folks, but to you," he mouthed, shocked to the core.

He was imagining the extent of the destruction if armies of ogres, trolls, älfar, bögnilim and other Tion-bred horrors marched in via Urgon with no warning, streaming out over the rest of Girdlegard. Nothing would remain.

So those cycles of deceptive calm they owed to the protection the undergroundlings had given them. And the undergroundlings were now at risk themselves. "Why did you do it? Why did you never show yourselves?"

"What for? None of your kind came over. We assumed you did not like us. And we knew that our brotherhood pact with the ubariu would cause trouble between us." She stood up and went to the door. "Now it's clear we were right to stay hidden. I must tell them that we're leaving for Weyurn," she said in the doorway. "You won't tell anyone what I've said?"

A thousand questions were burning on Tungdil's tongue but he controlled himself. "No one," he promised, touching his ax to strengthen the vow. "By Keenfire, I swear it." He smiled at her and she slipped out.

His thoughts raged in tumult. Unslayables, undergroundlings. It all sounded like unmitigated disaster.

It lay in his hands to prevent the catastrophe. Again. He did not feel particularly strong and was pleased to know there would soon be support. Soon he would be able to call on the help of his foster-father Lot-Ionan. A wise magus, older than any other soul in Girdlegard, he possessed a strong intellect with a wealth of experience. He had always stood Tungdil in good stead with his sound counsel. His assistance would be needed again. Or better still, Lot-Ionan should decide what to do. Tungdil did not want to be making decisions.

He caught sight of the last of the sealed letters.

He had refrained from reading this one out. It was from Glaïmbar Sharpax. Tungdil was afraid of what it would say. But read it he must.

He stood up, tearing it open.

Highly esteemed Tungdil Goldhand,

You were correct in thinking that I still am very attached to Balyndis. I summoned her to me as soon as I received your letter.

To my great joy she accepted the invitation and to my even greater delight she promised to return to my side. As my first wife she has every right to be there.

I am to tell you that she had been aware of your coldness toward her. For this reason she is prepared to give you up, on the understanding that she will never have to see you again. She says she would not be able to bear it.

I am sure that I shall be able to smooth things between Balyndis and her clan so that relations are as she deserves. I shall be a good husband to her and she will be the best royal consort the fifthling realm has ever seen.

I thank you for the openness you have shown. I respond in kind: true feelings do not admit of change. Balyndis has learned painfully that there is no stable commitment on your part. But we, children of the Smith . . .

Tungdil tore the letter through.

He did not need to go on reading. The important points had been made and he had no taste for a lecture on fidelity from Glaïmbar Sharpax. He knew full well what it entailed. Balyndis had read and understood his letter. He would always be grateful to her, and he was aware how much pain he had caused her. He could not rejoice over the parting.

He looked out into the courtyard to watch Sirka. He met his own reflection on the window glass. "You coward," he said.

His reflection seemed to nod in agreement.

XII

After the initial interruptions their journey now went smoothly. They boarded the two royal ships that had been placed at their disposal and headed for Mifurdania. On the way they put in at Windsport Island and left the sick elf in the care of Queen Wey's palace archivist.

But then their luck ran out.

The dwarves and their companions learned that even a lake could produce extremely high waves, that evening the goddess Elria started to play with their vessels. The waters were set in turbulent motion, and hurled against the stern of their ships.

Constantly tossed up and down they scudded over Weyurn's lake, with clouds of spray drenching them all. Apart from Tungdil not a single Girdlegard dwarf wasn't seasick. But the undergroundlings kept a firm footing on the swaying deck-planks.

Tungdil hurried down below to check on the statue in the hold. He would never forgive himself if any harm came to it now in this gale when they were so close to their destination. His legs set wide to help keep his balance, he walked round the blanket-clad stone figure of his foster-father, testing the support ropes. Then he drew back a corner of the blankets to reveal the face.

"Soon," he promised, taking a deep breath. First it had been a glimmer of hope, the thought he might one day see the familiar and well-loved magus come alive. Now it was as good as a certainty.

What will he say when he hears what has been happening? he wondered, touching the hem of the petrified robe that peeped out under the padded coverings. He caught himself thinking that Lot-Ionan might reproach him with something he had done during the past cycles.

Tungdil grinned. *No, he has no cause. Unless the acts of heroes can be condemned.* He tightened one of the ropes holding the statue in place and then climbed back up the companionway to the others.

"Elria's come up with a new curse for us," groaned Boïndil, leaning over the railing and belching up air. There was nothing in his stomach anymore. It was the first time he had spoken to Tungdil since the row back at the farm. Since then, he had preferred the company of Goda, the actor and the other dwarves.

"This is nothing," grinned Sirka. "Out on the ocean we've seen bigger storms than this."

"There's open sea in the Outer Lands?" Tungdil recalled the sketchy drawings he had seen of the land on the other side of the mountains. He did not remember reading about an ocean.

"Of course. We sail it." Sirka looked at the helmsman. "These ships and crews would be lost on our waters. They wouldn't survive the gales."

Furgas stood by, not bothered by the weather. "It must

have been somewhere near here," he conjectured, scanning the landscape. He called Rodario over: "The distance is right and there's an island over there. Is that the one you sailed round?"

Rodario hung on to the mast, water dripping from his clothes. "Could be. Let's hope the fisherman was correct when he was telling us about the älfar island."

"The storm's on our side," said Sirka. "We can get close without the thirdlings seeing us."

Tungdil surveyed his little group of diehards, remembering the nameless undergroundling who had taken them to Sûndalon that time. He asked Sirka about him. "What did those tattoos on his forehead signify? And the symbols on his clothing? Why wouldn't he give his name?"

"I think only seven people know it. I'm not one of them. He's a confidant of Sûndalon's and serves the acront of Letèfora. He was trained by him."

This information brought more questions than clarity. "But what—?"

"Mountain ahead!" the lookout shouted down. Tungdil had to suppress his curiosity.

Dergard, standing in the cabin doorway, waved Tungdil and Furgas out. "That's where the source is," he yelled against the wind. "I can feel it. No doubt about it."

"If the island has surfaced it means they're either expecting monsters or disembarking them," said Furgas.

Tungdil pursed his lips. Four monsters, possibly with a renewed intake of magic, would be impossible odds if they had not brought Lot-Ionan back to life first. "We don't have a choice," he said. "We have to storm the island and submerge it. Stand by, Dergard." He hurried up to the helmsman and captain to give orders. "Find a place we can land."

"Impossible. See that shoreline? Solid rock. It would slice our hull."

"There's no other way. We haven't got enough dinghies and we wouldn't be able to launch them in this weather anyway," insisted Tungdil. "If need be, run the ships aground and wreck them."

"You're no sailor, Tungdil Goldhand! Have you any idea what you're asking us to do? You're risking all our lives!"

"Just do it, Captain. There's more at stake than a couple of ships." *And a few lives.* He came off the bridge, then down below deck to chase the dwarves and Weyurn soldiers up top to start the onslaught on the island. Lot-Ionan's draped statue was brought up on deck and made ready for hoisting on the crane. Tungdil watched the preparations closely. There must be no mistakes.

They gathered in the bows. The nightmare älfar island grew in size as they approached.

Their ships ran aground on the basalt ledge, the spars of the keels bursting and splintering. None of the dwarves or undergroundlings made a sound; they clutched at ropes or the vessels' superstructure. The wooden planks sliced through as if a giant knife had severed them.

"All on shore!" shouted Tungdil, sounding a bugle to alert the dwarves on the second craft. He leaped off the deck and landed on the rock.

Most of the soldiers and dwarves did the same, although a dozen or so ended up in the water after the ship was forced away from the shore by the broiling waves. They sank without trace.

Tungdil cursed under his breath. Their lives must not have been lost in vain. "Let the statue down now!" he called. He could see water flooding into the open forward section of the ship.

The crane swung round as the sailors maneuvered the winch, and the stone magus left the deck.

When it was half over the shore the ship lurched again, splitting open on the rock like a loaf of bread torn apart.

The heavy weight danced and jumped around like a murderer in a hangman's noose. Then it proved too great a burden. The rope snapped and the statue plunged down.

Dwarves sprang out of the way to avoid being crushed to death. The figure tumbled to the shoreline shelf and started to roll toward the edge.

"Hold it fast!" bellowed Tungdil, running through water that came up to his middle. He pulled and tugged at the statue, together with five companions, but the blankets round it were sodden and it was heavier than ever. A wave threw three of the dwarves off balance. The stone figure of Lot-Ionan slipped over the edge and sank to the depths.

"No!" roared Tungdil, staring in horror at where the statue had disappeared. He stepped forward as if to dive after it.

"Let it be." Ireheart held him back. "Who knows whether you'd ever have been able to bring him back to life. We still have a magus, Scholar. We just have to get him to his magic."

The spell which had turned Lot-Ionan to stone was affecting Tungdil too, it seemed. He could not move. He could not speak. The wind howled in his face, and though he heard the cracking ships' timbers breaking up, his mind was at a standstill, his plans all over the place like liber-ated mercury, rolling and disappearing. *What happens now?* The words went round and round in his head. *I've lost him for all time. It's my fault.* This was no way to defeat the island.

"Tungdil!" bawled Ireheart in his ear, shaking him. "Come on, man. We need you."

"Damnation!" shouted Tungdil into the storm, spray washing away his tears of despair and disappointment. Then his resolute dwarf spirit took over and he exploded into action. "Let's get this blasted island conquered!" He raised his head. "Furgas!"

Furgas appeared, waved and jumped down off the remains of the ship. He took command and led them through the cave Rodario had encountered before. They were now faced with a massive wall. "There's a hidden entrance here," he explained, fiddling with a black stone let into the wall of the cliff.

Tungdil and the others stood back, checking in all direc-tions.

Looking back through the cave entrance Rodario saw another wave lift the damaged ships and smash them against the rock, breaking them into a thousand pieces in the foaming water. A few sailors crawled onto land, but most went to the bottom with the wreck. There was nothing left but to conquer and prevail. There was no going back.

In front of them the wall moved. "This'll take us to the corridor on the middle level of the forge," the actor told them.

"Some of you set the captives free," commanded

Tungdil, "but the rest go on. Follow Furgas and me, straight to the thirdlings." He nodded at them. "May Vraccas be with us. And make us once more the protectors of Girdlegard." He glanced at Sirka, smiled and then signaled to Furgas to set off.

Two hundred warriors ran through the narrow corridor toward an iron door fastened with metal bolts and bars. Furgas knew his way through these locks and contraptions and the door opened with ease.

Rodario recognized the place at once. They were near where he had fled to hide in the cave behind the furnaces.

Soldiers and dwarves spread out.

"Hey!" shouted one of the prisoners. "Who are you?"

Those standing near him heard the shout. The Girdlegard advance party had been sighted.

"By all the good gods: the queen's troops! Praise be to Elria! Will you save us?" the prisoner shouted, rattling his chains at them. Now there were shouts and calls on all sides. The men and women were afraid the soldiers would not free them.

Their cries brought the guards running, thinking there was a mutiny. They soon saw their mistake, but didn't bother to offer resistance. There were too few of them. Aware they stood no chance, they threw themselves on the mercy of the invading party.

But there were ten of the enemy placed in the galleries above, shooting arrows and throwing down red-hot coals. There were injuries, there were deaths. Their swift progress was halted.

Furgas, Rodario, Tungdil, Sirka, Ireheart and Goda meanwhile were leading a group of warriors to the furnace to attack the thirdlings. The sentries here did not run away or surrender. They fought with great spirit and were not to be subdued with a few random ax blows.

"Look out!" Tungdil noticed the forges on the platform above them were tipping, about to empty their molten contents. "Take cover! Get under the rock ledge, now!"

Liquid iron, glowing red, yellow and gold, poured down on them from above, sending sparks flying. Way below, others were caught by the red-hot splashes and were horribly burned. It was an awesome spectacle. A terrible sight—and a fatal one.

Several soldiers and chained workers sank screaming in the flood of red-hot iron; stinking fumes scorched airways and burned lungs. Hisses and screams filled the air.

"Where's Furgas?" Rodario saw that his friend was missing. "Furgas!" he yelled like a maniac. Tungdil had to stop him treading in a pool of molten metal. He would have lost his leg.

"There!" Ireheart pointed down to where he could see the magister's burning mantle smoldering on the liquid fire-death. A blackened arm was uplifted. "Vraccas has punished him for his deeds," he murmured.

"Aim at those archers hiding in the cliffs," commanded Tungdil furiously. They had lost yet another vital member of their invading force. Their ranks were thinning by the minute.

"Furgas," whispered Rodario, horrified at the loss. "My poor friend. The gods have been so cruel to you since the loss of Narmora. I thought they had taken pity on you when they allowed me to find you."

That blackened arm had been a last gesture of farewell

from the man with whom he had traveled the highways and byways for so many cycles, helping to make the *Curiosum* a magnificent success. He owed his friend so much. Gone, dead, incinerated. "We needed you still, Furgas." He wiped the tears from his eyes and drew his sword. "The thirdlings shall die to avenge your death." He stormed back along the gangway.

"Follow him!" Tungdil called to the dwarves. He ordered the last of the captive workers to be freed, telling them to keep the guards occupied. Then the group moved through a gap into a tall narrow cave.

Here was the island's heart. The room was full of valves, tubing and chains that disappeared up into the roof. There were five huge boilers, fifty paces high, taking up most of the floor room. Underneath the cauldrons enormous furnaces raged, producing the steam that made the island function.

Rodario saw the thirdlings next to the metal casing where narrow glass tubes emerged and led into wider funnels. A clear liquid was bubbling away. "You there!!" He brandished his sword in their direction. "You are going to pay for what you have done to my friend and to Girdlegard!" He flew down the steps to confront Veltaga and Bandilor.

Bandilor uttered an oath and moved the lever behind him. "You'll never get out of here alive!" Veltaga ran to one of the cauldrons, swung the lever and whirled the valve wheels.

"I hope the Incredible Showman knows there aren't any stage directions for this bit," said Ireheart, rushing down in his wake, followed by Goda and Tungdil and the rest of the warriors.

Bandilor lifted his ax and struck the lever to disable it. Then, calmly, he turned to parry Rodario's attack; he rammed his shoulder into Rodario's groin and slammed the handle of his ax into the actor's belly.

Rodario kept going. "Revenge for Furgas!" He kicked Bandilor in the privates and raised his sword to strike home. "Die!"

Distracted by the pain, the thirdling was unable to fend off the weapon. It entered his throat leaving a wound no medicus in Girdlegard would be able to treat. Blood spurted out, drenching levers and controls.

But it was not over yet.

Bandilor hit out at Rodario and struck him on the hip. The ax cut a long red swathe down the pelvis bone; clothing and flesh gaped open and the actor fell to the floor. Faster than a hammer hits iron on the forge the thirdling stood over him, aiming his dying blows at the injured man.

"No, you dwarf-hater!" Boïndil suddenly appeared, smashing his crow's beak against the other's weapon, striking it aside. It sang out like a bell as it hit the ground. "It's me you have to fight!" He used the impetus to whirl his weapon above his head before hitting home.

The blunt end collided with the side of Bandilor's head; his helmet could not protect him against the blow. Bone cracked, his face distorted and blood shot out from his nose. He was thrust against the wall and slid down beside Rodario who was lying there groaning.

"One less of you!" Ireheart spat on the thirdling and looked at Goda. "Nothing against your people. Just these blasted dwarf-haters."

Meanwhile Tungdil was trying to stop Veltaga's furious activity. Whatever she was doing at the controls was not good news for them. He felt the pressure in his ears and thought the floor under his feet was moving about less.

"Water!" yelled Dergard, pointing to the entrance. "They've let the water in!"

Tungdil guessed what that meant. The two thirdlings, faced with obvious defeat, had opened all the valves and started a dive. "Close up the vents! Close everything," he called to those behind him, and then he was hard on Veltaga's heels, chasing her up the iron stairway to the second floor. There were more levers up there she could wreak havoc with.

"You will die with us!" she screamed, grabbing two handles.

He reached her just as she was operating the wheel.

She hurled a dagger at him but he deflected it using Keenfire. Then she pulled out a sharp-edged cudgel for close-range combat—in her left hand a drawn sword.

From where he stood Tungdil could see a huge wave heading for the forge, and clouds of white steam swirled up, hissing wildly. The hot furnaces exploded in the cold water and metal fragments shot through the air.

"Get those blasted vents shut!" Tungdil commanded as he swerved to avoid a sweeping blow from her cudgel. It missed him and struck a valve instead.

At last the dwarves had managed to do what Tungdil had ordered. Some of the injured Weyurn soldiers crawled through and they got the iron doors closed. For the others there was no hope. Water still shot through tiny gaps in a fine spray.

"How did you find us?" hissed Veltaga, raising her weapon for the next blow.

"You dwarf-haters can't hide from us," he answered, blocking the attack aimed at his left shoulder. Then he sprang to the side to avoid her sword. "Furgas escaped. He helped us."

"The magister? He's here?" The dwarf-woman laughed. "Oh, he'll have thought up a special trap for you, if he's brought you here." She followed through with the blade of her sword and swiped at his arm, but his chain mail protected him. "You must be Tungdil Goldhand. The magister always said he wanted to kill you."

Tungdil could not understand what she was talking about. "A trap?" He aimed Keenfire at her middle.

Just in time she moved her cudgel to take the blow, but it bounced back and she was hurt as she swung it. Gasping, she fell backward against a wall of valves. "He always said everything that befell him was your fault. That's why the magister helped us with our plan."

"These are the lies of a dwarf-hater." Tungdil laughed at her. "You won't catch me out like that."

"Why should I lie to you?" Veltaga launched herself against him, attacking with both weapons at once. "You are here and you are going to die. What more proof do you want?"

Tungdil took the sword thrust on his chest. It was painful and broke one of his ribs, but it didn't kill him. The blade of Keenfire struck the metal head off the cudgel, rendering it useless.

As quick as lightning he hit Veltaga on the head with the haft, forcing her down to the iron floor-plate. "A fine plan to sow discord between Furgas and myself. But it won't work." He placed his boot on her breast and exerted pressure. "Do you surrender?"

The dwarf-woman was bleeding from her mouth and nose. The sigurdacia wood handle of the haft was hard as steel. "I don't have to invent anything, Goldhand. All this is the work of the magister. He thought it all up and built it. He created the monsters for the unslayables. They promised to use the power of the diamond against the dwarves."

She jerked her arm up and slashed at him with the sword she still held, but Tungdil swung the broad side of the ax, forcing its barbed hook into her forearm, holding her fast. "Will your lies never cease?"

Veltaga screamed with pain. "I'm not lying. The magister planned everything. He planned for you to be here. He wanted vengeance for his family."

A terrible metallic grinding noise filled the space.

"The doors!" yelled Goda. They're giving way!"

Ireheart stood facing the damaged levers and, with the other dwarves' assistance, tried to operate them; one broke off, another bent and moved the opposite way.

Tungdil turned the ax round and pushed down harder onto Veltaga's arm. "How deep are we going?"

"One thousand seven hundred paces. That's what the magister said. It's the deepest part of the lake," she howled. "You are going to your deaths. We've flooded all the chambers. You will die." She gave a tortured laugh. "Girdlegard's greatest hero and the only weapon that can hold back the unslayables and they'll both be lying at the bottom of the lake. That is a fine revenge." She spat bloody saliva at his face. "That's exactly what the magister wanted. He never needed the tunnel into the Outer Lands at all."

Tungdil gave a jerk on the barbed hook, jolting it free of her arm. Her lifeblood ran out onto the floor-plates. "You thirdlings are beneath contempt," he growled.

"You still don't believe me, do you?" Veltaga looked at her shattered arm. "Ask the actor. The magister sent Bandilor to pay him a visit in Mifurdania and threatened him so he wouldn't pursue him any further. He was too good-hearted. I would have killed the man straightaway, but the magister spared his life." Her eyelids were fluttering now, she was about to lose consciousness. "Girdlegard will perish, that's what he wanted. And you won't be able to stop it." She lowered her head, breathing only faintly. It would not be long before she died.

"What tunnel?" he asked, leaning over her, grabbing her by the collar of her leather jerkin and yanking her up. If there was a tunnel maybe it could be their escape from a watery grave. "Where is it?"

The mountain shuddered. They had arrived on the bed of the lake and the groaning of the iron watertight doors was getting louder.

"You can't reach the tunnel," she laughed through bloodied teeth. "You will . . ." Her gaze went straight through him and her eyes glazed over. She was dead.

Tungdil let go and her body fell back.

"Did she tell us anything?" asked Rodario. "Is there a way out?"

He shook his head. "We'll have to come up with something ourselves."

"Over here!" They heard the excitement in Sirka's voice. "Take a look at this!"

Six pillars ten paces high soared up from the floor, leading to a hexagonal platform, with chains and belts hanging from it. Next to it was a cage-like machine-lift operated by a pulley.

"What's the meaning of that?" murmured Goda, unconsciously copying her master's way of speaking. She touched one of the pillars. "Cold. Nothing special."

Dergard stepped forward. "That's it," he whispered in a voice full of awe. "That is the new source. I can feel the energy flowing through the iron."

"But it's not iron." Tungdil inspected the metal. "It's an alloy. It can conduct magic. Of course! Probably these pillars go down through the floor and stick out of the bottom of the island. They conduct energy from the new source up to that platform." He looked up. "Up there. That's where the unslayables' monsters were created."

"Now it's our turn," said Ireheart, pulling at Dergard's sleeve and pointing to the lift. "This will turn you into a proper magus. Have you thought up a nice wizard name?"

Dergard cleared his throat. "I shall call myself Knowledge-Lusty in honor of Nudin."

Tungdil tutted. "That's not a good idea, Dergard. It has bad connotations for us. Think of something else." He went over to the lift and went in. "Come on. The sooner you get the force inside you the sooner we get out of this prison of ours."

"You *will* be able to get us out of here, won't you?" Ireheart glowered at Dergard. "You magi can always do stuff like that. You have to!"

"I shall try," promised Dergard and he climbed up to join Tungdil. The others operated the pulley hoist and heaved the two of them into the air.

"The Lonely," the man said when they were halfway up. "I shall call myself Dergard the Lonely. There's no one left except me. No other famulus to use the magic. Only me."

"Sad but true," Tungdil agreed. He was watching the platform. Suddenly he perceived a slight glimmering.

Then they saw it clearly. Faint sparks were dancing along the edges, licking at the iron walls of the cauldrons.

"Magic!" said Dergard softly, with a trace of fear in his voice. "What will it be like, to be suffused with magic?"

Tungdil smiled at him encouragingly as the lift drew close to the platform. "Hundreds of magi in the past survived to live longer than any soul in Girdlegard." They slid up past the edge and looked down on its surface. "We . . ." He stopped abruptly "By Vraccas!" he exclaimed. Dergard retreated to the back of the lift.

One pace above the platform an älf floated, supported on a cloud of vapor and lightning bolts that flashed between his torso and the metal. For the most part his breast, belly, lower torso, shoulders and upper arms were covered with armor fused to his flesh. His hands were in armored gloves. The rest of him was naked. A slim narrow-bladed spear rotated next to him; runes on the blade were glowing green.

"Not a monster, but an älf," said Tungdil, trying to open the lift door. "Let us send him to his death before he wakes up." The door bolts were jammed. "Curses!"

He raised Keenfire and whacked it down on the lock. The fastenings shattered and the door swung open.

At the same moment the creature opened its eyes, showing nothing but black sockets under the lids. It hissed at them and showed its teeth, grabbed hold of the spear and sank down onto the platform. As soon as its naked feet touched the metal numerous symbols shone out on the armor.

"Come here!" Tungdil stormed out, his ax raised to strike.

The älf sprang up onto the nearest boiler, pushing off from there like a cat leaping. It catapulted itself up to a gap in the rock. It had gone for now. Sparks and lightning faded away.

"What's going on up there?"came Ireheart's worried voice.

Tungdil stepped over to the edge of the platform and looked down at his friends. "Watch out. There's an älf in the cave. It was on the platform bathing in magic. It was meant to be our enemies' little surprise." He turned cautiously to the walls again. "Dergard, come here."

"Where has it gone?" asked the famulus, feeling safer back in the cage.

"I don't know. We'll see it soon enough." Tungdil went round in a circle, searching; his eyesight was good in the half light. No trace of the enemy anywhere. Unusually for him he didn't mind. Apart from Keenfire they had nothing to match the power of a magic-empowered älf.

Dergard left the cage. He stepped onto the platform and walked into the center. He closed his eyes and raised his hands. Neither he nor Tungdil said a word.

There was a loud crash and a metallic grating sound destroyed the air of reverence. "The water's coming in!" Goda screamed. "The doors have burst! We're all going to drown!"

"Use the lift. Get up here to the platform." The cage clattered down to the ground. Tungdil called Dergard's name, but there was no response. "Wake up! You have to do something!" he demanded, giving him a push. "Dergard! Act now or we'll die!"

The magus staggered. Then he gasped for air and held his breast. "What power!" he breathed, overcome. "I can feel it! Tungdil, I can feel it in me!"

The dwarf grabbed him by the shoulders. "Then use it to save us from the flood here. Bring the island up to the surface!"

The cage appeared with the survivors from down below and they jumped one by one onto the platform. Foaming masses of water surged around the massive pillars, extinguishing the fires under the boilers in vast clouds of steam. The change in temperature put the hot metal under incredible stress and rivets burst, flying out in all directions.

The danger they were in grew by the moment, but all they could do was watch out for the älf and hope Dergard could save them.

The magus was acting as if in a trance. With a grin on his face and hands raised he mumbled something until his fingers started to write glowing symbols in the air. These jumbled about and came to rest on the inner walls of the mountain.

Again there was a shudder; they felt pressure in their ears. It could only mean one thing.

"He's doing it!" Rodario whooped, still holding his injured side. "He's actually doing it! That's what I call a proper test for a new magus!" He sat down again. "And when he's finished saving our lives, can he please sort out this wound for me if I've passed out," he added through clenched teeth.

"Keep watching the walls," Tungdil shouted, reminding them of the presence of the älf.

"Why are we doing it the favor of saving its life, too?" grumbled Ireheart. "Don't let it get away when we get up top!" He was deliberately sounding certain of success.

But the water had reached their thighs and had filled their boots. They could only hope that Dergard was going to pass his test and save them all. And as the water level started to sink there seemed no doubt that he was succeeding.

"Let's get down. And out! Who knows how long Dergard can hold the island?" exclaimed Tungdil. "Look for something we can use as a boat."

They hurried off the platform and ran back all the way to the cave—past ruined forges and the corpses of dwarves, soldiers and workers, over great lumps of rubble still radiating incredible heat. In the grotto they found some long boats tied up in a niche. Rodario remembered seeing guards rowing them, disguised as älfar.

Outside it was dark. Night had fallen. Elria spared them the trial of a new storm and let the stars shine down. They ran out onto the foreshore and launched the boats.

"Anyone seen that älf?" asked Tungdil, looking round.

"No idea where it's got to. But it'll go down with the island, I hope," said Ireheart. "Though I'd have preferred to split it down the middle."

Dergard, sitting in Tungdil's boat, suddenly collapsed wordlessly. The strain had been too much for him to bear. For a magus with absolutely no experience, he had achieved miracles.

But the island did not submerge. So long as the chambers were not flooded it would float on the waves like a cork refusing to sink.

"We must repair the mechanism," said Tungdil. "We'll need it again. Dergard will have to recharge."

"Without Furgas?" Rodario's boat came alongside. "How can we do that?"

Tungdil struggled with himself. Should he tell them what Veltaga had said? It was all lies, wasn't it?

On the other hand, even if some of it were true it made no difference now. Furgas and the thirdlings were dead; there was no danger of new machines. Thus far everyone thought Bandilor and Veltaga were the evil master-minds. He decided that was the way it should stay.

"We'll manage somehow," he told Rodario. "We don't have to do it all quite as perfectly as he did. We just have to be able to get down to the magic source and back up again. Perhaps force fields will form, extending as far as dry land. But until then Dergard will have to go diving from time to time." On his left he saw some lights and a dark silhouette. "There's an island with people on it. We'll row over there and then return with one of Queen Wey's ships. The soldiers can guard our conquest. We've got to get to Toboribor, or wherever the unslayables are now."

There were no objections. They rowed over to the island, found a little fishing harbor and asked their way to the village leader, who they hoped might be able to provide them with soldiers.

A fisherman took them to the brightly lit house of the village elder. "Come in!" He greeted them still in his night-shirt, his brown hair tousled. "It's quite a night, it seems."

"What do you mean?" asked Ireheart.

"You're not the first to visit me." He invited them into his official chamber and showed them the other visitor, wrapped in blankets in front of the stove, drying his wet hair and warming himself.

Tungdil knew the figure immediately from his gray beard, white hair and the light blue eyes, staring straight at him. Faced by the familiar friendly smile of one he thought he'd lost forever, he was completely overcome. He ran and embraced him. "Lot-Ionan," he sobbed with joy.

Girdlegard,
Kingdom of Idoslane,
Former Orc Realm of Toboribor,
Summer, 6241st Solar Cycle

The unslayable one stood in the shadows at the mouth of the cave. In his left hand he held a curved longbow. In front of him ten wire-reinforced arrows stuck upright in the rotting corpse of an overbold soldier, killed eleven orbits previously.

So far no further warriors had shown themselves.

I can smell you. Thirty soldiers: twenty-four men, six women. They were crouching behind a rock trying to work out how they could make it into the cave without incurring loss of life. These were scouts, sent out while the army was limiting its action to throwing a cordon around the hill. *As if you could fence me in.*

Every now and again small units would try to get inside Toboribor. In vain. No one was getting past him and the bastards.

The unslayable one was angry. Getting the diamond had taken much longer than he had thought. He was becoming uneasy. It was delaying their departure and prolonging the danger for his beloved sister. He was not stupid enough to think the human army would hang around forever. And if what the bastards on their travels had told him was true, strange things were happening involving the petrified statue of the old magus Lot-Ionan. He had not reckoned with that.

Three intrepid scouts were making their way up the hill, dodging from rock to rock, their paths intersecting.

"You shall die together," he mouthed. Pulling a black arrow out of the cadaver he notched it and drew back the string. Just before the paths of the three scouts crossed again he sent the arrow to its target.

It hit the first through the throat, killing the man behind and piercing the right eye of the smaller female soldier bringing up the rear.

Her shrill scream brought a smile to his lips. She fell backwards and crawled to the shelter of the nearest rock.

None of the support troop dared come to her aid. It was clear death was waiting in ambush. The unslayable one lowered his longbow and waited, watching the banners on the tents in the distance. *To think so many humans are needed to vanquish a handful of enemies*, he thought contemptuously. *How weak they are. They've always needed the help of others.* He saw two soldiers trying to reach the injured female. They will all be destroyed sooner or later. He picked out the next arrow, blew on the damp tip to dry off the decaying moist flesh from the corpse and prepared his next shot. *What a shame I shan't see it. I'll come back in a hundred cycles to see what has happened to the land.*

The two warriors were trying hard not to be observed. They nearly managed it but when the unslayable one took a step to the side he saw them. They were supporting the injured girl between them and helping her along. Exactly the right configuration to ensure they all died at once.

He ran out of the cave mouth, leaping onto a rock to achieve the height needed for a diagonal aim. He spanned the bow and loosed the feathered end of the arrow. *Fly and take their souls.*

The arrow hummed through the air like black lightning, pinning the legs of all three soldiers. They fell, stapled together by the arrow's shaft and screaming in pain: music to the ears of the unslayable one.

This masterful shot wakened the courage of the others.

"There he is!" He heard the angry shout of a woman and glimpsed the top of her helmet over the rock she was sheltering behind. "Quick! He's on his own and he can't get all of us! Or do we let him go on killing?" She stormed out toward him, her shield held high and sword drawn. The other twenty-four warriors followed her with war-whoops to give themselves courage.

He dropped the bow, unhurriedly drew out both swords

and waited for them to attack. This was just what he needed. Fresh blood to finish the next part of the ceremonial painting he had undertaken in order to welcome Nagsar Inàste back to life. He did not have the herbs from Dsôn Balsur that kept the tints fluid, so he had to keep getting new paint.

He did not move until their first wave was less than three paces away. Then, swiveling elegantly to avoid two arrows flying at him from a distance, he launched himself into his attackers' midst.

Humans moved more swiftly and flexibly in battle than dull orcs, but it still did not make them opponents to fear. Not these ones, anyway.

The unslayable one strode through them, distributing precise death-dealing blows left and right, so the men floundered and obstructed each other.

His two swords admirably delivered their fatal blows. Blood coated the blades and flew off, spattering the rocks, making patterns and lines on the black and gray.

The incidental art-work delighted him. Swinging his arms faster still, he savored the creation of this spontaneous fresco.

He dealt with the human attackers as if it were a routine execution. So superior was his strength that this slaughter could not be described as a battle. Mangled corpses and severed limbs lay all around and death cries provided a chorus audible to the waiting army. Back at base there was uproar as a cavalry unit rode off to the aid of the scouts.

The drumming of approaching hoofbeats did not disturb the unslayable one.

He faced the lone swordswoman who had egged the others on. The tip of his sword was directed at her quivering body as she lowered her own weapon. He read the horror in her green eyes.

"The name of your death is Nagsor Inàste," he addressed her, knowing she would not understand. The sound of his voice was enough to make her drop the shield and sword she bore. "I shall kill your body and soul so that nothing can remain of you." He stabbed her through the throat and she convulsed, clutching at the blade as if to postpone her end. "Expire, mortal." Drawing the blade downwards he sliced through her breast and belly. She fell with a sigh.

He grasped her helmet and, bending swiftly, used it to catch the dark blood spurting warm out of her neck. It would enable him to finish another swathe of the painting.

As he stood up he saw the riders approaching. There was no time for another fight now. Or his paint would clot.

Down in his quarters a blood-encrusted diamond lay on the table and next to it the decomposing severed forearm of a groundling. The golden bracelet on it showed the high status of its owner. He must have been holding the diamond when one of the bastards caught up with him.

By Samusin and Tion! The unslayable put the helmet on the table, picked up the diamond and rubbed the crumbling bits of dried blood off. *He's done it! He's brought me the diamond!*

It was of no consequence to him who had found the stone. There would be no words of praise. The bastards did not recognize any emotions other than contempt and hatred; they felt no pity in the face of pain caused by the machines. The existed for one purpose only: to obtain the diamond for Nagsar Inàste. He had even forbidden them to speak to him; the sound of their voices made him mad.

His right fist closed round the stone. *As soon as she opens her eyes the bastards shall die. Either I shall pitch them against the machines to cover our flight or I will finish them off with my own hands.*

The unslayable one hastened out, traversing the corridors until he came to the cavern where he had placed his sister. He ran up the steps to where she lay, pulling his helmet off from his black hair. "Look what I've brought you," he said lovingly as he knelt at her side. "This will make you better." Expectantly he placed the diamond between her folded hands and intoned the formula he had rehearsed in his mind all through the battle. Every syllable was enunciated with care. The rise and fall of the incantation followed exactly the instructions he had found in the old books.

Nothing happened.

"Blasted eoîl! What has she done to it?" He took the diamond in the tips of his fingers. "Obey me!" he told it. "I know the spell that makes your light subject to me. The parchment rolls in Dsôn revealed your secret to me. You cannot resist!" He brought the stone up to eye level and repeated the dark incantation.

Inside the artifact a reluctant glimmer appeared; the facets refracted the cavern's dull light and threw a pattern onto the walls, the ceiling, his own features and those of Nagsar Inàste.

"My God," he whispered, bending over her. "How

beautiful you are, my beloved sister!" He laid the stone back in her hands and touched her on the shoulder. "Awake from your sleep."

She did not move.

"Nagsar Inàste, rise up," he beseeched, placing his face close to hers. Her breast rose and fell imperceptibly. Warm air streamed gently out of her nostrils—but she remained as if dead.

The unslayable one stared at the stone. "You need more time? Is that it?" A spark of light ran over his sister's body, played on the altar and zoomed back into the diamond. "Then time you shall have," he promised darkly, standing up and replacing the helmet over his head cloth.

He walked backwards down the steps, turned away from his sibling and returned to the cave where he had killed the soldiers. This delay would give him time to complete the painting.

The diamond would carry out its healing work, he hoped. Somehow he would unlock its power for himself. *Out of light I shall create darkness.* There would soon be no more elves in Girdlegard. If need be the battle of Toboribor can run for another hundred cycles. *This is just the blink of an eye for me.*

Back at the cave entrance he saw that ten of the cavalry riders were busy loading the dead onto a wagon not forty paces away. Their horses waited impatiently, tethered to a rock.

How thoughtful of the humans. The unslayable one took his bow and moved over to the rotting cadaver which still held eight arrows ready for him. The woman fighter's blood would have coagulated by now. Time to collect fresh supplies.

His black gaze fastened on two men lifting a fallen comrade by the arms and legs. As soon as they straightened up they were in line, one behind the other. *Two at one shot.*

He pulled an arrow from the corpse and notched it slowly.

Girdlegard,
Queendom of Weyurn,
Twelve Miles Northwest of Mifurdania,
Late Summer, 6241st Solar Cycle

Tungdil's delight at being able to embrace his long-lost foster-father—something he would never have dared to do as his young apprentice—was difficult to express in words. "You are come alive again, resurrected from the stones, venerable Lot-Ionan! The gods were with us all!" he rejoiced.

Lot-Ionan smiled at him, the wrinkled face transformed. "Tungdil Bolofar! A familiar face amongst the strangers in Weyurn. You have grown strong. Strong and earnest. Like a warrior now, not my young smith and errand-boy." He looked round at the others by the door: he knew none of them. "I assume there's lots to tell? I have heard that Nudin was destroyed. More than six or seven cycles past."

"Aren't you too tired?"

"Not in the slightest. It's as if I've bathed in the fountain of eternal youth."

"What is the last thing you remember?"

The magus reflected. "It was the dispute with Nudin. I thought sand was running through my veins and my heart was turning to stone and dying. The next moment I awoke on the bottom of a lake and drowning. My magic saved me."

"We know there is a new magic source there, honored sir," said Tungdil. "But the other source has dried up forever." Before continuing, he turned to his companions. "It's best you go and rest now. Get your wounds attended to. On the morrow we shall all leave for Toboribor. I have a lot to talk about with my foster-father here, Lot-Ionan; I need to tell him what has been happening in Girdlegard." Then he looked at the village spokesman. "Be good enough to see we have somewhere to sleep. Queen Wey will reimburse you for the expense. Please bring us refreshment."

"Of course," replied the man, getting up to give the relevant instructions. A little later they were brought cheese, dried fish, bread and wine.

Tungdil smelled the wine but resisted the temptation. He shook Lot-Ionan's hand once more. "I am so glad to see you," he repeated, drawing up a chair next to him.

The magus noticed the golden mark on Tungdil's hand as it shimmered in the firelight. "What's this, then?" The eyes observed him sharply. "What is happening in Girdlegard?" Running his hands over Tungdil's short brown hair, he said, "And most of all I want to know how things have been for you."

Tungdil suppressed his weariness and related stories from the old times: battles with Nudin, and against the eoîl and her avatars. He told the magus she was an elf who had brought disaster to the land.

He kept it short, telling only the bare facts. But time sped by and when dawn showed rosy-red on the horizon, he was just coming to the most recent events. He told his foster-father about the diamonds, the thirdlings and the unslayable siblings. "Now they have got the diamond, they will try to use its power for evil. At the same time a huge army threatens the fourthlings' gates. It is made up of undergroundlings, orcs and others. They are the original owners of the diamond, and have the right to demand its return." He finished his report. "You have come back at the very best moment." He yawned, not able to resist the urge any longer.

Lot-Ionan was silent and stared at the flames in the fireplace. His hair and his beard were dry by now and he looked as if he had never been turned to stone. "The friends of yore are all dead, nothing is as I knew it." His light blue eyes looked out of the window. "Hardly am I free from Nôd'onn's curse, still trying to take in all the news, and already I must prepare to meet the next mighty foe." He sighed. "And my Tungdil Bolofar is now Tungdil Goldhand. A proper dwarf. A hero." He shook his white head. "Ye gods! What have you done to my world?"

"Your vaults are still there," smiled Tungdil. "The orcs did not destroy everything when they raged through."

"A little stability in these new times." Lot-Ionan turned and put his hand on Tungdil's shoulder. "But if Palandiell, and apparently Samusin as well, want me and the young magus to save Girdlegard from the unslayables, then so

be it. You made your real father more than proud. And
I am so proud of you, too."

Tungdil's eyes were swimming with emotion. "What
shall we do, venerable sir?"

"What you suggested. I will see the elf waiting on
Windsport Island and hear what he has to say. It is hard
to believe that the elves have left the path of light and
been dazzled by the forces of evil." He reached for some
of the cheese. As he did so, he took a sharp intake of
breath and stood up, clutching his back.

"Revered Lot-Ionan, what . . . ?"

He raised his hand. "It is nothing, Tungdil. It seems
not all of me is yet free of the petrifying curse." He made
another attempt to reach out for the cheese and this time
managed it. "It might be old age," he smiled. "I like to
forget how many cycles I have lived so far. I'm not counting
my statue-time." He ate the cheese and drank some wine.
"Then we'll be off to Toboribor to see about the
unslayables. On the way I'll test Dergard a bit so that I
can evaluate his talent. We should be able to vanquish the
älfar leaders. Unless they are able to employ the stone's
power."

"Should we give the diamond back to the undergroundlings?" asked Tungdil.

"I think so. It will save loss of life. If they really have
their own rune master and an army of that size—whatever the acronta might be—then Girdlegard has nothing
to oppose them with." He studied Tungdil's face. "On the
contrary. If they have preserved us in the past and never
tried to conquer our land despite their military superiority, it speaks in their favor. I am happy to explain this

to the kings and queens." He noted how tired-looking Tungdil's eyes had become. "Get some rest, Tungdil."

"No, I can sleep on the boat over to Windsport. At last we have all the vital people together—now is not the time to sleep. Time is on the side of the unslayables, not ours." He stood up and left the room with the magus.

The village spokesman awaited them with the message that two ships of the royal fleet had made harbor, enquiring about a shipwrecked party.

Impatiently Tungdil woke his companions and sent them off to the ship without their breakfast. Lot-Ionan summoned Dergard to his cabin and the two magi disappeared to talk away from prying eyes and ears.

One of the ships headed off to guard the älfar island. A contingent of soldiers was to land and hunt down the älf still at large. The second ship took Tungdil and his companions to Windsport Island to pick up the elf they had left at a shrine dedicated to Palandiell. They would cure his fever with Lot-Ionan's magic.

Now the summer showed itself from its best side. The fresh breeze filled the sails and drove the ship onwards.

Tungdil had closed his eyes as soon as they cast off. He spent the crossing asleep in a hammock until Sirka woke him in the evening.

"Are we there?" He rubbed his eyes, pleased to see her; the sight of her was still unfamiliar and exciting. He was astonished that he still felt shy about responding to her advances. Balyndis had agreed to set him free. Was he still bothered perhaps by the way he had gone about asking for his freedom? It seemed that not all the ties binding him and Balyndis had really been cut.

"Not yet. But soon." She held out her hand to help him up.

He looked at the end of the cliff where an imposing building stood. It now served less as a shrine and more as a house for Weyurn's royal archives. Palandiell was no longer the favorite deity here, as she was in the realms of Rân Ribastur or Tabaîn. Ever since the enormous increase in lake size in the country, the water goddess Elria had become more popular. But innumerable records were available in the shape of parchment rolls which held the memories of the old kingdom, its towns and villages.

The ship slid past while the waves pounded against the cliff fifty paces away. Veils of spray rose up and blew over to their vessel covering everything with a thin damp film. Tungdil was wide awake now.

"I'll tell Lot-Ionan," he said to Sirka and hurried off. It felt like running away almost. But deep inside he was burning to know more about her and her culture, before committing himself. Too many open questions had to be answered.

He knocked at the cabin door. "We have arrived, Lot-Ionan."

The magus could read the unspoken question about how Dergard was shaping up. "Come in," he invited, closing the door behind him.

Dergard was sitting on a bench, not looking very happy.

"My young friend here knows a few good formulae to make magic with, but he understandably lacks experience," Lot-Ionan began. "I, on the other hand, have plenty of experience but the time I spent turned to stone has left gaps in my memory." He touched himself on the temple.

"Sometimes there's a syllable missing, or my hands make the wrong movement. That can ruin any spell."

"What does that mean for our project, magus?"

"That Dergard and I need each other's help to confront the unslayables. One of us without the other won't be much use."

"You are more than one hundred cycles ahead of me, honored Lot-Ionan," said Dergard.

"It would be strange if that were not the case, but it does not alter the fact that my tongue or my hands may let me down. We don't have the time I would need to rectify the gaps in my memory." Lot-Ionan looked at Tungdil and the ax. "It will lie as ever in your hands to do all the fighting. Dergard and I will offer support, but probably no more than that." He was about to touch Tungdil's head but halted suddenly, caught by a flash of pain in his back. "Damned old age," he muttered. "Why have I got no spells for that?"

Tungdil considered the matter. "Let's not tell anyone about your state of health," he suggested. "The unslayables have to believe that you two are the ones to fear. Otherwise I shan't be able to get near enough to use Keenfire. Do you agree?"

Lot-Ionan smiled. "You are a good general, I see. We'll let friends and foe alike think that Dergard and I are the only ones up to taking on the älfar leaders."

The ship's progress slowed; shouts and trampling feet up on deck showed they were docking.

"Now let us see about the elf," said Lot-Ionan, stepping out of the cabin in the lead. The group left the ship, passed the little town and climbed up to the shrine, where its custodian was waiting: a man of about sixty cycles, slightly bald and with a red nose from too much wine. His clothing was in disarray as if flung on hastily.

"Welcome back." He bowed and led them past walls lined with bookshelves. Here were kept the ancient records of Weyurn's subjects: births, marriages and deaths. Queen Wey wanted to be able to trace the history of her land. "Your elf has not yet come round, but he still lives." The man put on an important air. "That is due to my care, of course, as well as to his own stamina." They stopped three paces short of tall double doors. "I am no medicus but I would say that a human would have died long since." His dull, drunkard's eyes swiveled to Lot-Ionan. "Is he your medicus?"

"Indeed," said the magus, to avoid further discussion. He opened the right-hand door and went in, accompanied by Dergard, Tungdil, Ireheart, Sirka, Goda and Rodario. The rest stayed in the halls of the shrine waiting to hear what the two magi might achieve.

The room was flooded with evening light and smelt of the lake and summer. Open windows let in the sound of the waves, fresh air and fine droplets of spray from the spume as the waters hit the cliffs below the building.

The elf lay, eyes closed, hands on blanket and torso wrapped in bandages.

"Thanks," said Lot-Ionan, closing the door firmly to leave the keeper outside. "What have you tried, Dergard?" asked the magus.

"I don't have much in the way of healing spells," he admitted ruefully.

The older magus undid the bandage and inspected the

puncture wounds in the elf's body. At the blackened edges the flesh was rotting. "You tried the formulae you found in Nudin's works?"

"Yes."

"Tell me which ones." Dergard reeled them off and the magus nodded. "These are good charms. Don't reproach yourself for anything. But the elf needs different magic."

He held his hands over the wounds, his eyes hazy. He intoned a spell until a bluish glow emerged from his finger-tips. The light dripped slowly like thick honey onto the damaged flesh, pooling on the elf's chest.

Lot-Ionan completed the charm, stepped back and gave a sign to Dergard, who carried on the procedure. The blue turned pale yellow now.

The magic caused the rotten flesh to be rejected. It shriveled up and fell off as dried skin onto the sheet. The holes left by the arrows closed up and healed over. Only lighter skin betrayed where the injuries had been.

"It is finished," breathed Dergard with relief, nodding at Lot-Ionan.

"Neither of us could have done this on our own," said the older of the two, smiling. "This is a good omen for our continued cooperation." He stepped over to the bed. "Let us wake him up."

Ireheart took a bowl of water and threw it on the elf's face. "Ho, wake up, there! You've been asleep long enough!"

The elf jerked his eyes open. Catching sight of the grinning dwarf he instinctively slid back, hitting his head on the bedstead. His hand flew to the side where he would normally have carried his weapon.

"Don't worry, friend," said Tungdil in elf language. "We found you in the groves of Âlandur with three arrows in you. Your own people had attacked you. We brought you with us here to Weyurn to look after you." He indicated his foster-father. "This is Lot-Ionan the Forbearing and next to him is Dergard the Lonely. These magi have saved your life. I am Tungdil Goldhand. Can you tell us what happened to you?"

"Tungdil Goldhand?" exclaimed the elf with relief. "Then I am in good company! I am Esdalân, Keeper of the Groves of Revenge."

"What's he saying?" grumbled Ireheart. "Scholar, tell him to speak so we can all understand."

"Are they all to be trusted?" asked Esdalân in his own language. He had understood the dwarf.

"Speak in elvish for now. I'll decide later who needs to know what."

The elf began his story. "I am Esdalân, baron of Jilsborn, and a good friend of Liútasil." He took a deep breath. "My prince is dead."

"We know. He died trying to defend the diamond, in battle with one of the monsters."

Esdalân's visage darkened in fury. "So *that's* the lie they're tricking you with? They're saying he fell fighting one of the unslayables' creatures?" He lowered his voice. "Liútasil was murdered. Four cycles ago."

XIII

Esdalân took a deep breath. Relating the murder of his prince had obviously affected him. "They kept it secret and gave us excuse after excuse to cover his disappearance, and by the time we learned the truth they had moved their own people into all the positions of power. Then they took over and wiped out the last of the right-thinking elves."

Tungdil was left speechless. "*They?*" he croaked. "Who are they?"

"The eoîl atár, followers of the eoîl. It's an obsessive cult. They accord the eoîl a godlike status just short of Sitalia's. They had demanded Liútasil join forces with the eoîl and set off to war in Girdlegard with her and her army against the creatures of Tion and Samusin. Liútasil refused and ordered them to do nothing."

"It sounds as if they did it anyway?"

"Yes. They sent messengers to the eoîl in secret, asking to speak with her and to find out how they could help. Nobody outside the atár cult knows what she told them. Ever since then they've been trying to take over power in Âlandur, to restore the elves to the pure race they once were, tolerating no evil, just like the eoîl."

In Tungdil this news broke through the last bastions of his mind like a battering ram. Sounding like an alarm in his head it made clear the significance the new elf buildings, the shrines that he and Ireheart had seen on their recent visit. It all stemmed from the eoîl's commands!

Esdalân lowered his gaze. "We underestimated them. Their views took hold and they soon had more followers than Liútasil thought good—as he told me. When he attempted to thwart them it was too late. Like most, I did not see through their machinations until recently. After that I listened in to several exchanges. I heard them talk about the future of the diamond. They had examined it, they said, and found it was not the genuine one."

"Examined it? How does that work?"

"I don't know. Perhaps the eoîl let them into the secret of the magic. Our people are able to use simple charms, but your magi would not call that proper magic. Maybe the eoîl changed all that?"

"Hmm. So it wasn't a bad thing that the stone fell into the hands of the unslayables."

Esdalân shook his head. "It never did fall into the monsters' hands. They made that up to explain the death of Liútasil. And they were planning to steal the rest of the diamonds from the fortress as soon as they had all been brought to Paland. Then they noticed me listening and turned to get me. I escaped in spite of their arrows." He pressed Tungdil's hand. "That I am still alive is thanks to you." He gave a wry smile. "A dwarf."

"No, not thanks to me alone. The magi have played the most important part in your recovery."

"But they couldn't have saved me if you hadn't taken

me with you." Esdalân's face grew serious. "Âlandur is under the sway of the atár. If I have understood correctly their intention is to carry out the eoîl's plans."

"They want to expel evil from Girdlegard. But . . . those few orcs and the unslayables—"

"You're making a mistake, Tungdil Goldhand," the elf interrupted. "The eoîl gave them the order to destroy *all* evil, in no matter what form."

"The envoys!" Tungdil remembered. "The elves sent envoys out to the various realms, apparently to exchange knowledge. But they won't have done anything except spy on the rulers and their subjects."

"The selection process has begun. In the end only a few races will survive in Girdlegard unless the atár are stopped. The dwarf folk have already suffered losses. The attacks on the villages and towns in Toboribor or near Borwôl are down to the atár as well. I am sure of it."

"But how can they do it? They are committing evil themselves. Don't they see that?" Tungdil thought of the children of the Smith whose wells had been poisoned.

"No, in their eyes it is not bad—on the contrary. When others can't understand they take it as proof that they're doing the right thing. As long as evil is working under-cover it must be combated by those who are able to perceive it." Esdalân took a deep breath. "They all want the diamond, Tungdil Goldhand. The diamond is the divine power of the eoîl made manifest. Even if it hurts me to say this and I must beg Sitalia's forgiveness, it is true: No one must trust my people any longer. Their offer of friend-ship is a pretense. In reality they are planning dark deeds."

Tungdil scratched his chin while his brain worked

feverishly. Girdlegard was faced with its most taxing situation. The elves, undergroundlings and unslayables all claimed ownership of the diamond. For now it seemed best for the undergroundlings to have it and take it away, far from Girdlegard's borders.

"Are there no elves left who aren't dazzled by the propaganda?" he asked Esdalân. "Is there no resistance movement?"

"No," he said. "I am afraid there are no clear-thinking elves anymore."

"And," Tungdil hesitated, "how many elves are there in Âlandur?"

"I don't know. I can see why you ask. If there is a war I assume all the warriors sent out from the groves of Âlandur will obey instructions and carry out the wishes of the atár."

Tungdil knew how skilled the elvish warriors and archers were. They were far superior in battle to the humans and even the dwarves faced an enormous challenge getting through their deadly hail of arrows in order to engage in close combat. Perhaps the undergroundling army would be fighting not Tion's creatures but Sitalia's, however strange the concept. Even stranger for the others.

"How much truth can Girdlegard tolerate?" he said, more to himself than to Esdalân.

"You should be asking how much of it they will believe," said the elf. "The elves have not done anything wrong in most eyes, and have always had the reputation of being noble, the noblest race in Girdlegard. They stand for beauty, art and goodness." His blue eyes measured Tungdil. "You believe my words because you have traveled and are wise. But put yourself in the place of the kings and queens whose support we shall be needing. They have only experienced what they see as generosity from my people. They will never believe us. The atár will think up a story that would brand me a traitor." He gave a sigh of desperation. "None of them will challenge the atár. Not at first. And afterwards it will be too late."

"You are right, Esdalân. None of the humans will believe it." Tungdil looked at Sirka. "But the dwarves will, as soon as we've got the diamond back from the älfar, and have placed it safely away from the elves. Unless they have it they will not dare reveal their true intentions. In the calm before the storm we shall use your help to rouse the people of Girdlegard and warn them about the atár plans."

The elf nodded. "I pray that Sitalia and all the ancestors may give their blessing to our endeavor. May the worst be avoided." Esdalân seemed relieved to have been able to impart this terrible knowledge to another. He let his gaze sweep the room. "Whom will you tell?"

Girdlegard,
Northeastern Part of the Brown Mountains,
Fourthling Kingdom,
Late Summer, 6241st Solar Cycle

Tandibur Pitpride of the clan of the Pit Prides raced along the long basalt planks over the series of defense ditches in front of the narrow pass into Girdlegard on the Silverfast side. Each trench was seven paces long and twenty deep and the sides had knife-sharp edges to slice any hapless body that fell in: sharp enough to sever chain mail links.

Tandibur turned his head. Behind the trenches stood the mighty Goldfast fortress ready to resist any invader with its unassailable gold-colored walls. The masons had built them with a finish like upended spears; here and there jewels sparkled, giving the construction an extravagant patina. Curtain walls soared thirty paces high and behind them the watchtower was in the form of a fifty-pace-tall dwarf, its forbidding head fully rotatable, turned by chains and pony-power. On top of the tower's stone helmet, and in the eye, ear and mouth cavities, guards stood watch, war machines to hand. Until now no monster had appeared at the gates and the catapults had never been needed.

It looked as if today might be different.

"Come on, get a move on!" he encouraged the five-score soldiers at his back. He was bringing reinforcements for the fortifications at Silverfast.

Tandibur had good reason for urgency. Silverfast was in trouble. It had been named after the silver shimmer of the stone it was built from. *Gnomes' silver*, the dwarves called it: attractive to look at but worthless apart from its durability. There was a similar rationale for Goldfast's designation.

The early fourthling builders had given Silverfast five towers pointing to the skies like the fingers of a hand, the tallest fifty paces high. From the gutter-spouts molten lead spewed onto the attackers at the gates and their screams rose up to the battlements.

A strong curtain wall connected the five towers, on

which defenders ran about, firing crossbows and throwing missiles over the parapet.

The orcs had been bombarding the iron gates, battering the fourthling front line, desperate to get through. They were applying all their strength, and were repulsed neither by molten lead, arrows or great lumps of rock.

If Tandibur had not known better he would have assumed something was hounding the green-skins that scared them more than fourthling axes. He glanced up at the towers where black smoke wafted. The burners under the smelting cauldrons were being fed constantly, but the troops would soon run out of lead. "We'll have to use gold to pour down instead," he said quietly.

The repeated thud of a battering ram echoed back from the surrounding mountains. The metal gates screamed in protest, bending under the onslaught.

"By Vraccas," shouted one of Tandibor's warriors. "Just listen to that! What kind of enemy makes all that din? What foe has Tion sent?"

"You'll see them soon enough," was Tandibur's terse reply. "Whatever it is in the ravine at Silverfast, you'll need courage, a stout heart and a sharp ax. They are the only things that can protect us from the monsters."

They saw rocks as big as a man hurled at and over the walls. In places the heavy missiles had damaged the battlements, crushing anyone sheltering behind. In other places smoking sacks filled with petroleum and pitch had burst against the walls, stinking terribly and making eyes and airways smart. Waves of blazing fire swallowed the dwarves on the walkways, incinerating them in seconds. And still the castle's defenders did not yield, but continued hurling stones down and setting off a hail of crossbow bolts.

What the newcomers saw spurred them on to fight. Reaching the broad stairs up to the encircling walkways, Tandibur split them into two groups, right and left. Dark red dwarf blood dripped down the steps as if to warn them not to go on.

A terrible sight awaited.

The walkways behind the thick fortress walls were covered in a grimly woven carpet of fast-cooling corpses: men and women they knew well. The bodies were piled so densely that they had no option but to plant their boots on flesh rather than stone. Most had been killed by arrows, others were victims of the missile showers from the catapults. The metallic reek of warm blood in puddles and streaming down the walls mixed with the stench of burned flesh and with the steaming vapors of the beasts besieging them.

Random objects flew smoking over their heads. Tandibur ducked automatically under his shield.

Silverfast's commander had been praying for them to arrive. With two arrow wounds in his right arm already, he had now been struck on the leg with a bolt and he could not remove it for fear of severe bleeding. He limped to a standstill some paces away, indicating a heap of stones. "Vraccas be thanked you have come! Take these and send them over the side." He hurried off. "Target the team on the battering ram."

Tandibur was motionless from shock. Then he picked up a rough boulder and heaved it on the battlements above the gate. He looked over. Spread out on the plains in front of Silverfast, monster was jostling monster. Thousands of them, mostly orcs, surged forward, yelling and storming the gates. Further back, horrible ogres, tall as giants, and their relations, big ugly hairy trolls, were constantly reloading the huge catapults to give the defenders not a moment's respite. They were also hurling smaller missiles into the gaps in the battlements. Their aim was depressingly good.

Tandibur froze. Only a few minutes before he had encouraged a fellow dwarf to action but his own spirit now failed him.

Directly underneath, maybe thirty paces down, a hundred ogres were wielding the biggest battering ram he had ever seen. Several trees must have been felled to make it and a huge iron monster head fronted the tip. Only ogres, with their titanic strength, were capable of lifting the dreadful siege weapon.

The gate was yielding inch by inch to the successive blows from the ram. The bolts and hinges were still holding but were so badly deformed that Silverfast would soon fall.

Tandibur shook off his fear and offered a prayer to Vraccas. The fortress must not be taken. He dropped his stone over the edge and pulled his head back in to avoid enemy fire. A shrill scream next to him told him not everyone had been so lucky. He bent over the victim. "Lie still. You'll be fine," he said, trying to sound convincing. A missile had shattered the other's face; the dwarf could scarcely breathe and blood was bubbling out of what was left of his nose.

"We do not give up," croaked the dwarf, trying to grasp Tandibur's hand, but as he made the movement his body went limp. The woven carpet of corpses had a new thread for its weft.

"Vraccas, take his soul." Tandibur brushed aside grief. Now was no time for tears.

He saw four heavy enemy rocks hit home, one after the other, in the center of the second highest tower, leaving a wide hole. Too wide. The building swayed and great fissures appeared in the masonry. Tandibur could see the warriors at the top scampering away from the edge in panic.

The top of the tower was poised over the left flank of the orc army; the tower broke in the middle. An eleven-pace section crashed down onto the foe and sent rubble bouncing back up behind the lines, bombarding orcs further back.

A gray dust cloud stopped Tandibor seeing what damage the hordes had suffered. The falling tower had killed many, and Silverfast's catapults were having some success against the enemy's infantry, who were screeching in terror.

"Tandibur!" Sigdal Rubiniam of the clan of the Gem Stones ran over and grabbed his arm. He was a young dwarf, not even fifty cycles, and one who tended to give up rather than see things through. That was when it was a matter of gem polishing. There was blood all over his mail tunic and he had a cut on his face which revealed white bone underneath. Where he had been standing, the battle still raged.

"We have to get back behind the ditches and retreat to Goldfast," he panted.

"We have orders," replied Tandibur, not able to wrench his eyes from the smoke-shrouded fallen tower.

"But it's useless," protested Sigdal, spreading his arms wide. "Look! The missiles have crushed three of my friends and I am drenched with their blood. It won't be long before

Silverfast falls. Let's save those who still live. We can combat
the next wave from the second fortress, in Goldfast."

Tandibur turned to find the defenders' commander. He
turned just in time to see that dwarf enveloped in a wall
of fire to fall like a burning comet from the castle walls.
The next meeting of battering ram and iron gate had the
stones under their feet shuddering so that wide cracks
opened up. The age-old granite was starting to give way.

The wind brought new low rumbles from the monsters.
These deep threatening tones reached Tandibur's ears for
the first time and no instrument he knew of could have
produced them.

Sigdal looked over the balustrade. "Look! They have
reinforcements!" There was no holding him now. "We've
got to abandon the stronghold."

Only a fool would have persisted in the face of what
was so obvious. "You are right," said Tandibur, reaching
for his bugle to call the troops. Now their commander
was no more, the army would follow his orders.

Then came the strident screeching of orc trombones and
the merciless bombardment stopped abruptly. No more
arrows or stones or firebombs hit Silverfast. All was as
still as the grave.

"What's going on?" Sigdal chanced a quick glance into
the distance. "A trick?"

"It sounds as if they're turning the catapults round,"
Tandibor interpreted, coming to stand next to him, his
shield held high as protection from stray arrows.

On the other side of the plain a broad black front was
rolling nearer. Compared to the numbers of monsters
round Silverfast this was not a whole army of fresh

replacement troops. Tandibur calculated it must be about two thousand. But each armor-suited warrior was double the height of a dwarf.

"What are they?" asked Sigdal, fascinated. "See how they run? By Vraccas, it looks like they've got bodies of iron but they're running like ponies!"

Meanwhile some of the catapults had been rotated. Frantic ogres and trolls were loading and firing at the advancing troops, but the missiles did no damage at all, hitting the ground harmlessly behind them. They were traveling too fast for the artillery to reload and adjust the trajectory.

The threatening metallic sound of crashing armor-plating got louder.

The monsters were still staring in disbelief at the approaching foe. Then the front line started to shriek and one of the orcs pushed back through the throng in the direction of Silverfast, where it tried to scale the walls using fingers and toes.

This was the sign the hordes had waited for. Their paralysis was over.

Grunting and screeching, the orcs renewed their onslaught on the stronghold, throwing up siege ladders, but now total confusion reigned. They hurled away whatever they carried: weapons or armor. Some broke their sword blades off to help them clamber up the sheer sides of the fortress. If their progress was impeded orcs wrenched slower colleagues off the walls. Two ogres made a run for it, trampling a band of orcs. They tried to scramble up the rungs of a ladder far too frail to carry their weight and the wood shattered, sending them plunging back down, to lie motionless at the foot of the walls, orc bodies crushed beneath them.

"Hang on! Drive them back!" Tandibur bellowed orders right and left. "It's easier than swatting flies. Don't let a single one pass." He raised his ax and struck an orc between neck and collarbone. Dark green blood spurted skywards and the orc fell back, pulling four of his kind with him to their deaths.

Fighting was easier now that the monsters, in their terror, had stopped using crossbows and covering fire from their catapults. This meant that the dwarves could risk showing themselves between the battlement merlons and use cudgels on the orcs' broad ugly heads as soon as they appeared.

Then the black-armored attackers arrived.

Shortly before the clash of the ranks they opened their visors and violet light streamed out.

Tandibur heard the bone-marrow-shaking noise of their hissing and growling, like an army of snakes and the thunder of a volcanic eruption. It warned of the danger and merciless bloodlust of these creatures before they tore through the orc mass like a sharp blade slicing rotten wood.

They did not halt but ran straight into the throng of monsters, each wielding two weapons. Crushed and mutilated or split in half, orcs littered the ground at Silverfast.

"By Vraccas! What beasts are these?" The dwarves felt the hairs on their necks rise in horror. Tandibur now shared the orcs' deadly fear. Instinctively he hid behind the battlements. What reached him was the ineradicable memory of the appalling noises: sharp screeches and bellows, pain stopped abruptly mid-howl. A chorus of dying so terrible that it ate away even at the mind of a dwarf.

Sigdal looked at Tandibur. "I have heard of a creature like this," he remembered. "It was the bodyguard of Andôkai the Tempestuous, the maga. No one knew where it was from but it was said to look like those things down there. They called it Djerûn. It was the king of all the monsters that Samusin and Tion ever created."

"But you can't see anything inside the armor?"

"No, it's that dazzling light." Sigdal pointed to the face.

Tandibur shook himself.

A third dwarf hurried up. "Shall I have the towers shoot at them, Tandibur?" he asked. "They make big targets—we can't miss."

Tandibur looked at Sigdal. "Andôkai's bodyguard, you think?"

"If the stories are true," said the dwarf, leaving a slight trace of doubt in the air.

The noise of battle on the other side surged closer to the walls. Tandibur looked down.

The black-plated beings had traversed the plain, cutting a bloody swathe through the orc army, now in disarray. It looked as if a wild animal had got into a chicken coop. The attackers had only lost a handful.

The orcs were so panic-stricken that their only urge was flight. They stormed away in small groups toward the far edge of the plain. Just before they reached the Outer Lands they were confronted by a new wall of black iron.

Tandibur yelled. "Look at that! They've drawn the green-skins into a trap! They're butchering them!"

"So do we fire or not?" asked the dwarf once more.

Tandibur shook his head. "Wait and see what they do next."

Until the evening fell they watched the unknown creatures harry and kill the orcs one by one; then ogres and trolls fell to their superior strength.

Night covered the narrow gorge that led to Girdlegard and with the darkness came silence.

There were no screams from the orcs. The dwarves heard no more groaning. Not a breath was left in the heap of bodies at the foot of Silverfast's high towers. The unknown beings wandered through the carnage, checking cadavers, and if anything twitched in the confusion of tangled limbs and heads, they followed through with a deadly blow from their blood-stained weapons.

The stars hid themselves behind thick clouds, unwilling to view the results of the massacre. Soon the dwarves noticed the sound of scraping and scrabbling.

"Any idea what they are up to?" asked Sigdal as he spied out at the scene. "It is so devilishly dark that even with eyes like mine I can't see."

Tandibur took a burning torch and tossed it down from the battlements.

The faint light showed black-armored warriors moving about, dragging two or three orcs by the feet from the field of slaughter.

"What will they do with them?" wondered Sigdal.

Tandibur pointed. To the left more of the strange beings were stripping the flesh from the bones of ogres and trolls. With great blows from their weapons they shattered the bones so that the marrow could be sucked out. Victory was providing its own celebration banquet.

"By Vraccas!" mouthed Sigdal in horror.

"The king of the monsters, eh?" said Tandibur, glad when the torch gave out, veiling these ghastly activities in darkness once more. "Then it seems we have here a whole folk of kings." He went to the steps. It was time to give Goldfast a full report of the action. "Get the gates repaired and have more rocks brought up here to the walkways. These creatures must be kept under constant observation. They may have freed us from the threat of the orcs' attack but we don't want them getting curious about the taste of dwarf flesh."

Tired and with aching limbs he walked down the stairway. Then, escorting the walking wounded, he moved off along the basalt planking toward the second fortress.

Tandibur was sensing they would have to confront whatever hid behind the black visors of these new warriors. "But with what weapons?" he whispered. "How can they be stopped?" He prayed to Vraccas that this small army of giants at Silverfast would not concern themselves with the dwarves. Not today, not tomorrow, not in ten thousand cycles.

Girdlegard,
Kingdom of Idoslane,
Ten Miles from the Caves of Toboribor,
Late Summer, 6241st Solar Cycle

Lot-Ionan sat quietly by the fire warming his hands. The nights had lost their summer mildness and after his six petrified cycles there was permanent cold within him;

neither hot tea, nor warm brandy nor thick blankets could drive it out.

Dergard was already asleep. Ireheart cut himself a piece of the rabbit from the spit-roast. He chewed away making unsatisfied noises.

"Magus, are you sure we can't get you those last few miles? It's not far now."

Lot-Ionan raised his white head. "Trust me, Boïndil. I would rather sleep in a warm tent than in the open air." He eased his back with his right hand. "My back is too painful to get back in the saddle."

Ireheart was calculating what the old man might weigh. "I could carry you."

Tungdil cut a morsel of meat for Sirka. During the journey he had spent hours thinking about Girdlegard's precarious situation. He had confided in Lot-Ionan but even with help from the magus no satisfactory course of action had emerged.

Otherwise he observed an iron silence. Not even Ireheart had been taken into their confidence. Since the incident on the farm there was a split in a friendship that had withstood tests in the past. This time it seemed difficult to get over. Not speaking meant an uncomfortable atmosphere between the two of them. "Leave it, Ireheart, let the magus get some rest. It's no good if he's thoroughly exhausted when we get there."

Sirka took the slice of meat and placed it between pieces of bread. She tasted it gingerly. "Now I know what I love about my own land," she said, fighting down a mouthful. "The meat tastes better."

"Probably how they feed the animals," grinned Tungdil.

"Well, I like it," mumbled Ireheart, making light work of the rest of the rabbit after Rodario had indicated he did not want any more. The playwright was sitting next to Lot-Ionan, scribbling away by candlelight.

"Say, Sirka, could you tell us about where you're from?" he said suddenly, dipping his pen in the ink. "We can see you, we saw your soldiers and we've heard about the adventures in Girdlegard . . ." The quill made circles in the air. "But what's it like back in . . . ?" He paused expectantly.

"Letèfora," she completed. "Why do you want to know?"

"To go in this play. And I'm curious." Rodario laughed. "Exotica goes down well on stage. The punters love a whiff of the Outer Lands."

Sirka's close-shaven head shimmered in the light, her dark skin enhancing the whiteness of her teeth. "Letèfora is a city where many races live: humans, acronta, ubariu and ourselves. The buildings are finer than any in Girdlegard. Not even the dwarves can match us for our architecture." She noted the indignation in Ireheart's face. "Don't look at me like that. I don't mean the dwarf buildings are not good. They are just . . ." She shrugged her shoulders. ". . . smaller."

"So what's the deal with monsters and things?" asked Rodario.

"Oh, I expect you'll find even their monsters are bigger than ours. And they probably fly. Their screams will deafen you and the mere sight of one will strike you dead," scoffed Boïndil. He wiped the meat juices off his over-short beard. "Just like Djerûn."

Sirka nodded, "You're right, Boïndil. Absolutely spot

on, even if I don't know what a Djerůn is. Our beasts are very varied. We have phottòr . . . winged orcs, and enough other creatures to make the bravest warriors quail and take flight."

"Only human soldiers, I'd wager," Goda joined in, earning a grateful look from her tutor. "Or elves, perhaps. But never the children of the Smith."

Before the harmless storytelling could develop into a fully fledged row about the dwarves and their courage, Tungdil threw in a question. So far he had listened with great interest, hanging on every word from Sirka's dark lips. "When we were traveling north through to the Outer Lands we found this rune on the wall." He sketched a shape in the sand.

Sirka reflected and drew a clearer version next to it. "It must have been this one. It's an ancient sign that indicates a safe mountain pass. Long ago our people reconnoitered the whole of the northern range."

"Aha," said Ireheart, pointing at her with the end of a rabbit bone he had been chewing at. "So you were preparing to attack Girdlegard."

"Yes," said Sirka, "but when we learned that dwarves were manning the gates, we gave up. We assumed the land behind the gates would be in your hands." She said all this in a tone of voice that could have been lies or truth. Nobody could work it out.

"Very enlightening," said Rodario and went on writing. "In view of the situation I'll be circumspect on the matter of invading Girdlegard." He put on a serious face. "The audience might not like it. We can do without upsetting people right now."

"That's if it's true," said Goda, taking firm hold of her night star to sharpen the blades with a whetstone. "Sounded to me like she was having us on."

Sirka grinned. "Who knows? Perhaps our scouts are still out there waiting for their opportunity?"

"Ho, a sense of humor. Do you know the one about the orc asking a dwarf the way?" Boïndil was starting to warm up.

"Hang on . . ." Tungdil had just remembered the young dwarf that had never returned. When Sirka mentioned the undergroundling scouts, an explanation occurred to him for the disappearance. He put the subject to her.

"Yes, I met one," came the reply.

"What?" Ireheart tossed the bone back over his shoulder. "What were you doing with the clan-dwarf? I thought he was a thirdling that had run off."

"A thirdling? No." Sirka asked for the water bottle, to rinse the last taste of rabbit away. "He had been following our scouts and got lost. It was too late when we found him. He was thin as a rake, talking rubbish about machines and saying he wanted to protect Girdlegard from them. He died of exhaustion soon after." Tungdil nodded. They had done the right thing telling Gremdulin Ironbite's mother her son had died. They had not wanted to awaken false hopes. "What were your scouts looking for at the gateway?"

"Seeing what was new." Sirka placed a log on the fire. "Seeing if things were all right."

They heard the sound of approaching hoof beats. A lantern swayed a couple of feet above the ground, illuminating the path for horse and rider.

"A messenger from Prince Mallen?" guessed Rodario,

getting up. "Good. He can tell the army we'll be with them tomorrow." The dwarves got to their feet as well, ready for a fight.

The rider saw the campfire and came over. "The blessings of Vraccas on you," came the greeting. "Good things come in threes!"

"Bramdal!" Ireheart cursed under his breath. "Now it's certain. He's spying on us," he whispered to Tungdil. "It's no coincidence we keep bumping into him."

The executioner rode up, and dismounted using his patent rope ladder. "There was far too good a smell of meat. I couldn't simply ride past."

Ireheart gleefully held up the rabbit carcass he had gnawed clean. "Too late, executioner. Death was way ahead of you this time. On your way."

Bramdal's dark clothing made it difficult to see where he ended and the darkness began. It helped that he had light blond beard braids and a pale face. "Looks like there's not much warmth at this fireside. What's the matter?"

"You need to ask?" Ireheart took a step forward and Goda did the same. "You turn up out of the blue once too often. Your business is with death and then to cap it all you sell off the dead bodies. What decent dwarf would do that?"

Bramdal wedged his thumbs under his belt. "I don't work as an executioner now, Boïndil Doubleblade. I told you before. And the fact we keep meeting is due to the fact we are both heading the same way. Why should I want to keep bumping into you?"

"My friend thinks you spy for the dwarf-haters." Tungdil watched the other's face very carefully.

"Then wouldn't I have my weapons drawn and be attacking you?" Bramdal sat down on the grass. "I could just stay quiet and pretend I don't mind being accused like that. Later on when you're all asleep I could slit your throats and rob Girdlegard of its greatest heroes." He looked at Lot-Ionan. "Did I forget something?"

"You forgot to mount up and ride off again," suggested Ireheart. "Be off with you, hangman. We don't want you here."

"What if I were bringing Trovegold news to the army?"

Tungdil moved over next to him. "If you like, give us your news and then be on your way. If you don't want to share it, then mount up and ride off now." He wanted to be rid of the executioner because he feared Boïndil was going to lose his temper.

Bramdal made a regretful face. "So that's the thanks I get for helping you reach the freelings that time? You drive me away from your fireside?"

"No." Ireheart drew himself up in front of the executioner, his war hammer in his hands. "It's me who's chasing you off."

Bramdal sighed. "I should have known you wouldn't be friendly. I got that impression last time we met." He stood up and went to his horse. "Trovegold is sending Prince Mallen money toward the expense of the siege. In return for that the freelings want to trade in Idoslane and have asked to negotiate with their largest towns." He climbed up onto his specially adapted saddle. "I would say there is a new alliance on its way there." From high up on his mount Bramdal nodded down at the others. "Because you never know how long the old ones will hold."

He cantered off toward the southeast. For a long time they could still see his lantern. Then he crested the brow of a hill and disappeared from view.

"Good riddance." Ireheart sat down again. He pulled a second rabbit out from behind a rock and skinned it. One puny little rabbit was never going to have been enough for him.

"What does that all mean?" Rodario asked himself and then the rest of them. "Are the freelings afraid the dwarf peoples will change their minds?"

"It looks like it." Lot-Ionan looked at Tungdil. "Can there be a reason?"

"No. I never saw anything in the talks to indicate a worsening of relationships. I don't know why they're looking for support like this." Tungdil threw himself down on the grass. Sirka joined him. "Do they know more than us?"

"We'll find out tomorrow." Lot-Ionan shivered and put more wood on the fire. "Let's not waste time worrying about it now. There are more important things. Let's get some sleep."

Goda was given first watch and the others bedded down by the fire. Tungdil thought for a long time about what the executioner had said.

Girdlegard, Kingdom of Idoslane,
Four Miles from the Toboribor Caves,
Late Summer, 6241st Solar Cycle

Tungdil and his companions halted on a small hill and surveyed the biggest siege ever mounted in Girdlegard.

The scene was impressive.

The joint armies of the Girdlegard kingdoms and the elf realm encircled the entrance to the orcs' underground domain. Nothing and no one could escape unseen. No less than seventy thousand warriors and volunteers had gathered here to confront the evil in the shape of the unslayables and their ghastly machine hybrids.

The deep green of field and orchard was marred by a black line of trenches; immediately behind lay the army encampments of the various kingdoms. Small portable bridges were available as need arose to cross the trenches.

The dwarves' numerous tents were pitched well behind the boundary. From there, units would set off to rage through the caves of Toboribor in search of the unslayables, one of the sentries told Tungdil's group. Nearly all the clans of the dwarf tribes had sent troops. A sea of standards and banners fluttered in the warm breeze and, a little way off, the flags of the freelings were flying.

"Isn't that splendid? The evil won't get through that lot." Ireheart surveyed the scene proudly.

"That's if the evil is in the caves in the first place." There was doubt in Lot-Ionan's voice.

Tungdil nodded. "Let's find out how successful they've been so far in eradicating the unslayable danger for all time." He spurred his pony on. The freelings had their camp set up too far away from the dwarves for his liking. Bramdal was proving to be correct.

Lot-Ionan rode next to him. "Have you got any further with your cogitations or are you still as much in the dark as I am?"

"I'm lost as well," he sighed. "It all stands or falls with how the elves behave. I won't risk a guess." He forced his gaze away from the banners of the town.

"I don't want to guess, either. Esdalân didn't seem the type to be telling lies, though there must be other reasons for elves to fire on elves. At any event it was better that we left him in the village back there. I want to make up my own mind." The magus indicated the tent bearing Mallen's standard. "Let's ride over. I think we should tell him everything. From what you say he is a level-headed ruler. Even if he is an Ido."

Bramdal must have given warning of their approach. They were received with shouted greetings and much approving pounding of fists on shields from the soldiers. Men bowed respectfully to the magus, delighted to see him returned.

The unusual noise drew Mallen out of his tent. He was attired in the impressive suit of armor his ancestors had worn and his fair hair streamed free. "Welcome to Idoslane, noble Lot-Ionan." The prince bowed. "And welcome to you all." He shook hands with Rodario and Ireheart. "Master Bramdal told us you would be joining us soon. The greatest heroes are now assembled. We will meet the unslayables head-on." Holding the tent flap open, the ruler invited them inside. "If you are not too tired I'd like to explain what we've achieved in the past few orbits." He sent messengers out to summon the dwarf commanders. Then he addressed Lot-Ionan. "You will forgive us for not putting on an adequate celebration in honor of your return, but we have no time to lose."

The magus nodded. "But of course, Prince Mallen.

There are more important matters. Celebrations can wait until our victory."

Like all the others he noticed the peculiar painting on the inside of the tent walls.

"A map," Mallen explained. "This is the dwarves' work. They have surveyed and drawn out all the caves they have penetrated here." He pointed to the blue-shaded area. "These parts they have taken over already. They have set up small strongholds within the cave complex."

"But are the unslayables really in the caves?" the magus wanted to know, seating himself at the table; the others followed suit.

"We're certainly working on that assumption. The dwarves have had sight of all their monsters. I think they are supposed to be diverting our attention from the unslayables themselves. That's why the dwarves are fighting their way in to the sections where resistance initially was low." Mallen showed them the part he was referring to, marked in green. "They were right. Suddenly, fierce resistance was encountered and it looks as if the last of the älfar are holed up in this cave area."

Gandogar strode in and Tungdil and the other Girdlegard dwarves bowed respectfully in greeting. A little way behind came the freeling commanders—and Bramdal. He gave them an inscrutable smile.

"What a pleasure to see all of you safe and well," Gandogar exclaimed. "And you, magus, I have only known as a stone statue. So you must be Lot-Ionan the Forbearing."

"Not all escaped with their lives. Far too many were carried off to Vraccas's Eternal Smithy," Tungdil interjected, giving a concise report of what had occurred in

Weyurn. "We lost Furgas on the island. He burned to death in molten iron. We saw it happen and could do nothing to save him."

Mallen and the high king both fell silent at this news.

"So Furgas is dead?" Mallen leaned forward on the table. "We shall miss his genius. In the past he wrought good as well as bad. I don't want to sound heartless, but did he at least say where his machine creatures' weak points might lie?"

"Yes." Rodario, eyes glistening at the thought of his dead friend, took out a folder he had carried in his saddlebag and put it on the table. "He left me several drawings to show where each monster will be most vulnerable." He cleared his throat, choked with emotion. "The points in question are small. Steady hands and a true aim will be needed when they are attacked."

Passing the folder of drawings to a servant to have copies made, Mallen said, "Trust me: I regret his death, but now is not the time to mourn the passing of friends. It will have to wait until the älfar have been defeated."

The tent opened again to admit Rejalin; she brought an escort of three guards and two unarmed elves.

"No one told me that a meeting had been arranged," she said with a gracious smile. "If I hadn't seen Gandogar entering the tent I would have missed it. Did you not wish to hear the view of the elves?"

Ireheart opened his mouth. "You can be—"

"Boïndil was about to say that you can be sure we would have called you," Tungdil interrupted smartly. "Because we need your warriors as soon as possible in Toboribor and not in the dwarf realms any more."

"Why is that? Surely you need us to keep the gateways safe while so much of your fighting force is here in Toboribor. The monsters still present an undeniable threat. The monsters and the undercover thirdlings in your own ranks." However charming and considerate her tone of voice, criticism was clear in Rejalin's message. It was her opinion that the thirdling traitors should have been assiduously sought out.

Tungdil was not surprised by what she said. Not anymore. She was walking the paths of the eoïl. "We have received information that the caves have a connection to the Outer Lands. Under the very feet of the besieging army a new horde is waiting. The dwarves in the caves are good warriors but even they and the army of humans would not be able to withstand this horde without the elves." He knew that she would fall for this lie. She would not be able to help herself, even if she had seen it coming.

"Where do you get this knowledge from, Tungdil Goldhand?" she asked in surprise.

"The thirdlings we captured told us." And he related the Weyurn adventures in an adapted version without mentioning the role Furgas had probably played. He left it with the thirdlings and unslayables being the evildoers. "Bandilor had made common cause with the älfar. He told us the unslayables' plans; they suited his own intentions."

The elf princess looked at him searchingly. "And you believe the word of a dwarf who allied himself with the evil?"

"I trust words spoken in fear of death," Tungdil corrected. "He thought that I would spare him. And Lot-Ionan tested the truth of his words with magic."

Tungdil looked at the others with silent pleading in his expression.

He received support from an unexpected quarter. "We shall be needing Âlandur's elf warriors here, Your Highness. Right now, before the enemy hordes spill out and swamp us. Do you want to carry the responsibility if Idoslane and the whole of Girdlegard fall under their sway?" It was more a demand than a request that Prince Mallen was putting to Rejalin. Two issues coincided. It was his own land that was threatened and he was starting to like the elf-woman less and less. And though it might not be wise to speak boldly, he did not hold back.

Tungdil was relieved. It made his own lie sound more credible.

"Now you are demanding my support, Prince Mallen?" Rejalin lifted her cup of water and sipped long and slow. "Did you not recently expel my envoys from your court?"

"There is a difference between a delegation and an army, princess," he said. "It was not in my mind to hold intellectually sophisticated conversations at a time when I am concerned with protecting our homeland from new and potentially disastrous threats." He leaned forward. "As soon as we have won, I shall be delighted to receive your delegates for a cultural exchange, but until then please understand that I cannot accept your offers. Instead please send an army. That I shall welcome with open arms."

Gandogar nodded. "Do not worry, Rejalin. We are aware of the value of your assistance, but we can defend ourselves well enough. And to reassure you further, we have already identified and imprisoned seven dwarf-haters who had been living under cover amongst us. We found them without the use of torture," he added. "The thirdlings who are intent on becoming assimilated helped us with this."

There was no way out for the elf princess. "Then let it be so," she decided, smiling away her defeat. "Messengers shall leave today to bring my warriors to Toboribor." She studied the cave-map. "The dwarves should move more quickly. The more we know about the tunnels and chambers underground, the better prepared we shall be to meet the hordes from the Outer Lands. It will be useful to be able to lay traps and ambushes."

"I agree with you." Gandogar raised his tankard and drank to her health. "The miners shall find the best places to set traps and start work at once."

"Do we know anything about when this new army might appear?" asked Rejalin. "Perhaps my forces will be too late?"

"No. Bandilor spoke of preparations. We still have time in hand," he reassured her. "Forgive me, but my friends and I are tired from the journey. We can hold an official meeting tomorrow to inform the other commanders. Now I would like to rest."

The elf princess concurred and withdrew, followed by the town commanders and Bramdal.

Hardly had they left than Tungdil arranged with Gandogar and Mallen to hold a secret meeting outside the camp at nightfall. "No guards, no retinue. Just you two," he insisted before he went. "Trust me. It is important, so tell no one."

Surprised by the urgency of his appeal the leaders agreed.

* * *

As the stars started to appear over Idoslane the three of them met at the appointed place. Mallen and Gandogar were both intrigued, but Tungdil asked them to be patient and he then stayed silent. Lot-Ionan soon joined them and the four of them rode off to the Deichseldorf inn, where they had left Esdalân.

Tungdil thought the elf was looking even more handsome since recovering from his fever. Better, he seemed fresher, more dazzling than any other living being in the vicinity. Just like Rejalin.

Gandogar and Mallen were sitting in the empty parlor of the inn listening to the elf's story by candlelight, their faces grave.

"Then I was right to distrust them," said the prince, "even if I would have preferred to be convinced of the goodness of the elves instead of hearing this news."

"It is appalling that they killed their leader." Gandogar could not credit it.

"And because I think the elf warriors are capable of anything, I invented a subterfuge to recall them to Toboribor," said Tungdil. "I prefer to have them all in one place, where we have our armies, rather than strewn throughout Girdlegard where they could do untold damage."

"You spoke of magic." Mallen raised his eyes and looked at Lot-Ionan. "Do you know anything about elf-magic, noble magus?"

"Not really. The elves, just like their dark cousins the älfar, are capable of casting minor spells in connection with their way of life. According to my old books these are mostly to do with the realm of flowers and decorative arts. Liútasil never mentioned his folk having the power to use magic in the same way as a magus or maga."

"That may be only partly so," Esdalân chimed in. His voice sounded impossibly pure to human ears. "The elves of Âlandur were never reputed to be very interested in magic. But others of my people, the elves of the Golden Plain, who were persecuted by the älfar, were more open to such arts. I remember hearing that the small number of Golden Plain elves that survived the älfar ravages fled to us in Âlandur."

Tungdil noticed that the elf's speech was changing, becoming more flowery and, to his ears, unbearable.

"That makes things different. So we cannot exclude the possibility of there being a descendant of these magically endowed elves in the ranks of the atár. Perhaps the eoîl gave him part of the knowledge." Lot-Ionan was summarizing. "That explains why they want the diamond."

Gandogar furrowed his brow. "Please don't think I am being unreasonable, noble magus, but what if you or Dergard had the power of the stone. How powerful would that make you?"

"If it is as Tungdil tells me, then this power would be . . ." He rubbed his white beard as he searched for the right word. "Immeasurable," he said finally. "The power would be immeasurable." He laughed slyly. "Have no fear, High King Gandogar. It does not entice me and for Dergard it is the same. We have the magic source to give us the same power. It would be nothing special for us. And then of course neither Dergard nor I are attracted to evil."

"Are you so sure?" Gandogar disappeared behind the

bar and poured them all some simple country wine. "He was one of Nudin's pupils. We know what happened to that magus."

"But don't forget the particular circumstances, Your Majesty," Lot-Ionan said, taking young Dergard's part. "There is no daemon, sending out insidious messages. Our opponents are mighty but they are physical enemies. And thus we can confront them." He held out his hand to receive the crockery mug, but gasped with pain. His back was troubling him with the movement. His eyes glazed and grew dim ... Then he thought he saw a figure by the door. A strangely familiar figure. "Nudin?"

"Noble Lot-Ionan, what is it?" The bearded face of Tungdil appeared suddenly in his field of vision, looking very worried. "Is it your back again?"

The magus shook his head, emptied the mug of wine and asked for more. "There are probably still tiny fragments of stone embedded in my body," he said slowly. "They affect my mind and make me see things that cannot be there." He stood up and went over into the dark corner of the room where he had seen his old friend. But however hard he looked, to his great relief he could find no trace.

"What is the matter, noble magus?"

"Nothing. I must stretch my legs. My back. It hurts. I never noticed when I was a statue." He returned to the group. "So what shall we do with the elves?" He picked up the thread again; he was cold now. "Shall we confront them and hear what they have to say, or shall we deal with the unslayables first?"

"My feeling is we should not postpone the conflict with the princess," said Mallen. "I'll tell you why. I don't like

534   *Markus Heitz*

the idea of the elves following their own ends in the middle of a battle with the älfar and their new creatures, snatching the diamond for themselves and then carrying out unimaginable deeds with its power. Of course, they will defeat the evil, I have no doubt." His gaze took in all of them. "But I don't think they will let us influence their decisions after that. I want to have Rejalin as a hostage. Before the battle starts."

"A good plan. If the elves go along with it," said Lot-Ionan, rubbing his eyes as if to punish his sight for the trick it had played on him.

"Now, Prince Mallen has just said exactly what I was thinking. If they refuse, it will be obvious they're up to no good," said Esdalân, raking his fine hair with his fingers. "I would suggest taking no risks at all. Let's impound all the elf warriors from Âlandur—there aren't many of them here at Toboribor."

"We'll take Esdalân with us and he can address the assembly in the morning," proposed Tungdil. "And then we'll see what the elves say in response to your story."

"Don't forget: We're all willing to listen to Esdalân because we have already had experience of the atár." Mallen turned to the elf. "But tomorrow you'll be addressing a less compliant audience. King Nate from Tabaîn and Queen Isika are both strong contenders for the elf support camp. You may not win them round."

Esdalân bent his head graciously as if he were a monarch acceding to a request. "Thank you for your warning, Prince Mallen. But I am sure I shall open the humans' eyes, though it cost me my life."

"Your life?" echoed Gandogar in horror. "No, no. We

do not wish that. We cannot lose the only right-thinking elf in the whole of Âlandur."

"It can't be helped." Esdalân was adamant. "I know Rejalin and can predict how she will react. I shall provoke her and from a certain point in my speech the line will have been crossed." He laid his hand on Tungdil's arm. "This I owe to you and to Girdlegard. My life was preserved by Sitalia when she sent a dwarf to me. I understand the will of the goddess. Our two peoples must proceed together against those who could bring about the destruction of the elves."

"Vraccas looks kindly on what is happening in this room." Gandogar spoke with emotion. His brown eyes encompassed the small group of conspirators. "Yet we should not forget to pray for the success of our venture. We urgently need the support of the gods." He planted his hand on the center of the table, and Esdalân laid his own hand on top. Mallen, Tungdil and Lot-Ionan followed suit.

"May we meet with success," the magus said gravely.

Girdlegard,
Kingdom of Idoslane,
Four Miles from the Caves of Toboribor,
Late Summer, 6241st Solar Cycle

Tungdil slept badly. He dreamed about Balyndis and Sirka. In the morning he awoke with only confused fragments still in his mind. Had the women been fighting about him or had he been fighting the women? Sirka had plunged her knife in his heart . . .

He sat up as soon as the first birds were singing. He felt his breast where the pain had brought his dream to life.

"A real nightmare," he sighed, rubbing the sore place while he got to his feet. He washed and put on his clothes and armor. The face in the polished silver mirror was old and tired. Of course this could all be the effect of the old drinking bouts. Or of the frustration in his soul. It had not left him. "Have I done the right thing?" he asked his reflection, as so often in the past.

"Are you sleep-walking or did you really get up this early?" said Ireheart, propping himself up on one elbow. "What's the trouble? Birds too loud?"

Tungdil turned round to face him. "Get up, Boïndil. I've got something to tell you." And so, while he dressed, the warrior received a summary of the previous night's events. "The assembly will be deciding today and I want you to keep an eye on Esdalân. Keep him safe from the elves. Protect *him*, not me."

Ireheart ran his hands through his black hair. It was still too short to braid. "Why didn't you take me along to your meeting?" he asked disappointedly. "How have I forfeited your trust?"

Tungdil was surprised. "I didn't think to, because . . ." He was searching for a reason and could not find one at first. Well, not one he could actually voice.

Boïndil was drawing his own conclusions. "It's Goda, isn't it?" He pulled on his boots. "You don't trust her and you think I'll tell her everything. You think she's a spy for the dwarf-haters. Since our quarrel at the farm things haven't been right. It's not how we were at the beginning of this adventure, Scholar. I keep wondering which of us has changed. How did it happen?"

"We have both changed, Ireheart." Tungdil hooked a stool with his foot and sat down by his friend. "You've lost your heart to a dwarf we don't know. She could be up to anything. You don't see the danger and I'm probably over-reacting." He smiled sadly. "And my heart is lost to a dwarf you absolutely abhor."

"Then it's the fault of the women, not us." The warrior grinned. "It's always the women."

Tungdil laughed quietly. "That's being too simplistic." He searched for the right words. "I'm not happy, Boïndil. Frustrated. In Girdlegard there's nowhere I feel at home. I don't belong with the humans. I don't belong with the dwarves."

"You'll be off to join the undergroundlings, then. I knew it."

"How . . ."

"You're the learned scholar, Tungdil. You sat around on your arse more than five cycles in Lot-Ionan's vaults trying to be a decent settled dwarf. For the sake of Balyndis. But your heart and soul weren't in it."

This took Tungdil by surprise. It was all true. He stared at his friend.

"Now, with the unslayables, there's a new challenge for you and then you'll be off, over the hills and far away." Ireheart smiled. "Whatever kind of dwarf you are, Tungdil, you're not the type that likes settling down. There are a few more characteristics of the children of the Smith that have passed you by as well. Good thing, too. You got the dwarves and freelings together. You united the dwarf tribes and Gindlegard has you to thank that it still exists in its present form." He patted Tungdil on the knee and stood up. "An ordinary dwarf like myself would never have managed all that. Vraccas made you like this to bring a bit of life into the race. Stay the way you are, Scholar. I'll have to get used to it, even if it takes some time. You'll have to excuse my grumbling. I am and remain your friend." He held out his hand. "If you want my friendship."

"How would I cope without a bad-tempered honest dwarf?" Tungdil grasped his hand and they embraced. He was glad they had had this exchange. The black curtains between them were now swept away.

Ireheart beamed with relief. "Now we've sorted that out, let's see how pointy-ears deals with Esdalân's accusations." He shouldered the crow's beak. "I said pointy-ears on purpose, because she's not one of the elves we have to get on with." He went over to where a canvas partition shielded Goda's sleeping quarters. "Ho, it's great to be able to say pointy-ears again."

Tungdil got himself a hearty breakfast. He sat quietly eating while Boïndil was briefing his trainee for the assembly session. It did not escape her notice that her mentor kept taking a sideways glance over to Tungdil. Finally she came over. "What can I do to convince you I am to be trusted? Give me a task, exact an oath from me—something to reassure you. I have Ireheart's confidence."

"It's not necessary, Goda," Tungdil replied.

"I want to get rid of these doubts you have about me," she insisted. "We are both of the thirdling tribe. You know what it is like not to be trusted."

He stayed silent about his and Gandogar's vague misgivings about letting the thirdlings reassemble as a tribe in their own right. "Yes, I do." The memory of the rejection he had met with from Balyndis's clan flashed through his mind. "And I don't like having you so near me and Ireheart, Goda, when I have these doubts. But I have a duty to be cautious. If you were a spy for the dwarf-haters you could cause immense damage with what you might learn."

She glared at him. "So your doubts can't be removed?"

Looking at Boïndil, Tungdil said, "You have convinced my friend, Goda. Give me time. Maybe I can come to the same conclusion."

"Not everyone is like Myr." Her words shot out.

Tungdil was shocked. "No, they are not all like her," he agreed softly, standing up and leaving the tent.

Outside, in the light of the rising sun, he marched sharply off, up and down the hillocks until he found the highest. Here he sat down on the dew-fresh grass, out of breath now.

He surveyed the scene spread out before him: smoke rose from a campfire or two. The army was starting to wake up, like the rest of Girdlegard.

Perhaps Balyndis, back in the Gray Range, was also waking. Was she looking at Glaïmbar and thinking of him? Was she cursing his memory? Did she still love him but understand it could lead nowhere? He hoped that she understood.

Tungdil snatched up a few blades of grass. What was going to happen to Sirka and him? Would he only disappoint her, too?

Turning these thoughts over in his mind he remained

on the hilltop until the sun climbed above the horizon. A fanfare signaled a meeting. He would arrive late, but no matter. They would not start without him.

"Vraccas, guide me," he begged, getting to his feet brushing the dew from his leather breeches and relishing the feel of the cool dawn air on his face.

He could not have said why he did so, but he turned toward the north. There he saw, ten miles away, the wide snake heading toward them over the hills of Idoslane. An army of considerable size was marching to Toboribor.

The ubariu: The thought shot through him. Without the fourthlings having noticed, Sundalôn had accompanied the army through the mountains to support his claim for the diamond. Tungdil tried to guess how many soldiers were involved. When Sirka had mentioned the number eighty thousand she had not been lying.

Now they had to hurry.

He started back down immediately. The meeting was going to be really interesting now. He wondered how Rejalin would react to the news of the approaching ubariu. Secretly Tungdil felt relieved to see the army. The elves would not dare to set out against such superior numbers.

Gandogar would be shaken to hear that the dwarves were not in sole charge of Girdlegard's safety. And had not been for several thousand cycles.

"Yes, this is going to be lively," he said to himself as he got near to the camp.

Sentries from the outposts were dashing in to inform Mallen of the approach of what they took to be an orc army that had appeared out of nowhere.

Tungdil went swiftly in, cutting a messenger off in mid-flow. "Your Highness. The approaching force is not an enemy," he explained. "These people have kept Girdlegard safe in the past just as my own have done. I shall send Sirka out to them. She will return to us with a delegation of the ubariu."

Prince Mallen, surrounded by tumult, tried to think. "I have stopped being surprised by anything," he said flatly. "Let us meet in the conference marquee."

Tugdil bowed and went off to give Sirka her instructions.

Girdlegard,
Kingdom of Idoslane,
Four Miles from the Caves of Toboribor,
Late Summer, 6241st Solar Cycle

The besieging armies were in complete uproar.

Four hundred ubariu standards had appeared on the hills behind the encircling siege. Each of the banners measured five paces in length and one pace in breadth; the bright fabrics with their unfamiliar symbols flapped and swirled in the wind. The poles they were suspended from bent with the weight of the material and each standard needed four bearers. The noise of the flags whipping in the breeze was audible from afar.

This sea of flags was enough to impress the humans, the dwarves and even the elves. For Tungdil there was, thanks to Sirka, the additional knowledge that each standard represented one thousand warriors encamped over the hills out of sight.

Depicted in the arms Tungdil noted stylized weapons, patterns like flowers, and images of animals; still others reminded him of elaborate elf designs. No two were the same. He cast a final admiring glance their way and then entered the tent where all the monarchs had foregathered. Arguments were already underway and it was no surprise to see Rejalin deep in conversation with Isika and Ortger.

Prince Mallen rose to his feet and rapped on the table for silence. "As we have all seen, something very unexpected has occurred," he said in carrying tones, suppressing the last of Isika's whispered comments. "Tungdil Goldhand, tell us what this means."

The dwarf got up. "The ubàriu have come to secure the return of their property. Their envoy Sundalôn explained at the previous session what vital importance the diamond has for them and for the whole of Girdlegard."

"It's a trick," exclaimed Rejalin, radiant as the morning. "These are creatures of Tion, disguised as lambs but with the nature of beasts."

"Did we not agree we should not judge purely on appearances, princess?" Tungdil's retort was still respectful in tone. "Must I remind you of your own relatives? If we followed your line of argument we would have to raise a hand against every elf in Girdlegard on the grounds that we cannot be sure there is no evil lurking in them." He had chosen these harsh words with care, to enrage and provoke her before Esdalân appeared. The more disturbed her behavior in front of the sovereigns of Girdlegard, the better.

The elf-woman was not going to do him the favor of

a wild retort, but her eyes flashed in his direction. She sensed the dwarf was up to something.

Before Tungdil could continue, a commotion at the entrance heralded seven of the unfamiliar ubariu. Sirka followed in their wake.

The ubariu differed in appearance from their close relatives, the orcs: their stature was broader and more muscular. However, their faces were more finely drawn, if hardly more attractive; sharpened tusks protruded from between their lips and their skin was the darkest of greens.

They wore skillfully fashioned iron armor quite unlike the crude harnesses the orcs would sport. Underneath was a layer of padded dark fabric and their feet were protected with boots. Their weapons were heavy curved swords, broad at the tip to enable a more powerful blow. They exuded a smell like lavender.

Ireheart cursed under his breath and took firm hold of his crow's beak. There was a sharp intake of breath from those present; Queen Wey was heard to groan.

"Our greetings to all the rulers of Girdlegard." The ubariu spokesman bowed. He surveyed the company with a pink-eyed gaze. The voice recalled that of an orc but his speech, though accented, was clearly enunciated. Like Sirka, of course, he was speaking a foreign language; Tungdil was astonished that the ubariu knew the common tongue the rest of them used. "My name is Flagur and I am here to help the ubariu," and he pointed to Sirka, "win back their stolen diamond."

"But I thought the orcs were the ubariu?" said Isika, thoroughly confused.

"We call each other ubariu," Sirka explained. "We are both creatures of the god Ubar."

"A nice family indeed," said Ortger, a flush of high emotion visible through the beard growth on his cheeks.

"We," said Flagur civilly but assertively, "are not the creatures that you call orcs and we refer to as phottòr. We may resemble them in looks but we fight them as fiercely as you in Girdlegard once had to do."

"Your army's approach can be read as a threat, Flagur," Isika said to him. She had gone very pale and her black hair emphasized this. "We have heard from the lookouts that you bring at least eighty thousand soldiers."

"One hundred thousand, Your Majesty. We will never threaten you. We are merely afraid that your own forces are not sufficient in number to retrieve the diamond from the hands of the unslayables. And we are afraid also because you tolerate the broka in your land." He indicated Rejalin.

"We have heard that you put them to the sword in the Outer Lands," Ortger exclaimed excitedly. "Don't try the same thing here!" He pointed to Lot-Ionan and Dergard. "We have powerful wise men that your warriors cannot win against. Magic, does that mean anything to you?"

Flagur, Rodario's skill and experience told him, was enjoying playing a simple mind; many here were treating him as if he were as backward as an orc. "Magic? No. Not me." He shook his head, then pointed to the ubariu in violet-hued clothing next to him. "He will know. He is our top rune master and he can do things that always astonish me." His companions laughed softly. "We must settle what is to happen about the diamond. Sundalôn told you how important it is for our land and for yours. For this reason I insist we receive the stone after the removal of the älfar."

"So there is a threat!" Isika exclaimed, smugly. "Your intentions are clear."

Flagur twisted his lips into a smile. Tungdil had faced a multitude of creatures in his time, yet he had never seen any looking quite so dangerous. "No, I give you my word that my soldiers and I will march out of Girdlegard without attacking a single one of your people."

A whisper ran through the assembly. They had heard the announcement but did not believe it.

Sirka raised her voice. "But what we *will* do is leave our own land, Fòn Gàla, and we shall no longer guard the secret pass into Girdlegard as our people have done for so long."

The lines in Gandogar's brow were deep channels rather than furrows. "Nonsense. There is no secret way through the mountains . . ." Then he hesitated, wondering the same thing as all the other rulers there. "How did you get through the ravine and past the two dwarf fortresses?" he demanded, his voice unsteady. "I swear by Vraccas I shall attack you myself, if . . ."

Flagur turned to Sirka. "You tell them."

"We led the ubariu into Girdlegard," she admitted. "We have known about the path for a long time and have protected it from the phottòr, who happened upon it by a grave mischance. We circumvented the fourthling strongholds while the acronta besieged your gates, creating a diversion."

"And this is the path that will be used by the most

ghastly of beings to invade your land," Flagur predicted. "You can prevent it. *If* you give us the diamond. With it we can awaken the artifact to life that will close up the Black Abyss."

"It's a trick!" Rejalin insisted.

Those were the words Tungdil had been waiting for. He pounced upon the elf-deceit. "A trick? If you speak of trickery, princess, how do you explain to these crowned heads the murder of Liútasil four cycles ago and the farce you stage here?"

Rejalin stared at him. For the space of a moment there was nothing elegant or wonderful about her. Then she recovered and replaced her mask of sheer beauty. "What nonsense are you spouting, Tungdil Goldhand? Is this how you repay my people's hospitality? You would tell lies about us?" The elves behind their leader conferred nervously. Her bodyguard pierced Tungdil with sharp looks, unable to take further action in the circumstances.

"It is true! I have witnesses, Your Majesties," he persisted, fending off her attempts to ridicule his evidence. "I need to tell you all something I had wanted to keep secret until the end of my days. The eoîl that Rodario and I destroyed in Porista was in reality an elf. Liútasil told me everything. The eoîl are the oldest and most powerful of the elves and none of the elf folk would dare take up arms against one. This was the reason elves would not help us in our struggle." And he reported what had really happened on top of the tower. Rodario, aware this was not his big moment, let Tungdil speak, then swore an oath on his own life as to the truth of each word. "Liútasil knew. Now that the eoîl followers have murdered him, it is impossible for me to remain silent." Rodario gave the signal for Ireheart and Sirka to go and fetch Esdalân.

Ortger turned to the elf-woman seated as still as a porcelain figurine, fists clenched in her lap. "Say it isn't true, what Tungdil Goldhand is telling us!"

"Wait to hear the witness you tried to have killed," said Tungdil, as the elf entered with Goda and Ireheart.

Esdalân's eyes were full of hatred and contempt for Rejalin. Again Tungdil was struck by the resemblance. "I stand here, Your Majesties, and take my oath before the goddess Sitalia that I heard her speak of Liútasil's murder with my own ears. She arranged it; she prepared the ground for treachery." As he spoke he indicated the princess with a graceful but accusatory gesture. "My sister and her followers are desperate to further the teachings of the eoîl who caused so much destruction and suffering here in Girdlegard and in the Outer Lands. Do not allow her, whatever happens, to gain possession of the diamond or your fate and that of your subjects will be terrible."

Siblings! This explained why Tungdil had been struck by the similarity. It also made Rejalin's attempt on the elf's life all the more dreadful a crime.

Esdalân reported of his experiences in Âlandur, about the new temples where the eoîl was worshipped, about the white stones that stood for purity and that were to be erected in each of the kingdoms; he told them about the plans to bring death to those who had, in distress and crisis, gone along with the evil, like the people of Toboribor; he spoke of how the elves would take over in Girdlegard, dictating to the citizens and allowing them no voice of their own, as soon as they had the diamond in their hands.

The assembled monarchs listened in horrified silence.

"The atár consider themselves the purest of the pure and as purity's champions as almost of the same status as the eoîl. They want authority over all these lands, to be moral protectors. But they are no better than vicious blinded creatures, killing so many in their own ranks that all opposition was eradicated." Esdalân swiveled round. His voice was unsteady now, choked with emotion. "And nobody saw. Not even I, her own brother. Now you all know. I beg you in the name of the dead of Âlandur, executed by the atár: Prevent this. Stop them!" He took a step back and met his sister's gaze.

Rejalin swallowed hard. His appearance here had thrown her.

Shocked silence reigned. Outside, soldiers' voices could be heard and the normal sounds of the town: The clink of harness, the noise of hammers and tools, the footsteps of citizens going about their daily business.

"By all the good gods," whispered Isika, laying her hand on Rejalin's white one. "Say something! You must answer these accusations!"

Revolted by the touch, the elf-woman haughtily pulled away her hand and wiped it on her cloak. "What is there to say?" she said contemptuously. "It is true. We want to give Girdlegard the purity and morality it deserves. The eoîl left us with this mission and we rejoice in fulfilling her wishes." She watched the faces that surrounded her. "It will not be long now and our time will come. Then the wheat will be sorted from the chaff. The new seed grain will grow more gloriously than anything that has been seen before. Now it is out in the open I appeal to you all: submit to our test and show that you are free of guilt."

"By Palandiell!" Queen Wey sprang forward. "How you have deceived me! You won my trust with falsehoods and empty promises in order to spy out my land!" She pointed an accusing finger. "Do you think that this confession will bring you a single supporter amongst these monarchs?"

"We knew you would react like this as soon as our good intentions to bring enlightenment and purity to Girdlegard became known. You cannot understand, Queen Wey." Rejalin smiled forgivingly. "You are not yet ready."

But Weyurn's sovereign was too deeply wounded to be calmed by such words. "Do not dare to speak to me as if you were my mother!" she cried indignantly.

"But that is what we are. We are the mothers calling Girdlegard to order. For the good of all," the elf princess attempted to explain. She stood up as if to go. "As so often with mothers, their actions are not understood by their disobedient children. Not until many cycles have passed and the seed of New Girdlegard has sprouted and grown will our efforts be acknowledged. Then shall we, the atár, and the wise teachings of the eoîl be recognized and praised."

Gandogar pushed in front of her, growling angrily. "Where are you off to, Rejalin? Face up to your responsibility. You have killed dwarves and humans."

She looked at him in surprise. "We have eradicated beings that were not pure enough to exist in the new order.

They were the chaff." Her bodyguards fanned out into a protective line to shield her.

"And why the firstlings? What had those dwarves done to hurt you?"

"You poor pitiful high king, with no idea what is happening in your own empire," she said. "It was a thirdling colony. Dwarf-haters. My spies were watching them and decided to act before they could carry out more evil deeds against you and any dwarves worthy of life." She smiled. "Only a few of you will remain, I fear. You have many dwarf-haters in your ranks. You do not understand."

"She is madder than I am," murmured Ireheart. "We must not let her escape, Scholar. She will destroy Girdlegard instead of vanquishing the unslayables and their bastard freaks."

Rejalin did not listen but strode off toward the entrance. The human monarchs were too confused by the revelations regarding the elf princess to know what to do.

But Gandogar did not move aside; he laid his hand on his cudgel. "You will stay here and answer for your deeds," he demanded in a determined voice.

Esdalân came to his side. "It is over, sister. I have warned Girdlegard about your evil plans and intrigues. You can never prevail in open warfare."

"And now, Highness?" Mallen moved over from the side. "You have brought death to too many. Including Alvaro, whose fears I was foolish to disregard. He was wiser than I."

"If you had believed him you would have died, too."

She surveyed him from head to toe. "As it seems you are all united with this unpleasant person from the Outer Lands against me, I have no choice but to open your eyes."

"You surely do not intend to wage war?" Ortger could not take this in, any more than could Isika. "I beg you . . ."

The elf-woman stared. "It is not *your* place to beg anything of me, young man. Whoever gets the diamond first will decide what happens in Girdlegard." She gave a sharp nod.

One of her bodyguards drew his sword as quick as lightning and made to thrust it into Esdalân's body.

But Gandogar had not missed a thing. His cudgel flew out to deflect the blade. The elf, however, followed through and struck the king in the chest as he tried to protect Esdalân.

The elves and Rejalin hurried out of the assembly. Suddenly, one of her guards turned round with a rapid arm movement and something whirred toward Esdalân.

Ireheart grabbed up a small stool and hurled it to intercept the knife that had been thrown. It fell harmlessly in the corner. In the meantime the princess made her escape.

"Let her go," said Mallen, seeing Goda setting out after her. "You would stand no chance against them." He rushed out and they heard him giving hasty orders. Horses whinnied and riders cantered off. The prince returned to the assembly. "My men will cut them off and hold them." He turned to Flagur. "We may be needing your warriors sooner than we thought. But not to attack the creatures of Tion."

Isika stood up. "I know when I have made a mistake," she admitted with humility. Recent events had changed her mind. "I would ask the dwarf people and Tungdil Goldhand to forgive me. The elves' skill in deception is too perfect. Without you this unthinkable plan would never have come to light. For this my heartfelt thanks." She looked at all the kings and queens. "I do not exaggerate when I say that once again we are indebted to the dwarves."

Tungdil was supporting Gandogar, who for some reason was having trouble staying on his feet. Ireheart helped him. "Gandogar, what's wrong? Did the sword get you in the ribs?" He checked the armor: there was a scratch and slight dent.

"That's what I call good dwarf armor," said Boïndil proudly.

Gandogar's eyes rolled back in his head. He tried to speak but his knees gave way and his arms hung limply by his sides.

"Quick, put him on the table," instructed Lot-Ionan. "Let me see to him."

They picked the high king up and stretched him out on the conference table. The dwarves took off his breastplate and the magus inspected where the impact had been.

"Nothing," he said, "no fractures." He touched a red mark underneath the ribs. "This area here is very vulnerable. It is possible to render someone unconscious with a single blow with one's hand. It is possible that the blade had a similar effect through the armor."

Tungdil saw a dark red spot appear on Gandogar's neck. "Blood!" he exclaimed, touching the dwarf's throat. At that moment he stopped breathing. Tungdil's hands explored the thick beard until he found the wound. Directly under the chin his fingers came across a sharp piece of metal. The broken sword blade had bounced up and pierced his skin there. He parted the king's jaws, fearing the worst.

"He's dying!" shouted Ireheart in horror, looking to Lot-Ionan. But when the magus began a spell, Tungdil stopped him.

"It is over," he said darkly and showed them Gandogar's mouth where the sword fragment had pierced right up into his skull. The high king's brain was irrevocably destroyed.

"By Vraccas," whispered a horrified Ireheart. He hung his head; Goda was doing likewise.

Tungdil shut the dead man's mouth and closed his eyes. "Put his armor back on," he ordered. "High King Gandogar Silverbeard, of the clan of the Silver Beards of Goïmdil's fourthlings, is on his way to the eternal smithy back into the hands of Vraccas, his creator. Take his body to the Brown Range where he shall find a resting place surrounded by his own clan and the majestic mountain peaks."

"The elves have slain the high king of the dwarves." Mallen looked at Esdalân. "This will not end well."

"Not the elves. It was the atár," said Tungdil, looking at the blood on his fingers. The death of his monarch suddenly made everything much worse.

"It will be hard to explain that difference to the tribes making their way here, and the dwarves already at Toboribor," predicted Ireheart. "Both have pointy ears." He looked over at Esdalân. "Saving your presence."

A soldier entered. He stared open-mouthed at the body of the high king. "Prince Mallen, the elf princess and her escort have escaped. They have vanished into thin air. Her soldiers have gone off to the caves."

"When was that?"

"Just after the beginning of the meeting. We thought they were following your orders."

Mallen uttered a curse. "Rejalin guessed she would be unmasked."

Lot-Ionan raised his arms. "Terrible though the death of Gandogar is, we have no time to mourn. The elves will try to find the unslayables and snatch the diamond." He glanced at Tungdil. "Go and tell the dwarves what has happened. Anger makes a dwarf invincible. Speed is of the essence. Vital if we are to survive." Then, to Mallen: "Send all your warriors into the caves and follow the dwarves. Guard all the entrances. Not a single elf must escape." Finally he turned to Flagur: "It is your task to defend the caves from without. We are expecting a huge army of atár."

Flagur nodded. "It will be an honor. We are experienced in stopping the broka and destroying them. Should it be necessary." He changed into a different language and his companions withdrew. "Shall we have the stone, Lot-Ionan?" he asked.

"Yes," spoke the magus without hesitating. "It has already caused enough trouble in Girdlegard. Take it and put it where at least it may do some good."

Flagur gave a sketchy bow and left.

Ireheart, Goda, Sirka and Tungdil took their leave and hurried out to inform the rest of the dwarves about the death of their high king. Tungdil felt a dull ache inside. He sensed this was not a good omen.

When they reached the camp the banners were already at half-mast. The news had spread quickly. And the anger of the warrior dwarves, men and women alike, gathering around to hear him confirm the rumor, was palpable. The commanders of the freelings stood somewhat apart.

Tungdil stepped onto an upended bucket brandishing Keenfire in the air. "High King Gandogar is dead . . ."

A furious dwarf pushed forward. "Murdered!" he screamed. "By the pointy-ears." There were shouts from all sides as indignation at the cowardly murder spread.

"Listen to me!" called Tungdil, as loud as he was able, to be heard over the noise of the throng. "The elves are not guilty of the king's death. Our foes are the atár. You must not make the mistake of treating them and the elves alike." The angry hubbub dwindled away and Tungdil was able to report what had happened in the tent. Then he pointed Keenfire at the caves of Toboribor. "The atár want to take over our homeland. Let us now fulfill the task Vraccas gave us. Stop them! For the sake of Girdlegard!"

No one spoke.

A dwarf in the first row went down on one knee, removed his helmet and leaned on the upright shaft of his war hammer. His lips moved silently. Warriors to the left and right followed his example. In a wave of clinking armor and clattering helmets the dwarves all knelt on the flattened grass. Only the dwarves of the free towns remained standing.

"What are they doing?" asked Sirka, surveying the sea

of bowed bare heads. "Are they calling you their new leader? Or are they praying?"

"No, they are not praying," answered Tungdil, all too conscious of what was happening. He could read their lips. "It is an oath of vengeance."

XIV

Girdlegard,
Kingdom of Gauragar,
The Blacksaddle,
Late Summer, 6241st Solar Cycle

Limasar stood contemplating the blackened remains of the table mountain from whence the eoîl and her army of light had issued. They had set the dark mountain on fire to show their power to the peoples of Girdlegard; even non-combustible elements had been transformed into sheets of bright flame.

The elf touched the rock reverently and scratched off some of the sooty deposit. Underneath, the stone was a startling white: the eoîl had driven out the evil and replaced it with purity. Only such pristine stone was fitted for the new holy shrines and palaces.

"A wonderful place to rest," said Itemara next to him. She was a member of the warrior division he was taking to Toboribor on the orders of their princess. "It's amazing that no one else has discovered the beauty to be found here."

"But how could they?" Limasar, the leader of the troop, looked at the elf-woman. "They think the place is cursed. Whereas, of course, nowhere is purer. It has been purified, cleansed right down to the depths of the earth." He raised his arms. "Can you imagine the magnificent palace we shall build for the eoîl and Rejalin?"

"Yes, Limasar," said Itemara, visibly moved. "It is the center of a pure . . ." She broke off, swayed and looked down at the crossbow bolt protruding from her breast bone.

Limasar quickly ducked behind a rock. "To arms!" he shouted to his warrior elves a hundred paces away camped under an overhang. Even creatures such as they, who preferred sunshine to night, needed to take shelter from the sun's scorching noontime rays.

Itemara wrenched the arrow out of her chest as if it had been a mere splinter, but blood spurted out onto the stone, trickling down. "Where was that . . ." And only then did the elf-woman collapse.

Limasar, scanning against the light, could hardly see his troops. He had led them from the Red Range of mountains in the southeast of Girdlegard. Finally he was able to make them out as they jumped to their feet.

At the same moment about fifty small creatures with huge two-handed quarrying hammers appeared on top of the rock they were sheltering under.

"Dwarves?" Limasar pressed himself against the rock. "Look out, overhead!"

The warning came too late. Above, where the rock was vulnerable, dwarves had been hammering away to split the stone. Limasar could hear the grinding sound as it gave way.

The enormous overhang crashed down in one piece, burying the company of warriors. Weighing many tons, the gigantic boulder crushed elves and horses like grapes in a wine press.

Just seventy of his four hundred soldiers survived the

attack. They crawled out of the debris. Others were pinned down and screaming for help.

The air was filled with the sound of arrows as crossbow bolts showered down on them, bringing swift death to thirty more.

With fearful roars the dwarves leaped down off the cliff and launched themselves without mercy on the wounded and helpless elves, taking no notice of pleas for help or gestures of surrender. Hammers that had made the rock face collapse were now smashing slender bones.

More and more dwarves appeared: the new arrivals, carrying axes, cudgels and shields. The remnants of Limasar's unit were hopelessly outnumbered.

"Accursed dwarves!" Limasar yelled. "May Sitalia strike them all!"

He heard footsteps and a shadow flew past. Suddenly a red-headed brawny dwarf with a bright beard was menacing him. "What coward is crawling around here in the dirt?" the dwarf laughed grimly. "Stand up, pointy-ears. I am Ginsgar Unforce of the clan of the Nail Smiths from Borengar's firstlings." He was wielding a two-headed hatchet and holding a shield. "You shall follow those you have led to ruin."

Limasar stood up and drew his sword. "How do you dare to attack us?"

"Your trickery has been exposed. All of you, you and your princess; you killed our high king—despicable treachery!" He made a great sweeping blow, but the elf dodged the ax. "We know your plans. Eoîl, huh! We destroyed her and we'll do the same to you."

Limasar stabbed at the dwarf, catching his shield. "*You?*

560   *Markus Heitz*

The dwarves think they will destroy us?" He laughed at him. "Not today, not tomorrow and not when the world comes to an end."

Ginsgar hacked at his opponent's right flank and, when the elf parried the blow, hit him on the head with the edge of his shield. The blow met bone and sent Limasar lurching into a block of stone. "You are wrong, as you see." He rammed the flat side of the shield onto the fist in which the elf held his sword. Putting his weight behind it he broke the fingers of the elf's hand. The weapon fell to the ground.

Limasar yelled and drew a dagger with his other hand. "You cannot prevail against purity."

Ginsgar struck the elf with his hatchet before he could be harmed by the dagger. The ax blade laid open the armor, and the chest beneath it. The elf collapsed.

"Bring me a hammer!" called Ginsgar, setting his foot against the elf's shoulder and wrenching his ax blade out of the elf's flesh. "Don't die yet, pointy-ears!" he laughed. "My hammer wants to smash your arrogant face. It's been waiting so long."

Five dwarves ran up with the weapon Ginsgar wanted. On their clothing could be seen the blood of countless elves. The head of the hammer was red and sticky and had fine hairs clinging to it.

"Tell me your name," Ginsgar demanded of Limasar, who shook his head weakly in protest. "No? then keep it to yourself and tell your false gods when you meet them." He lifted the hammer and dropped it vertically onto the skull of the wounded elf. The bone stood no chance against the strength of the blow. The skull burst open and blood streamed out through nostrils, ears and mouth before the head was crushed beyond recognition.

"That's for Gandogar!" he cried and spat on the mutilated corpse. He shouldered his hammer and went over to where the overhang had collapsed.

Pools of blood had formed on the rock; life-juices trickled out from underneath the huge slab of stone and from the bodies of those slain by arrow or club.

"A fine sight," Ginsgar laughed roughly, and the others joined in. "It was a good idea, paying the elves a visit and paying our respects to Gandogar, wasn't it?"

"Good thing you saw them coming," agreed Bilandel Lighthammer of the clan of the Hammer Heads, wiping blood off his face with a bit of rag. The two were alike, but his beard was brown whereas Ginsgar's was red. They would be taken for brothers were they not from different clans.

Ginsgar climbed onto the nearest rock to have a better view. He and his clan's five hundred warriors were the contingent from the Red Mountains sent as reinforcements for the Toboribor siege. The news of Gandogar's death had reached them as they marched. Dwarf spirit had flared up in fury and his soldiers were of one angry mind.

Seeing the numbers of elf dead did not cool his blood. He was eaten up by the thought that there were still elves alive. "What are these few paltry corpses? Âlandur is full of them," he murmured belligerently.

Bilandil looked up. "I agree. When it's over someone will find a way of explaining away what the pointy-ears have done and they won't get the punishment they deserve."

Ginsgar looked at his friend. "Hear me, children of the Smith!" he called. The dwarves thronged in front of him, not a trace of regret showing on any face. "Our high king has been taken from us. And we know who perpetrated his treacherous murder. They tell us the elves were dazzled and led astray by the avatars and the elf-woman that led them." He raised his hammer and pointed north. "Remember the wars our folk have waged against the elves over thousands of cycles. We never sought such wars but were forced into them by the aggression of the elves: their cruel deeds or malicious threats. Even the älfar are more honest than they are. I say the elves never wanted peace with our people. The slaying of Gandogar shows their true colors. We tried to negotiate reconciliation; may Vraccas be our witness that we tried. And this is how they repay us." He struck the rock a mighty blow with his hammer. "Enough! Let us make for Âlandur and tear the deceiving evil heart out of the elf-folk before another malevolent fruit ripens on the trees of their glades!"

And the dwarves roared approval in a frenzy of victory and blood-lust. They put aside the task they had been given.

"Long live Ginsgar!" shouted Bilandel, brandishing his morning star. "Let him lead us to Âlandur. And if our kind track down the diamond, we shall make sure no pointy-ears are alive to grab it!" He headed the march. "To Âlandur! Vengeance for Gandogar!"

Ginsgar was hoisted up and carried on a shield. "Vraccas is with us!" he promised his dwarf-following. "Death to all elves!"

Above the heads of the warrior throng he held his shield up with one hand and raised his warhammer in the other.

To see the impressive figure of the red-bearded dwarf was immediately to recognize the new high king of the dwarves—one who would preside over bitter and terrible times.

Girdlegard,
Kingdom of Idoslane,
The Caves of Toboribor,
Late Summer, 6241st Solar Cycle

Ireheart took a peek round the corner. The passageway, as yet unexplored, lay dark and abandoned before them. Or rather, it gave the impression of being abandoned.

"What happens if we meet elves, Scholar?" he said, before jumping round, his crow's beak raised.

"Depends how they behave. If they attack, we fight back," Tungdil answered. "But I don't want to see any of us lift a weapon first," he warned his companions.

He was leading one of the dwarf bands that in the last ten orbits had penetrated deep into the former orc territory. As well as Ireheart, Goda and Sirka, he had fifty heavily armored experienced warriors who had already shown their mettle in battles on the Blacksaddle and against the avatars and orcs in the Gray Range. Resolute veterans all, they feared no peril and would fight Tion himself if need be.

Lot-Ionan could not be with them. Instead, they had

Dergard to counter the magic of the unslayables or perhaps of the elves. The dwarves were taking over all the fighting.

Ireheart poked at a long thin object with the tip of his boot. "Orc bones. Not very old, but not very recent." He bent and picked up his find. "A snout-face's thigh bone. Severed with one blow." It was a clean cut. "Must have been an extremely sharp blade," he said, admiration in his voice. "Not a sword and certainly not the kind of ax the orcs use."

"The ubariu?" suggested Goda hesitantly. "Did they get in here secretly . . ."

"No." Tungdil moved forward cautiously, his right hand clasping Keenfire. "The unslayables. They killed the orcs."

Boïndil shook his head doubtfully. "Do you think they'd simply do away with the last of their allies for the hell of it?"

"No, not just for the hell of it. But they'd do it. Perhaps they'd carried out their task and weren't needed anymore."

From in front of them came a loud hiss and two large green spots glowed in the darkness. There was a rumbling sound as at terrifying creature made of tionium picked up a metal foot and moved toward them.

"That must be the thing King Ortger was describing," Ireheart called out, raising his crow's beak. "Anybody remember where the weak spot is for this particular freak?"

"No, don't look for a weak spot," Tungdil ordered. If Furgas was really the mastermind behind these monsters there wouldn't be any weak spots. "Let's get it another way."

Dergard pushed to the front, lifted his hands and started

to intone a spell, but Tungdil stopped him. "Keep your magic for when we face the unslayables," he said. "Don't forget that some of the parts are coated with an alloy that conducts magic."

"You are right." Dergard lowered his arms. "It would help rather than harm them." His gaze wandered upwards toward the roof. "But they presumably would be vulnerable to a rockfall?"

"Save the idea for emergencies. We'll try something else." He indicated to the dwarves who were carrying their climbing gear. "Take the ropes. Tie its legs together and trip it up."

The oversized suit of armor was pushing closer, rattling and hissing. The massive hands opened and closed with loud clicks as if it could not wait to grab hold of the dwarves. In the meantime they had glimpsed the monster's face behind the thick porthole at breast height. It was inwardly raging, the noise of the machinery drowning out its shouts.

"Can we get near enough before it realizes what we're up to?" one of the warriors wondered.

Tungdil gave a dark laugh. "We'll bring it to you. Get ready."

"Yes! That's what I like!" laughed Boïndil and gave the crow's beak a trial swing. "Let's knock. Maybe the thing inside will just open up and ask us in."

"Provoke it and get it to chase us. But be careful. We don't know if Ortger's told us everything it can do," warned Tungdil. "Take it in turns."

"I'll go first," demanded Ireheart and rushed off with half the dwarves after him. The others watched tensely as the first feigned attacks were made.

The creature was astonishingly flexible for its huge dimensions. Fatally flexible.

One overbold attacker lost his life. An iron-clad foot kicked him through the air and he collided with the wall of the tunnel, breaking his neck.

Over the creature's breast area openings became visible; then the monster bent forward and sent a hail of missiles shooting at the dwarves. All of them missed.

Ireheart was doing well. Although the fire of battle was raging in his veins and he was slamming away at the boots and joints of the monster, he was staying alert enough to keep walking backwards, luring the living suit of armor after him.

"Our turn now!" called Tungdil, raising Keenfire. It was time to find out what they could achieve. Would the alloy coating protect it?

Sirka bent and kissed Tungdil wordlessly, then smiled at him. "Just in case one of us doesn't make it out of the caves alive," she said, whirling her staff. "Shall we?"

He nodded and stormed ahead. Those few words of Sirka's echoed round his head and threatened to distract him from the task at hand. He pulled himself together and ducked to avoid the grasp of the machine's snapping fingers, feeling the draught as the blow narrowly missed. He attacked with Keenfire.

To his inordinate relief the ax head flamed into life, gathering power to strike the foe.

The blade hit home above the iron ankle. Lightning flashes blazed and the runes on the armor shone dark green. A jerk went through the machine and a new noise erupted inside like the twanging of a breaking bow string.

"It's still alive, Scholar!" Ireheart screamed from behind. "The thing in the glass case. It's still there. And I think it's laughing!"

Furious now, Tungdil drew back his weapon, there was dark green blood, nearly black, sticking to it. At least Keenfire was able to injure it. Then he saw the elf runes on the monster's right breast. The word he read was *deaths*.

"Take care," Sirka warned, but it was a second too late.

The flat iron hand hit him and catapulted him away. He lost his helmet and his belt came loose, tangling itself round his boots. Caught upside-down like a bound gugul he could see the monster stomping toward him, sharp iron nails underneath its boots, with fragments of bone and armor from previous encounters hung between them.

"Come here and I'll slit your tin can open!" he taunted the colossus, raising his ax.

Then Sirka was there, dragging him along by his belt. Their giant adversary followed them—and stepped into the trap.

Hardly had Tungdil and Sirka passed than the rope was tautened and the ends fastened round a rock.

It caught the monster's iron foot; its pace slackened. The rope burst apart but the beast had lost its balance. It managed to bring its arms forward to break the fall and to prevent itself falling onto its porthole.

"Now!" bellowed Ireheart sprinting off and using his momentum to swing the crow's beak upwards with tremendous force.

The blunt end hit the thick porthole in front of the

monster's face. Clunk! Four cracks appeared in the curved pane of glass. The three iron balls of Goda's night star completed the destruction. Shards fell down on her and Ireheart.

Sirka had freed Tungdil from his involuntary bondage. "Everything all right? Or have I dragged the skin off your bones?"

"No, you have stolen my heart." This time he was the one who planted a kiss, then he sprang up to help Boïndil, looking on in fury as the machine struggled up.

"Stay where you are, infernal bucket!" raged Ireheart, whacking the iron arms, in an attempt to break them, in spite of being underneath. "You have killed your last dwarf!" He struck an elbow joint.

The combination of the creature's massive weight and this well-aimed blow caused the material to yield. One of the holding bolts snapped, and the forearm broke off. The machine toppled and could not right itself.

"You're mad! Get out from under there!" called Tungdil.

But Ireheart was too far gone in his battle-lust to hear. "I'll smash your ugly nose and the rest of you to boot!" he promised the beast, thumping his crow's beak into its face. Blood sprayed out and the deformed features disappeared in a sea of black. The whole machine shuddered as if sharing the pain the creature within was suffering. "Ha! Now it's . . ."

The left arm gave way and the three-pace-long torso fell with a thud. Its fate was sealed.

Tungdil saw his friend disappear under the massive black armor. His cry of horror was drowned out by the terrible clanking and rattling, a noise that eclipsed any other sound in the tunnels. He did not dare look down to check for blood. "We'll have to hoist it up, to . . ."

"That was close," they heard Boïndil laugh. His helmet appeared on top of the armored monster, then he was up and standing on it swinging his crow's beak. "Ha! That's what Vraccas likes to see!" he called happily. "Now the unslayables have lost two of their beasts."

He stamped on the creature's metal back. "It wasn't actually the magister's weak point they told us about. But it wasn't bad, was it?"

Tungdil gestured him to come down. "Get off there before the altitude gets to your brain and you attempt more stupid suicidal stuff." He hid his relief behind the seemingly harsh words.

"Coming, Scholar." Ireheart stroked his weapon. "Crow's beak and I are in just the mood to take on another of these monsters." He looked down between his feet. "There's something like a lock here. Shall we break it open? It'll take us to the cogwheel innards, for sure."

With a high-pitched shriek steam gushed out of a vent next to Ireheart.

"No, let's get on." Tungdil did not like the sound at all. His own people's steam machines had valves to release a build-up of pressure. He did not know if this contraption had the same. "If the boiler blows I don't want to be next to it."

"Got you." He stepped over the iron hip, walked down the leg and jumped off the foot, brown eyes gleaming with a mixture of war-rage and triumphant delight: a dangerous combination of light-headed boldness and unshakeable self-confidence. "Do you know what? We'll have another of these down before the day is out."

"You are incorrigible," said Tungdil and left it at that. "Come on."

"Of course I'm incorrigible. But hesitation never gets you anywhere." He winked at Goda, who was gazing at him admiringly. She was proud he was her trainer and had completely forgotten the argument they had had in the barn.

Together they walked along the passage until they reached a fork. Tungdil mentally arranged the elf runes in the most likely order: *your deaths have*. Two more creatures were needed and they would have the riddle solved.

"And now?" Dergard wiped the sweat from his brow. He was the one least able to cope with the sultry heat, and these Toboribor caves were extremely hot, affected by the steaming simmering pools they found everywhere they went. The dwarves were not enjoying it much, either. It smelt too strongly of orc. Tungdil indicated a passageway where cooler air was emerging. "That one." He took the lead.

With every stride they took it got colder. Damp settled on their chain mail and the chilliness—welcome at first—soon had Dergard shivering.

"It's like a crypt." He spoke his thoughts out loud. "I don't like it here."

"Who do you think is enjoying this?" retorted Ireheart. "Just because I am a child of the Smith doesn't mean I feel happy in this pig-sty. Caves aren't all the same, you know, magus."

Tungdil had reached a cavern and realized that Dergard had not been far off the truth with his suggestion. "Quiet, he hissed back over his shoulder. A vague feeling of unease warned him against entering, but there was no choice. The diamond could be anywhere. "Come on, but quietly."

This cave was a good fifty paces long and broad and the walls curved above them in a dome at least forty paces high. Exactly in the middle a dark stalactite hung down; it was the length of two grown human men and the girth of an ancient tree.

The stalactite's tip pointed down to a woman with long black hair lying on an altar of basalt, her hands folded on her stomach and her eyes closed. Her black silk robes draped to the right and left of the bier partially obscured the älfar rune ornaments on the stone.

Under her crossed hands lay two long slender swords that Tungdil recognized at once. The unslayable siblings had used similar weapons to attack the eoîl in the battle on the tower.

A bluish light was emanating from the diamond on her breast. From time to time a silver flicker illuminated the signs and the countenance of the recumbent figure.

They had found the unslayable sister . . . and the stolen diamond.

On the floor round about them lay the skeletons of orcs: the remains of five hundred or more. The cut marks on the bones made no other interpretation possible: they had died by the same sharp blade.

"By Samusin!" whispered Dergard in fascination, unable to take his eyes off the älfar woman. "How exquisite she is." Even lying there like this, still and stiff, she had more grace, more elegance, more beauty than the elf princess Rejalin.

Tungdil and the other dwarves could not endure the sight of her features. It was like asking them to look into a dazzling reflection of a bar of gold. Or to go right up to a glowing furnace. They could have done none of these.

At last even Dergard had to lower his eyes. But the fascination had not left him. Blind to any danger, he approached the altar, lifting his trembling hands in his desire to touch the dark goddess. The brittle orc bones scrunched and crumbled under his feet.

"Leave the Creating Spirit alone." A voice as clear as a mountain spring sounded suddenly on all sides. "She has been tired for so very long."

Dergard stood stock still and looked to the right and left without seeing a soul. "I don't want to hurt her," he called in ecstatic tones. "Only . . . to be near to her. To kneel and gaze upon her."

"Can the pointy-ears have deprived our magus of his senses, Scholar?" asked Boïndil in dismay.

How Tungdil wished he had translated the runes in the inscriptions on the doors of the throne room in Dsôn Balsur. Perhaps it would have helped here. But he did not speak the älfar tongue. "I fear so," he replied under his breath.

"Shall we drag him away?" suggested Goda.

"No, stick together. And do nothing to provoke Dergard." He was afraid the magus would use magic to defend himself.

Dergard moved two paces closer to the altar. He lifted his gaze. The diamond illuminated the immaculate features, the sight of which burned itself into his brain. The magus was sobbing like a small child; he sank to his knees and crawled over toward the unslayable one through the mass of orc bones, unaffected by this ghastly detritus.

"Do not approach the Creating Spirit." The voice whipped him back.

"But I must," begged the awestruck Dergard, frightened at the thought of withdrawing.

They heard cogwheels clicking into action, the clanking of iron, the rattling of a drive mechanism and then a hissing sound. Out of a dark corner of the cavern swept a white cloud of vapor that wandered around randomly. Tungdil thought of the mist demons that had taken over Nudin.

"I shall not let you disturb her," said the elfish voice, with a terrifying hiss. The next in the series of machines made by the sick genius Furgas now approached, its many wheels turning the orc remains to dust.

Tungdil saw a mixture of vehicle and heavily armored beast: below the hip it disappeared into a box-like construction on wheels. The elf rune he was looking for was on the front plating: *faces.*

It had lifted the visor and yellow eyes watched Dergard from above: "Get out of here!"

"If it weren't so viciously dangerous, you'd have to give Furgas a medal for inventiveness," whispered Ireheart.

His words were picked up. The machine lifted its head suddenly and looked toward the cave entrance. "You have come to disturb the Creating Spirit." An armored hand shot up to slam the visor down. "I cannot permit that."

The vehicle picked up speed and came toward the dwarves through the sea of bones.

"Spread out!" Tungdil had seen the machine's long

tionium assault spikes, and the sharp wheels that would slice any victim lying on the ground. The trick with the rope was not going to work with this one.

Spotting that the dwarves were splitting into two groups, the machine operated a mechanism that let down two long blades right and left.

Ireheart grinned. "Not all the constructions are perfect. Those blades are set too high. We can easily . . ." With a loud clicking noise the blades were lowered down to mid-dwarf height.

"I should have kept my mouth shut." Ireheart was furious.

Then the monster machine started after them. Before long it had struck one brave warrior on the hip. The combination of the vehicle's speed and the blades' sharpness was enough to cut through chain mail and bone. Screaming and spurting blood, he collapsed onto the orc remains while the chase went on.

Three more dwarves were cut to pieces. The rest of the group swerved out of reach, pushing into a narrow cleft where the beast could not pass.

Tungdil made use of the distraction. With some of the other dwarves and Ireheart, Sirka and Goda, he ran through the cave, stopping at the altar on which the unslayable one lay. Their target was the diamond lying unguarded there.

"Ireheart, you get the diamond," Tungdil commanded. "I'm going to decapitate the älfar woman."

"Why not the other way round? I'd like to cut her head off."

"Because only Keenfire can put an end to the life of an unslayable."

Goda looked over her shoulder. "It's seen us and is coming this way." She slowed her pace and was about to confront the machine.

"No, keep going!" Ireheart grabbed her by the shoulder. "Behind the altar—it'll be safer there. Or it'll roll right over you." Running headlong he launched himself and leaped onto the älfar. If he wasn't going to get to take her head off at least he wanted to injure her.

A beam of green light hit him on the groin; the magic hurled him backwards and his crow's beak flew through the air, striking Sirka on the forehead. She sank to the ground, unconscious.

Goda whirled around to face the new attacker, but only found a very familiar face.

Dergard was crouching by the altar with one hand raised. "You must not disturb her, didn't you hear?" he hissed. "Don't you dare try again!"

Ireheart clambered to his feet, cursing. Apart from pins and needles all over and a few grazes on his hands he was all right. "You wait so long for a magus and when one finally arrives he's nothing but trouble." He looked to see how Sirka was. "She's alive, Scholar. You deal with the human."

But the machine rolled onward like a demented fiery bull, lowering the spear in its hand. The blade edges shimmered in the diamond's bluish light.

XV

Girdlegard,
Kingdom of Idolslane,
The Caves of Toboribor,
Late Summer, 6241st Solar Cycle

Tungdil confronted Dergard, thrusting Goda back. "Go and help your master," he told her. Then he made a feigned attack on the young magus, reckoning Keenfire would afford the protection he needed.

Dergard moved fast. From his fingertips he shot a light-ray toward Tungdil, but Keenfire attracted and then absorbed the magic beam's energy: its inlaid patterns lit up and the diamonds were transformed into brilliant miniature stars.

Tundil was unscathed; he felt the sigurdacia wood of the ax handle grow warm, that was all. Without further ado he struck the magus on the temple with the flat of the ax blade and Dergard passed out and sank to the ground.

"Look out, Scholar!" shouted Ireheart from behind. "Get down!"

Tungdil launched himself into a backwards dive.

The hybrid creature's long blade whirred past his face, missing him by the breadth of a beard-hair. The sharp metal edge clanged against the base of the altar and shattered. A roar of frustration was heard.

But the machine's powerful array of wheels continued

onwards, rolling over the unconscious Dergard and slicing him to pieces. Limbs were severed, and all that remained of the head was a shredded mass. Only the gods themselves could have revived him.

"I am going to kill you!" The monster hurled a spear at Ireheart, who had clambered onto the altar. The dwarf sprang back and with Goda dived under cover at the far end of the stone bier.

"I'll distract it," Tungdil called over his shoulder. "You two know what to do." He felt Dergard's death had been his fault. He had knocked the magus out and, unconscious, he had been easy prey.

The monster drew another spear stored lengthways on the vehicle's side. "Your ax is nothing to me," it said, slowly advancing. You cannot even reach me, groundling."

Tungdil ducked down to grab a loose blade fragment; he weighed it carefully, then cast it with all his strength at his adversary. The machine swiveled and struck him on the left shoulder with a jagged-edged knife. His own throw had not even damaged the machine's armor plating.

The creature laughed and sped onwards while Tungdil moved back from the altar to give himself more freedom of movement. "You will not defeat me," he vowed to the creature.

Now Goda tried her luck. She sprinted along the other side of the altar and jumped up in an attempt to get the diamond.

The fiendish creature turned its head and launched a spear in her direction. "Get away from the Creator Spirit!"

Goda was taken by surprise. The sharp point cut through her chain mail links and armor, piercing the collarbone and shoulder joint and forcing her to the floor. The weapon shaft protruded from her back.

Tungdil could not let himself think about her fate because the machine-monster was nearly upon him. He crouched down, did a shoulder roll to escape the lethal touch of the wheels and vicious blades, then jumped back on his feet.

With a mighty leap, he launched himself onto the broad platform of the vehicle. Above him towered the armored back of the creature.

Raising his arms he whacked Keenfire with tremendous force against the place he assumed the creature's spine to be. If this blow were not a death-dealer, his own life would shortly be over.

But the ax did not fail him. It tore into the tionium, hacking at the flesh and gouging through to the vertebrae giving off a dazzling glow as it did so, the diamonds pulsating as if they contained a heart.

The monster gave an ear-splitting screech, cringing and collapsing, its long arms convulsively grabbing at the dwarf on its back. "Get off me!"

"No!" Tungdil had already landed a second ax blow, despite difficulty in keeping his balance on the swaying metal deck. The next swipe was less powerful but hit the same spot, maximizing the injury.

With a bestial roar the creature waved its arms wildly and struck Tungdil on the chest. He flew through the air, landing with a thump on the ground, but without losing his grip on the ax handle. Dazed, he struggled to his feet and, as if through a veil, saw the creature lurching towards him again at high speed.

The other dwarves raced over to support their leader.

He glimpsed the spear that had narrowly missed Ireheart. "My life is in your hands, Vraccas!" Snatching up the spear he hurled it at the foe.

The machine drove on to its own destruction. Keenfire's strikes had rendered it incapable of taking evasive action or defending itself, and the spear-blade struck it full in the chest.

It swerved violently, then repeatedly somersaulted, each flip forcing the weapon deeper into its chest until the spear finally broke.

Tungdil vaulted aside to escape the heavy vehicle. It rumbled past him and burst open on impact with the cave wall, piercing the monster inside with the array of cogwheels, rods and gears that had propelled it. Blood poured down the rock.

Tungdil saw that the creature's legs had been amputated above the knee and the stumps fitted with hooks and chains to enable it to move along. It was a horrific sight.

Three dwarves helped Tungdil get over to the altar. Ireheart was standing in front, holding the diamond triumphantly in his right hand. "Here, Scholar," he called. "We've got it! Thank Vraccas! Come and hack off this pointy-ear's head so we can go and tend to our wounded." He got ready to throw it. "Here! Catch!"

An arrow whirred past and struck Ireheart on the left side. His hand was knocked sideways, the fingers opened and he dropped the stone; it fell onto the älfar's breast, rolled down onto her belly and came to rest by her folded hands.

Ireheart stared at the second arrow lodging in his forearm. "Treacherous elves!" he groaned. Then three more arrows hit him in the chest and he collapsed on top of the älfar woman.

Three dozen archer elves streamed out of the second entrance, raining arrows on the dwarves.

"Boïndil!" yelled Tungdil, distraught, as he stormed to meet them, ax held high. Now was no time to act out the role of scholar.

Before the other dwarves recovered from their surprise, fifteen of them had been felled. Those of Tungdil's band still alive hurtled to their leader's side to launch themselves at the hated foe and to stop the diamond being stolen.

These were the longest-lasting thirty-seven strides that Tungdil had ever taken in his entire life.

On all sides dwarf death-screams resounded. The skilled archers aimed at any gaps in the wall of shields and their deadly missiles repeatedly hit home.

Some of the arrows even penetrated the iron shields, nailing shields to forearms; or, going deeper still, they robbed a warrior of his life.

As the noise of war shouts, scurrying boots and rattling chain mail subsided, Tungdil, only three paces from the elves, realized he was the sole survivor. Behind him lay a trail of dwarf dead.

Eyes awash with tears of fury and hatred, he raised the ax and swung it at the nearest elf, only to receive a vicious blow on the head and a cut through his left eye. The pain was excruciating and erupted like a thunderstorm inside his head.

He lost all power in his muscles. Everything weighed a ton and Keenfire suddenly seemed as heavy as a mountain. Tungdil slid to the ground at the feet of an elf.

A boot turned him on his back and Rejalin's face floated above him. "The time of peace between our peoples, Tungdil Goldhand," she said icily, "is over. None of the groundlings will survive our test. You are all corrupt." She reached past him and lifted up Keenfire. "Heavy. But unique, in that it fights for good. It will serve us better than it has served your people." She stood tall. "We, the eoîl atár, will shepherd Girdlegard into an age of immaculate purity. The era of weakness and decay and dissolution is over."

Tungdil tried to reply but his senses deserted him. Death was knocking at his door ready to escort him to the eternal smithy.

Before he closed his eyes, giving in to an irresistible compulsion, Tungdil thought he saw a figure in black älfar armor step out of the shadows to approach the elf ranks from behind. In each raised hand a naked blade was clasped.

Warm rain . . . But was he imagining it? Where would warm rain come from in a cave?

Then his thoughts fragmented . . .

"Why have you done this to me?"

The unslayable one woke up, suddenly confronted by the beautiful face of his son, who was crouched down at his side, a spear in one armored glove, his hand touching the metal plates sewn into his perfect flesh.

"I have not harmed you. I have had you made mightier

than all other beings in Girdlegard." He sat up, rose swiftly from the couch and seized his helmet from the weapon stand. He had only intended to allow himself a moment's rest before returning to the fray. The battle seemed to be going increasingly against them. The dwarves and undergroundlings were fighting fiercely in the tunnels and for some reason the elves had also arrived in search of the diamond. This rivalry brought no advantage to himself and his sister Nagsar Inàste.

"Mightier than you, creator?"

"Why aren't you back in the tunnel where I told you to stay?" he censured his son.

"I needed to speak to you, creator father." His son stood up. "I don't wish to spill any more elf blood."

The unslayable froze. "Get back to your post at once," he said, his voice ice cold. "You are to kill every elf you meet."

"But they are just like us! We are killing them but they look like us. They must be friends . . ."

"We are not like them at all! Do friends come to your house and try to kill you? And try to steal your treasure?" He put on his helmet. "Do what you are told, boy. You are responsible for your creator mother." He turned abruptly toward his son. "Do you want her to die before she has ever clapped eyes on you?"

"Why are my brothers different from me?"

"They are not your brothers."

"But they said she is their creator mother too."

"They are lying. Have nothing to do with them." He made to thrust him out of the chamber into the passageway.

But the young älfar ducked under his arm and would

not yield. "Take these plates off me," he demanded harshly. "They hurt. I can't take them off by myself."

"No. You will need them. They will protect you in battle."

"Your armor goes on top, not right inside you. Why can't I have armor like that?" the young älfar argued stubbornly, his black gaze unwavering.

The unslayable hated such confrontations. "It is special metal that gets the powers working in you."

"But I still don't want it."

"I am supremely indifferent as to whether you want it or not. You are my son and you will do what I say."

"I . . ."

The unslayable one grabbed him by the throat. "Hold your tongue! We don't have time to argue about this nonsense. The safety of your creator mother is more important than any petty wish of yours. Have you understood?"

The black eye sockets of the young älfar sparked with anger. "But it hurts so much!"

"Deal with it!" The unslayable hurled him brutally out of the chamber. "You know where you're supposed to be." He wanted to waste no more time.

The älfar stumbled against the wall, growled and lifted his spear; immediately the runes on it blazed up, giving out a dark green light. "Take the metal out. I'm not asking, I'm telling you."

The unslayable stopped in his tracks. "Put down your weapon this instant!" he menaced, drawing his own two swords. "You do not threaten your father."

"You don't do this to me, either!" the älfar accused in reply, looking down at the black trickles of blood on the armor plating.

The unslayable one narrowed his eyes. "Did you go back to the island?"

"I wanted them to take the plates off, but the human wasn't there and the groundlings refused to help. All I could do was take some more of the power to make the pain less." He was watching the other's movements carefully. "I don't want to hurt you, creator father. Just let me be like you."

They stood wordlessly glaring at each other.

From nearby the clank of weapons could be heard. One of the bastards was screaming and bellowing amongst an uproar of dwarf yells.

"The enemy has found Nagsar Inàste's cavern. Happy now?" shouted the unslayable. "It was your task to guard that passage." He lifted his foot, but the spear was already leveled at his throat. "What is the meaning of this?"

"I've told you. You shall not leave until you have done what I want."

The creator father considered his handiwork: beauty and perfection on the outside, disappointing failure within. How had his sister borne him progeny such as this? Perhaps the fault could be traced back to the orcish violations she had been subjected to. His offspring's fine looks were no use to him at all. There was no place for a son who challenged him and made demands instead of obeying. The swords flashed swifter than arrows to find the gaps in the armor plating and pierce the breast and throat of the stupefied young älfar. "You are no longer any son of mine," declared the unslayable, with a sidestep deftly avoiding the leveled spear, behind which there was little force now. "Better ones will follow: sons who know how to obey their originator. Even if I and the creator mother have to wait another thousand cycles." He kicked his son in the belly, felling him; the swords slid back out of the torso, black blood spurting out of the wounds. "You wanted me to take the pain away?" He stabbed again with both swords.

The älfar reared up, then shrank down, attempting to ward off the slashing blades with his metal gauntlets. It was hopeless. The runes on his armor flickered and died as the slim body fell slack to the floor.

The unslayable wasted no more time. His beloved sister was in terrible danger and the bastards were not able to protect her.

As he drew nearer to her cavern the sounds of fighting ceased abruptly. It was not a good sign.

He entered at the rear of the cave and suppressed a cry of horror when he saw what had happened.

Elves. Elves in the white armor worn by the eoîl's followers had taken over the cave. One of their archers was finishing off the last of the groundlings with a shot through the eye as he reached the group. One bastard lay dead, surrounded by the ruins of his machine over by the wall, and the cave floor was littered with dwarf corpses.

No! Don't let them have taken you, beloved sister! He saw her beheaded torso lying on the altar. Her sacred black blood streamed down the sides, down the steps, and onto the floor of the cave. An elf woman held Nagsar Inàste's head in her hands and an elf was reverently holding out the diamond to her. The stone had ceased to shine.

Despair overwhelmed the unslayable. *My fault! It is my fault! If I had not failed she would be living still.* He leaned against the wall, feeling his strength ebb away, his limbs frozen.

The sight burned itself into his brain. He could smell her blood, see it still trickling still from the stump of her neck.

Images of the past rose up in his mind. Wonderful images. The time they had looked out from the highest window in the Dsôn tower to survey their realm in delighted pride; when they had celebrated their victories over the elves of the Golden Plain and Lesenteïl's followers; when they had made love—the pain and deep devotion— a passion that was never-ending . . .

Such memories were drowning in his sister's blood and being washed away. An elf strode up to the altar and prodded the corpse with a spear. It dropped down on the far side of the altar, rolled down the steps and came to rest awkwardly, like so much rubbish.

I shall avenge your death, my beloved Nagsar Inàste, as never a true wife was avenged by a loving spouse. Blind anger forced strength back into his muscles. Slowly he raised his swords. The elves by the altar were congratulating themselves on a presumed victory, praising the eoîl. *I shall leave Girdlegard. I shall take the diamond with me and decipher its secrets. And when I return nothing shall withstand my fury.* He circled slowly toward the elves. *Everything will perish in my storm. Like these elves.*

The unslayable one came up behind the first of them unobserved, their bloody destruction thus assured.

Those who had stowed their weapons fell first, with nothing to hand to fend off the attacker's double blades. Those still holding them were quickly overwhelmed.

Finally, with less than a third of their number still standing, outright slaughter turned into battle.

"The princess! Guard her!" echoed the cry. The elves put up tough resistance but were no match for the unslayable, powered as he was by his fury. Any injuries he took hardly slowed him. His whirring blades sliced at throats and arms, severing wrists and legs, plunging through skulls and chests. The old orc skeletons underfoot drank up the blood of new victims.

The unslayable lashed out furiously until only three warriors and the elf princess remained.

He fended off the first assault, spinning his assailant round so that the offending blade pierced the belly of the next foe. Swiftly he shattered the elf sword with his own; and with his other weapon he batted a sharp fragment into the third attacker's face.

He parried a thrust from the last elf coming at him with a jagged blade, severing the elf's arm below the elbow. Using his swords like scissors, he cut off the soldier's head, sending it flying through the air. Then he plunged his two blades with massive force right and left of the neck stump straight down into the warrior's body. Arms, shoulders and upper body parts were sliced off to fall on the heap of orc bones.

The screams and the scent of elf blood were still not enough to cool the raging fury within. "So you are their princess!" With one stride he was close, ducking under the elf woman's sword lunge and cutting through the tendons at the back of her knees with a swift right-handed swipe. She fell to the ground with a shriek of pain and he stood on her sword hand. "And Liútasil?"

She stared at him, mouthing something.

"Oh no, you'll put no eoîl curse on me." His left arm shot forward and he pierced her wrist, causing her to open her fingers so that the diamond rolled away with a clunk to land among the pile of old bones. "You, lady, have caused me more pain than I have ever felt; I shall distribute this pain among all the elves of Girdlegard." Withdrawing his sword, he rummaged around in the pile of bones until he had located the stone, lifting it up with a triumphant gesture. "It is mine now. As soon as I have learned how to put its powers fully to use I shall bring to your people the annihilation they so narrowly escaped before. Dsôn Balsur may have fallen but you will never be safe from the älfar."

In the princess's unwavering turquoise gaze, however, there was no trace of doubt: the blind faith of elves. "The eoîl will protect us. They will return. The symbols in the holy shrines promise . . ."

"Return? If they do I shall be here to destroy them. But you won't be around to see it happen, princess." The unslayable had caught the sounds of approaching foot-steps and gruff voices coming from the passage. A second wave of undergroundlings burst in. His wounds smarted badly and his limbs felt weak now. *Retreat. They are too many.* Pocketing the diamond and sheathing one of his swords, he took the handle of the second in both hands. "And there will be no more elves for the eoîl to find. Not in Girdlegard."

The blow he dealt Rejalin cut right through her torso, the blade slicing slantwise from shoulder to hip and crunching into the orc skeletons beneath her. He regretted that her end was swift. He would have preferred to torture her until the end of time, using her blood as a constantly renewable source of paint.

Beloved sister. He knelt by Nagsar Inàste's head and put out his hand gingerly to touch it . . . then stopped. He could not look at her features for a final time. The heartache would kill him.

Instead he stroked her long black hair and cut off a hank as a reminder. Then, clutching the lock in his blood-smeared hands, he bounded off into the tunnels as fast as his injuries would permit.

Girdlegard,
Kingdom of Idoslane,
The Caves of Toboribor,
Late Summer, 6241st Solar Cycle

Death was standing right in front of him, in the terrible image of the älfar that had escaped back on the island.

Towering proudly over the recumbent figure, death clasped a slender spear in one gloved fist while the other arm hung loose. The slim torso was partly naked and partly protected by armor.

The black depths of the eye sockets were trained on the dwarf. "You shall not die, Tungdil Goldhand," spoke death in friendly tones, bending over him. The long black hair framed a narrow face that was at one and the same time cruel and fascinating. death's right hand touched Tungdil's chest. "I still need you."

The älfar runes on armor and weapon gave off a greenish

glow and a sudden warmth suffused the dwarf's body. As the icy cold was displaced, his grateful heartbeat grew strong and his ears filled with the sound of rushing blood.

"Nagsor Inàste has escaped with the diamond you were seeking," death explained in a clear voice. "He will return to the island to reach the tunnel Furgas devised. It was nearly completed before you killed the magister. If Nagsor Inàste can finish the work he can get through to the Outer Lands. And the stone will be lost forever." Death stood up. "Nagsor Inàste will return with a huge army, greater than anything Girdlegard has ever seen. Neither you nor the orcs will be able to halt its progress."

Tungdil opened his mouth but could not speak.

Death turned away. "Stop him, Tungdil Goldhand. Stop him and his appalling offspring." Death stepped into the shadows and disappeared.

Tungdil tried to lift his head but a wave of pain enveloped him; he lost consciousness and fell back on the ground . . .

"Once upon a time death came for a dwarf and wanted to carry him off, but the dwarf stood firm on his rock, glowered and refused to go. So death passed him by."

Tungdil knew this saying from southern Sangpûr and he recognized the voice. He attempted to open his eyes but only the right one responded. The left consisted entirely of pain and refused to obey.

"Do you see? Did you see that?" a different voice rejoiced. "Didn't I tell you Vraccas would leave us at least one hero to save Girdlegard. Fantastic work, Lot-Ionan. Here's to your skill!"

Tungdil registered a bright light and blinked; he could see Rodario, Sirka and Lot-Ionan. "Where am I?" he croaked, raising his hand to touch his left eye.

The magus stopped him. "No, Tungdil, don't."

"An arrow," said Rodario, showing the item in question with blood still sticking to it. "We had to pull it out. Lot-Ionan turned up just in time to save your life. May the gods be thanked that they allowed you to live."

"But I could not save the sight of that eye," Lot-Ionan added regretfully.

Memory returned and Tungdil struggled up with the help of his friend. He had a bandage over one eye and half of his face.

"Be careful now," Sirka warned him. "You've only just come back from a meeting with your maker."

Around him in the cavern around a hundred dwarves were seeing to their wounded. "How are Ireheart and Goda?" he asked, leaning on Sirka's arm.

"We've taken them to the nearest camp," Rodario told him.

"That's not what I asked! How are they?"

"They are alive. Goda's injuries are not life-threatening but our hot-blooded friend is in a bad way. Your healers say it will be a few orbits before they know whether or not he'll make it." Rodario had lost his jocularity. "I'd never have thought the elves would do this."

As Tungdil clenched his fists in anger he noticed the dried blood on his hands and clothing. It could not all be his own? "Not the elves," he corrected. "It's the atár. Esdalân has nothing to do with all this." He caught sight of the remains of the älfar woman lying like garbage at the side of the altar, her head a good two paces off, with the long black hair obscuring her features.

Sirka followed his gaze. "That's elf handiwork; they did that presumably before they made the acquaintance of the second unslayable." She pointed to where the elf corpses lay soaking in their own blood.

Amongst the dead, all dispatched by the same murderous sword, lay the body of Rejalin. The diamond had been of no help to her.

"We've blocked off all the exits, but . . ."

Tungdil waved a hand dismissively. "Waste of time. He is on his way to Weyurn with his remaining offspring."

"The source? What does he need the magic source for if he's got the diamond?" Rodario wondered. "On the other hand, if he runs away from us he won't have the right spell to release its power."

Tungdil looked around for Keenfire: his specially forged ax was missing. The others had no idea what had happened to it. He assumed the unslayable had taken it, because death had left empty-handed. Now he had two reasons for hunting down the unslayable.

"I know why Fur . . . the thirdlings started to tunnel into the Outer Lands," he told them, swallowing the name of the magister because he still did not believe Bandilor's version. It could not be Furgás behind the whole ghastly plan. "They want to make a way through so that Tion's hordes can overrun Girdlegard. The tunnel must be nearly finished."

The others stared at him. This was the first they had heard of it. They looked hurt and surprised that he had kept it to himself.

"Bandilor told me during the fight," he explained. "I didn't think the tunnel was as important as the diamond."

"And how do you know the unslayable is heading there?" Rodario stroked his beard thoughtfully. "I don't want to pour cold water on the notion. I'm just surprised. Did he tell you before he left?"

"Yes," he lied. "The unslayable told me because he thought I was done for. He wanted me to die in despair." He looked at them determinedly. "He's on his way there. We've got to catch up with him before the elves find out and arrive in hot pursuit." Crusted elf blood flaked off his fingers as he moved them. He would have loved to get into a tub of warm water to rid himself of such filth.

"The elves have got other worries." Lot-Ionan signaled for a pony-drawn wagon. It would save them a long foot-slog underground, meaning they should reach the surface is about half an orbit. "We heard that the two elf missions Rejalin sent to Toboribor were ambushed and killed."

"Was it the ubariu?"

"No. Your lot," Rodario said without reproach. "One Ginsgar Unforce of the firstlings felt it incumbent on him to avenge the high king's death. He's marching on Âlandur. And apparently volunteers from the dwarf realms are swarming to his banner like flies. The atár will reap the storm they've sown."

They took their seats on the cart and the long journey up to the cave entrance began.

"I'm not joking, Tungdil. If you don't watch out and old Ginsgar is successful you'll have a new high king without a by your leave from your noble Xamtys and the other dwarf high and mighties. It won't come to a vote at all." Rodario waited for a reply.

Lot-Ionan nodded. "Just what I was thinking. And we don't want the dwarves led by a high king who's set on war. Who knows, perhaps he'll attack the freelings you were telling me about. Or the thirdlings?"

This was all too much for Tungdil. His eye—or what was left of it—was giving him acute pain, his best friend was fighting for his life, the diamond was lost and he had forfeited the magic ax. And now there's war with Âlandur—

"Be quiet, all of you," Sirka demanded. She had read his expression. "He needs rest. Let him sleep." She offered her lap as a pillow.

Exhausted, he laid his head on her knee, wishing fervently that when he woke up everything could be like before.

But Vraccas was not going to do him that favor. The wheel of time could not be halted and reversed.

When he woke up they were in the open and it was late afternoon. Autumn was near but the sun was giving up the last of its warmth as if there were no tomorrow.

Tungdil felt rested enough to visit Ireheart's sickbed and found Goda there, red-eyed and anxious, at her mentor's side, fingernails dug into her palms.

Tungdil needed no more evidence of Boïndil's parlous state of health or the strength of the thirdling's attachment.

The sight of his seriously injured comrade brought back the memory of the death of Boëndal, the twin brother. "May great Vraccas be magnanimous toward your hero here," he intoned, putting his hand on Goda's shoulder. "Goda, excuse all my harsh words and forgive me for not trusting you. I have no doubts now about your sincerity."

She raised her head and burst into tears. "I'm so afraid he'll die," she wept. "Isn't it crazy? I came to kill him to avenge Sanda's honor." She gave a sob and the feelings she had been concealing got the better of her. "Now he is near the death I so often wished on him. And it's my worst nightmare." Shyly she took hold of Ireheart's hand and bowed her head again.

Tungdil quickly wiped away his own tears. "Vraccas will not take him yet." He gave her shoulder a squeeze. "I saw death itself back there in the caves. He spoke to me and never mentioned summoning Ireheart."

She gave a faint smile. "Thank you. So you're not really surprised?"

"No. Balyndis told me what you two had talked about. I never thought you capable of treacherously killing either one of us." He turned around to go. "I was worried about maintaining secrecy. I was wrong, I can see that now." He pointed to the injured dwarf. "When he wakes up, Sirka, Rodario, Lot-Ionan and I will all have left. You stay here with him. Mind he stays in bed and tell him I shall be needing him when I go campaigning in the Outer Lands." He saw the shock in her face, and smiled reassuringly. "Only as an escort and for company on the way. I don't want to deprive you of him forever. One last journey, that's all. He more than anyone deserves to be with a loving companion." He went out quickly.

Goda laid her forehead on Ireheart's hand, closed her eyes and prayed to Vraccas. She had only ever once before asked her god so fervently for anything: the death of Sanda Flameheart's killer.

"Tell me, Vraccas, what you want of me in exchange for the life of your hero Boïndil?" she whispered unhappily. "I don't want him to die. Do you hear me, Creator of all Dwarves? Preserve his life and take mine instead."

"Vraccas had better not," grunted Ireheart softly. He pressed her hand. "You make sure you stay alive."

Goda's eyes shot open and she suppressed a gasp of delight. "Master!" she whispered ecstatically. The next moment she was wondering how long he had been conscious. She blushed and pulled her hand away, but he would not let go.

"So you came to kill me?" he asked; weakness forced him to speak slowly and carefully. Goda sobbed. "No, don't cry . . . I understand why. And believe me, there were times when I toyed with the thought of doing away with myself." He swallowed hard. "Vraccas knows how many nights I've lain awake regretting Sanda's death. I killed a magnificent dwarf. Like I had done once before." Ireheart forced himself to describe the painful events. There should be no more secrets from her. "Her name was Smeralda; she was a little younger than you. We were very fond of each other but our love ended harshly. I killed her in the heat of battle at the High Gate. I did not know what I was doing." Tears flowed. "I mistook her for one of the enemy . . ." He collected himself and paused. When his voice was steady again he sighed, "I thought I would never find love again after that. Until you came. I know we cannot be together, Goda. Killing your kinswoman is too great a barrier."

Goda stood up and sat on his bed. "I can see the torture

in your eyes, master. The pain is not from your wounds but in your soul. There can be no one in the whole of Girdlegard with more genuine regret than this." She had not let go of his hand. "I did not want to love you even when you stole into my thoughts. Yet, despite all my complaints about the training, I became fonder and fonder of you. I did not want to admit it. I forbade myself to love the dwarf that had killed Sanda. So I hid behind sarcasm and rejection. Until I thought I had lost you." Her shoulders shook. "When I saw you fall with all those arrows in you I should have rejoiced." She looked him in the eyes. "But the opposite happened. I wished I was the one lying there so badly injured."

Ireheart felt his throat constrict.

"Even if my great-grandmother's soul spins in fury, I can't help myself," she said softly. "With all my heart I long to be more to you than just a pupil, Boïndil Doubleblade of the secondling clan of Ax Swingers." Her gaze was as steady and honest as her words. "If I have not pushed you too far away with my unkindness, I want to ask you to let me remain close at your side. I don't care if we are fighting together in battle or sharing a home."

"The same goes for me," he croaked. "It would make me so very happy." A wave of joy shot through his body, washing all the pain away as he looked up at Goda's sweet face. The pale down on her cheeks reflected the candle-light's shimmer, and the warmest affection shone in her brown eyes. He hardly dared to believe what was happening. Perhaps it was just a feverish dream. If that was the case, he did not wish to be cured of the fever.

Goda lifted his hand to her lips and kissed it gently. "Yes, Boïndil. But promise me one thing: Let us fight the duel I demanded of you."

"What do you mean—?"

"Please," she interrupted him. "I made a vow to Sanda. I cannot break my promise to her. I've already broken my word by telling you of my feelings." Ireheart nodded and she breathed a sigh of relief. "I'll let you sleep now." And she made as if to leave his side.

Ireheart held her hand tightly. "Stay here," he begged, stroking her cheek.

She sat down again, and held his hand until he fell asleep.

She smiled, while a tear of despair escaped from her eye. She had betrayed her great-grandmother and yet felt enormously blessed. She had never felt such happiness.

Sirka was waiting for Tungdil outside the tent. "Do you feel up to another meeting?"

He nodded and she led him to Mallen's tent, where the blond Idoslane prince was standing in front of a map of Girdlegard. Around the table sat the kings and queens of the human realms; neither dwarves nor elves were present.

Mallen came over and bowed to Tungdil. "I want to show my gratitude and respect," he said. All the other men and women rose to their feet and followed suit. For Isika, Ortger and Wey it was also by way of an apology for things they had said in the past. Their consciences were not clear.

Tungdil heard the news about the dwarves' advance

under Ginsgar Unforce. It was of no concern to him. "There's no time to think about Âlandur. The important thing is the diamond. We cannot leave it in älfar hands." He told them what the unslayable had purportedly said. "I am sure he was not lying. He has made a pact with the thirdlings and presumably he knows very well what is waiting on the far side of the tunnel. When I was fighting the thirdlings Bandilor told me they had been negotiating with the monsters on the other side. In the worst possible scenario there may be an army already waiting for the tunnel into Girdlegard to open." Tungdil pointed to Âlandur on the map. "I don't approve of what Ginsgar Unforce has done. But I can understand why he has done it. He is acting like any dwarf would who sees no difference between elves and atàr."

Mallen looked at him. "I will have Ginsgar told of your disapproval, Tungdil Goldhand. I hope Xamtys will move soon and recall the rebellious warriors. There's nothing that I can do."

Bruron's expression was similarly rueful. "I am in the same situation. My best soldiers are in Toboribor. I won't be able to stop Ginsgar."

"It's regrettable that some of the elves Ginsgar will kill aren't actually involved in this atár madness. But it can't be helped." Tungdil bit his lip. "Don't get me wrong but you all know what is at stake."

Flagur entered the pavilion in full armor. "I have heard what is happening." He did not look happy at all and his light pink eyes reflected his dissatisfaction. "From now on allow us to support you. We shall escort you to the west. Our mounts are better than any of Girdlegard's horses, so we can get to the island ahead of the älfar. Unless he can fly."

"No, he can't do that," Lot-Ionan confirmed.

"Not yet, anyway," added Rodario. "As long as he hasn't accessed the diamond's power or got to the magic source."

"Let me have just one night's rest," Tungdil requested. "We'll set off in the morning."

"How many men should we take?" asked Flagur.

"How many will you need to destroy a creature that did for thirty elves and upward of a hundred orcs all by itself?" Tungdil would have loved to know exactly what had happened in the caves. And what the diamond had been doing in the hands of that sleeping beauty.

Flagur looked up. "We've seen a few of them where I'm from, but none anywhere near as dangerous as this one. Best if we take our rune master along and a dozen of our foremost warriors," he decided.

"A dozen?" Rodario was surprised. "You don't think you might be underestimating the opposition? There are still three monsters on the list. He's bound to have them with him."

Flagur only smiled, but his smile said more than any flowery assertions.

Isika pursued Tungdil's train of thought. "Just now you said the stone was lying on the älfar woman's chest and that she herself looked as if she were dead." She turned respectfully to the magus. "Do you know what this might signify, Lot-Ionan?"

"I can only hazard a guess." He thought hard. "The unslayable siblings escaped from Porista to the caves of

Toboribor by magic shortly before the Star of Judgment struck. Either their spell didn't work as planned or else it exacted a physical tribute that she was not equal to. I have read about magi being totally incapacitated if a spell goes wrong. It's extremely hard to revive them. Maybe by means of this diamond."

"It would explain her coma. But could she bear children in that state?" Isika looked round the circle. "I mean, these beasts must come from somewhere, even if they only fully turn into monsters after bathing in the magic source."

"And what if the male älfar had been struck down in the same way but had managed to free himself?" Rodario suggested. His eyes glinted with enthusiasm. "Maybe the two of them were found in the caves and the surviving orcs down there seized on the beautiful älfar and mated with her, overcome with animal lust. They violate her again and again, besotted by her beauty. Then the älfar wakes up, kills the orcs, makes common cause with the thirdlings and sends the misshapen bastards out into Girdlegard to serve his evil ends." He stopped for air, his eyes fixed on the far distance, actor that he was. An actor planning his next stage appearance. "And then, in order to create a pure being of his own flesh and blood, he takes the älfar beauty himself and impregnates her, creating the young one we saw on the island. A child born of siblings, purer than any other älfar and part of the highest dynasty. What a plot line."

Mallen smiled. "Your imagination is getting the better of you, my theatrical friend."

"Call it a variation on a possible truth, because we'll never find out what really happened. I don't suppose the unslayable is going to sit down and explain it all to us," Rodario admitted. "I think it's a tremendous story though."

"Well, it fits in with what the älfar are like," said Tungdil, tired now. "I must get some rest, if you don't mind. Pray for us all tonight."

The pavilion door-hanging flew aside and a dwarf came in and bowed to the company. His face was burned by the sun, his armor coated with dust and he smelled of sweat, horse and muck. "For the sake of Girdlegard, help the fourthlings!" he gasped, handing Prince Mallen a leather pouch. "I am Feldolin Whetstone of the Thyst Finders fourthling clan. I bring a message from the Brown Range. We are being besieged by incredible creatures."

"The size of two dwarves, wearing armor, and their eyes shining purple?" asked Sirka, to everyone's astonishment. "Voices like the whistle of the wind and the rumble of thunder at one and the same time?"

"By all the gods, you're describing Djerůn!" Rodario exclaimed. "Andôkai's bodyguard: a mountain of steel with many times the strength of a human."

Mallen took out a written account of the events at the pass and a sketch of the creatures laying siege to Silverfast. "More friends that look like enemies?" he remarked.

"It's the acronta," replied Flagur. "We got them to create a diversion so our own army could circumvent the dwarves without being seen. We didn't want a battle, because it would have meant killing dwarves. But they are Ubar's children, just as we are." The ubari grinned at the messenger, who had only just noticed him and was utterly terrified. "They won't harm you."

"The acronta," repeated Tungdil. "How many of them are there?"

"We don't know. But the army that protects us against some of the larger fiends has about three thousand sword-bearers."

"Ye gods," muttered Rodario. "Three thousand of them? What kind of creatures do you have in the Outer Lands if you need so many acronta to deal with them?"

"I never claimed life was easy in Letèfora." Flagur flexed his muscles in a display of strength that would have made any orc go pale with envy. "But that's nothing compared with what will issue from the Black Abyss. To vanquish them we would need thousands of acronta."

Tungdil nodded to the messenger. "You have heard the important part. Bring this good news to the fourthlings and to your . . ." He had been about to say *king* but remembered that the king of the fourthlings had been Gandogar. His corpse was on its way to the Brown Range to find its last resting place with the other fourthling rulers of the past. His soul was already with Vraccas at the eternal smithy and would be watching events from there.

"The throne is not empty," said Feldolin. "Gandogar's sister, Bylanta Slimfinger of the Silver Beards, administered all the duties of state while he traveled in his capacity as high king. As soon as peace is restored Gandogar's death can be duly mourned and Bylanta's regency celebrated."

"Bring her my homage and the blessings of Vraccas," said Tungdil. He raised his hand in salutation. "Now I must really go."

He and Sirka left the tent and crossed the human army base to get to the dwarf encampment. There, pale patches on the grass showed where some had already struck camp and left. Presumably they had gone to join Ginsgar Unforce.

"You will accompany me to the Black Abyss?" asked Sirka as they entered their tent.

"Yes, it's my duty to ensure the diamond arrives safely where it can do most good. And that is not here." He lay down carefully on the simple bed. His head hurt and the empty eye socket was throbbing so badly he could not think. He took her hand. "Sirka, I am the most unreliable dwarf in Girdlegard. I feel great affection for you, but . . ." He fell silent and stroked her bald head; her brown skin shimmered in the lamplight.

"I am not asking for more than that, Tungdil," she said.

"I cannot swear I will be faithful till the end of my days." He sighed. "I swore to Balyndis that I would always be true because I never thought my feelings would change, but it turned out to be a lie." He struck himself on the chest. "This accursed restlessness within me! I can't settle. I have the urge to keep searching for new horizons; I might do the same to you. I will never promise marriage to a woman again."

"Your restlessness is what has helped your homeland to survive. Without beings such as you nothing would move forward. Everyone would be frightened to attempt anything new; none would break new ground and abandon the familiar. It is good the way it is." She looked at him. "Is it true you dwarves live forever?"

"What? Oh no, we just live to a very great age, Sirka. I am seventy cycles now and that makes me a young dwarf still. The oldest of us can live more than six hundred cycles, they say." He saw the shock in her face. "What's the matter?"

"That's a big difference," she said quietly. "Our people never get past the age of sixty scycles. Most pass away at fifty."

"Fifty?" This was a surprise. "How old are you, Sirka?"

"I am twenty-one. My descendants are seven, five and three . . ."

"Your descendants." He spoke solemnly. "And where are they now?"

"I told you we love and part when it is over. We never force anyone to stay together if feelings have cooled and died. We are a passionate people." She gave him a kiss. "My children live in Letèfora. They are brought up by the community and I visit them regularly."

"Do they know you?"

"They call me their mother but it does not mean very much. They are children to all; everyone looks after everyone's children as if they were their own." She stroked his chest. "Rest. You have shown such fortitude today."

She stirred a powder into a small dish of water and handed it to him. "Drink this. It will ease your pain."

He did as he was bid and soon the throbbing in the eye socket grew fainter and allowed him to sleep. For the first time for ages he was not plagued by nightmares. He saw the Outer Lands in his mind's eye, full of beauty and new creatures. Sirka was his guide in this new land, one that fascinated and enticed him. Even if there was much he would not understand until he had seen it with his own eye.

*　　*　　*

The herd of befúns, the mounts that the ubariu had spoken of, were huge. They were like oversized orcs on four legs instead of two, with stumpy little tails. The body was muscular and as broad as that of a horse while the flat head had a snout with numerous protruding teeth. On their hands were three fingers apiece, covered in a hard layer of tough skin, with which they were able to pick up large objects.

To Tungdil the shape of the saddle seemed odd; it had a back support for the rider to rest against, relatively tall and curved like a small baldachin. He asked Sirka about the construction as someone pressed the reins into his hands. Stirrups were nowhere to be seen.

"The animals rear up in battle and help the rider by using their claws. The saddles are designed to stop us being thrown off." She shook the back rest. "We've had them lengthened. You slide into the correct position."

Rodario was getting to know his befún. "Stinks a bit, doesn't it?" He sniffed at its light gray skin. "Stinks quite a lot, in fact."

"It's from their glands. They secrete a substance to toughen the skin. They're safe against arrows and even a sword cut isn't a problem." Sirka showed him a damp shiny patch on the head. "A liquid also comes out there from time to time. Whatever you do, don't touch it."

"Is it acid?"

"No, it's a sex gland, so if you don't want to be jumped on by another befún for a bit of how's your father I suggest you leave it well alone."

"Aha!" Rodario slid right back in the saddle. "I enjoy making love but preferably not with this enchanting species. I probably wouldn't survive its attentions."

"Indeed. You wouldn't." Sirka vaulted up into the saddle and signaled to the troops behind her. She called out in a language her companions couldn't understand; it sounded elegant and was reminiscent of elvish.

Flagur rode at her side, if you could call it riding; the befúns' gait was nothing like that of a horse—more a series of rhythmical jumps, quite hard on the back and stomach if you were in the saddle. But they were swift and agile. Once equipped with an armored ubariu on its back, a befún would not be something Tungdil would want to face in battle. "Let's move on!" Flagur announced. "If the distance they told us is correct we'll be there in five orbits.

"That's very fast," said Tungdil. "That would be more than two hundred miles a day!"

Flagur grinned. "I keep forgetting things are different in Girdlegard. The befúns will run from sunup to sundown and they don't need any more rest than that, or to stop and feed. They're ideal for conditions back home." He clicked his tongue and made a strange noise that the befún responded to. They set off at a trot.

"It's amazing! I can hardly wait to escort the diamond back to your homeland," Tungdil said to Sirka.

"And I can't wait to show you around." She touched his hand gently and followed Flagur.

The little troop set off for Weyurn—a journey that would take them through the dry northlands of Sangpûr and forest margins of Rân Rîbastur: about a thousand miles all told. On the first orbit they crossed Idoslane. A more direct route would have led them through the burning desert heart of Sangpûr, but that was not a risk Tungdil wanted to take. Sandstorms and drought can be as deadly as any älfar.

Of them all it was Lot-Ionan who was finding it most difficult to adapt to the mounts. "I was a good rider once," he said, "and could always keep my seat. But these befúns are quite a challenge!" Like the others he was constantly being jolted forwards and backwards and from side to side. To be on the safe side he had tucked the end of his beard under one of the straps securing the luggage, so that it wouldn't blow in his face.

Tungdil was certainly feeling all the bones in his body. Often he would bite his tongue or his own cheek. No, if you weren't used to it, these animals made for uncomfortable riding. Sirka and Flagur and the rest of the troop were managing to look good in the saddle, thus earning respect in the eyes of the humans they passed on the road.

The strange picture they made not only aroused interest, but also instilled fear into some, who sought to defend themselves. They knew all too much about orcs from the old stories and these looked much more dangerous than the old versions. Only the royal banners of Mallen and Bruron kept the group immune from attack.

Flagur did not arrange any rest periods until after sunset, when almost immediately the befúns spontaneously came to a halt and lay down like dogs to rest; the saddles stayed on their backs.

Rodario jumped off rather than dismounting. "Why, by all the gods, do they do that?"

"They can't see very well in the dark and even at dusk their sight is bad. To stop themselves crashing into a tree or bumping into a rock they just lie down and wait for the sun to come up." Sirka took a net out of her saddlebag and went off to the stream. "Will one of you come with me to help catch their feed?"

"Fish?" Tungdil went with her. "These funny creatures eat fish? They look more like predator carnivores to me."

"You're right. They eat *everything*," she said, giving the word such emphasis that he preferred not to put further questions. "So it's vital they don't get hungry. If they set off to hunt on their own account the whole area could be devastated."

"I see." He waded into the water. "Throw me one end. We'll make a barrier," he suggested. "We can let the fish and the current do all the work rather than wear ourselves out continually tossing the net in." She agreed and together they set about collecting sticks and branches to secure the net as a kind of funnel.

Tungdil's empty eye socket was hurting badly, so Sirka gave him some more powder which he took with a handful of water from the stream.

The strangest insects were chirping away; soon the birds joined in with a twilight song. Tungdil realized it was one of very few evenings they had been spared any nasty surprises. "No älfar, no orcs," he sighed with relief, sinking down on the grassy bank.

"Like in Letèfora," said Sirka, propping herself up on one elbow so she could keep an eye on the net. "May Ubar help keep it that way. Too many sacrifices have been made; it would be awful if we don't succeed." She looked at him. "Balyndis. Is that her name?"

He nodded. "Yes, but I don't want to talk about her."

Sirka watched his solemn face. "I am so happy we've

found each other. It doesn't matter how long it lasts." She kissed him on the mouth.

He stroked the nape of her neck, pulling her close.

Laying her head on his shoulder she listened to the sound of his heart. "Sounds normal to me," she said after a while.

"What did you think it would sound like?"

"A heart that's going to beat for many hundred cycles should sound different. But it doesn't. It's not even any slower."

He sat up and pushed her gently to the ground, then placed his ear on her breast. The scent that rose in his nostrils was arousing, and he felt the warmth of her brown skin on his cheek.

"And what can *you* hear?"

"Same as with all dwarves," he said and kissed her throat. A sudden stabbing pain shot through his eye socket and he fell back. Any trace of desire abruptly disappeared. "Damn those atár," he cursed, clutching at the side of his face, but it only made it worse. "I feel like wishing Ginsgar success with his campaign."

"It's the best thing for broka," nodded Sirka earnestly. "Nobody is going to shed a tear for them. And there's more harmony among the peoples of Letèfora than ever now. No one there thinks they're above the rest. Just friends or enemies. But no more false friends." She stood up and went to check on their catch. "Come on, Tungdil. Let's take the befúns their feed before they start on Rodario."

They dragged the first load of fish over to their campsite in sacks, leaving the net in place in the stream to catch more. Later, when the befúns were fully fed, the two of them slipped under a blanket by the fire and fell asleep in each other's arms.

"Ah, love's young dream," said Rodario with a yawn. "I wonder what my own darling is up to?"

Flagur looked at him. "You've got a girl?"

"Yes."

"And how many children do you have with her?"

"With *her*? None, as far as I know." He gave a dirty grin. "But there may be a few boys and girls in Girdlegard that will do well on the stage." He waggled his eyebrows. "I am a friend to all women and women all love me. I am incredibly irresistible."

"And what does your girl have to say about that?"

"Have fun, she says; she's just the same as me," he laughed.

"Well, we seem to have more in common with humans than with dwarves," chuckled the ubariu.

"Don't jump to the wrong conclusion, my dear Flagur. Most people in Girdlegard are very keen on convention and like to live as married couples." Rodario smiled. "I make sure that the young wives don't find life too tedious, and I help prepare the daughters for love." He took a fish and grilled it over the fire on the end of a stick. "It's a shame there won't be much of an opportunity to learn more about your homeland. It would be illuminating to hear a couple of stories." He blinked. "But I'm far too sleepy to take notes."

"Why don't you come along with the diamond's escort? Then you can see my country," suggested Flagur.

"Do your people like theater? My repertoire of tales of heroes and their great deeds is enormous. I have the best range of props ..." His voice tailed away. "No, I *used to have* the best props possible. Magister Furgas made them all for me." He stared into the fire. "My friend is dead. I can't believe it. Can you? I spend five cycles searching for him; I free him from the clutches of his captors and then he melts away to nothing in a sea of red-hot iron. Killed by the treachery of thirdlings."

Flagur had been listening intently. "But not forgotten."

"No, I haven't forgotten him and I never will." He pulled the cooked fish off the bones and ate thoughtfully. Occasionally he looked over at Lot-Ionan, who was sitting on the grass some distance away from the fire talking to the ubariu rune master. "I wonder what they're discussing?"

"I expect they're talking about the different ways they each use magic." Flagur retrieved his fish from the fire, strewed some powder on it from a little bag, and started to eat his supper with evident relish.

"Can I try some?" asked Rodario, indicating the yellow spice.

"Of course."

The actor drizzled a little cautiously onto his fish, sniffed, and tasted it carefully. His expression moved from skeptical to delighted. "I think I should market this stuff," he enthused. "This mixture is ... unique! I've never tasted anything like it."

"I'm glad you like it. We used to wage war for it in the old days."

"Entirely reasonable," said Rodario. "And what agreement was reached?"

"We eradicated the other side." Flagur handed him the

little bag. "It's made from a particular stone, milled and ground, rinsed three times in salt water and then rubbed to a fine powder."

"You killed off a whole people for the spice?" He could not believe it.

"They were only phottòr. They have no brains. Not worth worrying about," the ubari reassured him. "But they were sitting on the biggest natural source of the spice, so we killed two birds with one stone: We had the meat and the spice."

Rodario lowered his fish. "You don't mean to say you ate the orcs?"

"Of course. They taste delicious, but the ones you had in Girdlegard were even better. I tried one who got lost and came over to our realm. It was the best ever taste." He closed his eyes. "Mmm; it's coming back to me now."

Suddenly the conversation was taking a frightening turn. There were not many occasions when orcs had managed to get out of Girdlegard through to the Outer Lands. "When was that? Where did you come across him?" Rodario enquired.

"It was ages ago. On the other side of the mountain you call the Gray Range. He was trying to persuade us to take arms against the ubariu . . . I mean, you dwarves." He laughed. "He was a stubborn fellow. He kept going on about immortality—something he'd drunk out of a little bottle."

Rodario put two and two together. It must have been one of the creatures subject to Ushnotz, the orc lord; part of a unit that had got cut off from the others and got through to the empty realm of the fifthlings at the stone gateway. In the early days it had not been guarded.

By Palandiell! The black water, he thought. Worried now, he watched Flagur and measured him up. Ushnotz's warriors had partaken of the black water and were immortal. What would happen if you ate the orc flesh? If the flesh was evil, would it pull you that way too? Was Flagur only pretending to be a friend? Perhaps he really wanted the diamond for his own rune master. Was he perhaps planning to take over Girdlegard with his hundred-thousand-strong army as soon as he had the stone?

The ubari watched him. "What's is the matter, Rodario? Why've you gone quiet?"

"I'm . . . tired." He avoided the question. "I'm sorry if I'm not good company. It always happens when . . . I eat fish." Quickly he wolfed down his meal and said goodnight. As if purely by chance he lay down next to Tungdil and tried to wake him gently.

"What is it, Fabuloso?" the dwarf asked, drunk with sleep.

"You'll never believe this but—"

"Then don't tell me," he interrupted, turning over. "I'm in pain."

"Our friend and ally has a secret. He's eaten an orc that had drunk from the black water," he whispered emphatically.

Now Tungdil was fully awake. "What are you talking about? Why would he do that?"

"Because they taste good. Apparently." Rodario shuddered.

Tungdil digested the news and considered the possibilities. "Even if it were true, Ushnotz and his orc folk are long dead."

"But *before that* Flagur ate one of them. He was from the Gray Range, he said." The actor was insistent and agitated.

Tungdil could just about work out what might have happened. Back then he and Ireheart had attacked a few orc scouts at the Stone Gateway and pursued three of them into the Outer Lands. One of these had escaped and must have run straight into Flagur's arms. "They eat orcs?"

It was not too far-fetched. He remembered that Djerûn met his nutritional needs from all sorts of Tion's creatures. The acronta and ubariu had a few characteristics in common.

He cast a look at Sirka's sleeping countenance and wondered whether the undergroundlings enjoyed certain dishes that might be based on less than conventional meat sources. If they worshipped the same god . . .

He found the idea revolting. Admittedly his own folk enjoyed eating insect larvae—something the humans found hard to understand. But there was still a difference between eating maggots and eating orcs. And the difference was not merely to do with the taste.

Rodario sighed. "What shall we do, Tungdil? Can we afford to trust Flagur or does he carry the seed of evil in him? Perhaps without being aware of it?"

The dwarf lifted his head a little to look at the ubari. He was sitting with his back to them in front of the flames of the campfire, his silhouette broad and impressive. "To be honest with you, I don't know," he answered the actor. "Keep an eye on him and tell me immediately if you get

the idea he's not behaving like an ally." He cradled his
head back on his arm. "But I shall trust him until we have
evidence to the contrary." He smiled. "Leave a few things
in the hands of the gods, Fabuloso. Give them something
to do and don't leave it all to the mortals."

"If you say so, Hero of Girdlegard," sighed Rodario,
closing his eyes."Let us hope the gods see everything."
Then he had a thought. "No, they don't have to see
absolutely everything. Otherwise my soul is never going
to get to the garden of the Creator Goddess."

"Why? Did she forbid humans to behave the way you
do?" asked Tungdil, his one eye firmly shut.

Rodario laughed softly. "It depends how you interpret
it. But she doesn't agree with making love to women who
really belong in the arms of another."

And there it was yet again: the thought of Balyndis.

Now he was free of her Tungdil found himself thinking
of her more often than when they had been a couple.
Guilty feelings nagged. He knew she would feel she had
been deceived. He knew how cowardly his conduct had
been. One letter. No more than that.

There he was, brave enough to vanquish Girdlegard's
most fiendish foes but unable to find the courage to face
his partner and admit that he no longer wanted to be with
her. No longer *could* be with her.

He opened his remaining eye and turned to Sirka,
contemplating her features, black in the starlight. He
listened to her even breathing, took in the smell of her
and felt her warmth.

At least Sirka would not suffer when one day he left
her. The undergroundling people seemed to be as rest-

less as his own wandering spirit when it came to emotional attachments. Perhaps she would be the one to leave first.

That thought made his heart lighter.

XVI

The befúns had proved their hardiness and stamina. In just a few orbits Tuagdil and his company had covered the distance to Weyurn—one that would have taken a rider on a horse three times as long.

They had increased their speed after meeting people on the road who spoke of having seen strange creatures ahead of them—or rather, stranger creatures than the ones in their own troop.

But nature was not on their side. Shortly before they reached the port of Shale night fell, bringing a shroud of thick fog. The befúns resolutely settled for their rest as usual, forcing Tungdil and his companions to cover the last four miles at a run. Flagur carried Lot-Ionan, who could not manage the pace.

By the time they reached the town gates of Shale, Tungdil and Rodario were bathed in perspiration and gasping for breath. They were admitted on the authority of Queen Wey, but the guards kept their weapons raised, not trusting the dangerous-looking orcs. How were they to know that the ubariu did not share the orcish appetite for human flesh?

The captain gave them an escort and ensured they were provided with everything they needed for their mission.

"This way to the port," called Tungdil, hurrying through one of the narrow alleyways that led down to the quay-side. A wide range of boats and ships lay at anchor, emerging like ghosts from the mist.

"Take this one," said the seafarer Sirka, indicating a small anonymous-looking sailing boat. "It's quite light, with a keel built for speed and a tall mast. We can hoist a lot of canvas and get to the island very quickly."

"Right. Off we go." Tungdil sent one of the guards on board the *Waveskimmer* to rouse the crew. The man ran up the gangway and jumped on deck, then disappeared from view.

They heard him call out and soon a second voice, rough and bad-tempered, answered. A short sharp argument ended with the guard unceremoniously flying over the railings into the harbor. Two fellow sentries helped haul him out.

"Let me guess. The captain said no?" An amused Rodario interpreted the situation.

"And said we could lick his arse," nodded the watchman, cursing and reaching for his sword. "I'll show the idiot."

Flagur made a face. "Let me speak to the captain," he said and stomped off up the gangway; the ramp creaked under his heavy steps.

"Someone's going to wish they had cooperated the first time," grinned Rodario.

There was no discussion. This time the captain was the one sent flying. He missed the corner of the pier, landed on the hard cobbles and lay there, befuddled.

"It's your own fault, Kordin," the guard told him, drenching the mariner with a bucket of water.

The cold water woke him out of his daze. With a bloody nose and a few abrasions Kordin stood up and looked out to his ship, where Flagur stood on deck, his stout arms on the rail. "What sort of a creature is that to let loose on an honest sailor? Why didn't you kill it? That would have been the decent thing to do."

"A friend," said Tungdil baldly. "Get the crew up. You have a vital mission for your queen."

"If she pays, no problem. Otherwise be off with you." Kordin was not in the least bit impressed, but that was about to change very quickly.

With a loud metallic clanking sound a spherical object comprised of two iron bands came rolling at high speed toward them and swept right through their midst.

The rune master and three of the watch, unable to step out of the way, were run down by the vehicle, crushed between iron and pier.

"That's the monster that robbed King Nate!" cried Rodario from behind the pillar where he had taken shelter. "At least we know we've caught up with them."

The ubariu drew their swords but quickly realized they were useless against such an attack.

The sphere had stopped rolling; then it changed course, heading for them again.

On the narrow pier there was little room to get out of the way; this time the victims were the captain, one of the ubariu and two guards. The harbor air was rent by their screams.

"Flagur!" Tungdil shouted up to the ubariu leader. "Use the hook on the freight crane, quickly!"

Flagur understood. He swiveled the crane so that it was

suspended over the pier, then released the winding mechanism just as the sphere launched its third attack. The rope unrolled with a whirr.

The hook clanged against the metal and the curved end caught in a gap between the iron bands. Creaking, the thick rope brought the huge ball to a standstill.

"Hoist it up!" Tungdil ordered and started for the ramp to help Flagur reel it in. Suddenly there was a loud click.

Some hidden fastenings in the sphere opened and the metal bands, broad as two fingers, slid closer to each other. The hook shot out, losing its grip. Now, instead of disappearing into the rucksack on the creature's body as they'd done back in Goldensheaf, they transformed themselves into a shield, protecting the monster.

It was the fourth of the bastards, a crossbred mixture of älfar and orc.

Its dark skin shimmered in the starlight, showing black wavy lines; the graceful but repellent features were mostly concealed behind locks of black hair. Opening its muzzle to show sharp teeth it growled aggressively. "I will kill you all," it vowed, drawing what appeared to be a multi-segmented sword. Abruptly it went into the attack, turning on the ubari standing nearest.

As the weapon swept in a wide curve the sword segments slipped apart. Inside, the weapon was hollow and contained a slender chain connecting the individual parts of the blade, giving the sword twice the normal range.

It struck the ubari unexpectedly and lethally, the flexible blade colliding with his sword, lifted in defense, and the sharp tip coiling round it like a snake and cutting him deep in the face. He fell dying to the ground.

The guards held their halberds ready but lacked the courage to advance on this terrifying enemy, whose lower body seemed to consist entirely of iron. Metal plates decorated with runes were sewn into its flesh to protect the upper body.

The monster moved forward, the iron foot grating against the stone. It was clearly extremely heavy. Again it brandished its cunning weapon and struck again, this time at Tungdil.

He managed to duck under the green-glowing blade, nearly falling off the wet slippery gangway as he did so.

The strange sword swung through the air and sliced through the ramp; the dwarf plunged into the water as the broken gang-plank fell. The waves met over his head and he sank like a stone.

He was overwhelmed with fear. This was Elria's element and suddenly he was reliving the terrible moment when he had fallen into the torrent that had drowned his young son. A thousand bubbles disorientated him; he could not see which way was up. He paddled around in a panic, splashing out wildly. Then he forced himself to be calm. It was panic that had robbed him of Balodil.

He abandoned trying to swim to the surface; his armor was probably too heavy for that anyway. Instead he felt his way along the wall to get to the quayside where, if his memory served, there were steps he should be able to climb up.

The bottom was soft and he sank into it. He was short of air already, but then his foot met the first step. Elria would not get him this time.

Above his head he heard the sound of metal striking metal; a flickering green light gave a ghostly glow to the stern of the ship. He could hear curses and shouts. This was no time to take a rest.

"There! There he is!" Rodario had leaned over the harbor wall and seen him. "Praise be to Palandiell—he's not food for fishes yet." He disappeared again, obviously keen to participate in the fighting.

Tungdil reached the pier; only eight ubariu were left standing now. The guards all lay dead or gravely injured. The creature had formed two small shields from its iron bands, and was using them to protect its flanks while it wielded its snake-sword, forcing the ubariu to keep their distance.

Tungdil lifted a halberd in both hands and ran straight for the creature's back.

It sensed his approach and whirled round to attack, but Tungdil was too far away to fall victim to the segmented sword. One of the shields was raised to protect the monster's face, but Tungdil thrust his halberd at the monster's right foot. The sharp tip penetrated the armor plating, and black blood gushed out of the wound. It wasn't a deadly wound but that hadn't been Tungdil's intention. He had something else in mind. A quick turn and a swift pulling movement and the long hook at the head of the weapon lodged between the armor plates.

"Take the halberds," he called to the ubariu. "Keep stabbing at its legs, then we'll have it over and into the water. Hold it fast so it doesn't escape."

The iron bands slammed down in an attempt to break off the halberd shaft, but it was sturdy enough to withstand the blow. Tungdil responded by shaking the weapon to and fro.

The ubariu picked up the weapons of the fallen guards and came to assist the dwarf, managing to force the monster ever closer to the edge of the pier. It hit out with the snake sword in fury, slicing through one halberd shaft after another. "I shall kill you," its clear voice called.

"For Girdlegard!" came a rallying cry above their heads and Rodario swung down on the crane's rope, feet outstretched, to crash into one of the monster's shields.

The irreverent assault took it by surprise. Weight and momentum allowed the actor to sweep the monster over the pier edge and into the harbor. As it fell it aimed a final blow at Rodario, cutting the calf of one leg. Then it sank below the surface.

"Oh, ye gods," groaned the actor, swinging back again, to be helped down by the ubariu. "Oh, that hurts like stink." He sat down on the pier. "But I was incredibly incredible again, wasn't I?" he joked, in spite of his injury.

"Yes, incredible," Lot-Ionan confirmed. There was nothing more he could do for the rune master, so he was kneeling next to the actor to inspect the wound. "That will have to have stitches," he said. "It will leave a fine scar."

"It's a good thing that accursed weapon didn't get me in the face. My good looks would have gone forever."

"Well done." Tungdil was staring into the water, and the ubariu were standing to his right and left, halberds raised, ready to hurl them at the monster should it resurface.

Bubbles came up and there was a glow from the depths.

"Sirka," called Tungdil, pointing at a heavy ship's anchor hanging from a nearby vessel. "Drop it. Quick!"

She took a plank, leaned it up against the side of the ship, ran up and along the deck to the bows, and released the anchor. It shot into the water with an enormous splash, and the next bubbles that rose brought black liquid with them.

"Right," said Tungdil to the waiting ubariu, "heave up the anchor and drop it again."

They did what he asked, noticing bent strips of iron with scraps of flesh attached to them caught on the tip of the anchor as they hauled it up. When they dropped it a second time, the water quickly changed color as though there were a thunder cloud directly under the surface.

They repeated the procedure a few more times until they could be positive there was no life left in the monster. Even if the injuries had not killed it, it would certainly have drowned by now.

More guards had arrived on the scene; Lot-Ionan described to their leader what had occurred, but he struggled to grasp what had befallen his men. They looked as though a millstone had flattened them.

For the ubariu rune master, too, the encounter with the monster had meant the end. This meant Lot-Ionan was the only being who could confront the unslayable with magic.

"Bring some nets and drag the bottom," he commanded.

Tungdil shook Rodario by the hand. "Excellently done, Incredible One. Without you it would have gone badly awry."

"Only a relatively small contribution. And only a slight wound." His gaze wandered over the bodies lying on the pier. "Compared with the toll of victims."

Lot-Ionan got to his feet. "We must make haste. I think the unslayable is already on his way to the island."

"Will you be all right?" Tungdil helped Rodario up.

"I'll have to be," he replied through clenched teeth. "Who else could put on a performance like that?" Together they made their way up the gangway and boarded the ship.

Sirka took command without further ado. The sailors were surprised but obeyed without question. There were forty of the royal guard on board now and the *Waveskimmer* had been commandeered in the queen's name. Mutiny was punishable by death.

"Here," called one of the soldiers in a rowing boat, making for the place where the monster had sunk. They threw hooks overboard and came up with a torn-off arm. The ironclad fingers moved with a clicking noise; to produce this monster thin bolts and rivets had forced the flesh to join metal and limb. Shrieking with disgust, the guard threw the find back into the water. Another man pulled up a distorted metal rucksack, lumps of bloody flesh clinging to the bands of metal that had previously transfixed the body of the monster. This catch was likewise tossed back into the waters of the port.

Sirka gave the order to cast off and for all sails to be set. They left harbor, taking course for the island.

"It's dead," sighed Rodario with relief. "One less of them."

"There's still one at large. And then there's the unslayable." Tungdil sat down and was given something to eat and drink. He was completely exhausted. The journey and fighting had taken everything out of him. And his empty eye socket was burning like red-hot coals.

After Sirka had dispensed a dose of pain-killing powder, he dozed. The fog worried him before he fell asleep: it was playing tricks. It looked as though the executioner Bramdal was standing on the quay.

Girdlegard,
Queendom of Weyurn,
Twenty Miles northeast of Mifurdania,
Late Summer, 6241st Solar Cycle

The fog refused to lift. On the contrary, it seemed keen to protect the unslayable one.

It was folly to head out over the lake in such visibility with all sails set. A collision with a floating log or rock could scupper them, yet, not knowing how far ahead their enemies were, they took the risk.

"If only I knew how they managed to overtake us." Flagur was infuriated.

"You saw what strength these creatures possess," Lot-Ionan consoled him. "And no one knows what an unslayable is capable of." On his own and about to face an opponent who could use magic, he was feeling apprehensive. There was no Dergard to help him out. And no rune master either. "Will you still be able to put the stone in the artifact?"

"How do you mean, Lot-Ionan?" asked Flagur, noticing that Sirka was getting the sails furled. The helmsman had told her they were approaching the place where the island had last been sighted.

"Your rune master is dead. Wouldn't you have needed him to activate the artifact?"

"Absolutely. *Our* rune master is dead. But there is another one. The acronta have one, though it won't be easy to get him to help." The ubari looked worried at the prospect. "They like the challenge of facing the Black Abyss beasts in battle. It's like telling a small child not to fight the older boys. They don't understand that they can't win in the long run." He looked at the wizard. "You are a magus. It would probably be simple for you to implant the diamond."

"I'm not familiar with these artifacts, you know," he confessed. "But I will certainly come with you. Otherwise it may be too late for both your homeland and ours."

Peering out into the mist, the watch called out a warning; then something collided with the sailing ship's bows.

"What was that?" shouted Sirka. "Any damage?"

"The planks are sound," came the reassuring reply. "It was driftwood probably. Maybe from another vessel; part of the hull, perhaps."

Tungdil was glad Sirka had reduced their sail area. If they had been traveling any faster the impact would have holed them.

As they got nearer to the island the *Waveskimmer* hit more floating wreckage. A troubling thought occurred to Tungdil: What was it they were sailing through?

"Where are Queen Wey's warships? The ones sent to protect the island?" a worried Rodario asked. "They should have . . ." He fell silent. "Curse the älfar!" he said, catching sight of Tungdil's expression. "He's sunk them?"

"Do you have another explanation, Fabuloso?" Land loomed up through the mist. "The island's still there. We . . ."

A column of blazing flame shot out from the mountainside, penetrating the mist; then a second one flashed bright fire into the night. Although they were a good hundred paces from the shoreline a wave of heat rolled over them. Smaller tongues of fire emerged from the main flame, forming a corona round the tip of the island. The light-show caught everyone's appalled attention.

"It's going down!" Tungdil could see what was happening. The unslayable was burning off gas and flooding the chambers to sink the island so that it would be out of reach. Would Lot-Ionan be able to magic himself down there to overcome the immortal enemy and the bastard? He thought it unlikely. "We've got to get there before it disappears. Full ahead, Sirka. Don't worry about the ship now."

The mariners looked at each other fearfully, uncertain what to do.

Tungdil went up to the nearest of them. "We must take this risk or else be blamed for all the misfortunes Girdlegard will suffer," he insisted. "We can only defeat the evil by landing on the island."

The sailors started to move, acting on his orders although aware it could mean the end for their ship. Tungdil recalled how the initial capture of the island had cost two ships. It must not happen again.

The *Waveskimmer* increased speed and with each new bump they feared they might be taking in water. Prayers to Elria were offered ceaselessly; the sailors would do nothing without asking the goddess for her protection.

The island sank quickly, flames extinguished now that the gas had been burned off.

Under Rodario's direction the helmsman maneuvered

them close enough for the ubariu, Tungdil and company to jump onto the slowly submerging island. The flat shoreline was already under water.

Rodario gasped in pain when he landed. His injured leg hurt hellishly. "That way," he said, indicating a narrow rock chimney. "Climb down there. It ends in a chamber leading inside."

The last bit they had to jump. It was a good twenty paces down but there was already enough ballast water at the bottom to make it safe for them to do so.

"What have I let myself in for?" sighed Rodario. Lot-Ionan nodded in silent sympathy.

One by one they dropped into the foaming water, then climbed the stone steps to get through a hatch to the passageway. Water was pouring from their clothing and shoes, the drops leaving a dark trail. A trail that could betray them.

"I know where we are." Tungdil had used his dwarf instincts well on his first visit: he pointed to the right. "That leads to the furnace, I think. If we go through it we come to the operating room for the boilers, don't we?"

Rodario nodded. "We should find the unslayable one there. Somebody must be using the controls."

They advanced cautiously, amazed at the appearance of the cave where once the furnaces had stood.

The molten iron that had cascaded down, threatening to engulf Tungdil and his friends, had hardened below into solid blocks like gray ice floes. Above, dripping ore had formed stalactites, or solidified on the rock in sheets of metal. It was a weird and wonderful sight.

"Go on," mouthed Tungdil, approaching the damaged

hatch in the boiler room. It had been struck by a heavy object of some kind; distorted, the round door hung from its hinges.

"Do you think the älfar is still here?" asked Rodario, drawing his sword. "Three to fight would be too many."

"No, I don't think he'll have waited for us," Tungdil said to allay his friend's anxiety. He entered the area that had once housed the gigantic furnaces and boilers.

Their first foe was already there.

A huge monster three and a half paces high stood next to the nearest furnace. Its arms were poles of glass and metal bars. On its head sat a tionium helmet formed like a death's head. It was whimpering and trying frantically to get the valve wheels to work, obviously trying to prevent the island from submerging. So far it had not noticed the intruders. Rune-adorned axes were stowed on its back in a large quiver resting on top of its black armor.

"What a giant," murmured Flagur, sounding delighted.

"Anyone see the unslayable?" asked Rodario, peering around in the half light.

"Let's deal with this misbegotten fiend first. Then we'll find the other one." Flagur licked his lips in anticipation. "I wonder what it tastes like. Never tried one."

The monster froze, its huge fingers still on the controls, and it looked back over its shoulder. A large tear slipped down from under the helmet and dripped over the lipless mouth.

"Why did he do it?" it whined. "I was a good son! I was always a good son." The long pins connecting helmet and skull banged against the iron cauldron above him. "He wants to kill me."

"No, *we* want to kill you," Flagur grinned and motioned his warriors forward.

"Stop!" Tungdil called them back. He approached the monster, recognizing its fear and wanting to turn this to their advantage. "Where is he, your father?" he asked softly.

"Gone," it sobbed. "He left me here to kill you. But I know he wants me dead. I'm supposed to die at the same time." It turned round, grabbing different valves now and spinning them randomly in its panic. The pressure indicators shot up and high over their heads came the screech of escaping steam. "I don't want to drown."

From where he stood, five weapon lengths away, Tungdil could read the rune on its helmet: *eight*. "Where did he go?" he asked the creature.

"He promised we'd go through the tunnel together," it muttered to itself, like a sulky child.

The contrast between its tremendous stature and the way it spoke and acted was almost pathetic, but the sight of the black gums and white fangs in its terrifying mouth made Tungdil shudder in revulsion. "Do you know where the tunnel is? We could take you there." He swallowed. "I'm a scientist. I know how the machine works."

The weird creature let go of the controls and swiveled round. "You do?" Under the oversized helmet its eyes sparkled green. "But the originator told me to kill you as soon as you arrive." It was overwhelmed. It could not reconcile its duty and its wish to survive.

Tungdil read the simple creature's mind. It intended to accept his suggestion, then kill them all as soon as they surfaced.

"Good. I'll take you there," it said, deception obvious in its voice. It stepped to one side and pointed to the controls. "Make it go up."

"Tell me where the tunnel is and we'll make the island go there." Tungdil's hand was on the lever. "But you must tell me the truth. The machine will know if you lie. It will screech and won't obey me. It doesn't like liars. It'll just let us all drown."

The creature had not expected that. Anxiously it surveyed the wall of controls, levers, wheels and indicators. "It's in the . . . south," it said, nervously.

Tungdil made the topmost valve expel whistling steam. "You're lying!" he exclaimed, as if outraged. "Now we'll all sink and drown."

"Northwest!" it yelled. "Northwest, I swear! It's in the cliff just under the giant's nose! There's a little sandbank with trees in front to hide the entrance." The creature dropped to its knees in front of the boiler, its armored legs clanking against the stone floor. "Please, dear machine, don't be angry. Bring us back up to the light!"

Tungdil was almost feeling sorry for it. "How does your father plan to get there?"

"Does it need to know?" The creature was astonished.

"Yes. The machine wants to get there first so that we can all go to the tunnel together."

"The originator took one of the warships that were floating round the island."

"And how did he destroy the other ones? With a diamond?"

"No." It turned to face the dwarf. "I destroyed them. All five of them." It lifted its shiny metal and green glass forearms as evidence of its ability. "With my special powers. I can use them whenever I want to."

"Five," murmured Rodario in dismay. "Would you credit it?"

The magus did not dare move. "It must be that alloy it has throughout its body. I've a feeling this monster may be the most dangerous and powerful of them all." He glanced over to Flagur. "Whatever you do, don't upset it. The weapons it's carrying are the least of our worries."

The ubari found it hard to do nothing, especially as the enemy seemed vulnerable, kneeling and not expecting an attack.

The island gave a shudder. It had reached the lake bed and the source.

"Make it go up," begged the terrified hybrid, taking its two axes out. As soon as it clasped the handles in its gloved fists the runes shone out on weapons and armor alike.

"Yes, I'm going to," Tungdil said calmly. "Watch." He pushed and pulled a few of the levers.

Just as the creature was about to stand up, Flagur saw his chance. The opportunity must not be missed. He lunged forward with his warriors.

The hybrid acted fast, throwing an ax at its assailants; it split open one of the ubariu down the whole length of his body, spewing blood and guts on the stones. Then the creature raised its free hand, the glass cylinder glowing green.

A beam of light shot from it, knocking Flagur to the ground and hurling him against the back wall by the entrance.

He leaped to his feet with a roar. His breastplate showed a black scorch mark.

"No!" yelled the monster, throwing its second ax, but the ubari dodged the missile. "Not now!"

Tungdil took his own ax and thrust it into the creature's naked shin while the monster's attention was elsewhere. He knew why the creature was so horrified. Its magic had been used up. Destroying all five of the warships had exhausted its power store, making the monster considerably less dangerous than they had been assuming.

As black blood sprayed out, it roared and yelled, wrenching an iron bar from the platform railings over its head, and launching it at the dwarf.

Tungdil had to drop his ax and jump out of the way. The massive iron stave missed him and pierced the control wall, smashing dozens of levers and wheels or bending them out of shape, to complete the work of destruction the thirdlings had begun in the previous battle.

"No!" it cried out. "Look what you've done! You've made me break the machine!" It launched itself from the floor, springing high onto the next platform and leaping away. "I'll kill you all!"

"Lot-Ionan!" Tungdil called. "Stop it recharging!"

The magician raised his hands and sent out a bright blue ray of light, missing the monster narrowly as it swerved at the last moment. The beam struck the middle of one of the boilers, releasing clouds of scalding steam from a hole the size of a mill stone.

Flagur and the ubariu stormed forward at Tungdil's command; Sirka, Rodario and Lot-Ionan followed at a slight distance.

The magus continued trying to zap the monster in an effort to prevent it reaching the platform and taking on more magic. He failed. Some invisible power was deflecting the beams.

Tungdil and some of the troop stepped onto the lift, while the others operated the winding gear. He heartily wished he still had Keenfire. "Let us hope it doesn't see us coming," he said to Flagur.

The monster climbed nimbly onto the nearest boiler and leaped from there to land on the platform.

As soon as its feet touched down, greenish flames flickered up and surrounded the armored figure; sparks sizzled along the rods on its glass forearms where the magic force was concentrated, and from inside the hollow glass, light blazed like small suns.

The swaying lift cage arrived at platform level, and Tungdil pushed the door open.

"You shall die!" screamed the beast in fury. "It's your fault I am stuck down here." It raised both arms toward the exhausted magus.

"Palandiell, give me strength," Lot-Ionan prayed, somehow managing to cast a protective spell. The enemy responded by shooting energy beams from its fingers.

Hissing, these beams encountered magic resistance. Lot-Ionan had conjured up a mirror spell, one of the simplest to effect. But even this straightforward incantation seemed to be failing in the face of some incomprehensible power. Was the creature tapping into the entire magic source and directing its power against him? His magic mirror cracked and splintered—with devastating consequences.

The beams were diffused into countless slender rays,

radiating out as if from the sun, destroying everything in the cave they touched.

"Lie down!" Tungdil shouted to his comrades, throwing himself flat onto the platform and hoping the special alloy it was made from would absorb the swirling fields of energy.

But nothing was able to withstand the rays.

The pressurized combustion chambers exploded, punching holes the size of a dwarf's fist into the rock walls; water started gushing in. Two of the ubariu fell victim to the sizzling death rays.

The monster itself suffered the same fate: randomly deflected beams hit him, one penetrating through its teeth into its mouth. Black smoke curled up from the impact spot. It uttered a roar of pain, fell backwards and plunged from the platform, several more deadly beams striking it before it crashed to the ground.

Tungdil stood up and surveyed the havoc all around him. Broad cracks were appearing on the cavern walls. The damaged rock would not withstand the pressure much longer. "Quick, everyone, get down again!" He leaped into the lift cage. "There's only one way to escape death."

Before they had reached ground level the roof fell in. A torrent of water cascaded in, threatening to engulf and drown them all: dwarves, ubariu and humans.

XVII

Girdlegard,
Queendom of Weyurn,
Thirty Miles Northeast of Mifurdania,
Late Summer, 6241st Solar Cycle

The *Waveskimmer* raced across the water toward the northern edge of the Red Mountain Range where the monster had said the tunnel entrance lay. The fog had lifted and those on deck were basking now in sunshine.

Sirka kissed Tungdil. "You are a very clever dwarf."

He relished the sensation of her soft lips on his own. "No, I just used my powers of observation," he said, watching out for the sandbank.

"Always so modest," complained Rodario from his hammock, where he was soaking up the invigorating rays. "If you hadn't had the idea of climbing into the empty boiler, we'd all have drowned." He shut his eyes against the bright light. "Even Lot-Ionan. Again, my deepest appreciation and heartiest thanks."

"It was the same principle as with the island. If something is full of air, it'll rise." Tungdil smiled and permitted himself a touch of pride.

Flagur, with a nasty cut on his shoulder from the sharp edges of the damaged boiler, nodded in agreement. He was seated on a barrel, naked to the waist, bandages to hand. One of his comrades was stitching the wound. "The actor is right. Things were looking very bad. As it is, most of us have survived." He did not appear to feel the needle.

Tungdil noticed Lot-Ionan was sitting in the shade on a coil of rope a little way off, near the main mast, and looking extremely ill at ease. He went over to his foster-father. "Revered sir, what is wrong?"

Lot-Ionan raised his white head and attempted a smile. He held out his hands. "Didn't you see? In the old days spells never went wrong. Never!" He clasped his hands as if he wanted to hide them from sight. "Now all I can do are silly little spells; my memory is playing tricks just when we need it most." He sighed heavily. "A mirror spell in a chamber surrounded by water and at the bottom of a lake. How stupid of me!"

"It's Nudin's fault, not yours," said Tungdil, trying to console him.

"I know that," the magus replied, "but it doesn't make it any better." He looked at the dwarf. "I am concerned about the future. About what happens after the battle with the unslayable."

Tungdil tried to guess at his thoughts. "The Outer Lands?"

"No. The future of magic in Girdlegard." He ran his fingers up the weathered timber of the mast. "The new magic wellspring lies so deep. Without the island nobody will ever get there to use it." He looked at the cliffs rearing up out of the water four miles ahead. One of them resembled a face, with a promontory like a nose. A giant's nose. "What's bothering me most is this: Is there anyone at all, apart from me, able to make use of it?"

"Perhaps one of Nudin's other initiates?" Tungdil played

with the free end of the rope. "Don't worry about getting to the lake bed. If you can get up to the surface in a boiler then you can get down again the same way. It's just a question of ballast. We don't need the island."

Lot-Ionan asked pensively, "But if any others trained under Nudin, why didn't they join Dergard and his friends?" He got to his feet and rubbed his back where stabs of pain were still troubling him. "What if I'm the last magus in Girdlegard?"

"They might have seen Dergard going with you instead of following in Nôd'onn's footsteps as a betrayal," Tungdil suggested. "Dergard located the source. We'll see if anyone else turns up in Weyurn suspiciously close to the same place." A call from the lookout warned they were nearing the cliff. "We're at our destination, venerable sir. Are you ready?"

"I don't know." His pale blue eyes seemed very tired. "But I have no choice." He smiled. "None of us have a choice, do we?"

The *Waveskimmer* ploughed through the waves toward the vegetation growing on the shore.

Tungdil wished his friend Ireheart were at his side for the coming confrontation. He was not only a good fighter but could lighten even the most critical of situations with a joke or scurrilous turn of phrase.

A squall pattern on the lake surface reminded Tungdil of the last of the rune messages: the one on the armor of the creature now at the bottom of the lake together with the remains of the island.

"*Eight*," he said quietly, mentally arranging the words. "*Your deaths have eight faces*." It was the unslayable's threat to the elves. *Would it prove to have been spoken too soon?* He was clear what the number eight meant. Five machine creatures, two unslayables and the älfar from Toboribor. Death in eight forms. Two were still around.

Rodario opened his eyes and got out of the hammock. "Where is the man o' war the unslayable used to get here? He can't have made it invisible."

Flagur—his injury stitched and bound, and his armor back on—pointed to starboard. "There's something over there." He looked up to the crow's nest. "What's that?" he called to the watch, indicating a shadow beneath the water.

"A ship," came the answer. "Sunk or scuppered and run aground on the sandbank. Looks like a warship."

"Well, that's that. The unslayable is here."

Sirka got the sails furled and launched the boats, not wanting to take their vessel too close in. Who could say how quickly they might have to make their escape?

They rowed over in silence, deep in thought. Walking over the soft sand they found a tunnel mouth three three paces high and two paces wide, concealed behind some thick bushes.

Cautiously they stepped into the cave, which soon became a stairway leading steeply down. Distant sounds echoed up out of the dark passage: hammering, stamping and banging.

They went down the steps and arrived in a tubular tunnel about ten paces in diameter. The floor was covered in a knee-deep layer of fine rock particles and the air was thick with dust, making Rodario sneeze. The polished tunnel walls shimmered in the faint light.

"Don't anyone light a torch," warned Tungdil. "The dust is too dense—it could easily combust."

"Yes, I've heard that can happen," nodded Rodario. "Didn't a flour mill in Porista once blow up? A candle flame igniting the flour dust?" He turned to where the tunnel met the lake. Solid supports with the girth of forest trees had been inserted to hold up the tunnel roof and walls of hefty shoring timbers and strong steel kept the water from pouring in and flooding the huge passage. "Bandilor certainly knew what he was doing when it comes to mining techniques," said Rodario. "And I thought the thirdlings were warriors first and foremost?"

"There's a lot to be learned from books, though," Tungdil replied with a grin. "Come on, let's go! We don't know how far ahead the unslayable is."

They hurried along the tunnel and reached a set of rails like those the dwarves were used to from back home. Three wagons stood ready; they could be propelled by muscle power.

Flagur pointed to marks on the ground where the dust was thinner: "So there was a fourth wagon."

"After him!" Tungdil jumped onto the vehicle, closely followed by the others. The journey began.

The ubariu operated the mechanism, and they soon reached considerable speed. Fine dust plagued them, getting into eyes, noses and mouths, the bitter-tasting grit grinding between their teeth and causing their eyes to burn and sting so that it was all they could do not to close them.

This tunnel took them in straight line through the heart of the Red Range.

"The monsters from the Outer Lands couldn't ask for

an easier way in," said Rodario, spitting out a mouthful of acrid dust. "No contending with mountain peaks, precipices, biting winds or ice and snow."

"True. But they would have to carry boats with them. Otherwise how would they get off that sandbank?" Sirka pointed out.

At the back of his mind Tungdil still had doubts about Bandilor being behind the whole plan. Though he did not want to believe it, he had to face up to the likelihood that it was Furgas, mad for revenge, who had planned the annihilation of Girdlegard's peoples. And he was sure the technical genius would have had some means up his sleeve to transport the army of monsters over the water. Perhaps they would have used the island or one of Weyurn's floating islets. There were plenty to choose from.

The mechanical expert's guilty involvement would have been indisputably proved if he had followed up the detailed hints Furgas had given them about the various monsters' weak points. But there had been no time to do that in the heat of battle. "Let's be glad we don't have to witness exactly how they would have done it," observed Tungdil. "Because that would have meant we were too late."

The tunnel was long but they were finally getting closer to the source of the rumbling, banging and hammering. The veil of dust was so thick it was like driving through an ash cloud; and the noise level increased until they could no longer hear themselves speak.

A huge black shadow suddenly appeared in front of them, completely filling the tunnel. It was a machine twenty paces long, rattling, clicking and grinding. At the front a drill was biting its way through the rock face, while dust and fine rubble spewed out behind. Rows of wheels, each the size of a hut, turned slowly to drive the drill.

Now Tungdil understood about the purpose of the tunnel. It must have been terribly complicated to fill it all in again behind them. They must have brought the excavation rig here to the Red Range via the floating nightmare island and of necessity have entered the cliff from under the water line to keep their activities secret. When they'd tunnelled far enough into the mountain, they'd been able to shore up their entrance hole behind them and then continue drilling their way down through the mountain range.

"The machine moves by itself," shouted Sirka into Tungdil's ear, yelling over the noise. "I can't see anyone operating it."

He nodded. This was by far the magister's greatest technical achievement. A machine that can eat its way through solid rock without being steered or directed, and can keep it up, cycle after cycle. Until it reached the Outer Lands, opening the door to death and destruction.

Rodario tugged at Tungdil's mail shirt and pointed to the missing wagon; it was tucked under the machine. The unslayable was not in it.

"He's somewhere on the machine," shouted Tungdil, climbing out and sinking nearly up to his armpits in the layer of dust. He made his way forward to the metal ladder near the hindmost wheel. It was like wading through powdery water.

His comrades followed him and one by one they climbed onto the machine. The iron frame shuddered and vibrated; rumbles continued unceasingly, as if there were heavy hammers at work on the inside. There was a strong smell of metal, oil and dust.

Soon they reached a narrow mesh platform: a walkway encircling the entire machine from which ladders led at regular intervals up and down to different levels. There was no sign of any levers or controls that might check the progress of the machine. Then they heard the noise level increase and noticed the juddering was getting faster. The drill was speeding up.

"We've got to stop it somehow," Tungdil roared. "The unslayable has—"

A figure in black armor landed immediately behind the ubari bringing up the rear. It used both its swords on the hapless victim. Cut into three pieces the warrior fell onto the metal walkway without even having glimpsed his killer. His blood washed the dust off the iron mesh and mixed with it to form damp grayish-red clumps.

The unslayable one moved swiftly and confidently forward in his magnificent suit of tionium armor—as if there was no weight to it at all. The pale, sulfur-colored light lent him an uncanny aura and the helmet's closed visor allowed no sight of his face. Tungdil stared at the foe and could only guess what was behind the protective armor.

The älfar did not want protracted combat at this stage. It hurried on up to the next level.

Flagur threw a dagger at him and caught the unslayable in mid-leap. The point penetrated the armor just above the right hip joint and dug its way halfway through the älfar's body. But he disappeared, nonetheless, as quickly as he had come.

Tungdil pointed overhead. "Up there! Perhaps there's a way in," he bellowed. "We must get the machine first. The älfar will come and find us."

Cautiously they clambered up from one level to the next, crawling over the back of the filth-covered mechanical digger. When they reached a hatch, Flagur went through first, followed by Tungdil and the others.

They saw that the unslayable had been busy. The machine, presumably, could be steered but there had been so much violent destruction in the hot, sticky, tight space that now it was impossible to see what levers and wheels were supposed to do what.

Sirka had found a wide door leading down to the engine room. She pointed to it, raising her eyebrows questioningly. Tungdil nodded.

Things were getting really uncomfortable. The heat had the sweat dripping off them all; oil on the rungs of the ladder made progress dangerous, and the gangways were even narrower than the one on the exterior of the machine. At least lanterns gave some light; not enough to help Rodario or Lot-Ionan, but sufficient for the dwarves and the ubariu.

They were overwhelmed by the sight that met their eyes. A collection of cogwheels of all sizes whirred round at different speeds. Rods and pistons rotated; chains and wide leather belts drove rollers, from which metal poles protruded, disappearing into iron cylinders. It was a living forest of metal. One false move and they would be dragged into the machinery.

"So what are we looking for?" Sirka yelled. "Or do we just try and break it?"

"Shouldn't think that would work. We need to find the driving mechanism. Then we have to destroy it."

She made a face. "And what does a driving mechanism look like?"

Rodario indicated something on the left: a huge iron block as big as a house. Chains emerged from it, distributed via a series of rollers and pulleys to other parts of the machine. "Let's start there and see what happens," he suggested.

One of the ubariu screamed and dropped its weapon. A narrow blade poking up through a gap in the iron mesh they were walking on had pierced the warrior's groin. Beneath their feet the unslayable was clinging like a spider to the underside of the walkway.

The dying ubari fell and the unslayable launched himself into the air, deftly landing on a slender cross-pole and then disappearing again into the dark.

Rodario gulped. They only had a handful of ubariu left to fight the enemy with. "Lot-Ionan, do something, for goodness' sake," he begged.

Tungdil could not blame the actor for such a reaction. "Over to the block, quickly," he commanded, racing ahead.

They reached the iron block. Chains were running past them at such a speed that they were only a blur causing an oil-laden draft. It would be almost impossible to halt them, Tungdil decided. They would have to concentrate on the pulleys.

But before he could tell the others what he wanted them to do the älfar turned up again out of the blue. He was targeting Flagur, but this time he faced an opponent who was expecting an attack.

Flagur parried the first blow with his own sword and caught hold of the arm bearing the second weapon. Then he kicked the unslayable one in the chest, making him hurtle backwards. He did not release the arm. The bone would fracture.

The älfar fell back like a doll, but pushed off again from the wall, slamming back into Flagur with twice the impetus. He thrust at Flagur with his sword, forcing the ubari to release the arm without having injured him at all.

His fellow ubariu rushed up and delivered blow after blow.

The unslayable one quickly realized his mistake. These opponents were not the normal kind of orc: strong but not very nimble. He took some punishment: two hits on the chest and on his left thigh. He tried to flee off into the shadows once more to try another surprise ambush.

Striking one of the ubariu down, he tricked a second with a feint that left his victim perilously close to a chain. After another lightning strike the ubari was tangled in the links and dragged off, his screams soon dying away. From somewhere inside the machine came a sickening clunk and the chain come back out of the engine room covered in blood.

"Grab him!" Lot-Ionan had seized the opportunity to weave a binding spell that he threw like a net over the unslayable one.

The runes on the black armor glowed in protest, but they could not protect the wearer from the effects of the magic. He froze stock still, issuing shouts of fury from behind his helmet.

"Force him to the ground!" Tungdil flung himself on the älfar. Flagur came to his aid and wrenched both weapons out of their enemy's grasp.

"Go ahead, you two." Rodario had no desire to join in. Instead he made for the engine. "I'll stop the motor." He had found a hatch that opened to reveal a whole row of cogwheels and a number of large fat metal springs constantly coiling and uncoiling.

Underneath them stood a tray full of oil; into which small lubricating ladles dipped prior to smearing the rapidly moving parts. The black liquid ran back along the rods to collect back in the same tray.

"Even I can work out what to do here." He laughed, then took his sword and punched a hole in the tray so that the oil ran out. The ladles had nothing to spoon up now.

Nothing happened. The machine went on running smoothly.

"That will take too long." To speed things up, Rodario chucked handfuls of powdered rock in through the hatch. The ladles picked it up and spread it over the circulating parts of the machinery.

Soon the first sharp tearing noises were heard. The metal was running hot and emitted a scorching smell. It would not be long before the machine came to a standstill.

"And once more the Incredible Rodario has an incredibly inspired idea." He congratulated himself. He closed the hatch and turned to see how Tungdil and the others were faring.

The first wheel came to a screeching stop. Some of the

parts that had been moving at very high speeds were suddenly halted. Others kept running but the transmission failed. Clanking and shuddering, some of the iron parts gave way. Fragments of shattered cogwheels shot through the air.

XVIII

"Let's see what's under that helmet," said Tungdil, reaching out to loosen the chinstrap. Loud crashes warned of trouble and fragments of shattered cogwheels flew past his ears. He swung round in shock to see what was happening. "What on earth have you done, Rodario?"

"I've wrecked the machine. Wasn't that what you wanted?" the Fabulous One retorted indignantly. "It'll all be over soon."

But the noise was telling a different story. Chains and drive belts were bursting and ripping apart and in the interior of the engine room havoc reigned. A symphony of destruction echoed from all sides, with projectiles shooting out from exploding machinery. It would have been safer to stand on a battlefield in a hail of arrows from a thousand enemy archers than to be in the iron belly of that machine.

"Everybody out!" yelled Tungdil. He had taken a painful hit on the back. Although the chain mail had stopped the metal bolt he was badly bruised.

They headed back. On the way Sirka spotted another hatch through which they got out onto a narrow iron walkway to a second exit. The unslayable one wasn't objecting. He had no desire to die inside an exploding machine.

It was not long before they got outside and could leap down into the dust on the tunnel floor and run for the wagons. Only then could they stop for breath.

"Remind me never to ask you to do any sabotage again," Tungdil said to Rodario, only half joking.

With a deafening screech like the death cry of some primeval creature the drill finally stopped turning and the machine stopped thudding. The last dust floated to the ground and the air grew still.

"We've done it!" Rodario gave a triumphant shout. He checked to see if he had been injured. "The old heroes are the new heroes of the day! Girdlegard is safe, my friends!"

"Not quite." Tungdil stretched out a hand, intending to take off the unslayable's helmet and interrogate him concerning the diamond, but the älfar's pointed boot shot out, catching the dwarf full on the forehead.

Either the unslayable one had only been pretending that Lot-Ionan's spell had worked, or the magus was no longer able to sustain the magic. The älfar grabbed a sword from the nearest ubari and elbowed away the soldier who had been restraining him; as the armored arm struck him in the face he fell senseless to the ground.

"How dare you stop me?" the älfar bellowed from behind his protective headgear, as he wielded his sword against Flagur, who fended off the blow but got punched on the nose instead. Blood spurted out to land glistening on the unslayable's metal gauntlet. "I'll slice your sinews and have you kneeling at my feet in your own blood!"

"Come on, wizard!" Rodario shouted to Lot-Ionan, swerving out of reach of the remarkably agile älfar.

Tungdil confronted the foe. "You have something that does not belong to you!"

The älfar did not deign to answer. Instead he launched a terrific blow, the momentum of which nearly had him down as Tungdil parried with his ax. A strike like that would have had even the strongest orc on its knees.

"What miserable creatures you are," said the älfar hollowly, disgust in his voice. "You deserve the destruction that awaits you all." Nonchalantly he sidestepped a blow from one of the ubariu whilst easily maintaining the pressure on his sword hand, and thus on Tungdil.

"The machine is useless now," the dwarf gasped, thrusting his opponent back toward Flagur's raised weapon.

"I don't need it anymore." The älfar was defiant. "The last section of quarrying I shall do with the diamond's power."

He swept the sword to one side, catching Tungdil off balance, and used the momentum to sink the blade into the belly of the last guardsman. "As soon as I have killed you." He sprang up into the air and onto the nearest of the wagons and catapulted off, his sword aimed at Lot-Ionan.

The magus lifted his hand toward the foe and closed his eyes. A single syllable was all that passed his lips— and suddenly the älfar hung suspended in mid-air.

Flagur leaped up with both of the enemy's own weapons, plunging them through his upper body. The razor-sharp steel pierced the armor and had the unslayable screaming in pain. "That's what my soldiers suffered, älfar!" Flagur growled, pleasure glinting in his pale pink eyes; he moved the blades from side to side to aggravate the creature's pain. "Suffer and die, monster! Suffer and die!"

But again the spell lost its effectiveness all too soon, and the unslayable dropped to the floor. With a furious bestial cry he pulled his swords out of his body and attacked Flagur with them.

Exactly what the älfar did next could not be followed with the naked eye. Blades whirled, blood sprayed out and then the ubari sank down into the gray dust that swamped him like water.

"I might have known," sighed Rodario. "Me up against a madman again. Like in Porista."

The älfar retreated, grabbing at a bag on his belt and taking the diamond out. His armored fist closed around the stone, grating and crackling.

"Destroy him!" called Tungdil, leaping forward. He had heard the enemy reciting älfar words: he must be attempting a spell. Sirka and Rodario attacked from different sides. The unslayable could not dodge all of their blows.

Then the diamond blazed out.

Dazzling beams shone through the armored fingers, illuminating the tunnel wall. The tionium became translucent, showing the bones of the hand holding the stone. The älfar pointed two fingers at Lot-Ionan.

Tungdil had no doubt that his foster-father was about to be hit by a ray from the diamond. "Vraccas! Help us!" He lowered his head and made a mighty leap toward his enemy, the blade of his ax directed at the unslayable's wrist.

The aim was true!

Tungdil felt the resistance offered by armor and bone, but neither could stop the blade's advance. The severed limb lay on the dusty ground and the stone's glare was extinguished.

Shrieking loudly, the injured älfar struck out at Tungdil.

The dwarf managed to lift the ax, but the älfar's sword sliced through the handle and dealt him a blow on his upper arm. It cut deep into armor plate and dwarf flesh, biting into the bone, where it lodged. If the sword had not first met the ax handle it would surely have cut off Tungdil's arm.

He gave a shout and staggered; his fingers opened involuntarily and he dropped the ax.

But Sirka did not abandon him. She leaped in front of him and attacked the älfar to drive him away from Tungdil. In the meantime Rodario and Lot-Ionan were scrabbling in the dust for the severed hand and the diamond it had held.

But even Sirka was no match for the unslayable one. He made as if to deliver a diagonal blow but instead pierced her shoulder. Then he pulled the blade sharply upwards and cut through her collarbone. Without a sound she fell to the ground and was swallowed up by the dust.

"No!" Blind with fury Tungdil stormed up to the älfar, who awaited his onslaught with sword raised ready to deliver a fatal blow.

"I've got it! I've got it!" Rodario had located the amputated hand and slammed it against the side of the wagon to break the grip on the stone, which he neatly caught as it fell. He handed the diamond to the magus, who accepted it with reverence.

Its appearance was no longer immaculate. There were now dark patches and dull places on its previously clear surface. Lot-Ionan even thought he could see cracks. Being touched by the älfar had not helped the stone at all. "Palandiell and Sitalia, I ask you for your aid," he said, enfolding the diamond in his hand. He searched for and found the power that slumbered deep within the gemstone.

Tungdil had reached the unslayable and had drawn his knife, aiming it at the lower of his opponent's wounds.

But he could not even get close. The älfar struck and the sword hit the dwarf on the left side, slicing through on a slant under the arm, between the iron rings of the armor, between the ribs, and into the heart.

Tungdil's blood turned into molten ore of the mountain; his whole body glowed with heat. But his heart was ice cold.

"Your death bears the name Nagsòr Inàste," the älfar intoned clearly before he moved the blade and pulled it out. Dark red dwarven blood gushed out of the gaping wound, pouring down Tungdil's clothing and soaking into the dust. "I shall have your life, groundling. There will be no grave for your bones, and your soul will wander, eternally lost. As lost as the whole of Girdlegard will be on my return."

"I . . ." Tungdil frowned, took two steps and lifted his knife. "Sirka . . ." He collapsed at the feet of his älfar murderer and sank up to the neck in the thick dust. The iciness spread into every last corner of his body, robbing him of movement. Everything grew dark. The älfar merged with the shadows and disappeared into the gray.

Rodario had witnessed the death of his friend. "Magus, you must perform a miracle," he said in lifeless tones, and raised his weapon. "I will ensure a few moments' grace for you."

Lot-Ionan could feel the strength of the diamond, but it was refusing to do his bidding.

"It's not as easy as it looks, is it?" said a familiar voice next to him.

The magus shivered, not daring to turn his head. "Nudin?"

"What is left of him, old friend."

Lot-Ionan swallowed with apprehension as he saw the älfar approaching again, keen to complete his handiwork and regain the diamond.

Rodario pushed forward in front of the magus and brandished his sword, even if he knew that he was likely to be the first to fall. The other two seemed incredibly slow—as if their limbs were tied down to the heaviest of weights.

"You have to open yourself up to the stone," said Nudin, speaking from Lot-Ionan's other side this time. "Let it see inside your soul. If it sees you are worthy, its power will help you against the unslayable."

"Get away from me! You are a specter!" Lot-Ionan hissed, deep in concentration.

"Only in part, old friend," he heard the long-dead magus say, now from behind where he stood. "I continue to live in you."

"How could that be?"

Nudin gave a quiet laugh. "How is your back, Lot-Ionan the Forbearing? Does it still hurt when you make certain movements?"

Lot-Ionan turned round and thought he could see a man by the machine, but he could not make out the features. He blinked and the figure had disappeared. "How do you know that?"

"Shouldn't you be helping Rodario rather than chasing ghosts?" The friendly admonition echoed from all sides. "The good man will die and then the unslayable will cut you to pieces."

"How was it possible for *him* to use the diamond?"

"Later, Lot-Ionan! If you want to save Girdlegard you have to make an effort." After a short pause the voice added, "Or do you want *me* to help you, old friend?"

"No," Lot-Ionan shot back the answer. He closed his eyes tight and pressed the diamond with both hands, trying to force the power out of it like squeezing the juice out of a fruit. Nothing happened. Then came a shout from Rodario and the crash of a body falling.

"Too slow, old friend. Now there is no one between the unslayable and yourself. The bravest heroes of Girdlegard are all vanquished," said Nudin. "My offer still stands, Long-Sufferer. You won't get far today with your famous patience, believe you me."

Lot-Ionan opened his eyes and saw the älfar two paces away. Visions of a devastated Girdlegard flamed up in his mind. Innumerable beasts were streaming in hordes from the north, escaped from the confines of the Black Abyss, and they were joining forces with the monsters from the west. Together they were raging through the defenseless land and inching it toward annihilation. Nothing remained except for enclaves of horror, scorched and violated, all the people reduced to servants of evil.

The älfar pushed up his visor and showed the magus his even-featured face where, instead of eyes, only two dark holes were to be seen.

The beauty of that face was arresting and impossible to resist. Lot-Ionan recognized that he wished only to fulfill every demand the creature might put on him. It would only have to ask him for the stone and . . .

"No," he shouted at the älfar, stiffening every sinew against the remorseless attraction—even if he would not be able to sustain the effort. "Help me, Nudin," he said quietly.

"Gladly, my friend."

A vicious sharp pain stabbed Lot-Ionan's spine, traveling up and shooting through the shoulder into the arm, spreading into the fingertips. Suddenly the diamond blazed with green fire.

And at once the magus knew all his powers were returning. He remembered the spells. Many spells. They rushed into his mind of their own accord, and his mouth formed the words as his hands made the magic gestures, to fling at the älfar.

The creature was staggered by this magic onslaught. Enclosed within a sphere of malachite fire there was no escape. A single thought from Lot-Ionan sufficed to make the ball-like structure shrink around the älfar until it touched the tip of his helmet.

He crouched down and tried to strike a hole in his prison, but his efforts were in vain. The globe grew tighter around him, until his skeleton crunched under the pressure. The tionium bent out of shape, bones fractured and pierced the skin and internal organs of the unslayable; his blood flowed down onto the dust. His shrill screams reverberated through the tunnels.

By this time the globe's diameter was that of a small wagon wheel; it shrank and shrank to the size of a crystal divining ball, then to the size of a child's marble. Magic turned the unslayable into a bloody thing of flesh and metal devoid of any life.

Lot-Ionan made the sphere disappear, and the tiny ball rolled into the dust. With the aid of his new-found powers he raised it up without having to touch the revolting object; he sent it flying into the heart of the machine.

"Are you pleased with me, Forbearing One?" asked Nudin's voice. "I think we worked very well together."

The magus paid no heed and instead gave swift attention to his companions. For Tungdil any help was now too late. The älfar sword had cut his heart into pieces. "No," Lot-Ionan whispered, aghast. Memories of the past, happier cycles, rose in his mind: Tungdil working at the forge, or laughing in the kitchen with the maid Frala and her children, while the dwarf read them stories. What would he not have given to return to those far-off days. With everything he had since lost.

"Try!" whispered Nudin enticingly.

"Try what?"

"To bring him back to life."

"To make him one of the undead? I cannot do that. And even if I could, no, it's better he should . . ."

Nudin laughed, as an adult will laugh at the naiveté of

a child. "Lot-Ionan the Forbearing. There is no limit to the power in your hands. The gods will be jealous. Go on, try."

"No."

"Try it. You won't be disappointed."

Lot-Ionan placed his left hand gingerly on the dwarf's lifeless body while in his right he grasped the diamond. Healing spells combined with images of a vital Tungdil.

The magic worked!

As the wound closed up and the heart began to beat under his fingertips, the magus could hardly take it in. He had acquired dominion over life and death, the fervent desire of magi and magae for generations. The power was his, so simply, with no need for cycles of research, invention of new spells, and countless experiments. All that was needed he held in his hands.

Tungdil's eyelids fluttered and opened. He looked at his foster-father. "Revered Lot-Ionan? Am I dead?" Coughing, he sat up, spitting out dust and blood. In disbelief he ran his fingers over the ripped chain mail shirt; he could see exactly where the älfar's sword had struck. "I *must* be dead." His brow furrowed. "He hit me . . ." He hastily looked around for the älfar, getting to his feet. Then he noticed that even the severe injury to his arm had gone. "Where is the unslayable?"

"Dead." Lot-Ionan stroked Tungdil's hair as he used to do when he was young. "The diamond, Tungdil. It is incredibly powerful and it can . . . heal wounds like nothing else in the whole of Girdlegard." He did not wish his foster-child to know that of rights he should be in the eternal forge with Vraccas.

"Dead?" Tungdil felt giddy. He had to put a hand on the wagon to steady himself. "Where is the body?"

"I have destroyed it. It is in the machine somewhere."

"Are you certain that . . ."

"Yes." The magus went over to treat Rodario's injuries. The actor, too, would of rights have been with his ancestors, his belly sliced open by the älfar's blade so the entrails spilled out. But the diamond and the magic power restored everything to its rightful place and the deadly wound had closed up before Tungdil could see it.

After that, Sirka and Flagur were attended to. The other freed souls Lot-Ionan left in the hands of the god Ubar. He did not want to be profligate with the force of the diamond. It surely would come to an end at some time.

Tungdil searched the wagon the älfar had used to reach the tunnel's end, hoping he might locate Keenfire. No luck. This time the enemy had ensured the legendary weapon would not be found.

His boot met something sharp, something metal. He bent down and picked up one of the unslayable one's swords.

"A trophy?" commented Rodario, extremely surprised at his own survival.

Tungdil was admiring the blade's quality and decided to take it with him. "I'll make myself an ax from this metal. It will stand me in good stead until I find Keenfire." He went to Sirka and embraced her. "We've done it," he whispered with relief. "The diamond is safe."

"Let's get out of the tunnels," said Rodario. He indicated his shredded clothing. "I have no idea how I survived all that, but I'm not asking." He nodded to the magus. "At last I appreciate the wonders of magic, revered magus."

Climbing into the wagon he started to crank. "All aboard, heroes of Girdlegard! I want to see the sun."

Tungdil saw from their faces that none of them understood what had happened. Nobody had witnessed what had occurred between Lot-Ionan and the unslayable. But joy took over from speculation and laid itself over all the open questions like a fire blanket over flames. It killed his own doubts, too.

Flagur and Rodario cranked the handle, and the journey to the tunnel mouth began.

Lot-Ionan glanced over his shoulder. Again he saw the vague figure of a man standing by the machine, his arm raised in salute, as if he were going to stay there to await their return. The magus quickly turned; as he did so he was aware again of an acute pain in his spine.

They were all tired when they reached the point where this part of their adventure had started. Not a single beam of light fell through the tunnel entrance; it was nighttime. In darkness they climbed the broad steps.

"Imagine: if it weren't for us, armies of orcs would have been marching up here," said Rodario when they were halfway up. "It's so good to know what we have achieved. What a fight! Me, in combat with an unslayable! Who'd have thought it?"

"So why did you come?" Tungdil asked.

Rodario winked at him. "I thought you might need not my sword but my store of knowledge. And my way with words: my best weapon. Closely followed, of course, by what only the prettiest girls get to see."

"I knew that was coming," said Tungdil, laughing. In spite of their exhaustion, their spirits rose.

"Isn't it great?" Rodario was on a high. "The toughest of all missions, to defeat the unslayable—and we've done it! Now for the Outer Lands: a long journey, but one with no danger."

Tungdil grinned. "What makes you say 'with no danger', Fabuloso?"

"What could go wrong with an escort of a hundred thousand warriors and a powerful magus on your side?" He tripped on a step and fell forwards. "Cursed darkness! This is no good." He searched in his pocket.

"What are you doing, Rodario?" asked Tungdil.

Stone scraped on metal and sparks ignited, catching the wick of a lamp. The warm glow illuminated the actor's fine features. "Light, Tungdil. I don't want to have survived combat with the älfar, only to break my neck on some stairs." He looked round. "What do we do with the tunnel?"

Whoompf! The air was full of flame and a smell of burning.

With a loud whistle the fire shot down into the depths. The tiny flame had brought about the event most dreaded by miners and dwarves everywhere.

"You are so stupid, Rodario!" hissed Tungdil, batting out flames in his hair. Luckily, the explosion had not set their clothes alight. He grabbed Sirka's hand and ran.

They rushed frantically to escape the inferno that threatened to engulf them. Just as they raced out of the tunnel an enormous vibration shook the ground, hurling them onto the sandbank.

In front of them the whole surface of the lake exploded, with a huge water spout shooting up into the dark night sky. When it had reached its zenith at a height of one hundred paces, a jet of flame illuminated the geyser from within. The hissing steam reminded Tungdil of the hot springs in mountain areas. The magnitude of the detonation caused by the dust igniting had destroyed the shoring, and the lake waters had gushed into the tunnel.

The water ebbed away and then rushed back in waves that swamped the sandbank, carrying all of them away with it. They heard loud gurgling as it cascaded down into the tunnel, flooding the whole excavation. With all their strength they clung to the cliff face to avoid being swept off and sucked down into the tunnel to drown.

At last the cave was full and the noise of the water died away. The foaming waves quietened and the last of the eddies on the surface calmed.

Then, to their intense relief the *Waveskimmer* approached to take them on board and with all sails set they headed east.

Girdlegard,
Kingdom of Gauragar.
Floodland,
Late Summer, 6241st Solar Cycle

"I suggest we join up with the ubariu army in Pendleburg." It was evening. Tungdil was in the captain's cabin with his friends, poring over a map of Girdlegard as they discussed strategy.

The *Waveskimmer* had passed the Gauragar border; now they were in Floodland, the part of the kingdom that had become submerged five cycles previously when Weyurn's lakes spread. Where the inundation had brought death and destruction, now the water made travel easier. They had crossed directly to the east and were approaching the Brown Mountains.

Flagur nodded. "That will be best. There's no one in Girdlegard trying to get the stone now, so we can take the risk and go to Urgon without an escort." He looked at Lot-Ionan, who was holding the diamond in one hand and gazing absent-mindedly through the tiny window. "What is your view, revered magus? Is there still any danger?"

The magus gave no answer.

Instead Tungdil spoke up: "There is still one älfar on the loose. He was on the island the thirdlings used as a base. But he did not join the unslayable one and I've heard no rumors about him recently."

"That's a good start." Flagur rested broad forearms on the table and the wood creaked in response to his weight.

"I'm not afraid of him," the dwarf repeated.

"But I am, my noble fellow hero," murmured Rodario. "The last älfar slit my belly open and it was not a nice feeling. I don't think this one will be any more kindly disposed to me. Don't forget. We murdered its parents. That is reason enough for hostility over and above natural viciousness."

"I'm for an escort guard," Sirka chipped in. "King Bruron should send troops. The more swords we have, the better defended we are."

"Agreed," said Tungdil.

Rodario scribbled it all down. He had been nominated

scribe. The messages would be duly sent off as soon as they reached dry land. He sorted through his notes. "One letter for Bylanta, queen of the fourthlings, to say we're on our way; a message for Ireheart, and one for the ubariu army, and one for all the monarchs to tell them we're taking the diamond over the border, and . . ." he said, indicating the last piece of paper " . . . a message to Bruron asking for an escort." He dipped the nib into the ink again to write the final sentences.

Lot-Ionan sighed. "It's no good trying to hide it any longer." He placed the stone on the table. "Flagur, what do you see?"

Rodario said nothing. He glanced at Tungdil and hoped he was remembering what they had talked about the other night. "No, don't touch it," he said when the ubari stretched out a hand. "Just look at it, like the magus said."

Flagur was hurt. "Why shouldn't I touch it?"

"You ate orc flesh, Flagur, and it will have been contaminated with Black Water," he explained.

"I understand," said the ubari without malice. "So he's afraid—so *you're* afraid—the badness might have infected me and that I might have quite different reasons for wanting to hold the stone?" He grinned wickedly. "A nice thought!"

"Don't get me wrong. We had another visitor to Girdlegard once, supposed to be on the side of goodness," Rodario pointed out. He felt it was his duty to explain. "I have great respect for you and for Sirka, but," he inclined his head, "so far we've had to take your word for everything. I mean, how do we know the Black Abyss and its terrible threat even exists? Maybe the diamond isn't really needed for activating the artifact?" He cleared his throat. "Ever since that night these doubts have been around. Forgive me, Flagur."

"Accursed actor!" Swift as lightning Flagur seized the diamond. He stared at his own fist; from deep down, dark laughter sounded and his pink eyes flashed with cruelty. "At last!" he bawled, jumping up. "The trick worked! Ubar be praised!" Sirka went to his side, brandishing her battlestick at the showman. "See what a magnificent rune master I am," he continued. "Feel my power!" Then his countenance transformed itself. He grinned at Rodario, who had drawn his sword courageously. "What do you think of my acting skills?"

"What?" The theater man blinked. His breath was labored and he looked as if someone had just yelled in his ear to rouse him from deep sleep.

"My performance. How was it?"

"Your . . . your *performance*? Very funny! I nearly cut your throat!" Rodario gave a rueful glance in Tungdil's direction. "Great hero! You're looking particularly relaxed." Tungdil grinned, then he laughed out loud and all the others joined in. "Right, I understand! You've rehearsed this little scene to get me really scared?" He pulled a face. "I'll have my own back for that one, I promise. Nobody challenges the Emperor of the Stage with impunity! Nobody."

Tungdil patted him on the shoulder. "You're right. I'd already spoken to him about our worries. Lot-Ionan examined him with magic and couldn't find anything untoward."

"It was good of you to alert us," said Lot-Ionan,

smiling. "But you deserved a fright after your idiocy back there—"

"Thanks, thanks. Got it now." Rodario cut him short. Can we get back to what's important?"

Sirka and Flagur sat down again, grinning. But Flagur's mirth quickly disappeared. "The diamond never used to look like that before!" He passed it to Sirka.

"Cracks, black patches," she observed. "Where are they from? The unslayable's touch?" She held it to the light. "It looks as if it could shatter at any moment."

"That's the only explanation I can come up with," Lot-Ionan stroked his snowy beard—or at least what was left of it after the fireblast in the cave. "I expect the älfar forced it; he must have used the last of his own magic to break its protective shield."

"And the glow we saw: was it the power of the stone or the unslayable's magic?" wondered Tungdil.

"It was the diamond. It was a pure, clear light. The contamination must have happened shortly after that." Lot-Ionan looked at Flagur and Sirka. "It's vital to know whether the artifact will work with the diamond in this state or not."

"Might it not produce the very opposite effect?" Rodario asked to inspect the stone and rubbed it gently with one finger. Even though it seemed uneven, the surface was as smooth as glass. He could not detect the cracks. "If the evil is in there, won't we just risk waking it up? Or to put it another way," he said, putting the stone in the middle of the table, "what if the artifact summons up evil instead of repressing it?"

They fell silent and watched the diamond follow the

movement of the waves, tipping this way and that. It looked so harmless; however mighty and significant, it betrayed no sign of the power stored within. No one knew what its effect might be.

"Did you feel anything when you used the stone, revered magus?" asked Sirka. "You know about magic. You've studied it. Was there anything odd?"

Lot-Ionan recalled Nudin's voice and mysterious appearance. "No," he lied calmly. He assumed the events related to himself rather than to the diamond. "No, it allowed me to use it. And I'm a long way from being on the side of evil." He took a quick gulp of his wine and, as he bent forward, felt a stabbing pain in his back. He nearly dropped the beaker.

Tungdil took a deep breath. "It's probably best not to tell the rulers our doubts."

Rodario had got over his sulk and was joining in again. "I quite agree. They would rather send an army to the Black Abyss against the monsters rather than risk using an artifact that can't be trusted." He flicked the diamond. "I'm for trying it out. It might speed things up. Either it will work and no one will realize we were skeptical about it here tonight on the *Waveskimmer*, or it won't work. Then they can still send out their army."

"To put it another way: we have no choice," said Flagur. "It won't be long before the monsters notice the barrier is down. The diamond must be put back in its place."

Lot-Ionan raised his head and gazed out at the sunset-lit waters. "As a last resort there's still me. The force of the diamond can still provide magic enough to repel the first attack wave."

"You are sure you have regained all your previous knowledge?" said Sirka carefully, trying to reduce the half insult to a quarter insult.

The magus smiled at her. It was a confident smile, and completely convincing. "I feel I have the power of two magi," he responded. "Blood has reached all parts of my body now and has washed away the last traces of the stone I was turned to." He touched himself on the temple. "Here, too. I can see the formulae clearly again like in my heyday." After a short pause he added, "This *is* my heyday. The fight with the unslayable has shaken me awake."

"Then let's leave it at that," Tungdil summed up and then stretched. "We'll go to the Outer Lands and we'll employ the diamond. After that, may the gods Vraccas and Ubar show what they can do for us, because we will have done everything we can to avert disaster." He stood up and strode to the door. "Excuse me for a moment."

"Dwarf-water offering for Elria?" Rodario joked. "Be kind to the goddess. She has let us off lightly more than once."

Tungdil laughed and left the cabin for a pee. He had chosen to do it from the bows of the ship. Elria's good-will or not, his own water was determined to leave him now.

When he had relieved himself he stayed at the railing, experiencing the gentle rise and fall of the vessel and enjoying the cool air.

For him water was still an uncanny element. Many of his kind would steadfastly refuse to go near a lake or even a stream. Or even to step into a big puddle. They believed

Elria had cursed them. The undergroundlings, on the other hand, seemed to relish travel on water. What a difference.

He gazed over the light swell on the lake's surface. It looked like liquid night that had dripped down from the sky and collected on the earth.

"I'd like to congratulate you on defeating my creator," said a clear quiet voice behind him. Tungdil recognized it at once. Death had returned.

Swiveling slowly, he saw the älfar seated cross-legged near the chest where the extra canvas was kept. His spear lay at his feet. His armor showed black against skin that was otherwise pale. Long hair hung down over his face. His gauntleted hands were resting on his knees and in one armored fist he held a lock of black hair. "What will you do now?"

Tungdil knew he himself was only carrying a knife. "What is your name?"

"My begetter never gave me one. He said my enemies would find a name to suit me." He did not take his eyes off Tungdil. He seemed alert but not aggressive or nervous, as if aware of his superior strength. "But the names I've heard don't please me. Nobody wants to be known by a curse. And so I have chosen Aiphatòn. Like the star." He raised his right arm and pointed to the sky, where it glittered against the dark. "It is the life-star of the elves. My begetter said the star would grow dim whenever an elf died in Girdlegard. In the last few orbits I could hardly see it at all. Something's happening with the elves."

"Most of them are waging war and are probably being wiped out. Because they are guilty of treason against

Girdlegard," Tungdil explained. "Do you consider your-self an elf?"

"I look like an elf. Am I not an elf?" came the surprising question.

"What did your begetter tell you that you were?"

"He told me nothing. But he and the creating spirit mother looked like elves." He lowered his head and his face was hidden under the curtain of hair. "I am glad he is dead. He demanded and committed atrocities." His metal hand scraped over the tionium plates sewn into his flesh.

"Is that why you told us where your begetter was heading?"

"Yes. I sensed you would defeat him. I was not able to." He raised his head once more. "What will you do now?"

"We . . ." Tungdil hesitated. The älfar did not know that he had been born as the elves' deadliest enemy. It might well be that he was playing a low trick and that he was pursuing the same despicable ends as his father before him. But if he wanted the diamond, why was he not attacking?

"You don't trust me, although I spared your life in Toboribor? Although I told you where to find my begetter? And you are still alive although I could so easily have killed you and tossed you overboard?" He stood up with a swift and elegant movement that combined strength and agility. "Then I shall tell you what I want. Take me to the elves that are different from my creator father. I know there are elves that are good and peace-loving. I wish to live amongst them." He stepped out of the shadows toward the dwarf.

Tungdil saw his dark eyes. "You are not an elf," he said solemnly. "You are an älfar. They are merciless enemies of the elves, Aiphatòn. You cannot live with them. They would kill you outright. "

"Why? I have not harmed them."

"But you belong to the race that persecuted their kind for a very long time and nearly wiped them out. They will never forgive you your lineage."

The älfar clicked his tongue. "Let me speak to them and we'll see." He folded the black lock of hair into a piece of waxed cloth and slid it inside his glove.

Tungdil shook his head. "Aiphatòn, listen to me. I advise you to hide away from dwarves and humans and elves. No one will see you without feeling fear and hatred. Leave Girdlegard and seek your own kind."

"But I don't want to join those you call älfar," he hissed, baring his teeth. "If they are like my begetter it's best I kill them all." He raised his hand and reached for the spear that was still lying on the deck. The runes on the weapon started to glow. It leaped into his hand. "I don't want to be like them."

Tungdil still did not have the slightest idea whether the älfar could be trusted. Everything pointed to the opposite: both what he knew from stories and what he had personal experience of. Sinthoras, Caphalor and Ondori were the älfar he had met in combat himself. But then there had been Narmora, the half-älfar woman who had been Furgas's companion. In spite of her ancestry she had fought for the good and had paid a high price: she had surrendered her happiness and the lives of her children. Her own life, too.

"What can you tell me about your begetter and the

dwarves?" he asked, to turn the conversation in a different direction.

"They are dead. What is there to say?"

Tungdil hesitated. "Did you see Furgas? The man who was kept captive by the dwarves?"

"Yes." Aiphatòn raised his armored hand. "It was he who turned me into what I am. My begetter asked him to. He made me like I am. He was their . . ." He struggled to find the word. "They did what he said and they followed his orders," was how he expressed it. "There was a lot that I heard."

"He was their leader?"

"Yes, that's it. He discovered the island together with the dwarves, and he came with soldiers to take it over. The humans all had to work for him. The magister made machines that he gave to the dwarves and they took them away. He made the constructions he sent through the mountain. They were to locate the monsters. And it was for the monsters that he built the tunnel." The älfar sat next to Tungdil at the gunwale. "He was in Toboribor, too, looking for orcs to use with his other machines. That's when he found my creators and the orcs. My creators gave him my siblings and he took them away and made new creatures out of them."

"How did he know about the magic source? He's a magister technicus, not a magus."

"I don't know. I just know *that* he did."

However painful it was, Tungdil had to believe the älfar. He had heard the truth first from the mouth of Bandilor and now Aiphatòn was confirming it. Tungdil had wished to hear a different version.

The älfar looked out over the waves. "I've told you what I want, I've told you what I know and where I'm from. Now tell me what you are going to do."

"We're going to the Outer Lands—"

"To the monsters Furgas spoke of?" he interrupted.

"No, not to the west. To the north." And before Aiphatòn could ask, he said, "You cannot come with us."

Aiphatòn shrugged his shoulders helplessly. It was difficult to read his state of mind from his face: the black eyes hid all feeling. But his body language spoke of deep distress. "What shall I do here in Girdlegard where nobody will have me?" A red teardrop ran down his cheek, leaving a pink smear. "I have nowhere to go. I only have enemies."

By now Tungdil was convinced that Aiphatòn was genuine. "Come with me, I'll introduce you—"

"No." Aiphatòn's attitude was determined. He had reached a decision. "If there is no place for me in Girdlegard, then I will make a place for myself." He smiled kindly. "Whatever you are planning, I wish you success. I am sure we will meet again." He vaulted over the side of the ship and slipped silently down into the water, the waves closing over his head.

Tungdil leaned over the side. He could not see anything. Aiphatòn was gone as if he had never existed.

"Hey, what's up?" the watch called out, noticing the dwarf. "Man overboard?" The man came nearer.

"No. A fish jumping." Tungdil turned around and went back to the cabin.

Like the first time, he decided to tell his friends nothing of the encounter.

He would not have been able to explain to them where the älfar had suddenly appeared from. He prayed to Vraccas that he and the älfar would never have to face each other as adversaries.

And yet he was almost certain that sooner or later they would.

Girdlegard
Kingdom of Urgon,
Pendleburg,
Early Autumn, 6241st Solar Cycle

From his fortress walls Ortger was watching the black-clad troops of the advance guard approach. "The people here in Urgon all went into hiding when they heard that this allied army was on its way," he told Prince Mallen. "And I know why. No one wants friends like these." He surveyed the head of the silent procession. These creatures were taller and broader than orcs; they were terrifying and were heavily armed.

"I can see why they're afraid. It was the same in Idoslane." Mallen headed down to the hall for the ceremony. Tungdil and his friends had arrived in Pendleburg in the course of the previous orbit, together with Lot-Ionan and the diamond.

"We've had five cycles free of Tion's monsters and now they come marching through Girdlegard. That's what the people are saying." Ortger accompanied him. "The common people have no faith in their professed peaceful intentions. I'm glad the ubariu will be leaving again.

Otherwise I'm afraid there'd be incidents. Too many people have suffered at orc hands."

The generals entered the castle courtyard; undergroundlings and ubariu presented a strange picture marching side by side. By Girdlegard standards it was a case of sworn enemies becoming brothers; it seemed unnatural.

Flagur and Sirka stepped out from an adjacent building to welcome them; Tungdil was with them.

Ortger said nothing, but his face showed what he thought. He was disturbed to see Tungdil showing interest in these mixtures of dwarf and orc. Worse still, rumor said he had even chosen one of them as his new partner.

"Come, let us go into the armory." He strode off, followed by Mallen.

"You are the host. Aren't you going to greet them?"

"I don't want them to feel welcome, Prince Mallen. One hundred thousand mouths won't be easy to feed; the sooner they go, the better. We will hold the leave-taking ceremony, that is all."

They entered the chamber where Ireheart, Goda, Lot-Ionan, Rodario, the fourthling queen Bylanta, Ginsgar Unforce, Esdalân and the ambassadors were gathered round a table.

The other kings and queens had not thought it necessary to come to Pendleburg in person. Everything had been said and they had all accepted the decision of the magus. The diamond was to leave Girdlegard. The royal ambassadors were there out of courtesy, because Mallen had requested this final session.

Soon Tungdil, Flagur and Sirka returned to the conference room.

Ortger got up. "Welcome to Pendleburg. We are here to discuss recent events and to honor the heroes." He sketched a bow in the direction of Flagur and Sirka. "Accept my thanks, Flagur, for your part in protecting Girdlegard; I know that you will continue to work for our benefit in your own land." He turned to Tungdil and the magus. "And all honor to those who will be crossing the border and embarking on the rigors of a journey into the unknown. And now, Prince Mallen, the floor is yours."

The Idoslane prince rose. "I want to show our appreciation." He addressed them with all due form. "A small ceremony to honor your departure. Of course it bears no relation to the celebrations we shall hold on your return." He smiled at Tungdil. "May Vraccas guide your steps and protect you."

One by one the ambassadors conveyed their sovereigns' messages of goodwill, promising praise, recognition and lasting gratitude on their return.

Outwardly noncommittal, Tungdil listened and smiled. But inside he was simmering like boiling mountain blood. So the heroes were of no importance to the rulers; having risked life and limb they were to be greeted by substitutes offering formulaic phrases.

Bylanta stood up and fixed her brown eyes on Tungdil. On the diminutive side, she had the classic stature of a fourthling woman dwarf; compared to Sirka she seemed as small as a gnome. Her long blond hair hung forward over her shoulder in a braid, her light chain mail tunic was decorated extravagantly with jewels and on her head she wore a skillfully worked crown sparkling with diamonds.

"I am Balynta Slimfinger of the Silver Beard clan, queen over the fourthlings and sovereign in the Brown Range of Mountains." Her voice was steady, clear and confident. "I shall accompany your procession to the gates of Silverfast. It will be an honor, Tungdil Goldhand, to ride with you. I offer you my friendship just as you gave your own to Gandogar." She sat down.

Ginsgar Unforce got to his feet. No dwarf could be of more impressive appearance; not even Glaïmbar, king of the fifthlings, came close. His fine red beard, broad shoulders, resolute attitude and the determination in his eyes, all made of him a rare figure of a dwarf.

"I salute you, Tungdil Goldhand. I am Ginsgar Unforce of the Nail Smith clan of Borengar's firstlings. As high king I bring you the greetings of the dwarf folks," he said in a sonorous bass. "May you return safe and sound from the Outer Lands . . ."

Bylanta turned her head. "How is it that here we apparently have a new high king, when he has not been chosen by myself or my clans? I have not heard of an assembly being called?" she said with surprise in her tone. "I thought a high king would be high king of all the dwarf folks, and not just of some?"

"There was an assembly *and* an election," replied Ginsgar, unmoved. "The warriors following me to Âlandur to punish the elves for their treachery appointed me their high king. And there were dwarves from your clans, Bylanta, among them. So accordingly it is right that I be high king."

This came as news to Mallen and Ortger and the ambassadors. Lot-Ionan threw Tungdil a knowing look. Exactly what he and Rodario had feared now seemed to have happened: a war hero had declared himself ruler.

Esdalân regarded Ginsgar with menace. "What have you done to Âlandur, dwarf? The atár were your enemies, not my people. Not the green groves and the beautiful buildings. Not the ground on which you marched."

"We were hunting down the atár and we found them everywhere. They ambushed us from the protection of their temples and attacked us from the shelter of the woods and villages." Ginsgar met and held the elf's accusatory gaze. "And so we laid waste the land to destroy any cover."

"And the cradles of new-born infants? You thought them potential hiding-places?" Esdalân exclaimed furiously.

"We slew the atár offspring. This must have been in your interest too, elf. They would only have created new perdition." Ginsgar laid his hand on his war hammer. "When we have done with cleaning up Âlandur the elves may return. Trees can regrow. So can your people."

"How many innocent victims have you murdered?"

"We murdered none. We executed those who deserved death," came Ginsgar's swift retort. "You should be grateful. On your own you would never have defeated the atár."

Esdalân leaped up, knocking his chair over with a loud crash. "Support I would have welcomed, but what you have done, Ginsgar Unforce, was senseless slaughter! You are no better than orcs!" Leaning on the table in front of him, he whispered in despair, "Do you know how many of my people are still alive?"

In a bored voice the dwarf answered, "I should think about a hundred."

"Thirty-seven," shouted Esdalân. "Thirty-seven! And of those, ten are women and nine are children."

Ginsgar's red eyebrows crunched together. "We were thorough. So now at least you present no threat to Girdlegard."

"It was blind vengeance. No more, no less." The elf straightened with a jerk, tears streaming down his harmonious features, now a mask of hatred. He pointed at Ginsgar and continued in his own language until he turned and stalked out of the hall without looking right or left.

"By Palandiell," whispered Lot-Ionan. Rodario grew pale as a white-washed wall. "And we did nothing to stop them." He put his hand on his belt where the diamond hung in a leather purse. "We let it happen."

"What else could we have done?" exclaimed Ortger. "It is a crying shame, of course, but tell me what choice we had?"

Tungdil could not grasp it, either. What Ginsgar had done was unforgiveable. It was living proof of the cruelty of this self-appointed high king. "We are all guilty. Our joint armies should have set out from Toboribor to Âlandur with all dispatch to prevent this wholesale slaughter." He bestowed a withering glance on Ginsgar. "Do you know what you have done? You have thrown away our best opportunity of ever winning the elves' gratitude. Instead of that you have ensured their renewed enmity."

"I'm really scared." Ginsgar smiled and gave himself a little shake. "Thirty-seven pointy-ears are a true army to put the wind up the dwarf folks."

Bylanta spat at his feet. "You are as nothing, Ginsgar Unforce. I shall have you impeached before all the assembled clans of the five dwarf folks, so that you may be properly punished. I pray to Vracrass that the elves may one day become reconciled to us in some future orbit. Whether or not this involves your death."

"Now there's a far better candidate for the throne," Rodario murmured to Tungdil. "How about a high queen for a change? She has charisma, don't you think?"

Ginsgar regarded the blob of spittle by his boot. "Spit out your poison, Bylanta. It won't kill me. I was chosen by all of the clans. That's what counts. It doesn't matter where or how." He addressed the conference. "We're done here. I've told you my wishes and I'm off. Perhaps I should go back to Âlandur and check under all the bushes. Thoroughness is one of our best qualities." He nodded, shouldered his war hammer and left the hall with his characteristic rolling gait.

Now Tungdil had his certainty: in this land, where dwarves such as Ginsgar ruled in hatred, he did not wish to stay.

He took hold of Sirka's hand and pressed it firmly.

XIX

Girdlegard,
Kingdom of Urgon,
Pendleburg,
Early Autumn, 6241st Solar Cycle

Resounding hammer blows and complaining screams of metal on anvil could be heard all over the cloud-hung stronghold. Squadrons of gray rain clouds were driving across the land and not stopping at the castle walls. The cloud contents poured onto the stones as if wanting to wash out all the mortar and bring down the defenses.

Tungdil, in breeches, boots and leather apron, was spending most of his time in the forge turning the unslayable's sword into a new weapon. With all his strength he was beating out the last trace of evil. He had written off the possibility of finding Keenfire, just as he had dismissed the possibility of a future in Girdlegard. The dwarf folks he had discarded from his mind as well.

There was nothing to keep him here. Twice he had averted the impending downfall and destruction of Girdlegard, and this was his third and last mission. After that the dwarves could see how they coped without him. No matter what he did and how many lives were lost along the way, reason would not prevail. Not here and not with any of the peoples of Girdlegard.

Anger strengthened his arm and sent his hammer blows off true. He interrupted his labors to wipe the sweat from his remaining eye; he no longer wore a bandage over the left where a simple white patch now covered the empty socket.

He brandished the fruits of his toil toward the entrance. As yet he was not sure what was emerging from his handiwork. It was neither ax nor sword, nor club. He left it up to the fire, the hammer and the skill of his hands to form something completely new without a specific design.

The metal must be an alloy he had not met before. He could hear as much from the sound it made; it sang in response to his forging. It had incredible stability, long refusing to give up its original shape to take on another. It was an age since he had been given such a challenge at the anvil.

Hasty footsteps came splashing through puddles and over the wet flagstones. Sirka stumbled in at the threshold. Her sight was not as good as his own in this smoky twilight. "Tungdil?"

He tapped the vice with his hammer to indicate where he stood. "Over here. By the furnace."

"We won't be able to leave yet," she said, feeling her way. "This rain has turned Urgon's mountain streams to raging torrents. The king's scouts report some of the roads have been washed away." She had located him now and when she kissed him rainwater dripped from her nose down onto his. "We won't be leaving for another seven orbits."

Tungdil nodded. Ortger would have to feed the hundred thousand for longer than he had bargained; provisions would have to be brought in from all over the kingdom. It was an enormous task. Gauragar and Idoslane were

helping out with grain supplies. "I'm not ready, either."
He showed her what he had done so far.

"Strange," she said. "I've never seen a weapon like
that."

"It will be worthy of a hero like myself," he said, mock-
ingly. "What are Goda and Ireheart up to?"

"Now that they are committed to each other they are
never apart," grinned Sirka. "Dwarves, rain, a warm bed—
you can work it out, can't you? No better excuse than
the weather for staying in. The master and his apprentice
will be in training, I presume."

"Good, so no one will notice that I've been in the forge
all this time."

Sirka watched the flames. "I shan't ever really understand the fascination with forging like this." She wiped
her hand across her brow to remove the sweat now blended
with raindrops. "I wonder what you'll think of the way
we make our metal goods."

Tungdil put the unfinished weapon back in the fire and
laid his hammer down on the anvil before taking the dwarf-
woman in his arms. She was wearing only a thin leather
garment and her bodice lacing allowed him a good view
of her brown skin. He stroked her shorn head tenderly
and kissed her slowly as desire flamed up within him.

He threw the hammer at the door to close it. The catch
slipped down into place. She grinned and opened the
fastenings of his leather apron.

They made love for a long time on a blanket spread
on the floor next to the furnace. Tungdil could never get
enough of Sirka. He loved to stroke her dark skin and to
feel the heat of her inner fire in the course of their love-

play increasing until the sweat poured off her. The under-groundling woman had once spoken of belonging to a passionate folk. This did not merely apply to fighting.

Afterwards they rested by the fire, watching the flickering tongues of flame.

"It will be hard for you to leave your kinsfolk, Tungdil."

"I have no kinsfolk," he countered. "I have been thinking a lot and have arrived at the conclusion that my heart only belongs to one other." He kissed her throat. "That's you. Otherwise, I'm like . . ." He had nearly betrayed his secret and spoken the name of the young älf. ". . . otherwise there's no one. Do I go to the dwarves who are fighting under Ginsgar Unforce, making old enemies into new ones? Or do I go the humans? I wouldn't feel at home with the elves, either."

"I'll give you a new home for as long as you want. It'll be up to you. You can always go away again, Tungdil. I know how you are—restless. You did warn me." Sirka smiled and slipped her clothes on. Tungdil admired her sinewy body; it was tough and flexible enough for combat or for this kind of gymnastics. "And I in my turn warned you. There's no *forever* for us. No *eternally yours*. Not usually, anyway."

"Your eternity, Sirka, would only be one or two cycles for me," he said thoughtfully. "I'm likely to live up to ten times longer than you."

She threaded the laces back through the leather, fastening her bodice tight and depriving him of the last glimpse of her naked flesh. "That's weird. If we have children you could outlive nine generations!"

When he heard the word children he gave a start. Then

he remembered that undergroundlings brought up their offspring quite differently from the traditions of his own kind. He relaxed again. If he were tempted to roam again he would not have to worry about the care of his own children. He was rather taken by the thought of leaving descendants in the land of the undergroundlings: a line of offspring that would live longer than all their neighbours.

He got to his feet and started to dress. "Yes, it's a weird thought," he said, echoing her words. He kissed her again on the nape of her neck. "I can't tell you how I'm looking forward to all the new things."

"Yes, as soon as we have restored the artifact," she agreed, opening the door to let dull light into the workshop. It was still raining. "Afterwards it will all be very exciting," she promised enticingly. "Not just because of me." Then she hurried out and ran through the cloudburst to her quarters.

Tungdil's mood had improved and his fury had gone. "Oh, shit!" He had forgotten to take the metal out of the fire. If it had gone molten he would have wasted all his efforts.

Swiftly he pulled it out with tongs, drawing it carefully from its burial place in the red-hot coals. Sparks whizzed and flew through the air until they cooled and fell to the ground as ash.

The metal was now as soft as sun-warmed wax. It shone golden yellow like honey and there were long threads that cooled in the air and turned gray.

"So, that's what you want to look like?" he said to his new weapon, dousing it in a tub of water. The liquid bubbled and boiled and quickly reduced to half its volume while the metal cooled. Tungdil had never seen such an effect.

He took the weapon out and turned it from side to side in wonder: it was black as the night and longer than the arm of a full-grown man. It was thicker on one side and had long drawn-out needle-thin points so that it looked like fish bones or a comb. On the other side it slimmed down like a blade and its center of gravity lay high up on the haft, which gave each swipe added momentum without detracting from its ease of wielding.

"Right, so let's give you your final form, shall we?" Tungdil pushed it into the furnace, heating it through once more. He worked to finesse the weapon until evening, giving it a rounded handle that he could clasp in both hands. It seemed to him that the metal had surrendered its resistance to him now.

Night had long fallen and still he sat at work, sharpening the blade with a small grindstone. Bright sparks flew off in a sizzling arc, bouncing against the door. Tungdil tested the edge by taking a lump of coal and stroking the metal across it gently without applying any pressure. It sliced through the black stone as easily as if it had been air. He was satisfied for now.

Tired and hungry he stomped across the site through the rain, his new weapon at his side. He needed food and drink.

"Is it too late to bring you greetings from the towns of the freelings?"

Tungdil stopped short and raised his weapon. A dwarf stood by the smithy in the pouring rain. His cape and hood were soaked and he must have been waiting by the window a long while. For a messenger this behavior was unusual. "Show me your face!"

The dwarf approached, pulling back his hood. "I thought you would recognize my voice."

Tungdil found himself face to face with Bramdal Masterstroke. "You again?" Suspicion made him keep the blade raised diagonally before him. "What is it you want?"

"I am to bring greetings from King Gordislan and the other town rulers and to wish you well for the journey to the Outer Lands." Bramdal pointed to a roof overhang. "Can we go somewhere dry?"

Tungdil did not believe the one-time executioner. "You've waited all this time outside the forge watching me and you grab me out here in the rain, just to say bon voyage?" Tungdil did not move. The rain did not bother him. "You'll allow that's a trifle odd?"

"Nobody must know I'm speaking to you. My mission isn't over when I've given you the good wishes."

"Have you got anything to back your story up, Bramdal?"

Carefully Bramdal put a hand under his cape and pulled out a roll of leather. Then he handed Tungdil a signet ring. "This authenticates what I'm about to tell you. And this is Gordislan's signet ring." Water dripped from his yellow beard. "Come on, can we go inside?"

Tungdil indicated the forge door with the tip of his weapon. In its dark warmth they refrained from lighting a lamp. Tungdil read the missive by the glow from the furnace and examined the ring minutely. Bramdal was in truth a trusted adviser to the king of Trovegold. "Perhaps you were always more than an executioner?"

Bramdal nodded. "Gemmil and others before him used to send me out on missions to observe the humans and report what they said about the dwarves. We were waiting for the right moment for the towns to start trading with them." He installed himself on the anvil, drawing his cape off and hanging it up to dry. "We knew the dwarves would resent it and that we would have to think carefully about this move. Your visit helped. But the future isn't going to be easy."

"It seems to me that recently the free towns have chosen to align themselves with the humans."

"Your impression is correct. We are very concerned about developments up in the mountains. I heard the exchange between Ginsgar and Balyndis. What Ginsgar thinks of the towns is an open secret. That's the reason we'll soon be making open advances to the humans. The death of Gandogar was the last straw."

"You're here to tell me that?"

Bramdal nodded slowly. "Yes. The town kings think you are a sensible smith-child and they're placing their hopes on you. They expect you will be the facilitator between the dwarf folks in the coming dispute about the high kingship. There is no hero greater than yourself, so they want you to be the first to learn their plans. It's pretty certain that the dwarf folks won't understand our motives."

"The freelings are afraid of their own kinsmen? And so they are looking to the humans for allies? Is that how far it's come?"

"If Ginsgar is the new high king, yes." Bramdal picked up his cape and reversed it to dry the other side. "We heard Ginsgar wants to annex the free towns and get his hands on their wealth."

"And you want to increase trade with the humans so they'll come to your aid if you're in trouble. I can see what you're driving at. But why must no one know we're talking?"

"Gordislan is afraid Ginsgar already has a plan up his sleeve and will implement it at once if he hears the towns are preparing for an attack. We'd have no time to arrange an alliance with the humans."

Tungdil fed the furnace, stirring the glowing coals and using the bellows to encourage the flames. There was a crackling response and the temperature started to rise. "Tell the monarchs that I'm honored by their trust. But I don't intend to come back to Girdlegard any time soon." Tungdil saw the fire's glow reflected in Bramdal's pale brown eyes. "And that's a secret, too. The free kings must know I won't be there for them if there is a clash. They will have to sort things out by themselves."

"You're going to abandon your responsibilities?" Bramdal was astonished.

"I have no more responsibilities here. It is enough. I have saved Girdlegard twice and together with my friends I'm about to do it for a third time. Others must take over. I am for distant horizons."

The executioner returned his gaze. "How would you feel if you came back and saw war had broken out? War amongst the children of the Smith? That the gates were broken and hordes of monsters had overrun Girdlegard?"

He strode nearer. "And knowing you could have prevented it?"

Tungdil smiled, unmoved by his words. "I would say that others had failed to think and act. I have been Girdlegard's protector for so long now and I am not the only dwarf with a head on his shoulders. Tell the kings that they may rely on Bylanta's wisdom. They should appeal to her for support."

"But your word is weightier with the clans."

"I am a thirdling, Bramdal, and have never sought to conceal my lineage. Ginsgar would use that to undermine my reputation." He went to the door and stepped across the threshold. "Give Gordislan my message. I shall not change my mind." He nodded goodbye. "So it was never just coincidence that we kept meeting?"

"Nothing in life is pure coincidence, Tungdil Goldhand." Bramdal moved closer to the fire. "I shall take them your message. And I shall pray to Vraccas that he will change your mind."

"You're welcome to try. It's not going to work." Tungdil closed the door behind him and marched through the puddles to cross the yard. He knew this exchange was going to trouble him but he was determined to leave Girdlegard to its fate. Deep in thought he entered the room where his meal had been waiting for him. He still avoided beer and wine and took only water.

"There he is, our scholar!" Ireheart entered, for a change not wearing his mail shirt but only the leather undertunic. And it had not been properly fastened. It looked as if he had put it on in a hurry. Tungdil showed him the weapon he had been forging. "So is that the unslayable's sword?"

Wordlessly chewing his food, Tungdil pushed the blade over to his friend, handle first.

"It's sharp. I've never seen anything like it. What are you calling it?"

Tungdil shrugged his shoulders.

The warrior lifted it up, weighing it in his hands, attempted a few swipes and looked round for something to try it out on. A footstool fell victim to the blade.

The cutting edge had sliced through the finger-thick wood without a splinter.

"By Vraccas!" Ireheart laid the blade on the table. "Extraordinary. Light as a dagger, cuts like the sharpest of swords and behaves like an ax." He contemplated his own hand and saw a drop of blood on the ball of his thumb. "And it's thirsty for my blood," he laughed. "There are sharp metal bits still to be filed off."

Tungdil's brow furrowed. He knew it had been smooth as marble to hold just now. That was why rough-textured leather was used to wrap the grip. He took a deep breath. "I'll have to give it another going-over."

"Why not Bloodthirster?" Ireheart joked. "It would be a good name." He took some of the water and grabbed a large slice of ham.

"What particular exercise are you and Goda working on at the moment?" Tungdil liked the name Ireheart had suggested. "Wrestling moves?"

Boïndil felt himself go red. "Very observant, scholar."

"You're practicing enough to make the walls shake." Behind them they heard the scornful voice of Rodario, who was joining them at table.

"I shan't be taking instruction from you," said the twin, sinking his teeth into the ham. "You are a master of a different sort of wrestling."

"There hasn't been any wrestling with anyone for some time, Master Hot Blood." Rodario sat down at his side. "I'm staying true to my Tassia."

"Of course you are." Ireheart waved aside the protest. "If that's the truth then this piece of meat will fly." He picked it up and let go. It dropped straight onto the table. "Not looking good, sir actor."

Tungdil laughed and Rodario joined in. "I'm happy for you, Ireheart," he said. "A lady at last to soften your warrior soul and to harden other parts."

Boïndil grinned broadly. "It's all ended well. I would never have thought it possible."

"There can't only be bad things in life, otherwise the world would cease," said Tungdil. "Enjoy what you have."

"They're doing that all the time," said Rodario, poking fun again. His well-meant mockery revealed the friends' joy at the young love of these two dwarves.

"We're wrestling. That's all. We want to keep fit for the adventures that await us in the Outer Lands. I shall be going with you," Ireheart told Tungdil. "This adventure will be my greatest yet."

Rodario clapped. "Before either of you asks: I too would deem it an honor to accompany you. In those far-off lands there are scenes and stories with which I shall delight my valued audiences."

"You too?" Ireheart exclaimed. "Vraccas help us! He'll talk us to death. Or make something explode at the wrong time."

"Huh, very funny."

"Word gets round. Like what you did in the belly of the machine. Could all have been done differently, you know."

"Yes, mock away, you destroyer of bedsteads. But I tell you I shall be of supreme use on the trip." He stood up, pretending to be offended. "Just so's you know: Ortger has chosen a different route. The roads are narrower but they're passable. We can leave in the morning, Lot-Ionan says. Chop chop, off to bed now, my heroes. And no more wrestling, Ireheart. Not tonight. Or at least pull the bed away from the wall." Rodario disappeared with a grin on his face.

Tungdil was pleased. The delay had been long enough to finish making the weapon. Excellent.

"If it's true what the Emperor of Boasters and Big Mouths has just said," Ireheart said, "I'll get some rest." He laid his hand on Tungdil's shoulder "Are you sure you want to leave Girdlegard forever?" he asked, his voice earnest now.

"Yes, Ireheart. I don't want to see them slip into the next catastrophe, and this time one they've made for themselves."

"You mean Ginsgar's work?"

"What else? In the worst case it'll mean dispute amongst the dwarf folks. Some will join Ginsgar the Self-Appointed and the others will insist on their traditions, call an assembly and choose a different high king." He took a drink of water and thought of what Bramdal had said. "Where will it end, Boïndil? Can you tell me?"

Ireheart lowered his head. "Ginsgar asked me to take command of his bodyguard," he admitted quietly. "I told him I'd think about it."

"That you'd think about it?" Tungdil was about to reproach his friend but stopped. "Yes, you are right. You must work it out for yourself. I have no right to tell you what you should do. I'm leaving here."

Ireheart sat down again. "It's not easy, Scholar. Some of Ginsgar's views are sensible but on the other hand he is a warmonger. He will prove a high king devoid of any mercy." Ireheart ran a hand over his short black plait.

"Think on my words: the freelings and the thirdlings will be his new foes." Tungdil cut off a slice of cheese. "If you take command you'll be fighting all the time. I know it's what you love to do but shouldn't you be happier fighting orcs and monsters, not your own kind?" He put the food in his mouth and got up. "Think about that while you're deciding. Ginsgar Unforce will be going down in the chronicles as a notorious figure. Not as a good high king." He patted him on the shoulder. "Good night, Ireheart. Speak to Goda and make up your mind. You've time enough before you return to Girdlegard." He picked up his weapon and walked out past his friend.

On the way he ran his hands over the blade and tested the sharpness, but now it felt rough on his hands. He had not been careful enough and it had cut him—not deep but enough to draw blood.

"That name is the right one for you," he said to his weapon. "From now on you shall be known as *Bloodthirster*. You will drink the blood of many monsters, I promise. And you shall serve me well." He studied the red drops on the blade. "But you shall never taste dwarven blood. If you do, I shall shatter you into a thousand pieces."

A soft shimmer was visible down the length of the blade. It may have been a reflection of the lamplight but Tungdil chose to read it as acceptance. The pact had been made.

Girdlegard,
Fourthling Realm,
Brown Mountains, Fortress Silverfast,
Early Autumn, 6241st Solar Cycle

Bylanta held out her hand to Tungdil. "May Vraccas protect you from all the dangers of the Outer Lands and bring you safely back to us."

"He will indeed," he replied courteously as he shook the queen's slender hand. He was not about to let her know that he didn't intend to return.

They were standing beneath the four intact towers on the stronghold walls at Silverfast. This was where the acronta had long maintained the illusion of an enemy siege. There was no trace of their presence now. All you could see were piles of orc bones with the flesh chewed off them. The fourthlings had decided to leave them as a deterrent.

"I hope that Ginsgar Unforce may soon meet his death." He expressed his thoughts openly. "If not, there will be grim times ahead for the dwarves."

"Honestly spoken." Balyanta looked at him appraisingly. "Then let us be frank, Tungdil Goldhand: the dwarf folks need someone who can stand up to Ginsgar. Not easy after his victories in Âlandur. He has so many followers and much clandestine support in the dwarf realms."

"Glaïmbar . . ."

"No, it's you who are needed, I think. Balendilîn the Second is not strong enough anymore; with one arm he doesn't stand a chance. No one will listen to Malbalor because he's from the thirdlings and Ginsgar has spread poison about them."

"I'm a thirdling, too . . ."

Bylanta remained as resolute as toughened gold. "You are a hero, Tungdil. Nobody doubts you. You have done great deeds. And Glaïmbar makes no secret of his admiration of Ginsgar, so I can't rely on him." She smiled. "That leaves Xamtys and myself. Two dwarf queens against unreason a hundred times stronger than we are. We could use a hero at our side." She pressed his hand and laid her other hand on his arm. "So come back quickly, Tungdil."

He bowed to her and mounted his pony to catch up with the head of the march. Tungdil wished he had been spared her softly spoken words; they had touched him more than he wanted. They went on working where Bramdal's from the evening before had left off. Bylanta had appealed to his sense of responsibility, calling on him to accept the duties in Girdlegard that could be expected of a dwarf of his heroic stature.

"Damn," he cursed out loud and dug his heels so fiercely into his pony's sides that the animal gave a startled leap, galloping off as if a pack of wolves were at their heels. The heavy scent of the ubariu and their steeds had already spooked it.

"Someone's in a hurry to see new lands," Rodario commented as Tungdil rushed up to join his friends. He wrapped the cape Ortger had given him tighter round himself. "My goodness, it was cold enough in Urgon's mountains, but here it feels like winter."

Flagur sat up tall in the saddle and gave the trumpeter a sign. The bugle call echoed back from the mountainside and the army set off at once, with the stamp of nailed boots, the sounds of the horses, the bumping and jangling of the baggage train.

"They may fight monsters, but . . ." said Ireheart, turning back to look at the long column "but they're enough to put the wind up anyone." When he caught Tungdil's and Sirka's disapproving looks he quickly added, "But I know they're all right, of course."

Goda rolled her eyes. She insisted on riding behind him and to one side, out of respect, as in her view he was still her weapons master, whatever love she bore him and whatever they now shared. She said, "You are hopeless."

"That's right, you lot. Have a go at me. I might as well be a snout-faced orc." He rode off, grumbling. "I do try. Vraccas and Ubar are my witnesses."

Rodario laughed. "Progress indeed. He actually got the name of the foreigners' god right!"

"But it took second place to Vraccas, of course. That'll never change."

"I'm off to check on my troops. See you later!" Sirka rode back to join the undergroundling ranks.

Tungdil followed her with his eyes then looked ahead. The tension was mounting. Soon he would be seeing things no dwarf had seen before.

Every twist in the mountain roads made him hope for some revelation but it was several orbits before they had left the tortuous chasms behind.

By now he was riding out to reconnoiter with the ubariu scouts, so keen was he to catch a first glance of Sirka's land.

He was so obsessed by the need to explore that he

forgot everything else. He only wanted to get out of Girdlegard, away from a responsibility he now totally rejected.

They travelled through the maze of rocks and somber gorges, along giddying precipices, with dank fog swirling round them so that each step was a deadly risk.

The route for their return would have to be located anew, because the mountains refused to accept any guiding marks they tried to set, whether a painted or a chiseled sign. Some of the scouts claimed the rock walls even moved.

Tungdil caught himself wondering about turning back, but without a real reason. It was not that he was afraid. But there was something round him and the scouts that made him nervous. Impatience was getting the better of him. It demanded that he either arrive in Letéfora immediately or else that they return to Girdlegard. If he turned round he could clearly see the path inviting him. Turning forward again, there was only fog and vague outlines of cloud and rocks. He must pull himself together.

From time to time the scouts pointed out dark side paths from where perhaps the monsters might have emerged to march off to the pass and toward Silverfast. Probably one of these paths led to the Black Abyss.

Tungdil sensed that he would have got hopelessly lost without their guidance. So it was with enormous relief that after fifteen orbits he noticed the landscape gradually changing.

The mountains became hills and grew broader and greener while bare rock was replaced by verdant slopes studded with windswept trees. A final twist in their road revealed a new world.

They were standing on a plateau, maybe two miles high, and the view took Tungdil's breath away.

A broad plain spread at their feet and in the center lay a city of gigantic size. He had never seen so many buildings in one place. It was far bigger than any of the human cities in Girdlegard and was threaded through with wide straight streets bustling with activity; concentric rings of thick walls provided defensive ramparts. The highest buildings were in the middle; round, oval, or rectangular. The tallest must have been at least three hundred paces high. You could see the birds circling overhead and diving in great flocks down into the artificial canyons.

"How is that possible?" Tungdil was amazed. "Who lives there? Giants?"

A scout pointed out particular areas in the cityscape. "That is Letèfora directly in front of us. There are some humans there, a few of my own kin, but mostly ubariu and a handful of acronta. All in all I'd say there were about two hundred thousand." His hand was raised toward the west where, close to the horizon, they could see another city. "That one is the largest city this side of the ocean. It's called Hòphoca and it offers shelter to ten times a hundred thousand." He turned to the east. "Over there is the region of the monsters. They've taken over the ruins of old settlements where humans used to live; they were abandoned when Letèfora was built. The monsters defend the area stubbornly. We let them live there because the acronta enjoy hunting them."

Tungdil surveyed the harvested fields, roads and streets

running between the cities. There did not appear to be any villages to speak of, but a few extensive farmsteads here and there. Small forest areas ensured a green panorama.

"Where is the acronta army?" asked one of the guides.

"I don't know. Perhaps they're taking the mountain route and looking out for more monsters."

In the far distance Tungdil could make out a silvery shimmer. That must be the sea. Sirka had told him about it: an endless expanse of water with storm winds and waves high enough to make ships and whole islands disappear without trace.

"Our first destination is Letèfora," said the ubari. "From there the road leads straight through monster territory toward the Black Abyss."

"Why not use the paths you showed me back there? If we march up with all these troops the monsters might be alerted to the fact the artifact is not working."

The ubari shook his head and patted the neck of his mount. "The paths are dangerous. You can easily get lost— worse than the roads we took—and then you won't ever find the way out. The ubariu once lost a complete army. So did we. The ones who survived somehow were lucky enough to find their way back with tales of rocks that came alive, evil vapors and the most ghastly creatures that lay in wait for them. That's why we took the other route. Nobody but the acronta dare go that way." He grinned. "The monsters whose land we'll go through are much too cowardly to stand up to us. *Nobody* challenges an army of one hundred thousand." He dismounted. "We'll wait here." He sent two of his men back to inform Flagur and to guide them through the labyrinth.

"Where is the hidden road to Girdlegard?" Tungdil asked, sitting down on the ground, while the scout started laying a fire. He could not take his eyes off the city. He had noticed high masts with ropes spanned between them carrying cages above the streets. The wind, he fancied, was bringing him new sounds and smells.

"You'd have to go back half a star course toward the west, just short of the monsters' land. The entrance is easy to miss in spite of the bastion we and the ubariu have erected. We don't want it looking too obvious, otherwise there'd be even more of the beasts turning up."

Tungdil was as excited as a small child, looking forward to the orbits he would be spending here with Sirka. Not for a moment did he regret having turned his back on Girdlegard. Forever, it seemed.

"What are those cages?" he asked.

The scout blew into the fire again to bring the flames to life. Blue and green flickered up. "Must be the wood," he surmised, seeing the dwarf's surprise. "I've seen yellow and red fire too." Then he nodded over at the masts. "That's how we get around. We've got these platforms in Letèfora and the transport's really easy going in straight lines. Saves a lot of time you'd waste going on foot. specially when the roads are crowded. You can get about fifty humans in one of those cages—less if it's us, of course. And acronta prefer to walk."

Tungdil had spotted a bridge of titanic proportions running directly to Letèfora from the mountains in the southwest. "That connects with the mines, does it?"

The scout grinned. "Only a dwarf would ask about mines. No, it's a water channel supplying the city. There are distribution points in the city itself taking the water in pipes to the various districts."

"And how . . . ?"

The ubari lifted a hand. "Tungdil, let me see to my mount. Then we can talk some more. But I'm sure Flagur and Sirka will want to explain the delights of Letèfora to you." He stood up to see to the wants of his befún.

Tungdil went over to his pony, lifted off its saddle and led it to where it could graze. Then he took out paper, inkwell and a quill pen and began to make a drawing of the strange town.

The Outer Lands,
City of Letèfora,
Early Autumn, 6241st Solar Cycle

Tungdil was only to have this one short fascinating insight into life in Letèfora for now.

Flagur took him and his friends into town to introduce him to the ruler, who watched over the fate of his subjects from his residence in the most impressive of the buildings.

As the group rode along the broad street the gates were opened for them promptly when the sentries recognized Flagur's standard.

The inhabitants bowed, clapped spontaneously or called out. Not understanding the words, Tungdil nevertheless assumed they were being congratulated and welcomed.

The exterior walls of the local houses were covered with a clay layer bearing ornate decorations executed by skillful artisans. Some of the houses were colorfully painted while others were duller in hue but striking because of the use of tiles and ceramic ware; there seemed to be a liking for rounded archways and window frames.

Buildings here were on a par with the standard set by his own kin, but differed from the type of houses favored by humans. Oval and round shapes were popular: many took the form of globes set half in the earth, a style not seen in Girdlegard.

Details were picked out in colored glass; mosaics showed ornamental shapes or hunting and battle scenes. On some facades there were candid depictions of the physical act of union, such as would have made Girdlegarders blush.

"Very nice indeed," Rodario commented, trying to get a better view.

"So you still have something to learn, Fabuloso?" Ireheart laughed. He pretended not to mind this civic lack of prudishness, but he avoided looking too closely. It was not fitting.

"Of course. There are always new ideas." Rodario smiled in greeting at some of the women passing by and when they inclined their heads in response he had a generous view into their décolleté. "It's even better to learn from a mistress of the art, of course." He smiled at the warrior. "You know what I mean, don't you? You favor a swift stroke, I believe."

"Keep your smutty ideas well away from my relationship," Ireheart warned him without a trace of humor. "I won't have you dragging things down to your level." His fists were clenched.

"We'll discuss it another time, then," Rodario conceded

defeat, but winked at a passing maiden, who immediately averted her eyes.

They approached a square building that tapered off toward the top with wide staircases on each side. Above, the construction had a flattened oval shape which supported four towers.

"I'm used to great buildings, Scholar," said Ireheart, "but this is more impressive than anything I've ever seen." His eyes wandered over the stone walls. "I can't decide whether this used to be a mountain or whether they've formed it out of enormous blocks of stone. There are no joins to be seen."

They rode into a hall which was a good hundred paces square. Servants hurried over, humans and ubariu, to take care of the animals, while an undergroundling in a light blue silken dress appeared and bowed before them. Her dark brown hair was long and wavy and her skin nearly black; around her waist she wore a decorative bejeweled chain, fashioned from some unfamiliar metal.

Tungdil and Goda were astonished but tactful, while Ireheart voiced his surprise without inhibition. "By Vraccas, has she burned herself?" he asked, with much sympathy and no volume control.

Flagur laughed outright and Sirka grinned. "No, Boïndil. She will have had black skin from birth. Our people come in all kinds of different colors. Not like you."

He made a face. "What on earth for? So their enemies can't see them in the tunnels, perhaps?"

"I can't tell you what Ubar intended. It's just the way it is." Sirka answered.

"You are being rude," Goda mouthed to her mentor. "Don't stare."

"Jolly good thing they don't understand our language," said Rodario. "Otherwise you'd have to be apologizing all the time."

"Why? Just because I'm curious?" Ireheart shouldered his crow's beak. "It's difficult to imagine a dwarf wearing that pale blue. Or a deep red."

"That's not what I meant when I said different colors." Sirka looked to Tungdil for help.

"So what colors did you mean?"

"Wait and see." Flagur put an end to the conversation. "They're expecting us." He exchanged a few words with the undergroundling, then they followed her.

The party strode through rectangular galleries five paces high, climbed steps to a floor where the corridors were semicircular, then moved on to the next level where the walls and ceilings of the walkways had a lozenge shape. Tungdil had to ask Sirka about this.

"The building depicts our belief system, which encompasses underworlds and overworlds. Each of these worlds has a different symbol. We climb up through each of the worlds up to where the ruler of the city is; he was chosen by Ubar and is his representative."

"So is he a god as well?"

"He is the voice and the hand of Ubar. To ignore or challenge what he says would invite punishment from the hand of the god."

The undergroundling in the blue silk approached a gate that was five paces by three, fashioned out of polished silver and guarded by two heavily armed acronta.

THE REVENGE OF THE DWARVES 709

Tungdil, Rodario and Ireheart immediately thought of Djerûn.

Round the gate was a garland of chiseled runes, and paintings of warriors and fabulous beasts. Tungdil assumed they must be the gods of the upper and lower worlds.

Above them all, larger than life, was the picture of a being that he knew well: broad jaws with rows of protruding needle-sharp incisors and an oversize bony head a bit like a human skull, and covered with a thin layer of unhealthy-looking skin with veins painted in yellow. Instead of a nose there were three large holes.

"*Djerûn! By . . . the gods*" stammered Tungdil quietly.

Lot-Ionan took the diamond out of the pouch on his belt but even he could not take his eyes off the portrait. "What sort of creature did Andôkai have at her side?"

"We're there now," said Flagur, taking a deep breath. "Are you ready to meet the ruler of Letèfora?" He pointed to the picture. "To your eyes he may look like a monster but don't forget he is the image of our god Ubar. Show respect." He nodded to the undergroundling and she gave a signal to the acronta guards.

The sentries sprang to life, took hold of the gate's iron handles placed two paces above floor level, and flung wide the double doors.

Light streamed through the tall room; countless windows, each as high and wide as one of the tall armed guards, permitted the ruler a view over the eastern part of Letèfora in the early morning sunshine.

The chamber walls bore enchanting painted friezes, with inlays of gold, silver and other precious metals adding opulence.

On the regal stool on the throne dais there sat the mightiest acront they had ever seen. Now they knew why the corridors all needed such high ceilings; the monarch must have been a good four paces tall.

He wore neither armor nor helmet but instead a flowing garment of white fabric embroidered in gold and black. The similarity to the details of his portrait in the entrance hall was striking: according to Girdlegard standards a long way from a beauty.

His large violet-colored eyes appraised the visitors. With a deafening crack the wings on his back unfolded, blocking out some of the light. It had been with that very noise that Djerůn had so terrified the orcs and all other creatures of Tion.

The undergroundling in blue went to stand at the acront's side. She addressed Flagur.

"He says you are welcome here in Letèfora and he is delighted our mission has had a positive outcome." Sirka translated for Tungdil and his friends.

"So she can understand him?" Ireheart stroked his black beard, puzzled. "I thought it was supposed to be impossible."

"She is his consort. She needs to be able to understand him," Sirka answered simply. "In each generation there is one of us born able to understand an acront and she has been chosen to be his wife and to rule at his side."

Rodario bent over to the warrior. "How does it feel when you've just insulted the mightiest woman in the land, Master Foot in Mouth?"

"I did not insult her, Big Mouth," Ireheart insisted, quietly, but he was furious. Goda placed her hand restrain-ingly on his arm. This was not the moment for an argument.

The acront was speaking again and, as his spouse transmitted his words, Sirka translated for the others. "It seems the news of the army's destruction was false?"

"Who brought that news, Celestial Acront?" asked Flagur.

"It was a stranger, a woman who knew magic. She came to Letèfora some time ago and told us how badly things were going in Girdlegard. She said she had managed to get here with the last of her strength. *With* the diamond."

"She showed it to you, Celestial Acront?"

"She did. I gave her an escort to go to the Black Abyss."

"But that cannot be," exclaimed Lot-Ionan in agitation, opening his palm and displaying the true diamond. "You have been tricked by a forgery. *We* have the real stone!"

Rodario took a deep breath. "I have absolutely no idea what is happening but it's not going to be good."

Tungdil stepped forward. "Did she give her name, Celestial Acront?"

The acront's uncanny eyes focused on the dwarf and the creature spoke once more, its voice transfixing Tungdil; the import was transmitted to the consort and then translated by Sirka.

"Yes. She called herself Narmora. Narmora the Forgotten."

XX

The Outer Lands,
East of the City of Letèfora,
One Mile from the Black Abyss,
Early Autumn, 6241st Solar Cycle

The noise created by twenty thousand swift-moving befúns and the jangling of weapons and armor was enough to send the monsters crawling deeper into their hiding places in the ruins of the old houses. Not one dared emerge.

The acront of Letèfora was not relying purely on the combined strength of ubariu and undergroundlings. With the army he sent war machines as complex as any Furgas had devised. Four armored vehicles, each forty paces long, ten wide and ten high, rolled at the head of the march and four at its rear. Iron plating across wooden frames made them look like hulls of overturned ships.

Catapults in the bellies of the machines were ready to launch flurries of spears and arrows through the slits; placed high up, these afforded a superior range of around three hundred paces and could fire in three hundred and sixty degrees and so cover any part of the battlefield.

These colossi were driven by a simple but efficient system of wind sails. On the upper side there were large rotating towers and sails to catch the wind's power, which was transmitted by shafts to the driving axle, much as wind power drives a miller's wheel. The machines labored along on a series of small rollers and could match the speed of a furious dwarf. Not to be sneezed at.

"Impressive, aren't they?" Rodario said to Tungdil. He, too, had changed mounts and was now riding a befún; they were so much quicker than other animals. "Did you see how quickly the vehicles change direction? The rollers work individually, so they can turn on the spot and even go sideways."

At the roadside Tungdil noted the corpses of creatures shot in encounters with the first wave of troops. The beasts had learned not to attempt the same thing again. "With just one of those vehicles the orcs could have been cleared out of Girdlegard ages ago."

Rodario seemed to be studying the wagon but he was preoccupied with what the acront had told them. "It can't be Narmora. We saw what was left of her. The Star of Judgment burned away all that was älfish in her. She can't possibly have survived."

"Magic and love are powerful forces—and not always benign," Lot-Ionan chimed in, riding at Tungdil's side. "Don't forget it was Furgas who located the magic well-spring. In his madness he might have constructed a machine out of her remains, similar to those he made out of the unslayable's beasts."

Rodario gave himself a shake. "Narmora turning up again—a dead thing with a mechanical heart made of iron springs and cogs, and only moving because of magic in her veins? Furgas could never have done that to her. He loved her too much for that."

"He loved her so much *that* he could do it. He did not

want to be without her," contradicted Tungdil. "Let's hope we can stop her before she destroys the artifact."

"What terrible vengeance to wreak on Girdlegard. What would be the motive?" asked the magus.

"But it's exactly what he swore in Porista that he would do," Tungdil recalled, thinking back to when he had broken the news to Furgas of the deaths of his daughter and his life-partner. The hatred in the magister's eyes had been greater than any smoldering in a thirdling.

"The Judgment Star cost her all she held dear: her children, her whole life." Rodario looked at where the ground fell away and no grass grew: only sand and dead earth, as if life itself were afraid to approach what lay below.

The armored vehicles at the head of the column broke formation now, slowing down and fanning out so that the ones from the rear could join them.

Sirka had been listening in silence. Now she heard the fanfare. "We'll soon be at the Black Abyss. We need to take the diamond up to the front."

The befúns altered their pace to powerful leaps. Strangely enough, the unpleasant swaying motion was reduced at these high speeds.

A wide bare indentation appeared in the landscape with the chasm at its center. The Black Abyss was a good half-mile in length and a hundred paces wide and looked like a slash cut in the body of the earth, its edges dark and smooth. Steep paths led up on either side.

"Like a gangrenous wound," commented Ireheart, spitting in disgust. "The beasts are the pus."

Flagur gestured south to a strange device at the entrance.

"That's the artifact." He gave a sigh of relief. "It seems to be intact. I had feared the worst."

Tungdil forced himself to say nothing; he must not kill their optimism. Narmora had been a powerful maga. Who knew what a demi-älf was capable of? "Have those exits guarded," he said to the ubari. "To be on the safe side. We don't want to be ambushed while we're activating the diamond." He turned to Lot-Ionan. "Are you prepared, honored magus?"

He studied the vast crater. "If it is possible to be prepared for what awaits here."

Ireheart looked around him. "What's happened to the advance party? We've seen no trace of them."

"The escort will have gone down the ravine. But I can't think why. Perhaps a battle? Or maybe Narmora had a trick in store and she's woken the beasts of the abyss."

The army split into two sections, with ten thousand ubariu and undergroundlings positioned in front of the exits from the Black Abyss, a living barrier to whatever might come storming out. They kept a hundred-pace safety margin from the precipice edges of the dread ravine.

The armored vehicles moved into position sideways-on behind the troops. Inside the tanks adjustments were made; the wind sail-wheels were running but as yet not engaged.

Flagur had explained that the sails were not just a driving mechanism but also produced energy for additional cata-pults. If the wagons were stationary it was possible to activate mechanical slings. These could fire off constantly using wind power and the crew only had to ensure the aim was correctly adjusted. They used their own supply of munitions or could scoop stones up from the ground below the vehicle through small hatches.

The vehicles were ready.

In the meantime Sirka, Tungdil and friends had reached the artifact. It consisted of several upright linked metal rings in roughly the form of a globe with a diameter approaching twenty paces. Symbols, runes and chiseled marks and patterns adorned the rings. A series of reinforcing rods radiated out to the circumference from a central decorated hub.

"The diamond needs to go in there, I assume," said Lot-Ionan, getting down.

Ireheart shaded his eyes against the sun and looked up. "How do we get up? I can't see a ladder."

"That's why we need a rune master." Flagur bowed to Lot-Ionan. "Or our magus, of course. You must have a flying spell?"

"No, why would I?"

"Then you'll have to climb."

"Wouldn't it be better if you carried him on your back into the center?" Rodario ventured. "You look stronger."

Flagur shook his head. "I can't touch the artifact. Only a rune master or a magus who is pure in spirit. Anyone else will be pulverized if they try."

At that moment a horn sounded. It was a leaden tone issuing from the depths of the ravine, a dark, ear-splitting screech full of hatred and elation. It summoned its subjects with the promise of freedom, murder and destruction.

The friends could do nothing until the last echoes died away.

"It's been heard," Sirka mouthed fearfully. "We . . ."

Out of the ravine surged an angry chorus from thousands of throats.

"Here they come!" Flagur leaped onto his befún. "I must join my warriors. They must see I am not deserting them." He drew his sword and nodded to Lot-Ionan. "Revered sir, it was an honor to meet you." Flagur raced off; his commands could soon be heard in the distance.

The first rows of soldiers knelt down holding long iron spears to impale the first wave of beasts; in the ranks behind, the archers made ready their bows, while others held their huge shields to form a protective cover for their heads. The wagons opened up their shooting flaps.

Lot-Ionan approached the artifact, which was sending out enough energy to make the individual white hairs of his beard and on his head bristle and stand out. His steps slowed the nearer he got to it. He glanced behind to where the others were waiting and following his every move.

"I . . ." He was trying to say something, but he felt a blow in his chest. He stumbled backwards and fell in the dust, a black älf arrow in his breast. It had struck him right in the heart.

A shadow fell over him and a man leaped over his body, grabbing the bag at his belt that held the precious stone.

Warm blood spread as Lot-Ionan's damaged heart continued to pump. Then it stopped. With a groan, Lot-Ionan closed his eyes . . .

"Furgas?" Rodario had recognized the man who had sprung from behind one of the iron rings.

"We are in the Outer Lands. Here the dead return." The magister snatched the diamond from the dying magus and walked slowly backwards. "I tricked even you, Incredible Rodario," he smiled in satisfaction. When Tungdil took a step forward, Furgas raised his arm. "Stay where you are! Or the arrow will get you." He indicated the other end of the artifact where a woman was standing with a bow spanned ready. "We shall see evil released from the Black Abyss. With my assistance it will march into the heart of Girdlegard." He put the diamond in his mouth and swallowed it.

Ireheart raised his weapon slowly. "What a stupid idea," he growled. "Now I'm really going to hurt him."

"You can't prevent it." Furgas looked over at the ravine. "*That* is the revenge I wanted for Girdlegard. The land will be submerged in waves of the beasts and will be annihilated. A fitting punishment for its arrogance and for having followed the dwarves and their false beliefs." He stared at Tungdil. "The eoîl were never a danger. It was you misbegotten dwarves interfering that robbed me of my family."

"That isn't Narmora," murmured Ireheart. "She would be doing magic."

Rodario said nothing but knew he was right. It could be the woman he had seen on the boat in Mifurdania. He was cross with himself for not having thought about her again. Now that the name of Narmora had been mentioned he was clear who she had resembled. That was why Furgas would have selected her as his ally. Perhaps in his twisted mind he actually thought she was his beloved spouse come back to life? "All that, the destruction of a whole land, all for the sake of vengeance? Do you think that's what Narmora would have wanted? She fought with us against the danger."

"She did not want to die!" Furgas cut in. "No, you will all pay by mourning your loved ones as I have been mourning mine. For over five cycles now." He shook his fist and moved away. "In Girdlegard there will be not a single soul who does not experience the pain I feel."

"And then?" Rodario carried on the train of thought. "Then Girdlegard is finished."

"Why not? For all I care the lands can go hang." He shrugged. "None of the worlds are anything without her; she gave me children and she saved my life."

"You deceived me, Furgas." Rodario went up to him.

The archer let her arrow loose and it hit Rodario in the right thigh. He fell next to Lot-Ionan. The archer woman notched a second arrow with lightning-swift and practiced moves.

"I told you. Stay there and watch." Furgas stared at his former friend without a trace of remorse. "It's your own fault you were hit."

From out of the ravine the roar continued to belch.

An ugly hail fell on the allies: the remains, severed limbs and heads and chopped flesh, of the advance party, whom Furgas and his assistant had lured to their deaths. The dull thuds were sickening as the gruesome missiles fell on upturned shields and armor plating. The spraying blood and appalling smell did not fail in the intended effect.

Sirka became resolute. She had lost friends and relations and was determined to avenge their deaths.

"You have made terrible mistakes," Rodario groaned, clasping his hand over the arrow wound. "Don't make it worse."

"No one will forgive me what I have done. There's no

making it worse," Furgas cut in. "I built the machines to hound the dwarves. I didn't take a lot of persuading when Bandilor suggested it. And I was happy enough to side with the unslayable. I knew exactly what I was doing and I planned it all in detail. Now I am at my goal. Why would I stop now?"

"We've found your tunnel. Evil won't be getting through there anymore," Tungdil told him, as he gave Goda a signal; Ireheart understood as well. "How ever did you manage to make those bastard hybrids out of machines and monsters?"

"There's always room for coincidence in my plans," he smiled. "When we were prospecting for iron ore on the lake bed we noticed the rocks were quite different. I thought of the source in Porista and started to suspect a connection. And it occurred to me we had found the metal that conducts magic." He looked over to the abyss. The shower of body parts did not seem to be drying up. "I wondered if the machines could use it. Narmora had told me about the magic dormant in älfar. When the unslayable left his bastards with me I just tried it out." Pride shone in his eyes. "The two thirdlings smelted me the special metal and then I created the new machines. Nobody before me had ever thought of combining magic, iron and living bodies."

"You turned them into well-nigh undefeatable monsters."

"That was my plan, Tungdil." He folded his hands and was deathly calm. "I just wanted a distraction. While you were chasing the machines nobody worried about me. My tunnel could have been finished without anyone noticing. But the Black Abyss serves my purposes better." Furgas turned to the mighty incision in the earth and nodded. "Hard to credit, isn't it? I was playing you this farce all along, ever since Rodario turned up on the island." Furgas turned to the actor. "My simulated suicide made it all perfect. You believed me and you told me all your secrets. Because of you my revenge will be sweeter than I could ever have imagined. Yes, if we did but know certain things in advance . . . Like the existence of the Black Abyss."

The thudding had stopped and the horn sounded once more. The Black Abyss launched its horrors onto the defenders.

Tungdil was too far away to see exactly, but the monsters surging out of the chasm seemed far worse than anything known previously in Girdlegard: some had four arms and claws, others had two long necks and heads like snakes.

He noted a big fat creature as tall as a tree, with a red body shimmering moistly like raw meat, and half a dozen tentacles waving in the air, grabbing at anything in range. When it caught its prey it simply squashed it up against its own flesh until clouds of steam rose. The victims were dissolved in acid and ingested directly via countless mouths.

Similar ghastly beings came running and riding out of the ravine; large and small, unspeakably ugly and horrific to see.

Winged monsters as tall as a house crawled up the ravine sides and threw themselves off to take advantage of updraughts and prevailing winds. They sailed over the heads of the ubariu and with their long claws ripped open the scalps of the defending warriors.

The catapults had opened fire now and were keeping up an answering barrage on the attackers.

Flying beasts attacked the armored wagons, landing on them or climbing on top to destroy the wind sails, or to strip off the iron plates to get inside. The allied army had to support the vehicles under attack.

Suddenly the shrillest of screams issued from the depths of the chasm; it was louder than any other noise. The voice was so loud that it cracked the rocks at the side of the chasm. Friend and foe alike stopped in their tracks in utter horror and the monsters ceased their onslaught. They were terrified of their own kind.

"Ubar protect us," whispered Sirka, flinching and stepping back involuntarily. "A kordrion! Only the cry of a kordrion can split rocks, it says in the books. Nothing can hold it back if it escapes."

Furgas scuffed. "And there isn't anyone to hold it back, Sirka." He pointed to Lot-Ionan. "Your last hope lies there. The old man has failed."

The hand of the magus moved. Assumed dead, he still managed to direct a dark green beam at Furgas.

It swept the technical genius off his feet and sent him flying up toward the hub until suspended exactly above it. Then the wizard broke off the ray and Furgas sank down. At the last moment he put out a hand to grab one of the reinforcements.

The woman took a shot at Lot-Ionan but the arrow never made it. Magic forced it to hang in the air. Lot-Ionan had been prepared for the attack.

"Great! The stone is up there now. It's just got to get into the setting." Ireheart ran to confront the archer-woman, Goda at his heels. "I'll take her, Scholar. You find a way to get Lot-Ionan up to the diamond."

Tungdil and Sirka helped the magus to his feet.

Lot-Ionan drew the arrow out of his flesh and discarded it. "It's not so easy to kill a magus," he said with a peculiar smile. "Evil will not prevail." He grasped the iron rings to start the climb.

A bolt of lightning struck from the center of the artifact, sending the wizard sailing through the air to land four paces away. He lay groaning as smoke poured out of his body.

"Lot-Ionan!" Tungdil ran to his side. The wizard's hand was badly burned and the skin was flaking off onto the ground. Blood seeped out of the blackened flesh. His eyes had turned back in his head and he was convulsing.

Sirka stared. "It's because his soul is not true," she realized with horror. She watched the battle rage. "What now?"

Their army was holding their ground on nearly all sides, but a few of the creatures had broken through the defense line. And it was these misbegotten beings that were now heading toward the artifact. They were well aware what had held them prisoner for so long in their black ravine. They were desperate to destroy it.

"I don't know," Tungdil replied quietly. Raising *Bloodthirster* he mounted his befún and rode to confront the monsters. "I'll keep them busy. Then we'll have to see. Look after the magus."

Ireheart had reached the archer and smashed her bow just as she was notching her next arrow. It fell harmlessly to the ground and she leaped back in fury, drawing her sword.

His eyes flashed. "So, you cowardly murderess. Let us

see what battle skills you have now that I've broken your favorite toy." He dealt her a blow with his crow's beak.

She sidestepped deftly and launched a kick but he was able to ward it off with the handle of his ax. He drove the jagged point, where the spike had broken off, deep into her flank, tearing a gaping wound. She fell back, gasping.

"You ain't seen nothing yet, you crafty bitch," he crowed and, whirling his ax, was about to strike when she threw her sword.

It missed him and he heard Goda cry out.

Up until recently there would have been nothing that could have distracted him in combat, but his concern for Goda did so now. He turned.

The archer's sword was stuck deep in Goha's arm, and the impact had forced her backwards—right up against the rings of the artifact.

"Vraccas! No!" yelled Boïndil, thinking of what Flagur had said. In his mind's eye he saw Goda transformed to ashes, torn by lightning bolts, consumed by flames . . .

But nothing happened.

Before he could realize how surprised he was, he felt a sharp pain in his side. It had a hellish kick. Turning, he faced the flying fist of the archer-woman.

"Not so fast!" he exclaimed and hit at her hand with the flat of his battleax. There was a loud crack on contact and the finger bones crunched. Without waiting to see what she was doing, he dealt her an uppercut with the jagged edge, shattering her chin.

She fell to the ground but still slashed out with her dagger.

Ireheart sprang to one side and the glistening knife-tip missed him. "My turn," he laughed, lifting his weapon high over his head to slam it down with all his strength. "What does a skull do when it bursts?"

The woman had no answer. Under the blow from his ax her head demonstrated the solution to his riddle.

From far above Furgas shouted. He had found his footing on one of the cross-bars and sat there, condemned to watch and wait, which was what he had demanded the others should do.

"We'll deal with you in a minute," Ireheart called up. He raced to Goda's side. "Are you all right?"

"Yes," she said. "I was careful, master." Laying his hand on the sword handle he pulled it out of her arm. Goda gave a quiet moan. He showed her the sword. "Never throw your weapon unless you have a second one," he reminded her. "She still had her little toothpick."

Goda noticed the blood trickling out of his side. "I can see."

"That? Only a scratch." He inspected her back for any scorch marks on the armor. Nothing. A slight giddiness forced him to plant his feet firmly on the ground.

"Goda, Ireheart!" called Sirka. "Come over here. The magus has something to say."

It was only now that the two dwarves saw Lot-Ionan stretched out on the ground next to Rodario. "Oh no! Did he fall?" asked Boïndil somberly. "Now we'll need a catapult to get him up there."

They ran to the magus. His breath was short and he was obviously in great pain. Sweat glistened on his forehead. "I didn't fall. The artifact rejected me," he explained.

Ireheart looked up at Furgas. "Fine artifact this one is. Why doesn't it grill him instead of you?"

Lot-Ionan turned his pale blue gaze on Goda. "You must go and complete the task."

"Me?" The dwarf-maiden raised her night star as if in excuse. "I'm a warrior and—"

"The rune master knew and I saw it with my own eyes, too," he interrupted, speaking hoarsely. "Goda, you bear within you the gift to use magic. And unlike mine your soul will be pure and innocent."

"Innocent?" Rodario scoffed. "It's a good thing the artifact does not have ears, after what I heard in Pendleburg."

Goda blushed. Ireheart looked sternly at Rodario. "We were doing wrestling drills, actor. She is still untouched."

Lot-Ionan gazed steadily into Goda's brown eyes. "I don't know how—perhaps from the magic source, or perhaps you've had it from birth."

"Is that what you and the rune master were talking about at the campfire that night?" Rodario remembered the evening he had shared the strange spice with Flagur and seen the two men talking.

"Yes. I did not want to tell Goda until we had completed our mission. You might have been my famula." He shut his eyes, and his teeth were chattering. "Climb up, Goda." His words could hardly be heard now. "Kill Furgas, put the diamond in the setting and save Girdlegard."

"And my homeland, too," added Sirka.

On the left more and more beasts were breaking through, heading for the artifact. Tungdil rode back and forth, felling one creature after another, but there were far too many. Three dozen were coming their way.

Sirka pillowed Lot-Ionan's head on her mantle, then she took her combat stick and nodded to Ireheart. "I think we've got work to do."

Rodario broke the arrow off close to the entry wound and got to his feet. "Well, you'll be needing me, as well. I can't miss a third opportunity to be a hero."

Ireheart gave Goda a tender kiss. "Hurry. But not too fast. Leave a few for me and my crow's beak." He turned to face the foe. Again the world seemed to waver in front of his eyes and he needed to blink before his sight cleared.

"Irrepressible," was all Goda said. She went to the nearest ring and sought a hold for her fingers as she started to climb.

"Just you try," shouted Furgas. "I'll kill you."

Sirka twirled her weapon and looked at Ireheart. "Can I ask a favor?"

"Sure."

"Tell me the joke about the orc and the dwarf?"

"Now?"

"Might be our last chance." Sirka grinned. The first monster was ten paces away, swinging a huge sword.

"Hurry."

"Well, one orbit, a dwarf meets an orc at the Stone Gateway." Ireheart raised his crow's beak. "The orc saw him and said, 'Little man, can you tell me where . . . ?'"

Sirka's adversary arrived and grabbed her attention with a hefty swipe.

"Later," she called to Ireheart as she put her heart and soul into the fight.

Tungdil spurred his befún across the battlefield, striking at the monsters' heads with *Bloodthirster*. Each strike took a life.

The refashioned älfish blade raged amongst the enemy throng. It seemed as if the sword were helping of its own accord, directing its own attack, and seeking out the most vulnerable places to strike. The weapon was uncanny but fascinating.

But whatever efforts the ubariu and the under-groundlings made, more and more creatures broke through the defenses, as soldiers were lost.

The winged monsters could not be stopped. They seemed immune against attack by arrow or crossbow bolt and had overturned two of the armored wagons, falling in swarms on the others. Swift as the wind they tore off the heavy plating to slaughter the crew inside.

The remaining vehicles gave the infantry some cover and kept up a spear attack, but they too were damaged.

"Curses!" Tungdil halted his befún to study the arti-fact. He saw Furgas was at the top and that a small figure was making its way up on the outside ring. "Goda?"

The befún cowered and emitted a furious roar. All at once it was dark round Tungdil, and a foul-smelling wind touched him. Claws slashed to the right and the left, lodging in the flesh of his steed, then up he soared . . .

The ground fell back and he was hovering over the battlefield witnessing the butchery on both sides of the chasm; it was a miniaturized version of what he had been experiencing himself.

"What . . . ?" Tungdil turned to see the hideous face of one of the winged monsters, its muzzle agape.

His first thought was to plunge *Bloodthirster* between the teeth of the beast to kill it. But it would have meant his own death. From one hundred paces up in the air a fall was certain death.

Instead, he leaped off his injured steed to land on a claw of the flying beast, who dropped the befún and uttered a fearful cry. The animal tumbled to earth, smashing four ubariu beneath itself as it fell into their own ranks.

"You won't shake me off," snarled Tungdil, stabbing the monster in the belly, making a gash half a pace long, out of which a stinking liquid gushed to drench him.

Screeching, the dying beast tried to land, coming down over the line of undergroundlings and skimming over the spears of the Black Abyss army before it came to earth with widespread wings, blundering through the ranks and killing or maiming maybe fifty.

Vraccas protected Tungdil. Apart from a few scratches and a shallow gouge on his right calf from a spear tip, there was nothing. So he struggled out from under the wing and found himself standing right in the middle of the opposing army. He had not been noticed.

The foremost ranks of the ubariu and undergroundlings were an arrow's flight away, and the entrance to the chasm fifty paces from him.

"Well, Vraccas, whatever your plan is," he said, looking round, "I'm very keen to know how it all ends."

Again he heard the sound of the kordrion. Stone cracked and a landslide of rubble buried several beasts. Immediately there was stillness and the warriors' eyes all turned to the entrance to the ravine.

A pale claw as wide as three fortress gates shot up out

of the blackness of the abyss and took hold of the outer edge of the ravine, trying for a hold. Cracks formed and rock crumbled under the pressure and weight of the creature that was still down there in the dark attempting to free itself. Its claw fastened into the rock again, the long nails taking hold.

The most dwarven of Tungdil's virtues came to the fore. When all about him was hopelessness, he kept his head and drew on the qualities of steadfast stubbornness and pigheadedness or whatever other folk thought of when they spoke of the dwarves.

He climbed up the corpse of the winged beast so that both friend and foe should see he was there. He took his bugle from his belt, placed it to his lips and replied to the call of the kordrion, sounding the battle signal into the horrified silence.

"I shall not allow you out of your prison," he bellowed down into the chasm. He raised *Bloodthirster*, drenched as it was with the black lifeblood of all the creatures he had vanquished. "The weapon I snatched from evil shall be the one to stop you, whatever you are. Fire fights fire."

He stormed straight through the ranks of the beasts, and hacked to pieces every assailant that dared to cross his path; it was as if their armor was but butter and their bodies but straw.

Behind him he heard Flagur's voice, then the ubariu yelled and the undergroundlings hallooed, joining their efforts with his own.

Hope began to blossom.

* * *

Flagur saw Tungdil suddenly appear between the enemy ranks and the cadaver of the monster. He had sounded his horn as fearlessly as if standing in safety behind the walls of Letèfora. His words resounded clearly, echoing over the death-filled field. Then he sprang forward.

"Ubar, you have sent us a true hero, whose courage surpasses even that of an acront," he avowed, lifting his sword. "Let us follow him!" He sent his rallying cry to right and to left. "We shall be the first to defeat a kordrion. For Ubar!" Stepping forward, his weapon grasped in both hands, he cut the beast that reared up before him into two halves, slicing from skull to groin. He was covered in its dark blood and the smell of it spurred him on.

His warriors joined their voices to his own and sallied forth. Turning their enormous shields they charged ten paces deep into enemy lines. There they halted: the first ubariu formed a protective metal wall, cutting off the antagonists now behind them from the main army of monsters.

Following in the wake of the ubariu, the undergroundlings bombarded this isolated section, felling monsters so swiftly with their combat batons that the creatures could not coordinate any defense.

Meanwhile, pressure was increasing at the shield barrier where the Black Abyss hordes were menacing the ubariu.

"Again!" yelled Flagur, calling for the lance with his banner affixed. They repeated the maneuver: turn shields aside, let some of the assailants through, hem them in and butcher them.

"Take care!" called Flagur to the front line overlooking the field, holding his banner aloft to ensure the enemy knew what name death bore.

At that moment he felt a searing pain in his side. Suddenly there was an arrow sticking out between his ribs, making breathing a torture. Yet Flagur did not surrender to the pain. His fingers contracted around the shaft of his lance and he used it to support himself. Show no weakness. The battle must first be won. "And change . . . now!"

Those fighting at the front withdrew and were neatly replaced by a second line of fresh warriors, so that the onslaught kept up its momentum. Their enemy floundered when faced with well-drilled strategy like this. The monsters were exhausting themselves in their relentless attack.

Losses, however, were many.

More than once Flagur saw a good friend fall, heard a death cry and chimed with it in his soul.

On the outside no weakness could be seen, even though he would have wished his fallen warriors out from underneath the carcasses of slaughtered monsters. They deserved a better resting place. Several of them he had known for countless star cycles; he had trained them himself. To watch them die like this hurt as badly as the arrow in his side. Mourning would have to wait, as always in battle.

Flagur saw that one of the armored vehicles was set sideways-on to provide cover for their advance. Flurries of arrows and spears were whizzing out over the heads of their own troops. The archers knew their stuff. Five whole rows of the enemy were felled by these missiles, and a second salvo mowed a wide path through the heaving, screaming throng.

"Onwards and forwards!" commanded Flagur, his spear

aloft and the pennant cracking in the breeze, signaling the major assault.

Goda climbed up. Now she had reached a crossbar and slid along on it toward Furgas. Beneath her, Sirka and Ireheart were thumping the life out of the beasts; Rodario had a short bow and a quiver taken from one of the creatures and was loosing arrows at the foe. No matter if your aim was not very good—in this crush you would always hit a target.

Ireheart gave full vent to his battle rage. He used the madness coursing through his veins to make him insuperable in combat. The crow's beak whirred without rest, denting helmets, shattering bones, slicing through armor and hurling the victims a good two paces through the air.

Sirka for her part was fighting like the water element, slipping into gaps and using the barb on her slim weapon to strike and the hook to fend off blows, to wrench swords out of assailants' hands, or to thrust into unprotected flesh. She never stayed long in one position, but moved with flowing grace.

Goda had nearly reached Furgas.

He was watching her. "What do you think you are doing?" he asked. "I'm curious to see . . ."

Goda drew out her night star, her favorite weapon, with its three hefty spiked globes. She would have to be careful not to lose her footing if she missed her mark. She balanced cautiously, stepping out along the narrow strut, and raising her right hand.

Furgas pushed himself backwards out of range. "You won't get me like that." He squinted down, looking for the next reinforcing bar. "Time is on my side, dwarf. Always the most reliable of allies." When Goda came closer still, he jumped off and dropped down, his fingers outstretched to catch the next bar.

Even though she only had one weapon with her Goda decided to contravene the first rule of combat: she hurled the night star at Furgas.

The three spiked balls hit his hands and smashed his fingers; screaming, he plunged, landing on his belly in the very setting the diamond was destined for—a central setting ringed with spikes.

"No!" He shrieked in agony, working the spikes even deeper into his flesh as he struggled. His blood flowed down over the hub and cascaded to the ground. His movements became gradually weaker. Finally his screams died away.

Goda sent a prayer of thanks to Vraccas, climbed carefully down to the central hub where Furgas's body hung. The next problem would be to locate the stone. "How do I find it?" she called out to Ireheart.

Her dwarf mentor was whacking a monster on the paw with his crow's beak, and ramming his own sharp helmet into its abdomen, so that black blood streamed down over his head and shoulders. "Slit him open. Top part of his belly. It's only a little while since he swallowed it." Hopping back to avoid a spear thrust, he sliced the head off his assailant.

Goda drew her dagger and forced the body into a sitting position, hauling it off the spikes. The hole in the magister's chest would not be big enough so she was just placing the knife tip underneath his ribs when he opened his eyes.

"I won't give it up," he croaked, blood gushing out of his mouth, dripping down his chin. "I shall have my revenge." He pushed her and she lost her balance.

She fell.

Tungdil stormed into the darkness of the chasm where light was afraid to go.

In front of him reared up a being beyond the wit of Tion to create. It would have needed gods such as Girdlegard had never known.

The kordrion was a vast tower of horror. Its wings were folded close in to its huge muscular body, for there was no space in this ravine for the mountainous creature to spread them. Four huge dog-like paws bore its stupendous weight, though the front two limbs seemed more like arms. The rest of its naked body lay in shadow.

Its neck was comparatively short and it had a head like a dragon, but festooned with horns and spikes. Behind the long bony snout glinted four gray eyes. Further back, two blue ones. It was half upright and struggling to place its claws into fissures in the rock to drag itself up.

A three-armed beast leaped shrieking toward Tungdil, long muzzle agape, with a dark red barbed tongue snaking out.

The dwarf confronted that tongue quite simply by holding up *Bloodthirster*, whose wicked cutting edge sliced the flesh, sending the creature whimpering back, its bleeding tongue segments recoiled into its maw.

But Tungdil followed through, cutting the monster in two from top to bottom. Then he turned *Bloodthirster* on the kordrion. "Get back in the abyss you crawled out of," he commanded. "I don't believe anything is insuperable, whether my opponents look like you or even worse."

The creature's blue eyes focused on him. It dropped down onto its forepaws, but this still meant that its head hovered a good ten paces above Tungdil. It opened its powerful jaws and roared at the dwarf. Each and every tooth in its head was as big as one ubariu standing on top of a second.

From behind he heard the rattle and clash of weapons and armor, and then Flagur stood at his back with his ubariu and undergroundlings. With the aid of their armored vehicles they had managed to defeat the beasts and had stopped up the entrance. The kordrion was making things easy for them now because none of the other monsters still in the ravine dared force their way past it.

"Ubar, help us now," was Flagur's prayer. "How can we deal with this one?"

"I can see the acrontas might be needed for a monster like this." Tungdil experienced no fear. With *Bloodthirster* in his grasp he was a bundle of confidence, tenacity and cussedness. "But if we don't make a start we'll never know if it can be done without them." He raced forwards, aiming for the claws which were now down on the rocky floor. "While he's stuck in this cleft we have the advantage. Cut through the tendons—hack at anything you can reach. Sooner or later we'll have him down!"

Flagur watched the dwarf go. "He's not afraid at all," he murmured admiringly as he lifted his own spear. Shaft and banner fabric were now drenched in the blood of monsters he had slain. "Onwards!" he called out, and cantered off, his breath shallow as he battled with the wound in his side.

His warriors followed him and rushed towards the kordrion with weapons held high—until they heard the infamous roar. But it was not the being in front of them that made the horrendous sound.

Flagur's steps slackened and the blood froze in his veins. The ecstasy of battle dispersed and gave way to fear. "Tungdil! Come back! There are two of them!"

Then the kordrion opened its great muzzle and swept the warriors with a wave of white fire.

With enormous presence of mind Goda managed to hook her leg over one of the bars. She pulled herself up again, panting hard. She could never have imagined herself capable of these acrobatic *tours de force*. All that exercise, all those drills, all that training with heaving and hauling—it was all paying off now. She would never complain again about the harshness of that regime.

Ropes with grappling hooks flew past her, fastening themselves to the bars. Some of the monsters were attempting to demolish the artifact, while their comrades, at risk to their own lives, tried to provide cover from attacks by Ireheart and Sirka.

"Faster!" Boïndil called up to her. He knew what was making him feel giddy; the woman's dagger had been coated with poison and it was starting to work.

Goda crawled over to Furgas. "You did not get rid of me."

He drew a rattling breath and drew out his dagger. "And you have not killed me."

"I'm going to make up for that." She avoided his lunge, grabbed his useless arm and removed the knife. It was easy for her now to overcome the fatally wounded Furgas and to ram his own dagger into his body. The man gave one final groan and died.

Now she was faced with the part of her task she was not happy about. She fumbled around in the magister's warm vitals until she found the hard object she was searching for.

"I have it!" she yelled triumphantly, to boost the morale of the defenders below. She cut the diamond out, then gave the corpse a shove so it plummeted to the ground.

Goda did not bother to clean the stone but pressed it, filthy though it was, into the setting, then closed the four fastenings. She stared at the stone. "Come on now! Do something!" She rubbed it to make it work.

A new roar sounded from the chasm and a wall of white fire shot out of the cleft, surging across the ground. The burning bodies of ubariu and undergroundlings were hurled through the air before slamming into the cliff face and extinguishing like sparks. The armored vehicle that was nearest was consumed with fire so that the iron plating peeled off and the wooden frame beneath turned to ash.

The kordrion pushed itself out into the light. With a louder roar than ever, which broke whole boulders off, it forced its way free and was approaching on all fours. It gave another roar of victory as it left the darkness of the abyss. Goda couldn't gauge its size accurately. Twenty paces high and sixty paces long?

The army ran back from the chasm's edge, overwhelmed by horror . . .

The kordrion reared up and unfolded its pale wings. The world grew dark, as if a cloud had covered the sun.

"Goda!" yelled Ireheart, as he felled his last opponent by slamming into its ribcage. Ribs broke puncturing heart and innards. The three of them, he, Sirka and Rodario, had managed to prevent the destruction of the artifact. "We're waiting!" His legs gave way and he collapsed, sinking down onto the body of his victim. His sight was going, colors swimming together confusedly.

Sirka stared at the huge pale mass of the kordrion. "Tungdil," she whispered in horror, grasping the fact that her companion could not have survived. That white fire melted stone and steel.

"He'll be OK," said Ireheart, fighting the effects of the poison and rallying. "The scholar always survives. He is a friend of the gods." But his face too darkened in concern. A monster like this had never been seen before. It was trampling the ubariu and undergroundlings, sending out another plume of white fire, killing five hundred fighters at one stroke. The last of the armed vehicles was over-turned and burnt. Nothing remained but a glowing hulk. The kordrion was growing stronger with every moment it was able to spend outside its prison-gorge.

Goda hit out in despair and fury at the stone that was failing them so. She heard a slight click and it slipped down into place in the setting.

A bright silver light shot along the bars of the artifact, slamming into the mighty rings: the symbols started to glow faintly and then increased in brightness with an opal sheen that made Goda think she was losing her sight.

When her vision cleared she saw a glittering sphere had

overlaid the rings of the artifact. A second globe enclosed the opening to the Black Abyss.

She could no longer see the first kordrion, a severed claw and part of a wing being the only evidence that it had ever emerged from its dungeon. A second version raged wildly behind the delicate but impenetrable barrier; as if possessed it hurled itself against the thin membrane, to no avail.

"I've done it," she whispered, hardly daring to believe it. She gazed at the diamond's matt shimmer. She laughed out loud. "I've done it!"

"Yes, you have!" Ireheart returned her joyful words. He tried to stand up, but felt very wobbly. "Come down carefully so I can hug you!"

Rodario placed his hand on Sirka's shoulder. "Tungdil will have made it, too," he encouraged.

She let her eyes roam across the sunken battlefield, now filled with the cadavers of beasts and the corpses of her own people. A number of monsters had escaped the axes and swords of their opponents and were fleeing over the edges of the crater to disappear into the distance.

"But the kordrion has got away," she stammered. "The artifact did not work in time. What now?" She looked at Rodario. "There's no hope. The books say—"

"Don't give up, let's wait and see. The old books aren't always right, you know." He leaned on her shoulder for support. "Come, let's go over to the ravine to find Tungdil."

She gave him a grateful smile. Together with Goda and an unusually pale Ireheart they made their way over the mountain of bodies.

But neither Tungdil nor Flagur returned from that battle.

XXI

The Outer Lands,
East of Letèfora, At the Black Abyss,
Early Autumn, 6241st Solar Cycle

Sirka was standing by the protective globe, with one hand on its shining surface. She could feel a tingling in her fingers from the energy it contained.

On the other side she could see the kordrion's head; it had slunk back into the ravine to rest and was observing her with its topmost pair of eyes. Its ugly skull lay on its claws; every so often it selected an ubariu corpse and swallowed it with obvious enjoyment, before taking up its original position. And waiting.

Ireheart joined her. "It's waiting for the barrier's strength to let up."

"That one and a thousand others," said Sirka sadly. "I know we can't open the barrier even for a few minutes to go and look for Tungdil. The kordrion would be out like a shot. One of them free is bad enough."

Ireheart watched her face. "You've been keeping watch for three orbits now. You've hardly eaten or drunk anything. Come over to the camp," he begged. "The scholar wouldn't want you to starve yourself to death on his account." He wiped a tear from his eye.

She swallowed hard. "I'm coming," she said and turned round.

The banners of the ubariu fluttered over the crater.

Reinforcements had arrived and a temporary camp had been set up where their injured could be cared for and from which any monsters remaining at large could be pursued and hunted down.

"They say the kordrion has taken to the hills," he told her, to break the silence and to take her thoughts and his own away from their pain.

"Do you think he's dead?"

"Who do you mean?"

"Tungdil."

Ireheart took a deep breath but found breathing ever more difficult. He was relying on his dwarven constitution to help him recover from the poison. It had not killed him outright, so it was not going to do so now. "Common sense would say yes. Only four hundred warriors have survived out of twenty thousand." He fought down his despair. "But I haven't seen his body with my own eyes. And no one has been able to tell me how he died. So I don't give an orc's fart for common sense. I say he's still alive. He's cutting a path through the ranks of the beasts and is looking for the way out. He will cleanse the ravine of evil and he won't stop until they're all dead. One fine orbit, there he'll be, all of a sudden. And if it takes five hundred cycles." A new tear trickled down through his beard.

"I shan't be able to wait that long, Ireheart," said Sirka, her voice choked with emotion. "If he comes back and asks you about me, then . . ." She wept.

Ireheart stood ramrod stiff at first, then he relented and took her in his arms. Her tears mixed with his own: undergroundling and dwarf united in grief.

"Tell him," she said quietly, "that I never chose another after him. Even if this is not the way of my people. I know I can never have another companion like him at my side." She freed herself from his brotherly embrace and dried her tears on her sleeve.

"I shall tell him," he promised gruffly.

In silence they made their way to the mess tent, where Lot-Ionan, Goda and Rodario were waiting, together with the city-king's consort.

Opposite them sat the acront, dressed in strange raiment, his head hidden under a light veil. The garment he wore was like the apparel of an ubariu rune master.

The monarch's wife looked at Sirka and said something to her. "They have been waiting for me," she translated. "The acront wishes to speak to Goda about the future."

Ireheart regarded the mountain of fabric with more than a degree of suspicion. "What is there to discuss?" A rush of heat overwhelmed him: he was perspiring from every pore. His body was sweating out the poison. That had to be good.

The acront raised his voice and his consort translated the uncanny sounds; in turn, Sirka rendered the words into the language spoken in Girdlegard.

"He says the ubariu have not yet got a new rune master. He says that you, Goda, should remain in Letèfora to guard the artifact until the ubariu have appointed and trained a rune master from among their ranks. He has noted minute cracks in the sphere containing the Black Abyss, because something had affected the diamond's purity." She waited until the acront's partner had interpreted some more words. "Thus it is essential that someone watches and if necessary steps in to strengthen it. It would only be for . . ." Sirka did some calculations ". . . four cycles. After that she could return to her own country."

"And what if she doesn't want to?" Ireheart wanted to know.

"You can of course leave. But consider well. A fracture in the protection would mean disaster for Girdlegard," Sirka translated. "It would only be for a transitional period. All requests will be met; Goda shall have everything she needs. And she will be rewarded for her services."

Goda sat next to her master, feeling very unsure of herself. "I am not a maga," she said.

"Yes, you are," contradicted Lot-Ionan, who had his injured arm in a sling. "You have not received the training but deep inside you are indeed a maga."

"You honor me to speak so, venerable sire. But at the moment I am not even a famula." Goda was unhappy. "What could I achieve without Lot-Ionan's knowledge store?"

The acront spoke once more.

"He says you are the only one allowed to touch the diamond and the artifact. You are connected to both and you are vital. If anything were to happen to the artifact to make the protection sphere collapse, nobody but you would be capable of erecting it again." Sirka lent the acront her voice. "He asks you to give him four cycles."

Goda looked up at Ireheart, but he shook his head so vehemently that his short black braid flipped back and forth. "No, it's absolutely your decision. But if you want to stay I shall not leave your side," he vowed. "I shall never leave you alone again. And who knows. Perhaps the scholar will return. Then it's fitting there should be two familiar faces to greet him," he grinned.

"Then it is agreed," Goda confirmed. It was obvious that the decision was not an easy one for her. "I shall stay until the ubariu have a new rune master."

The acront inclined his head and his eyes glowed purple under the veil. Then he got to his feet and left the tent with his royal consort. He had said all there was to be said.

Rodario watched him depart. "So that means that he is not innocent and pure in spirit, either," he concluded. He adjusted the bandage on his leg. "As for me, dear friends, don't be offended, but I'm for heading back to Girdlegard in a few orbits' time. Someone's got to report what has been happening here, and that we're safe now. Safe until the next adventure," he added, stroking his beard. He was looking forward to taking Tassia in his arms again and to relating his own heroic story. "I tell you, the theater tents will be overflowing with people wanting to see these events on stage."

Ireheart lifted his eyebrow quizzically. "*Tents*, impresario? Since when have you owned more than one?"

"*Not yet*, Boïndil, my friend, not yet. But it's time I started to expand my little troupe into a theater empire known throughout the lands." He nodded to Goda. "I shall come back at intervals to get your news, you'll see."

"You'll get lost and end up with the monsters," the warrior teased, wiping the sweat from his brow.

The hint was enough to unsettle Rodario. "Mm, I'll have to think of how to get home in one piece. Maybe I should try out that secret path, the invisible mysterious pass that leads to Girdlegard." He got up. "They'll be striking camp tomorrow to return to Letèfora, I understand. And I hope very much that there might be the odd conquest on the way. There are pretty women on the streets." He raised his hand in farewell and left the mess tent.

"I, too, shall be leaving the Outer Lands," said the magus to the three dwarves. "I have the feeling that I am needed back home. It is time to find new famuli and to spread the high art of magic in Girdlegard." When he moved, his back gave him a sharp twinge again. He thought he had spied Nudin's silhouette at the doorway, but the dark shape had disappeared quickly. "It won't be easy to use the magic wellspring at the bottom of the lake, but it will be possible. Tungdil had some brilliant idea about a metal diving bell."

Goda smiled. "Girdlegard will be glad to have your support. Will you take me on as your famula when the four cycles have passed?"

He stroked her blond hair. "Who knows what you will have learned in that time?" he hinted. "Perhaps you will discover a style of magic all your own. I know nothing about ubariu magic. You will be way ahead of me in that. Even for one such as myself the ways of magic are unfathomable. It likes to keep something up its sleeve. I can only warn you not to be prodigal with your powers." He stood up and shook hands with each in turn. "We shall surely meet again. And we shall see Tungdil again. I feel it in the depths of my soul, and so my spirits are high." He turned his bright blue gaze on Sirka. "You will live to see him again. Don't despair. Look forward to the dawn when he returns to you from the Abyss." He nodded and left.

Sirka also bade her friends farewell. Boïndil let her depart, even though he still had not told her the punchline. It was not the right time for jokes at the moment.

The two dwarves were alone.

"Do you know what's bothering me?" said Ireheart thoughtfully, after the last steps had died away. "Why did the artifact reject Lot-Ionan?"

"Well, if anyone is pure in spirit then it has to be Lot-Ionan," said Goda springing to the defense of the magus. "And who expects a magus to sacrifice his life to chastity? I'm sure he doesn't get up to anything like that now, but I'm sure he remembers what he did when he was younger . . ." She took his hand. "He is good."

Ireheart was thinking. "Yes, you're right." He let himself be persuaded. Then his face took on a worried expression. "You know what this means for our iron band?"

"We shall have to wait another four cycles."

He sighed. "That will be hard. As hard as any diamond."

Goda laughed. "In the meantime you can train me up to be the very best warrior maiden there's ever been in Girdlegard or the Outer Lands. Your efforts and your noble restraint will receive their reward after four cycles." She gave him a long kiss. "And we're not forbidden to kiss." She smiled. For a second it crossed her mind that they still had to fight the duel she had vowed to her dead grandmother. That could wait.

Ireheart touched her cheek, stroking the pale down on her skin. "It will be the best and the worst four cycles of my life," he joked. "Vraccas hates me for some reason." He kissed her and then became earnest. "I pray daily to our creator that he may keep Tungdil safe." He stood up and went to the doorway, opened it and looked over toward the Black Abyss under its shimmering globe. "I wonder where he is? And what he's doing, alone with the misbegotten offspring of strange gods?" Again he wiped the perspiration from his brow.

Goda took his hand. She could give him no answer and she certainly did not share his optimism about Tungdil's fate. She presumed him dead. But she was not going to say so.

In silence they both watched the glowing sphere under which lay both hope and horror. You could not have the one without the other.

Girdlegard,
Porista, Royal Capital of Gauragar,
Winter, 6241st Solar Cycle

Once more Girdlegard's rulers were meeting to confer.

King Bruron escorted his guests into the first completed chamber of his royal residence. Huge stoves ensured a pleasant temperature despite wintry blizzards without.

Bruron had ordered sumptuous decoration of the hall, commissioning furnishings, frescoes, tapestries and sculptures with taste and care. The impression given was that the rest of the palace was already in place. However, only the outlines of the main structure were visible. The elf Esdalân, the monarchs of the human realms, lords of the dwarven kingdoms and heads of the freeling cities were gathered to hear Rodario's reports from the Outer Lands:

eloquently and with compelling and colorful detail he described recent events at the Black Abyss.

". . . and so—with the sacrifice brought by Tungdil Goldhand—the battle ended. We have lost a great hero. He gave his life for Girdlegard . . ." he bowed to his audience ". . . for your sake and to enable you to sleep soundly in your beds. May this courageous dwarf forever remain in your thoughts, and let us ensure that it is not only the children of the Smith who mourn him." With these words he took his seat to deafening applause, in particular from the dwarves, on whose faces many a tear glistened.

Lot-Ionan rose to his feet. Dressed in a light blue robe, he wore white gloves to hide the disfiguring burns he had received from touching the artifact. In his left hand he held a long, superbly carved walking stick of birchwood. "I see it as our task to utilize this new peace accorded us by the sacrifice of my foster-son Tungdil and his companions, some of whom remain in the Outer Lands. It is time for reconciliation." He looked at Esdalân. "The elves have been subjected to horrendous treatment meted out in anger. Are you prepared to let bygones be bygones and excuse the deeds targeted at the atár?"

Esdalân looked at Ginsgar calmly. "I insist on an apology for the cruelties received and for the devastation suffered in Âlandur. The grand palaces and temples were laid waste, and this was fitting. But it was not right that settlements were torched and destroyed when the inhabitants had nothing to do with the blinkered obsessions of some of my people. Sincere words of atonement and some redress are essential here." His gaze wandered over the faces of the assembled dwarves. "With your help we shall reconstruct our elf realm. When that is done, then there shall be forgiveness for the children of the Smith."

Ginsgar opened his mouth to let out a hearty laugh. "Sure thing, Esdalân. We can build a few houses for thirty-seven elves, no bother. That forgiveness will be winging its way to us."

If offended by the words and tone, Esdalân chose not to show it. He was too sensible to allow himself to respond in kind. "And how about the words of apology from you, Ginsgar Unforce? You led your troops through our groves, plundering and killing."

The laughter ceased abruptly. "And your own apology for the poisoning of the dwarves?"

"That was the atár, not the elves." Esdalân looked past Ginsgar and appealed to Xamtys. "Atár and elves have nothing in common."

"Hair-splitting," said Ginsgar with contempt. "If I don't hear an apology, then you'll have to wait, too."

"In that case I don't want the dwarves' help in Âlandur." Esdalân nodded to the self-appointed high king. "As soon as you are ready to apologize our two peoples may make a fresh start. But not until then." The elf leaned back in his seat, making it obvious that he had no more to say. But the door of reconciliation had not been slammed shut.

Lot-Ionan sent a disapproving look Ginsgar's way. "How can you do this, Ginsgar Unforce?"

"Easily," he replied curtly. He, too, had no more to add. The gulf between the two peoples had not grown any narrower. The dead heaped in that gulf prevented any peace.

"You will come to your senses," predicted Lot-Ionan.

He addressed the whole assembly. "We have heard that the kordrion has escaped and taken to the hills. It is feared that it will be hiding somewhere between the fifthling and fourthling territories, to lick its wounds. It is vital that the dwarves patrol not only the passes but also the remote mountain regions. As soon as the kordrion is sighted, I must be told."

"Didn't Master Rodario say the creature cannot be over-powered?" Isika asked.

"As far as the ubariu and the undergroundlings are concerned, yes." Lot-Ionan indicated his wand. "I am looking into acquiring new famuli and famulae to train. We shall soon have young people versed in the high art of magic. No one has tried to combat the kordrion with magic. The rune masters of the ubariu used their powers differently from my own ways." He smiled reassuringly. "You see, Queen Isika, I am optimistic."

Queen Wey started to speak. "Then let me add something here, venerable magus, to make you more confident still, even if it has been with great concern that I and my subjects have observed it." She went to the map of Girdlegard and indicated her own realm. "The water level in the lake is sinking all the time. It's as if someone had pulled the plug out of a bath tub."

Rodario and Lot-Ionan exchanged swift glances.

"How much has been lost?" the actor asked. He was aware of a possible reason. The force and weight of water gushing in had foiled the magister's attempt to complete the tunnel. Somewhere in the western part of the Outer Lands a mighty river must be bringing potential devastation.

"My citizens who live on solid islands report the level has fallen by as much as ten paces. Ports and harbors are having to be resited. In some places the lake waters have shrunk so much that people have to walk a whole day to collect fresh water for their homes." Queen Wey surveyed the assembly solemnly. "The lake is running dry. Soon, my subjects will be living not on islands but on mountain peaks soaring a thousand paces up into the sky. It may be good news for you, Lot-Ionan, because access to the magic source will be easier, but my people are distraught. You can't make farmers out of fishermen."

"I think I can guess what has caused the water to vanish," said the magus. He explained his theory. It coincided with Rodario's ideas. "We could deal with the cause if we collapsed the tunnels. I would prefer to undertake a dive to the bottom of the lake for the magic before I see a water-based country turned to desert laid bare. Weyurn without its lakes is unthinkable. The whole of Girdlegard would suffer: its lakes give rise to our rivers and streams. The consequences would be dire indeed."

Mallen asked to be allowed to speak. "In the name of the human kingdoms I suggest the dwarves permit our warriors to share guard duties at each of the passes into Girdlegard." He stood up. "It is only fair that we don't leave the defense of the whole of Girdlegard up to the dwarves. We too want to make our contribution to our safety and security. It will be our gesture of acknowledgement and thanks for them having stood guard loyally these thousands of cycles, losing thousands of their people in the course of that defense."

"No," interrupted Ginsgar. "We'll have no humans in

our mountains. We are carrying out our duties properly on our own. Humans would get in the way. They understand neither our way of life nor our way of thinking and fighting. If there were an attack our soldiers would be hindered by them, not helped."

"*You* have no kingdom under you," Xamtys corrected him. "You have appointed yourself high king, that's all." She inclined her head toward Mallen. "As for the firstlings, let me say that humans are welcome to join their efforts to our own. We have suffered too many losses recently and would be grateful for more soldiers to help fill the gaps in our ranks, until our own new recruits are trained up."

Bylanta and Balendilîn agreed with her, but Glaïmbar and Malbalor refused to cooperate. From the looks exchanged between Ginsgar and Xamtys it seemed the dwarven folks were headed for a massive clash of wills about who should have overall power. Never had their enmity been displayed so openly. In the past they had given outsiders the impression of unity or had formed a common front of silence when disputes occurred.

Mallen expressed his thanks. "Let us discuss numbers tomorrow: how many soldiers the firstlings, secondlings and fourthlings will take."

The council now moved to the topic of what line to take with the ubariu and the mighty empire in the northeast of the Outer Lands. Against Ginsgar's will— unsurprisingly—it was decided to invite initial contact, if for no other reason than to tackle the kordrion. The monarchs resolved to leave it in the lap of the gods as to how the relationship developed after that.

As it was already late Bruron closed the meeting. The potentates of Girdlegard were to reconvene in the morning. The kings and queens of the human realms left the hall and the dwarves remained behind to continue negotiations.

Immediately Xamtys slammed her fist down on the table and hissed accusingly at Ginsgar, "How can you dare to appear here as high king?"

"The matter is settled," he snorted, dismissing her with a smile and gesture.

"You *think* it is settled. You have a handful of followers, Ginsgar, and they swore loyalty to you when they were high on battle victory. Not more than that."

"Not in my view." Glaïmbar spoke. "Ginsgar did what we should have done. Elves or atár, what's the difference? When the next eoîl turns up, the thirty-seven pointy-ears will go mad and try to found another empire of purity. We're better off without the elves." He pushed back his chair and knelt before Ginsgar, proffering his weapon. He bowed his head. "I acknowledge you as my high king, Ginsgar Unforce."

Malbalor also rose and dropped to one knee, repeating the ceremony.

Xamtys jumped up. "So much hot-headed madness from my own realm is insufferable!" She looked at Glaïmbar. "I can't think why you are supporting him." Then she turned her eyes to Malbalor. "You are afraid of losing authority because you are a thirdling. You think you'll hang on to power and your people will be left in peace if you join the dwarf who calls freelings and thirdlings his enemies." Her eyes narrowed. "You are both wrong. You have split the dwarf folks with your decision. I will never accept Ginsgar as high king." She stood up and knelt before Bylanta, to be joined by Balendilìn. "We swear allegiance to you, High Queen Bylanta Slimfinger of the clan of the Silver Beards," they chorused.

Then the freeling city representatives, Bramdal amongst their number, rose and stood at the side of the fourthling queen. They swore no oath but made their commitment plain.

Ginsgar jerked to his feet. "By Vraccas! Rebellion!" he bellowed, reaching for his battle hammer. Malbalor and Glaïmbar stood stock still. "And you," he shouted at the freelings, "I'll have you back with the dwarves as Vraccas decreed. Your realms outside Girdlegard have seen their last days."

Bramdal gave him a contemptuous look.

"You and your two friends will be responsible for what happens," said Bylanta somberly. "We can prevent the feud," she insisted to Malbalor and Glaïmbar, "if you give me your oath of fealty! Avert this rift!"

"They have acknowledged me as their ruler," thundered Ginsgar. "And I shall not rest until I am high king of all the dwarven folks. It is your fault! You are the traitors for not supporting my claim."

Bylanta drew back. "It is better if we leave," she said to the dwarves under her banner. "I pray that Vraccas may instill some sense in you, Ginsgar Unforce."

"That he has done, as my deeds testify." He laughed scornfully as they left the hall. "We shall force them to swear allegiance," he told the two kings, laying his hands on their shoulders. "You will not regret having supported me." He indicated they should rise.

"I hope you are right." Glaïmbar was on his feet. "They'll soon understand that what you have done was the only solution for Âlandur." He lowered his voice. "It's just you stopped too soon, high king."

Ginsgar laughed cruelly and ran his hand over his fire-red beard. "Plenty of time . . ." he hinted with mirth. "Let us drink to my confirmation as high king."

Malbalor thanked him but gave his excuses. "I am too tired, Your Majesty. I should be but poor company and I am not in the mood to celebrate a victory that is nothing of the kind."

"Make no mistake, Malbalor. It will be a great victory and we shan't have to wait long." He gave him a friendly tap on the chest. "And then we shall drink together."

"Yes. *Then* we shall," he responded weakly, taking his cup of water as Glaïmbar and Ginsgar led the way.

Malbalor was not happy with this stirring of unrest. Xamtys had seen through his motives immediately. As king of the thirdlings, in joining forces with Ginsgar, he felt he would be gaining security for himself and his folk. He must use the intervening time to prepare for Ginsgar's endeavors.

If leaders did not soon become more clear-sighted, the feud about the high king's title would end in internecine strife. It would be the first time dwarves fought each other without the thirdlings being the cause, as had been the case under Lorimbas.

A hazy suspicion rose in his mind. "Vraccas, give us reason or give us Ginsgar's defeat," he murmured, downing the contents of his cup. "Save your children."

*   *   *

Girdlegard,
Gray Mountains,
Realm of the Fifthlings,
Winter, 6241st Solar Cycle

Balyndis was seated in the throne room surrounded by the old fifthling grandeur, and the new fifthling magnificence. She interrupted the talks with the clan elders and opened the letter she had just been handed.

It was from Rodario and contained many pages detailing recent events and in particular how Tungdil had met his end. Even if no one could say with certainty that he had died, the descriptions of the monsters in the Black Abyss made it impossible that he could have survived.

"Dead," she mouthed. Tears sprang to her eyes, and the words on the paper became illegible through the mist.

"Queen Balyndis," one of the dwarves prompted cautiously. "What has happened? Is King Glaïmbar not well?"

"No. No, he is fine." She forced herself to smile, although her heart was mourning the dwarf she was once linked to with the iron band. She had released him from their union, aware that his soul was restless. It had changed nothing in her feelings toward him.

She had returned to Glaïmbar's side more or less by default. She had not wanted to go back to her firstling clan and certainly had not wanted to go to the freelings. Glaïmbar's invitation had reached her at a time when few other options were open. He had accepted her back as his spouse without a word about the past; and for this she truly loved him. It was a different love from the one she had for Tungdil. And would always have.

"Would you like to rest?" one of the dwarves suggested. "Perhaps in your condition . . . ?"

"Indeed," she said, grateful for the excuse. She got up to leave. "Forgive me. I should go and lie down. We will meet again shortly before sunset."

The clan leaders bowed and Balyndis walked through the throne room to the door. Her attention was otherwise engaged but she still noticed she was being stared at. Geroïn Leadenring was looking at her with malice; he was the brother of Syndalis Leadenring, the king's second wife. Glaïmbar had rejected her in favor of Balyndis and this had aroused much ill-feeling.

Balyndis avoided the gaze and hurried through the corridors, past her own chambers and directly into the small forge where she was often to be found creating all manner of items in the little leisure time at her disposal. The furnace was always burning, fed from the Dragon Fire.

She cast the pages of the letter one by one onto the glowing coals, observing how they curled in the heat and caught, then turned to ash. The featherlight black flakes flew up the chimney and off, far over the peaks of the Gray Mountains and beyond.

Balyndis watched them go; she threw a shovelful of coal into the furnace and set the bellows to work. Soon white flames were dancing, sending out tremendous heat. She did not want these lines anywhere near her if they spoke of Tungdil's death. She needed nothing to remind her of him or of his heroic deeds.

The finest remembrance he could have left her with she

carried beneath her heart. All the fifthlings presumed the child was Glaïmbar's.

They should continue to think so.

Girdlegard,
Queendom of Weyurn,
Near the Tunnel,
Winter, 6241st Solar Cycle

It was early afternoon but it looked as if night had fallen. A winter storm covered the western part of Weyurn, bringing icy rain and the first flakes of snow.

Algin saw the foresail belly out dangerously with the storm wind which was chasing the little fishing boat over the crests of the waves. They were traveling so fast that the man was afraid the hull would lift clean out of the water. "Take it down," he yelled to his friend Retar the helmsman, pointing at the threatened wind-filled canvas.

"No—if we do that the lake will get us," he shouted back against the roar of the storm.

"If that sail rips we're done for." Algin staggered across the rearing deck and with cold wet fingers tried to undo the knots to drop the topsail. That would be simpler than furling the canvas. "We must head back to harbor."

"One more buoy," Retar called, holding fast to the tiller. "The net at the old sandbank must be full to bursting. This storm will have fair driven the fish in for us."

Algin hesitated. Their catch so far had been poor for a whole orbit's fishing. Elria must have guided the shoals out to the very depths of the lake. "All right, then," he agreed, taking his hand from the rope. Retar grinned and set the course.

That was when the fisherman noticed the cavernous hole in the cliff, opening like the circular gullet of a huge worm. It measured a good ten paces in diameter and was one third under water.

He jabbed Retar with his elbow to show him. "Take a look at that!" he yelled. "Now I know why the lake water is disappearing out from under our keel. That tunnel must lead straight to the Red Mountains."

Retar stared at it. "What do the dwarves want with all our water?" He was furious. "I don't get it. Why are they digging . . . ?"

Both of them saw a monstrous shape fill the entrance. An extended neck with an elongated skull was slowly emerging and the nostrils flared at the front of the slim muzzle. The creature was testing the air for scents. Its dark green skin was covered in shimmering damp scales.

"Elria!" ejaculated Algin. "What on earth . . . ?"

The monster looked their way, drew in a huge breath and raised its head, its eyes blazing red. Steam shot from its nose.

Retar swore and swung the helm around. The buoy he'd been so keen to reach was bobbing on the surface by the creature's feet. He abandoned all thoughts of it.

"It's . . . a dragon," stammered Algin. "By Elria! It's exactly like the ones in the stories." Fascinated, he watched the creature launch itself gracefully into the water.

Its broad shadowy shape was approaching them now, just under the surface, and moving fast, faster than any fish they'd ever seen. The nearer it got, the better able they were to judge its size: from head to tail-tip fifty paces at least, they thought, and ten wide.

"Hard to port! By all the gods, hard to port!" he screamed at Retar, the fear of death in him. "Quick! It's going to ram us."

The dragon ducked down under their boat and disappeared.

"It's dived! It's spared us."

"Who's going to believe that?" croaked Retar.

"There's been so much happening in Girdlegard, they'll have to take our word for it." Algin looked at the gaping hole in the cliff. "We must let Queen Wey know about the tunnel and the dragon right away." He was not certain whether dwarves or dragons were responsible for digging the tunnel. "To think that one of these creatures has come back after so long. The sagas speak of dragons as being cruel and clever. What does it want here?"

"I don't care. I'll be offering ten of my best fish to the goddess for saving me and my boat," a pale-faced Retar muttered. "For her protection . . ."

Algin observed the waters beneath their craft filling with light. Their boat was suddenly enveloped in a curtain of blood-red fire. Flames shot around the gunwales three paces high; the heat was intolerable. Algin and Retar screamed in helpless panic. To jump overboard was certain death.

All at once flames burst up through the hull, enrobing mast, sails and men, and incinerating flesh, skin and bone. Not a smudge of ash remained.

The boat broke apart. The blackened pieces of the wreck tossed on the waves and were driven off by the current.

Nothing would be found.

No trace of Algin, of Retar, of their boat . . .

Nor of any dragon.

Dramatis Personae

Fidelgar Strikefast

Baigar Fourhand

Gremdulin Ironbite of the clan of the Iron Biters.

Saphira Ironbite of the clan of the Iron Biters.

Bilba Chiselstrike of the clan of the Stone Teasers.

Thirdling Kingdom

Tungdil Goldhand, warrior and scholar.

Balodil, his son.

Goda Flameheart, warrior maiden.

Manon Hardfoot of the clan of the Death Ax.

Malbalor White-Eye of the clan of the Bone Breakers, king of the thirdlings.

Diemo Deathblade of the clan of the Death Blades, commander of the guard.

Veltaga and **Bandilor**, dwarf-haters.

Fourthling Kingdom

Goïmdil's folk

Gandogar Silverbeard of the clan of the Silver Beards, king of the fourthlings and high king of all the dwarves.

Bylanta Slimfinger of the clan of the Silver Beards, sister to Gandogar.

Ingbar Onyx-Eye of the clan of the Stone Turners, lift master.

Glaïmbli Sparkeye of the clan of the Spark Eyes.

Tandibur Pitpride of the clan of the Pit Prides.

Sigdal Rubiniam of the clan of the Gem Stones.

Feldolin Whetstone of the clan of the Thyst Finders.

Freelings
Bramdal Masterstroke, executioner.
Gordislan Hammerfist, king of Trovegold.

HUMANS
The fabulous Rodario, actor and impresario.
Furgas, theatre technician and prop-master.
Nolik, rich man.
Tassia, his wife.
Gesa, comely matron.
Reimar, worker.
Lambus, a smith from Mifurdania.
Gilspan, innkeeper.
Ilgar, worker.
Lia, treasure seeker.
Franek, treasure seeker.
Deifrich, merchant.
Kartev, merchant.
Kea, female assistant.
Tamás, building master.
Ove, building master.
Meinart, captain of the Urgon guard.
Hakulana, spear leader, female lieutenant.
Torant, scout and equerry.
Alvaro, commander of bodyguard to Prince Mallen.
Kordin, captain of the *Waveskimmer*.
Retar and **Algin,** fishermen of Weyurn.
Flira and **Ormardin,** children of fisher family.
Talena, fisherman's wife.
Mendar, sloop captain.
Risava, famula.

Dergard, famulus.

Lomostin, famulus.

Prince Mallen of Ido, sovereign of Idoslane.

Ortger, King of Urgon.

Bruron, King of Gauragar.

Umilante, Queen of Sangpûr.

Wey IV, Queen of Weyurn.

Isika, Queen of Rân Ribastur.

Nate, King of Tabaîn.

OTHERS

Liútasil, Lord of the elves of Âlandur.

Rejalin, envoy from Âlandur.

Eldrur, envoy from Âlandur.

Irdosíl, envoy from Âlandur.

Antamar, envoy from Âlandur.

Vilanoîl and **Tiwalún,** elves from Âlandur.

Esdalân, Baron of Jilsbon from Âlandur.

Limasar, elf warrior.

Itemara, elf warrior maiden.

Hui, dog.

Gronsha, orc.

Kamdra, ubari warrior.

Flagur, ubari prince.

Acknowledgments

Who would have thought it? A third volume with Tungdil and his companions!

I am happy for the dwarves in their success and am particularly glad that my diminutive friends have enjoyed and still enjoy such popularity. With this they have achieved my dream: they made it possible for me to earn my bread exclusively as an author. Small creatures, great effect.

Apparently, the thing to do when it is all going really well is—stop. In this case it is time to do just that.

Why?

I should like to allow Girdlegard some privacy to order affairs between its various peoples.

Let us see what emerges in a few years' time. Perhaps one day I shall open the gates to Girdlegard once more, and who knows how it may look then and what fates awaited the heroes? In the meantime I am traveling in Ulldart, my fantasy continent, forging peace and causing mayhem.

My thanks are due to the many dwarf friends who laughed along with Tungdil and his companions when things were good and sighed for them when times were hard. I should like to thank the loyal team of test readers: Nicole Schuhmacher, Sonja and Jan Rüther, and Tanja

Karmann. For their staunch support on previous volumes, thanks to Dr. Patrick Müller and Meike Sewering. Much praise and many thanks to my German editor Angela Kuepper, who has looked after the dwarves with me for the last three years.

extras

orbit

www.orbitbooks.net

about the author

Markus Heitz was born in 1971 in Germany. He studied history, German language, and literature and won the German Fantasy Award in 2003 for his debut novel, *Shadows Over Ulldart*. His *Dwarves* series is a bestseller in Europe. Markus Heitz lives in Zweibrücken.

Find out more about Markus Heitz and other Orbit authors by registering for the free monthly newsletter at www.orbitbooks.net

if you enjoyed
THE REVENGE OF THE DWARVES
look out for

THE EDGE OF THE WORLD

by

Kevin J. Anderson

I

Off the Coast of Uraba

These foreign seas looked much the same as the waters of home, but Criston Vora knew the lands were different, the people were different, and their religion was contrary to everything he had been taught in the Aidenist kirk. For a twenty-year-old sailor eager to see the world, those differences could be either wondrous or frightening—he wouldn't know which until he met the people of Uraba, which he was about to do.

The *Fishhook* had made this voyage several times, and Criston's captain, Andon Shay, was confident in his abilities to negotiate another trade deal with the Uraban merchants. The young man kept his eyes open and studied the unfolding coastline as the ship sailed far, far south of everything he had known.

From his fishing village of Windcatch, he had always felt the call of the sea, wanting to see what lay beyond the horizon, yearning to explore. Though he had signed on for only a short trading voyage, at least he was seeing the other continent: *Uraba*. A place of legends and mystery.

Though connected by a narrow isthmus, the world's two main continents, Uraba and Tierra, were separated by a wide gulf of history and culture. Ages ago, at the beginning of time, when Ondun—God—had sent two of his sons in separate sailing ships to explore the world, the descendants of Aiden's crew had settled Tierra, while those from Urec's vessel colonized Uraba. Over the centuries, the followers of Aiden and the followers of Urec developed separate civilizations, religions, and traditions; despite their differences, they were bound together by ties of trade and necessity.

On a bright sunny day with a brisk breeze, Captain Shay called for the sails to be trimmed for a gentle approach to the city of Ouroussa, where they hoped to find eager customers. The hold of the *Fishhook* contained barrels of whale oil from Soeland Reach, large spools of hemp rope from Erietta, grain from Alamont, and, in a special locked chest in the captain's cabin, beautiful metal-worked jewelry made by the skilled smiths of Corag Reach. Though the bangles and ornaments would be sold to the followers of Urec, the Corag metalworkers had subtly hidden a tiny Aidenist fishhook on each piece of jewelry.

Captain Shay would sell his cargo at prices greatly reduced from what the other Uraban merchants and middlemen could offer. With fast vessels, intrepid Tierran sailors braved the uncharted currents and sailed directly to Uraba's coastal cities, bypassing the much slower over-land merchants (much to their consternation).

Near the ship's wheel, Criston paused to look at the two compasses mounted on a sheltered pedestal, a traditional magnetic compass that always pointed toward magnetic north and a magical Captain's Compass that always pointed *home*. The silver needle of the Captain's Compass came from the same piece of precious metal as an identical needle in the Tierran capital city of Calay. These twinned needles remained linked to each other by sympathetic magic, as all things in Ondun's creation were said to be linked.

Now, as the *Fishhook* closed in on Ouroussa, the crew saw a flurry of activity in the distant harbor; a ship with a bright red sail set out to meet them, sailing toward the open water. Captain Shay gestured to Criston. "Go aloft and have a look, Seaman Vora." Shay's dark hair ran to his shoulders, and instead of wearing a full bushy beard like most ship captains, he kept his neatly trimmed.

Nimble and unafraid of heights, the young man scrambled up the shroud lines to reach the lookout nest. During the voyage, Criston had enjoyed spending time high atop the main mast overlooking the waters; he had even seen several fearsome-looking sea serpents, but only at a distance.

As the Uraban ship approached, Criston noted its central painted icon on its square mainsail, the Eye of Urec. He spied additional movement in the harbor, where two fast Uraban galleys launched, their oars extended, beating across the water at a good clip. They spread apart, approaching the *Fishhook* from opposite directions.

Captain Shay called for a report, and Criston scrambled back down the lines to relate what he had seen to Captain Shay. "I couldn't see many crewmen aboard the main ship, Captain. Maybe they just want to escort us into port."

"Never needed an escort before. These aren't waters that require a pilot." Shay snapped orders to his crew, and all twenty-eight men came out on deck to stand ready. "Once they know what we're offering, they'll welcome us with open arms, but don't let your guard down." He turned back to the young sailor. "This could be a very interesting first voyage for you, Seaman."

"It's not my first voyage, sir. I've spent most of my life on boats."

"It's your first voyage with *me*, and that's what counts."

Criston's father, a fisherman, had been lost at sea, and

Criston himself had served aboard many boats, working the local catch but dreaming of more ambitious voyages. Though young, Criston owned his own small boat for carrying cargo up to the Tierran capital of Calay, but the prospect of paying off the money-lenders seemed daunting. So when the *Fishhook* had passed through Windcatch on her way south and Captain Shay asked for short-term sailors to accompany him on a two-month trip to Ouroussa, offering wages higher than he could make on his own boat, Criston had jumped at the chance.

Not only would it help him pay off the debt, but it would give Criston a chance to see far-off lands. And when he returned to Windcatch with his purse full of coins, he would finally be able to marry Adrea, whom he had loved for years. Once the *Fishhook* unloaded her cargo in Ouroussa, Criston could be on his way home. . . .

As the scarlet-sailed Uraban ship closed to within hailing distance, he spotted a man standing near the bow dressed in loose cream-colored robes, his head wrapped in a pale olba. Only five crewmen stood with the man on the foreign vessel's deck. The robed man shouted across to them in heavily accented Tierran. "I am Fillok, Ouroussa's city leader. What goods have you brought us?"

Shay lowered his voice to Criston. "Fillok . . . I know that name. I think he's the brother of the soldan of Outer Wahilir, an important man. Why would *he* come to meet us?" He frowned in consternation. "Men who consider themselves important sometimes do brash things, and it's rarely a good sign." The captain raised his voice and called back across the water, "We are on our way to port. I can give your harbormaster a full list."

"It is my right to inspect your cargo here and now!

How do we know your boat is not filled with soldiers to attack Ouroussa?"

"Why would we do that?" Shay asked, genuinely perplexed.

If Fillok did not change course, his ship would collide with the *Fishhook* within minutes. Captain Shay eyed the two swift war galleys coming toward them from both port and starboard. "This doesn't feel right, Vora. Go up there and have another look." The young sailor slipped away and scrambled back up the ropes to the lookout nest.

Tierran traders often made great profit from selling to Uraban cities, but many vessels vanished, more than could reasonably be accounted for by storms and reefs. If Fillok were an ambitious and unprincipled man, he could have attacked those traders and seized their cargoes. No one in Tierra would know.

When Criston reached the lookout nest and peered down at the foreign ship, he was astonished to see far more than just the five Uraban sailors standing at the ropes. At least a dozen armed men crouched out of sight behind crates and sailcloth on the deck; the hatches were open, and even more Uraban men crowded below, holding bright scimitars. Criston cupped his hands around his mouth and yelled at the top of his lungs, "Captain, it's a trap! The ship is full of armed men!"

Shay shouted to his crew, "Set sails! All canvas, take the wind *now!*" Already on edge, the men jumped to untie knots, pull ropes, and drop sails abruptly into place.

Criston's warning forced Fillok into abrupt action. The Ouroussan city leader screamed something in his own language, and hidden men burst into view, lifting their swords. Shrill trumpets sounded a call to battle. Ropes with grappling hooks flew across the narrow gap between the two ships; several fell into the water, but three caught the *Fishhook*'s deck rail. Answering horns and drum-beats came from the two closing war galleys, and the rowers picked up their pace.

Shay reached down to grab a long harpoon stowed just below the starboard bow of the *Fishhook*. The Tierran men armed themselves with boat-hooks, oars, and stunning clubs. Criston clambered back down to the deck, ready to join the fight. He held a long boat-knife to defend himself, though its reach was much shorter than that of a Uraban scimitar.

Criston ran to the straining ropes that bound the ships together, just as five Urabans jumped across the gap with an eerie inhuman howl. Ducking the wide swing of a Uraban sword, he sawed at the first rope until it snapped and immediately set to work on the second one.

The *Fishhook*'s sails were fully extended now, giving her a much greater canvas area than Fillok's small Uraban ship. The ropes creaked as the Tierran vessel tried to break away. One of the Tierran sailors went down, bleeding from a deep gash in his head.

Ignoring the mayhem around him, Captain Shay cocked his arm back and let the long harpoon fly toward the other ship. Where its sharp iron tip plunged directly through Fillok's chest. The Ouroussan city leader staggered backward, grabbing the harpoon's shaft in astonishment, before he collapsed into a pool of blood on his own deck.

The Uraban attackers howled in rage upon seeing their leader killed. They piled against one another, preparing to leap across and slaughter the Tierrans. Racing in from shore, the two war galleys closed in a pincer maneuver.

Criston sawed with his knife until he severed the third grappling rope, and like a freed stallion, the *Fishhook* lunged free, separating from the Uraban ship as many of the enemy fighters leaped across. A dozen men tumbled into the deep water, and only two managed to cling to the side of the *Fishhook*, clutching nets and an anchor rope. Leaning over the rail, Criston lopped off fingers with a knife slash, and the screaming men slid into the water.

Though he was as white as a sheet, Captain Shay's voice did not waver as he shouted, "All speed—head north! Out to open sea!" The *Fishhook* began to pull away.

Only three enemy soldiers remained on the deck. Captain Shay's crew quickly dispatched them and dumped the bodies overboard.

With Fillok killed—the brother of the local soldan!— the remaining Uraban sailors were in a frenzy aboard his ship. The drums of the approaching war galleys beat furiously, but the *Fishhook*'s sails pushed the cargo ship faster. The coastline began to dwindle in the distance, but Criston knew the uproar would not die down. "Captain, what just happened? Why did they do that? We came only to trade."

"They wanted our cargo, and now they'll want our hides as well." Shay looked sick. "Fillok's brother will go to Soldan-Shah Imir and demand blood. I suppose the blood of any Tierran will do. We have to get to King Korastine as quickly as possible." He gave the young sailor a weary smile as he turned the wheel and aligned the course with the Captain's Compass. "When we pass Windcatch, I can drop you off, Mr. Vora. But for the rest of us . . ." He shook his head, still frowning. "I think we just started a war."

II

The Royal Cog, Sailing to Ishalem Three Months Later
The royal ship sailed southward through the night, following the Tierran coastline. She was a single-masted cog with her square sails trimmed so that she made slow headway under the stars. Because the route down to the holy city of Ishalem was so well charted, with lighthouses to mark hazardous stretches, the captain was comfortable with proceeding in the dark.

Even so, King Korastine of Tierra could not sleep, caught between hope and anxiety about the upcoming meeting with Soldan-Shah Imir. After the disastrous clash between Captain Shay's trading ship and the Uraban privateers, he could just as easily have been leading warships down to ransack Ouroussa and sink enemy ships in the harbor.

Instead of leaping headfirst into war, the Uraban leader had dispatched his best ambassador, a man named Giladen, to search for a peaceful solution. Though neither leader would admit it, both knew that Captain Shay should not have gone where he did; they also knew that Fillok should not have attacked a peaceful trading ship, and that a harpoon in the heart was exactly what he deserved. Though their respective populations were inflamed, both the king and the soldan-shah believed they had a chance to salvage the situation.

Long past midnight, Korastine stood on the raised bow platform and gazed into the misty shadows that lay ahead, imagining their destination. *Ishalem*. The sacred city built on the narrow isthmus that connected the continents . . . the most ancient settlement in the known world, considered holy by both the Aidenist religion and the rival Urecari religion.

Korastine wrapped weathered hands around the wooden balustrade. He was a thin man, wise-looking, barely forty. His long hair and neatly trimmed beard were light brown, salted with graying strands. He could already see what he would look like when he grew old, and times like these aged a man more swiftly.

In Ishalem, he and the soldan-shah would sign a treaty blessed by the Aidenist prester-marshall and the head sikara priestess of the Urecari church. After so many years of turmoil, they would divide the known world in half, clearly defining the two spheres of influence. That would settle the matter for all time, and at last there would be peace.

So why couldn't he sleep? Why did his stomach insist upon knotting itself with doubts? With a heavy sigh, he tried to convince himself that he was just being a fool, stung by too many disappointments, too many misplaced dreams.

The mist intensified the salt-and-seaweed smell in the air. The whispering laughter of gentle waves against the hull planks was soothing. Though there were hammocks below, most crewmen chose to sleep on the open deck. A puff of breeze luffed the sailcloth, making the masts and rigging creak.

Korastine barely heard the soft barefoot tread ascending the steps to the forecastle platform. He turned to see his beloved eleven-year-old daughter rubbing sleep from her eyes. "Are we almost to Ishalem, Father?"

"We'll be there in the morning." He reached out to hug her, and she comfortably folded herself into his arms.

Princess Anjine had straight brown hair, parted in the middle. When she was at court in Calay, she brushed her hair many times nightly, as her mother had once insisted, but on the five-day voyage, the girl didn't bother with such silliness, and the king couldn't blame her.

Though Queen Sena had been dead from pneumonia for half a year now, Korastine and his wife had often disagreed on the raising of their only child; the queen insisted that Anjine ought to be ladylike and courtly, while Korastine wanted the girl to focus more on leadership—while also being allowed some measure of her own childhood. As an uneasy compromise, the princess had learned both.

Knowing how much was at stake with the upcoming treaty, the king insisted that Anjine accompany him now. He could never forget the responsibility he had to his people and to his daughter. One day, he would leave Tierra in Anjine's care, and he did not want to give her a broken, war-torn land.

Korastine glanced around for his daughter's constant companion. "Where is Mateo?" One year older than Anjine, the young man was Korastine's ward by virtue of a heartfelt promise made when Mateo's father, a captain of the royal guard, had died in the line of duty.

"Oh, *he* has no trouble sleeping." Anjine lounged back against the rail. "Should I go splash a bucket of seawater in his face?"

"Let him sleep. We're going to have a busy day when we reach port."

As the royal cog had sailed out of Calay Harbor, Anjine and Mateo had chattered with excitement about the exotic things they were going to see. Neither had ever been to Ishalem, though they had heard plenty of stories from sailors, presters, and teachers. By the second day, however, the excitement of the voyage faded, and Mateo made it his personal mission to entertain Anjine. After the king had scolded the two children for scrambling up the mast and hanging on the rigging, Mateo devoted himself to playing strategy games with her. They hunkered down together on the deck boards, sketching out a chalk grid and making their marks. Korastine noted, proudly, that Anjine won more often than the boy did.

Queen Sena would have argued against bringing Mateo Bornan along at all, claiming that the king had gone far beyond the requirements of his promise to care for the boy. Though he did not like to think ill of the dead, stuffy Sena was no longer with them, and Korastine could raise his daughter as he pleased.

Now, wide-awake and eager as the ship sailed on, Anjine stood next to her father. Though her head barely came to his chin, he could think only of how tall, how mature his little girl was becoming. Where had the years gone? He felt a hint of tears welling in his eyes. By signing the Edict, he would leave her—and all his people—with a better, safer world.

Anjine strained to see through the fog, then pointed. "Is that Aiden's Lighthouse?"

Korastine did see a flicker, like an ember suspended in the air. "If it isn't, then we're far off course." The tall tower of sturdy rock had been erected on a jutting point of land outside of Ishalem. Its light burned constantly, not just to warn ships of the reefs that lay farther south, but to represent the light of Aiden's wisdom.

A groggy Mateo hurried across the deck, and the twelve-year-old sprang onto the forecastle platform to stand between Anjine and Korastine. So full of energy, like his father had been! The dark-haired young man would make a fine soldier someday—a high-ranking officer, if Korastine had anything to do with it.

Before long, they could see a silvery fringe of dawn on the eastern horizon. The off-watch crewmen began to awaken, and the cook stoked his stove in the gallery to begin cooking breakfast. Men worked the rigging, pulling ropes to stretch the sails, now that the captain could see his heading. Ahead and to port, the shore loomed out of the shadows.

Korastine stared at the western edge of the isthmus that separated the vast Oceansea from the calmer Middlesea. He remembered the first time he'd sailed down the coast at his own father's side, being trained to lead Tierra. . . . He had made the voyage six times now, always on matters of state, always in response to a major or minor political emergency. After this time, though . . .

Finally the warm sun burned off the rest of the morning fog, and the whitewashed buildings of sprawling, majestic Ishalem came into view. Ah, he remembered the amazement and wonder with which he had first viewed the holy city. Anjine would be seeing the same thing now, through the clarity and optimism of youth.

On the Aidenist side of the city, the architecture showed familiar Tierran influence, similar to what one might find in any coastal village, while in the Uraban District on the opposite side of the isthmus, the buildings looked alien, with unusual curves and angles, stuccoed rather than timbered, the roofs tiled rather than thatched.

On the highest hill in the center of Ishalem stood the ruins of the Arkship, little more than a skeletal hull with one broken mast, like a giant beached sea beast, lying far from the water. Anjine pointed as soon as she spotted it. "That's the ship! Aiden's ship."

Korastine uttered an automatic awed prayer. "Yes, the actual one."

Prester-Marshall Baine appeared on deck, wearing a long, dark brown robe trimmed with purple silk. An Aidenist fishhook pendant hung at his throat, nearly covered by his unruly red beard. King Korastine not only revered the energetic religious leader, he *respected* Baine as an intelligent, thoughtful friend. Though he was only in his mid-thirties, Baine had reached a high position of authority and responsibility, thanks to his forceful personality and his persuasive words. The prester-marshall closed his blue eyes as he bowed in silent prayer. "The holy Arkship."

"But how could such a big ship get so far from the water?" Mateo asked pragmatically, and Anjine gave him a brisk kick in the shin.

The prester-marshall chided her. "Some presters might tell you never to question, but that is tantamount to telling you not to *think*. Ondun created us to explore, to experience. There is no harm in raising questions, and Mateo has asked a good one. That conundrum has puzzled scholars for many generations."

Mateo flashed a vindicated grin at Anjine, but the prester-marshall didn't exactly answer his query. "Now would be a good time to reflect upon where our people came from. You have heard the story all your life, but when you gaze upon Ishalem, you can see in your heart that it is more than just a *story*.

"At the beginning of the world, Ondun created the continents and the seas and the skies. He made His own perfect holy land, which He called Terravitae, and Ondun filled the land with crops and orchards, forests, animals, birds, and insects. He populated it with His own people. Then He made other people and scattered them across the remaining continents. When He was finished with all His work, Ondun created three special sons—Aiden, Urec, and Joron.

"Satisfied with all that He had done, Ondun bequeathed stewardship of the world to His heirs, for He had other worlds to create, and He would soon depart. Ondun instructed Aiden, Urec, and Joron that they must keep this world intact, improve it, make it thrive. While the youngest son, Joron, remained behind to rule Terravitae, Ondun commanded that His two older sons go out in separate ships to explore His creation."

Baine related the tale to Anjine and Mateo with an earnestness that village presters could never match. Korastine smiled: No wonder the man had risen so quickly in the church hierarchy. "Before the voyage, Ondun gave Urec a special map to show him how to find the mysteries of the world, and the key to creation. To Aiden, he gave a special compass to facilitate his return to Terravitae, for its needle was charmed always to point home."

"Like a Captain's Compass," Mateo interrupted.

"The very first Captain's Compass," Anjine corrected.

"Aiden and Urec each constructed a giant Arkship, and taking their crews and families with them, sailed away from Terraviae on separate routes. But Urec was arrogant and sure of himself. He would explore the world, but considered the map an insult to his bravery, a way of cheating. Urec threw the chart overboard and chose his own course." Baine raised his bushy red eyebrows for dramatic effect. "Now, the Urecari will tell it differently, because such foolishness does not reflect well upon the man they consider their prophet! But we have the Book of Aiden to tell us the truth."

The prester-marshall looked up as the cog sailed toward

the crowded maze of wharves. "We know that one of Aiden's crew members was secretly a spy for Urec, though the Urecari deny it. As soon as Aiden's ship passed well beyond sight of Terravitae, the Urecari spy damaged the sacred compass so that Aiden, too, became lost.

"After voyaging aimlessly for years, Aiden's ship came to rest here. The crew intermarried with the people of Tierra, and their descendants now populate half the world. When Urec's ship landed, he, his crew, and their children settled in Uraba to the south."

As the royal ship pulled into the harbor, Korastine saw the buildings clustered like devout worshippers kneeling before the many-spired Aidenist kirk built on the western side of the Arkship hill. The cog drifted up to a long dock festooned with pennants and garlands. Gulls greeted them with a raucous fanfare. Ishalem looked so glorious that Korastine could almost believe that their meeting was blessed by Ondun.

Anjine glanced up toward the gigantic wreck on the hill. "So how do we know that's Aiden's ship, instead of Urec's—as the Urecari say?"

"Because we *know*. Yes, we know."